Contents

BOOKS BY AGATHA CHRISTIE

The ABC Murders
The Adventure of the Christmas Pudding
After the Funeral
And Then There Were None
Appointment with Death
At Bertram's Hotel
The Big Four
The Body in the Library
By the Pricking of My Thumbs
Cards on the Table
A Caribbean Mystery
Cat Among the Pigeons
The Clocks
Crooked House
Curtain: Poirot's Last Case
Dead Man's Folly
Death Comes as the End
Death in the Clouds
Death on the Nile
Destination Unknown
Dumb Witness
Elephants Can Remember
Endless Night
Evil Under the Sun
Five Little Pigs
4.50 from Paddington
Hallowe'en Party
Hercule Poirot's Christmas
Hickory Dickory Dock
The Hollow
The Hound of Death
The Labours of Hercules
The Listerdale Mystery
Lord Edgware Dies
The Man in the Brown Suit
The Mirror Crack'd from Side to Side
Miss Marple's Final Cases
The Moving Finger
Mrs McGinty's Dead
The Murder at the Vicarage
Murder in Mesopotamia
Murder in the Mews
A Murder is Announced
Murder is Easy
The Murder of Roger Ackroyd
Murder on the Links
Murder on the Orient Express
The Mysterious Affair at Styles

The Mysterious Mr Quin
The Mystery of the Blue Train
Nemesis
N or M?
One, Two, Buckle My Shoe
Ordeal by Innocence
The Pale Horse
Parker Pyne Investigates
Partners in Crime
Passenger to Frankfurt
Peril at End House
A Pocket Full of Rye
Poirot Investigates
Poirot's Early Cases
Postern of Fate
Problem at Pollensa Bay
Sad Cypress
The Secret Adversary
The Secret of Chimneys
The Seven Dials Mystery
The Sittaford Mystery
Sleeping Murder
Sparkling Cyanide
Taken at the Flood
They Came to Baghdad
They Do It With Mirrors
Third Girl
The Thirteen Problems
Three-Act Tragedy
Towards Zero
Why Didn't They Ask Evans

Novels under the Nom de Plume of 'Mary Westmacott'
Absent in the Spring
The Burden
A Daughter's A Daughter
Giant's Bread
The Rose and the Yew Tree
Unfinished Portrait

Books under the name of Agatha Christie Mallowan
Come Tell me How You Live
Star Over Bethlehem

Autobiography
Agatha Christie: An Autobiography

Nemesis

to Dauphne Honeybone

Contents

CHAPTER 1

Overture

In the afternoons it was the custom of Miss Jane Marple to unfold her second newspaper. Two newspapers were delivered at her house every morning. The first one Miss Marple read while sipping her early morning tea, that is, if it was delivered in time. The boy who delivered the papers was notably erratic in his management of time. Frequently, too, there was either a new boy or a boy who was acting temporarily as a stand-in for the first one. And each one would have ideas of his own as to the geographical route that he should take in delivering. Perhaps it varied monotony for him. But those customers who were used to reading their paper early so that they could snap up the more saucy items in the day's news before departing for their bus, train or other means of progress to the day's work were annoyed if the papers were late, though the middle-aged and elderly ladies who resided peacefully in St Mary Mead often preferred to read a newspaper propped up on their breakfast table.

Today, Miss Marple had absorbed the front page and a few other items in the daily paper that she had nicknamed 'the Daily All-Sorts', this being a slightly satirical allusion to the fact that her paper, the *Daily Newsgiver*, owing to a change of proprietor, to her own and to other of her friends' great annoyance, now provided articles on men's tailoring, women's dress, female heart-throbs, competitions for children, and complaining letters from women and had managed pretty well to shove any real news off any part of it but the front page, or to some obscure corner where it was impossible to find it. Miss Marple, being old-fashioned, preferred her newspapers to *be* newspapers and give you news.

In the afternoon, having finished her luncheon, treated herself to twenty minutes' nap in a specially purchased, upright armchair which catered for the demands of her rheumatic back, she had opened *The Times*, which lent itself still to a more leisurely perusal. Not that *The Times* was what it used to be. The maddening thing about *The Times* was that you couldn't *find* anything any more. Instead of going through from the front page and knowing where everything else was so that you passed easily to any special articles on subjects in which you were interested, there were now extraordinary interruptions to this time-honoured programme. Two pages were suddenly devoted to travel in Capri with illustrations. Sport appeared with far more prominence than it had ever had in the old days. Court news and obituaries were a little more faithful to routine. The births, marriages and deaths which had at one time occupied Miss Marple's attention first of all owing to their prominent position had migrated to a different part of *The Times*, though of late, Miss Marple noted, they had come almost permanently to rest on the back page.

Miss Marple gave her attention first to the main news on the front page. She did not linger long on that because it was equivalent to what she had already read this morning, though possibly couched in a slightly more dignified manner. She cast her eye down the table of contents. Articles, comments, science, sport; then she pursued her usual plan, turned the paper over and had a quick run down the births, marriages and deaths, after which she proposed to turn to the page given to correspondence, where she nearly always found something to enjoy; from that she passed on to the Court Circular, on which page today's news from the Sale Rooms could also be found. A short article on Science was often placed there but she did not propose to read that. It seldom made sense for her.

Having turned the paper over as usual to the births, marriages and deaths, Miss Marple thought to herself, as so often before,

'It's sad really, but nowadays one is only interested in the *deaths*!'

People had babies, but the people who had babies were not likely to be even known by name to Miss Marple. If there had been a column dealing with babies labelled as grandchildren, there might have been some chance of a pleasurable recognition. She might have thought to herself,

'Really, Mary Prendergast has had a *third* granddaughter!', though even that perhaps might have been a bit remote.

She skimmed down Marriages, also with not a very close survey, because most of her old friends' daughters or sons had married some years ago already. She came to the Deaths column, and gave that her more serious attention. Gave it enough, in fact, so as to be sure she would not miss a name. Alloway, Angopastro, Arden, Barton, Bedshaw, Burgoweisser – (dear me, what a *German* name, but he seemed to be late of Leeds). Carpenter, Camperdown, Clegg. Clegg? Now was that one of the Cleggs she knew? No, it didn't seem to be. Janet Clegg. Somewhere in Yorkshire. McDonald, McKenzie, Nicholson. Nicholson? No. Again not a Nicholson she knew. Ogg, Ormerod – that must be one of the aunts, she thought. Yes, probably so. Linda Ormerod. No, she hadn't known her. Quantril? Dear me, that must be Elizabeth Quantril. Eighty-five. Well, really! She had thought Elizabeth Quantril had died some years ago. Fancy her having lived so long! So delicate she'd always been, too. Nobody had expected *her* to make old bones. Race, Radley, Rafiel. Rafiel? Something stirred. That name was familiar. Rafiel. Belford Park, Maidstone. Belford Park, Maidstone. No, she couldn't recall that address. No flowers. Jason Rafiel.

Oh well, an unusual name. She supposed she'd just heard it somewhere. Ross-Perkins. Now that might be – no, it wasn't. Ryland? Emily Ryland? No. No, she'd never known an Emily Ryland. *Deeply loved by her husband and children.* Well, very nice or very sad. Whichever way you liked to look at it.

Miss Marple laid down her paper, glancing idly through the crossword while she puzzled to remember why the name Rafiel was familiar to her.

'It will come to me,' said Miss Marple, knowing from long experience the way old people's memories worked.

'It'll come to me, I have no doubt.'

She glanced out of the window towards the garden, withdrew her gaze and tried to put the garden out of her mind. Her garden had been the source of great pleasure and also a great deal of hard work to Miss Marple for many, many years. And now, owing to the fussiness of doctors, working in the garden was forbidden to her. She'd once tried to fight this ban, but had come to the conclusion that she had, after all, better do as she was told. She had arranged her chair at such an angle as not to be easy to look out in the garden unless she definitely and clearly wished to see something in particular. She sighed, picked up her knitting bag and took out a small child's woolly jacket in process of coming to a conclusion. The back was done and the front. Now she would have to get on with the sleeves. Sleeves were always boring. Two sleeves, both alike. Yes, very boring. Pretty coloured pink wool, however. Pink wool. Now wait a minute, where did that fit in? Yes – yes – it fitted in with that name she'd just read in the paper. Pink wool. A blue sea. A Caribbean sea. A sandy beach. Sunshine. Herself knitting and – why, of course, Mr Rafiel. That trip she had made to the Caribbean. The island of St Honoré. A treat from her nephew Raymond. And she remembered Joan, her niece-in-law, Raymond's wife, saying:

'Don't get mixed up in any more murders, Aunt Jane. It isn't good for you.'

Well, she hadn't *wished* to get mixed up in any murders, but it just happened. That was all. Simply because of an elderly Major with a glass eye who had insisted on telling her some very long and boring stories. Poor Major – now what was *his* name? She'd forgotten that now. Mr Rafiel and his secretary, Mrs – Mrs Walters, yes, Esther Walters, and his masseur-attendant, Jackson. It all came back. Well, well. Poor Mr Rafiel. So Mr Rafiel was dead. He had known he was going to die before very long. He had practically told her so. It seemed as though he had lasted longer than the doctors had thought. He was a strong man, an obstinate man – a very rich man.

Miss Marple remained in thought, her knitting needles working regularly, but her mind not really on her knitting. Her mind was on the late Mr Rafiel, and remembering what she could remember about him. Not an easy man to forget, really. She could conjure his appearance up mentally quite well. Yes, a very definite personality, a difficult man, an irritable man, shockingly rude sometimes. Nobody ever resented his being rude, though. She remembered that also. They didn't resent his being rude because he was so rich. Yes, he had been very rich. He had had his secretary with him and a valet attendant, a qualified masseur. He had not been able to get about very well without help.

Rather a doubtful character that nurse-attendant had been, Miss Marple thought. Mr Rafiel had been very rude to him sometimes. He had never seemed to mind. And that, again, of course was because Mr Rafiel was so rich.

'Nobody else would pay him half what I do,' Mr Rafiel had said, 'and he knows it. He's good at his job, though.'

Miss Marple wondered whether Jackson? – Johnson? had stayed on with Mr Rafiel. Stayed on for what must have been – another year? A year and three or four months. She thought probably not. Mr Rafiel was one who liked a change. He got tired of people, tired of their ways, tired of their faces, tired of their voices.

Miss Marple understood that. She had felt the same sometimes. That companion of hers, that nice, attentive, maddening woman with her cooing voice.

'Ah,' said Miss Marple, 'what a change for the better since –' oh dear, she'd forgotten *her* name now – Miss – Miss Bishop? – no, not Miss Bishop. Oh dear, how difficult it was.

Her mind went back to Mr Rafiel and to – no, it wasn't Johnson, it had been Jackson, Arthur Jackson.

'Oh, dear,' said Miss Marple again, 'I always get *all* the names wrong. And of course, it was Miss *Knight* I was thinking of. Not Miss *Bishop*. Why do I think of her as Miss Bishop?' The answer came to her. Chess, of course. A chess piece. A knight. A bishop.

'I shall be calling her Miss Castle next time I think of her, I suppose, or Miss Rook. Though, really, she's not the sort of person who would ever rook anybody. No, indeed. And now what was the name of that nice secretary that Mr Rafiel had. Oh yes, Esther Walters. That was right. I wonder what has happened to Esther Walters? She'd inherited money? She would probably inherit money now.'

Mr Rafiel, she remembered, had told her something about that, or she had – oh, dear, what a muddle things were when you tried to remember with any kind of exactitude. Esther Walters. It had hit her badly, that business in the Caribbean, but she would have got over it. She'd been a widow, hadn't she? Miss Marple hoped that Esther Walters had married again, some nice, kindly, reliable man. It seemed faintly unlikely. Esther Walters, she thought, had had rather a genius for liking the wrong kind of men to marry.

Miss Marple went back to thinking about Mr Rafiel. No flowers, it had said. Not that she herself would have dreamed of sending flowers to Mr Rafiel. He could buy up all the nurseries in England if he'd wanted to. And anyway, they hadn't been on those terms. They hadn't been – friends, or on terms of affection. They had been – what was the word she wanted? – allies. Yes, they had been allies for a very short time. A very exciting time. And he had been an ally worth having. She had known so. She'd known it as she had gone running through a dark, tropical night in the Caribbean and had come to him. Yes, she remembered, she'd been wearing that pink wool – what used they to call them when she was young? – a fascinator. That nice pink wool kind of shawl-scarf that she'd put round her head, and he had looked at her and laughed, and later when she had said – she smiled at the remembrance – one word she had used and he had laughed, but he hadn't laughed in the end. No, he'd done what she asked him and therefore – 'Ah!' Miss Marple sighed, it had been, she had to admit it, all very exciting. And she'd never told her nephew or dear John about it because, after all, it was what they'd told her not to do, wasn't it? Miss Marple nodded her head. Then she murmured softly,

'Poor Mr Rafiel, I hope he didn't – suffer.'

Probably not. Probably he'd been kept by expensive doctors under sedatives, easing the end. He had suffered a great deal in those weeks in the Caribbean. He'd nearly always been in pain. A brave man.

A brave man. She was sorry he was dead because she thought that though he'd been elderly and an invalid and ill, the world had lost something through his going. She had no idea what he could have been like in business. Ruthless, she thought, and rude and over-mastering and aggressive. A great attacker. But – but a good friend, she thought. And somewhere in him a deep kind of kindness that he was very careful never to show on the surface. A man she admired and respected. Well, she was sorry he was gone and she hoped he hadn't minded too much and that his passing had been easy. And now he would be cremated no doubt and put in some large, handsome marble vault. She didn't even know if he'd been married. He had never mentioned a wife, never mentioned children. A lonely man? Or had his life been so full that he hadn't needed to feel lonely? She wondered.

She sat there quite a long time that afternoon, wondering about Mr Rafiel. She had never expected to see him again after she had returned to England and she never *had* seen him again. Yet in some queer way she could at any moment have felt she was in touch with him. If he had approached her or had suggested that they meet again, feeling perhaps a bond because of a life that had been saved between them, or of some other bond. A bond –

'Surely,' said Miss Marple, aghast at an idea that had come into her mind, 'there can't be a bond of *ruthlessness* between us? Was she, Jane Marple – could she ever be – ruthless? 'D'you know,' said Miss Marple to herself, 'it's extraordinary, I never thought about it before. I believe, you know, I *could* be ruthless . . .'

The door opened and a dark, curly head was popped in. It was Cherry, the welcome successor to Miss Bishop – Miss Knight.

'Did you say something?' said Cherry.

'I was speaking to myself,' said Miss Marple, 'I just wondered if I could ever be ruthless.'

'What, you?' said Cherry. 'Never! You're kindness itself.'

'All the same,' said Miss Marple, 'I believe I *could* be ruthless if there was due cause.'

'What would you call due cause?'

'In the cause of justice,' said Miss Marple.

'You did have it in for little Gary Hopkins I must say,' said Cherry. 'When you caught him torturing his cat that day. Never knew you had it in you to go for anyone like that! Scared him stiff, you did. He's never forgotten it.'

'I hope he hasn't tortured any more cats.'

'Well, he's made sure you weren't about if he did,' said Cherry. 'In fact I'm not at all sure as there isn't other boys as got scared. Seeing you with your wool and the pretty things you knits and all that – anyone would think you were gentle as a lamb. But there's times I could say you'd behave like a lion if you was goaded into it.'

Miss Marple looked a little doubtful. She could not quite see herself in the rôle in which Cherry was now casting her. Had she ever – she paused on the reflection, recalling various moments – there had been intense irritation with Miss Bishop – Knight. (Really, she must *not* forget names in this way.) But her irritation had shown itself in more or less ironical remarks. Lions, presumably, did not use irony. There was nothing ironical about a lion. It sprang. It roared. It used its claws, presumably it took large bites at its prey.

'Really,' said Miss Marple, 'I don't think I have ever behaved *quite* like that.'

Walking slowly along her garden that evening with the usual feelings of vexation rising in her, Miss Marple considered the point again. Possibly the sight of a plant of snap-dragons recalled it to her mind. Really, she had *told* old George again and again that she only wanted sulphur-coloured

14

antirrhinums, *not* that rather ugly purple shade that gardeners always seemed so fond of. 'Sulphur yellow,' said Miss Marple aloud.

Someone the other side of the railing that abutted on the lane past her house turned her head and spoke.

'I beg your pardon? You said something?'

'I was talking to myself, I'm afraid,' said Miss Marple, turning to look over the railing.

This was someone she did not know, and she knew most people in St Mary Mead. Knew them by sight even if not personally. It was a thickset woman in a shabby but tough tweed skirt, and wearing good country shoes. She wore an emerald pullover and a knitted woollen scarf.

'I'm afraid one does at my age,' added Miss Marple.

'Nice garden you've got here,' said the other woman.

'Not particularly nice now,' said Miss Marple. 'When I could attend to it myself –'

'Oh I know. I understand just what you feel. I suppose you've got one of those – I have a lot of names for them, mostly very rude – elderly chaps who say they know all about gardening. Sometimes they do, sometimes they don't know a thing about it. They come and have a lot of cups of tea and do a little very mild weeding. They're quite nice, some of them, but all the same it does make one's temper rise.' She added, 'I'm quite a keen gardener myself.'

'Do you live here?' asked Miss Marple, with some interest.

'Well, I'm boarding with a Mrs Hastings. I think I've heard her speak of you. You're Miss Marple, aren't you?'

'Oh yes.'

'I've come as a sort of companion-gardener. My name is Bartlett, by the way. Miss Bartlett. There's not really much to do there,' said Miss Bartlett. 'She goes in for annuals and all that. Nothing you can really get your teeth into.' She opened her mouth and showed her teeth when making this remark. 'Of course I do a few odd jobs as well. Shopping, you know, and things like that. Anyway, if you want any time put in here, I could put in an hour or two for you. I'd say I might be better than any chap you've got now.'

'That would be easy,' said Miss Marple. 'I like flowers best. Don't care so much for vegetables.'

'I do vegetables for Mrs Hastings. Dull but necessary. Well, I'll be getting along.' Her eyes swept over Miss Marple from head to foot, as though memorizing her, then she nodded cheerfully and tramped off.

Mrs Hastings? Miss Marple couldn't remember the name of any Mrs Hastings. Certainly Mrs Hastings was not an old friend. She had certainly never been a gardening chum. Ah, of course, it was probably those newly built houses at the end of Gibraltar Road. Several families had moved in in the last year. Miss Marple sighed, looked again with annoyance at the antirrhinums, saw several weeds which she yearned to root up, one or two exuberant suckers she would like to attack with her secateurs, and finally, sighing, and manfully resisting temptation, she made a detour round by the lane and returned to her house. Her mind recurred again to Mr Rafiel. They had been, he and she – what was the title of that book they used to quote so much when she was young? *Ships that pass in the night.* Rather apt it was really, when she came to think of it. Ships that pass in the night . . . It was in the night that she had gone to him to ask – no, to demand – help. To insist, to say no time must be lost. And he had agreed, and put things in train at once! Perhaps she *had* been rather lion-like on that occasion? No. No, that was quite wrong. It had not been anger she had felt. It had been insistence on something that was absolutely imperative to be put in hand at once. And he'd understood.

Poor Mr Rafiel. The ship that had passed in the night had been an interesting ship. Once you got used to his being rude, he might have been quite an agreeable man? No! She shook her head. Mr Rafiel could never have been an agreeable man. Well, she must put Mr Rafiel out of her head.

Ships that pass in the night, and speak each other in passing;
Only a signal shown and a distant voice in the darkness.

She would probably never think of him again. She would look out perhaps to see if there was an obituary of him in *The Times*. But she did not think it was very likely. He was not a very well known character, she thought. Not famous. He had just been very rich. Of course, many people did have obituaries in the paper just because they were very rich; but she thought that Mr Rafiel's richness would possibly not have been of that kind. He had not been prominent in any great industry, he had not been a great financial genius, or a noteworthy banker. He had just all his life made enormous amounts of money . . .

CHAPTER 2

Code Word Nemesis

It was about a week or so after Mr Rafiel's death that Miss Marple picked up a letter from her breakfast tray, and looked at it for a moment before opening it. The other two letters that had come by this morning's post were bills, or just possibly receipts for bills. In either case they were not of any particular interest. This letter might be.

A London postmark, typewritten address, a long, good quality envelope. Miss Marple slit it neatly with the paper knife she always kept handy on her tray. It was headed, Messrs Broadribb and Schuster, Solicitors and Notaries Public, with an address in Bloomsbury. It asked her, in suitable courteous and legal phraseology, to call upon them one day in the following week, at their office, to discuss a proposition that might be to her advantage. Thursday, the 24th was suggested. If that date was not convenient, perhaps she would let them know what date she would be likely to be in London in the near future. They added that they were the solicitors to the late Mr Rafiel, with whom they understood she had been acquainted.

Miss Marple frowned in some slight puzzlement. She got up rather more slowly than usual, thinking about the letter she had received. She was escorted downstairs by Cherry, who was meticulous in hanging about in the hall so as to make sure that Miss Marple did not come to grief walking by herself down the staircase, which was of the old-fashioned kind which turned a sharp corner in the middle of its run.

'You take very good care of me, Cherry,' said Miss Marple.

'Got to,' said Cherry, in her usual idiom. 'Good people are scarce.'

'Well, thank you for the compliment,' said Miss Marple, arriving safely with her last foot on the ground floor.

'Nothing the matter, is there?' asked Cherry. 'You look a bit rattled like, if you know what I mean.'

'No, nothing's the matter,' said Miss Marple. 'I had rather an unusual letter from a firm of solicitors.'

'Nobody is suing you for anything, are they?' said Cherry, who was inclined to regard solicitors' letters as invariably associated with disaster of some kind.

'Oh no, I don't think so,' said Miss Marple. 'Nothing of that kind. They just asked me to call upon them next week in London.'

'Perhaps you've been left a fortune,' said Cherry, hopefully.

'That, I think, is *very* unlikely,' said Miss Marple.

'Well, you never know,' said Cherry.

Settling herself in her chair, and taking her knitting out of its embroidered knitting bag, Miss Marple considered the possibility of Mr Rafiel having left her a fortune. It seemed even more unlikely than when Cherry had suggested it. Mr Rafiel, she thought, was not that kind of a man.

It was not possible for her to go on the date suggested. She was attending a meeting of the Women's Institute to discuss the raising of a sum for building a small additional couple of rooms. But she wrote, naming a day in the following week. In due course her letter was answered and the appointment definitely confirmed. She wondered what Messrs Broadribb and Schuster were like. The letter had been signed by J. R. Broadribb who was, apparently, the senior partner. It was possible, Miss Marple thought, that Mr Rafiel *might* have left her some small memoir or souvenir in his will. Perhaps some book on rare flowers that had been in his library and which he thought would please an old lady who was keen on gardening. Or perhaps a cameo brooch which had belonged to some great-aunt of his. She amused herself by these fancies. They were only fancies, she thought, because in either case it would merely be a case of the Executors – if these lawyers were the Executors – forwarding her by post any such object. They would not have wanted an interview.

'Oh well,' said Miss Marple, 'I shall know next Tuesday.'

II

'Wonder what she'll be like?' said Mr Broadribb to Mr Schuster, glancing at the clock as he did so.

'She's due in a quarter of an hour,' said Mr Schuster. 'Wonder if she'll be punctual?'

'Oh, I should think so. She's elderly, I gather, and much more punctilious than the young scatter-brains of today.'

'Fat or thin, I wonder?' said Mr Schuster.

Mr Broadribb shook his head.

'Didn't Rafiel ever describe her to you?' asked Mr Schuster.

'He was extraordinarily cagey in everthing he said about her.'

'The whole thing seems very odd to me,' said Mr Schuster. 'If we only knew a bit more about what it all meant . . .'

'It might be,' said Mr Broadribb thoughtfully, 'something to do with Michael.'

'What? After all these years? Couldn't be. What put that into your head? Did he mention –'

'No, he didn't mention anything. Gave me no clue at all as to what was in his mind. Just gave me instructions.'

'Think he was getting a bit eccentric and all that towards the end?'

'Not in the least. Mentally he was as brilliant as ever. His physical ill-health never affected his brain, anyway. In the last two months of his life he made an extra two hundred thousand pounds. Just like that.'

'He had a *flair*,' said Mr Schuster with due reverence. 'Certainly, he always had a flair.'

'A great financial brain,' said Mr Broadribb, also in a tone of reverence suitable to the sentiment. 'Not many like him, more's the pity.'

A buzzer went on the table. Mr Schuster picked up the receiver. A female voice said,

'Miss Jane Marple is here to see Mr Broadribb by appointment.'

Mr Schuster looked at his partner, raising an eyebrow for an affirmative or a negative. Mr Broadribb nodded.

'Show her up,' said Mr Schuster. And he added, 'Now we'll see.'

Miss Marple entered a room where a middle-aged gentleman with a thin, spare body and a long rather melancholy face rose to greet her. This apparently was Mr Broadribb, whose appearance somewhat contradicted his name. With him was a rather younger middle-aged gentleman of definitely more ample proportions. He had black hair, small keen eyes and a tendency to a double chin.

'My partner, Mr Schuster,' Mr Broadribb presented.

'I hope you didn't feel the stairs too much,' said Mr Schuster. 'Seventy if she is a day – nearer eighty perhaps,' he was thinking in his own mind.

'I always get a little breathless going upstairs.'

'An old-fashioned building this,' said Mr Broadribb apologetically. 'No lift. Ah well, we are a very long established firm and we don't go in for as many of the modern gadgets as perhaps our clients expect of us.'

'This room has very pleasant proportions,' said Miss Marple, politely.

She accepted the chair that Mr Broadribb drew forward for her. Mr Schuster, in an unobtrusive sort of way, left the room.

'I hope that chair is comfortable,' said Mr Broadribb. 'I'll pull that curtain slightly, shall I? You may feel the sun a little too much in your eyes.'

'Thank you,' said Miss Marple, gratefully.

She sat there, upright as was her habit. She wore a light tweed suit, a string of pearls and a small velvet toque. To himself Mr Broadribb was saying, 'The Provincial Lady. A good type. Fluffy old girl. May be scatty – may not. Quite a shrewd eye. I wonder where Rafiel came across her. Somebody's aunt, perhaps, up from the country?' While these thoughts passed through his head, he was making the kind of introductory small talk

19

relating to the weather, the unfortunate effects of late frosts early in the year and such other remarks as he considered suitable.

Miss Marple made the necessary responses and sat placidly awaiting the opening of preliminaries to the meeting.

'You will be wondering what all this is about,' said Mr Broadribb, shifting a few papers in front of him and giving her a suitable smile. 'You've heard, no doubt, of Mr Rafiel's death, or perhaps you saw it in the paper.'

'I saw it in the paper,' said Miss Marple.

'He was, I understand, a friend of yours.'

'I met him first just over a year ago,' said Miss Marple. 'In the West Indies,' she added.

'Ah. I remember. He went out there, I believe, for his health. It did him some good, perhaps, but he was already a very ill man, badly crippled, as you know.'

'Yes,' said Miss Marple.

'You knew him well?'

'No,' said Miss Marple, 'I would not say that. We were fellow visitors in a hotel. We had occasional conversations. I never saw him again after my return to England. I live very quietly in the country, you see, and I gather that he was completely absorbed in business.'

'He continued transacting business right up – well, I could almost say right up to the day of his death,' said Mr Broadribb. 'A very fine financial brain.'

'I am sure that was so,' said Miss Marple. 'I realized quite soon that he was a – well, a very remarkable character altogether.'

'I don't know if you have any idea – whether you've been given any idea at some time by Mr Rafiel – as to what this proposition is that I have been instructed to put up to you?'

'I cannot imagine,' said Miss Marple, 'what possible kind of proposition Mr Rafiel might have wanted to put up to me. It seems most unlikely.'

'He had a very high opinion of you.'

'That is kind of him, but hardly justified,' said Miss Marple. 'I am a very simple person.'

'As you no doubt realize, he died a very rich man. The provisions of his Will are on the whole fairly simple. He had already made dispositions of his fortune some time before his death. Trusts and other beneficiary arrangements.'

'That is, I believe, very usual procedure nowadays,' said Miss Marple, 'though I am not at all cognizant of financial matters myself.'

'The purpose of this appointment,' said Mr Broadribb, 'is that I am instructed to tell you that a sum of money has been laid aside to become yours absolutely at the end of one year, but conditional on your accepting a certain proposition, with which I am to make you acquainted.'

He took from the table in front of him a long envelope. It was sealed. He passed it across the table to her.

'It would be better, I think, that you should read for yourself of what this consists. There is no hurry. Take your time.'

Miss Marple took her time. She availed herself of a small paper knife which Mr Broadribb handed to her, slit up the envelope, took out the enclosure, one sheet of typewriting, and read it. She folded it up again, then re-read it and looked at Mr Broadribb.

'This is hardly very definite. Is there no more definite elucidation of any kind?'

'Not so far as I am concerned. I was to hand you this, and tell you the amount of the legacy. The sum in question is twenty thousand pounds free of legacy duty.'

Miss Marple sat looking at him. Surprise had rendered her speechless. Mr Broadribb said no more for the moment. He was watching her closely. There was no doubt of her surprise. It was obviously the last thing Miss Marple had expected to hear. Mr Broadribb wondered what her first words would be. She looked at him with the directness, the severity that one of his own aunts might have done. When she spoke it was almost accusingly.

'That is a very large sum of money,' said Miss Marple.

'Not quite so large as it used to be,' said Mr Broadribb (and just restrained himself from saying, 'Mere chicken feed nowadays').

'I must admit,' said Miss Marple, 'that I am amazed. Frankly, quite amazed.'

She picked up the document and read it carefully through again.

'I gather you know the terms of this?' she said.

'Yes. It was dictated to me personally by Mr Rafiel.'

'Did he not give you any explanation of it?'

'No, he did not.'

'You suggested, I suppose, that it might be better if he did,' said Miss Marple. There was a slight acidity in her voice now.

Mr Broadribb smiled faintly.

'You are quite right. That is what I did. I said that you might find it difficult to – oh, to understand exactly what he was driving at.'

'Very remarkable,' said Miss Marple.

'There is no need, of course,' said Mr Broadribb, 'for you to give me an answer now.'

'No,' said Miss Marple, 'I should have to reflect upon this.'

'It is, as you have pointed out, quite a substantial sum of money.'

21

'I am old,' said Miss Marple. 'Elderly, we say, but old is a better word. Definitely old. It is both possible and indeed probable that I might not live as long as a year to earn this money, in the rather doubtful case that I *was* able to earn it.'

'Money is not to be despised at any age,' said Mr Broadribb.

'I could benefit certain charities in which I have an interest,' said Miss Marple, 'and there are always people. People whom one wishes one could do a little something for but one's own funds do not admit of it. And then I will not pretend that there are not pleasures and desires – things that one has not been able to indulge in or to afford – I think Mr Rafiel knew quite well that to be able to do so, quite unexpectedly, would give an elderly person a great deal of pleasure.'

'Yes, indeed,' said Mr Broadribb. 'A cruise abroad, perhaps? One of these excellent *tours* as arranged nowadays. Theatres, concerts – the ability to replenish one's cellars.'

'My tastes would be a little more moderate than that,' said Miss Marple. 'Partridges,' she said thoughtfully, 'it is very difficult to get partridges nowadays, and they're very expensive. I should enjoy a partridge – a whole partridge – to myself, very much. A box of *marrons glacés* is an expensive taste which I cannot often gratify. Possibly a visit to the opera. It means a car to take one to Covent Garden and back, and the expense of a night in a hotel. But I must not indulge in idle chat,' she said. 'I will take this back with me and reflect upon it. Really, what on earth made Mr Rafiel – you have no idea *why* he should have suggested this particular proposition, and why he should think that I could be of service to him in any way? He must have known that it was over a year, nearly two years since he had seen me and that I might have got much more feeble than I have, and much more unable to exercise such small talents as I might have. He was taking a risk. There are other people surely much better qualified to undertake an investigation of this nature?'

'Frankly, one would think so,' said Mr Broadribb, 'but he selected *you*, Miss Marple. Forgive me if this is idle curiosity but have you had – oh, how shall I put it? – any connection with crime or the investigation of crime?'

'Strictly speaking I should say no,' said Miss Marple. 'Nothing professional, that is to say. I have never been a probation officer or indeed sat as a magistrate on a Bench or been connected in any way with a detective agency. To explain to you, Mr Broadribb, which I think it is only fair for me to do and which I think Mr Rafiel ought to have done, to explain it in any way all I can say is that during our stay in the West Indies, we both, Mr Rafiel and myself, had a certain connection with a crime that took place there. A rather unlikely and perplexing murder.'

'And you and Mr Rafiel solved it?'

'I should not put it quite like that,' said Miss Marple. 'Mr Rafiel, by the force of his personality, and I, by putting together one or two obvious indications that came to my notice, were successful in preventing a second murder just as it was about to take place. I could not have done it alone, I was physically far too feeble. Mr Rafiel could not have done it alone, he was a cripple. We acted as allies, however.'

'Just one other question I should like to ask you, Miss Marple. Does the word "Nemesis" mean anything to you?'

'*Nemesis*,' said Miss Marple. It was not a question. A very slow and unexpected smile dawned on her face. 'Yes,' she said, 'it does mean something to me. It meant something to me and it meant something to Mr Rafiel. I said it to him, and he was much amused by my describing myself by that name.'

Whatever Mr Broadribb had expected it was not that. He looked at Miss Marple with something of the same astonished surprise that Mr Rafiel had once felt in a bedroom by the Caribbean sea. A nice and quite intelligent old lady. But really – Nemesis!

'You feel the same, I am sure,' said Miss Marple.

She rose to her feet.

'If you should find or receive any further instructions in this matter, you will perhaps let me know, Mr Broadribb. It seems to me extraordinary that there should not be *something* of that kind. This leaves me entirely in the dark really as to what Mr Rafiel is asking me to do or try to do.'

'You are not acquainted with his family, his friends, his –'

'No. I told you. He was a fellow traveller in a foreign part of the world. We had a certain association as allies in a very mystifying matter. That is all.' As she was about to go to the door she turned suddenly and asked: 'He had a secretary, Mrs Esther Walters. Would it be infringing etiquette if I asked if Mr Rafiel left her fifty thousand pounds?'

'His bequest will appear in the press,' said Mr Broadribb. 'I can answer your question in the affirmative. Mrs Walter's name is now Mrs Anderson, by the way. She has re-married.'

'I am glad to hear that. She was a widow with one daughter, and she was a very adequate secretary, it appears. She understood Mr Rafiel very well. A nice woman. I am glad she has benefited.'

That evening, Miss Marple, sitting in her straight-backed chair, her feet stretched out to the fireplace where a small wood fire was burning owing to the sudden cold spell which, as is its habit, can always descend on England at any moment selected by itself, took once more from the long envelope the document delivered to her that morning. Still in a state of partial unbelief

23

she read, murmuring the words here and there below her breath as though to impress them on her mind,

'To Miss Jane Marple, resident in the village of St Mary Mead.

This will be delivered to you after my death by the good offices of my solicitor, James Broadribb. He is the man I employ for dealing with such legal matters as fall in the field of my private affairs, not my business activities. He is a sound and trustworthy lawyer. Like the majority of the human race he is susceptible to the sin of curiosity. I have not satisfied his curiosity. In some respects this matter will remain between you and myself. Our code word, my dear lady, is Nemesis. I don't think you will have forgotten in what place and in what circumstances you first spoke that word to me. In the course of my business activities over what is now quite a long life, I have learnt one thing about a man whom I wish to employ. He has to have a flair. A flair for the particular job I want him to do. It is not knowledge, it is not experience. The only word that describes it is *flair*. A natural gift for doing a certain thing.

You, my dear, if I may call you that, have a natural *flair* for justice, and that has led to your having a natural *flair* for crime. I want you to investigate a certain crime. I have ordered a certain sum to be placed so that if you accept this request and as a result of your investigation this crime is properly elucidated, the money will become yours absolutely. I have set aside a year for you to engage on this mission. You are not young, but you are, if I may say so, tough. I think I can trust a reasonable fate to keep you alive for a year at least.

I think the work involved will not be distasteful to you. You have a natural genius, I should say, for investigation. The necessary funds for what I may describe as working capital for making this investigation will be remitted to you during that period, whenever necessary. I offer this to you as an alternative to what may be your life at present.

I envisage you sitting in a chair, a chair that is agreeable and comfortable for whatever kind or form of rheumatism from which you may suffer. All persons of your age, I consider, are likely to suffer from some form of rheumatism. If this ailment affects your knees or your back, it will not be easy for you to get about much and you will spend your time mainly in knitting. I see you, as I saw you once one night as I rose from sleep disturbed by your urgency, in a cloud of pink wool.

I envisage you knitting more jackets, head scarves and a good many other things of which I do not know the name. If you prefer to continue knitting, that is your decision. If you prefer to serve the cause of justice, I hope that you may at least find it interesting.

Let justice roll down like waters.

And righteousness like an everlasting stream.
Amos.

CHAPTER 3

Miss Marple Takes Action

Miss Marple read this letter three times – then she laid it aside and sat frowning slightly while she considered the letter and its implications.

The first thought that came to her was that she was left with a surprising lack of definite information. Would there be any further information coming to her from Mr Broadribb? Almost certainly she felt that there would be no such thing. That would not have fitted in with Mr Rafiel's plan. Yet how on earth could Mr Rafiel expect her to do anything, to take any course of action in a matter about which she knew nothing. It was intriguing. After a few minutes more for consideration, she decided that Mr Rafiel had meant it to be intriguing. Her thoughts went back to him, for the brief time that she had known him. His disability, his bad temper, his flashes of brilliance, of occasional humour. He'd enjoy, she thought, teasing people. He had been enjoying, she felt, and this letter made it almost certain, baffling the natural curiosity of Mr Broadribb.

There was nothing in the letter he had written her to give her the slightest clue as to what this business was all about. It was no help to her whatsoever. Mr Rafiel, she thought, had very definitely not meant it to be of any help. He had had – how could she put it? – other ideas. All the same, she could not start out into the blue knowing nothing. This could almost be described as a crossword puzzle with no clues given. There would *have* to be clues. She would *have* to know what she was wanted to do, where she was wanted to go, whether she was to solve some problem sitting in her armchair and laying aside her knitting needles in order to concentrate better. Or did Mr Rafiel intend her to take a plane or a boat to the West Indies or to South America or to some other specially directed spot? She would either have to find out for herself what it was she was meant to do, or else she would have to receive definite instructions. He might think she had sufficient ingenuity to guess at things, to ask questions, to find out that way? No, she couldn't quite believe *that*.

'If he does think that,' said Miss Marple aloud, 'he's gaga. I mean, he was gaga before he died.'

But she didn't think Mr Rafiel would have been gaga.

'I shall receive instructions,' said Miss Marple. 'But what instructions and when?'

It was only then that it occurred to her suddenly that without noticing it she had definitely accepted the mandate. She spoke aloud again, addressing the atmosphere.

'I believe in eternal life,' said Miss Marple. 'I don't know exactly where you are, Mr Rafiel, but I have no doubt that you are *somewhere* – I will do my best to fulfil your wishes.'

II

It was three days later when Miss Marple wrote to Mr Broadribb. It was a very short letter, keeping strictly to the point.

'Dear Mr Broadribb,

I have considered the suggestion you made to me and I am letting you know that I have decided to accept the proposal made to me by the late Mr Rafiel. I shall do my best to comply with his wishes, though I am not at all assured of success. Indeed, I hardly see how it is possible for me to be successful. I have been given no direct instructions in his letter and have not been – I think the term is briefed – *in any way*. If you have any further communication you are holding for me which sets out definite instructions, I should be glad if you will send it to me, but I imagine that as you have not done so, that is not the case.

I presume that Mr Rafiel was of sound mind and disposition when he died? I think I am justified in asking if there has been recently in his life any criminal affair in which he might possibly have been interested, either in the course of his business or in his personal relations. Has he ever expressed to you any anger or dissatisfaction with some notable miscarriage of justice about which he felt strongly? If so, I think I should be justified in asking you to let me know about it. Has any relation or connection of his suffered some hardship, lately been the victim of some unjust dealing, or what might be considered as such?

I am sure you will understand my reasons for asking these things. Indeed, Mr Rafiel himself may have expected me to do so.'

III

Mr Broadribb showed this to Mr Schuster, who leaned back in his chair and whistled.

'She's going to take it on, is she? Sporting old bean,' he said. Then he added, 'I suppose she knows something of what it's all about, does she?'

'Apparently not,' said Mr Broadribb.

'I wish we did,' said Mr Schuster. 'He was an odd cuss.'

'A difficult man,' said Mr Broadribb.

'I haven't got the least idea,' said Mr Schuster, 'have you?'

'No, I haven't,' said Mr Broadribb. He added, 'He didn't want me to have, I suppose.'

'Well, he's made things a lot more difficult by doing that. I don't see the least chance that some old pussy from the country can interpret a dead man's brain and know what fantasy was plaguing him. You don't think he was leading her up the garden path? Having her on? Sort of joke, you know. Perhaps he thinks that she thinks she's the cat's whiskers at solving village problems, but he's going to teach her a sharp lesson –'

'No,' said Mr Broadribb, 'I don't quite think that. Rafiel wasn't that type of man.'

'He was a mischievous devil sometimes,' said Mr Schuster.

'Yes, but not – I think he was serious over this. *Something* was worrying him. In fact I'm quite sure something was worrying him.'

'And he didn't tell you what it was or give you the least idea?'

'No, he didn't.'

'Then how the devil can he expect –' Schuster broke off.

'He can't really have expected anything to come of this,' said Mr Broadribb. 'I mean, how is she going to set about it?'

'A practical joke, if you ask me.'

'Twenty thousand pounds is a lot of money.'

'Yes, but if he knows she can't do it?'

'No,' said Mr Broadribb. 'He wouldn't have been as unsporting as all that. He must think she's got a chance of doing or finding out whatever it is.'

'And what do we do?'

'Wait,' said Mr Broadribb. 'Wait and see what happens next. After all, there has to be some development.'

'Got some sealed orders somewhere, have you?'

'My dear Schuster,' said Mr Broadribb, 'Mr Rafiel had implicit trust in my discretion and in my ethical conduct as a lawyer. Those sealed instructions are to be opened only under certain circumstances, none of which has yet arisen.'

'And never will,' said Mr Schuster.

That ended the subject.

IV

Mr Broadribb and Mr Schuster were lucky in so much as they had a full professional life to lead. Miss Marple was not so fortunate. She knitted and she reflected and she also went out for walks, occasionally remonstrated with by Cherry for so doing.

'You know what the doctor said. You weren't to take too much exercise.'

'I walk very slowly,' said Miss Marple, 'and I am not doing anything. Digging, I mean, or weeding. I just – well, I just put one foot in front of the other and wonder about things.'

'What things?' asked Cherry, with some interest.

'I wish I knew,' said Miss Marple, and asked Cherry to bring her an extra scarf as there was a chilly wind.

'What's fidgeting her, that's what I would like to know,' said Cherry to her husband as she set before him a Chinese plate of rice and a concoction of kidneys. 'Chinese dinner,' she said.

Her husband nodded approval.

'You get a better cook every day,' he said.

'I'm worried about her,' said Cherry. 'I'm worried because she's worried a bit. She had a letter and it stirred her all up.'

'What she needs is to sit quiet,' said Cherry's husband. 'Sit quiet, take it easy, get herself new books from the library, get a friend or two to come and see her.'

'She's thinking out something,' said Cherry. 'Sort of plan. Thinking out how to tackle something, that's how I look at it.'

She broke off the conversation at this stage and took in the coffee tray and put it down by Miss Marple's side.

'Do you know a woman who lives in a new house somewhere here, she's called Mrs Hastings?' asked Miss Marple. 'And someone called Miss Bartlett, I think it is, who lives with her –'

'What – do you mean the house that's been all done up and repainted at the end of the village? The people there haven't been there very long. I don't know what their names are. Why do you want to know? They're not very interesting. At least I shouldn't say they were.'

'Are they related?' asked Miss Marple.

'No. Just friends, I think.'

'I wonder why –' said Miss Marple, and broke off.

'You wondered why what?'

'Nothing,' said Miss Marple. 'Clear my little hand desk, will you, and give me my pen and the notepaper. I'm going to write a letter.'

'Who to?' said Cherry, with the natural curiosity of her kind.

'To a clergyman's sister,' said Miss Marple. 'His name is Canon Prescott.'

'That's the one you met abroad, in the West Indies, isn't it? You showed me his photo in your album.'

29

'Yes.'

'Not feeling bad, are you? Wanting to write to a clergyman and all that?'

'I'm feeling extremely well,' said Miss Marple, 'and I am anxious to get busy on something. It's just possible Miss Prescott might help.'

'Dear Miss Prescott,' wrote Miss Marple, 'I hope you have not forgotten me. I met you and your brother in the West Indies, if you remember, at St Honoré. I hope the dear Canon is well and did not suffer much with his asthma in the cold weather last winter.

I am writing to ask you if you can possibly let me have the address of Mrs Walters – Esther Walters – whom you may remember from the Caribbean days. She was a secretary to Mr Rafiel. She did give me her address at the time, but unfortunately I have mislaid it. I was anxious to write to her as I have some horticultural information which she asked me about but which I was not able to tell her at the time. I heard in a round-about way the other day that she had married again, but I don't think my informant was very certain of these facts. Perhaps you know more about her than I do.

I hope this is not troubling you too much. With kind regards to your brother and best wishes to yourself,

Yours sincerely,

Jane Marple.'

Miss Marple felt better when she had despatched this missive.

'At least,' she said, 'I've started *doing* something. Not that I hope much from this, but still it might help.'

Miss Prescott answered the letter almost by return of post. She was a most efficient woman. She wrote a pleasant letter and enclosed the address in question.

'I have not heard anything directly about Esther Walters,' she said, 'but like you I heard from a friend that they had seen a notice of her re-marriage. Her name now is, I believe, Mrs Alderson or Anderson. Her address is Winslow Lodge, near Alton, Hants. My brother sends his best wishes to you. It is sad that we live so far apart. We in the north of England and you south of London. I hope that we may meet on some occasion in the future.

Yours sincerely,

Joan Prescott.'

'Winslow Lodge, Alton,' said Miss Marple, writing it down. 'Not so far away from here, really. No. Not so far away. I could – I don't know what would be the best method – possibly one of Inch's taxis. Slightly extravagant, but if anything results from it, it could be charged as expenses quite legitimately. Now do I write to her beforehand or do I leave it to chance? I think it would be better really, to leave it to chance. Poor Esther. She could hardly remember me with any affection or kindliness.'

Miss Marple lost herself in a train of thought that arose from her thoughts. It was quite possible that her actions in the Caribbean had saved Esther Walters from being murdered in the not far distant future. At any rate, that was Miss Marple's belief, but probably Esther Walters had not believed any such thing. 'A nice woman,' said Miss Marple, uttering the words in a soft tone aloud, 'a very nice woman. The kind that would so easily marry a bad lot. In fact, the sort of woman that would marry a murderer if she were ever given half a chance. I still consider,' continued Miss Marple thoughtfully, sinking her voice still lower, 'that I probably saved her life. In fact, I am almost sure of it, but I don't think she would agree with that point of view. She probably dislikes me very much. Which makes it more difficult to use her as a source of information. Still, one can but try. It's better than sitting here, waiting, waiting, waiting.'

Was Mr Rafiel perhaps making fun of her when he had written that letter? He was not always a particularly kindly man – he could be very careless of people's feelings.

'Anyway,' said Miss Marple, glancing at the clock and deciding that she would have an early night in bed, 'when one thinks of things just before going to sleep, quite often ideas come. It may work out that way.'

'Sleep well?' asked Cherry, as she put down an early morning tea tray on the table at Miss Marple's elbow.

'I had a curious dream,' said Miss Marple.

'Nightmare?'

'No, no, nothing of that kind. I was talking to someone, not anyone I knew very well. Just talking. Then when I looked, I saw it wasn't that person at all I was talking to. It was somebody else. Very odd.'

'Bit of a mix up,' said Cherry, helpfully.

'It just reminded me of something,' said Miss Marple, 'or rather of someone I once knew. Order Inch for me, will you? To come here about half past eleven.'

Inch was part of Miss Marple's past. Originally the proprietor of a cab, Mr Inch had died, been succeeded by his son 'Young Inch,' then aged forty-four, who had turned the family business into a garage and acquired two aged cars. On his decease the garage acquired a new owner. There had been since then Pip's Cars, James's Taxis and Arthur's Car Hire – old inhabitants still spoke of Inch.

'Not going to London, are you?'

'No, I'm not going to London. I shall have lunch perhaps in Haslemere.'

'Now what are you up to now?' said Cherry, looking at her suspiciously.

'Endeavouring to meet someone by accident and make it seem purely natural,' said Miss Marple. 'Not really very easy, but I hope that I can manage it.'

At half past eleven the taxi waited. Miss Marple instructed Cherry.

'Ring up this number, will you, Cherry? Ask if Mrs Anderson is at home. If Mrs Anderson answers or if she is going to come to the telephone, say a Mr Broadribb wants to speak to her. You,' said Miss Marple, 'are Mr Broadribb's secretary. If she's out, find out what time she will be in.'

'And if she is in and I get her?'

'Ask what day she could arrange to meet Mr Broadribb at his office in London next week. When she tells you, make a note of it and ring off.'

'The things you think of! Why all this? Why do you want *me* to do it?'

'Memory is a curious thing,' said Miss Marple. 'Sometimes one remembers a voice even if one hasn't heard it for over a year.'

'Well, Mrs What's-a-name won't have heard mine at any time, will she?'

'No,' said Miss Marple. 'That is why *you* are making the call.'

Cherry fulfilled her instruction. Mrs Anderson was out shopping, she learned, but would be in for lunch and all the afternoon.

'Well, that makes things easier,' said Miss Marple. 'Is Inch here? Ah yes. Good morning, Edward,' she said, to the present driver of Arthur's taxis whose actual name was George. 'Now this is where I want you to go. It ought not to take, I think, more than an hour and a half.'

The expedition set off.

CHAPTER 4

Esther Walters

Esther Anderson came out of the Supermarket and went towards where she had parked her car. Parking grew more difficult every day, she thought. She collided with somebody, an elderly woman limping a little who was walking towards her. She apologized, and the other woman made an exclamation.

'Why, indeed, it's – surely – it's Mrs Walters, isn't it? Esther Walters? You don't remember me, I expect. Jane Marple. We met in the hotel in St Honoré, oh – quite a long time ago. A year and half.'

'Miss Marple? So it is, of course. Fancy seeing you!'

'How very nice to see you. I am lunching with some friends near here but I have to pass back through Alton later. Will you be at home this afternoon? I should so like to have a nice chat with you. It's so nice to see an old friend.'

'Yes, of course. Any time after 3 o'clock.'

The arrangement was ratified.

'Old Jane Marple,' said Esther Anderson, smiling to herself. 'Fancy her turning up. I thought she'd died a long time ago.'

Miss Marple rang the bell of Winslow Lodge at 3.30 precisely. Esther opened the door to her and brought her in.

Miss Marple sat down in the chair indicated to her, fluttering a little in the restless manner that she adopted when slightly flustered. Or at any rate, when she was seeming to be slightly flustered. In this case it was misleading, since things had happened exactly as she had hoped they would happen.

'It's so nice to see you,' she said to Esther. 'So very nice to see you again. You know, I do think things are so very odd in this world. You hope you'll meet people again and you're quite sure you will. And then time passes and suddenly it's all such a surprise.'

'And then,' said Esther, 'one says it's a small world, doesn't one?'

'Yes, indeed, and I think there *is* something in that. I mean it does *seem* a very large world and the West Indies are such a very long way away from England. Well, I mean, of course I might have met you anywhere. In London or at Harrods. On a railway station or in a bus. There are so many possibilities.'

'Yes, there are a lot of possibilities,' said Esther. 'I certainly shouldn't have expected to meet you just here because this isn't really quite your part of the world, is it?'

'No. No, it isn't. Not that you're really so very far from St Mary Mead where I live. Actually, I think it's only about twenty-five miles. But twenty-five miles in the country, when one hasn't got a car – and of course I couldn't afford a car, and anyway, I mean, I can't drive a car – so it wouldn't be much to the point, so one really only does see one's neighbours on the bus route, or else go by a taxi from the village.'

'You're looking wonderfully well,' said Esther.

'I was just going to say *you* were looking wonderfully well, my dear. I had no idea you lived in this part of the world.'

'I have only done so for a short time. Since my marriage, actually.'

'Oh, I didn't know. How interesting. I suppose I must have missed it. I always do look down the marriages.'

'I've been married four or five months,' said Esther. 'My name is Anderson now.'

'Mrs Anderson,' said Miss Marple. 'Yes. I must try and remember that. And your husband?'

It would be unnatural, she thought, if she did not ask about the husband. Old maids were notoriously inquisitive.

'He is an engineer,' said Esther. 'He runs the Time and Motion Branch. He is,' she hesitated – 'a little younger than I am.'

'Much better,' said Miss Marple immediately. 'Oh, much better, my dear. In these days men age so much quicker than women. I known it used not to be said so, but actually it's true. I mean they get more things the matter with them. I think, perhaps, they worry and work too much. And then they get high blood pressure or low blood pressure or sometimes a little heart trouble. They're rather prone to gastric ulcers, too. I don't think *we* worry so much, you know. I think we're a tougher sex.'

'Perhaps we are,' said Esther.

She smiled now at Miss Marple, and Miss Marple felt reassured. The last time she had seen Esther, Esther had looked as though she hated her and probably she had hated her at that moment. But now, well now, perhaps, she might even feel slightly grateful. She might have realized that she, herself, might even have been under a stone slab in a respectable churchyard, instead of living a presumably happy life with Mr Anderson.

'You look very well,' she said, 'and very gay.'

'So do you, Miss Marple.'

'Well, of course, I am rather older now. And one has so many ailments. I mean, not desperate ones, nothing of that kind, but I mean one has always some kind of rheumatism or some kind of ache and pain somewhere. One's feet are not what one would like feet to be. And there's usually one's back or a shoulder or painful hands. Oh, dear, one shouldn't talk about these things. What a very nice house you have.'

'Yes, we haven't been in it very long. We moved in about four

34

months ago.'

Miss Marple looked round. She had rather thought that that was the case. She thought, too, that when they had moved in they had moved in on quite a handsome scale. The furniture was expensive, it was comfortable, comfortable and just this side of luxury. Good curtains, good covers, no particular artistic taste displayed, but then she would not have expected that. She thought she knew the reason for this appearance of prosperity. She thought it had come about on the strength of the late Mr Rafiel's handsome legacy to Esther. She was glad to think that Mr Rafiel had not changed his mind.

'I expect you saw the notice of Mr Rafiel's death,' said Esther, speaking almost as if she knew what was in Miss Marple's mind.

'Yes. Yes, indeed I did. It was about a month ago now, wasn't it? I was so sorry. Very distressed really, although, well, I suppose one knew – he almost admitted it himself, didn't he? He hinted several times that it wouldn't be very long. I think he was quite a brave man about it all, don't you?'

'Yes, he was a very brave man, and a very kind one really,' said Esther. 'He told me, you know, when I first worked for him, that he was going to give me a very good salary but that I would have to save out of it because I needn't expect to have anything more from him. Well, I certainly didn't expect to have *anything* more from him. He was very much a man of his word, wasn't he? But apparently he changed his mind.'

'Yes,' said Miss Marple. 'Yes. I am very glad of that. I thought perhaps – not that he, of course, said anything – but I wondered.'

'He left me a very big legacy,' said Esther. 'A surprisingly large sum of money. It came as a very great surprise. I could hardly believe it at first.'

'I think he wanted it to be a surprise to you. I think he was perhaps that kind of man,' said Miss Marple. She added: 'Did he leave anything to – oh, what was his name? – the man attendant, the nurse-attendant?'

'Oh, you mean Jackson? No, he didn't leave anything to Jackson, but I believe he made him some handsome presents in the last year.'

'Have you even seen anything more of Jackson?'

'No. No, I don't think I've met him once since the time out in the islands. He didn't stay with Mr Rafiel after they got back to England. I think he went to Lord somebody who lives in Jersey or Guernsey.'

'I would like to have seen Mr Rafiel again,' said Miss Marple. 'It seems odd after we'd all been mixed up so. He and you and I and some others. And then, later, when I'd come home, when six months had passed – it occurred to me one day how closely associated we had been in our time of stress, and yet how little I really knew about Mr Rafiel. I was thinking it only the other day, after I'd seen the notice of his death. I wished I could know a little more. Where he was born, you know, and his parents. What they were like. Whether he had any children, or nephews or cousins or any family. I would so like to know.'

Esther Anderson smiled slightly. She looked at Miss Marple and her expression seemed to say 'Yes, I'm sure you always want to know everything of that kind about everyone you meet.' But she merely said:

'No, there was really only one thing that everyone *did* know about him.'

'That he was very rich,' said Miss Marple immediately. 'That's what you mean, isn't it? When you know that someone is very rich, somehow, well, you don't ask any more. I mean you don't ask to *know* any more. You say "He is very rich" or you say "He is enormously rich," and your voice just goes down a little because it's so impressive, isn't it, when you meet someone who *is* immensely rich.'

Esther laughed slightly.

'He wasn't married, was he?' asked Miss Marple. 'He never mentioned a wife.'

'He lost his wife many years ago. Quite soon after they were married, I believe. I believe she was much younger than he was – I think she died of cancer. Very sad.'

'Had he children?'

'Oh yes, two daughters, and a son. One daughter is married and lives in America. The other daughter died young, I believe. I met the American one once. She wasn't at all like her father. Rather a quiet, depressed looking young woman.' She added, 'Mr Rafiel never spoke about the son. I rather think that there had been trouble there. A scandal or something of that kind. I believe he died some years ago. Anyway – his father never mentioned him.'

'Oh dear. That was very sad.'

'I think it happened quite a long time ago. I believe he took off for somewhere or other abroad and never came back – died out there, wherever it was.'

'Was Mr Rafiel very upset about it?'

'One wouldn't know with him,' said Esther. 'He was the kind of man who would always decide to cut his losses. If his son turned out to be unsatisfactory, a burden instead of a blessing, I think he would just shrug the whole thing off. Do what was necessary perhaps in the way of sending him money for support, but never thinking of him again.'

'One wonders,' said Miss Marple. 'He never spoke of him or said anything?'

'If you remember, he was a man who never said anything much about

36

personal feelings or his own life.'

'No. No, of course not. But I thought perhaps, you having been – well, his secretary for so many years, that he might have confided any troubles to you.'

'He was not a man for confiding troubles,' said Esther. 'If he had any, which I rather doubt. He was wedded to his business, one might say. He was father to his business and his business was the only kind of son or daughter that he had that mattered, I think. He enjoyed it all, investment, making money. Business coups –'

'Call no man happy until he is dead –' murmured Miss Marple, repeating the words in the manner of one pronouncing them as a kind of slogan, which indeed they appeared to be in these days, or so she would have said.

'So there was nothing especially worrying him, was there, before his death?'

'No. Why should you think so?' Esther sounded surprised.

'Well, I didn't actually think so,' said Miss Marple, 'I just wondered because things do worry people more when they are – I won't say getting old – because he really wasn't old, but I mean things worry you more when you are laid up and can't do as much as you did and have to take things easy. Then worries just come into your mind and make themselves *felt*.'

'Yes, I know what you mean,' said Esther. 'But I don't think Mr Rafiel was like that. Anyway,' she added, 'I ceased being his secretary some time ago. Two or three months after I met Edmund.'

'Ah yes. Your husband. Mr Rafiel must have been very upset at losing you.'

'Oh I don't think so,' said Esther lightly. 'He was not one who would be upset over that sort of thing. He'd immediately get another secretary – which he did. And then if she didn't suit him he'd just get rid of her with a kindly golden handshake and get somebody else, till he found somebody who suited him. He was an intensely sensible man always.'

'Yes. Yes, I can see that. Though he could lose his temper very easily.'

'Oh, he enjoyed losing his temper,' said Esther. 'It made a bit of drama for him, I think.'

'Drama,' said Miss Marple thoughtfully. 'Do you think – I have often wondered – do you think that Mr Rafiel had any particular interest in criminology, the study of it, I mean? He – well, I don't know . . .'

'You mean because of what happened in the Caribbean?' Esther's voice had gone suddenly hard.

Miss Marple felt doubtful of going on, and yet she must somehow or other try and get a little helpful knowledge.

'Well, no, not because of that, but afterwards, perhaps, he wondered about the psychology of these things. Or he got interested in the cases where justice had not been administered properly or – oh, well . . .'

She sounded more scatty every minute.

'Why should he take the least interest in anything of that kind? And don't let's talk about that horrible business in St Honoré.'

'Oh no, I think you are *quite* right. I'm sure I'm very sorry. I was just thinking of some of the things that Mr Rafiel sometimes *said*. Queer turns of phrase, sometimes, and I just wondered if he had any theories you know . . . about the causes of crime?'

'His interests were always entirely financial,' said Esther shortly. 'A really clever swindle of a criminal kind might have interested him, nothing else –'

She was looking coldly still at Miss Marple.

'I am sorry,' said Miss Marple apologetically. 'I – I shouldn't have talked about distressing matters that are fortunately past. And I must be getting on my way,' she added. 'I have got my train to catch and I shall only just have time. Oh dear, what did I do with my bag – oh yes, here it is.'

She collected her bag, umbrella and a few other things, fussing away until the tension had slightly abated. As she went out of the door, she turned to Esther who was urging her to stay and have a cup of tea.

'No thank you, my dear, I'm so short of time. I'm very pleased to have seen you again and I do offer my best congratulations and hopes for a very happy life. I don't suppose you will be taking up any post again now, will you?'

'Oh, some people do. They find it interesting, they say. They get bored when they have nothing to do. But I think I shall rather enjoy living a life of leisure. I shall enjoy my legacy, too, that Mr Rafiel left me. It was very kind of him and I think he'd want me – well, to enjoy it even if I spent it in what he'd think of perhaps as a rather silly, female way! Expensive clothes and a new hairdo and all that. He'd have thought that sort of thing very silly.' She added suddenly, 'I was fond of him, you know. Yes, I was quite fond of him. I think it was because he was a sort of challenge to me. He was difficult to get on with, and therefore I enjoyed managing it.'

'And managing him?'

'Well, not quite managing him, but perhaps a little more than he knew I was.'

Miss Marple trotted away down the road. She looked back once and waved her hand – Esther Anderson was still standing on the doorstep, and she waved back cheerfully.

'I thought this might have been something to do with her or something she knew about,' said Miss Marple to herself. 'I think I'm wrong. No, I don't think she's concerned in this business, whatever it is, *in any way*. Oh dear, I feel Mr Rafiel expected me to be much *cleverer* than I am being. I think he expected me to put things together – but what things? And what do I do next, I wonder?' She shook her head.

She had to think over things very carefully. This business had been, as it were, left to her. Left to her to refuse, to accept, to understand what it was all about? Or *not* understand anything, but to go forward and hope that some kind of guidance might be given to her. Occasionally she closed her eyes and tried to picture Mr Rafiel's face. Sitting in the garden of the hotel in the West Indies, in his tropical suit; his bad-tempered corrugated face, his flashes of occasional humour. What she really wanted to know was what had been in his mind when he worked up this scheme, when he set out to bring it about. To lure her into accepting it, to persuade her to accept it, to – well, perhaps one should say – to bully her into accepting it. The third was much the most likely, knowing Mr Rafiel. And yet, take it that he had wanted something done and he had chosen her, settled upon her to do it. Why? Because she had suddenly come into his mind? But why should she have come into his mind?

She thought back to Mr Rafiel and the things that had occurred at St Honoré. Had perhaps the problem he had been considering at the time of his death sent his mind back to that visit to the West Indies? Was it in some way connected with someone who had been out there, who had taken part or been an onlooker there and was that what had put Miss Marple into his mind? Was there some link or some connection? If not, why should he suddenly think of her? What was it about her that could make her useful to him, in any way at all? She was an elderly, rather scatty, quite ordinary person, physically not very strong, mentally not nearly as alert as she used to be. What had been her special qualifications, if any? She couldn't think of any. Could it possibly have been a bit of *fun* on Mr Rafiel's part? Even if Mr Rafiel had been on the point of death he might have wanted to have some kind of joke that suited his peculiar sense of humour.

She could not deny that Mr Rafiel could quite possibly wish to have a joke, even on his death-bed. Some ironical humour of his might be satisfied.

'I must,' said Miss Marple to herself firmly, 'I *must* have some qualification for something.' After all, since Mr Rafiel was no longer in this world, he could not enjoy his joke at first hand. What qualifications *had* she got? 'What qualities have I got that could be useful to anyone for *anything*?' said Miss Marple.

She considered herself with proper humility. She was inquisitive, she asked questions, she was the sort of age and type that could be expected to ask questions. That was one point, a possible point. You could send a private detective round to ask questions, or some psychological investigator, but it was true that you could much more easily send an elderly lady with a habit of snooping and being inquisitive, of talking too much, of wanting to find out about things, and it would seem perfectly natural.

'An old pussy,' said Miss Marple to herself. 'Yes, I can see I'm quite recognizable as an old pussy. There are so many old pussies, and they're all so much alike. And, of course, yes, I'm very ordinary. An ordinary rather scatty old lady. And that of course is very good *camouflage*. Dear me, I wonder if I'm thinking on the right lines. I do, sometimes, know what people are *like*. I mean, I know what people are like, because they remind me of certain other people I have known. So I know some of their faults and some of their virtues. I know what kind of people *they* are. There's that.'

She thought again of St Honoré and the Hotel of the Golden Palm. She had made one attempt to enquire into the possibilities of a link, by her visit to Esther Walters. That had been definitely non-productive, Miss Marple decided. There didn't seem any further link leading from there. Nothing that would tie up with his request that Miss Marple should busy herself with something, the nature of which she still had no idea!

'Dear me,' said Miss Marple, 'What a tiresome man you are, Mr Rafiel!' She said it aloud and there was definite reproach in her voice.

Later, however, as she climbed into bed and applied her cosy hot water bottle to the most painful portion of her rheumatic back, she spoke again – in what might be taken as a semi-apology.

'I've done the best I could,' she said.

She spoke aloud with the air of addressing one who might easily be in the room. It is true he might be anywhere, but even then there might be some telepathic or telephonic communication, and if so, she was going to speak definitely and to the point.

'I've done all I could. The best according to my limitations, and I must now leave it up to *you*.'

With that she settled herself more comfortably, stretched out a hand, switched off the electric light, and went to sleep.

CHAPTER 5

Instructions From Beyond

It was some three or four days later that a communication arrived by the second post. Miss Marple picked up the letter, did what she usually did to letters, turned it over, looked at the stamp, looked at the handwriting, decided that it wasn't a bill and opened it. It was typewritten.

'Dear Miss Marple,

By the time you read this I shall be dead and also buried. *Not* cremated, I am glad to think. It has always seemed to me unlikely that one would manage to rise up from one's handsome bronze vase full of ashes and haunt anyone if one wanted so to do! Whereas the idea of rising from one's grave and haunting anyone is quite possible. Shall I want to do that? Who knows. I might even want to communicate with *you*.

By now my solicitors will have communicated with you and will have put a certain proposition before you. I hope you will have accepted it. If you have not accepted it, don't feel in the least remorseful. It will be your choice.

This should reach you, if my solicitors have done what they were told to do, and if the posts have done the duty they are expected to perform, on the 11th of the month. In two days from now you will receive a communication from a travel bureau in London. I hope what it proposes will not be distateful to you. I needn't say more. I want you to have an open mind. Take care of yourself. I think you will manage to do that. You are a very shrewd person. The best of luck and may your guardian angel be at your side looking after you. You may need one.

Your affectionate friend,

J.B. Rafiel.'

'Two days!' said Miss Marple.

She found it difficult to pass the time. The Post Office did their duty and so did the Famous Houses and Gardens of Great Britain.

'Dear Miss Jane Marple,

Obeying instructions given us by the late Mr Rafiel we send you particulars of our Tour No 37 of the Famous Houses and Gardens of Great Britain which starts from London on Thursday next – the 17th.

If it should be possible for you to come to our office in London, our

Mrs Sandbourne who is to accompany the tour, will be very glad to give you all particulars and to answer all questions.

Our tours last for a period of two to three weeks. This particular tour, Mr Rafiel thinks, will be particularly acceptable to you as it will visit a part of England which as far as he knows you have not yet visited, and takes in some really very attractive scenery and gardens. He has arranged for you to have the best accommodation and all the luxury available that we can provide.

Perhaps you will let us know which day would suit you to visit our office in Berkeley Street?'

Miss Marple folded up the letter, put it in her bag, noted the telephone number, thought of a few friends whom she knew, rang up two of them, one of whom had been for tours with the Famous Houses and Gardens, and spoke highly of them, the other one had not been personally on a tour but had friends who had travelled with this particular firm and who said everything was very well done, though rather expensive, and not too exhausting for the elderly. She then rang up the Berkeley Street number and said she would call upon them on the following Tuesday.

The next day she spoke to Cherry on the subject.

'I may be going away, Cherry,' she said. 'On a Tour,'

'A Tour?' said Cherry, 'One of these travel tours? You mean a package tour abroad?'

'Not abroad. In this country,' said Miss Marple. 'Mainly visiting historic buildings and gardens.'

'Do you think it's all right to do that at your age? These things can be very tiring, you know. You have to walk miles sometimes.'

'My health is really very good,' said Miss Marple, 'and I have always heard that in these tours they are careful to provide restful intervals for such people who are not particularly strong.'

'Well, be careful of yourself, that's all,' said Cherry. 'We don't want you falling down with a heart attack, even if you are looking at a particularly sumptuous fountain or something. Your're a bit old, you know, to do this sort of thing. Excuse me saying it, it sounds rude, but I don't like to think of you passing out because you've done too much or anything like that.'

'I can take care of myself,' said Miss Marple, with some dignity.

'All right, but you just be careful,' said Cherry.

Miss Marple packed a suitcase bag, went to London, booked a room at a modest hotel – ('Ah, Bertram's Hotel,' she thought in her mind, 'what a wonderful hotel *that* was! Oh dear, I must forget all those things, the St George is quite a pleasant place.') At the appointed time she was at Berkeley

Street and was shown in to the office where a pleasant woman of about thirty-five rose to meet her, explained that her name was Mrs Sandbourne and that she would be in personal charge of this particular tour.

'Am I to understand,' said Miss Marple, 'that this trip is in my case –' she hesitated.

Mrs Sandbourne, sensing slight embarrassment, said:

'Oh yes, I ought to have explained perhaps better in the letter we sent you. Mr Rafiel has paid all expenses.'

'You *do* know that he is dead?' said Miss Marple.

'Oh yes, but this was arranged before his death. He mentioned that he was in ill health but wanted to provide a treat for a very old friend of his who had not had the opportunity of travelling as much as she could have wished.'

II

Two days later, Miss Marple, carrying her small over-night bag, her new and smart suitcase surrendered to the driver, had boarded a most comfortable and luxurious coach which was taking a north-westerly route out of London; she was studying the passenger list which was attached to the inside of a handsome brochure giving details of the daily itinerary of the coach, and various information as to hotels and meals, places to be seen, and occasional alternatives on some days which, although the fact was not stressed, actually intimated that one choice of itinerary was for the young and active and that the other choice would be peculiarly suitable for the elderly, those whose feet hurt them, who suffered from arthritis or rheumatism and who would prefer to sit about and *not* walk long distances or up too many hills. It was all very tactful and well arranged.

Miss Marple read the passenger list and surveyed her fellow passengers. There was no difficulty about doing this because the other fellow passengers were doing much the same themselves. They were surveying her, amongst others, but nobody as far as Miss Marple could notice was taking any particular interest in her.

> Mrs Riseley-Porter
> Miss Joanna Crawford
> Colonel and Mrs Walker
> Mr and Mrs H. T. Butler
> Miss Elizabeth Temple
> Professor Wanstead
> Mr Richard Jameson

43

Miss Lumley
Miss Bentham
Mr Casper
Miss Cooke
Miss Barrow
Mr Emlyn Price
Miss Jane Marple

There were four elderly ladies. Miss Marple took note of them first, as it were, to clear them out of the way. Two were travelling together. Miss Marple put them down as about seventy. They could roughly be considered as contemporaries of her own. One of them was very definitely the complaining type, one who would want to have seats at the front of the coach or else would make a point of having them at the back of the coach. Would wish to sit on the sunny side or could only bear to sit on the shady side. Who would want more fresh air, or less fresh air. They had with them travelling rugs and knitted scarves and quite an assortment of guide books. They were slightly crippled and often in pain from feet or backs or knees but were nevertheless of those whom age and ailments could not prevent from enjoying life while they still had it. Old pussies, but definitely *not* stay-at-home old pussies. Miss Marple made an entry in the little book she carried.

Fifteen passengers not including herself, or Mrs Sandbourne. And since she had been sent on this coach tour, one at least of those fifteen passengers must be of importance in some way. Either as a source of information or someone concerned with the law or a law case, or it might even be a murderer. A murderer who might have already killed or one who might be preparing to kill. Anything was possible, Miss Marple thought, with Mr Rafiel! Anyway, she must make notes of these people.

On the right-hand page of her notebook, she would note down who might be worthy of attention from Mr Rafiel's point of view and on the left she would note down or cross off those who could only be of any interest if they could produce some useful information for her. Information, it might be, that they did not even know they possessed. Or rather that even if they possessed it, they did not know it could possibly be useful to her or to Mr Rafiel or to the law or to Justice with a capital 'J'. At the back of her little book, she might this evening make a note or two as to whether anyone had reminded her of characters she had known in the past at St Mary Mead and other places. Any similarities might make a useful pointer. It had done so on other occasions.

The other two elderly ladies were apparently separate travellers. Both of

44

them were about sixty. One was a well preserved, well-dressed woman of obvious social importance in her own mind, but probably in other people's minds as well. Her voice was loud and dictatorial. She appeared to have in tow a niece, a girl of about eighteen or nineteen who addressed her as Aunt Geraldine. The niece, Miss Marple noted, was obviously well accustomed to coping with Aunt Geraldine's bossiness. She was a competent girl as well as being an attractive one.

Across the aisle from Miss Marple was a big man with square shoulders and a clumsy-looking body, looking as though he had been carelessly assembled by an ambitious child out of chunky bricks. His face looked as though nature had planned it to be round but the face had rebelled at this and decided to achieve a square effect by developing a powerful jaw. He had a thick head of greyish hair and enormous bushy eyebrows which moved up and down to give point to what he was saying. His remarks seemed mainly to come out in a series of barks as though he was a talkative sheepdog. He shared his seat with a tall dark foreigner who moved restlessly in his seat and gesticulated freely. He spoke a most peculiar English, making occasional remarks in French and German. The bulky man seemed quite capable of meeting these onslaughts of foreign language, and shifted obligingly to either French or German. Taking a quick glance at them again, Miss Marple decided that the bushy eyebrows must be Professor Wanstead and the excitable foreigner was Mr Caspar.

She wondered what it was they were discussing with such animation, but was baffled by the rapidity and force of Mr Caspar's delivery.

The seat in front of them was occupied by the other woman of about sixty, a tall woman, possibly over sixty, but a woman who would have stood out in a crowd anywhere. She was still a very handsome woman with dark grey hair coiled high on her head, drawn back from a fine forehead. She had a low, clear, incisive voice. A personality, Miss Marple thought. Someone! Yes, she was decidedly someone. 'Reminds me,' she thought to herself, 'of Dame Emily Waldron.' Dame Emily Waldron had been the Principal of an Oxford College and a notable scientist, and Miss Marple, having once met her in her nephew's company, had never quite forgotten her.

Miss Marple resumed her survey of the passengers. There were two married couples, one American, middle-aged, amiable, a talkative wife and a placidly agreeing husband. They were obviously dedicated travellers and sightseers. There was also an English middle-aged couple whom Miss Marple noted down without hesitation as a retired military man and wife. She ticked them off from the list as Colonel and Mrs Walker.

In the seat behind her was a tall, thin man of about thirty with a highly technical vocabulary, clearly an architect. There were also two middle-aged ladies travelling together rather further up the coach. They were discussing the brochure and deciding what the tour was going to hold for them in the way of attractions. One was dark and thin and the other was fair and sturdily built and the latter's face seemed faintly familiar to Miss Marple. She wondered where she had seen or met her before. However, she could not recall the occasion to mind. Possibly someone she had met at a cocktail party or sat opposite to in a train. There was nothing very special about her to remember.

Only one more passenger remained for her to appraise, and this was a young man, possibly of about nineteen or twenty. He wore the appropriate clothes for his age and sex; tight black jeans, a polo necked purple sweater and his head was an outsize rich mop of non-disciplined black hair. He was looking with an air of interest at the bossy woman's niece, and the bossy woman's niece also, Miss Marple thought, was looking with some interest at him. In spite of the preponderance of elderly pussies and middle-aged females there were, at any rate, two *young* people among the passengers.

They stopped for lunch at a pleasant riverside hotel, and the afternoon sight-seeing was given over to Blenheim. Miss Marple had already visited Blenheim twice before, so she saved her feet by limiting the amount of sight-seeing indoors and coming fairly soon to the enjoyment of the gardens and the beautiful view.

By the time they arrived at the hotel where they were to stay the night, the passengers were getting to know each other. The efficient Mrs Sandbourne, still brisk and unwearied by her duties in directing the sight-seeing, did her part very well; creating little groups by adding anyone who looked as if they were left out to one or other of them, murmuring, 'You *must* make Colonel Walker describe his garden to you. Such a wonderful collection of fuchsias he has.' With such little sentences she drew people together.

Miss Marple was now able to attach names to all the passengers. Bushy eyebrows turned out to be Professor Wanstead, as she had thought, and the foreigner was Mr Caspar. The bossy woman was Mrs Riseley-Porter and her niece was called Joanna Crawford. The young man with the hair was Emlyn Price and he and Joanna Crawford appeared to be finding out that certain things in life, such as decided opinions, they had in common, on economics, art, general dislikes, politics and such topics.

The two eldest pussies graduated naturally to Miss Marple as a kindred elderly pussy. They discussed happily arthritis, rheumatism, diets, new doctors, remedies both professional, patent, and reminiscences of old wives' treatments which had had success where all else failed. They discussed the many tours they had been on to foreign places in Europe; hotels, travel agencies and finally the County of Somerset where Miss

Lumley and Miss Bentham lived, and where the difficulties of getting suitable gardeners could hardly be believed.

The two middle-aged ladies travelling together turned out to be Miss Cooke and Miss Barrow. Miss Marple still felt that one of these two, the fair one, Miss Cooke, was faintly familiar to her, but she still could not remember where she had seen her before. Probably it was only her fancy. It might also be just fancy but she could not help feeling that Miss Barrow and Miss Cooke appeared to be avoiding her. They seemed rather anxious to move away if she approached. That, of course, *might* be entirely her imagination.

Fifteen people, one of whom at least must matter in some way. In casual conversation that evening she introduced the name of Mr Rafiel, so as to note if anyone reacted in any way. Nobody did.

The handsome woman was identified as Miss Elizabeth Temple, who was the retired Headmistress of a famous girl's school. Nobody appeared to Miss Marple likely to be a murderer except possibly Mr Casper, and that was probably foreign prejudice. The thin young man was Richard Jameson, an architect.

'Perhaps I shall do better tomorrow,' said Miss Marple to herself.

III

Miss Marple went to bed definitely tired out. Sight-seeing was pleasant but exhausting, and trying to study fifteen or sixteen people at once and wondering as you did so which of them could possibly be connected with a murder, was even more exhausting. It had a touch of such unreality about it that one could not, Miss Marple felt, take it seriously. These seemed to be all perfectly nice people, the sort of people who go on cruises and on tours and all the rest of it. However, she took another quick and cursory glance at the passenger list, making a few little entries in her notebook.

Mrs Risley-Porter? *Not* connected with crime. Too social and self-centred.

Niece, Joanna Crawford? The same? But very efficient.

Mrs Riseley-Porter, however, might have information of some kind which Miss Marple might find had a bearing on matters. She must keep on agreeable terms with Mrs Riseley-Porter.

Miss Elizabeth Temple? A personality. Interesting. She did not remind Miss Marple of any murderer she'd ever known. 'In fact,' said Miss Marple to herself, 'she really radiates integrity. *If* she had committed a murder, it would be a very popular murder. Perhaps for some noble reason or for some reason that she thought noble?' But that wasn't satisfactory either. Miss Temple, she thought, would always know what she was doing and why she was doing it and would not have any silly ideas about nobility when merely evil existed. 'All the same,' said Miss Marple. 'she's *someone* and she might – she just *might* be a person Mr Rafiel wanted me to meet for some reason.' She jotted down these thoughts on the right hand side of her notebook.

She shifted her point of view. She had been considering a possible murderer – what about a prospective victim? Who was a possible victim? No one very likely. Perhaps Mrs Riseley-Porter might qualify – rich – rather disagreeable. The efficient niece might inherit. She and the anarchistic Emlyn Price might combine in the cause of anti-capitalism. Not a very credible idea, but no other feasible murder seemed on offer.

Professor Wanstead? An interesting man, she was sure. Kindly, too. Was he a scientist or was he medical? She was not as yet sure, but she put him down on the side of science. She herself knew nothing of science, but it seemed not at all unlikely.

Mr and Mrs Butler? She wrote them off. Nice Americans. No connections with anyone in the West Indies or anyone she had known. No, she didn't think that the Butlers could be relevant.

Richard Jameson? That was the thin architect. Miss Marple didn't see how architecture could come into it, though it might, she supposed. A priest's hole, perhaps? One of the houses they were going to visit might have a priest's hole which would contain a skeleton. And Mr Jameson, being an architect, would know just where the priest's hole was. He might aid her to discover it, or she might aid him to discover it and then they would find a body. 'Oh really,' said Miss Marple, 'What nonsense I am talking and thinking.'

Miss Cooke and Miss Barrow? A perfectly ordinary pair. And yet she'd certainly seen one of them before. At least she'd seen Miss Cooke before. Oh well, it would come to her, she supposed.

Colonel and Mrs Walker? Nice people. Retired Army folk. Served abroad mostly. Nice to talk to, but she didn't think there'd be anything for her there.

Miss Bentham and Miss Lumley? The elderly pussies. Unlikely to be criminals, but, being elderly pussies, they might know plenty of gossip, or have some information, or might make some illuminating remark even if it happened to come about in connection with rheumatism, arthritis or patent medicine.

Mr Caspar? Possibly a dangerous character. Very excitable. She would keep him on the list for the present.

Emlyn Price? A student presumably. Students were very violent. Would

Mr Rafiel have sent her on the track of a student? Well, it would depend perhaps on what the student had done or wished to do or was going to do. A dedicated anarchist, perhaps.

'Oh dear,' said Miss Marple, suddenly exhausted, 'I *must* go to bed.'

Her feet ached, her back ached and her mental reactions were not, she thought, at their best. She slept at once. Her sleep was enlivened by several dreams.

One where Professor Wanstead's bushy eyebrows fell off because they were not his own eyebrows, but false ones. As she woke again, her first impression was that which so often follows dreams, a belief that the dream in question had solved everything. 'Of course,' she thought, 'of *course!*' His eyebrows were false and that solved the whole thing. *He* was the criminal.

Sadly, it came to her that nothing was solved. Professor Wanstead's eyebrows coming off was of no help at all.

Unfortunately now, she was no longer sleepy. She sat up in bed with some determination.

She sighed and slipped on her dressing-gown, moved from her bed to an upright chair, took a slightly larger notebook from her suitcase and started work.

'The project I have undertaken,' she wrote, 'is connected certainly with crime of some kind. Mr Rafiel has distinctly stated that in his letter. He said I had a *flair* for justice and that necessarily included a flair for crime. So crime is involved, and it is presumably not espionage or fraud or robbery, because such things have never come my way and I have no connection with such things, or knowledge of them, or special skills. What Mr Rafiel knows of me is only what he knew during the period of time when we were both in St Honoré. We were connected there with a murder. Murders as reported in the press have never claimed my attention. I have never read books on criminology as a subject or really been interested in such a thing. No, it has just happened that I have found myself in the vicinity of murder rather more often than would seem normal. My attention has been directed to murders involving friends or acquaintances. These curious coincidences of connections with special subjects seem to happen to people in life. One of my aunts, I remember, was on five occasions shipwrecked and a friend of mine was what I believe is officially called accident-prone. I know some of her friends refused to ride in a taxi with her. She had been in four taxi accidents and three car accidents and two railway accidents. Things like this seem to happen to certain people for no appreciable reason. I do not like to write it down but it does appear that murders seem to happen, not to me myself, thank goodness, but seem to happen in my vicinity.'

Miss Marple paused, changed her position, put a cushion in her back, and continued:

'I must try to make as logical a survey as I can of this project which I have undertaken. My instructions, or my 'briefing' as naval friends of mine put it, are so far quite inadequate. Practically non-existent. So I must ask myself one clear question. What is all this *about*? Answer! *I do not know*. Curious and interesting. An odd way for a man like Mr Rafiel to go about things, especially when he was a successful business and financial operator. He wants me to guess, to employ my instinct, to observe and to obey such directions as are given to me or are hinted to me.

'So: Point 1. Directions will be given me. Direction from a dead man. Point 2. What is involved in my problem is *justice*. Either to set right an injustice or to avenge evil by bringing it to justice. This is in accord with the code word Nemesis given to me by Mr Rafiel.

'After explanations of the principle involved, I received my first factual directive. It was arranged by Mr Rafiel before his death that I was to go on Tour No 37 of Famous Houses and Gardens. Why? That is what I have to ask myself. Is it for some geographical or territorial reason? A connection or a clue? Some particular famous house? Or something involving some particular garden or landscape connected? This seems unlikely. The more likely explanations lies on the *people* or one of the people on this particular coach party. None of them is known to me personally, but one of them at least must be connected with the riddle I have to solve. Somebody among our group is connected or concerned with a murder. Somebody has information or a special link with the victim of a crime, or someone personally is himself or herself a murderer. A murderer as yet unsuspected.'

Miss Marple stopped here suddenly. She nodded her head. She was satisfied now with her analysis so far as it went.

And so to bed.

Miss Marple added to her notebook.

'Here endeth the First Day.'

CHAPTER 6

Love

The following morning they visited a small Queen Anne Manor House. The drive there had not been very long or tiring. It was a very charming-looking house and had an interesting history as well as a very beautiful and unusually laid out garden.

Richard Jameson, the architect, was full of admiration for the structural beauty of the house and being the kind of young man who is fond of hearing his own voice, he slowed down in nearly every room that they went through, pointing out every special moulding of fireplace, and giving historical dates and references. Some of the group, appreciative at first, began to get slightly restive, as the somewhat monotonous lecturing went on. Some of them began to edge carefully away and fall behind the party. The local caretaker, who was in charge, was not himself too pleased at having his occupation usurped by one of the sightseers. He made a few efforts to get matters back into his own hands but Mr Jameson was unyielding. The caretaker made a last try.

'In this room, ladies and gentlemen, the White Parlour, folks call it, is where they found a body. A young man it was, stabbed with a dagger, lying on the hearthrug. Way back in the seventeen hundred and something it was. It was said that the Lady Moffat of that day had a lover. He came through a small side door and up a steep staircase to this room through a loose panel there was to the left of the fireplace. Sir Richard Moffat, her husband, you see, was said to be across the seas in the Low Countries. But he come home, and in he came unexpectedly and caught 'em there together.'

He paused proudly. He was pleased at the response from his audience, glad of a respite from the architectural details which they had been having forced down their throats.

'Why, isn't that just too romantic, Henry?' said Mrs Butler in her resonant trans-Atlantic tones. 'Why, you know, there's quite an *atmosphere* in this room. I feel it. I certainly can feel it.'

'Mamie is very sensitive to atmospheres,' said her husband proudly to those around him. 'Why, once when we were in an old house down in Louisiana ...'

The narrative of Mamie's special sensitivity got into its swing and Miss Marple and one or two others seized their opportunity to edge gently out of the room and down the exquisitely moulded staircase to the ground floor.

'A friend of mine,' said Miss Marple to Miss Cooke and Miss Barrow who

51

were next to her, 'had a most nerve-racking experience only a few years ago. A dead body on their library floor one morning.'

'One of the family?' asked Miss Barrow. 'An epileptic fit?'

'Oh no, it was a murder. A strange girl in evening dress. A blonde. But her hair was dyed. She was really a brunette; and – oh . . .' Miss Marple broke off, her eyes fixed on Miss Cooke's yellow hair where it escaped from her headscarf.

It had come to her suddenly. She knew why Miss Cooke's face was familiar and she knew where she had seen her before. But when she had seen her then, Miss Cooke's hair had been dark – almost black. And now it was bright yellow.

Mrs Riseley-Porter, coming down the stairs, spoke decisively as she pushed past them and completed the staircase and turned into the hall.

'I really cannot go up and down any more of those stairs,' she declared, 'and standing around in these rooms is very tiring. I believe the gardens here, although not extensive, are quite celebrated in horticultural circles. I suggest we go there without loss of time. It looks as though it might cloud over before long. I think we shall get rain before morning is out.'

The authority with which Mrs Riseley-Porter could enforce her remarks had its usual result. All those near at hand or within hearing followed her obediently out through french doors in the dining-room into the garden. The gardens had indeed all that Mrs Riseley-Porter had claimed for them. She herself took possession firmly of Colonel Walker and set off briskly. Some of the others followed them, others took paths in the opposite direction.

Miss Marple herself made a determined bee-line for a garden seat which appeared to be of comfortable proportions as well as of artistic merit. She sank down on it with relief, and a sigh matching her own was emitted by Miss Elizabeth Temple as she followed Miss Marple and came to sit beside her on the seat.

'Going over houses is always tiring,' said Miss Temple. 'The most tiring thing in the world. Especially if you have to listen to an exhaustive lecture in each room.'

'Of course, all that we were told is very interesting,' said Miss Marple, rather doubtfully.

'Oh, do you think so?' said Miss Temple. Her head turned slightly and her eyes met those of Miss Marple. Something passed between the two women, a kind of *rapport* – of understanding tinged with mirth.

'Don't you?' asked Miss Marple.

'No,' said Miss Temple.

This time the understanding was definitely established between them.

52

They sat there companionably in silence. Presently Elizabeth Temple began to talk about gardens, and this garden in particular. 'It was designed by Holman,' she said, 'somewhere about 1800 or 1798. He died young. A pity. He had great genius.'

'It is so sad when anyone dies young,' said Miss Marple.

'I wonder,' said Elizabeth Temple.

She said it in a curious, meditative way.

'But they miss so much,' said Miss Marple. 'So many things.'

'Or escape so much,' said Miss Temple.

'Being as old as I am now,' said Miss Marple, 'I suppose I can't help feeling that early death means missing things.'

'And I,' said Elizabeth Temple, 'having spent nearly all my life amongst the young, look at life as a period in time complete in itself. What did T. S. Eliot say: *The moment of the rose and the moment of the yew tree are of equal duration*.'

Miss Marple said, 'I see what you mean . . . A life of whatever length is a complete experience. But don't you –' she hesitated, '– ever feel that a life could be incomplete because it has been cut unduly short?'

'Yes, that *is* so.'

Miss Marple said, looking at the flowers near her, 'How beautiful peonies are. That long border of them – so proud and yet so beautifully fragile.'

Elizabeth Temple turned her head towards her.

'Did you come on this trip to see the houses or to see gardens?' she asked.

'I suppose really to see the houses,' said Miss Marple. 'I shall enjoy the gardens most, though, but the houses – they will be a new experience for me. Their variety and their history, and the beautiful old furniture and the pictures.' She added: 'A kind friend gave me this trip as a gift. I am very grateful. I have not seen very many big and famous houses in my life.'

'A kind thought,' said Miss Temple.

'Do you often go on these sight-seeing tours?' asked Miss Marple.

'No. This is not for me exactly a sight-seeing tour.'

Miss Marple looked at her with interest. She half opened her lips to speak but refrained from putting a question. Miss Temple smiled at her.

'You wonder why I am here, what my motive is, my reason. Well, why don't you make a guess?'

'Oh, I wouldn't like to do that,' said Miss Marple.

'Yes, do do so.' Elizabeth Temple was urgent. 'It would interest me. Yes, really interest me. Make a guess.'

Miss Marple was silent for quite a few moments. Her eyes looked at Elizabeth Temple steadily, ranging over her thoughtfully in her appraisement. She said,

'This is not from what I know about you or what I have been told about you. I know that you are quite a famous person and that your school is a very famous one. No. I am only making my guess from what you look like. I should – write you down as a pilgrim. You have the look of one who is on a pilgrimage.'

There was a silence and then Elizabeth said,

'That describes it very well. Yes, I am on a pilgrimage.'

Miss Marple said after a moment or two,

'The friend who sent me on this tour and paid all my expenses is now dead. He was a Mr Rafiel, a very rich man. Did you by any chance know him?'

'Jason Rafiel? I know him by name, of course. I never knew him personally, or met him. He gave a large endowment once to an educational project in which I was interested. I was very grateful. As you say, he was a very wealthy man. I saw the notice of his death in the papers a few weeks ago. So he was an old friend of yours?'

'No,' said Miss Marple. 'I had met him just over a year ago abroad. In the West Indies. I never knew much about him. His life or his family or any personal friends that he had. He was a great financier but otherwise, or so people always said, he was a man who was very reserved about himself. Did you know his family or anyone ...?' Miss Marple paused. 'I often wondered, but one does not like to ask questions and seem inquisitive.'

Elizabeth was silent for a minute – then she said:

'I knew a girl once ... A girl who had been a pupil of mine at Fallowfield, my school. She was no actual relation to Mr Rafiel, but she *was* at one time engaged to marry Mr Rafiel's son.'

'But she didn't marry him?' Miss Marple asked.

'No.'

'Why not?'

Miss Temple said,

'One might hope to say – like to say – because she had too much sense. He was not the type of a young man one would want anyone one was fond of to marry. She was a very lovely girl and a very sweet girl. I don't know why she didn't marry him. Nobody has ever told me.' She sighed and then said, 'Anway, she died ...'

'Why did she die?' said Miss Marple.

Elizabeth Temple stared at the peonies for some minutes. When she spoke she uttered one word. It echoed like the tone of a deep bell – so much so that it was startling.

'Love!' she said.

Miss Marple queried the word sharply. 'Love?'

'One of the most frightening words there is in the world,' said Elizabeth Temple.

Again her voice was bitter and tragic.

'Love . . .'

CHAPTER 7

An Invitation

Miss Marple decided to miss out on the afternoon's sightseeing. She admitted to being somewhat tired and would perhaps give a miss to an ancient church and its 14th-century glass. She would rest for a while and join them at the tea-room which had been pointed out to her in the main street. Mrs Sandbourne agreed that she was being very sensible.

Miss Marple, resting on a comfortable bench outside the tea-room, reflected on what she planned to do next and whether it would be wise to do it or not.

When the others joined her at tea-time it was easy for her to attach herself unobtrusively to Miss Cooke and Miss Barrow and sit with them at a table for four. The fourth chair was occupied by Mr Caspar whom Miss Marple considered as not sufficiently conversant with the English language to matter.

Leaning across the table, as she nibbled a slice of Swiss roll, Miss Marple said to Miss Cooke,

'You know, I am *quite* sure we have met before. I have been wondering and wondering about it – I'm not as good as I was at remembering faces, but I'm sure I have met you somewhere.'

Miss Cooke looked kindly but doubtful. Her eyes went to her friend, Miss Barrow. So did Miss Marple's. Miss Barrow showed no signs of helping to probe the mystery.

'I don't know if you've ever stayed in my part of the world,' went on Miss Marple, 'I live in St Mary Mead. Quite a small village, you know. At least, not so small nowadays, there is so much building going on everywhere. Not very far from Much Benham and only twelve miles from the coast at Loomouth.'

'Oh,' said Miss Cooke, 'let me see. Well, I know Loomouth quite well and perhaps –'

Suddenly Miss Marple made a pleased exclamation.

'Why, of *course*! I was in my garden one day at St Mary Mead and you spoke to me as you were passing by on the footpath. You said you were staying down there, I remember, with a friend –'

'Of course,' said Miss Cooke. 'How stupid of me. I do remember you now. We spoke of how difficult it was nowadays to get anyone – to do job gardening, I mean – anyone who was any *use*.'

'Yes. You were not living there, I think? You were staying

56

with someone.'

'Yes, I was staying with . . . with . . .' for a moment Miss Cooke hesitated, with the air of one who hardly knows or remembers a name.

'With a Mrs Sutherland, was it?' suggested Miss Marple.

'No, no, it was . . . er . . . Mrs –'

'Hastings,' said Miss Barrow firmly as she took a piece of chocolate cake.

'Oh yes, in one of the new houses,' said Miss Marple.

'Hastings,' said Mr Caspar unexpectedly. He beamed. 'I have been to Hastings – I have been to Eastbourne, too.' He beamed again. 'Very nice – by the sea.'

'Such a coincidence,' said Miss Marple, 'meeting again so soon – such a small world, isn't it?'

'Oh, well, we are all so fond of gardens,' said Miss Cooke vaguely.

'Flowers very pretty,' said Mr Caspar. 'I like very much –' He beamed again.

'So many rare and beautiful shrubs,' said Miss Cooke.

Miss Marple went full speed ahead with a gardening conversation of some technicality – Miss Cooke responded. Miss Barrow put in an occasional remark.

Mr Caspar relapsed into smiling silence.

Later, as Miss Marple took her usual rest before dinner, she conned over what she had collected. Miss Cooke *had* admitted being in St Mary Mead. She *had* admitted walking past Miss Marple's house. Had agreed it was quite a coincidence. Coincidence? thought Miss Marple meditatively, turning the word over in her mouth rather as a child might do to a certain lollipop to decide its flavour. Was it a coincidence? Or had she had some reason to come there? Had she been *sent* there? Sent there – for what reason? Was that a ridiculous thing to imagine?

'Any coincidence,' said Miss Marple to herself, 'is *always* worth noticing. You can throw it away later if it *is* only a coincidence.'

Miss Cooke and Miss Barrow appeared to be a perfectly normal pair of friends doing the kind of tour which, according to them, they did every year. They had been on an Hellenic cruise last year and a tour of bulbs in Holland the year before, and Northern Ireland the year before that. They seemed perfectly pleasant and ordinary people. But Miss Cooke, she thought, had for a moment looked as though she were about to disclaim her visit to St Mary Mead. She had looked at her friend, Miss Barrow, rather as though she were seeking instruction as to what to say. Miss Barrow was presumably the senior partner –

'Of course, really, I may have been imagining all these things,' thought Miss Marple. 'They may have no significance whatever.'

The word danger came unexpectedly into her mind. Used by Mr Rafiel in his first letter – and there had been some reference to her needing a guardian angel in his second letter. Was she going into danger in this business? – and why? From whom?

Surely not from Miss Cooke and Miss Barrow. Such an ordinary-looking couple.

All the same Miss Cooke *had* dyed her hair and altered her style of hairdressing. Disguised her appearance as much as she could, in fact. Which was odd, to say the least of it! She considered once more her fellow travellers.

Mr Caspar, now, it would have been much easier to imagine that *he* might be dangerous. Did he understand more English than he pretended to do? She began to wonder about Mr Caspar.

Miss Marple had never quite succeeded in abandoning her Victorian view of foreigners. One never *knew* with foreigners. Quite absurd, of course, to feel like that – she had many friends from various foreign countries. All the same . . .? Miss Cooke, Miss Barrow, Mr Caspar, that young man with the wild hair – Emlyn Something – a revolutionary – a practising anarchist? Mr and Mrs Butler – such nice Americans – but perhaps – too good to be true?

'Really,' said Miss Marple, 'I *must* pull myself together.'

She turned her attention to the itinerary of their trip. Tomorrow, she thought, was going to be rather strenuous. A morning's sight-seeing drive, starting rather early: a long, rather athletic walk on a coastal path in the afternoon. Certain interesting marine flowering plants – it would be tiring. A tactful suggestion was appended. Anyone who felt like a rest could stay behind in their hotel, the Golden Boar, which had a very pleasant garden or could do a short excursion which would only take an hour, to a beauty spot nearby. She thought perhaps that she would do that.

But though she did not know it then, her plans were to be suddenly altered.

As Miss Marple came down from her rooms in the Golden Boar the next day after washing her hands before luncheon, a woman in a tweed coat and skirt came forward rather nervously and spoke to her.

'Excuse me, are you Miss Marple – Miss Jane Marple?'

'Yes, that is my name,' said Miss Marple, slightly surprised.

'My name is Mrs Glynne. Lavinia Glynne. I and my two sisters live near here and – well, we heard you were coming, you see –'

'You heard I was coming?' said Miss Marple with some slight surprise.

'Yes. A very old friend of ours wrote to us – oh, quite some time ago, it must have been three weeks ago, but he asked us to make a note of this date.

58

The date of the Famous Houses and Gardens Tour. He said that a great friend of his – or a relation, I'm not quite sure which – would be on that tour.'

Miss Marple continued to look surprised.

'I'm speaking of a Mr Rafiel,' said Mrs Glynne.

'Oh! Mr Rafiel,' said Miss Marple – 'you – you know that –'

'That he died? Yes. So sad. Just after his letter came. I think it must have been certainly very soon after he wrote to us. But we felt a special *urgency* to try to do what he had asked. He suggested, you know, that perhaps you would like to come and stay with us for a couple of nights. This part of the tour is rather strenuous. I mean, it's all right for the young people, but it is very trying for anyone older. It involves several miles of walking and a certain amount of climbing up difficult cliff paths and places. My sisters and I would be so very pleased if you could come and stay in our house here. It is only ten minutes' walk from the hotel and I'm sure we could show you many interesting things locally.'

Miss Marple hesitated a minute. She liked the look of Mrs Glynne, plump, good-natured, and friendly though a little shy. Besides – here again must be Mr Rafiel's instructions – the next step for her to take? Yes, it must be so.

She wondered why she felt nervous. Perhaps because she was now at home with the people in the tour, felt part of the group although as yet she had only known them for three days.

She turned to where Mrs Glynne was standing, looking up at her anxiously.

'Thank you – it is most kind of you. I shall be very pleased to come.'

59

CHAPTER 8

The Three Sisters

Miss Marple stood looking out of a window. Behind her, on the bed, was her suitcase. She looked out over the garden with unseeing eyes. It was not often that she failed to see a garden she was looking at, in either a mood of admiration or a mood of criticism. In this case it would presumably have been criticism. It was a neglected garden, a garden on which little money had been spent possibly for some years, and on which very little work had been done. The house, too, had been neglected. It was well proportioned, the furniture in it had been good furniture once, but had had little in late years of polishing or attention. It was not a house, she thought, that had been, at any rate of late years, loved in any way. It lived up to its name: The Old Manor House. A house, built with grace and a certain amount of beauty, lived in once, cherished. The daughters and sons had married and left and now it was lived in by Mrs Glynne who, from a word she had let fall when she showed Miss Marple up to the bedroom appointed to her, had inherited it with her sisters from an uncle and had come here to live with her sisters after her husband had died. They had all grown older, their incomes had dwindled, labour had been more difficult to get.

The other sisters, presumably, had remained unmarried, one older, one younger than Mrs Glynne, two Miss Bradbury-Scotts.

There was no sign of anything which belonged to a child in the house. No discarded ball, no old perambulator, no little chair or a table. This was just a house with three sisters.

'Sounds very Russian,' murmured Miss Marple to herself. She did mean The Three Sisters, didn't she? Chekhov, was it? or Dostoyevsky? Really, she couldn't remember. Three sisters. But these would certainly not be the kind of three sisters who were yearning to go to Moscow. These three sisters were presumably, she was almost sure they were, content to remain where they were. She had been introduced to the other two who had come, one out of the kitchen and one down a flight of stairs, to welcome her. Their manners were well bred and gracious. They were what Miss Marple would have called in her youth by the now obsolete terms 'ladies' – and what she once recalled calling 'decayed ladies'. Her father had said to her:

'No, dear Jane, not *decayed*. Distressed gentlewomen.'

Gentlewomen nowadays were not so liable to be distressed. They were aided by Government or by Societies or by a rich relation. Or, perhaps – by someone like Mr Rafiel. Because, after all, that was the whole point, the

60

whole reason for her being here, wasn't it? Mr Rafiel had arranged all this. He had taken, Miss Marple thought, a good deal of trouble about it. He had known, presumably, some four or five weeks before his death, just when that death was likely to be, give and take a little, since doctors were usually moderately optimistic, knowing from experience that patients who ought to die within a certain period very often took an unexpected lease of life and lingered on, still doomed, but obstinately declining to take the final step. On the other hand, hospital nurses when in charge of patients, had, Miss Marple thought from her experience, always expected the patients to be dead the next day, and were much surprised when they were not. But in voicing their gloomy views to Doctor, when he came, they were apt to receive in reply as the doctor went out of the hall door, a private aside of, 'Linger a few weeks yet, I shouldn't wonder.' Very nice of Doctor to be so optimistic, Nurse would think, but surely Doctor was wrong. Doctor very often wasn't wrong. He knew that people who were in pain, helpless, crippled, even unhappy, still liked living and wanting to live. They would take one of Doctor's pills to help them pass the night, but they had no intention of taking a few more than necessary of Doctor's pills, just in order to pass the threshold to a world that they did not as yet know anything about!

Mr Rafiel. That was the person Miss Marple was thinking about as she looked across the garden with unseeing eyes. Mr Rafiel? She felt now that she was getting a little closer to understanding the task laid upon her, the project suggested to her. Mr Rafiel was a man who made plans. Made them in the same way that he planned financial deals and take-overs. In the words of her servant, Cherry, he had had a problem. When Cherry had a problem, she often came and consulted Miss Marple about it.

This was a problem that Mr Rafiel could not deal with himself, which must have annoyed him very much, Miss Marple thought, because he could usually deal with any problem himself and insisted on doing so. But he was bedridden and dying. He could arrange his financial affairs, communicate with his lawyers, with his employees and with such friends and relations as he had, but there was something or someone that he had not arranged for. A problem he had not solved, a problem he still wanted to solve, a project he still wanted to bring about. And apparently it was not one that could be settled by financial aid, by business dealings, by the services of a lawyer.

'So he thought of me,' said Miss Marple.

It still surprised her very much. Very much indeed. However, in the sense she was now thinking of it, his letter had been quite explicit. He had thought she had certain qualifications for doing something. It had to do, she thought once again, with something in the nature of crime or affected by

61

crime. The only other thing he knew about Miss Marple was that she was devoted to gardens. Well it could hardly be a gardening problem that he wanted her to solve. But he might think of her in connection with crime. Crime in the West Indies and crimes in her own neighbourhood at home.

A crime – where?

Mr Rafiel had made arrangements. Arrangements, to begin with, with his lawyers. They had done their part. After the right interval of time they had forwarded to her his letter. It had been, she thought, a well considered and well thought out letter. It would have been simpler, certainly, to tell her exactly what he wanted her to do and why he wanted it. She was surprised in a way that he had not, before his death, sent for her, probably in a somewhat peremptory way and more or less lying on what he would have assured her was his deathbed, and would then have bullied her until she consented to do what he was asking her. But no, that would not really have been Mr Rafiel's way, she thought. He *could* bully people, none better, but this was not a case for bullying, and he did not wish either, she was sure, to appeal to her, to beg her to do him a favour, to urge her to redress a wrong. No. That again would not have been Mr Rafiel's way. He wanted, she thought, as he had probably wanted all his life, to pay for what he required. He wanted to pay her and therefore he wanted to interest her enough to enjoy doing certain work. The pay was offered to intrigue her, not really to tempt her. It was to arouse her interest. She did not think that he had said to himself, 'Offer enough money and she'll leap at it' because, as she knew very well herself, the money sounded very agreeable but she was not in urgent need of money. She had her dear and affectionate nephew who, if she was in straits for money of any kind, if she needed repairs to her house or a visit to a specialist or special treats, dear Raymond would always provide them. No. The sum he offered was to be excited. It was to be exciting in the same way as it was exciting when you had a ticket for the Irish Sweep. It was a fine big sum of money that you could never achieve by any other means except luck.

But all the same, Miss Marple thought to herself, she would need some luck as well as hard work, she would require a lot of thought and pondering and possibly what she was doing might involve a certain amount of danger. But she'd got to find out herself what it was all about, he wasn't going to tell her, partly perhaps because he did not want to influence her? It is hard to tell anyone about something without letting slip your own point of view about it. It could be that Mr Rafiel had thought that his own point of view might be wrong. It was not very like him to think such a thing, but it could be possible. He might suspect that his judgment, impaired by illness, was not quite as good as it used to be. So she, Miss Marple, his agent, his employee, was to make her own guesses, come to her own conclusions.

Well, it was time she came to a few conclusions now. In other words, back to the old question, *what was all this about?*

She had been directed. Let her take that first. She had been directed by a man who was not dead. She had been directed away from St Mary Mead. Therefore, the task, whatever it must be, could not be attacked from there. It was not a neighbourhood problem, it was not a problem that you could solve just by looking through newspaper cuttings or making enquiries, not, that is, until you found what you had to make enquiries about. She had been directed, first to the lawyer's office, then to read a letter – two letters – in her home, then to be sent on a pleasant and well run tour round some of the Famous Houses and Gardens of Great Britain. From that she had come to the next stepping stone. The house she was in at this moment. The Old Manor House, Jocelyn St Mary, where lived Miss Clotilde Bradbury-Scott, Mrs Glynne and Miss Anthea Bradbury-Scott. Mr Rafiel had arranged that, arranged it beforehand. Some weeks before he died. Probably it was the next thing he had done after instructing his lawyers and after booking a seat on the tour in her name. Therefore, she was in this house for a purpose. It might be for only two nights, it might be for longer. There might be certain things arranged which would lead her to stay longer or she would be asked to stay longer. That brought her back to where she stood now.

Mrs Glynne and her two sisters. They must be concerned, implicated in whatever this was. She would have to find out what it was. The time was short. That was the only trouble. Miss Marple had no doubt for one moment that she had the capacity to find out things. She was one of those chatty, fluffy old ladies whom other people expect to talk, to ask questions that were, on the face of it, merely gossipy questions. She would talk about her childhood and that would lead to one of the sisters talking about theirs. She'd talk about food she had eaten, servants she had had, daughters and cousins and relations, travel, marriages, births and – yes – deaths. There must be no show of special interest in her eyes when she heard about a death. Not at all. Almost automatically she was sure she could come up with the right response such as, 'Oh dear me, how *very* sad!' She would have to find out relationships, incidents, life stories, see if any suggestive incidents would pop up, so to speak. It might be some incidents in the neighbourhood, not directly concerned with these three people. Something they could know about, talk about, or were pretty sure to talk about. Anyway, there would be *something* here, some clue, some pointer. The second day from now she would rejoin the tour, unless she had by that time some indication that she was *not* to rejoin the tour. Her mind swept from the house to the coach and the people who had sat in it. It might be that what she was seeking had been there in the coach, and would be there again when she rejoined it. One person, several people, some innocent (some not so innocent), some long past story. She frowned a little, trying to remember something. Something that had flashed in her mind that she had thought: Really I am sure – of what had she been sure?

Her mind went back to the three sisters. She must not be too long up here. She must unpack a few modest needs for two nights, something to change into this evening, night clothes, sponge bag, and then go down and rejoin her hostesses and make pleasant talk. A main point had to be decided. Were the three sisters to be her allies or were the three sisters enemies? They might fall into either catgory. She must think about that carefully.

There was a tap on the door and Mrs Glynne entered.

'I do hope you will be quite comfortable here. Can I help you to unpack? We have a very nice woman who comes in but she is only here in the morning. But she'll help you with anything.'

'Oh no, thank you,' said Miss Marple. 'I only took out just a few necessities.'

'I thought I'd show you the way downstairs again. It's rather a rambling house, you know. There are two staircases and it does make it a little difficult. Sometimes people lose their way.'

'Oh, it's very kind of you,' said Miss Marple.

'I hope then you will come downstairs and we will have a glass of sherry before lunch.'

Miss Marple accepted gratefully and followed her guide down the stairs. Mrs Glynne, she judged, was a good many years younger than she herself was. Fifty, perhaps. Not much more. Miss Marple negotiated the stairs carefully, her left knee was always a little uncertain. There was, however, a banister at one side of the stairs. Very beautiful stairs they were, and she remarked on them.

'It is really a very lovely house,' she said. 'Built I suppose in the 1700s. Am I right?'

'1780,' said Mrs Glynne.

She seemed pleased with Miss Marple's appreciation. She took Miss Marple into the drawing-room. A large graceful room. There were one or two rather beautiful pieces of furniture. A Queen Anne desk and a William and Mary oyster-shell bureau. There were also some rather cumbrous Victorian settees and cabinets. The curtains were of chintz, faded and somewhat worn, the carpet was, Miss Marple thought, Irish. Possibly a Limerick Aubusson type. The sofa was ponderous and the velvet of its much worn. The other two sisters were already sitting there. They rose as Miss Marple came in and approached her, one with a glass of sherry, the other directing her to a chair.

'I don't know whether you like sitting rather high? So many people do.'

'I do,' said Miss Marple. 'It's so much easier. One's back, you know.'

The sisters appeared to know about the difficulties of backs. The eldest of the sisters was a tall handsome woman, dark with a black coil of hair. The other one might have been a good deal younger. She was thin with grey hair that had once been fair hanging untidily on her shoulders and a faintly wraith-like appearance. She could be cast successfully as a mature Ophelia, Miss Marple thought.

Clotilde, Miss Marple thought, was certainly no Ophelia, but she would have made a magnificent Clytemnestra – she could have stabbed a husband in his bath with exultation. But since she had never had a husband, that solution wouldn't do. Miss Marple could not see her murdering anyone else but a husband – and there had been no Agamemnon in this house.

Clotilde Bradbury-Scott, Anthea Bradbury-Scott, Lavinia Glynne. Clotilde was handsome, Lavinia was plain but pleasant-looking, Anthea had one eyelid which twitched from time to time. Her eyes were large and grey and she had an odd way of glancing round to right and then to left, and then suddenly, in a rather strange manner, behind her over her shoulder. It was as though she felt someone was watching her all the time. Odd, thought Miss Marple. She wondered a little about Anthea.

They sat down and conversation ensued. Mrs Glynne left the room, apparently for the kitchen. She was, it seemed, the active domestic one of the three. The conversation took a usual course. Clotidle Bradbury-Scott explained that the house was a family one. It had belonged to her great-uncle and then to her uncle and when he had died it was left to her and her two sisters who had joined her there.

'He only had one son, you see,' explained Miss Bradbury-Scott, 'and he was killed in the war. We are really the last of the family, except for some very distant cousins.'

'A beautifully proportioned house,' said Miss Marple. 'Your sister tells me it was built about 1780.'

'Yes, I believe so. One could wish, you know, it was not quite so large and rambling.'

'Repairs too,' said Miss Marple, 'come very heavy nowadays.'

'Oh yes, indeed,' Clotilde sighed. 'And in many ways we have to let a lot of it just fall down. Sad, but there it is. A lot of the outhouses, for instance, and a greenhouse. We had a very beautiful big greenhouse.'

'Lovely muscat grapevine in it,' said Anthea. 'And Cherry Pie used to grow all along the walls inside. Yes, I really regret that very much. Of course, during the war one could not get any gardeners. We had a very young gardener and then he was called up. One does not of course grudge that, but all the same it was impossible to get things repaired and so the whole greenhouse fell down.'

'So did the little conservatory near the house.'

Both sisters sighed, with the sighing of those who have noted time passing, and times changing – but not for the better.

There was a melancholy here in this house, thought Miss Marple. It was impregnated somehow with sorrow – a sorrow that could not be dispersed or removed since it had penetrated too deep. It had sunk in . . . She shivered suddenly.

CHAPTER 9

Polygonum Baldschuanicum

The meal was conventional. A small joint of mutton, roast potatoes, followed by a plum tart with a small jug of cream and rather indifferent pastry. There were a few pictures round the dining-room wall, family pictures, Miss Marple presumed, Victorian portraits without any particular merit, the sideboard was large and heavy, a handsome piece of plum-coloured mahogany. The curtains were of dark crimson damask and at the big mahogany table ten people could easily have been seated.

Miss Marple chattered about the incidents of the tour in so far as she had been on it. As this, however, had only been three days, there was not very much to say.

'Mr Rafiel, I suppose, was an old friend of yours?' said the eldest Miss Bradbury-Scott.

'Not really,' said Miss Marple. 'I met him first when I was on a cruise to the West Indies. He was out there for his health, I imagine.'

'Yes, he had been very crippled for some years,' said Anthea.

'Very sad,' said Miss Marple. 'Very sad indeed. I really admired his fortitude. He seemed to manage to do so much work. Every day, you know, he dictated to his secretary and was continually sending off cables. He did not seem to give in at all kindly to being an invalid.'

'Oh no, he wouldn't,' said Anthea.

'We have not seen much of him of late years,' said Mrs Glynne. 'He was a busy man, of course. He always remembered us at Christmas very kindly.'

'Do you live in London, Miss Marple?' asked Anthea.

'Oh no,' said Miss Marple. 'I live in the country. A very small place half way between Loomouth and Market Basing. About twenty-five miles from London. It used to be a very pretty old-world village but of course like everything else, it is becoming what they call developed nowadays.' She added, 'Mr Rafiel, I suppose, lived in London? At least I noticed that in the St Honoré hotel register his address was somewhere in Eaton Square, I think, or was it Belgrave Square?'

'He had a country house in Kent,' said Clotilde. 'He used to entertain there, I think, sometimes. Business friends, mostly you know, or people from abroad. I don't think any of us ever visited him there. He nearly always entertained us in London on the rare occasions when we happened to meet.'

'It was very kind of him,' said Miss Marple, 'to suggest to you that you should invite me here during the course of this tour. Very thoughtful. One

67

wouldn't really have expected a busy man such as he must have been to have had such kindly thoughts.'

'We have invited before friends of his who have been on these tours. On the whole they are very considerate the way they arrange these things. It is impossible, of course, to suit everybody's taste. The young ones naturally wish to walk, to make long excursions, to ascend hills for a view, and all that sort of thing. And the older ones who are not up to it, remain in the hotels, but hotels round here are not really at all luxurious. I am sure you would have found today's trip and the one to St Bonaventure tomorrow also, very fatiguing. Tomorrow I believe there is a visit to an island, you know, in a boat and sometimes it can be very rough.'

'Even going round houses can be very tiring,' said Mrs Glynne.

'Oh, I know,' said Miss Marple. 'So much walking and standing about. One's feet get very tired. I suppose really I ought not to take these expeditions, but it is such a temptation to see beautiful buildings and fine rooms and furniture. All these things. And of course some splendid pictures.'

'And the gardens,' said Anthea. 'You like gardens, don't you?'

'Oh yes,' said Miss Marple, 'specially the gardens. From the description in the prospectus I am really looking foward very much to seeing some of the really finely kept gardens of the historic houses we have still to visit.' She beamed round the table.

It was all very pleasant, very natural, and yet she wondered why for some reason she had a feeling of strain. A feeling that there was something unnatural here. But what did she mean by unnatural? The conversation was ordinary enough, consisting mainly of platitudes. She herself was making conventional remarks and so were the three sisters.

The Three Sisters, thought Miss Marple once again considering that phrase. Why did anything thought of in threes somehow seem to suggest a sinister atmosphere? The Three Sisters. The Three Witches of Macbeth. Well, one could hardly compare these three sisters to the three witches. Although Miss Marple had always thought at the back of her mind that the theatrical producers made a mistake in the way in which they produced the three witches. One production which she had seen, indeed, seemed to her quite absurd. The witches had looked more like pantomine creatures with flapping wings and ridiculously spectacular steeple hats. They had danced and slithered about. Miss Marple remembered saying to her nephew, who was standing her this Shakespearean treat, 'You know, Raymond, my dear, if *I* were ever producing this splendid play I would make the three witches *quite* different. I would have them three ordinary, normal old women. Old Scottish women. They wouldn't dance or caper. They would look at each

68

other rather slyly and you would feel a sort of menace just behind the ordinariness of them.'

Miss Marple helped herself to the last mouthful of plum tart and looked across the table at Anthea. Ordinary, untidy, very vague-looking, a bit scatty. Why should she feel that Anthea was sinister?

'I am imagining things,' said Miss Marple to herself. 'I mustn't do that.'

After luncheon she was taken on a tour of the garden. It was Anthea who was deputed to accompany her. It was, Miss Marple thought, rather a sad progress. Here, there had once been a well kept, though certainly not in any way an outstanding or remarkable, garden. It had had the elements of an ordinary Victorian garden. A shrubbery, a drive of speckled laurels, no doubt there had once been a well kept lawn and paths, a kitchen garden of about an acre and a half, too big evidently for the three sisters who lived here now. Part of it was unplanted and had gone largely to weeds. Ground elder had taken over most of the flower beds and Miss Marple's hands could hardly restrain themselves from pulling up the vagrant bindweed asserting its superiority.

Miss Anthea's long hair flapped in the wind, shedding from time to time a vague hairpin on the path or the grass. She talked rather jerkily.

'*You* have a very nice garden, I expect,' she said.

'Oh, it's a very small one,' said Miss Marple.

They had come along a grass path and were pausing in front of a kind of hillock that rested against the wall at the end of it.

'Our greenhouse,' said Miss Anthea, mournfully.

'Oh yes, where you had such a delightful grapevine.'

'Three vines,' said Anthea. 'A Black Hamburg and one of those small white grapes, very sweet, you know. And a third one of beautiful muscats.'

'And a heliotrope, you said.'

'Cherry Pie,' said Anthea.

'Ah yes, Cherry Pie. Such a lovely smell. Was there any bomb trouble round here? Did that – er – knock the greenhouse down?'

'Oh no, we never suffered from anything of that kind. This neighbourhood was quite free of bombs. No, I'm afraid it just fell down from decay. We hadn't been here so very long and we had no money to repair it, or to build it up again. And in fact, it wouldn't have been worth it really because we couldn't have kept it up even if we did. I'm afraid we just let it fall down. There was nothing else we could do. And now you see, it's all grown over.'

'Ah that, completely covered by – what is that flowering creeper just coming into bloom?'

'Oh yes. It's quite a common one,' said Anthea. 'It begins with a P. Now

69

what is the name of it?' she said doubtfully. 'Poly something, something like that.'

'Oh yes. I think I do know the name. Polygonum Baldschuanicum. Very quick growing, I think, isn't it? Very useful really if one wants to hide any tumbledown building or anything ugly of that kind.'

The mound in front of her was certainly thickly covered with the all-enveloping green and white flowering plant. It was, as Miss Marple well knew, a kind of menace to anything else that wanted to grow. Polygonum covered everything, and covered it in a remarkably short time.

'The greenhouse must have been quite a big one,' she said.

'Oh yes – we had peaches in it, too – and nectarines.' Anthea looked miserable.

'It looks really very pretty now,' said Miss Marple in a consoling tone. 'Very pretty little white flowers, aren't they?'

'We have a very nice magnolia tree down this path to the left,' said Anthea. 'Once I believe there used to be a very fine border here – a herbaceous border. But that again one cannot keep up. It is too difficult. Everything is too difficult. Nothing is like it used to be – it's all spoilt – everywhere.'

She led the way quickly down a path at right-angles which ran along a side wall. Her pace had increased. Miss Marple could hardly keep up with her. It was, thought Miss Marple, as though she were deliberately being steered away from the Polygonum mound by her hostess. Steered away as from some ugly or displeasing spot. Was she ashamed perhaps that the past glories no longer remained? The Polygonum certainly was growing with extraordinary abandonment. It was not even being clipped or kept to reasonable proportions. It made a kind of flowery wilderness of that bit of the garden.

She almost looks as though she was running away from it, thought Miss Marple, as she followed her hostess. Presently her attention was diverted to a broken down pig-sty which had a few rose tendrils round it.

'My great-uncle used to keep a few pigs,' explained Anthea, 'but of course one would never dream of doing anything of that kind nowadays, would one? Rather too noisome, I am afraid. We have a few floribunda roses near the house. I really think floribundas are such a great answer to difficulties.'

'Oh, I know,' said Miss Marple.

She mentioned the names of a few recent productions in the rose line. All the names, she thought, were entirely strange to Miss Anthea.

'Do you often come on these tours?'

The question came suddenly.

'You mean the tours of houses and of gardens?'

'Yes. Some people do it every year.'

'Oh I couldn't hope to do that. They're rather expensive, you see. A friend very kindly gave me a present of this to celebrate my next birthday. So kind.'

'Oh. I wondered. I wondered *why* you came. I mean – it's bound to be rather tiring, isn't it? Still, if you usually go to the West Indies, and places like that . . .'

'Oh, the West Indies was the result of kindness, too. On the part of a nephew, that time. A dear boy. So very thoughtful for his old aunt.'

'Oh, I see. Yes, I see.'

'I don't know what one would do without the younger generation,' said Miss Marple. 'They are so kind, are they not?'

'I – I suppose so. I don't really know. I – we haven't – any young relations.'

'Does your sister, Mrs Glynne, have any children? She did not mention any. One never likes to ask.'

'No. She and her husband never had any children. It's as well perhaps.'

'And what do you mean by that?' Miss Marple wondered as they returned to the house.

CHAPTER 10

'Oh! Fond, Oh! Fair, The Days That Were'

At half past eight the next morning there was a smart tap on the door, and in answer to Miss Marple's 'Come in' the door was opened and an elderly woman entered, bearing a tray with a teapot, a cup and a milk jug and a small plate of bread and butter.

'Early morning tea, ma'am,' she said cheerfully. 'It's a nice day, it is. I see you've got your curtains drawn back already. You've slept well then?'

'Very well indeed,' said Miss Marple, laying aside a small devotional book which she had been reading.

'Well, it's a lovely day, it is. They'll have it nice for going to the Bonaventure Rocks. It's just as well you're not doing it. It's cruel hard on the legs, it is.'

'I'm really very happy to be here,' said Miss Marple. 'So kind of Miss Bradbury-Scott and Mrs Glynne to issue this invitation.'

'Ah well, it's nice for them too. It cheers them up to have a bit of company come to the house. Ah, it's a sad place nowadays, so it is.'

She pulled the curtains at the window rather more fully, pushed back a chair and deposited a can of hot water in the china basin.

'There's a bathroom on the next floor,' she said, 'but we think it's better always for someone elderly to have their hot water here, so they don't have to climb the stairs.'

'It's very kind of you, I'm sure – you know this house well?'

'I was here as a girl – I was the housemaid then. Three servants they had – a cook, a housemaid – a parlour-maid – kitchen maid too at one time. That was in the old Colonel's time. Horses he kept too, and a groom. Ah, those were the days. Sad it is when things happen the way they do. He lost his wife young, the Colonel did. His son was killed in the war and his only daughter went away to live on the other side of the world. Married a New Zealander she did. Died having a baby and the baby died too. He was a sad man living alone here, and he let the house go – it wasn't kept up as it should have been. When he died he left the place to his niece Miss Clotilde and her two sisters, and she and Miss Anthea came here to live – and later Miss Lavinia lost her husband and came to join them –' she sighed and shook her head. 'They never did much to the house – couldn't afford it – and they let the garden go as well –'

'It all seems a great pity,' said Miss Marple.

'And such nice ladies as they all are, too – Miss Anthea is the scatty one,

72

but Miss Clotilde went to university and is very brainy – she talks three languages – and Mrs Glynne, she's a very nice lady indeed. I thought when she came to join them as things might go better. But you never know, do you, what the future holds? I feel sometimes, as though there was a doom on this house.'

Miss Marple looked enquiring.

'First one thing and then another. The dreadful plane accident – in Spain it was – and everybody killed. Nasty things, aeroplanes – I'd never go in one of them. Miss Clotilde's friends were both killed, they were husband and wife – the daughter was still at school, luckily, and escaped, but Miss Clotilde brought her here to live and did everything for her. Took her abroad for trips – to Italy and France, treated her like a daughter. She was such a happy girl – and a very sweet nature. You'd never dream that such an awful thing could happen.'

'An awful thing. What was it? Did it happen here?'

'No, not here, thank God. Though in a way you might say it *did* happen here. It was here that she met him. He was in the neighbourhood – and the ladies knew his father, who was a very rich man, so he came here to visit – that was the beginning –'

'They fell in love?'

'Yes, she fell in love with him right away. He was an attractive-looking boy, with a nice way of talking and passing the time of day. You'd never think – you'd never think for one moment –' she broke off.

'There was a love affair? And it went wrong? And the girl committed suicide?'

'Suicide?' The old woman stared at Miss Marple with startled eyes.

'Whoever now told you *that*? Murder it was, bare-faced murder. Strangled and her head beaten to pulp. Miss Clotilde had to go and identify her – she's never been quite the same since. They found her body a good thirty miles from here – in the scrub of a disused quarry. And it's believed that it wasn't the first murder he'd done. There had been other girls. Six months she'd been missing. And the police searching far and wide. Oh! A wicked devil he was – a bad lot from the day he was born or so it seems. They say nowadays as there are those as can't help what they do – not right in the head, and they can't be held responsible. I don't believe a word of it! Killers are killers. And they won't even hang them nowadays. I know as there's often madness as runs in old families – there was the Derwents over at Brassington – every second generation one or other of them died in the loony bin – and there was old Mrs Paulett; walked about the lanes in her diamond tiara saying she was Marie Antoinette until they shut her up. But there wasn't anything really wrong with her – just silly like. But this boy.

Yes, he was a devil right enough.'

'What did they do to him?'

'They'd abolished hanging by then – or else he was too young. I can't remember it all now. They found him guilty. It may have been Bostol or Broadsand – one of those places beginning with 'B' as they sent him to.'

'What was the name of the boy?'

'Michael – can't remember his last name. It's ten years ago that it happened – one forgets. Italian sort of name – like a picture. Someone who paints pictures – Raffle, that's it –'

'Michael Rafiel?'

'That's right! There was a rumour as went about that his father being so rich got him wangled out of prison. An escape like the Bank Robbers. But I think as that was just talk –'

So it had not been suicide. It had been murder. 'Love!' Elizabeth Temple had named as the cause of a girl's death. In a way she was right. A young girl had fallen in love with a killer – and for love of him had gone unsuspecting to an ugly death.

Miss Marple gave a little shudder. On her way along the village street yesterday she had passed a newspaper placard: EPSOM DOWNS MURDER, SECOND GIRL'S BODY DISCOVERED, YOUTH ASKED TO ASSIST POLICE.

So history repeated itself. An old pattern – an ugly pattern. Some lines of forgotten verse came haltingly into her brain:

> Rose white youth, passionate, pale,
> A singing stream in a silent vale,
> A fairy prince in a prosy tale,
> Oh there's nothing in life so finely frail
> As Rose White Youth

Who was there to guard Youth from Pain and Death? Youth who could not, who had never been able to, guard itself. Did they know too little? Or was it that they knew too much? And therefore thought they knew it all.

II

Miss Marple, coming down the stairs that morning, probably rather earlier than she had been expected, found no immediate sign of her hostesses. She let herself out at the front door and wandered once round the garden. It was not because she'd really enjoyed this particular garden. It was some vague feeling that there was something here that she ought to notice, something that would give her some idea, or that had given her some idea only she had

74

not – well, frankly, she had not been bright enough to realize just what the bright idea had been. Something she ought to take note of, something that had a bearing.

She was not at the moment anxious to see any of the three sisters. She wanted to turn a few things over in her mind. The new facts that had come to her through Janet's early tea chat.

A side gate stood open and she went through it to the village street and along a line of small shops to where a steeple poked up announcing the site of the church and its churchyard. She pushed open the lych-gate and wandered about among the graves, some dating from quite a while back, some by the far wall later ones, and one or two beyond the wall in what was obviously a new enclosure. There was nothing of great interest among the older tombs. Certain names recurred as they do in villages. A good many Princes of village origin had been buried. Jasper Prince, deeply regretted. Margery Prince, Edgar and Walter Prince, Melanie Prince, 4 years old. A family record. Hiram Broad – Ellen Jane Broad, Eliza Broad 91 years.

She was turning away from the latter when she observed an elderly man moving in slow motion among the graves, tidying up as he walked. He gave her a salute and a 'good morning.'

'Good morning,' said Miss Marple. 'A very pleasant day.'

'It'll turn to rain later,' said the old man.

He spoke with the utmost certainty.

'There seem to be a lot of Princes and Broads buried here,' said Miss Marple.

'Ah yes, there've always been Princes here. Used to own quite a bit of land once. There have been Broads a good many years, too.'

'I see a child is buried here. Very sad when one sees a child's grave.'

'Ah, that'll be little Melanie that was. Mellie, we called her. Yes, it was a sad death. Run over, she was. Ran out into the street, went to get sweets at the sweet shop. Happens a lot nowadays with cars going through at the pace they do.'

'It is sad to think,' said Miss Marple, 'that there are so many deaths all the time. And one doesn't really notice it until one looks at the inscriptions in the churchyard. Sickness, old age, children run over, sometimes even more dreadful things. Young girls killed. Crimes, I mean.'

'Ah, yes, there's a lot of that about. Silly girls, I call most of 'em. And their mums haven't got time to look after them properly nowadays – what with going out to work so much.'

Miss Marple rather agreed with his criticism, but had no wish to waste time in agreement on the trend of the day.

'Staying at The Old Manor House, aren't you?' the old man asked. 'Come

75

here on the coach tour I saw. But it got too much for you, I suppose. Some of those that are gettin' on can't always take it.'

'I *did* find it a little exhausting,' confessed Miss Marple, 'and a very kind friend of mine, a Mr Rafiel, wrote to some friends of his here and they invited me to stay for a couple of nights.'

The name, Rafiel, clearly meant nothing to the elderly gardener.

'Mrs Glynne and her two sisters have been very kind,' said Miss Marple. 'I suppose they've lived here a long time?'

'Not so long as that. Twenty years maybe. Belonged to old Colonel Bradbury-Scott, The Old Manor House did. Close on seventy he was when he died.'

'Did he have any children?'

'A son what was killed in the war. That's why he left the place to his nieces. Nobody else to leave it to.'

He went back to his work amongst the graves.

Miss Marple went into the church. It had felt the hand of a Victorian restorer, and had bright Victorian glass in the windows. One or two brasses and some tablets on the walls were all that was left of the past.

Miss Marple sat down in an uncomfortable pew and wondered about things.

Was she on the right track now? Things were connecting up – but the connections were far from clear.

A girl had been murdered – (actually several girls had been murdered) – suspected young men (or 'youths' as they were usually called nowadays) had been rounded up by the police, to 'assist them in their enquiries.' A common pattern, but this was an old history, dating back ten or twelve years. There was nothing to find out – now, no problems to solve. A tragedy labelled Finis.

What could be done by her? What could Mr Rafiel possibly want her to do?

Elizabeth Temple ... She must get Elizabeth Temple to tell her more. Elizabeth had spoken of a girl who had been engaged to be married to Michael Rafiel. But was that really so? That did not seem to be known to those in The Old Manor House.

A more familiar version came into Miss Marple's mind – the kind of story that had been reasonably frequent in her own village. Starting as always, 'Boy meets girl'. Developing in the usual way –

'And then the girl finds she is pregnant,' said Miss Marple to herself, 'and she tells the boy and she wants him to marry her. But he, perhaps, doesn't want to marry – he has never had any idea of marrying her. But things may be made difficult for him in this case. His father, perhaps, won't hear of

76

such a thing. Her relations will insist that he "does the right thing". And by now he is tired of the girl – he's got another girl perhaps. And so he takes a quick brutal way out – strangles her, beats her head to a pulp to avoid identification. It fits with his record – a brutal sordid crime – *but* forgotten and done with.'

She looked round the church in which she was sitting. It looked so peaceful. The reality of Evil was hard to believe in. A *flair* for Evil – that was what Mr Rafiel had attributed to her. She rose and walked out of the church and stood looking round the churchyard again. Here, amongst the gravestones and their worn inscriptions, no sense of Evil moved in her.

Was it Evil she had sensed yesterday at The Old Manor House? That deep depression of despair, that dark desperate grief. Anthea Bradbury-Scott, her eyes gazing fearfully back over *one* shoulder, as though fearing some presence that stood there – always stood there – behind her.

They knew something, those Three Sisters, but what was it that they knew?

Elizabeth Temple, she thought again. She pictured Elizabeth Temple with the rest of the coach party, striding across the downs at this moment, climbing up a steep path and gazing over the cliffs out to sea.

Tomorrow, when she rejoined the tour, she would get Elizabeth Temple to tell her more.

Miss Marple retraced her steps to The Old Manor House, walking rather slowly because she was by now tired. She could not really feel that her morning had been productive in any way. So far The Old Manor House had given her no distinctive ideas of any kind, a tale of a past tragedy told by Janet, but there were always past tragedies treasured in the memories of domestic workers and which were remembered quite as clearly as all the happy events such as spectacular weddings, big entertainments and successful operations or accidents from which people had recovered in a miraculous manner.

As she drew near the gate she saw two female figures standing there. One of them detached itself and came to meet her. It was Mrs Glynne.

'Oh, there you are,' she said. 'We wondered, you know. I thought you must have gone out for a walk somewhere and I did so hope you wouldn't overtire yourself. If I had known you had come downstairs and gone out, I would have come with you to show anything there is to show. Not that there is very much.'

'Oh, I just wandered around,' said Miss Marple. 'The churchyard, you know, and the church. I'm always very interested in churches. Sometimes there are very curious epitaphs. Things like that. I make quite a collection of them. I suppose the church here was restored in Victorian times?'

'Yes, they did put in some rather ugly pews, I think. You know, good quality wood, and strong and all that, but not very artistic.'

'I hope they didn't take away anything of particular interest.'

'No, I don't think so. It's not really a very old church.'

'There did not seem to be many tablets or brasses or anything of that kind,' agreed Miss Marple.

'You are quite interested in ecclesiastical architecture?'

'Oh, I don't make a study of it or anything like that, but of course in my own village, St Mary Mead, things do rather revolve round the church. I mean, they always have. In my young days, that was so. Nowadays of course it's rather different. Were you brought up in this neighbourhood?'

'Oh, not really. We lived not very far away, about thirty miles or so. At Little Herdsley. My father was a retired serviceman – a Major in the Artillery. We came over here occasionally to see my uncle – indeed to see my great-uncle before him. No. I've not even been here very much of late years. My other two sisters moved in after my uncle's death, but at that time I was still abroad with my husband. He only died about four or five years ago.'

'Oh, I see.'

'They were anxious I should come and join them here and really, it seemed the best thing to do. We had lived in India for some years. My husband was still stationed there at the time of his death. It is very difficult nowadays to know where one would wish to – should I say, put one's roots down.'

'Yes, indeed. I can quite see that. And you felt, of course, that you had roots here since your family had been here for a long time.'

'Yes. Yes, one did feel that. Of course, I'd always kept up with my sisters, had been to visit them. But things are always very different from what one thinks they will be. I have bought a small cottage near London, near Hampton Court, where I spend a good deal of my time, and I do a little occasional work for one or two charities in London.'

'So your time is fully occupied. How wise of you.'

'I have felt of late that I should spend more time here, perhaps. I've been a little worried about my sisters.'

'Their health?' suggested Miss Marple. 'One *is* rather worried nowadays, especially as there is not really anyone competent whom one can employ to look after people as they become rather feebler or have certain ailments. So much rheumatism and arthritis about. One is always so afraid of people falling down in the bath or an accident coming down stairs. Something of that kind.'

'Clotilde has always been very strong,' said Mrs Glynne. 'Tough, I should

78

describe her. But I am rather worried sometimes about Anthea. She is vague, you know, very vague indeed. And she wanders off sometimes – and doesn't seem to know where she is.'

'Yes, it is sad when people worry. There is so much to worry one.'

'I don't really think there is much to worry Anthea.'

'She worries about income tax, perhaps, money affairs,' suggested Miss Marple.

'No, no, not that so much but – oh, she worries so much about the garden. She remembers the garden as it used to be, and she's very anxious, you know, to – well, to spend money in putting things right again. Clotilde has had to tell her that really one can't afford that nowadays. But she keeps talking of the hot-houses, the peaches that used to be there. The grapes – and all that.'

'And the Cherry Pie on the walls?' suggested Miss Marple, remembering a remark.

'Fancy your remembering that. Yes. Yes, it's one of the things one does remember. Such a charming smell, heliotrope. And such a nice name for it, Cherry Pie. One always remembers that. And the grapevine. The little, small, early sweet grapes. Ah well, one must not remember the past too much.'

'And the flower borders too, I suppose,' said Miss Marple.

'Yes. Yes, Anthea would like to have a big well kept herbaceous border again. Really *not* feasible now. It is as much as one can do to get local people who will come and mow the lawns every fortnight. Every year one seems to employ a different firm. And Anthea would like pampas grass planted again. And the Mrs Simpkin pinks. White, you know. All along the stone edge border. And a fig tree that grew just outside the greenhouse. She remembers all these and talks about them.'

'It must be difficult for you.'

'Well, yes. Arguments, you see, hardly appeal in any way. Clotilde, of course, is very downright about things. She just refuses point-blank and says she doesn't want to hear another word about it.'

'It is difficult,' said Miss Marple, 'to know how to take things. Whether one should be firm. Rather authoritative. Perhaps, even, well, just a little – a little *fierce*, you know, or whether one should be sympathetic. Listen to things and perhaps hold out hopes which one knows are not justified. Yes, it's difficult.'

'But it's easier for me because you see I go away again, and then come back now and then to stay. So it's easy for me to pretend things may be easier soon and that something may be done. But really, the other day when I came home and I found that Anthea had tried to engage a most expensive firm of landscape gardeners to renovate the garden, to build up the greenhouse again – which is *quite* absurd because even if you put vines in they would not bear for another two or three years. Clotilde knew nothing about it and she was extremely angry when she discovered the estimate for this work on Anthea's desk. She was really quite unkind.'

'So many things are difficult,' said Miss Marple.

It was a useful phrase which she used often.

'I shall have to go rather early tomorrow morning, I think,' said Miss Marple. 'I was making enquiries at the Golden Boar where I understand the coach party assembles tomorrow morning. They are making quite an early start. Nine o'clock, I understand.'

'Oh dear. I hope you will not find it too fatiguing.'

'Oh, I don't think so. I gather we are going to a place called – now wait a minute, what was it called? – Stirling St Mary. Something like that. And it does not seem to be very far away. There's an interesting church to see on the way and a castle. In the afternoon there is a quite pleasant garden, not too many acres, but some special flowers. I feel sure that after this very nice rest that I have had here, I shall be quite all right. I understand now that I would have been very tired if I had had these days of climbing up cliffsides and all the rest of it.'

'Well, you must rest this afternoon, so as to be fresh for tomorrow,' said Mrs Glynne, as they went into the house. 'Miss Marple has been to visit the church,' said Mrs Glynne to Clotilde.

'I'm afraid there is not very much to see,' said Clotilde. 'Victorian glass of a most hideous kind, I think myself. No expense spared. I'm afraid my uncle was partly to blame. He was very pleased with those rather crude reds and blues.'

'Very crude. Very vulgar, I always think,' said Lavinia Glynne.

Miss Marple settled down after lunch to have a nap, and she did not join her hostesses until nearly dinner time. After dinner a good deal of chat went on until it was bedtime. Miss Marple set the tone in remembrances ... Remembrances of her own youth, her early days, places she had visited, travels or tours she had made, occasional people she had known.

She went to bed tired, with a sense of failure. She had learned nothing more, possibly because there was nothing more to learn. A fishing expedition where the fish did not rise – possibly because there were no fish there. Or it could be that she did not know the right bait to use?

CHAPTER 11

Accident

Miss Marple's tea was brought at seven-thirty the following morning so as to allow her plenty of time to get up and pack her few belongings. She was just closing her small suitcase when there was a rather hurried tap on the door and Clotilde came in, looking upset.

'Oh dear, Miss Marple, there is a young man downstairs who has called to see you. Emlyn Price. He is on the tour with you and they sent him here.'

'Of course, I remember him. Yes. Quite young?'

'Oh yes. Very modern-looking, and a lot of hair and all that, but he has really come to – well, to break some bad news to you. There has been, I am sorry to say, an accident.'

'An accident?' Miss Marple stared. 'You mean – to the coach? There has been an accident on the road? Someone has been hurt?'

'No. No, it was not the coach. There was no trouble there. It was in the course of the expedition yesterday afternoon. There was a great deal of wind you may remember, though I don't think that had anything to do with it. People strayed about a bit, I think. There is a regular path, but you can also climb up and go across the downs. Both ways lead to the Memorial Tower on the top of Bonaventure – where they were all making for. People got separated a bit and I suppose, really, there was no one actually guiding them or looking after them which, perhaps, there ought to have been. People aren't very surefooted always and the slope overhanging the gorge is very steep. There was a bad fall of stones or rocks which came crashing down the hillside and knocked someone out on the path below.'

'Oh dear,' said Miss Marple, 'I am sorry. I am most terribly sorry. Who was it who was hurt?'

'A Miss Temple or Tenderdon, I understand.'

'Elizabeth Temple,' said Miss Marple. 'Oh dear, I am sorry. I talked to her a good deal. I sat in the next seat to her on the coach. She is, I believe, a retired school-mistress, a very well known one.'

'Of course,' said Clotilde, 'I know her quite well. She was Headmistress of Fallowfield, quite a famous school. I'd no idea she was on this tour. She retired as Headmistress, I think a year or two ago, and there is a new, rather young Headmistress there now with rather advanced progressive ideas. But Miss Temple is not very old, really, she's about sixty, I should think, and very active, fond of climbing and walking and all the rest of it. This really seems *most* unfortunate. I hope she's not badly hurt. I haven't heard any details yet.'

'This is quite ready now,' said Miss Marple, snapping down the lid of her suitcase. 'I will come down at once and see Mr Price.'

Clotilde seized the suitcase.

'Let me. I can carry this perfectly. Come down with me, and be careful of the stairs.'

Miss Marple came down. Emlyn Price was waiting for her. His hair was looking even wilder than usual and he was wearing a splendid array of fancy boots and a leather jerkin and brilliant emerald green trousers.

'Such an unfortunate business,' he said, seizing Miss Marple's hand. 'I thought I'd come along myself and – well, break it to you about the accident. I expect Miss Bradbury-Scott has told you. It's Miss Temple. You know. The school dame. I don't know quite what she was doing or what happened, but some stones, or rather boulders, rolled down from above. It's rather a precipitous slope and it knocked her out and they had to take her off to hospital with concussion last night. I gather she's rather bad. Anyway, the tour for today is cancelled and we are stopping on here tonight.'

'Oh dear,' said Miss Marple, 'I am sorry. I'm very sorry.'

'I think they've decided not to go on today because they really have to wait and see what the medical report is, so we are proposing to spend one more night here at the Golden Boar and to rearrange the tour a little, so that perhaps we shall miss out altogether going to Grangmering which we were going to do tomorrow, and which is not very interesting really, or so they say. Mrs Sandbourne has gone off early to the hospital to see how things are this morning. She's going to join us at the Golden Boar for coffee at 11 o'clock. I thought perhaps you'd like to come along and hear the latest news.'

'I'll certainly come along with you,' said Miss Marple. 'Of course. At once.'

She turned to say goodbye to Clotilde and Mrs Glynne who had joined her.

'I must thank you so much,' she said. 'You have been so kind and it has been so delightful to have these two nights here. I feel so rested and everything. Most unfortunate this has occurred.'

'If you would like to spend another night,' said Mrs Glynne, 'I am sure –' She looked at Clotilde.

It occurred to Miss Marple, who had as sharp a sideways glance as anyone could desire, that Clotilde had a slightly disapproving look. She almost shook her head, though it was such a small movement that it was hardly noticeable. But she was, Miss Marple thought, hushing down the

82

suggestion that Mrs Glynne was making.

'. . . although of course I expect it would be nicer for you to be with the others and to –'

'Oh yes, I think it would be better,' said Miss Marple. 'I shall know then what the plans are and what to do about things, and perhaps I could be of help in some way. One never knows. So thank you again very much. It will not be difficult, I expect, to get a room at the Golden Boar.' She looked at Emlyn, who said reassuringly,

'That'll be all right. Several rooms have been vacated today. They won't be full at all. Mrs Sandbourne, I think, has booked for all the party to stay there tonight, and tomorrow we shall see – well, we shall see how this all goes on.'

Goodbyes were said again and thanks. Emlyn Price took Miss Marple's belongings and started out at a good striding pace.

'It's really only just round the corner, and then the first street to the left,' he said.

'Yes, I passed it yesterday, I think. Poor Miss Temple. I do hope she's not badly hurt.'

'I think she is rather,' said Emlyn Price. 'Of course, you know what doctors are, and hospital people. They say the same thing always: "as well as can be expected". There's no local hospital – they had to take her to Carristown which is about eight miles away. Anyway, Mrs Sandbourne will be back with the news by the time we've fixed you up at the hotel.'

They got there to find the tour assembled in the coffee room and coffee and morning buns and pastries were being served. Mr and Mrs Butler were talking at the moment.

'Oh, it's just too, too tragic this happening,' said Mrs Butler. 'Just too upsetting, isn't it? Just when we were all so happy and enjoying everything so much. Poor Miss Temple. And I always thought she was very sure-footed. But there, you know, you never can tell, can you, Henry?'

'No, indeed,' said Henry. 'No, indeed. I am wondering really – yes, our time's very short you know – whether we hadn't better – well, give up this tour at this point here. Not continue with it. It seems to me that there's bound to be a bit of difficulty resuming things until we know definitely. If this was – well – I mean, if this should be so serious that it could prove fatal, there might – well – I mean there might have to be an inquest or something of that kind.'

'Oh Henry, don't say dreadful things like that!'

'I'm sure,' said Miss Cooke, 'that you are being a little too pessimistic, Mr Butler. I am sure that things couldn't be as serious as that.'

In his foreign voice Mr Caspar said: 'But yes, they are serious. I hear yesterday. When Mrs Sandbourne talk on telephone to doctor. It is very, very serious. They say she has concussion bad – very bad. A special doctor he is coming to look at her and see if he can operate or if impossible. Yes – it is all very bad.'

'Oh dear,' said Miss Lumley. 'If there's any doubt, perhaps we ought to go home, Mildred. I must look up the trains, I think.' She turned to Mrs Butler. 'You see, I have made arrangements about my cats with the neighbours, and if I was delayed a day or two it might make great difficulties for *everyone*.'

'Well, it's no good our working ourselves up too much,' said Mrs Risely-Porter, in her deep, authoritative voice, 'Joanna, put this bun in the waste-paper basket, will you? It is really quite uneatable. Most unpleasant jam. But I don't want to leave it on my plate. It might make for bad feeling.'

Joanna got rid of the bun. She said:

'Do you think it would be all right if Emlyn and I went out for a walk? I mean, just saw something of the town. It's not much good our sitting about here, making gloomy remarks, is it? We can't *do* anything.'

'I think you'd be very wise to go out,' said Miss Cooke.

'Yes, you go along,' said Miss Barrow before Mrs Risely-Porter could speak.

Miss Cooke and Miss Barrow looked at each other and sighed, shaking their heads.

'The grass was very slippery,' said Miss Barrow. 'I slid once or twice myself, you know, on that very short turf.'

'And the stones, too,' said Miss Cooke. 'Quite a shower of small stones fell down just as I was turning a corner on the path. Yes, one struck me on the shoulder quite sharply.'

Tea, coffee, biscuits and cakes despatched, everyone seemed somewhat dissociated and ill at ease. When a catastrophe has occurred, it is very difficult to know what is the proper way to meet it. Everyone had given their view, had expressed surprise and distress. They were now awaiting news and at the same time had a slight hankering after some form of sight-seeing, some interest to carry them through the morning. Lunch would not be served until one o'clock and they really felt that to sit around and repeat their same remarks would be rather a gloomy business.

Miss Cooke and Miss Barrow rose as one woman and explained that it was necessary for them to do a little shopping. One or two things they needed, and they also wished to go to the post office and buy stamps.

'I want to send off one or two postcards. And I want to enquire about postal dues on a letter to China,' said Miss Barrow.

'And I want to match some wools,' said Miss Cooke. 'And also it seemed to me there was rather an interesting building on the other side of the Market Square.'

'I think it would do us all good to get out,' said Miss Barrow.

Colonel and Mrs Walker also rose, and suggested to Mr and Mrs Butler that they too might go out and see what there was to see. Mrs Butler expressed hopes of an antique shop.

'Only I don't really mean a real antique shop. More what you would call a junk shop. Sometimes you can pick up some really interesting things there.'

They all trooped out. Emlyn Price had already sidled to the door and disappeared in pursuit of Joanna without troubling to use conversation to explain his departure. Mrs Risely-Porter, having made a belated attempt to call her niece back, said she thought that at least the lounge would be rather more pleasant to sit in. Miss Lumley agreed – Mr Caspar escorted the ladies with the air of a foreign equerry.

Professor Wanstead and Miss Marple remained.

'I think myself,' said Professor Wanstead, addressing Miss Marple, 'that it would be pleasant to sit outside the hotel. There is a small terrace giving on the street. If I might persuade you?'

Miss Marple thanked him and rose to her feet. She had hardly exchanged a word so far with Professor Wanstead. He had several learned looking books with him, one of which he was usually perusing. Even in the coach he continued to try and read.

'But perhaps you too want to shop,' he said. 'For myself, I would prefer to wait somewhere peacefully for the return of Mrs Sandbourne. It is important, I think, that we should know exactly what we are in for.'

'I quite agree with you, as to that,' said Miss Marple. 'I did a certain amount of walking round the town yesterday and I don't feel any necessity to do so again today. I'd rather wait here in case there is anything I can do to help. Not that I suppose there is, but one never knows.'

They moved together through the hotel door and round the corner to where there was a little square of garden with a raised stone walk close to the wall of the hotel and on which there were various forms of basket chairs. There was no one there at the moment so they sat down. Miss Marple looked thoughtfully at her vis-à-vis. At his corrugated and wrinkled face, his bushy brows, his luxuriant head of grey hair. He walked with a slight stoop. He had an interesting face, Miss Marple decided. His voice was dry and caustic, a professional man of some kind, she thought.

'I am not wrong, am I,' said Professor Wanstead. 'You *are* Miss Jane Marple?'

'Yes, I am Jane Marple.'

She was slightly surprised, though for no particular reason. They had not been long enough together for people to be identified by the other travellers. The last two nights she had not been with the rest of the party. It was quite natural.

'I thought so,' said Professor Wanstead, 'from a description I have had of you.'

'A description of me?' Miss Marple was again slightly surprised.

'Yes, I had a description of you –' he paused for a moment. His voice was not exactly lowered, but it lost volume, although she could still hear it quite easily '– from Mr Rafiel.'

'Oh,' said Miss Marple, startled. 'From Mr Rafiel.'

'You are surprised?'

'Well, yes, I am rather.'

'I don't know that you should be.'

'I didn't expect –' began Miss Marple and then stopped.

Professor Wanstead did not speak. He was merely sitting, looking at her intently. In a minute or two, thought Miss Marple to herself, he will say to me, 'What symptoms exactly, dear lady? Any discomfort in swallowing? Any lack of sleep? Digestion in good order?' She was almost sure now that he was a doctor.

'When did he describe me to you? That must have been –'

'You were going to say some time ago – some weeks ago. Before his death – that is so. He told me that you would be on this tour.'

'And he knew that you would be on it too – that you were going on it.'

'You can put it that way,' said Professor Wanstead. 'He said,' he continued, 'that you would be travelling on this tour, that he had in fact arranged for you to be travelling on this tour.'

'It was very kind of him,' said Miss Marple. 'Very kind indeed. I was most surprised when I found he'd booked me. Such a treat. Which I could not have afforded for myself.'

'Yes,' said Professor Wanstead. 'Very well put.' He nodded his head as one who applauds a good performance by a pupil.

'It is sad that it has been interrupted in this fashion,' said Miss Marple. 'Very sad indeed. When I am sure we were all enjoying ourselves so much.'

'Yes,' said Professor Wanstead. 'Yes, very sad. And unexpected, do you think, or not unexpected?'

'Now what do you mean by that, Professor Wanstead?'

His lips curled in a slight smile as he met her challenging look.

'Mr Rafiel,' he said, 'spoke to me about you at some length, Miss Marple. He suggested that I should be on this tour with you. I should in due course almost certainly make your acquaintance, since members in a tour

86

inevitably do make each other's acquaintance, though it usually takes a day or two for them to split up, as it were, into possible groupings led by similar tastes or interests. And he further suggested to me that I should, shall we say, keep an eye on you.'

'Keep an eye on me?' said Miss Marple, showing some slight displeasure. 'And for what reason?'

'I think reasons of protection. He wanted to be quite sure that nothing should happen to you.'

'Happen to me? What should happen to me, I should like to know?'

'Possibly what happened to Miss Elizabeth Temple,' said Professor Wanstead.

Joanna Crawford came round the corner of the hotel. She was carrying a shopping basket. She passed them, nodding a little, she looked towards them with slight curiosity and went on down the street. Professor Wanstead did not speak until she had gone out of sight.

'A nice girl,' he said, 'at least I think so. Content at present to be a beast of burden to an autocratic aunt, but I have no doubt will reach the age of rebellion fairly soon.'

'What did you mean by what you said just now?' said Miss Marple, uninterested for the moment in Joanna's possible rebellion.

'That is a question which, perhaps, owing to what has happened, we shall have to discuss.'

'You mean because of the accident?'

'Yes. If it was an accident.'

'Do you think it *wasn't* an accident?'

'Well, I think it's just possible. That's all.'

'I don't of course know anything about it,' said Miss Marple, hesitating.

'No. You were absent from the scene. You were – shall I put it this way – were you just possibly on duty elsewhere?'

Miss Marple was silent for a moment. She looked at Professor Wanstead once or twice and then she said:

'I don't think I know exactly what you mean.'

'You are being careful. You are quite right to be careful.'

'I have made it a habit,' said Miss Marple.

'To be careful?'

'I should not put it exactly like that, but I have made a point of being always ready to disbelieve as well as believe anything that is told to me.'

'Yes, and you are quite right too. You don't know anything about me. You know my name from the passenger list of a very agreeable tour visiting castles and historic houses and splendid gardens. Possibly the gardens are what will interest you most.'

87

'Possibly.'

'There are other people here too who are interested in gardens.'

'Or profess to be interested in gardens.'

'Ah,' said Professor Wanstead. 'You have noticed that.'

He went on. 'Well, it was my part, or at any rate to begin with, to observe you, to watch what you were doing, to be near at hand in case there was any possibility of – well, we might call it roughly – dirty work of any kind. But things are slightly altered now. You must make up your mind if I am your enemy or your ally.'

'Perhaps you are right,' said Miss Marple. 'You put it very clearly but you have not given me any information about yourself yet on which to judge. You were a friend, I presume, of the late Mr Rafiel?'

'No,' said Professor Wanstead, 'I was not a friend of Mr Rafiel. I had met him once or twice. Once on a committee of a hospital, once at some other public event. I knew about him. He, I gather, also knew about me. If I say to you, Miss Marple, that I am a man of some eminence in my own profession, you may think me a man of bounding conceit.'

'I don't think so,' said Miss Marple. 'I should say, if you say that about yourself, that you are probably speaking the truth. You are, perhaps, a medical man.'

'Ah. You are perceptive, Miss Marple. Yes, you are quite perceptive. I have a medical degree, but I have a speciality too. I am a pathologist and psychologist. I don't carry credentials about with me. You will probably have to take my word up to a certain point, though I can show you letters addressed to me, and possibly official documents that might convince you. I undertake mainly specialist work in connection with medical jurisprudence. To put it in perfectly plain everyday language, I am interested in the different types of criminal brain. That has been a study of mine for many years. I have written books on the subject, some of them violently disputed, some of them which have attracted adherence to my ideas. I do not do very arduous work nowadays, I spend my time mainly writing up my subject, stressing certain points that have appealed to me. From time to time I come across things that strike me as interesting. Things that I want to study more closely. This I am afraid must seem rather tedious to you.'

'Not at all,' said Miss Marple. 'I am hoping perhaps, from what you are saying now, that you will be able to explain to me certain things which Mr Rafiel did not see fit to explain to me. He asked me to embark upon a certain project but he gave me no useful information on which to work. He left me to accept it and proceed, as it were, completely in the dark. It seemed to me extremely foolish of him to treat the matter in that way.'

'But you accepted it?'

'I accepted it. I will be quite honest with you. I had a financial incentive.'

'Did that weigh with you?'

Miss Marple was silent for a moment and then she said slowly,

'You may not believe it, but my answer to that is, "Not really".'

'I am not surprised. But your interest was aroused. That is what you are trying to tell me.'

'Yes. My interest was aroused. I had known Mr Rafiel not well, casually, but for a certain period of time – some weeks in fact – in the West Indies. I see you know about it, more or less.'

'I know that that was where Mr Rafiel met you and where – shall I say – you two collaborated.'

Miss Marple looked at him rather doubtfully. 'Oh,' she said, 'he said that, did he?' She shook her head.

'Yes, he did,' said Professor Wanstead. 'He said you had a remarkable flair for criminal matters.'

Miss Marple raised her eyebrows as she looked at him.

'And I suppose that seems to you most unlikely,' she said. 'It surprises you.'

'I seldom allow myself to be surprised at what happens,' said Professor Wanstead. 'Mr Rafiel was a very shrewd and astute man, a good judge of people. He thought that you, too, were a good judge of people.'

'I would not set myself up as a good judge of people,' said Miss Marple. 'I would only say that certain people remind me of certain other people that I have known, and that therefore I can presuppose a certain likeness between the way they would act. If you think I know all about what I am supposed to be doing here, you are wrong.'

'By accident more than design,' said Professor Wanstead, 'we seem to have settled here in a particularly suitable spot for discussion of certain matters. We do not appear to be overlooked, we cannot easily be overheard, we are not near a window or a door and there is no balcony or window overhead. In fact, we can talk.'

'I should appreciate that,' said Miss Marple. 'I am stressing the fact that I am myself completely in the dark as to what I am doing or supposed to be doing. I don't know why Mr Rafiel wanted it that way.'

'I think I can guess that. He wanted you to approach a certain set of facts, of happenings, unbiased by what anyone would tell you first.'

'So you are not going to tell me anything either?' Miss Marple sounded irritated. 'Really!' she said, 'there are limits.'

'Yes,' said Professor Wanstead. He smiled suddenly. 'I agree with you. We must do away with some of these limits. I am going to tell you certain facts that will make certain things fairly clear to you. You in turn may be able to tell me certain facts.'

'I rather doubt it,' said Miss Marple. 'One or two rather peculiar indications perhaps, but indications are not facts.'

'Therefore –' said Professor Wanstead, and paused.

'For goodness' sake, tell me something,' said Miss Marple.

CHAPTER 12

A Consultation

'I'm not going to make a long story of things. I'll explain quite simply how I came into this matter. I act as confidential adviser from time to time for the Home Office. I am also in touch with certain institutions. There are certain establishments which, in the event of crime, provide board and lodging for certain types of criminal who have been found guilty of certain acts. They remain there at what is termed Her Majesty's pleasure, sometimes for a definite length of time and in direct association with their age. If they are below a certain age they have to be received in some places of detention specially indicated. You understand that, no doubt.'

'Yes, I understand quite well what you mean.'

'Usually I am consulted fairly soon after whatever the – shall we call it – crime has happened, to judge such matters as treatment, possibilities in the case, prognosis favourable or unfavourable, all the various words. They do not mean much and I will not go into them. But occasionally also I am consulted by a responsible Head of such an institution for a particular reason. In this matter I received a communication from a certain Department which was passed to me through the Home Office. I went to visit the Head of this institution. In fact, the Governor responsible for the prisoners or patients or whatever you like to call them. He was by way of being a friend of mine. A friend of fairly long standing though not one with whom I was on terms of great intimacy. I went down to the institution in question and the Governor laid his troubles before me. They referred to one particular inmate. He was not satisfied about this inmate. He had certain doubts. This was the case of a young man or one who had been a young man, in fact little more than a boy, when he came there. That was now several years ago. As time went on, and after the present Governor had taken up his own residence there (he had not been there at the original arrival of this prisoner), he became worried. Not because he himself was a professional man, but because he was a man of experience of criminal patients and prisoners. To put it quite simply, this had been a boy who from his early youth had been completely unsatisfactory. You can call it by what term you like. A young delinquent, a young thug, a bad lot, a person of diminished responsibility. There are many terms. Some of them fit, some of them don't fit, some of them are merely puzzling. He was a criminal type. That was certain. He had joined gangs, he had beaten up people, he was a thief, he had stolen, he had embezzled, he had taken part in swindles, he had initiated certain frauds. In fact, he was a son who would be any father's despair.'

'Oh, I see,' said Miss Marple.

'And what do you see, Miss Marple?'

'Well, what I think I see is that you are talking of Mr Rafiel's son.'

'You are quite right. I am talking of Mr Rafiel's son. What do you know about him?'

'Nothing,' said Miss Marple. 'I only heard – and that was yesterday – that Mr Rafiel had a delinquent, or unsatisfactory, if we like to put it mildly, son. A son with a criminal record. I know very little about him. Was he Mr Rafiel's only son?'

'Yes, he was Mr Rafiel's only son. But Mr Rafiel also had two daughters. One of them died when she was fourteen, the elder daughter married quite happily but had no children.'

'Very sad for him.'

'Possibly,' said Professor Wanstead. 'One never knows. His wife died young and I think it possible that *her* death saddened him very much, though he was never willing to show it. How much he cared for his son and daughters I don't know. He provided for them. He did his best for them. He did his best for his son, but what his feelings were one cannot say. He was not an easy man to read that way. I think his whole life and interest lay in his profession of making money. It was the making of it, like all great financiers, that interested him. Not the actual money which he secured by it. That, as you might say, was sent out like a good servant to earn more money in more interesting and unexpected ways. He enjoyed finance. He loved finance. He thought of very little else.

'I think he did all that was possible for his son. He got him out of scrapes at school, he employed good lawyers to get him released from Court proceedings whenever possible, but the final blow came, perhaps presaged by some early happenings. The boy was taken to Court on a charge of assault against a young girl. It was said to be assault and rape and he suffered a term of imprisonment for it, with some leniency shown because of his youth. But later, a second and really serious charge was brought against him.'

'He killed a girl,' said Miss Marple. 'It that right? That's what I heard.'

'He lured a girl away from her home. It was some time before her body was found. She had been strangled. And afterwards her face and head had been disfigured by some heavy stones or rocks, presumably to prevent her identity being made known.'

'Not a very nice business,' said Miss Marple, in her most old-ladylike tone.

Professor Wanstead looked at her for a moment or two.

'You describe it that way?'

'It is how it seems to me,' said Miss Marple. 'I don't like that sort of thing. I never have. If you expect me to feel sympathy, regret, urge an unhappy childhood, blame bad environment; if you expect me in fact to weep over him, this young murderer of yours, I do not feel inclined so to do. I do not like evil beings who do evil things.'

'I am delighted to hear it,' said Professor Wanstead. 'What I suffer in the course of my profession from people weeping and gnashing their teeth, and blaming everything on some happening in the past, you would hardly believe. If people knew the bad environments that people had had, the unkindness, the difficulties of their lives and the fact that nevertheless they can come through unscathed, I don't think they would so often take the opposite point of view. The misfits are to be pitied, yes, they are to be pitied if I may say so for the genes with which they are born and over which they have no control themselves. I pity epileptics in the same way. If you know what genes are –'

'I know, more or less,' said Miss Marple. 'It's common knowledge nowadays, though naturally I have no exact chemical or technical knowledge.'

'The Governor, a man of experience, told me exactly why he was so anxious to have my verdict. He had felt increasingly in his experience of this particular inmate that, in plain words, the boy was *not* a killer. He didn't think he was the type of a killer, he was like no killer he had ever seen before, he was of the opinion that the boy was the kind of criminal type who would never go straight no matter what treatment was given to him, would never reform himself; and for whom nothing in one sense of the word could be done, but at the same time he felt increasingly certain that the verdict upon him had been a wrong one. He did not believe that the boy had killed a girl, first strangled her and then disfigured her after rolling her body into a ditch. He just couldn't bring himself to believe it. He'd looked over the facts of the case, which seemed to be fully proved. This boy had known the girl, he had been seen with her on several different occasions before the crime. They had presumably slept together and there were other points. His car had been seen in the neighbourhood. He himself had been recognized and all the rest of it. A perfectly fair case. But my friend was unhappy about it, he said. He was a man who had a very strong feeling for justice. He wanted a different opinion. He wanted, in fact, not the police side which he knew, he wanted a professional medical view. That was my field, he said. My line of country entirely. He wanted me to see this young man and talk with him, visit him, make a professional appraisal of him and give him my opinion.'

'Very interesting,' said Miss Marple. 'Yes, I call that very interesting.

After all, your friend – I mean your Governor – was a man of experience, a man who loved justice. He was a man whom you'd be willing to listen to. Presumably then, you did listen to him.'

'Yes,' said Professor Wanstead, 'I was deeply interested. I saw the subject, as I will call him, I approached him from several different attitudes. I talked to him, I discussed various changes likely to occur in the law. I told him it might be possible to bring down a lawyer, a Queen's Counsel, to see what points there might be in his favour, and other things. I approached him as a friend but also as an enemy so that I could see how he responded to different approaches, and I also made a good many physical tests, such as we use very frequently nowadays. I will not go into those with you because they are wholly technical.'

'Then what did you think in the end?'

'I thought,' said Professor Wanstead, 'I thought my friend was likely to be right. I did not think that Michael Rafiel was a murderer.'

'What about the earlier case you mentioned?'

'That told against him, of course. Not in the jury's mind, because of course they did not hear about that until after the judge's summing up, but certainly in the judge's mind. It told against him, but I made a few enquiries myself afterwards. He had assaulted a girl. He had conceivably raped her, but he had not attempted to strangle her and in my opinion – I have seen a great many cases which come before the Assizes – it seems to me highly unlikely that there was a very definite case of rape. Girls, you must remember, are far more ready to be raped nowadays than they used to be. Their mothers insist, very often, that they should call it rape. The girl in question had had several boy-friends who had gone further than friendship. I did not think it counted very greatly as evidence against him. The actual murder case – yes, that was undoubtedly murder – but I continued to feel by all tests, physical tests, mental tests, psychological tests, none of them accorded with this particular crime.'

'Then what did you do?'

'I communicated with Mr Rafiel. I told him that I would like an interview with him on a certain matter concerning his son. I went to him. I told him what I thought, what the Governor thought, that we had no evidence, that there were no grounds of appeal, at present, but that we both believed that a miscarriage of justice had been committed. I said I thought possibly an enquiry might be held, it might be an expensive business, it might bring out certain facts that could be laid before the Home Office, it might be successful, it might not. There might be something there, some evidence if you looked for it. I said it would be expensive to look for it but I presumed that would make no difference to anyone in his position. I had realized by that time that he was a sick man, a very ill man. He told me so himself. He told me that he had been in expectation of an early death, that he'd been warned two years ago that death could not be delayed for what they first thought was about a year, but later they realized that he would last rather longer because of his unusual physical strength. I asked him what he felt about his son.'

'And what did he feel about his son?' said Miss Marple.

'Ah, you want to know that. So did I. He was, I think, extremely honest with me even if –'

'– even if rather ruthless?' said Miss Marple.

'Yes, Miss Marple. You are using the right word. He was a ruthless man, but he was a just man and an honest man. He said, "I've known what my son was like for many years. I have not tried to change him because I don't believe that anyone could change him. He is made a certain way. He is crooked. He's a bad lot. He'll always be in trouble. He's dishonest. Nobody, nothing could make him go straight. I am well assured of that. I have in a sense washed my hands of him. Though not legally or outwardly; he has always had money if he required it. Help legal or otherwise if he gets into trouble. I have done always what I could do. Well, let us say if I had a son who was a spastic, who was sick, who was epileptic, I would do what I could for him. If you have a son who is sick morally, shall we say, and for whom there is no cure, I have done what I could also. No more and no less. What can I do for him now?" I told him that it depended what he wanted to do. "There's no difficulty about that," he said. "I am handicapped but I can see quite clearly what I want to do. I want to get him vindicated. I want to get him released from confinement. I want to get him free to continue to lead his own life as best he can lead it. If he must lead it in further dishonesties, then he must lead it that way. I will leave provision for him, to do for him everything that can be done. I don't want him suffering, imprisoned, cut off from his life because of a perfectly natural and unfortunate mistake. If somebody else, some other man killed that girl, I want the fact brought to light and recognized. I want justice for Michael. But I am handicapped. I am a very ill man. My time is measured now not in years or months but in weeks."

'Lawyers, I suggested – I know a firm – He cut me short. "Your lawyers will be useless. I must arrange what I can arrange in such a limited time." He offered me a large fee to undertake the search for the truth and to undertake everything possible with no expense spared. "I can do next to nothing myself. Death may come at any moment. I empower you as my chief help, and to assist you at my request I will try to find a certain person." He wrote down a name for me. Miss Jane Marple. He said "I don't want to give you her address. I want you to meet her in surroundings of my own choosing," and he then told me of this tour, this charming, harmless, innocent tour of historic houses, castles and gardens. He would provide me with a reservation on it ahead for a certain date. "Miss Jane Marple," he said, "will also be on that tour. You will meet her there, you will encounter her casually, and thus it will be seen clearly to be a casual meeting."

'I was to choose my own time and moment to make myself known to you if I thought that that would be the better way. You have already asked me if I or my friend, the Governor, had any reason to suspect or know of any other person who might have been guilty of the murder. My friend the Governor certainly suggested nothing of the kind, and he had already taken up the matter with the police officer who had been in charge of the case. A most reliable detective-superintendent with very good experience in these matters.'

'No other man was suggested? No other friend of the girl's? No other former friend who might have been supplanted?'

'There was nothing of that kind to find. I asked him to tell me a little about you. He did not however consent to do so. He told me you were elderly. He told me that you were a person who knew about people. He told me one other thing.' He paused.

'What's the other thing?' said Miss Marple. 'I have some natural curiosity, you know. I really can't think of any other advantage I conceivably could have. I am slightly deaf. My eyesight is not quite as good as it used to be. I cannot really think that I have any advantages beyond the fact that I may, I suppose, seem rather foolish and simple, and am in fact, what used to be called in rather earlier days an "old pussy". I *am* an old pussy. Is that the sort of thing he said?'

'No,' said Professor Wanstead. 'What he said was he thought you had a very fine sense of evil.'

'Oh,' said Miss Marple. She was taken aback.

Professor Wanstead was watching her.

'Would you say that was true?' he said.

Miss Marple was quiet for quite a long time. At last she said,

'Perhaps it is, Yes, perhaps. I have at several different times in my life been apprehensive, have recognized that there was evil in the neighbourhood, the surroundings, that the environment of someone who was evil was near me, connected with what was happening.'

She looked at him suddenly and smiled.

'It's rather, you know,' she said, 'like being born with a very keen sense of smell. You can smell a leak of gas when other people can't do so. You can distinguish one perfume from another very easily. I had an aunt once,'

96

continued Miss Marple thoughtfully, 'who said she could smell when people told a lie. She said there was quite a distinctive odour came to her. Their noses twitched, she said, and then the smell came. I don't know if it was true or not, but – well, on several occasions she was quite remarkable. She said to my uncle once, "Don't Jack, engage that young man you were talking to this morning. He was telling you lies the whole time he was talking." That turned out to be quite true.'

'A sense of evil,' said Professor Wanstead. 'Well, if you do sense evil, tell me. I shall be glad to know. I don't think I have a particular sense of evil myself. Ill-health, yes, but not – not evil up here.' He tapped his forehead.

'I'd better tell you briefly how I came into things now,' said Miss Marple. 'Mr Rafiel, as you know, died. His lawyers asked me to come and see them, apprised me of his proposition. I received a letter from him which explained nothing. After that I heard nothing more for some little time. Then I got a letter from the company who run these tours saying that Mr Rafiel before his death had made a reservation for me knowing that I should enjoy a trip very much, and wanting to give it me as a surprise present. I was very astonished but took it as an indication of the first step that I was to undertake. I was to go on this tour and presumably in the course of the tour some other indication or hint or clue or direction would come to me. I think it did. Yesterday, no, the day before, I was received on my arrival here by three ladies who live at an old manor house here and who very kindly extended an invitation to me. They had heard from Mr Rafiel, they said, who had written some time before his death, saying that a very old friend of his would be coming on this tour and would they be kind enough to put her up for two or three days as he thought she was not fit to attempt the particular ascent of this rather difficult climb up the headland to where there was a memorial tower which was the principal event of yesterday's tour.'

'And you took that also as an indication of what you were to do?'

'Of course,' said Miss Marple. 'There can be no other reason for it. He was not a man to shower benefits for nothing, out of compassion for an old lady who wasn't good at walking up hills. No. He *wanted* me to go there.'

'And you went there? And what then?'

'Nothing,' said Miss Marple. 'Three sisters.'

'Three weird sisters?'

'They ought to have been,' said Miss Marple, 'but I don't think they were. They didn't seem to be anyway. I don't know yet. I suppose they may have been – they may be, I mean. They seem ordinary enough. They didn't belong to this house. It had belonged to an uncle of theirs and they'd come here to live some years ago. They are in rather poor circumstances, they are amiable, not particularly interesting. All slightly different in type. They do not appear to have been well acquainted with Mr Rafiel. Any conversation I have had with them appears to yield nothing.'

'So you learnt nothing during your stay?'

'I learnt the facts of the case you've just told me. Not from them. From an elderly servant, who started her reminiscences dating back to the time of the uncle. She knew of Mr Rafiel only as a name. But she was eloquent on the theme of the murder: it had all started with the visit here of a son of Mr Rafiel's who was a bad lot, of how the girl had fallen in love with him and that he'd strangled the girl, and how sad and tragic and terrible it all was. "With bells on", as you might say,' said Miss Marple, using a phrase of her youth. 'Plenty of exaggeration, but it was a nasty story, and she seemed to believe that the police view was that this hadn't been his only murder –'

'It didn't seem to you to connect up with the three weird sisters?'

'No, only that they'd been the guardians of the girl – and had loved her dearly. No more than that.'

'They might know something – something about another man?'

'Yes – that's what we want, isn't it? The other man – a man of brutality, who wouldn't hesitate to bash in a girl's head after he'd killed her. The kind of man who could be driven frantic with jealousy. There are men like that.'

'No other curious things happened at The Old Manor?'

'Not really. One of the sisters, the youngest I think, kept talking about the garden. She sounded as though she was a very keen gardener, but she couldn't be because she didn't know the names of half the things. I laid a trap or two for her, mentioning special rare shrubs and saying did she know it? and yes, she said, wasn't it a wonderful plant? I said it was not very hardy and she agreed. But she didn't know anything about plants. That reminds me –'

'Reminds you of what?'

'Well, you'll think I'm just silly about gardens and plants, but I mean one does *know* things about them. I mean, I know a few things about birds and I know some things about gardens.'

'And I gather that it's not birds but gardens that are troubling you.'

'Yes. Have you noticed two middle-aged women on this tour? Miss Barrow and Miss Cooke.'

'Yes. I've noticed them. Pair of middle-aged spinsteres travelling together.'

'That's right. Well, I've found out something odd about Miss Cooke. That is her name, isn't it? I mean it's her name on the tour.'

'Why – has she got another name?'

'I think so. She's the same person who visited me – I won't say visited me

98

exactly, but she was outside my garden fence in St Mary Mead, the village where I live. She expressed pleasure at my garden and talked about gardening with me. Told me she was living in the village and working in somebody's garden, who'd moved into a new house there. I rather think,' said Miss Marple, 'yes, I rather think that the whole thing was lies. There again, she knew nothing about gardening. She pretended to but it wasn't true.'

'Why do you think she came there?'

'I'd no idea at the time. She said her name was Bartlett – and the name of the woman she said she was living with began with "H", though I can't remember it for the moment. Her hair was not only differently done but it was a different colour and her clothes were of a different style. I didn't recognize her at first on this trip. Just wondered why her face was vaguely familiar. And then suddenly it came to me. Because of the dyed hair. I said where I had seen her before. She admitted that she'd been there – but pretended that she, too, hadn't recognized *me*. All lies.'

'And what's your opinion about all that?'

'Well, one thing certainly – Miss Cooke (to give her her present name) came to St Mary Mead just to have a look at me – so that she'd be quite sure to be able to recognize me when we met again –'

'And why was that felt to be necessary?'

'I don't know. There are two possibilities. I'm not sure that I like one of them very much.'

'I don't know,' said Professor Wanstead, 'that I like it very much either.'

They were both silent for a minute or two, and then Professor Wanstead said –

'I don't like what happened to Elizabeth Temple. You've talked to her during this trip?'

'Yes, I have. When she's better I'd like to talk to her again – she could tell me – us – things about the girl who was murdered. She spoke to me of this girl – who had been at her school, who had been going to marry Mr Rafiel's son – but didn't marry him. Instead she died. I asked how or why she died – and she answered with the word "Love". I took it as meaning a suicide – but it was murder. Murder through jealousy would fit. Another man. Some other man we've got to find. Miss Temple may be able to tell us who he was.'

'No other sinister possibilities?'

'I think, really, it is casual information we need. I see no reason to believe that there is any sinister suggestion in any of the coach passengers – or any sinister suggestion about the people living in The Old Manor House. But one of those three sisters may have known or remembered something that the girl or Michael once said. Clotilde used to take the girl abroad. Therefore, she may know of something that occurred on some foreign trip perhaps. Something that the girl said or mentioned or did on some trip. Some man that the girl met. Something which has nothing to do with The Old Manor House here. It is difficult because only by talking, by casual information, can you get any clue. The second sister, Mrs Glynne, married fairly early, has spent time, I gather, in India and in Africa. She may have heard of something through her husband, or through her husband's relations, through various things that are unconnected with The Old Manor House here although she has visited it from time to time. She knew the murdered girl presumably, but I should think she knew her much less well than the other two. But that does not mean that she may not know some significant *facts* about the girl. The third sister is more scatty, more localized, does not seem to have known the girl as well. But still, she too *may* have information about possible lovers – or boy-friends – seen the girl with an unknown man. That's her, by the way, passing the hotel now.'

Miss Marple, however occupied by her tête-à-tête, had not relinquished the habits of a lifetime. A public thoroughfare was always to her an observation post. All the passers-by, either loitering or hurrying, had been noticed automatically.

'Anthea Bradbury-Scott – the one with the big parcel. She's going to the post office, I suppose. It's just round the corner, isn't it?'

'Looks a bit daft to me,' said Professor Wanstead, 'all that floating hair – grey hair too – a kind of Ophelia of fifty.'

'I thought of Ophelia too, when I first saw her. Oh dear, I wish I knew what I ought to do next. Stay here at the Golden Boar for a day or two, or go on with the coach tour. It's like looking for a needle in a haystack. If you stick your fingers in it long enough, you ought to come up with something – even if one does get pricked in the process.'

CHAPTER 13

Black and Red Check

Mrs Sandbourne returned just as the party was sitting down to lunch. Her news was not good. Miss Temple was still unconscious. She certainly could not be moved for several days.

Having given the bulletin, Mrs Sandbourne turned the conversation to practical matters. She produced suitable timetables of trains for those who wished to return to London and proposed suitable plans for the resumption of the tour on the morrow or the next day. She had a list of suitable short expeditions in the near neighbourhood for this afternoon – small groups in hired cars.

Professor Wanstead drew Miss Marple aside as they went out of the dining-room –

'You may want to rest this afternoon. If not, I will call for you here in an hour's time. There is an interesting church you might care to see –?'

'That would be very nice,' said Miss Marple.

II

Miss Marple sat quite still in the car that had come to fetch her. Professor Wanstead had called for her at the time he had said.

'I thought you might enjoy seeing this particular church. And a very pretty village, too,' he explained. 'There's no reason really why one should not enjoy the local sights when one can.'

'It's very kind of you, I'm sure,' Miss Marple had said.

She had looked at him with that slightly fluttery gaze of hers.

'*Very* kind,' she said, 'It just seems – well, I don't want to say it seems heartless, but well, you know what I mean.'

'My dear lady, Miss Temple is not an old friend of yours or anything like that. Sad as this accident has been.'

'Well,' said Miss Marple again, 'this is very kind of you.'

Professor Wanstead had opened the door of the car and Miss Marple got into it. It was, she presumed, a hired car. A kindly thought to take an elderly lady to see one of the sights of the neighbourhood. He might have taken somebody younger, more interesting and certainly better looking. Miss Marple looked at him thoughtfully once or twice as they drove through the village. He was not looking at her. He was gazing out of his own window.

When they had left the village behind and were on a second class country road twisting round the hillside, he turned his head and said to her,

'We are not going to a church, I am afraid.'

'No,' said Miss Marple, 'I thought perhaps we weren't.'

'Yes, the idea would have come to you.'

'Where are we going, may I ask?'

'We are going to a hospital, in Carristown.'

'Ah yes, that was where Miss Temple was taken?'

It was a question, though it hardly needed to be one.

'Yes,' he said. 'Mrs Sandbourne saw her and brought me back a letter from the Hospital Authorities. I have just finished talking to them on the telephone.'

'Is she going on well?'

'No. Not going on very well.'

'I see. At least – I hope I don't see,' said Miss Marple.

'Her recovery is very problematical but there is nothing that can be done. She may not recover consciousness again. On the other hand she may have a few lucid intervals.'

'And you are taking *me* there? Why? I am not a friend of hers, you know. I only just met her for the first time on this trip.'

'Yes, I realize that. I'm taking you there because in one of the lucid intervals she has had, she asked for you.'

'I see,' said Miss Marple. 'I wonder why she should ask for *me*, why she should have thought that I – that I could be useful in any way to her, or do anything. She is a woman of perception. In her way, you know, a great woman. As Headmistress of Fallowfield she occupied a prominent position in the educational world.'

'The best girls' school there is, I suppose?'

'Yes. She was a great personality. She was herself a woman of considerable scholarship. Mathematics were her speciality, but she was an "all round" – what I should call an educator. Was interested in education, what girls were fitted for, how to encourage them. Oh, many other things. It is sad and very cruel if she dies,' said Miss Marple. 'It will seem such a waste of a life. Although she had retired from her Headmistress-ship she still exercised a lot of power. This accident –' She stopped. 'Perhaps you do not want us to discuss the accident?'

'I think it is better that we should do so. A big boulder crashed down the hillside. It has been known to happen before though only at very long divided intervals of time. However, somebody came and spoke to me about it,' said Professor Wanstead.

'Came and spoke to you about the accident? Who was it?'

'The two young people. Joanna Crawford and Emlyn Price.'

'What did they say?'

'Joanna told me that she had the impression there was someone on the hillside. Rather high up. She and Emlyn were climbing up from the lower main path, following a rough track that wound round the curve of the hill. As they turned a corner she definitely saw, outlined against the skyline, a man or a woman who was trying to roll a big boulder forward along the ground. The boulder was rocking – and finally it started to roll, at first slowly and then gathering speed down the hillside. Miss Temple was walking along the main path below, and had come to a point just underneath it when the boulder hit her. If it was done deliberately it might not, of course, have succeeded; it might have missed her – but it did succeed. If what was being attempted was a deliberate attack on the woman walking below it succeeded only too well.'

'Was it a man or a woman they saw?' asked Miss Marple.

'Unfortunately, Joanna Crawford could not say. Whoever it was, was wearing jeans or trousers, and had on a lurid poloneck pullover in red and black checks. The figure turned and moved out of sight almost immediately. She is inclined to think it was a man but cannot be certain.'

'And she thinks, or you think, that it was a deliberate attempt on Miss Temple's life?'

'The more she mulls it over, the more she thinks that that was exactly what it was. The boy agrees.'

'You have no idea who it might have been?'

'No idea whatever. No more have they. It might be one of our fellow travellers, someone who went for a stroll that afternoon. It might be someone completely unknown who knew that the coach was making a halt here and chose this place to make an attack on one of the passengers. Some youthful lover of violence for violence's sake. Or it might have been an enemy.'

'It seems very melodramatic if one says "a secret enemy",' said Miss Marple.

'Yes, it does. Who would want to kill a retired and respected Headmistress? That is a question we want answered. It is possible, faintly possible that Miss Temple herself might be able to tell us. She might have recognized the figure above her or she might more likely have known of someone who bore her ill-will for some special reason.'

'It still seems unlikely.'

'I agree with you,' said Professor Wanstead. 'She seems a totally unlikely person to be a fit victim of attack, but yet when one reflects, a Headmistress knows a great many people. A great many people, shall we put it this way,

103

have passed through her hands.'

'A lot of girls you mean have passed through her hands.'

'Yes. Yes, that is what I meant. Girls and their families. A Headmistress must have knowledge of many things. Romances, for instance, that girls might indulge in, unknown to their parents. It happens very often. Especially in the last ten or twenty years. Girls are said to mature earlier. That is physically true, though in a deeper sense of the word, they mature late. They remain childish longer. Childish in the clothes they like to wear, childish with their floating hair. Even their mini skirts represent a worship of childishness. Their Baby Doll nightdresses, their gymslips and shorts – all children's fashions. They wish *not* to become adult – *not* to have to accept our kind of responsibility. And yet like all children, they want to be *thought* grown up, and free to do what they think are grown up things. And that leads sometimes to tragedy and sometimes to the aftermath of tragedy.'

'Are you thinking of some particular case?'

'No. No, not really. I'm only thinking – well, shall we say letting possibilities pass through my mind. I cannot believe that Elizabeth Temple had a *personal* enemy. An enemy ruthless enough to wish to take an opportunity of killing her. What I do think –' he looked at Miss Marple, '– would you like to make a suggestion?'

'Of a possibility? Well, I think I know or guess what you *are* suggesting. You are suggesting that Miss Temple knew something, knew some fact or had some knowledge that would be inconvenient or even dangerous to somebody if it was known.'

'Yes, I do feel exactly that.'

'In that case,' said Miss Marple, 'it seems indicated that there is someone on our couch tour who recognized Miss Temple or knew who she was, but who perhaps after the passage of some years was not remembered or might even not have been recognized by Miss Temple. It seems to throw it back on our passengers, does it not?' She paused. 'That pullover you mentioned – red and black checks, you said?'

'Oh yes? The pullover –' He looked at her curiously. 'What was it that struck you about that?'

'It was very noticeable,' said Miss Marple. 'That is what your words led me to infer. It was very mentionable. So much so that the girl Joanna mentioned it specifically.'

'Yes. And what does that suggest to you?'

'The trailing of flags,' said Miss Marple thoughtfully. 'Something that will be seen, remembered, observed, recognized.'

'Yes.' Professor Wanstead looked at her with encouragement.

'When you describe a person you have seen, seen not close at hand but from a distance, the first thing you will describe will be their clothes. Not their faces, not their walk, not their hands, not their feet. A scarlet tam-o'-shanter, a purple cloak, a bizarre leather jacket, a pullover of brilliant reds and blacks. Something very recognizable, very noticeable. The object of it being that when that person removes that garment, gets rid of it, sends it by post in a parcel to some address, say, about a hundred miles away, or thrusts it in a rubbish bin in a city or burns it or tears it up or destroys it, she or he will be the one person modestly and rather drably attired who will not be suspected or looked at or thought of. It must have been *meant*, that scarlet and black check jersey. Meant so that it will be recognized again though actually it will never again be seen on that particular person.'

'A very sound idea,' said Professor Wanstead. 'As I have told you,' continued the Professor, 'Fallowfield is situated not very far from here. Sixteen miles, I think. So this is Elizabeth Temple's part of the world, a part she knows well with people in it that she also might know well.'

'Yes. It widens the possibilities,' said Miss Marple. 'I agree with you,' she said presently, 'that the attacker is more likely to have been a man than a woman. That boulder, if it was done with intent, was sent on its course very accurately. Accuracy is more a male quality than a female one. On the other hand there might easily have been someone on our coach, or possibly in the neighbourhood, who saw Miss Temple in the street, a former pupil of hers in past years. Someone whom she herself might not recognize after a period of time. But the girl or woman would have recognized her, because a Headmaster or Headmistress of over sixty is not unlike the same Headmaster or Headmistress at the age of fifty. She is recognizable. Some woman who recognized her former mistress and also knew that her mistress knew something damaging about her. Someone who might in some way prove a danger to her.' She sighed. 'I myself do not know this part of the world at all. Have you any particular knowledge of it?'

'No,' said Professor Wanstead. 'I could not claim a personal knowledge of this part of the country. I know something, however, of various things that have happened in this part of the world entirely because of what you have told me. If it had not been for my acquaintanceship with you and the things you have told me I could have been more at sea than I am.

'What are you yourself actually doing here? You do not know. Yet you were sent here. It was deliberately arranged by Rafiel that you should come here, that you should take this coach tour, that you and I should meet. There have been other places where we have stopped or through which we have passed, but special arrangements were made so that you should actually stay for a couple of nights here. You were put up with former friends of his who would not have refused any request he made. Was there a reason for that?'

'So that I could learn certain facts that I had to know,' said Miss Marple.

'A series of murders that took place a good many years ago?' Professor Wanstead looked doubtful. 'There is nothing unusual in that. You can say the same of many places in England and Wales. These things seem always to go in a series. First a girl found assaulted and murdered. Then another girl not very far away. Then something of the same kind perhaps twenty miles away. The same pattern of death.

'Two girls were reported missing from Jocelyn St Mary itself, the one that we have been discussing whose body was found six months later, many miles away and who was last seen in the company of Michael Rafiel –'

'And the other?'

'A girl called Nora Broad. *Not* a "quiet girl with no boy-friends". Possibly with one boy-friend too many. Her body was never found. It will be – one day. There have been cases when twenty years have passed,' said Wanstead. He slowed down: 'We have arrived. This is Carristown, and here is the Hospital.'

Shepherded by Professor Wanstead, Miss Marple entered. The Professor was obviously expected. He was ushered into a small room where a woman rose from a desk.

'Oh yes,' she said, 'Professor Wanstead. And – er – this is – er –' She hesitated slightly.

'Miss Jane Marple,' said Professor Wanstead. 'I talked to Sister Barker on the telephone.'

'Oh yes. Sister Barker said that she would be accompanying you.'

'How is Miss Temple?'

'Much the same, I think. I am afraid there is not much improvement to report.' She rose. 'I will take you to Sister Barker.'

Sister Barker was a tall, thin woman. She had a low, decisive voice and dark grey eyes that had a habit of looking at you and looking away almost immediately, leaving you with the feeling that you had been inspected in a very short space of time, and judgment pronounced upon you.

'I don't know what arrangements you have in mind,' said Professor Wanstead.

'Well, I had better tell Miss Marple just what we have arranged. First I must make it clear to you that the patient, Miss Temple, is still in a coma with very rare intervals. She appears to come to occasionally, to recognize her surroundings and to be able to say a few words. But there is nothing one can do to stimulate her. It has to be left to the utmost patience. I expect Professor Wanstead has already told you that in one of her intervals of consciousness she uttered quite distinctly the words "Miss Jane Marple". And then: "*I want to speak to her. Miss Jane Marple.*" After that she relapsed into unconsciousness. Doctor thought it advisable to get in touch with the other occupants of the coach. Professor Wanstead came to see us and explained various matters and said he would bring you over. I am afraid that all we can ask you to do is to sit in the private ward where Miss Temple is, and perhaps be ready to make a note of any words she should say, if she does regain consciousness. I am afraid the prognosis is not very helpful. To be quite frank, which is better I think, since you are not a near relative and are unlikely to be disturbed by this information, Doctor thinks that she is sinking fast, that she may die without recovering consciousness. There is nothing one can do to relieve the concussion. It is important that someone should hear what she says and Doctor thinks it advisable that she should not see too many people round her if she regains consciousness. If Miss Marple is not worried at the thought of sitting there alone, there will be a nurse in the room, though not obviously so. That is, she will not be noticed from the bed, and will not move unless she's asked for. She will sit in a corner of the room shielded by a screen.' She added, 'We have a police official there also, ready to take down anything. The Doctor thinks it advisable that he also should not be noticed by Miss Temple. One person alone, and that possibly a person she *expects* to see, will not alarm her or make her lose knowledge of what she wants to say to you. I hope this will not be too difficult a thing to ask you?'

'Oh no,' said Miss Marple, 'I'm quite prepared to do that. I have a small notebook with me and a Biro pen that will not be in evidence. I can remember things by heart for a very short time, so I need not appear to be obviously taking notes of what she says. You can trust my memory and I am not deaf – not deaf in the real sense of the word. I don't think my hearing is quite as good as it used to be, but if I am sitting near a bedside, I ought to be able to hear anything she says quite easily even if it is whispered. I am used to sick people. I have had a good deal to do with them in my time.'

Again the lightning glance of Sister Barker went over Miss Marple. This time a faint inclination of the head showed satisfaction.

'It is kind of you,' she said, 'and I am sure that if there is any help you can give, we can rely on you to give it. If Professor Wanstead likes to sit in the waiting-room downstairs, we can call him at any moment if it should be necessary. Now, Miss Marple, perhaps you will accompany me.'

Miss Marple followed Sister along a passage and into a small well appointed single room. In the bed there, in a dimly-lighted room since the blinds were half drawn, lay Elizabeth Temple. She lay there like a statue, yet she did not give the impression of being asleep. Her breath came uncertainly in slight gasps. Sister Barker bent to examine her patient, motioned Miss Marple into a chair beside the bed. She then crossed the room to the door again. A young man with a notebook in his hand came from behind the screen there.

'Doctor's orders, Mr Reckitt,' said Sister Barker.

A nurse also appeared. She had been sitting in the opposite corner of the room.

'Call me if necessary, Nurse Edmonds,' said Sister Barker, 'and get Miss Marple anything she may need.'

Miss Marple loosened her coat. The room was warm. The nurse approached and took it from her. Then she retired to her former position, Miss Marple sat down in the chair. She looked at Elizabeth Temple thinking, as she had thought before when looking at her in the coach, what a fine shaped head she had. Her grey hair drawn back from it, fitted her face in a perfect cap-like effect. A handsome woman, and a woman of personality. Yes, a thousand pities, Miss Marple thought, a thousand pities if the world was going to lose Elizabeth Temple.

Miss Marple eased the cushion at her back, moved the chair a fraction of an inch and sat quietly to wait. Whether to wait in vain or to some point, she had no idea. Time passed. Ten minutes, twenty minutes, half an hour, thirty-five minutes. Then suddenly, quite unexpectedly as it were, a voice came. Low, but distinct, slightly husky. None of the resonance it had once held. 'Miss Marple.'

Elizabeth Temple's eyes were open now. They were looking at Miss Marple. They looked competent, perfectly sensible. She was studying the face of the woman who was sitting by her bed, studying her without any sign of emotion, of surprise. Only, one would say, of scrutiny. Fully conscious scrutiny. And the voice spoke again.

'Miss Marple. You are Jane Marple?'

'That is right. Yes.' said Miss Marple, 'Jane Marple.'

'Henry often spoke of you. He said things about you.'

The voice stopped. Miss Marple said with a slight query in her voice, 'Henry?'

'Henry Clithering, an old friend of mine – very old friend.'

'An old friend of mine too,' said Miss Marple. 'Henry Clithering.'

Her mind went back to the many years she had known him, Sir Henry Clithering, the things he had said to her, the assistance he had asked from her sometimes, and the assistance that she had asked from him. A very old friend.

'I remembered your name. On the passenger list. I thought it must be you. You could help. That's what he – Henry, yes – would say if he were

108

here. You might be able to help. To find out. It's important. Very important although – it's a long time ago now – a – long – time – ago.'

Her voice faltered a little, her eyes half closed. Nurse got up, came across the room, picked up a small glass and held it to Elizabeth Temple's lips. Miss Temple took a sip, nodded her head dismissively. Nurse put down the glass and went back to her chair.

'If I can help, I will,' said Miss Marple. She asked no further questions. Miss Temple said, 'Good,' and after a minute or two, again, 'Good.'

For two or three minutes she lay with her eyes closed. She might have been asleep or unconscious. Then her eyes opened again suddenly.

'Which,' she said, 'which of them? That's what one has got to know. Do you know what I am talking about?'

'I think so. A girl who died – Nora Broad?' A frown came quickly to Elizabeth Temple's forehead.

'No, no, no. The other girl. Verity Hunt.'

There was a pause and then, 'Jane Marple. You're old – older than when he talked about you. You're older, but you can still find out things, can't you?'

Her voice became slightly higher, more insistent.

'You can, can't you? Say you can. I've not much time. I know that. I know it quite well. One of them, but which? Find out. Henry would have said you can. It may be dangerous for you – but you'll find out, won't you?'

'With God's help, I will,' said Miss Marple. It was a vow.

'Ah.'

The eyes closed, then opened again. Something like a smile seemed to try and twitch the lips.

'The big stone from above. The Stone of Death.'

'Who rolled that stone down?'

'Don't know. No matter – only – Verity. Find out about Verity. Truth. Another name for truth, Verity.'

Miss Marple saw the faint relaxation of the body on the bed. There was a faintly whispered: 'Goodbye. Do your best . . .'

Her body relaxed, the eyes closed. The nurse came again to the bedside. This time she took up the pulse, felt it, and beckoned to Miss Marple. Miss Marple rose obediently and followed her out of the room.

'That's been a big effort for her,' said the nurse. 'She won't regain consciousness again for some time. Perhaps not at all. I hope you learnt something?'

'I don't think I did,' said Miss Marple, 'but one never knows, does one.'

'Did you get anything?' asked Professor Wanstead, as they went out to the car.

'A name,' said Miss Marple. 'Verity. Was that the girl's name?'

'Yes. Verity Hunt.'

Elizabeth Temple died an hour and a half later. She died without regaining consciousness.

Mr Broadribb Wonders

'Seen *The Times* this morning?' said Mr Broadribb to his partner, Mr Schuster.

Mr Shuster said he couldn't afford *The Times*, he took the *Telegraph*.

'Well, it may be in that too,' said Mr Broadribb. 'In the deaths, Miss Elizabeth Temple, D.Sc.'

Mr Schuster looked faintly puzzled.

'Headmistress of Fallowfield. You've heard of Fallowfield, haven't you?'

'Of course,' said Schuster. 'Girls' school. Been going for fifty years or so. First class, fantastically expensive. So she was the Headmistress of it, was she? I thought the Headmistress had resigned some time ago. Six months at least. I'm sure I read about it in the paper. That is to say there was a bit about the Headmistress. Married woman. Youngish. Thirty-five to forty. Modern ideas. Give the girls lessons in cosmetics, let 'em wear trouser suits. Something of that kind.'

'Hum,' said Mr Broadribb, making the noise that solicitors of his age are likely to make when they hear something which elicits criticism based on long experience. 'Don't think she'll ever make the name that Elizabeth Temple did. Quite someone, she was. Been there a long time, too.'

'Yes,' said Mr Schuster, somewhat uninterested. He wondered why Broadribb was so interested in defunct school-mistresses.

Schools were not really of particular interest to either of the two gentlemen. Their own offspring were now more or less disposed of. Mr Broadribb's two sons were respectively in the Civil Service and in an oil firm, and Mr Schuster's rather younger progeny were at different universities where both of them respectively were making as much trouble for those in authority as they possibly could do. He said,

'What about her?'

'She was on a coach tour,' said Mr Broadribb.

'Those coaches,' said Mr Schuster. 'I wouldn't let any of my relations go on one of those. One went off a precipice in Switzerland last week and two months ago one had a crash and twenty were killed. Don't know who drives these things nowadays.'

'It was one of those Country Houses and Gardens and Objects of Interest in Britain – or whatever they call it – tours,' said Mr Broadribb. 'That's not quite the right name, but you know what I mean.'

'Oh yes, I know. Oh the – er – yes, that's the one we sent Miss

What's-a-name on. The one old Rafiel booked.'

'Miss Jane Marple was on it.'

'She didn't get killed too, did she?' asked Mr Schuster.

'Not so far as I know,' said Mr Broadribb. 'I just wondered a bit, though.'

'Was it a road accident?'

'No. It was at one of the beauty spot places. They were walking on a path up a hill. It was a stiff walk. Up a rather steep hill with boulders and things on it. Some of the boulders got loose and came rushing down the mountainside. Miss Temple was knocked out and taken to hospital with concussion and died –'

'Bad luck,' said Mr Schuster, and waited for more.

'I only wondered,' said Mr Broadribb, 'because I happened to remember that – well, that Fallowfield was the school where the girl was at.'

'What girl? I don't really know what you're talking about, Broadribb.'

'The girl who was done in by young Michael Rafiel. I was just recalling a few things which might seem to have some slight connection with this curious Jane Marple business that old Rafiel was so keen on. Wish he'd told us more.'

'What's the connection?' said Mr Schuster.

He looked more interested now. His legal wits were in process of being sharpened, to give a sound opinion on whatever it was that Mr Broadribb was about to confide to him.

'That girl. Can't remember her last name now. Christian name was Hope and Faith or something like that. Verity, that was her name. Verity Hunter, I think it was. She was one of that series of murdered girls. Found her body in a ditch about thirty miles away from where she'd gone missing. Been dead six months. Strangled apparently, and her head and face had been bashed in – to delay recognition, they thought, but she *was* recognized all right. Clothes, handbag, jewellery nearby – some mole or scar. Oh yes, she was identified quite easily –'

'Actually, she was the one the trial was all about, wasn't she?'

'Yes. Suspected of having done away with perhaps three other girls during the past year, Michael was. But evidence wasn't so good in the other deaths – so the police went all out on this one – plenty of evidence – bad record. Earlier cases of assault and rape. Well, we all know what rape is nowadays. Mum tells the girl she's got to accuse the young man of rape even if the young man hasn't had much chance, with the girl at him all the time to come to the house while mum's away at work or dad's gone on holiday. Doesn't stop badgering him until she's forced him to sleep with her. Then, as I say, mum tells the girl to call it rape. However, that's not the point,' said Mr Broadribb. 'I wondered if things mightn't tie up a bit, you know. I

112

thought this Jane Marple business with Rafiel might have something to do with Michael.'

'Found guilty, wasn't he? And given a life sentence?'

'I can't remember now – it's so long ago. Or did they get away with a verdict of diminished responsibility?'

'And Verity Hunter or Hunt was educated at that school. Miss Temple's school? She wasn't still a schoolgirl though, was she, when she was killed? Not that I can remember.'

'Oh no. She was eighteen or nineteen, living with relations or friends of her parents, or something like that. Nice house, nice people, nice girl by all accounts. The sort of girl whose relations always say "she was a very quiet girl, rather shy, didn't go about with strange people and had no boy-friends." Relations never know what boy-friends a girl has. The girls take mighty good care of that. And young Rafiel was said to be very attractive to girls.'

'Never been any doubt that he did it?' asked Mr Schuster.

'Not a scrap. Told a lot of lies in the witness box, anyway. His Counsel would have done better not to have let him give evidence. A lot of his friends gave him an alibi that didn't stand up, if you know what I mean. All his friends seemed to be fluent liars.'

'What's your feeling about it, Broadribb?'

'Oh, I haven't got any feelings,' said Mr Broadribb, 'I was just wondering if this woman's death might tie up.'

'In what way?'

'Well, you know – about these boulders that fall down cliff sides and drop on top of someone. It's not always in the course of nature. Boulders usually stay where they are, in my experience.'

CHAPTER 15

Verity

'Verity,' said Miss Marple.

Elizabeth Margaret Temple had died the evening before. It had been a peaceful death. Miss Marple, sitting once more amidst the faded chintz of the drawing-room in The Old Manor House, had laid aside the baby's pink coat which she had previously been engaged in knitting and had substituted a crocheted purple scarf. This half-mourning touch went with Miss Marple's early Victorian ideas of tactfulness in face of tragedy.

An inquest was to be held on the following day. The vicar had been approached and had agreed to hold a brief memorial service in the church as soon as arrangements could be made. Undertakers suitably attired, with proper mourning faces, took general charge of things in liaison with the police. The inquest was to take place on the following morning at 11 o'clock. Members of the coach tour had agreed to attend the inquest. And several of them had chosen to remain on so as to attend the church service also.

Mrs Glynne had come to the Golden Boar and urged Miss Marple to return to The Old Manor House until she finally returned to the tour.

'You will get away from all the reporters.'

Miss Marple had thanked all three sisters warmly and had accepted.

The coach tour would be resumed after the memorial service, driving first to South Bedestone, thirty-five miles away, where there was a good class hotel which had been originally chosen for a stopping place. After that the tour would go on as usual.

There were, however, as Miss Marple had considered likely, certain persons who were disengaging themselves and returning home, or were going in other directions and not continuing on the tour. There was something to be said in favour of either decision. To leave what would become a journey of painful memories, or to continue with the sight-seeing that had already been paid for and which had been interrupted only by one of those painful accidents that may happen on any sight-seeing expedition. A lot would depend, Miss Marple thought, on the outcome of the inquest.

Miss Marple, after exchanging various conventional remarks proper to the occasion with her three hostesses, had devoted herself to her purple wool and had sat considering her next line of investigation. And so it was that with her fingers still busy, she had uttered the one word, 'Verity'. Throwing it as one throws a pebble into a stream, solely to observe what the

114

result – if any – would be. Would it mean something to her hostesses? It might or it might not. Otherwise, when she joined the members of the tour at their hotel meal this evening, which had been arranged, she would try the effect of it there. It had been, she thought to herself, the last word or almost the last word that Elizabeth Temple had spoken. So therefore, thought Miss Marple (her fingers still busy because she did not need to look at her crocheting, she could read a book or conduct a conversation while her fingers, though slightly crippled with rheumatism, would proceed correctly through their appointed movements). So therefore, 'Verity'.

Like a stone into a pool, causing ripples, a splash, something? Or nothing. Surely there would be a reaction of one sort or another. Yes, she had not been mistaken. Although her face registered nothing, the keen eyes behind her glasses had watched three people in a simultaneous manner as she had trained herself to do for many years now, when wishing to observe her neighbours either in church, mothers' meetings, or at other public functions in St Mary Mead when she had been on the track of some interesting piece of news or gossip.

Mrs Glynne had dropped the book she was holding and had looked across towards Miss Marple with slight surprise. Surprise, it seemed, at the particular word coming from Miss Marple, but not surprised really to hear it.

Clotilde reacted differently. Her head shot up, she leant forward a little, then she looked not at Miss Marple but across the room in the direction of the window. Her hands clenched themselves, she kept very still. Miss Marple, although dropping her head slightly as though she was not looking any more, noted that her eyes were filling with tears. Clotilde sat quite still and let the tears roll down her cheeks. She made no attempt to take out a handkerchief, she uttered no word. Miss Marple was impressed by the aura of grief that came from her.

Anthea's reaction was different. It was quick, excited, almost pleasurable.

'Verity? Verity, did you say? Did you know her? I'd no idea. It is Verity Hunt you mean?'

Lavinia Glynne said, 'It's a Christian name?'

'*I* never knew anyone of that name,' said Miss Marple, 'but I *did* mean a Christian name. Yes. It is rather unusual, I think. Verity.' She repeated it thoughtfully.

She let her purple wool ball fall and looked round with the slightly apologetic and embarrassed look of one who realizes she has made a serious *faux pas*, but is not sure why.

'I – I am so sorry. Have I said something I shouldn't? It was only

115

because . . .'

'No, of course not,' said Mrs Glynne. 'It was just that it is – it is a name we know, a name with which we have – associations.'

'It just came into my mind,' said Miss Marple, still apologetic, 'because, you know, it was poor Miss Temple who said it. I went to see her, you know, yesterday afternoon. Professor Wanstead took me. He seemed to think that I might be able to – to – I don't know if it's the proper word – to *rouse* her, in some way. She was in a coma and they thought – not that I was a friend of hers at any time, but we had chattered together on the tour and we often sat beside each other, as you know, on some of the days and we had talked. And he thought perhaps I might be of some use. I'm afraid I wasn't though. Not at all. I just sat there and waited and then she did say one or two words, but they didn't seem to mean anything. But finally, just when it was time for me to go, she did open her eyes and looked at me – I don't know if she was mistaking me for someone – but she did say that word. Verity! And, well of course it stuck in my mind, especially with her passing away yesterday evening. It must have been someone or something that she had in her mind. But of course it might just mean – well, of course it might just mean Truth. That's what verity means, doesn't it?'

She looked from Clotilde to Lavinia to Anthea.

'It was the Christian name of a girl we knew,' said Lavinia Glynne. 'That is why it startled us.'

'Especially because of the awful way she died,' said Anthea.

Clotilde said in her deep voice, 'Anthea! there's no need to go into these details.'

'But after all, everyone knows quite well about her,' said Anthea. She looked towards Miss Marple. 'I thought perhaps you might have known about her because you knew Mr Rafiel, didn't you? Well, I mean, he wrote to us about you so you must have known him. And I thought perhaps – well, he'd mentioned the whole thing to you.'

'I'm so sorry,' said Miss Marple, 'I'm afraid I don't quite understand what you're talking about.'

'They found her body in a ditch,' said Anthea.

There was never any holding Anthea, Miss Marple thought, not once she got going. But she thought that Anthea's vociferous talk was putting additional strain on Clotilde. She had taken out a handkerchief now in a quiet, non-committal way. She brushed tears from her eyes and then sat upright, her back very straight, her eyes deep and tragic.

'Verity,' she said, 'was a girl we cared for very much. She lived here for a while. I was very fond of her –'

'And she was very fond of you,' said Lavinia.

116

'Her parents were friends of mine,' said Clotilde. 'They were killed in a plane accident.'

'She was at school at Fallowfield,' explained Lavinia. 'I suppose that was how Miss Temple came to remember her.'

'Oh I see,' said Miss Marple. 'Where Miss Temple was Headmistress, is that it? I have heard of Fallowfield often, of course. It's a very fine school, isn't it?'

'Yes,' said Clotilde. 'Verity was a pupil there. After her parents died she came to stay with us for a time while she could decide what she wanted to do with her future. She was eighteen or nineteen. A very sweet girl and a very affectionate and loving one. She thought perhaps of training for nursing, but she had very good brains and Miss Temple was very insistent that she ought to go to university. So she was studying and having coaching for that when – when this terrible thing happened.'

She turned her face away.

'I – do you mind if we don't talk about it any more just now?'

'Oh, of course not,' said Miss Marple. 'I'm so sorry to have impinged on some tragedy. I didn't know. I – I haven't heard ... I thought – well I mean ...' She became more and more incoherent.

That evening she heard a little more. Mrs Glynne came to her bedroom when she was changing her dress to go out and join the others at the hotel.

'I thought I ought to come and explain a little to you,' said Mrs Glynne, 'about – about the girl Verity Hunt. Of course you couldn't know that our sister Clotilde was particularly fond of her and that her really horrible death was a terrible shock. We never mention her if we can help it, but – I think it would be easier if I told you the facts completely and you will understand. Apparently Verity had, without our knowledge, made friends with an undesirable – a more than undesirable – it turned out to be a dangerous – young man who already had a criminal record. He came here to visit us when he was passing through once. We knew his father very well.' She paused. 'I think I'd better tell you the whole truth if you don't know, and you don't seem to. He was actually Mr Rafiel's son, Michael –'

'Oh dear,' said Miss Marple, 'not – not – I can't remember his name but I do remember hearing that there was a son – and, that he hadn't been very satisfactory.'

'A little more than that,' said Mrs Glynne. 'He'd always given trouble. He'd been had up in court once or twice for various things. Once assaulting a teenager – other things of that type. Of course I consider myself that the magistrates are too lenient with that kind of thing. They don't want to upset a young man's university career. And so they let them off with a – I forget

117

what they call it – a suspended sentence, something of that kind. If these boys were sent to gaol at once it would perhaps warn them off that type of life. He was a thief, too. He had forged cheques, he pinched things. He was a thoroughly bad lot. We were friends of his mother's. It was lucky for her, I think, that she died young before she had time to be upset by the way her son was turning out. Mr Rafiel did all he could, I think. Tried to find suitable jobs for the boy, paid fines for him and things like that. But I think it was a great blow to him, though he pretended to be more or less indifferent and to write it off as one of those things that happen. We had, as probably people here in the village will tell you, we had a bad outbreak of murders and violence in this district. Not only here. They were in different parts of the country, twenty miles away, sometimes fifty miles away. One or two, it's suspected by the police, were nearly a hundred miles away. But they seemed to centre more or less on this part of the world. Anyway, Verity one day went out to visit a friend and – well, she didn't come back. We went to the police about it, the police sought for her, searched the whole countryside but they couldn't find any trace of her. We advertised, they advertised, and they suggested that she'd gone off with a boy-friend. Then word began to get round that she had been seen with Michael Rafiel. By now the police had their eye on Michael as a possibility for certain crimes that had occurred, although they couldn't find any direct evidence. Verity was said to have been seen, described by her clothing and other things, with a young man of Michael's appearance and in a car that corresponded to a description of his car. But there was no further evidence until her body was discovered six months later, thirty miles from here in a rather wild part of wooded country, in a ditch covered with stones and piled earth. Clotilde had to go to identify it – it was Verity all right. She'd been strangled and her head beaten in. Clotilde has never quite got over the shock. There were certain marks, a mole and an old scar and of course her clothes and the contents of her handbag. Miss Temple was very fond of Verity. She must have thought of her just before she died.'

'I'm sorry,' said Miss Marple. 'I'm really very, very sorry. Please tell your sister that I didn't know. I had no idea.'

CHAPTER 16

The Inquest

Miss Marple walked slowly along the village street on her way towards the market place where the inquest was to take place in the old-fashioned Georgian building which had been known for a hundred years as the Curfew Arms. She glanced at her watch. There was still a good twenty minutes before she need be there. She looked into the shops. She paused before the shop that sold wool and babies' jackets, and peered inside for a few moments. A girl in the shop was serving. Small woolly coats were being tried on two children. Further along the counter there was an elderly woman.

Miss Marple went into the shop, went along the counter to a seat opposite the elderly woman, and produced a sample of pink wool. She had run out, she explained, of this particular brand of wool and had a little jacket she needed to finish. The match was soon made, some more samples of wool that Miss Marple had admired were brought our for her to look at, and soon she was in conversation. Starting with the sadness of the accident which had just taken place. Mrs Merrypit, if her name was identical with that which was written up outside the shop, was full of the importance of the accident, and the general difficulties of getting local governments to do anything about the dangers of footpaths and public rights of way.

'After the rain, you see, you get all the soil washed off and then the boulders get loose and then down they comes. I remember one year they had three falls – three accidents there was. One boy nearly killed, he was, and then later that year, oh six months later, I think, there was a man got his arm broken, and the third time it was poor old Mrs Walker. Blind she was and pretty well deaf too. She never heard nothing or she could have got out of the way, they say. Somebody saw it and they called out to her, but they was too far away to reach her or to run to get her. And so she was killed.'

'Oh how sad,' said Miss Marple, 'how tragic. The sort of thing that's not easily forgotten, is it.'

'No indeed. I except the Coroner'll mention it today.'

'I expect he will,' said Miss Marple. 'In a terrible way it seems quite a natural thing to happen, doesn't it, though of course there are accidents sometimes by pushing things about, you know. Just pushing, making stones rock. That sort of thing.'

'Ah well, there's boys as be up to anything. But I don't think I've ever seen them up that way, fooling about.'

119

Miss Marple went on to the subject of pullovers. Bright coloured pullovers.

'It's not for myself,' she said, 'it's for one of my great-nephews. You know he wants a polo-necked pullover and very bright colours he'd like.'

'Yes, they do like bright colours nowadays, don't they?' agreed Mrs Merrypit. 'Not in jeans. Black jeans they like. Black or dark blue. But they like a bit of brightness up above.'

Miss Marple described a pullover of check design in bright colours. There appeared to be quite a good stock of pullovers and jerseys, but anything in red and black did not seem to be on display, nor even was anything like it mentioned as having been lately in stock. After looking at a few samples Miss Marple prepared to take her departure, chatting first about the former murders she had heard about which had happened in this part of the world.

'They got the fellow in the end,' said Mrs Merrypit. 'Nice-looking boy, hardly have thought it of him. He'd been well brought up, you know. Been to university and all that. Father was very rich, they say. Touched in the head, I suppose. Not that they sent him to Broadway, or whatever the place is. No, they didn't do that, but I think myself he must have been a mental case – there was five or six other girls, so they said. The police had one after another of the young men round here-abouts to help them. Geoffrey Grant they had up. They were pretty sure it was him to begin with. He was always a bit queer, ever since he was a boy. Interfered with little girls going to school, you know. He used to offer them sweets and get them to come down the lanes with him and see the primroses, or something like that. Yes, they had very strong suspicions about him. But it wasn't him. And then there was another one. Bert Williams, but he'd been far away on two occasions, at least – what they call an alibi, so it couldn't be him. And then at last it came to this – what's-is-name, I can't remember him now. Luke I think his name was – no Mike Something. Very nice-looking, as I say, but he had a bad record. Yes, stealing, forging cheques, all sorts of things like that. And two what-you-call 'em paternity cases, no, I don't mean that, but you know what I mean. When a girl's going to have a baby. You know and they make an order and make the fellow pay. He'd got two girls in the family way before this.'

'Was this girl in the family way?'

'Oh yes, she was. At first we thought when the body was found it might have been Nora Broad. That was Mrs Broad's niece, down at the mill shop. Great one for going with the boys, she was. She'd gone away missing from home in the same way. Nobody knew where she was. So when this body turned up six months later they thought at first it was her.'

120

'But it wasn't?'

'No – someone quite different.'

'Did her body ever turn up?'

'No. I suppose it might some day, but they think on the whole it was pushed into the river. Ah well, you never know, do you? You never know what you may dig up off a ploughed field or something like that. I was taken once to see all that treasure. Luton Loo was it – some name like that? Somewhere in the East Counties. Under a ploughed field it was. Beautiful. Gold ships and Viking ships and gold plate, enormous great platters. Well, you never know. Any day you may turn up a dead body or you may turn up a gold platter. And it may be hundreds of years old like that gold plate was, or it may be a three- or four-years-old body, like Mary Lucas who'd been missing for four years, they say. Somewhere near Reigate she was found. Ah well, all these things! It's a sad life. Yes, it's a very sad life. You never know what's coming.'

'There was another girl who'd lived here, wasn't there?' said Miss Marple, 'who was killed.'

'You mean the body they thought was Nora Broad's but it wasn't? Yes. I've forgotten her name now. Hope, it was, I think. Hope or Charity. One of those sort of names, if you know what I mean. Used to be used a lot in Victorian times but you don't hear them so much nowadays. Lived at the Manor House, she did. She'd been there for some time after her parents were killed.'

'Her parents died in an accident, didn't they?'

'That's right. In a plane going to Spain or Italy, one of those places.'

'And you say she came to live here? Were they relations of hers?'

'I don't know if they were relations, but Mrs Glynne as she is now, was I think a great friend of her mother's or something that way. Mrs Glynne, of course, was married and gone abroad but Miss Clotilde – that's the eldest one, the dark one – she was very fond of the girl. She took her abroad, to Italy and France and all sorts of places, and she had her trained a bit of typewriting and shorthand and that sort of thing, and art classes too. She's very arty, Miss Clotilde is. Oh, she was mighty fond of the girl. Broken-hearted she was when she disappeared. Quite different to Miss Anthea –'

'Miss Anthea is the youngest one, isn't she?'

'Yes. Not quite all there, some people say. Scatty like, you know, in her mind. Sometimes you see her walking along, talking to herself, you know, and tossing her head in a very queer way. Children get frightened of her sometimes. They say she's a bit queer about things. I don't know. You hear everything in a village, don't you? The great-uncle who lived here before, he was a bit peculiar too. Used to practise revolver shooting in the garden. For no reason at all so far as anyone could see. Proud of his marksmanship, he said he was, whatever marksmanship is.'

'But Miss Clotilde is not peculiar?'

'Oh no, she's clever, she is. Knows Latin and Greek, I believe. Would have liked to go to university but she had to look after her mother who was an invalid for a long time. But she was very fond of Miss – now, what was her name? – Faith perhaps. She was very fond of her and treated her like a daughter. And then along comes this young what's-his-name, Michael I think it was – and then one day the girl just goes off without saying a word to anyone. I don't know if Miss Clotilde knew as she was in the family way.'

'But you knew,' said Miss Marple.

'Ah well, I've got a lot of experience. I usually know when a girl's that way. It's plain enough to the eye. It's not only the shape, as you might say, you can tell by the look in their eyes and the way they walk and sit, and the sort of giddy fits they get and sick turns now and again. Oh yes, I thought to myself, here's another one of them. Miss Clotilde had to go and identify the body. Nearly broke her up, it did. She was like a different woman for weeks afterwards. Fairly loved that girl, she did.'

'And the other one – Miss Anthea?'

'Funnily enough, you know, I thought she had a kind of pleased look as though she was – yes, just pleased. Not nice, eh? Farmer Plummer's daughter used to look like that. Always used to go and see pigs killed. Enjoyed it. Funny things goes on in families.'

Miss Marple said goodbye, saw she had another ten minutes to go and passed on to the post office. The post office and general store of Jocelyn St Mary was just off the Market Square.

Miss Marple went into the post office, bought some stamps, looked at some of the postcards and then turned her attention to various paperback books. A middle-aged woman with rather a vinegary face presided behind the postal counter. She assisted Miss Marple to free a book from the wire support in which the books were.

'Stick a bit sometimes, they do. People don't put them back straight, you see.'

There was by now no one else in the shop. Miss Marple looked with distaste at the jacket of the book, a naked girl with blood-stained markings on her face and a sinister-looking killer bending over her with a blood-stained knife in his hand.

'Really,' she said, 'I don't like these horrors nowadays.'

'Gone a bit too far with some of their jackets, haven't they,' said Mrs Vinegar. 'Not everyone as likes them. Too fond of violence in every way, I'd say nowadays.'

Miss Marple detached a second book. '*Whatever Happened to Baby Jane*,' she read. 'Oh dear, it's a sad world one lives in.'

'Oh yes, I know. Saw in yesterday's paper, I did, some woman left her baby outside a supermarket and then someone else comes along and wheels it away. And all for no reason as far as one can see. The police found her all right. They all seem to say the same things, whether they steal from a supermarket or take away a baby. Don't know what came over them, they say.'

'Perhaps they really don't,' suggested Miss Marple.

Mrs Vinegar looked even more like vinegar.

'Take me a lot to believe that, it would.'

Miss Marple looked round – the post office was still empty. She advanced to the window.

'If you are not too busy, I wonder if you could answer a question of mine,' said Miss Marple. 'I have done something extremely stupid. Of late years I make so many mistakes. This was a parcel addressed to a charity. I sent them clothes – pullovers and children's woollies, and I did it up and addressed it and it was sent off – and only this morning it came to me suddenly that I'd made a mistake and written the wrong address. I *don't* suppose any list is kept of the addresses of parcels – but I thought someone might have just happened to remember it. The address I meant to put was The Dockyard and Thames Side Welfare Association.'

Mrs Vinegar was looking quite kindly now, touched by Miss Marple's patent incapacity and general state of senility and dither.

'Did you bring it yourself?'

'No, I didn't – I'm staying at The Old Manor House – and one of them, Mrs Glynne, I think – said she or her sister would post it. Very kind of her –'

'Let me see now. It would have been on Tuesday, would it? It wasn't Mrs Glynne who brought it in, it was the youngest one, Miss Anthea.'

'Yes, yes, I think that was the day –'

'I remember it quite well. In a good sized dress box – and moderately heavy. I think. But not what you said, Dockyard Association – I can't recall anything like that. It was the Reverend Matthews – The East Ham Women and Children's Woollen Clothing Appeal.'

'Oh yes.' Miss Marple clasped her hands is an ecstasy of relief. 'How clever of you – I see now how I came to do it. At Christmas I *did* send things to the East Ham Society in answer to a special appeal for knitted things, so I must have copied down the wrong address. Can you just repeat it?' She entered it carefully in a small notebook.

'I'm afraid the parcel's gone off, though –'

'Oh yes, but I can write, explaining the mistake and ask them to forward the parcel to the Dockyard Association instead. Thank you *so* much.'

Miss Marple trotted out.

Mrs Vinegar produced stamps for her next customer, remarking in an aside to a colleague – 'Scatty as they make them, poor old creature. Expect she's always doing that sort of thing.'

Miss Marple went out of the post office and ran into Emlyn Price and Joanna Crawford.

Joanna, she noticed, was very pale and looked upset.

'I've got to give evidence,' she said. 'I don't know – what will they ask me? I'm so afraid. I – I don't like it. I told the police sergeant, I told him what I thought we saw.'

'Don't you worry, Joanna,' said Emlyn Price. 'This is just a coroner's inquest, you know. He's a nice man, a doctor, I believe. He'll just ask you a few questions and you'll say what you saw.'

'You saw it too,' said Joanna.

'Yes, I did,' said Emlyn. 'At least I saw there was someone up there. Near the boulders and things. Now come on, Joanna.'

'They came and searched our rooms in the hotel,' said Joanna. 'They asked our permission but they had a search warrant. They looked in our rooms and among the things in our luggage.'

'I think they wanted to find that check pullover you described. Anyway, there's nothing for you to worry about. If you'd had a black and scarlet pullover yourself you wouldn't have talked about it, would you. It was black and scarlet, wasn't it?'

'I don't know,' said Emlyn Price. 'I don't really know the colours of things very well. I think it was a sort of bright colour. That's all I know.'

'They didn't find one,' said Joanna. 'After all, none of us have very many things with us. You don't when you go on a coach travel. There wasn't anything like that among anybody's things. I've never seen anyone – of our lot, I mean, wearing anything like that. Not so far. Have you?'

'No, I haven't, but I suppose – I don't know that I should know if I *had* seen it,' said Emlyn Price. 'I don't always know red from green.'

'No, you're a bit colour blind, aren't you,' said Joanna. 'I noticed that the other day.'

'What do you mean, you noticed it.'

'My red scarf. I asked if you'd seen it. You said you'd seen a green one somewhere and you brought me the red one. I'd left it in the dining-room. But you didn't really know it was red.'

'Well, don't go about saying I'm colour blind. I don't like it. Puts people off in some way.'

124

'Men are more often colour blind than women,' said Joanna. 'It's one of those sex-link things,' she added, with an air of erudition. 'You know, it passes through the female and comes out in the male.'

'You make it sound as though it was measles,' said Emlyn Price. 'Well, here we are.'

'You don't seem to mind,' said Joanna, as they walked up the steps.

'Well, I don't really. I've never been to an inquest. Things are rather interesting when you do them for the first time.'

Dr Stokes was a middle-aged man with greying hair and spectacles. Police evidence was given first, then the medical evidence with technical details of the concussion injuries which had caused death. Mrs Sandbourne gave particulars of the coach tour, the expedition as arranged for that particular afternoon, and particulars of how the fatality had occurred. Miss Temple, she said, although not young, was a very brisk walker. The party were going along a well known footpath which led round the curve of a hill which slowly mounted to the old Moorland Church originally built in Elizabethan times, though repaired and added to later. On an adjoining crest was what was called the Bonaventure Memorial. It was a fairly steep ascent and people usually climbed it at different paces from each other. The younger ones very often ran or walked ahead and reached their destination much earlier than the others. The elderly ones took it slowly. She herself usually kept at the rear of the party so that she could, if they liked, go back. Miss Temple, she said, had been talking to a Mr and Mrs Butler. Miss Temple, though she was over sixty, had been slightly impatient at their slow pace and had outdistanced them, had turned a corner and gone on ahead rather rapidly, which she had done often before. She was inclined to get impatient if waiting for people to catch up for too long, and preferred to make her own pace. They had heard a cry ahead, and she and the others had run on, turned a curve of the pathway and had found Miss Temple lying on the ground. A large boulder detached from the hillside above where there were several others of the same kind, must, they had thought, have rolled down the hillside and struck Miss Temple as she was going along the path below. A most unfortunate and tragic accident.

'You had no idea there was anything but an accident?'

'No, indeed. I can hardly see how it could have been anything but an accident.'

'You saw no one above you on the hillside?'

'No. This is the main path round the hill but of course people do wander about over the top. I did not see anyone that particular afternoon.'

Then Joanna Crawford was called. After particulars of her name and age

125

Dr Stokes asked,

'You were not walking with the remainder of the party?'

'No, we had left the path. We'd gone round the hill a little higher up the slope.'

'You were walking with a companion?'

'Yes. With Mr Emlyn Price.'

'There was no one else actually walking with you?'

'No. We were talking and we were looking at one or two of the flowers. They seemed of rather an uncommon kind. Emlyn's interested in botany.'

'Were you out of sight of the rest of the party?'

'Not all the time. They were walking along the main path – some way below us, that is.'

'Did you see Miss Temple?'

'I think so. She was walking ahead of the others, and I think I saw her turn a corner of the path ahead of them after which we didn't see her because the contour of the hill hid her.'

'Did you see someone walking above you on the hillside?'

'Yes. Up amongst a good many boulders. There's a sort of great patch of boulders on the side of the hill.'

'Yes,' said Dr Stokes, 'I know exactly the place you mean. Large granite boulders. People call them the Wethers, or the Grey Wethers sometimes.'

'I suppose they might look like sheep from a distance but we weren't so very far away from them.'

'And you saw someone up there?'

'Yes. Someone was more or less in the middle of the boulders, leaning over them.'

'Pushing them, do you think?'

'Yes. I thought so, and wondered why. He seemed to be pushing at one on the outside of the group near the edge. They were so big and so heavy I would have thought it was impossible to push them. But the one he or she was pushing seemed to be balanced like a rocking stone.'

'You said first *he*, now you say *he* or *she*, Miss Crawford. Which do you think it was?'

'Well, I thought – I suppose – I suppose I thought it was a man, but I wasn't actually thinking at the time. It was – he or she was – wearing trousers and a pullover, a sort of man's pullover with a polo neck.'

'What colour was the pullover?'

'Rather a bright red and black in checks. And there was longish hair at the back of a kind of beret, rather like a woman's hair, but then it might just as well have been a man's.'

'It certainly might,' said Dr Stokes, rather drily. 'Identifying a male or

126

female figure by their hair is certainly not easy these days.' He went on, 'What happened next?'

'Well, the stone began to roll over. It sort of toppled over the edge and then it began to gain speed. I said to Emlyn, 'Oh it's going to go right over down the hill.' Then we heard a sort of crash as it fell. And I think I heard a cry from below but I might have imagined it.'

'And then?'

'Oh, we ran on up a bit and round the corner of the hill to see what happened to the stone.'

'And what did you see?'

'We saw the boulder below on the path with a body underneath it – and people coming running round the corner.'

'Was it Miss Temple who uttered the cry?'

'I think it must have been. It might have been one of the others who was catching up and turned the corner. Oh! it was – it was horrible.'

'Yes, I'm sure it was. What had happened to the figure you'd seen above? The man or woman in the red and black pullover? Was that figure still there among the stones?'

'I don't know. I never looked up there. I was – I was busy looking at the accident, and running down the hill to see if one could do anything. I did just look up, I think, but there wasn't anyone in sight. Only the stones. There were a lot of contours and you could lose anyone quite easily from view.'

'Could it have been one of your party?'

'Oh, no. I'm sure it wasn't one of us. I would have known because, I mean, one would have known by their clothes. I'm sure nobody was wearing a scarlet and black pullover.'

'Thank you, Miss Crawford.'

Emlyn Price was called next. His story was practically a replica of Joanna's.

There was a little more evidence which did not amount to much.

The Coroner brought in that there was not sufficient evidence to show how Elizabeth Temple had come to her death, and adjourned the inquest for a fortnight.

CHAPTER 17

Miss Marple Makes a Visit

As they walked back from the inquest to the Golden Boar hardly anyone spoke. Professor Wanstead walked beside Miss Marple, and since she was not a very fast walker, they fell slightly behind the others.

'What will happen next?' Miss Marple asked at last.

'Do you mean legally or to us?'

'I suppose both,' said Miss Marple, 'because one will surely affect the other.'

'It will be presumably a case of the police making further enquiries, arising out of the evidence given by those two young people.'

'Yes.'

'Further enquiry will be necessary. The inquest was bound to be adjourned. One can hardly expect the Coroner to give a verdict of accidental death.'

'No, I understand that.' She said, 'What did you think of their evidence?'

Professor Wanstead directed a sharp glance from under his beetling eyebrows.

'Have you any ideas on the subject, Miss Marple?' His voice was suggestive. 'Of course,' said Professor Wanstead, 'we knew beforehand what they were going to say.'

'Yes.'

'What you mean is that you are asking what I thought about them themselves, their feelings about it.'

'It was interesting,' said Miss Marple. 'Very interesting. The red and black check pullover. Rather important, I think, don't you? Rather striking?'

'Yes, exactly that.'

He shot again that look at her under his eyebrows. 'What does it suggest to you exactly?'

'I think,' said Miss Marple. 'I think the description of that might give us a valuable clue.'

They came to the Golden Boar. It was only about half past twelve and Mrs Sandbourne suggested a little refreshment before going in to luncheon. As sherry and tomato juice and other liquors were being consumed, Mrs Sandbourne proceeded to make certain announcements.

'I have taken advice,' she said, 'both from the Coroner and Inspector Douglas. Since the medical evidence has been taken fully, there will be at the church a funeral memorial service tomorrow at eleven o'clock. I'm going to make arrangements with Mr Courtney, the local vicar, about it. On the following day it will be best, I think, to resume our tour. The programme will be slightly altered, since we have lost three days, but I think it can be re-organized on rather simpler lines. I have heard from one or two members of our party that they would prefer to return to London, presumably by rail. I can quite understand the feelings lying behind this, and would not like to try and influence you in any way. This death has been a very sad occurrence. I still cannot help but believe that Miss Temple's death *was* the result of an accident. Such a thing has happened before on that particular pathway, though there do not appear in this case to have been any geological or atmospherical conditions causing it. I think a good deal more investigation will have to be made. Of course, some hiker on a walking tour – that kind of thing – may have been pushing about boulders quite innocently, not realizing that there was a danger for someone walking below in what he or she was doing. If so, if that person comes forward, the whole thing may be cleared up quite quickly, but I agree one cannot take that for granted at present. It seems unlikely that the late Miss Temple could have had an enemy, or anyone who wished her harm of any kind. What I should suggest is, that we do not discuss the accident any further. Investigations will be made by the local authorities whose business it is. I think we will probably all like to attend the memorial service in the church tomorrow. And after that, on continuing the tour, I hope that it may distract our minds from the shock we have had. There are still some very interesting and famous houses to see and some very beautiful scenery also.'

Luncheon being announced shortly after that, the subject was not discussed any further. That is to say, not openly. After lunch, as they took coffee in the lounge, people were prone to get together in little groups, discussing their further arrangements.

'Are you continuing on the tour?' asked Professor Wanstead of Miss Marple.

'No,' said Miss Marple. She spoke thoughtfully. 'No. I think – I think that what has happened inclines me to remain here a little longer.'

'At the Golden Boar or at The Old Manor House?'

'That rather depends as to whether I receive any further invitation to go back to The Old Manor House. I would not like to suggest it myself because my original invitation was for the two nights that the tour was to have stayed here originally. I think possibly it would be better for me to remain at the Golden Boar.'

'You don't feel like returning to St Mary Mead?'

'Not yet,' said Miss Marple. 'There are one or two things I could do there,

I think. One thing I have done already.' She met his enquiring gaze. 'If you are going on,' she said, 'with the rest of the party, I will tell you what I have put in hand, and suggest a small side-line of enquiry that might be helpful. The other reason that I wish to stay here I will tell you later. There are certain enquiries – local enquiries – that I want to make. They may not lead anywhere so I think it as well not to mention them now. And you?'

'I should like to return to London. I have work there waiting to be done. Unless, that is, I can be helpful to you here?'

'No,' said Miss Marple, 'I do not think so at present. I expect you have various enquiries of your own that you wish to put in hand.'

'I came on the tour to meet you, Miss Marple.'

'And now you have met me and know what I know, or practically all that I know, you have other enquiries to put in hand. I understand that. But before you leave here, I think there are one or two things – well, that might be helpful, might give a result.'

'I see. You have ideas.'

'I am remembering what you said.'

'You have perhaps pinned down the smell of evil?'

'It is difficult,' said Miss Marple, 'to know exactly what something wrong in the atmosphere really means.'

'But you do feel that there is something wrong in the atmosphere?'

'Oh yes. Very clearly.'

'And especially since Miss Temple's death which, of course, was not an accident, no matter what Mrs Sandbourne hopes.'

'No,' said Miss Marple, 'it was not an accident. What I don't think I have told you is that Miss Temple said to me once that she was on a pilgrimage.'

'Interesting,' said the Professor. 'Yes, interesting. She didn't tell you what the pilgrimage was, to where or to whom?'

'No,' said Miss Marple, 'if she'd lived just a little longer and not been so weak, she might have told me. But unfortunately, death came a little too soon.'

'So that you have not any further ideas on that subject.'

'No. Only a feeling of assurance that her pilgrimage was put an end to by malign design. Someone wanted to stop her going wherever she was going, or stop her going to whomever she was going to. One can only hope that chance or Providence may throw light on that.'

'That's why you're staying here?'

'Not only that,' said Miss Marple. 'I want to find out something more about a girl called Nora Broad.'

'Nora Broad.' He looked faintly puzzled.

'The other girl who disappeared about the same time as Verity Hunt did.

130

You remember you mentioned her to me. A girl who had boy-friends and was, I understand, very *ready* to *have* boy-friends. A foolish girl, but attractive apparently to the male sex. I think,' said Miss Marple, 'that to learn a little more about her might help me in my enquiries.'

'Have it your own way, Detective-Inspector Marple,' said Professor Wanstead.

The service took place on the following morning. All the members of the tour were there. Miss Marple looked round the church. Several of the locals were there also. Mrs Glynne was there and her sister Clotilde. The youngest one, Anthea, did not attend. There were one or two people from the village also, she thought. Probably not acquainted with Miss Temple but there out of a rather morbid curiosity in regard to what was not spoken of by the term 'foul play'. There was, too, an elderly clergyman; in gaiters, well over seventy, Miss Marple thought, a broad-shouldered old man with a noble mane of white hair. He was slightly crippled and found it difficult both to kneel and to stand. It was a fine face, Miss Marple thought, and she wondered who he was. Some old friend of Elizabeth Temple, she presumed, who might perhaps have come from quite a long distance to attend the service?

As they came out of the church Miss Marple exchanged a few words with her fellow travellers. She knew now pretty well who was doing what. The Butlers were returning to London.

'I told Henry I just couldn't go on with it,' said Mrs Butler. 'You know – I feel all the time that any minute just as we might be walking round a corner, someone, you know, might shoot us or throw a stone at us. Someone who has got a down on the Famous Houses of England.'

'Now then, Mamie, now then,' said Mr Butler, 'don't you let your imagination go as far as that!'

'Well, you just don't know nowadays. What with hijackers about and kidnapping and all the rest of it, I don't feel really protected anywhere.'

Old Miss Lumley and Miss Bentham were continuing with the tour, their anxieties allayed.

'We've paid very highly for this tour and it seems a pity to miss anything just because this very sad accident has happened. We rang up a very good neighbour of ours last night, and they are going to see to the cats, so we don't need to worry.'

It was going to remain an accident for Miss Lumley and Miss Bentham. They had decided it was more comfortable that way.

Mrs Riseley-Porter was also continuing on the tour. Colonel and Mrs Walker were resolved that nothing would make them miss seeing a particularly rare collection of fuschsias in the garden due to be visited the day after tomorrow. The architect, Jameson, was also guided by his wish to see various buildings of special interest for him. Mr Caspar, however, was departing by rail, he said. Miss Cooke and Miss Barrow seemed undecided.

'Pretty good walks round here,' said Miss Cooke. 'I think we'll stay at the Golden Boar for a little. That's what you're going to do, isn't it, Miss Marple?'

'I really think so,' said Miss Marple. 'I don't feel quite equal to going on travelling and all that. I think a day or two's rest would be helpful to me after what's happened.'

As the little crowd dispersed, Miss Marple took an unostentatious route of her own. From her handbag she took out a leaf torn from her notebook on which she had entered two addresses. The first, a Mrs Blackett, lived in a neat little house and garden just by the end of the road where it sloped down towards the valley. A small neat woman opened the door.

'Mrs Blackett?'

'Yes, yes, ma'am, that's my name.'

'I wonder if I might just come in and speak to you for a minute or two. I have just been to the service and I am feeling a little giddy. If I could just sit down for a minute or two?'

'Dear me, now, dear me. Oh, I'm sorry for that. Come right in, ma'am, come right in. That's right. You sit down here. Now I'll get you a glass of water – or maybe you'd like a pot of tea?'

'No, thank you,' said Miss Marple, 'a glass of water would put me right.'

Mrs Blackett returned with a glass of water and a pleasurable prospect of talking about ailments and giddiness and other things.

'You know, I've got a nephew like that. He oughtn't to be at his age, he's not much over fifty but now and then he'll come over giddy all of a sudden and unless he sits down at once – why you don't know, sometimes he'll pass out right on the floor. Terrible, it is. Terrible. And doctors, they don't seem able to do anything about it. Here's your glass of water.'

'Ah,' said Miss Marple, sipping, 'I feel much better.'

'Been to the service, have you, for the poor lady as got done in, as some say, or accident as others. I'd say it's accident every time. But these inquests and coroners, they always want to make things look criminal, they do.'

'Oh yes,' said Miss Marple. 'I've been so sorry to hear of a lot of things like that in the past. I was hearing a great deal about a girl called Nora. Nora Broad, I think.'

'Ah, Nora, yes. Well, she was my cousin's daughter. yes. A long while ago, that was. Went off and never come back. These girls, there's no holding them. I said often, I did, to Nancy Broad – that's my cousin – I said

132

to her, "You're out working all day," and I said, "What's Nora doing? You know she's the kind that likes the boys. Well," I said, "there'll be trouble. You see if there isn't." And sure enough, I was quite right.'

'You mean –?'

'Ah, the usual trouble. Yes, in the family way. Mind you, I don't think as my cousin Nancy knew about it. But of course, I'm sixty-five and I know what's what and I know the way a girl looks and I think I know who it was, but I'm not sure. I might have been wrong because he went on living in the place and he was real cut up when Nora was missing.'

'She went off, did she?'

'Well, she accepted a lift from someone – a stranger. That's the last time she was seen. I forget the make of the car now. Some funny name it had. An Audit or something like that. Anyway, she'd been seen once or twice in that car. And off she went in it. And it was said it was that same car that the poor girl what got herself murdered used to go riding in. But I don't think as that happened to Nora. If Nora'd been murdered, the body would have come to light by now. Don't you think so?'

'It certainly seems likely,' said Miss Marple. 'Was she a girl who did well at school and all that?'

'Ah no, she wasn't. She was idle and she wasn't too clever at her books either. No. She was all for the boys from the time she was twelve-years-old onwards. I think in the end she must have gone off with someone or other for good. But she never let anyone know. She never sent as much as a postcard. Went off, I think, with someone as promised her things. You know. Another girl I knew – but that was when I was young – went off with one of them Africans. He told her as his father was a Shake. Funny sort of word, but a shake I think it was. Anyway it was somewhere in Africa or in Algiers. Yes, in Algiers it was. Somewhere there. And she was going to have all sorts of wonderful things. He had six camels, the boy's father, she said and a whole troop of horses and she was going to live in a wonderful house, she was, with carpets hanging up all over the walls, which seems a funny place to put carpets. And off she went. She come back again three years later. Yes. Terrible time, she'd had. Terrible. They lived in a nasty little house made of earth. Yes, it was. And nothing much to eat except what they call cos-cos which I always thought was lettuce, but it seems it isn't. Something more like semolina pudding. Oh terrible it was. And in the end he said she was no good to him and he'd divorce her. He said he'd only got to say "I divorce you" three times, and he did and walked out and somehow or other, some kind of Society out there took charge of her and paid her fare home to England. And there she was. Ah, but that was about thirty to forty years ago, that was. Now Nora, that was only about seven or eight years ago.

But I expect she'll be back one of these days, having learnt her lesson and finding out that all these fine promises didn't come to much.'

'Had she anyone to go to here except her – her mother – your cousin, I mean? Anyone who –'

'Well, there's many as was kind to her. There was the people at The Old Manor House, you know. Mrs Glynne wasn't there then, but Miss Clotilde, she was always one to be good to the girls from school. Yes, many a nice present she's given Nora. She gave her a very nice scarf and a pretty dress once. Very nice, it was. A summer frock, a sort of foulard silk. Ah, she was very kind, Miss Clotilde was. Tried to make Nora take more interest in her schooling. Lots of things like that. Advised her against the way she was going on because, you see – well, I wouldn't like to say it, not when she's my cousin's child though, mark you, my cousin is only one who married my boy cousin, that is to say – but I mean it was something terrible the way she went on with all the boys. Anyone could pick her up. Real sad it is. I'd say she'll go on the streets in the end. I don't believe she has any future but that. I don't like to say these things, but there it is. Anyway, perhaps it's better than getting herself murdered like Miss Hunt did, what lived at The Old Manor House. Cruel, that was. They thought she'd gone off with someone and the police, they was busy. Always asking questions and having the young men who'd been with the girl up to help them with their enquiries and all that. Geoffrey Grant there was, Billy Thompson, and the Landfords' Harry. All unemployed – with plenty of jobs going if they'd want to take them. Things usedn't to be like that when I was young. Girls behaved proper. And the boys knew they'd got to work if they wanted to get anywhere.'

Miss Marple talked a little more, said that she was now quite restored, thanked Mrs Blackett, and went out.

Her next visit was to a girl who was planting out lettuces.

'Nora Broad? Oh, *she* hasn't been in the village for years. Went off with someone, she did. She was a great one for boys. I always wondered where she'd end up. Did you want to see her for any particular reason?'

'I had a letter from a friend abroad,' said Miss Marple, untruthfully. 'A very nice family and they were thinking of engaging a Miss Nora Broad. She'd been in some trouble, I think. Married someone who was rather a bad lot and had left her and gone off with another woman, and she wanted to get a job looking after children. My friend knew nothing about her, but I gathered she came from this village. So I wondered if there was anyone here who could – well, tell me something about her. You went to school with her, I understand?'

'Oh yes, we were in the same class, we were. Mind you, I didn't approve

134

of all Nora's goings-on. She was boy mad, she was. Well, I had a nice boy-friend myself that I was going steady with at the time, and I told her she'd do herself no good going off with every Tom, Dick and Harry that offered her a lift in a car or took her along to a pub where she told lies about her age, as likely as not. She was a good mature girl as looked a lot older than she was.'

'Dark or fair?'

'Oh, she had dark hair. Pretty hair it was. Always loose like, you know, as girls do.'

'Were the police worried about her when she disappeared?'

'Yes. You see, she didn't leave no word behind. She just went out one night and didn't come back. She was seen getting into a car and nobody saw her. Just at that time there'd been a good many murders, you know. Not specially round here, but all over the country. The police, they were rounding up a lot of young men and boys. Thought as Nora might be a body at the time we did. But not she. She was all right. I'd say as likely as not she's making a bit of money still in London or one of these big towns doing a strip-tease, something of that kind. That's the kind she was.'

'I don't think,' said Miss Marple, 'that if it's the same person, that she'd be very suitable for my friend.'

'She'd have to change a bit if she was to be suitable,' said the girl.

CHAPTER 18

Archdeacon Brabazon

When Miss Marple, slightly out of breath and rather tired, got back to the Golden Boar, the receptionist came out from her pen and across to meet her.

'Oh, Miss Marple, there is someone here who wants to speak to you. Archdeacon Brabazon.'

'Archdeacon Brabazon?' Miss Marple looked puzzled.

'Yes. He's been trying to find you. He had heard you were with this tour and he wanted to talk to you before you might have left or gone to London. I told him that some of them were going back to London by the later train this afternoon, but he is very, very anxious to speak to you before you go. I have put him in the television lounge. It is quieter there. The other is very noisy just at this moment.'

Slightly surprised, Miss Marple went to the room indicated. Archdeacon Brabazon turned out to be the elderly cleric whom she had noticed at the memorial service. He rose and came towards her.

'Miss Marple. Miss Jane Marple?'

'Yes, that is my name. You wanted –'

'I am Archdeacon Brabazon. I came here this morning to attend the service for a very old friend of mine, Miss Elizabeth Temple.'

'Oh yes?' said Miss Marple. 'Do sit down.'

'Thank you, I will, I am not quite as strong as I was.' He lowered himself carefully into a chair.

'And you –'

Miss Marple sat down beside him.

'Yes,' she said, 'you wanted to see me?'

'Well, I must explain how that comes about. I'm quite aware that I am a complete stranger to you. As a matter of fact I made a short visit to the hospital at Carristown, talking to the matron before going on to the church here. It was she who told me that before she died Elizabeth had asked to see a fellow member of the tour. Miss Jane Marple. And that Miss Jane Marple had visited her and sat with her just a very, very short time before Elizabeth died.'

He looked at her anxiously.

'Yes,' said Miss Marple, 'that is so. It surprised me to be sent for.'

'You are an old friend of hers?'

'No,' said Miss Marple. 'I only met her on this tour. That's why I was surprised. We had expressed ideas to each other, occasionally sat next to

136

each other in the coach, and had struck up quite an acquaintanceship. But I was surprised that she should have expressed a wish to see me when she was so ill.'

'Yes. Yes, I can quite imagine that. She was, as I have said, a very old friend of mine. In fact, she was coming to see me, to visit me. I live in Fillminster, which is where your coach tour will be stopping the day after tomorrow. And by arrangement she was coming to visit me there, she wanted to talk to me about various matters about which she thought I could help her.'

'I see,' said Miss Marple. 'May I ask you a question? I hope it is not too intimate a question.'

'Of course, Miss Marple. Ask me anything you like.'

'One of the things Miss Temple said to me was that her presence on the tour was *not* merely because she wished to visit historic homes and gardens. She described it by a rather unusual word to use, as a pilgrimage.'

'Did she,' said Archdeacon Brabazon. 'Did she indeed now? Yes, that's interesting. Interesting and perhaps significant.'

'So what I am asking you is, do you think that the pilgrimage she spoke of was her visit to you?'

'I think it must have been,' said the Archdeacon. 'Yes, I think so.'

'We had been talking,' said Miss Marple, 'about a young girl. A girl called Verity.'

'Ah yes. Verity Hunt.'

'I did not know her surname. Miss Temple, I think, mentioned her only as Verity.'

'Verity Hunt is dead,' said the Archdeacon. 'She died quite a number of years ago. Did you know that?'

'Yes,' said Miss Marple. 'I knew it. Miss Temple and I were talking about her. Miss Temple told me something that I did not know. She said she had been engaged to be married to the son of a Mr Rafiel. Mr Rafiel is, or again I must say was, a friend of mine. Mr Rafiel has paid the expenses of this tour out of his kindness. I think, though, that possibly he wanted – indeed, intended – me to meet Miss Temple on this tour. I think he thought she could give me certain information.'

'Certain information about Verity?'

'Yes.'

'That is why she was coming to me. She wanted to know certain facts.'

'She wanted to know,' said Miss Marple, 'why Verity broke off her engagement to marry Mr Rafiel's son.'

'Verity,' said Archdeacon Brabazon, 'did *not* break off her engagement. I am certain of that. As certain as one can be of anything.'

'Miss Temple did not know that, did she?'

'No. I think she was puzzled and unhappy about what happened and was coming to me to ask me why the marriage did not take place.'

'And why did it not take place?' asked Miss Marple. 'Please do not think that I am unduly curious. It's not idle curiosity that is driving me. I too am on – not a pilgrimage – but what I should call a mission. I too want to know why Michael Rafiel and Verity Hunt did not marry.'

The Archdeacon studied her for a moment or two.

'You are involved in some way,' he said. 'I see that.'

'I am involved,' said Miss Marple, 'by the dying wishes of Michael Rafiel's father. He asked me to do this for him.'

'I have no reason not to tell you all I know,' said the Archdeacon slowly. 'You are asking me what Elizabeth Temple would have been asking me, you are asking me something I do not know myself. Those two young people, Miss Marple, intended to marry. They had made arrangements to marry. I was going to marry them. It was a marriage, I gather, which was being kept a secret. I knew both these young people, I knew that dear child Verity from a long way back. I prepared her for confirmation, I used to hold services in Lent, for Easter, on other occasions, in Elizabeth Temple's school. A very fine school it was, too. A very fine woman she was. A wonderful teacher with a great sense of each girl's capabilities – for what she was best fitted for in studies. She urged careers on girls she thought would relish careers, and did not force girls that she felt were not really suited to them. She was a great woman and a very dear friend. Verity was one of the most beautiful children – girls, rather – that I have come across. Beautiful in mind, in heart, as well as in appearance. She had the great misfortune to lose her parents before she was truly adult. They were both killed in a charter plane going on a holiday to Italy. Verity went to live when she left school with a Miss Clotilde Bradbury-Scott whom you know, probably, as living here. She had been a close friend of Verity's mother. There are three sisters, though the second one was married and living abroad, so there were only two of them living here. Clotilde, the eldest one, became extremely attached to Verity. She did everything possible to give her a happy life. She took her abroad once or twice, gave her art lessons in Italy and loved and cared for her dearly in every way. Verity, too, came to love her probably as much as she could have loved her own mother. She depended on Clotilde. Clotilde herself was an intellectual and well educated woman. She did not urge a university career on Verity, but this I gather was really because Verity did not really yearn after one. She preferred to study art and music and such subjects. She lived here at The Old Manor House and had, I think, a very happy life. She always seemed to be happy. Naturally, I did not see her after she came here

138

since Fillminister, where I was in the cathedral, is nearly sixty miles from here. I wrote to her at Christmas and other festivals, and she remembered me always with a Christmas card. But I saw nothing of her until the day came when she suddenly turned up, a very beautiful and fully grown young woman by then, with an attractive young man whom I also happened to know slightly, Mr Rafiel's son, Michael. They came to me because they were in love with each other and wanted to get married.'

'And you agreed to marry them?'

'Yes, I did. Perhaps, Miss Marple, you may think that I should not have done so. They had come to me in secret, it was obvious. Clotilde Bradbury-Scott, I should imagine, had tried to discourage the romance between them. She was well within her rights in doing so. Michael Rafiel, I will tell you frankly, was not the kind of husband you would want for any daughter or relation of yours. She was too young really, to make up her mind, and Michael had been a source of trouble ever since his very young days. He had been had up before junior courts, he had had unsuitable friends, he had been drawn into various gangster activities, he'd sabotaged buildings and telephone boxes. He had been on intimate terms with various girls, had maintenance claims which he had had to meet. Yes, he was a bad lot with the girls as well as in other ways, yet he was extremely attractive and they fell for him and behaved in an extremely silly fashion. He had served two short jail sentences. Frankly, he had a criminal record. I was acquainted with his father, though I did not know him well, and I think that his father did all that he could – all that a man of his character could – to help his son. He came to his rescue, he got him jobs in which he might have succeeded. He paid up his debts, paid out damages. He did all this. I don't know –'

'But he could have done more, you think?'

'No,' said the Archdeacon, 'I've come to an age now when I know that one must accept one's fellow human beings as being the kind of people and having the kind of, shall we say in modern terms, genetic make-up which gives them the characters they have. I don't think that Mr Rafiel had affection for his son, a great affection at any time. To say he was reasonably fond of him would be the most you could say. He gave him no love. Whether it would have been better for Michael if he had had love from his father, I do not know. Perhaps it would have made no difference. As it was, it was sad. The boy was not stupid. He had a certain amount of intellect and talent. He could have done well if he had wished to do well, and had taken the trouble. But he was by nature – let us admit it frankly – a delinquent. He had certain qualities one appreciated. He had a sense of humour, he was in various ways generous and kindly. He would stand by a friend, help a friend out of a scrape. He treated his girl-friends badly, got them into trouble as the local

139

saying is, and then more or less abandoned them and took up with somebody else. So there I was faced with those two and – yes – I agreed to marry them. I told Verity, I told her quite frankly, the kind of boy she wanted to marry. I found that he had not tried to deceive her in any way. He'd told her that he'd always been in trouble both with the police, and in every other way. He told her that he was going, when he married her, to turn over a new leaf. Everything would be changed. I warned her that that would not happen, he would not change. People do not change. He might *mean* to change. Verity, I think, knew that almost as well as I did. She admitted that she knew it. She said, "I know what Mike is like. I know he'll probably always be like it, but I love him. I may be able to help him and I may not. But I'll take that risk." And I will tell you this, Miss Marple. I know – none better, I have done a lot with young people, I have married a lot of young people and I have seen them come to grief, I have seen them unexpectedly turn out well – but I know this and recognize it. I know when a couple are really in love with each other. And by that I do not mean just sexually attracted. There is too much talk about sex, too much attention is paid to it. I do not mean that anything about sex is wrong. That is nonsense. But sex cannot take the place of love, it goes *with* love but it cannot succeed by itself. To love means the words of the marriage service. For better, for worse, for richer for poorer, in sickness and in health. That is what you take on if you love and wish to marry. Those two loved each other. To love and to cherish until death do us part. And that,' said the Archdeacon, 'is where my story ends. I cannot go on because *I do not know what happened*. I only know that I agreed to do as they asked, that I made the necessary arrangements; we settled a day, an hour, a time, a place. I think perhaps that I was to blame for agreeing to the secrecy.'

'They didn't want anyone to know?' said Miss Marple.

'No. Verity did not want anyone to know, and I should say most certainly Mike did not want anyone to know. They were afraid of being stopped. To Verity, I think, besides love, there was also a feeling of escape. Natural, I think, owing to the circumstances of her life. She had lost her real guardians, her parents, she had entered on her new life after their death, at an age when a school girl arrives at having a "crush" on someone. An attractive mistress. Anything from the games mistress to the mathematics mistress, or a prefect or an older girl. A state that does not last for very long, is merely a natural part of life. Then from that you go on to the next stage when you realize that what you want in your life is what complements yourself. A relationship between a man and a woman. You start then to look about you for a mate. The mate you want in life. And if you are wise, you take your time, you have friends, but you are looking, as the old nurses used to say to children, for Mr Right to come along. Clotilde Bradbury-Scott was exceptionally good to Verity, and Verity, I think, gave her what I should call hero-worship. She was a personality as a woman. Handsome, accomplished, interesting. I think Verity adored her in an almost romantic way and I think Clotilde came to love Verity as though she were her own daughter. And so Verity grew to maturity in an atmosphere of adoration, lived an interesting life with interesting subjects to stimulate her intellect. It was a happy life, but I think little by little she was conscious – conscious without knowing she was conscious, shall we say – of a wish to escape. Escape from being loved. To escape, she didn't know into what or *where*. But she did know after she met Michael. She wanted to escape to a life where male and female come together to create the next stage of living in this world. But she knew that it was impossible to make Clotilde understand how she felt. She knew that Clotilde would be bitterly opposed to her taking her love for Michael seriously. And Clotilde, I fear, was right in her belief . . . I know that now. He was not a husband that Verity ought to have taken or had. The road that she started out on led not to life, not to increased living and happiness. It led to shock, pain, death. You see, Miss Marple, that I have a grave feeling of guilt. My motives were good, but I didn't know what I ought to have known. I knew Verity, *but I didn't know Michael.* I understood Verity's wish for secrecy because I knew what a strong personality Clotilde Bradbury-Scott had. She might have had a strong enough influence over Verity to persuade her to give up the marriage.'

'You think then that that was what she did do? You think Clotilde told her enough about Michael to persuade her to give up the idea of marrying him?'

'No, I do *not* believe that. I still do not. Verity would have told me if so. She would have got word to me.'

'What did actually happen on that day?'

'I haven't told you that yet. The day was fixed. The time, the hour and the place, and I waited. Waited for a bride and bridegroom who didn't come, who sent no word, no excuse, *nothing*. I didn't know why! I never *have* known why. It still seems to me unbelievable. Unbelievable, I mean, not that they did not come, that could be explicable easily enough, but that they sent no word. Some scrawled line of writing. And that is why I wondered and hoped that Elizabeth Temple, before she died, might have told *you* something. Given you some message perhaps for me. If she knew or had any idea that she was dying, she might have wanted to get a message to me.'

'She wanted information *from* you,' said Miss Marple. 'That, I am sure, was the reason she was coming to you.'

'Yes. Yes, that is probably true. It seemed to me, you see, that Verity would have said nothing to the people who could have stopped her. Clotilde and Anthea Bradbury-Scott, but because she had always been very devoted to Elizabeth Temple – and Elizabeth Temple had had great influence over her – it seems to me that she would have written and given her information of some kind.'

'I think she did,' said Miss Marple.

'Information, you think?'

'The information she gave to Elizabeth Temple,' said Miss Marple, 'was this. That she was going to marry Michael Rafiel. Miss Temple knew that. It was one of the things she said to me. She said: "I knew a girl called Verity who was going to marry Michael Rafiel" and the only person who could have told her that was Verity herself. Verity must have written to her or sent some word to her. And then when I said "Why didn't she marry him?" she said: "She died." '

'Then we come to a full stop,' said Archdeacon Brabazon. He sighed. 'Elizabeth and I know no more than those two facts. Elizabeth, that Verity was going to marry Michael. And I that those two were going to marry, that they had arranged it and that they were coming on a settled day and time. And I waited for them, but there was no marriage. No bride, no bridegroom, no word.'

'And you have no idea what happened?' said Miss Marple.

'I do not for one minute believe that Verity or Michael definitely parted, broke off.'

'But *something* must have happened between them? Something that opened Verity's eyes perhaps, to certain aspects of Michael's character and personality, that she had not realized or known before.'

'That is not a satisfying answer because still she would have let me know. She would not have left me waiting to join them together in holy matrimony. To put the most ridiculous side of it, she was a girl with beautiful manners, well brought up. She would have sent word. No. I'm afraid that only one thing could have happened.'

'Death?' said Miss Marple. She was remembering that one word that Elizabeth Temple had said which had sounded like the deep tone of a bell.

'Yes.' Archdeacon Bradazon sighed. 'Death.'

'Love,' said Miss Marple thoughtfully.

'By that you mean –' he hesitated.

'It's what Miss Temple said to me. I said "What killed her?" and she said "Love" and that love was the most frightening word in the world. The most frightening word.'

'I see,' said the Archdeacon. 'I see – or I think I see.'

'What is your solution?'

'Split personality,' he sighed. 'Something that is not apparent to other people unless they are technically qualified to observe it. Jekyll and Hyde are real, you know. They were not Stevenson's invention as such. Michael Rafiel was a – must have been schizophrenic. He had a dual personality. I have no medical knowledge, no psychoanalytic experience. But there must have been in him the two parts of two identities. One, a well-meaning, almost lovable boy, a boy perhaps whose principal attraction was his wish for happiness. But there was also a second personality, someone who was forced by some mental deformation perhaps – something we as yet are not sure of – to kill – not an enemy, but the person he loved, and so he killed Verity. Not knowing perhaps *why* he had to or *what* it meant. There are very frightening things in this world of ours, mental quirks, mental disease or deformity of a brain. One of my parishioners was a very sad case in point. Two elderly women living together, pensioned. They had been friends in service together somewhere. They appeared to be a happy couple. And yet one day one of them killed the other. She sent for an old friend of hers, the vicar of her parish, and said: "I have killed Louisa. It is very sad," she said, "but I saw the devil looking out of her eyes and I knew I was being commanded to kill her." Things like that make one sometimes despair of living. One says why? and how? and yet one day knowledge will come. Doctors will find out or learn just some small deformity of a chromosome or gene. Some gland that overworks or leaves off working.'

'So you think that's what happened?' said Miss Marple.

'It *did* happen. The body was not found, I know, for some time afterwards. Verity just disappeared. She went away from home and was not seen again ...'

'But it must have happened *then* – that very day –'

'But surely at the trial –'

'You mean after the body was found, when the police finally arrested Michael?'

'He had been one of the first, you know, to be asked to come and give assistance to the police. He had been seen about with the girl, she had been noticed in his car. They were sure all along that he was the man they wanted. He was their first suspect, and they never stopped suspecting him. The other young men who had known Verity were questioned, and one and all had alibis or lack of evidence. They continued to suspect Michael, and finally the body was found. Strangled and the head and face disfigured with heavy blows. A mad frenzied attack. He wasn't sane when he struck those blows. Mr Hyde, let us say, had taken over.'

Miss Marple shivered.

The Archdeacon went on, his voice low and sad. 'And yet, even now sometimes, I hope and feel that it was some other young man who killed her. Someone who was definitely mentally deranged, though no one had any idea of it. Some stranger, perhaps, whom she had met in the neighbourhood. Someone who she had met by chance, who had given her a lift in a car, and then –' He shook his head.

'I suppose that *could* have been true.' said Miss Marple.

'Mike made a bad impression in court,' said the Archdeacon. 'Told foolish and senseless lies. Lied as to where his car had been. Got his friends to give him impossible alibis. He was frightened. He said nothing of his plan to marry. I believe his Counsel was of the opinion that that would tell against him – that she might have been forcing him to marry her and that he didn't want to. It's so long ago now, I remember no details. But the evidence was dead against him. He was guilty – and he looked guilty.

'So you see, do you not, Miss Marple, that I'm a very sad and unhappy man. I made the wrong judgment, I encouraged a very sweet and lovely girl to go to her death, because I did not know enough of human nature. I was ignorant of the danger she was running. I believed that if she had had any fear of him, any sudden knowledge of something evil in him, she would have broken her pledge to marry him and have come to me and told me of her fear, of her knowledge of him. But nothing of that ever happened. Why *did* he kill her? Did he kill her because perhaps he knew she was going to have a child? Because by now he had formed a tie with some other girl and did not want to be forced to marry Verity? I can't believe it. Or was it some entirely different reason. Because *she* had suddenly felt a fear of him, a knowledge of danger from him, and had broken off her association with him? Did that rouse his anger, his fury, and did that lead him to violence and to killing her? One does not know.'

'You do not know?' said Miss Marple, 'but you *do* still know and believe one thing, don't you?'

'What do you mean exactly by "believe"? Are you talking from the religious point of view?'

'Oh no,' said Miss Marple, 'I didn't mean that. I mean, there seems to be in you, or so I feel it, a very strong belief that those two loved each other, that they meant to marry, but that *something* happened that prevented it. Something that ended in her death, but you still really believe that they *were* coming to you to get married that day?'

'You are quite right, my dear. Yes, I cannot help still believing in two lovers who wished to get married, who were ready to take each other on for better, for worse, for richer or poorer, in sickness and in health. She loved him and she would have taken him for better or for worse. As far as she had gone, she took him for worse. It brought about her death.'

144

'You must go on believing as you do,' said Miss Marple. 'I think, you know, that *I* believe it too.'

'But then what?'

'I don't know yet,' said Miss Marple. 'I'm not sure, but I think Elizabeth Temple did know or was beginning to know what happened. A frightening word, she said. *Love.* I thought when she spoke that what she meant was that because of a love affair Verity committed suicide. Because she found out something about Michael, or because something about Michael suddenly upset her and revolted her. But it couldn't have been suicide.'

'No,' said the Archdeacon, 'that couldn't be so. The injuries were described very fully at the trial. You don't commit suicide by beating in your own head.'

'Horrible!' said Miss Marple. 'Horrible! And you couldn't do that to anyone you loved even if you had to kill "for love", could you? If he'd killed her, he couldn't have done it that way. Strangling – perhaps, but you wouldn't beat in the face and the head that you loved.' She murmured, 'Love, love – a frightening word.'

CHAPTER 19

Goodbyes Are Said

The coach was drawn up in front of the Golden Boar on the following morning. Miss Marple had come down and was saying goodbye to various friends. She found Mrs Riseley-Porter in a state of high indignation.

'Really, girls nowadays,' she said. 'No vigour. No stamina.'

Miss Marple looked at her enquiringly.

'Joanna, I mean. My niece.'

'Oh dear. Is she not well?'

'Well, she says not. I can't see anything much the matter with her. She says she's got a sore throat, she feels she might have a temperature coming on. All nonsense, I think.'

'Oh, I'm very sorry,' said Miss Marple. 'Is there anything I can do? Look after her?'

'I should leave her alone, if I were you,' said Mrs Riseley-Porter. 'If you ask me, it's all an excuse.'

Miss Marple looked enquiringly at her once more.

'Girls are so silly. Always falling in love.'

'Emlyn Price?' said Miss Marple.

'Oh, so you've noticed it too. Yes, they're really getting to a stage of spooning about together. I don't much care for him anyway. One of these long-haired students, you know. Always going on demos or something like that. Why can't they say demonstration properly? I hate abbreviations. And how am *I* going to get alone? Nobody to look after me, collect my luggage, take it in, take it out. Really. I'm paying for this complete trip and everything.'

'I thought she seemed so attentive to you,' said Miss Marple.

'Well, not the last day or two. Girls don't understand that people have to have a little assistance when they get to middle age. They seem to have some absurd idea – she and the Price boy – of going to visit some mountain or some land-mark. About a seven or eight mile walk there and back.'

'But surely if she has a sore throat and a temperature . . .'

'You'll see, as soon as the coach is gone the sore throat will get better and the temperature will go down,' said Mrs Riseley-Porter. 'Oh dear, we've got to get on board now. Oh, goodbye, Miss Marple, it's nice to have met you. I'm sorry you're not coming with us.'

'I'm very sorry myself,' said Miss Marple, 'but really you know, I'm not so young and vigorous as you are, Mrs Riseley-Porter, and I really feel after

146

all the – well, shock and everything else the last few days, I really must have a complete twenty-four hours' rest.'

'Well, hope to see you somewhere in the future.'

They shook hands. Mrs Riseley-Porter climbed into the coach.

A voice behind Miss Marple's shoulder said:

'*Bon Voyage* and Good Riddance.'

She turned to see Emlyn Price. He was grinning.

'Was that addressed to Mrs Riseley-Porter?'

'Yes. Who else.'

'I'm sorry to hear that Joanna is under the weather this morning.'

Emlyn Price grinned at Miss Marple again.

'She'll be all right,' he said, 'as soon as that coach is gone.'

'Oh really!' said Miss Marple, 'do you mean –?'

'Yes, I do mean,' said Emlyn Price. 'Joanna's had enough of that aunt of hers, bossing her around all the time.'

'Then you are not going in the coach either?'

'No. I'm staying on here for a couple of days. I'm going to get around a bit and do a few excursions. Don't look so disapproving, Miss Marple. You're not really as disapproving as all that, are you?'

'Well,' said Miss Marple, 'I have known such things happen in my own youth. The excuses may have been different, and I think we had less chance of getting away with things than you do now.'

Colonel and Mrs Walker came up and shook Miss Marple warmly by the hand.

'So nice to have known you and had all those delightful horticultural talks,' said the Colonel. 'I believe the day after tomorrow we're going to have a real treat, if nothing else happens. Really it's too sad, this very unfortunate accident. I must say I think myself it *is* an accident. I really think the Coroner was going beyond everything in his feelings about this.'

'It seems very odd,' said Miss Marple, 'that nobody has come forward, if they were up on top there, pushing about rocks and boulders and things, that they haven't come forward to say so.'

'Think they'll be blamed, of course,' said Colonel Walker. 'They're going to keep jolly quiet, that's what they're going to do. Well, goodbye. I'll send you a cutting of that Magnolia highdownensis and one of the Mahonia japonica too. Though I'm not quite sure if it would do as well where you live.'

They in turn got into the coach. Miss Marple turned away. She turned to see Professor Wanstead waving to the departing coach. Mrs Sandbourne came out, said goodbye to Miss Marple and got in the coach and Miss Marple took Professor Wanstead by the arm.

'I want you,' she said. 'Can we go somewhere where we can talk?'

'Yes. What about the place where we sat the other day?'

'Round here there's a very nice verandah place, I think.'

They walked round the corner of the hotel. There was some gay horn-blowing, and the coach departed.

'I wish, in a way, you know,' said Professor Wanstead, 'that you weren't staying behind. I'd rather have seen you safely on your way in the coach.' He looked at her sharply. 'Why are you staying here? Nervous exhaustion or something else?'

'Something else,' said Miss Marple. 'I'm not particularly exhausted, though it makes a perfectly natural excuse for somebody of my age.'

'I feel really I ought to stay here and keep an eye on you.'

'No,' said Miss Marple, 'there's no need to do that. There are other things you ought to be doing.'

'What things?' He looked at her. 'Have you got ideas or knowledge?'

'I think I have knowledge, but I'll have to verify it. There are certain things that I can't do myself. I think you will help to do them because you're in touch with what I refer to as the authorities.'

'Meaning Scotland Yard, Chief Constables and the Governors of Her Majesty's Prisons?'

'Yes. One or other or all of them. You might have the Home Secretary in your pocket, too.'

'You certainly do have ideas! Well, what do you want me to do?'

'First of all I want to give you this address.'

She took out a notebook and tore out one page and handed it to him.

'What's this? Oh yes, well known charity, isn't it?'

'One of the better ones, I believe. They do a lot of good. You send them clothes,' said Miss Marple, 'children's clothes and women's clothes. Coats. Pullovers, all those sort of things.'

'Well, do you want me to contribute to this?'

'No, it's an appeal for charity, it's a bit of what belongs to what we're doing. What you and I are doing.'

'In what way?'

'I want you to make enquiries there about a parcel which was sent from here two days ago, posted from this post office.'

'Who posted it – did you?'

'No,' said Miss Marple. 'No. But I assumed responsibility for it.'

'What does that mean?'

'It means,' said Miss Marple, smiling slightly, 'that I went into the post office here and I explained rather scattily and – well, like the old pussy I am – that I had very foolishly asked someone to take a parcel for me and post it, and I had put the wrong address on it. I was very upset by this. The postmistress very kindly said she remembered the parcel, but the address on it was not the one I was mentioning. It was this one, the one I have just given to you. I explained that I had been very foolish and written the wrong address on it, confusing it with another one I sometimes send things to. She told me it was too late to do anything about it now because the parcel, naturally, had gone off. I said it was quite all right, that I would send a letter to the particular charity to which the parcel had been sent, and explain that it had been addressed to them by mistake. Would they very kindly forward it on to the charity that I had meant to receive it.'

'It seems rather a roundabout way.'

'Well,' said Miss Marple, 'one has to say *something*. I'm not going to do that at all. *You* are going to deal with the matter. We've got to know what's inside that parcel! I have no doubt you can get means.'

'Will there be anything inside the parcel to say who actually sent it?'

'I rather think not. It may have a slip of paper saying "from friends" or it may have a fictitious name and address – something like Mrs Pippin, 14 Westbourne Grove – and if anyone made enquiries there, there'd be no person of such a name living there.'

'Oh. Any other alternatives?'

'It might possibly, most unlikely but possible, have a slip saying "From Miss Anthea Bradbury-Scott" –'

'Did she –?'

'She took it to the post,' said Miss Marple.

'And you had asked her to take it there?'

'Oh no,' said Miss Marple. 'I hadn't asked anyone to post anything. The first I saw of the parcel was when Anthea passed the garden of the Golden Boar where you and I were sitting talking, carrying it.'

'But you went to the post office and represented that the parcel was yours.'

'Yes,' said Miss Marple, 'which was quite untrue. But post offices are careful. And, you see, I wanted to find out where it had been sent.'

'You wanted to find out if such a parcel had been sent, and if it had been sent by one of the Bradbury-Scotts – or especially Miss Anthea?'

'I knew it would be Anthea,' said Miss Marple, 'because we'd seen her.'

'Well?' He took the paper from her hand. 'Yes, I can set this in motion. You think this parcel will be interesting?'

'I think the contents of it might be quite important.'

'You like keeping your secrets, don't you?' said Professor Wanstead.

'Not exactly secrets,' said Miss Marple, 'they are only *probabilities* that I am exploring. One does not like to make definite assertions unless one has a little more definite knowledge.'

'Anything else?'

'I think – I think that whoever's in charge of these things, ought to be warned that there might be a second body to be found.'

'Do you mean a second body connected with the particular crime that we have been considering? A crime that took place ten years ago?'

'Yes,' said Miss Marple. 'I'm quite sure of it, as a matter of fact.'

'Another body. Whose body?'

'Well,' said Miss Marple, 'it's only my idea so far.'

'Any idea where this body is?'

'Oh! Yes,' said Miss Marple, 'I'm quite sure I know where it *is*, but I have to have a little more time before I can tell you that.'

'What kind of a body? Man's? Woman's? Child's? Girl's?'

'There's another girl who is missing,' said Miss Marple. 'A girl called Nora Broad. She disappeared from here and she's never been heard any more of. I think her body might be in a particular place.'

Professor Wanstead looked at her.

'You know, the more you say, the less I like leaving you here,' he said. 'Having all these ideas – and possibly doing something foolish – either –' He stopped.

'Either it's all nonsense? –' said Miss Marple.

'No, no, I didn't mean that. But either you know too much – which might be dangerous . . . I think I am going to stay here to keep an eye on you.'

'No, you're not,' said Miss Marple. 'You've got to go to London and set certain things moving.'

'You spoke as though you knew a good deal now, Miss Marple.'

'I think I do know a good deal now. But I have got to be sure.'

'Yes, but if you make sure, that may be the last thing you do make sure of! We don't want a third body. Yours.'

'Oh, I'm not expecting anything like that,' said Miss Marple.

'There might be danger, you know, if any of your ideas are right. Have you suspicions of any one particular person?'

'I think I have certain knowledge as to one person. I have got to find out – I have got to stay here. You asked me once if I felt an atmosphere of evil. Well, that atmosphere is here all right, an atmosphere of evil, of danger if you like – of great unhappiness, of fear . . . I've got to do something about that. The best I can do. But an old woman like me can't do very much.'

Professor Wanstead counted under his breath. 'One – two – three – four –'

'What are you counting?' asked Miss Marple.

'The people who left in the coach. Presumably you're not interested in

150

them, since you've let them go off and you're staying here.'

'Why should I be interested in them?'

'Because you said Mr Rafiel had sent you in the coach for a particular reason and sent you on this tour for a particular reason and sent you to The Old Manor House for a particular reason. Very well then. The death of Elizabeth Temple ties up with someone in the coach. Your remaining here ties up with The Old Manor House.'

'You're not quite right,' said Miss Marple. 'There are connections between the two. I want someone to tell me things.'

'Do you think you can make anyone tell you things?'

'I think I might. You'll miss your train if you don't go soon.'

'Take care of yourself,' said Professor Wanstead.

'I mean to take care of myself.'

The door into the lounge opened and two people came out. Miss Cooke and Miss Barrow.

'Hullo' said Professor Wanstead, 'I thought you'd gone off with the coach.'

'Well, we changed our minds at the last moment,' said Miss Cooke cheerfully. 'You know we've just discovered that there are some very agreeable walks near here and there are one or two places I'm very anxious to see. A church with a very unusual Saxon font. Only four or five miles away and quite easily reached by the local bus, I think. You see, it's not only houses and gardens. I'm very interested in church architecture.'

'So am I,' said Miss Barrow. 'There's also Finley Park which is a very fine piece of horticultural planting not far from here. We really thought that it would be much pleasanter to stay here for a day or two.'

'You're staying here at the Golden Boar?'

'Yes. We were fortunate enough to be able to get a very nice double room. Really a better one than the one we have had for the last two days.'

'You will miss your train,' said Miss Marple again.

'I wish,' said Professor Wanstead, 'that you –'

'I shall be quite all right,' said Miss Marple urgently. 'Such a kind man,' she said, as he disappeared round the side of the house, 'who really takes so much care of me – I might be a great-aunt of his or something like that.'

'It's all been a great shock, hasn't it,' said Miss Cooke. 'Perhaps you may like to come with us when we go to visit St Martins in the Grove.'

'You're very kind,' said Miss Marple, 'but I don't think today I feel quite strong enough for expeditions. Perhaps tomorrow if there is anything interesting to see.'

'Well, we must leave you then.'

Miss Marple smiled at them both and went into the hotel.

151

CHAPTER 20

Miss Marple Has Ideas

Having had lunch in the dining-room, Miss Marple went out on the terrace to drink her coffee. She was just sipping her second cup when a tall, thin figure came striding up the steps, and approached her, speaking rather breathlessly. She saw that it was Anthea Bradbury-Scott.

'Oh, Miss Marple, we've only just heard, you know, that you didn't go with the coach, after all. We thought you were going on with the tour. We had no idea you were staying on here. Both Clotilde and Lavinia sent me here to say we do so hope you will come back to The Old Manor House and stay with us. I'm sure it will be nicer for you to be there. There are so many people coming and going here always, especially over a weekend and things like that. So we'd be very, very glad – we really would – if you would come back to us.'

'Oh, that's very kind of you,' said Miss Marple. 'Really very kind, but I'm sure – I mean, you know it was just a two-day visit. I meant originally to go off with the coach. I mean, after the two days. If it hadn't been for this very, very tragic accident but – well, I really felt I couldn't go on any longer. I thought I must have at least, well at least one night's rest.'

'But I mean it would be so much better if you came to us. We'd try and make you comfortable.'

'Oh, there's no question of that,' said Miss Marple. 'I was extremely comfortable staying with you. Oh yes, I did enjoy it very much. Such a beautiful house. And all your things are so nice. You know, your china and glass and furniture. It's such a pleasure to be in a home and not a hotel.'

'Then you must come with me now. Yes, you really must. I could go and pack your things for you.'

'Oh – well, that's very kind of you. I can do that myself.'

'Well, shall I come and help you?'

'That would be very kind,' said Miss Marple.

They repaired to her bedroom where Anthea, in a somewhat slap-dash manner, packed Miss Marple's belongings together. Miss Marple, who had her own ways of folding things, had to bite her lip to keep an air of complacency on her face. Really, she thought, she can't fold *anything* properly.

Anthea got hold of a porter from the hotel and he carried the suitcase round the corner and down the street to The Old Manor House. Miss Marple tipped him adequately and, still uttering fussy little speeches of thanks and pleasure, rejoined the sisters.

'The Three Sisters!' she was thinking, 'here we are again.' She sat down in the drawing-room, and closed her eyes for a minute, breathing rather fast. She appeared to be somewhat out of breath. It was only natural, she felt at her age, and after all Anthea and the hotel porter had set a fast pace. But really she was trying to acquire through her closed eyes what the feeling was she had on coming into this house again. Was something in it sinister? No, not so much sinister as unhappy. Deep unhappiness. So much so it was almost frightening.

She opened her eyes again and looked at the two other occupants of the room. Mrs Glynne had just come in from the kitchen, bearing an afternoon tea tray. She looked as she had looked all along. Comfortable, no particular emotions or feelings. Perhaps almost too devoid of them, Miss Marple thought. Had she accustomed herself, through perhaps a life of some stress and difficulty, to show nothing to the outer world, to keep a reserve and let no-one know what her inner feelings were?

She looked from her to Clotilde. She had a Clytemnestra look, as she had thought before. She had certainly not murdered her husband for she had never had a husband to murder and it seemed unlikely that she had murdered the girl to whom she was said to have been extremely attached. That, Miss Marple was quite sure, was true. She had seen before how the tears had welled from Clotilde's eyes when the death of Verity had been mentioned.

And what about Anthea? Anthea had taken that cardboard box to the post office. Anthea had come to fetch her. Anthea – she was very doubtful about Anthea. Scatty? Too scatty for her age. Eyes that wandered and came back to you. Eyes that seemed to see things that other people might not see, over your shoulder. She's frightened, thought Miss Marple. Frightened of something. What was she frightened of? Was she perhaps a mental case of some kind? Frightened perhaps of going back to some institution or establishment where she might have spent part of her life? Frightened of those two sisters of hers feeling that it was unwise for her to remain at liberty? Were they uncertain, those two, what their sister Anthea might do or say?

There was *some* atmosphere here. She wondered, as she sipped the last of her tea, what Miss Cooke and Miss Barrow were doing. Had they gone to visit that church or was that all talk, meaningless talk? It was odd. Odd the way they had come and looked at her at St Mary Mead so as to know her again on the coach, but not to acknowledge that they had ever seen or met her before.

There were quite a lot of difficult things going on. Presently Mrs Glynne

153

removed the tea tray, Anthea went out into the garden and Miss Marple was left alone with Clotilde.

'I think,' said Miss Marple, 'that you know an Archdeacon Brabazon, do you not?'

'Oh yes,' said Clotilde, 'he was in church yesterday at the service. Do you know him?'

'Oh no,' said Miss Marple, 'but he did come to the Golden Boar and he came and spoke to me there. I gather he had been to the hospital and was enquiring about poor Miss Temple's death. He wondered if Miss Temple had sent any message to him. I gather she was thinking of paying him a visit. But of course I told him that although I did go there in case I could do anything there was nothing that could be done except sit by poor Miss Temple's bed. She was unconscious, you know. I could have done nothing to help her.'

'She didn't say – say anything – any explanation of what had happened?' asked Clotilde.

She asked without much interest. Miss Marple wondered if she felt more interest than she expressed, but on the whole she thought not. She thought Clotilde was busy with thoughts of something quite different.

'Do you think it *was* an accident?' Miss Marple asked, 'Or do you think there is something in that story that Mrs Riseley-Porter's niece told? About seeing someone pushing a boulder.'

'Well, I suppose if those two said so, they must have seen it.'

'Yes. They both said so, didn't they,' said Miss Marple, 'though not quite in the same terms. But perhaps that's quite natural.'

Clotilde looked at her curiously.

'You seem to be intrigued by that.'

'Well, it seems so very unlikely,' said Miss Marple, 'an unlikely story, unless –'

'Unless what?'

'Well, I just wondered,' said Miss Marple.

Mrs Glynne came into the room again.

'You just wondered what?' she asked.

'We're talking about the accident, or the non-accident,' said Clotilde.

'But who –'

'It seems a very odd story that they told,' said Miss Marple again.

'There's something about this place,' said Clotilde suddenly. 'Something about this atmosphere. We never got over it here. Never. Never since – since Verity died. It's years but it doesn't go away. A shadow's here.' She looked at Miss Marple. 'Don't you think so too? Don't you feel a shadow here?'

154

'Well, I'm a stranger,' said Miss Marple. 'It's different for you and your sisters who've lived here and who knew the dead girl. She was, I gather, as Archdeacon Brabazon was saying – a very charming and beautiful girl.'

'She was a lovely girl. A dear child too,' said Clotilde.

'I wish I'd known her better,' said Mrs Glynne. 'Of course I was living abroad at that time. My husband and I came home on leave once, but we were mostly in London. We didn't come down here often.'

Anthea came in from the garden. She was carrying in her hand a great bunch of lilies.

'Funeral flowers,' she said. 'That's what we ought to have here today, isn't it? I'll put them in a great jar. Funeral flowers,' and she laughed suddenly. A queer, hysterical little giggle.

'Anthea,' said Clotilde, 'don't – don't do that. It's not – its not right.'

'I'll go and put them in water,' said Anthea, cheerfully. She went out of the room.

'Really,' said Mrs Glynne, 'Anthea! I do think she's –'

'She's getting worse,' said Clotilde.

Miss Marple adopted an attitude of not listening or hearing. She picked up a small enamel box and looked at it with admiring eyes.

'She'll probably break a vase now,' said Lavinia.

She went out of the room. Miss Marple said,

'You are worried about your sister, about Anthea?'

'Well yes, she's always been rather unbalanced. She's the youngest and she was rather delicate as a girl. But lately, I think, she's got definitely worse. She hasn't got any idea, I think, of the gravity of things. She has these silly fits of hysteria. Hysterical laughter at things one ought to be serious about. We don't want to – well, to send her anywhere or – you know. She ought to have treatment, I think, but I don't think she would like to go away from home. This is her home, after all. Though sometimes it's – it's very difficult.'

'All life is difficult sometimes,' said Miss Marple.

'Lavinia talks of going away,' said Clotilde. 'She talks of going to live abroad again. At Taormina, I think. She was there with her husband a lot and they were very happy. She's been at home with us now for many years, but she seems to have this longing to get away and to travel. Sometimes I think – sometimes I think she doesn't like being in the same house as Anthea.'

'Oh dear,' said Miss Marple. 'Yes, I have heard of cases like that where these difficulties do arise.'

'She's afraid of Anthea,' said Clotilde. 'Definitely afraid of her. And really, I keep telling her there's nothing to be afraid of. Anthea's just rather

155

silly at times. You know, has queer ideas and says queer things. But I don't think there's any danger of her – well, I mean of – oh, I don't know what I mean. Doing anything dangerous or strange or queer.'

'There's never been any trouble of that kind?' enquired Miss Marple.

'Oh no. There's never been anything. She gets nervous fits of temper sometimes and she takes rather sudden dislikes to people. She's very jealous, you know, over things. Very jealous of a lot of – well, fuss being made over different people. I don't know. Sometimes I think we'd better sell this house and leave it altogether.'

'It is sad for you, isn't it,' said Miss Marple. 'I think I can understand that it must be very sad for you living here with the memory of the past.'

'You understand that, do you? Yes, I can see that you do. One cannot help it. One's mind goes back to that dear, lovable child. She was like a daughter to me. She was the daughter, anyway, of one of my best friends. She was very intelligent too. She was a clever girl. She was a good artist. She was doing very well with her art training and designing. She was taking up a good deal of designing. I was very proud of her. And then – this wretched attachment, this terrible mentally afflicted boy.'

'You mean Mr Rafiel's son, Michael Rafiel?'

'Yes. If only he'd never come here. It just happened that he was staying in this part of the world and his father suggested he might look us up and he came and had a meal with us. He could be very charming, you know. But he always had been a sad delinquent, a bad record. He'd been in prison twice, and a very bad history with girls. But I never thought that Verity . . . just a case of infatuation. I suppose it happens to girls of that age. She was infatuated with him. Insisted that everything that had happened to him had not been his fault. You know the things girls say. "Everyone is against him," that's what they always say. Everyone's against him. Nobody made allowances for him. Oh, one gets tired of hearing these things said. Can't one put a little sense into girls?'

'They have not usually very much sense, I agree,' said Miss Marple.

'She wouldn't listen. I – I tried to keep him away from the house. I told him he was not to come here any more. That of course was stupid. I realized that afterwards. It only meant that she went and met him outside the house. I don't know where. They had various meeting places. He used to call for her in his car at an agreed spot and bring her home late at night. Once or twice he didn't bring her home until the next day. I tried to tell them it must stop, that it must all cease, but they wouldn't listen. Verity wouldn't listen. I didn't expect him to, of course.'

'She intended to marry him?' asked Miss Marple.

'Well, I don't think it ever got as far as that. I don't think he ever wanted

156

to marry her or thought of such a thing.'

'I am very sorry for you,' said Miss Marple. 'You must have suffered a lot.'

'Yes. The worst was having to go and identify the body. That was some time after – after she'd disappeared from here. We thought of course that she'd run away with him and we thought that we'd get news of them some time. I knew the police seemed to be taking it rather seriously. They asked Michael to go to the police station and help them with enquiries and his account of himself didn't seem to agree with what local people were saying.

'Then they found her. A long way from here. About thirty miles away. In a kind of ditchy hedgy spot down an unfrequented lane where hardly anyone ever went. Yes, I had to go and view the body in the mortuary. A terrible sight. The cruelty, the force that had been used. What did he want to do that to her for? Wasn't it enough that he strangled her? He strangled her with her own scarf. I can't – I can't talk about it any more. I can't bear it, I can't bear it.'

Tears rained suddenly down her face.

'I'm sorry for you,' said Miss Marple. 'I'm very, very sorry.'

'I believe you are.' Clotilde looked at her suddenly. 'And even you don't know the worst of it.'

'In what way?'

'I don't know – I don't know about Anthea.'

'What do you mean about Anthea?'

'She was so queer at that time. She was – she was very jealous. She suddenly seemed to turn against Verity. To look at her as though she hated her. Sometimes I thought – I thought perhaps – oh no, it's an awful thing to think, you can't think that about your own sister – she did once attack someone. You know, she used to get these storms of rage. I wondered if it *could* have been – oh, I mustn't say such things. There's no question of any such thing. Please forget what I've said. There's nothing in it, nothing at all. But – but – well, she's not quite normal. I've got to face that. When she was quite young queer things happened once or twice – with animals. We had a parrot. A parrot that said things, silly things like parrots do say and she wrung its neck and I've never felt the same since. I've never felt that I could trust her. I've never felt *sure*. I've never felt – oh, goodness, I'm getting hysterical, too.'

'Come, come,' said Miss Marple, 'don't think of these things.'

'No. It's bad enough to know – to know that Verity died. Died in that horrible way. At any rate, other girls are safe from that boy. Life sentence he got. He's still in prison. They won't let him out to do anything to anyone else. Though why they couldn't bring it in as some mental trouble –

diminished responsibility – one of these things they use nowadays. He ought to have gone to Broadmoor. I'm sure he wasn't responsible for anything that he did.'

She got up and went out of the room. Mrs Glynne had come back and passed her sister in the doorway.

'You mustn't pay any attention to Clotilde,' she said. 'She's never quite recovered from that ghastly business years ago. She loved Verity very much.'

'She seems to be worried about your other sister.'

'About Anthea? Anthea's all right. She's – er – well, she's scatty, you know. She's a bit – hysterical. Apt to get worked up about things, and she has queer fancies, imagination sometimes. But I don't think there's any need for Clotilde to worry so much. Dear me, who's that passing the window?'

Two apologetic figures suddenly showed themselves in the french window.

'Oh do excuse us,' said Miss Barrow, 'we were just walking round the house to see if we could find Miss Marple. We had heard she'd come here with you and I wonder – oh, there you are, my dear Miss Marple. I wanted to tell you that we didn't get to that church after all this afternoon. Apparently it's closed for cleaning, so I think we shall have to give up any other expedition today and go on one tomorrow. I do hope you don't mind us coming in this way. I did ring at the front-door bell but it didn't seem to be ringing.'

'I'm afraid it doesn't sometimes,' said Mrs Glynne. 'You know, it's rather temperamental. Sometimes it rings and sometimes it doesn't. But do sit down and talk to us a little. I'd no idea that you hadn't gone with the coach.'

'No, we thought we would do a little sight-seeing round here, as we had got so far, and going with the coach would really be rather – well, rather painful after what has happened just a day or two ago.'

'You must have some sherry,' said Mrs Glynne.

She went out of the room and presently returned. Anthea was with her, quite calm now, bringing glasses and a decanter of sherry, and they sat down together.

'I can't help wanting to know,' said Mrs Glynne, 'what really is going to happen in this business. I mean of poor Miss Temple. I mean, it seems so very impossible to know what the police think. They still seem to be in charge, and I mean the inquest being adjourned, so obviously they are not satisfied. I don't know if there's anything in the nature of the wound.'

'I shouldn't think so,' said Miss Barrow. 'I mean a blow on the head, bad concussion – well, I mean that came from the boulder. The only point is,

Miss Marple, if the boulder rolled itself down or somebody rolled it.'

'Oh,' said Miss Cooke, 'but surely you can't think that – who on earth would want to roll a boulder down, do that sort of thing? I suppose there are always hooligans about. You know, some young foreigners or students. I really wonder, you know, whether – well –'

'You mean,' said Miss Marple, 'you wondered if that someone was one of our fellow travellers.'

'Well, I – I didn't say that,' said Miss Cooke.

'But surely,' said Miss Marple, 'we can't help – well, thinking about that sort of thing. I mean, there must be some explanation. If the police seem sure it wasn't an accident, well then it must have been done by somebody and – well, I mean, Miss Temple was a stranger to this place here. It doesn't seem as if anyone could have done it – anyone local I mean. So it really comes back to – well, I mean, to all of us who were in the coach, doesn't it?'

She gave a faint, rather whinnying old lady's laugh.

'Oh surely!'

'No, I suppose I ought not to say such things. But you know, really crimes are very interesting. Sometimes the most extraordinary things have happened.'

'Have you any definite feeling yourself, Miss Marple? I should be interested to hear,' said Clotilde.

'Well, one does think of possibilities.'

'Mr Caspar,' said Miss Cooke. 'You know, I didn't like the look of that man from the first. He looked to me – well, I thought he might have something to do with espionage or something. You know, perhaps come to this country to look for atomic secrets or something.'

'I don't think we've got any atomic secrets round here,' said Mrs Glynne.

'Of course we haven't,' said Anthea. 'Perhaps it was someone who was following her. Perhaps it was someone who was tracking her because she was a criminal of some kind.'

'Nonsense,' said Clotilde. 'She was the Headmistress, retired, of a very well known school, she was a very fine scholar. Why should anyone be trying to track her down?'

'Oh, I don't know. She might have gone peculiar or something.'

'I'm sure,' said Mrs Glynne, 'that Miss Marple has some ideas.'

'Well, I have some ideas,' said Miss Marple. 'It seems to me that – well, the only people that could be ... Oh dear, this is so difficult to say. But I mean there are two people who just spring into one's mind as possibilities logically. I mean, I don't think that it's really so at all because I'm sure they're both very nice people, but I mean there's nobody else really logically who could be suspected, should I say.'

'Who do you mean? This is very interesting.'

'Well, I don't think I ought to say such things. It's only a – sort of wild conjecture.'

'Who do you think might have rolled the boulder down? Who do you think could have been the person that Joanna and Emlyn Price saw?'

'Well, what I did think was that – that perhaps they hadn't seen anybody.'

'I don't quite understand,' said Anthea, 'they hadn't seen anybody?'

'Well, perhaps they might have made it all up.'

'What – about seeing someone?'

'Well, it's possible, isn't it.'

'Do you mean as a sort of joke or a sort of unkind idea? What *do* you mean?'

'Well, I suppose – one does hear of young people doing very extraordinary things nowadays,' said Miss Marple. 'You know, putting things in horses' eyes, smashing Legation windows and attacking people. Throwing stones, at people, and it's usually being done by somebody young, isn't it? And they were the only young people, weren't they?'

'You mean Emlyn Price and Joanna might have rolled over that boulder?'

'Well, they're the only sort of obvious people, aren't they?' said Miss Marple.

'Fancy!' said Clotilde. 'Oh, I should never have thought of that. But I see – yes, I just see that there could be something in what you say. Of course, I don't know what those two were like. I haven't been travelling with them.'

'Oh, they were very nice,' said Miss Marple. 'Joanna seemed to me a particularly – you know, capable girl.'

'Capable of doing anything?' asked Anthea.

'Anthea,' said Clotilde, 'do be quiet.'

'Yes. Quite capable,' said Miss Marple. 'After all, if you're going to do what may result in murder, you'd have to be rather capable so as to manage not to be seen or anything.'

'They must have been in it together, though,' suggested Miss Barrow.

'Oh yes,' said Miss Marple. 'They were in it together and they told roughly the same story. They are the – well, they are the obvious suspects, that's all I can say. They were out of sight of the others. All the other people were on the lower path. They could have gone up to the top of the hill, they could have rocked the boulder. Perhaps they didn't mean to kill Miss Temple specially. They may have meant it just as a – well, just as a piece of anarchy or smashing something or someone – anyone in fact. They rolled it over. And then of course they told the story of seeing someone there. Some rather peculiar costume or other which also sounds very unlikely and – well,

I oughtn't to say these things but I *have* been thinking about it.'

'It seems to me a very interesting thought,' said Mrs Glynne. 'What do you think, Clotilde?'

'I think it's a possibility. I shouldn't have thought of it myself.'

'Well,' said Miss Cooke, rising to her feet, 'we must be going back to the Golden Boar now. Are you coming with us, Miss Marple?'

'Oh no,' said Miss Marple. 'I suppose you don't know. I've forgotten to tell you. Miss Bradbury-Scott very kindly asked me to come back and stay another night – or two nights – here.'

'Oh, I see. Well, I'm sure that'll be very nice for you. Much more comfortable. They seem rather a noisy lot that have arrived at the Golden Boar this evening.'

'Won't you come round and have some coffee with us after dinner?' suggested Clotilde. 'It's quite a warm evening. We can't offer you dinner because I'm afraid we haven't got enough in the house, but if you'll come in and have some coffee with us . . .'

'That would be very nice,' said Miss Cooke. 'Yes, we will certainly avail ourselves of your hospitality.'

CHAPTER 21

The Clock Strikes Three

Miss Cooke and Miss Barrow arrived very promptly at 8.45. One wore beige lace and the other one a shade of olive green. During dinner Anthea had asked Miss Marple about these two ladies.

'It seems very funny of them,' she said, 'to want to stay behind.'

'Oh, I don't think so,' said Miss Marple. 'I think it is really quite natural. They have a rather exact plan, I imagine.'

'What do you mean by a plan?' asked Mrs Glynne.

'Well, I should think they are always prepared for various eventualities and have a plan for dealing with them.'

'Do you mean,' said Anthea, with some interest, 'do you mean that they had a plan for dealing with murder?'

'I wish,' said Mrs Glynne, 'that you wouldn't talk of poor Miss Temple's death as murder.'

'But of course it's murder,' said Anthea. 'All I wonder is who wanted to murder her? I should think probably some pupil of hers at the school who always hated her and had it in for her.'

'Do you think hate can last as long as that?' asked Miss Marple.

'Oh, I should think so. I should think you could hate anyone for years.'

'No,' said Miss Marple, 'I think hate would die out. You could try and keep it up artificially, but I think you would fail. It's not as strong a force as love,' she added.

'Don't you think that Miss Cooke or Miss Barrow or both of them might have done the murder?'

'Why should they?' said Mrs Glynne. 'Really, Anthea! They seemed very nice women to me.'

'*I* think there's something rather mysterious about them,' said Anthea. 'Don't you, Clotilde?'

'I think perhaps you're right,' said Clotilde. 'They seemed to me to be slightly artificial, if you know what I mean.'

'*I* think there's something very sinister about them,' said Anthea.

'You've got such an imagination always,' said Mrs Glynne. 'Anyway, they were walking along the bottom path, weren't they? You saw them there, didn't you?' she said to Miss Marple.

'I can't say that I noticed them particularly,' said Miss Marple. 'In fact, I had no opportunity of doing so.'

'You mean –?'

162

'She wasn't there,' said Clotilde. 'She was here in our garden.'

'Oh, of course. I forgot.'

'A very nice, peaceful day it was,' said Miss Marple. 'I enjoyed it very much. Tomorrow morning I would like to go out and look again at that mass of white flowers coming into bloom at the end of the garden near that raised up mound. It was just beginning to come out the other day. It must be a mass of bloom now. I shall always remember that as part of my visit here, you know.'

'I hate it,' said Anthea. 'I want it taken away. I want to build up a greenhouse again there. Surely if we save enough money we can do that, Clotilde?'

'We'll leave that alone,' said Clotilde. 'I don't want that touched. What use is a greenhouse to us now? It would be years before grapes would bear fruit again.'

'Come,' said Mrs Glynne, 'we can't go on arguing over that. Let us go into the drawing-room. Our guests will be coming shortly for coffee.'

It was then that the guests had arrived. Clotilde brought in the tray of coffee. She poured out the cups and distributed them. She placed one before each guest and then brought one to Miss Marple. Miss Cooke leaned forward.

'Oh, do forgive me, Miss Marple, but really, do you know, I shouldn't drink that if I were you. Coffee, I mean, at this time of night. You won't sleep properly.'

'Oh, do you think so?' said Miss Marple. 'I am quite used to coffee in the evening.'

'Yes, but this is very strong, good coffee. I should advise you not to drink it.'

Miss Marple looked at Miss Cooke. Miss Cooke's face was very earnest, her fair, unnatural-looking hair flopped over one eye. The other eye blinked slightly.

'I see what you mean,' said Miss Marple. 'Perhaps you are right. You know something, I gather, about diet.'

'Oh yes, I make quite a study of it. I had some training in nursing, you know, and one thing and another.'

'Indeed.' Miss Marple pushed the cup away slightly. 'I suppose there is no photograph of this girl?' she asked. 'Verity Hunt, or whatever her name was? The Archdeacon was talking about her. He seemed to have been very fond of her.'

'I think he was. He was fond of all young people,' said Clotilde.

She got up, went across the room and lifted the lid of a desk. From that she brought a photograph and brought it over for Miss Marple to see.

'That was Verity,' she said.

'A beautiful face,' said Miss Marple. 'Yes, a very beautiful and unusual face. Poor child.'

'It's dreadful nowadays,' said Anthea, 'these things seem to be happening the whole time. Girls going out with every kind of young man. Nobody taking any trouble to look after them.'

'They have to look after themselves nowadays,' said Clotilde, 'and they've no idea of how to do it, heaven help them!'

She stretched out a hand to take back the photograph from Miss Marple. As she did so her sleeve caught the coffee cup and knocked it to the floor.

'Oh dear!' said Miss Marple. 'Was that my fault? Did I jog your arm?'

'No,' said Clotilde, 'it was my sleeve. It's rather a floating sleeve. Perhaps you would like some hot milk, if you are afraid to take coffee?'

'That would be very kind,' said Miss Marple. 'A glass of hot milk when I go to bed would be very soothing indeed, and always gives one a good night.'

After a little more desultory conversation, Miss Cooke and Miss Barrow took their departure. A rather fussy departure in which first one and then the other came back to collect some article they'd left behind. A scarf, a handbag and a pocket handkerchief.

'Fuss, fuss, fuss,' said Anthea, when they had departed.

'Somehow,' said Mrs Glynne, 'I agree with Clotilde that those two don't seem *real*, if you know what I mean,' she said to Miss Marple.

'Yes,' said Miss Marple, 'I *do* rather agree with you. They *don't* seem very real. I have wondered about them a good deal. Wondered, I mean, why they came on this tour and if they were really enjoying it. And what was their reason for coming.'

'And have you discovered the answers to all those things?' asked Clotilde.

'I think so,' said Miss Marple. She sighed. 'I've discovered the answers to a lot of things,' she said.

'Up to now I hope you've enjoyed yourself,' said Clotilde.

'I am glad to have left the tour now,' said Miss Marple. 'I don't think I should have enjoyed much more of it.'

'No. I can quite understand that.'

Clotilde fetched a glass of hot milk from the kitchen and accompanied Miss Marple up to her room.

'Is there anything else I can get you?' she asked. 'Anything at all?'

'No, thank you,' said Miss Marple. 'I have everything I want. I have my little night bag here, you see, so I need not do any more unpacking. Thank you,' she said, 'it is very kind of you and your sisters to put me up again tonight.'

'Well, we couldn't do much less, having had Mr Rafiel's letter. He was a very thoughtful man.'

'Yes,' said Miss Marple, 'the kind of man who – well, thinks of everything. A good brain, I should think.'

'I believe he was a very noted financier.'

'Financially and otherwise, he thought of a lot of things,' said Miss Marple. 'Oh well, I shall be glad to get to bed. Goodnight, Miss Bradbury-Scott.'

'Shall I send you breakfast up in the morning, you'd like to have it in bed?'

'No, no, I wouldn't put you out for the world. No, no, I would rather come down. A cup of tea, perhaps, would be very nice, but I want to go out in the garden. I particularly want to see that mound all covered with white flowers, so beautiful and so triumphant –'

'Goodnight,' said Clotilde, 'sleep well.'

II

In the hall of The Old Manor House the grandfather clock at the bottom of the stairs struck two o'clock. The clocks in the house did not all strike in unison and some of them, indeed, did not strike at all. To keep a house full of antique clocks in working order was not easy. At three o'clock the clock on the first floor landing struck a soft-chimed three o'clock. A faint chink of light showed through the hinge of the door.

Miss Marple sat up in bed and put her fingers on the switch of the electric lamp by her bed. The door opened very softly. There was no light outside now but the soft footstep came through the door into the room. Miss Marple switched the light on.

'Oh,' she said, 'it's you, Miss Bradbury-Scott. Is there anything special?'

'I just came to see if you wanted anything,' said Miss Bradbury-Scott.

'Miss Marple looked at her. Clotilde had on a long purple robe. What a handsome woman she was, thought Miss Marple. Her hair framing her forehead, a tragic figure, a figure of drama. Again Miss Marple thought of Greek plays. Clytemnestra again.

'You're sure there is nothing I can bring you?'

'No, thank you,' said Miss Marple. 'I'm afraid,' she said apologetically, 'that I have not drunk my milk.'

'Oh dear, why not?'

'I did not think it would be very good for me,' said Miss Marple.

Clotilde stood there, at the foot of the bed, looking at her.

165

'Not wholesome, you know,' said Miss Marple.

'Just what do you mean by that?' Clotilde's voice was harsh now.

'I think you know what I mean,' said Miss Marple. 'I think you've known all the evening. Perhaps before that.'

'I have no idea what you are talking about.'

'No?' There was a faint satirical note to the questioning monosyllable.

'I am afraid the milk is cold now. I will take it away and get you some hot.'

Clotilde stretched out a hand and took the glass of milk from the bedside.

'Don't trouble yourself,' said Miss Marple. 'Even if you brought it me, I should not drink it.'

'I really cannot understand the point of what you're saying. Really,' said Clotilde, looking at her. 'What a very extraordinary person you are. What sort of a woman are you? Why are you talking like this? Who are you?'

Miss Marple pulled down the mass of pink wool that encircled her head, a pink wool scarf of the same kind that she had once worn in the West Indies.

'One of my names,' she said, 'is Nemesis.'

'Nemesis? And what does that mean?'

'I think you know,' said Miss Marple. 'You are a very well educated woman. Nemesis is long delayed sometimes, but it comes in the end.'

'What are you talking about?'

'About a very beautiful girl whom you killed,' said Miss Marple.

'Whom I killed? What do you mean?'

'I mean the girl Verity.'

'And why should I kill her?'

'Because you loved her,' said Miss Marple.

'Of course I loved her. I was devoted to her. And she loved me.'

'Somebody said to me not very long ago that love was a very frightening word. It *is* a frightening word. You loved Verity too much. She meant everything in the world to you. She was devoted to you until something else came into her life. A different kind of love came into her life. She fell in love with a boy, a young man. Not a very suitable one, not a very good specimen, not anyone with a good record, but she loved him and he loved her and she wanted to escape. To escape from the burden of the bondage of love she was living in with you. She wanted a normal woman's life. To live with the man of her choice, to have children by him. She wanted marriage and the happiness of normality.'

Clotilde moved. She came to a chair and sat down in it, staring at Miss Marple.

'So,' she said, 'you seem to understand very well.'

'Yes, I do understand.'

'What you say is quite true. I shan't deny it. It doesn't matter if I do or do not deny it.'

'No,' said Miss Marple, 'you are quite right there. It will not matter.'

'Do you know at all – can you imagine – how I have suffered?'

'Yes,' said Miss Marple, 'I can imagine it. I've always been able to imagine things.'

'Did you imagine the agony, the agony of thinking, of knowing you are going to lose the thing you love best in the world. And I was losing it to a miserable, depraved delinquent. A man unworthy of my beautiful, splendid girl, I had to stop it. I had to – I had to.'

'Yes,' said Miss Marple. 'Sooner than let the girl go, you killed her. Because you loved her, you killed her.'

'Do you think I could ever do a thing like that? Do you think I could strangle the girl I loved? Do you think I could bash her face in, crush her head to a pulp? Nothing but a vicious, depraved man would do a thing like that.'

'No,' said Miss Marple, 'you wouldn't do that. You loved her and you would not be able to do that.'

'Well then, you see, you are talking nonsense.'

'You didn't do that to her. The girl that happened to was not the girl you loved. Verity's here still, isn't she? She's here in the garden. I don't think you strangled her. I think you gave her a drink of coffee or of milk, you gave her a painless overdose of sleeping stuff. And then when she was dead, you took her out into the garden, you pulled aside the fallen bricks of the greenhouse, and you made a vault for her there, under the floor with the bricks, and covered it over. And then the polygonum was planted there and has flowered ever since, growing bigger and stronger every year. Verity has remained here with you. You never let her go.'

'You fool! You crazy old fool! Do you think you are ever going to get away to tell this story?'

'I think so,' said Miss Marple. 'I'm not quite sure of it. You are a strong woman, a great deal stronger than I am.'

'I'm glad you appreciate that.'

'And you wouldn't have any scruples,' said Miss Marple. 'You know one doesn't stop at one murder. I have noticed that in the course of my life and in what I have observed of crime. You killed two girls, didn't you? You killed the girl you loved and you killed a different girl.'

'I killed a silly little tramp, an adolescent tart. Nora Broad. How did you know about her?'

'I wondered,' said Miss Marple. 'I didn't think from what I saw of you that you could have borne to strangle and disfigure the girl you loved. But another girl disappeared also about that time, a girl whose body has never

167

been found. But I thought the body *had* been found, only they hadn't known that the body was Nora Broad's. It was dressed in Verity's clothes, it was identified as Verity by the person who would be the first applied to, the person who knew her better than anyone else. You had to go and say if the body found was the body of Verity. You recognized it. You said that that dead body was Verity's.'

'And why should I do that?'

'Because you wanted the boy who had taken Verity away from you, the boy whom Verity had loved and who had loved Verity, you wanted him tried for murder. And so you hid that second body in a place where it would not be too easily discovered. When that was discovered, it would be thought to be the wrong girl. You would make sure that it was identified in the way you wanted. You dressed it in Verity's clothes, put her handbag there; a letter or two, a bangle, a little cross on a chain – you disfigured her face.

'A week ago you committed a third murder, the murder of Elizabeth Temple. You killed her because she was coming to this part of the world, and you were afraid of what she might have known, from what Verity might have written to her or told her, and you thought that if Elizabeth Temple got together with Archdeacon Brabazon, they might with what they both knew come at some appraisal of the truth. Elizabeth Temple must not be allowed to meet the Archdeacon. You are a very powerful woman. You could have rolled that boulder down the hillside. It must have taken some doing, but you are a very strong woman.'

'Strong enough to deal with you,' said Clotilde.

'I don't think,' said Miss Marple, 'that you will be allowed to do that.'

'What do you mean, you miserable, shrivelled up old woman?'

'Yes,' said Miss Marple, 'I'm an elderly pussy and I have very little strength in my arms or my legs. Very little strength anywhere. But I am in my own way an emissary of justice.'

Clotilde laughed, 'And who'll stop me from putting an end to you?'

'I think,' said Miss Marple, 'my guardian angel.'

'Trusting to your guardian angel, are you?' said Clotilde, and laughed again.

She advanced towards the bed.

'Possibly two guardian angels,' said Miss Marple. 'Mr Rafiel always did things on a lavish scale.'

Her hand slipped under the pillow and out again. In it was a whistle which she put to her lips. It was something of a sensation in whistles. It had the shrill fury which would attract a policeman from the end of a street. Two things happened almost simultaneously. The door of the room opened. Clotilde turned. Miss Barrow was standing in the doorway. At the same

168

moment the large wardrobe hanging cupboard opened and Miss Cooke stepped out of it. There was a grim air of professionalism about them both which was very noticeable, in contrast to their pleasant social behaviour a little earlier in the evening.

'Two guardian angels,' said Miss Marple happily. 'Mr Rafiel has done me very proud! as one used to say.'

CHAPTER 22

Miss Marple Tells Her Story

'When did you find out,' asked Professor Wanstead, 'that those two women were private agents accompanying you for your protection?'

He leaned forward in his chair looking thoughtfully at the white-haired old lady who sat in an upright position in the chair opposite him. They were in an official Government building in London, and there were four other persons present.

An official from the Public Prosecutor's Office; the Assistant Commissioner of Scotland Yard, Sir James Lloyd, the Governor of Manstone Prison, Sir Andrew McNeil. The fourth person was the Home Secretary.

'Not until the last evening,' said Miss Marple. 'I wasn't actually sure until then. Miss Cooke had come to St Mary Mead and I found out fairly quickly that she was not what she represented herself to be, which was a woman knowledgeable in gardening who had come there to help a friend with her garden. So I was left with the choice of deciding what her real object had been, once she had acquainted herself with my appearance, which was obviously the only thing she could have come for. When I recognized her again, on the coach, I had to make up my mind if she was accompanying the tour in the rôle of guardianship, or whether those two women were enemies enlisted by what I might call the other side.

'I was only really sure that last evening when Miss Cooke prevented me, by very distinct words of warning, from drinking the cup of coffee that Clotilde Bradbury-Scott had just set down in front of me. She phrased it very cleverly, but the warning was clearly there. Later, when I was wishing those two goodnight, one of them took my hand in both of hers giving me a particularly friendly and affectionate handshake. And in doing so she passed something into my hand, which, when I examined it later, I found to be a high-powered whistle. I took it to bed with me, accepted the glass of milk which was urged upon me by my hostess, and wished her goodnight, being careful not to change my simple and friendly attitude.'

'You didn't drink the milk?'

'Of course not,' said Miss Marple. 'What do you take me for?'

'I beg your pardon,' said Professor Wanstead. 'It surprises me that you didn't lock your door.'

'That would have been quite the wrong thing to do,' said Miss Marple. 'I wanted Clotilde Bradbury-Scott to come in. I wanted to see what she would say or do. I thought it was almost certain that she *would* come in when sufficient time had elapsed, to make sure that I had drunk the milk, and was in an unconscious sleep from which presumably I would not have woken up again.'

'Did you help Miss Cooke to conceal herself in the wardrobe?'

'No. It was a complete surprise when she came out of that suddenly. I suppose,' said Miss Marple thoughtfully, thinking it over, 'I suppose she slipped in there just when I had gone down the passage to the – er – to the bathroom.'

'You knew the two women were in the house?'

'I thought they would be at hand somewhere after they'd given me the whistle. I do not think it was a difficult house to which to gain access, there were no shuttered windows or burglar alarms or anything of that kind. One of them came back on the pretext of having left a handbag and a scarf. Between them they probably managed to leave a window unfastened, and I should imagine they came back into the house almost as soon as they left it, while the inhabitants inside were going up to bed.'

'You took a big risk, Miss Marple.'

'I hoped for the best,' said Miss Marple. 'One cannot go through life without attracting certain risks if they are necessary.'

'Your tip about the parcel dispatched to that charity, by the way, was entirely successful. It contained a brand new brightly coloured man's polo-necked jumper in scarlet and black checks. Most noticeable. What made you think of that?'

'Well,' said Miss Marple, 'that was really very simple. The description that Emlyn and Joanna gave of the figure they had seen made it seem almost certain that these very bright coloured and noticeable clothes were *meant* to be noticed, and that therefore it would be very important that they should not be hidden locally or kept among the person's own belongings. They must be got out of the way as soon as could be. And really there is only one way successfully of disposing of something. That is through the general post. Anything in the nature of clothes can be very easily dispatched to charities. Think how pleased the people who collect winter garments for Unemployed Mothers, or whatever the name of the charity, would be to find a nearly brand new woollen jumper. All I had to do was to find out the address where it had been sent.'

'And you *asked* them that at the post office?' The Home Secretary looked slightly shocked.

'Not directly, of course. I mean, I had to be a little flustered and explain how I'd put the wrong address on some clothes that I was sending to a charity and could they by any chance tell me if the parcel one of my kind hostesses had brought up there, had been sent off. And a very nice woman there did her best and remembered that it was *not* the address I was hoping it had been sent to, and she gave me the address that she *had* noted. She had no suspicion, I think, that I had any wish for the information apart from being – well, rather muddle-headed, elderly, and very worried about where my parcel of worn clothes had gone.'

'Ah,' said Professor Wanstead, 'I see you are an actress, Miss Marple, as well as an avenger.' Then he said, 'When did you first begin to discover what had happened ten years ago?'

'To begin with,' said Miss Marple, 'I found things very difficult, almost impossible. In my mind I was blaming Mr Rafiel for not having made things clear to me. But I see now that he'd been very wise not to do so. Really, you know, he *was* extraordinarily clever. I can see why he was such a big financier and made so much money so easily. He laid his plans so well. He gave me just enough information in small packets each time. I was, as it were, directed. First my guardian angels were alerted to note what I looked like. Then I was directed on the tour and to the people on it.'

'Did you suspect, if I may use that word, anyone on the tour at first?'

'Only as possibilities.'

'No feeling of evil?'

'Ah, you have remembered that. No, I did not think there was any definite atmosphere of evil. I was not told who my contact was there, but *she* made herself known to *me*.'

'Elizabeth Temple?'

'Yes. It was like a searchlight,' said Miss Marple, 'illuminating things on a dark night. So far, you see, I had been in the dark. There were certain things that must be, must logically be, I mean, because of what Mr Rafiel had indicated. There must be somewhere a victim and somewhere a murderer. Yes, a killer was indicated because that was the only liaison that had existed between Mr Rafiel and myself. There had been a murder in the West Indies. Both he and I had been involved in it and all he knew of me was my connection with that. So it could not be any other type of crime. And it could not, either, be a casual crime. It must be, and show itself definitely to be, the handiwork of someone who had accepted evil. Evil instead of good. There seemed to be two victims indicated. There must be someone who had been killed and there must be clearly a victim of injustice. A victim who had been accused of a crime he or she had not committed. So now, while I pondered these things, I had no light upon them until I talked to Miss Temple. She was very intense, very compelling. There came the first link which I had with Mr Rafiel. She spoke of a girl she had known, a girl who had once been engaged to Mr Rafiel's son. Here then was my first ray of light. Presently she also told me that the girl had not married him. I asked why not and she said "because she died". I asked then how she died, what had killed her, and she said very strongly, very compellingly – I can hear her voice still, it was like the sound of a deep bell – she said *Love*. And she said after that "the most frightening word there can be is Love". I did not know then exactly what she meant. In fact the first idea that came to me was that the girl had committed suicide as a result of an unhappy love affair. It can happen often enough, and a very sad tragedy it is when it does happen. That was the most I knew then. That and the fact that the journey she herself was engaged upon was no mere pleasure tour. She was going, she told me, on a pilgrimage. She was going to some place or to some person. I did not learn then who the person was, that only came later.'

'Archdeacon Brabazon?'

'Yes. I had no idea then of his existence. But from then on I felt that the chief characters – the chief actors – in the drama, whichever way you like to put it, were not on the tour. They were not members of the coach party. I hesitated just for a short time, hesitated over some particular persons. I hesitated, considering Joanna Crawford and Emlyn Price.'

'Why fix on them?'

'Because of their youth,' said Miss Marple. 'Because youth is so often associated with suicide, with violence, with intense jealousy and tragic love. A man kills his girl – it happens. Yes, my mind went to them but it did not seem to me there was any association there. No shadow of evil, of despair, of misery. I used the idea of them later as a kind of false pointer when we were drinking sherry at The Old Manor House that last evening. I pointed out how they could be the most easy suspects in the death of Elizabeth Temple. When I see them again,' said Miss Marple, punctiliously, 'I shall apologize to them for having used them as useful characters to distract attention from my real ideas.'

'And the next thing was the death of Elizabeth Temple?'

'No,' said Miss Marple. 'Actually the next thing was my arrival at The Old Manor House. The kindness of my reception and taking up my stay there under their hospitable roof. That again had been arranged by Mr Rafiel. So I knew that I must go there, but not for what reason I was go to there. It might be merely a place where more information would come to me to lead me onwards in my quest. I am sorry,' Miss Marple said, suddenly becoming her normal apologetic and slightly fussy self, 'I am talking at much too great a length. I really must not inflict on you all that I thought and . . .'

'Please go on,' said Professor Wanstead. 'You may not know it but what you are telling me is particularly interesting to me. It ties up with so much I have known and seen in the work I do. Go on giving me what you felt.'

'Yes, go on,' said Sir Andrew McNeil.

'It *was* feeling,' said Miss Marple. 'It wasn't really, you know, logical deduction. It was based on a kind of emotional reaction or susceptibility to – well, I can only call it atmosphere.'

'Yes,' said Wanstead, 'there is atmosphere. Atmosphere in houses, atmosphere in places, in the garden, in the forest, in a public house, in a cottage.'

'The three sisters. That is what I thought and felt and said to myself when I went into The Old Manor House. I was so kindly received by Lavinia Glynne. There's something about the phrase – the three sisters – that springs up in your mind as sinister. It combines with the three sisters in Russian literature, the three witches on Macbeth's heath. It seemed to me that there was an atmosphere there of sorrow, of deep felt unhappiness, also an atmosphere of fear and a kind of struggling different atmosphere which I can only describe as an atmosphere of normality.'

'Your last word interests me,' said Wanstead.

'It was due, I think, to Mrs Glynne. She was the one who came to meet me when the coach arrived and explained the invitation. She was an entirely normal and pleasant woman, a widow. She was not very happy, but when I say she was not very happy it was nothing to do with sorrow or deep unhappiness, it was just that she had the wrong atmosphere for her own character. She took me back with her and I met the other two sisters. The next morning I was to hear from an aged housemaid who brought my early morning tea, a story of past tragedy, of a girl who had been killed by her boyfriend. Of several other girls in the neighbourhood who'd fallen victims to violence, or sexual assault. I had to make my second appraisal. I had dismissed the people in the coach as not being personally concerned in my search. Somewhere still there was a killer. I had to ask myself if one of the killers could be here. Here in this house where I had been sent, Clotilde, Lavinia, Anthea. Three names of three weird sisters, three happy – unhappy – suffering – frightened – what were they? My attention was caught first by Clotilde. A tall, handsome woman. A personality. Just as Elizabeth Temple had been a personality. I felt that here where the field was limited, I must at least sum up what I could about the three sisters. Three Fates. Who could be a killer? What kind of a killer? What kind of a killing? I could feel then rising up rather slowly, rather slowly like a miasma does, an atmosphere. I don't think there is any other word that expresses it except evil. Not necessarily that any of these three was evil, but they were certainly living in an atmosphere where evil had happened, had left its shadow or was still threatening them. Clotilde, the eldest, was the first one I considered. She was handsome, she was strong, she was, I thought, a woman of intense emotional feeling. I saw her, I will admit, as a possible Clytemnestra. I had recently,' Miss Marple dropped into her everyday tones, 'been taken very kindly to a Greek play performed at a well-known boys' public school not far from my home. I had been very, very impressed by the acting of the Agamemnon and particularly the performance of the boy who had played Clytemnestra. A very remarkable performance. It seemed to me that in Clotilde I could imagine a woman who could plan and carry out the killing of a husband in his bath.'

For a moment Professor Wanstead had all he could do to repress a laugh. It was the seriousness of Miss Marple's tone. She gave him a slight twinkle from her eyes.

'Yes, it sounds rather silly, does it not, said like that? But I could *see* her that way, playing that part, that is to say. Very unfortunately, she had no husband. She had never had a husband, and therefore did not kill a husband. Then I considered my guide to the house. Lavinia Glynne. She seemed an extremely nice, wholesome and pleasant woman. But alas, certain people who have killed have produced much that effect on the world round them. They have been charming people. Many murderers have been delightful and pleasant men and people have been astonished. They are what I call the respectable killers. The ones who would commit murder from entirely utilitarian motives. Without emotion, but to gain a required end. I didn't think it was very likely and I should be highly surprised if it was so, but I could not leave out Mrs Glynne. She had had a husband. She was a widow and had been a widow for some years. It could be. I left it at that. And then I came to the third sister. Anthea. She was a disquieting personality. Badly co-ordinated, it seemed to me, scatter-brained, and in a condition of some emotion which I thought on the whole was fear. She was frightened of something. Intensely frightened of something. Well, that could fit in too. If she had committed a crime of some kind, a crime which she had thought was finished with and past, there might have been some recrudescence, some raising up of old problems, something perhaps connected with the Elizabeth Temple enquiries; she might have felt fear that an old crime would be revived or discovered. She had a curious way of looking at you, and then looking sharply from side to side over one shoulder as though she saw something standing behind her. Something that made her afraid. So she too was a possible answer. A possibly slightly mentally unhinged killer who could have killed because she considered herself persecuted. Because she was afraid. These were only ideas. They were only a rather more pronounced assessment of possibilities that I had already gone through on the coach. But the atmosphere of the house was on me more than ever. That next day I walked in the garden with Anthea. At the end of the principal grass path was a mound. A mound created by the falling down of a former greenhouse. Owing to a lack of repairs and of gardeners at the end of the war it had fallen into disuse, come to pieces, bricks had been piled up surmounted with earth and turf, and had been planted with a certain creeper. A creeper well known when you want to hide or cover some ugly pieces of building in your garden. Polygonum it is called. One of the quickest flowering shrubs which swallows and kills and dries up and gets rid of everything it grows over. It grows over everything. It is in a way a rather frightening plant. It has beautiful white flowers, it can look very lovely. It was not yet in bloom but it was going to be. I stood there with Anthea, and she seemed to be desperately unhappy over the loss of the greenhouse. She said it had had such lovely grapes, it seemed to be the thing she remembered most about the garden when she had been a child there. And she wanted, she wanted desperately to have enough money so as to dig up the mound, level the ground and rebuild the greenhouse and stock it with muscat grapes and peaches as the old greenhouse had been. It was a terrible nostalgia for the past she was feeling. It was more than that. Again, very clearly, I felt an atmosphere of fear. Something about the mound made her frightened. I couldn't then think what it was. You know the next thing that happened. It was Elizabeth Temple's death and there was no doubt from the story told by Emlyn Price and Joanna Crawford that there could be only one conclusion. It was no accident. It was deliberate murder.

'I think it was from then on,' said Miss Marple, 'that I knew. I came to the conclusion there had been three killings. I heard the full story of Mr Rafiel's son, the delinquent boy, the ex-jailbird and I thought that he was all those things, but none of them showed him as being a killer or likely to be a killer. All the evidence was against him. There was no doubt in anyone's mind that he had killed the girl whose name I had now learned as being Verity Hunt. But Archdeacon Brabazon put the final crown on the business, as it were. He had known those two young people. They had come to him with their story of wanting to get married and he had taken it upon himself to decide that they should get married. He thought that it was not perhaps a wise marriage, but it was a marriage that was justified by the fact that they both loved each other. The girl loved the boy with what he called a true love. A love as true as her name. And he thought that the boy, for all his bad sexual reputation, had truly loved the girl and had every intention of being faithful to her and trying to reform some of his evil tendencies. The Archdeacon was not optimistic. He did not, I think, believe it would be a thoroughly happy marriage, but it was to his mind what he called a necessary marriage. Necessary because if you love enough you will pay the price, even if the price is disappointment and a certain amount of unhappiness. But one thing

I was quite sure of. That disfigured face, that battered-in head could not have been the action of a boy who really loved the girl. This was not a story of sexual assault. I was ready to take the Archdeacon's word for that. But I knew, too, that I'd got the right clue, the clue that was given me by Elizabeth Temple. She had said that the cause of Verity's death was Love – one of the most frightening words there is.

'It was quite clear then,' said Miss Marple. 'I think I'd known for some time really. It was just the small things that hadn't fitted in, but now they did. They fitted in with what Elizabeth Temple had said. The cause of Verity's death. She had said first the one word "Love" and then that "Love could be the most frightening word there was". It was all mapped out so plainly then. The overwhelming love that Clotilde had had for this girl. The girl's hero-worship of her, dependency on her, and then as she grew a little older, her normal instincts came into play. She wanted Love. She wanted to be free to love, to marry, to have children. And along came the boy that she could love. She knew that he was unreliable, she knew he was what was technically called a bad lot, but that,' said Miss Marple, in a more ordinary tone of voice, 'is not what puts any girl off a boy. No. Young women like bad lots. They always have. They fall in love with bad lots. They are quite sure they can change them. And the nice, kind, steady, reliable husbands got the answer, in my young days, that one would be "a sister to them", which never satisfied them at all. Verity fell in love with Michael Rafiel, and Michael Rafiel was prepared to turn over a new leaf and marry this girl and was sure he would never wish to look at another girl again. I don't say this would have been a happy-ever-after thing, but it was, as the Archdeacon said quite surely, it *was* real love. And so they planned to get married. And I think Verity wrote to Elizabeth and told her that she was going to marry Michael Rafiel. It was arranged in secret because I think Verity did realize that what she was doing was essentially an escape. She was escaping from a life that she didn't want to live any longer, from someone whom she loved very much but not in the way she loved Michael. And she would not be allowed to do so. Permission would not be willingly given, every obstacle would be put in their way. So, like other young people, they were going to elope. There was no need for them to fly off to Gretna Green, they were of sufficiently mature age to marry. So she appealed to Archdeacon Brabazon, her old friend who had confirmed her – who was a real friend. And the wedding was arranged, the day, the time, probably even she bought secretly some garment in which to be married. They were to meet somewhere, no doubt. They were to come to the rendezvous separately. I think he came there, but she did *not* come. He waited perhaps. Waited and then tried to find out, perhaps, why she didn't come. I think then a message may have been given him, even a letter sent him, possibly in her forged handwriting, saying she had changed her mind. It was all over and she was going away for a time to get over it. I don't know. But I don't think he ever dreamt of the real reason of why she hadn't come, of why she had sent no word. He hadn't thought for one moment that she had been deliberately, cruelly, almost madly perhaps, destroyed. Clotilde was not going to lose the person she loved. She was not going to let her escape, she was not going to let her go to the young man whom she herself hated and loathed. She would keep Verity, keep her in her own way. But what I could not believe was – I did not believe that she'd strangled the girl and had then disfigured her face. I don't think she could have borne to do that. I think that she had re-arranged the bricks of the fallen greenhouse and piled up earth and turf over most of it. The girl had already been given a drink, an over-dose of sleeping draught probably. Grecian, as it were, in tradition. One cup of hemlock – even if it wasn't hemlock. And she buried the girl there in the garden, piled the bricks over her and the earth and the turf –'

'Did neither of the other sisters suspect it?'

'Mrs Glynne was not there then. Her husband had not died and she was still abroad. But Anthea was there. I think Anthea did know *something* of what went on. I don't know that she suspected death at first, but she knew that Clotilde had been occupying herself with the raising up of a mound at the end of the garden to be covered with flowering shrubs, to be a place of beauty. I think perhaps the truth came to her little by little. And then Clotilde, having accepted evil, done evil, surrendered to evil, had no qualms about what she would do next. I think she enjoyed planning it. She had a certain amount of influence over a sly, sexy little village girl who came to her cadging for benefits now and then. I think it was easy for her to arrange one day to take the girl on a picnic or an expedition a good long way away. Thirty or forty miles. She'd chosen the place beforehand, I think. She strangled the girl, disfigured her, hid her under turned earth, leaves and branches. Why should anyone ever suspect her of doing any such thing? She put Verity's handbag there and a little chain Verity used to wear round her neck and possibly dressed her in clothes belonging to Verity. She hoped the crime would not be found out for some time but in the meantime she spread abroad rumours of Nora Broad having been seen about in Michael's car, going about with Michael. Possibly she spread a story that Verity had broken off the engagement to be married because of his infidelity with this girl. She may have said anything and I think everything she said she enjoyed, poor lost soul.'

'Why do you say "poor lost soul," Miss Marple?'

'Because,' said Miss Marple, 'I don't suppose there can be any agony so great as what Clotilde has suffered all this time – ten years now – living in eternal sorrow. Living, you see, with the thing she *had* to live with. She had kept Verity, kept her there at The Old Manor House, in the garden, kept her there for ever. She didn't realize at first what that meant. Her passionate longing for the girl to be alive again. I don't think she ever suffered from remorse. I don't think she had even that consolation. She just suffered – went on suffering year after year. And I know now what Elizabeth Temple meant. Better perhaps than she herself did. Love *is* a very terrible thing. It is alive to evil, it can be one of the most evil things there can be. And she had to live with that day after day, year after year. I think, you know, that Anthea was frightened of that. I think she knew more clearly the whole time what Clotilde had done and she thought that Clotilde knew that she knew. And she was afraid of what Clotilde might do. Clotilde gave that parcel to Anthea to post, the one with the pullover. She said things to me about Anthea, that she was mentally disturbed, that if she suffered from persecution or jealousy Anthea might do anything. I think – yes – that in the not so distant future – something might have happened to Anthea – an arranged suicide because of a guilty conscience –'

'And yet you are sorry for that woman?' asked Sir Andrew. 'Malignant evil is like cancer – a malignant tumour. It brings suffering.'

'Of course,' said Miss Marple.

'I suppose you have been told what happened that night,' said Professor Wanstead, 'after your guardian angels had removed you?'

'You mean Clotilde? She had picked up my glass of milk, I remember. She was still holding it when Miss Cooke took me out of the room. I suppose she – drank it, did she?'

'Yes. Did you know that might happen?'

'I didn't think of it, no, not at the moment. I suppose I could have known it if I'd thought about it.'

'Nobody could have stopped her. She was so quick about it, and nobody quite realized there was anything wrong in the milk.'

'So she drank it.'

'Does that surprise you?'

'No, it would have seemed to her the natural thing to do, one can't really wonder. It had come by this time that she wanted to escape – from all the things she was having to live with. Just as Verity had wanted to escape from the life that she was living there. Very odd, isn't it, that the retribution one brings on oneself fits so closely with what has caused it.'

'You sound sorrier for her than you were for the girl who died.'

'No,' said Miss Marple, 'it's a different kind of being sorry. I'm sorry for Verity because of all that she missed, all that she was so near to obtaining. A

179

life of love and devotion and service to the man she had chosen, and whom she truly loved. Truly and in all verity. She missed all that and nothing can give that back to her. I'm sorry for her because of what she *didn't* have. But she escaped what Clotilde had to suffer. Sorrow, misery, fear and a growing cultivation and imbibing of evil. Clotilde had to live with all those. Sorrow, frustrated love which she could never get back, she had to live with the two sisters who suspected, who were afraid of her, and she had to live with the girl she had kept there.'

'You mean Verity?'

'Yes. Buried in the garden, buried in the tomb that Clotilde had prepared. She was *there* in The Old Manor House and I think Clotilde *knew* she was there. It might be that she even saw her or thought she saw her, sometimes when she went to pick a spray of polygonum blossom. She must have felt very close to Verity then. Nothing worse could happen to her, could it, than that? Nothing worse ...'

CHAPTER 23

End Pieces

'That old lady gives me the creeps,' said Sir Andrew McNeil, when he had said goodbye and thanks to Miss Marple.

'So gentle – and so ruthless,' said the Assistant Commissioner.

Professor Wanstead took Miss Marple down to his car which was waiting, and then returned for a few final words.

'What do you think of her, Edmund?'

'The most frightening woman I ever met,' said the Home Secretary.

'Ruthless?' asked Professor Wanstead.

'No, no, I don't mean that but – well, a very frightening woman.'

'Nemesis,' said Professor Wanstead thoughtfully.

'Those two women, said the P.P.D. man, 'you know, the security agents who were looking after her, they gave a most extraordinary description of her that night. They got into the house quite easily, hid themselves in a small downstairs room until everyone went upstairs, then one went into the bedroom and into the wardrobe and the other stayed outside the room to watch. The one in the bedroom said that when she threw open the door of the wardrobe and came out, there was the old lady sitting up in bed with a pink fluffy shawl round her neck and a perfectly placid face, twittering away and talking like an elderly school marm. They said she gave them quite a turn.'

'A pink fluffy shawl,' said Professor Wanstead. 'Yes, yes, I do remember –'

'What do you remember?'

'Old Rafiel. He told me about her, you know, and then he laughed. He said one thing he'd never forget in all his life. He said it was when one of the funniest scatter-brained old pussies he'd ever met came marching into his bedroom out in the West Indies, with a fluffy pink scarf round her neck, telling him he was to get up and do something to prevent a murder. And he said, "What on earth do you think you're doing?" And she said she was Nemesis. Nemesis! He could not imagine anything less like it, he said. I like the touch of the pink woolly scarf.' said Professor Wanstead, thoughtfully, 'I like that, very much.'

'Michael,' said Professor Wanstead, 'I want to introduce you to Miss Jane Marple, who's been very active on your behalf.'

The young man of thirty-two looked at the white-haired, rather dicky old lady with a slightly doubtful expression.

'Oh – er –' he said, 'well, I guess I have heard about it. Thanks very much.'

He looked at Wanstead.

'It's true, is it, they're going to give me a free pardon or something silly like that?'

'Yes. A release will be put through quite soon. You'll be a free man in a very short time.'

'Oh.' Michael sounded slightly doubtful.

'It will take a little getting used to, I expect,' said Miss Marple kindly.

She looked at him thoughtfully. Seeing him in retrospect as he might have been ten years or so ago. Still quite attractive – though he showed all the signs of strain. Attractive, yes. Very attractive, she thought he would have been once. A gaiety about him then, there would have been, and a charm. He'd lost that now, but it would come back perhaps. A weak mouth and attractively shaped eyes that could look you straight in the face, and probably had been always extremely useful for telling lies that you really wanted to believe. Very like – who was it? – she dived into past memories – Jonathan Birkin, of course. He had sung in the choir. A really delightful baritone voice. And how fond the girls had been of him! Quite a good job he'd had as a clerk in Messrs Gabriel's firm. A pity there had been that little matter of the cheques.

'Oh,' said Michael. He said, with even more embarrassment, 'It's been very kind of you, I'm sure, to take so much trouble.'

'I've enjoyed it,' said Miss Marple. 'Well, I'm glad to have met you. Goodbye. I hope you've got a very good time coming to you. Our country is in rather a bad way just now, but you'll probably find some job or other that you might quite enjoy doing.'

'Oh yes. Thanks, thanks very much. I – I really am very grateful, you know.'

His tone sounded still extremely unsure about it.

'It's not me you ought to be grateful to,' said Miss Marple, 'you ought to be grateful to you father.'

'Dad? Dad never thought much of me.'

Your father, when he was a dying man, was determined to see that you got justice.'

'Justice.' Michael Rafiel considered it.

'Yes, your father thought Justice was important. He was, I think, a very just man himself. In the letter he wrote me asking me to undertake this proposition, he directed me to a quotation:

"Let Justice roll down like waters
And Righteousness like an everlasting stream." '

'Oh! What's it mean? Shakespeare?'

'No, the Bible – one has to think about it – I had to.'

Miss Marple unwrapped a parcel she had been carrying.

'They gave me this,' she said. 'They thought I might like to have it – because I had helped to find out the truth of what had really happened. I think, though, that you are the person who should have first claim on it – that is if you really want it. But maybe you do *not* want it –'

She handed him the photograph of Verity Hunt that Clotilde Bradbury-Scott had shown her once in the drawing-room of The Old Manor House.

He took it – and stood with it, staring down on it . . . His face changed, the lines of it softened, then hardened. Miss Marple watched him without speaking. The silence went on for some little time. Professor Wanstead also watched – he watched them both, the old lady and the boy.

It came to him that this was in some way a crisis – a moment that might affect a whole new way of life.

Michael Rafiel sighed – he stretched out and gave the photograph back to Miss Marple.

'No, you are right, I do not want it. All that life is gone – she's gone – I can't keep her with me. Anything I do now has got to be new – going forward. You –' he hesitated, looking at her – 'You understand?'

'Yes,' said Miss Marple – 'I understand – I think you are right. I wish you good luck in the life you are now going to begin.'

He said goodbye and went out.

'Well,' said Professor Wanstead, 'not an enthusiastic young man. He could have thanked you a bit more enthusiastically for what you did for him.'

'Oh, that's quite all right,' said Miss Marple. 'I didn't expect him to do so. It would have embarrassed him even more. It is, you know,' she added, 'very embarrassing when one has to thank people and start life again and see everything from a different angle and all that. I think he might do well. He's not bitter. That's the great thing. I understand quite well why that girl loved him –'

'Well, perhaps he'll go straight this time.'

'One rather doubts that,' said Miss Marple. 'I don't know that he'd be able to help himself unless – of course,' she said, 'the great thing to hope for

183

is that he'll meet a really nice girl.'

'What I like about you,' said Professor Wanstead, 'is your delightfully practical mind.'

III

'She'll be here presently,' said Mr Broadribb to Mr Schuster.

'Yes. The whole thing's pretty extraordinary, isn't it?'

'I couldn't believe it at first,' said Broadribb. 'You know, when poor old Rafiel was dying, I thought this whole thing was – well, senility or something. Not that he was old enough for that.'

The buzzer went. Mr Schuster picked up the phone.

'Oh, she's here, is she? Bring her up,' he said. 'She's come,' he said. 'I wonder now. You know, it's the oddest thing I ever heard in my life. Getting an old lady to go racketing round the countryside looking for she doesn't know what. The police think, you know, that that woman committed not just one murder but three. Three! I ask you! Verity Hunt's body was under the mound in the garden, just as the old lady said it was. She hadn't been strangled and the face was not disfigured.'

'I wonder the old lady herself didn't get done in,' said Mr Broadribb. 'Far too old to be able to take care of herself.'

'She had a couple of detectives, apparently, looking afer her.'

'What, *two* of them?'

'Yes, I didn't know that.'

Miss Marple was ushered into their room.

'Congratulations, Miss Marple,' said Mr Broadribb, rising to greet her.

'Very best wishes. Splendid job,' said Mr Schuster, shaking hands.

Miss Marple sat down composedly on the other side of the desk.

'As I told you in my letter,' she said, 'I think I have fulfilled the terms of the proposition that was made to me. I have succeeded in what I was asked to do.'

'Oh I know. Yes, we've heard already. We've heard from Professor Wanstead and from the legal department and from the police authorities. Yes, it's been a splendid job, Miss Marple. We congratulate you.'

'I was afraid,' said Miss Marple, 'that I would not be able to do what was required of me. It seemed so very difficult, almost impossible at first.'

'Yes indeed. It seems quite impossible to me. I don't know how you did it, Miss Marple.'

'Oh well,' said Miss Marple, 'it's just perseverance, isn't it, that leads to things.'

'Now about the sum of money we are holding. It's at your disposal at any time now. I don't know whether you would like us to pay it into your bank or whether you would like to consult us possibly as to the investment of it? It's quite a large sum.'

'Twenty thousand pounds,' said Miss Marple. 'Yes, it is a very large sum by my way of thinking. Quite extraordinary,' she added.

'If you would like an introduction to our brokers, they could give you possibly some ideas about investing.'

'Oh, I don't want to invest any of it.'

'But surely it would be –'

'There's no point in saving at my age,' said Miss Marple. 'I mean the point of this money – I'm sure Mr Rafiel meant it that way – is to enjoy a few things that one thought one never would have the money to enjoy.'

'Well, I see your point of view,' said Mr Broadribb. 'Then your instructions would be that we pay this sum of money into your bank?'

'Middleton's Bank, 132 High Street, St Mary Mead,' said Miss Marple.

'You have a deposit account, I expect. We will place it to your deposit account?'

'Certainly not,' said Miss Marple. 'Put it into my current account.'

'You don't think –'

'I do think,' said Miss Marple. 'I want it in my current account.'

She got up and shook hands.

'You could ask your bank manager's advice, you know, Miss Marple. It really is – one never knows when one wants something for a rainy day.'

'The only thing I shall want for a rainy day will be my umbrella,' said Miss Marple.

She shook hands with them both again.

'Thank you so much, Mr Broadribb. And you too, Mr Schuster. You've been so kind to me, giving me all the information I needed.'

'You really want that money put into your current account?'

'Yes,' said Miss Marple. 'I'm going to spend it, you know. I'm going to have some fun with it.'

She looked back from the door and she laughed. Just for one moment Mr Schuster, who was a man of more imagination than Mr Broadribb, had a vague impression of a young and pretty girl shaking hands with the vicar at a garden party in the country. It was, as he realized a moment later, a recollection of his own youth. But Miss Marple had, for a minute, reminded him of that particular girl, young, happy, going to enjoy herself.

'Mr Rafiel would have liked me to have fun,' said Miss Marple.

She went out of the door.

'Nemesis,' said Mr Broadribb. 'That's what Rafiel called her. Nemesis. Never seen anybody less like Nemesis, have you?'

Mr Schuster shook his head.

'It must have been another of Mr Rafiel's little jokes,' said Mr Broadribb.

Sleeping Murder

Miss Marple's Last Case

Contents

CHAPTER 1

A House

Gwenda Reed stood, shivering a little, on the quayside.

The docks and the custom sheds and all of England that she could see, were gently waving up and down.

And it was in that moment that she made her decision – the decision that was to lead to such very momentous events.

She wouldn't go by the boat train to London as she had planned.

After all, why should she? No one was waiting for her, nobody expected her. She had only just got off that heaving creaking boat (it had been an exceptionally rough three days through the Bay and up to Plymouth) and the last thing she wanted was to get into a heaving swaying train. She would go to a hotel, a nice firm steady hotel standing on good solid ground. And she would get into a nice steady bed that didn't creak and roll. And she would go to sleep, and the next morning – why, of course – what a splendid idea! She would hire a car and she would drive slowly and without hurrying herself all through the South of England looking about for a house – a nice house – the house that she and Giles had planned she should find. Yes, that was a splendid idea.

In that way she would see something of England – of the England that Giles had told her about and which she had never seen; although, like most New Zealanders, she called it Home. At the moment, England was not looking particularly attractive. It was a grey day with rain imminent and a sharp irritating wind blowing. Plymouth, Gwenda thought, as she moved forward obediently in the queue for Passports and Customs, was probably not the best of England.

On the following morning, however, her feelings were entirely different. The sun was shining. The view from her window was attractive. And the universe in general was no longer waving and wobbling. It had steadied down. This was England at last and here she was, Gwenda Reed, young married woman of twenty-one, on her travels. Giles's return to England was uncertain. He might follow her in a few weeks. It might be as long as six months. His suggestion had been that Gwenda should precede him to England and should look about for a suitable house. They both thought it would be nice to have, somewhere, a permanency. Giles's job would always entail a certain amount of travelling. Sometimes Gwenda would come too, sometimes the conditions would not be suitable. But they both liked the idea of having a home – some place of their own. Giles had inherited some

191

furniture from an aunt recently, so that everything combined to make the idea a sensible and practical one.

Since Gwenda and Giles were reasonably well off the prospect presented no difficulties.

Gwenda had demurred at first at choosing a house on her own. 'We ought to do it together,' she had said. But Giles had said laughingly: 'I'm not much of a hand at houses. If *you* like it, *I* shall. A bit of a garden, of course, and not some brand-new horror – and not too big. Somewhere on the south coast was my idea. At any rate, not too far inland.'

'Was there any particular place?' Gwenda asked. But Giles said No. He'd been left an orphan young (they were both orphans) and had been passed around to various relations for holidays, and no particular spot had any particular association for him. It was to be Gwenda's house – and as for waiting until they could choose it together, suppose he were held up for six months? What would Gwenda do with herself all that time? Hang about in hotels? No, she was to find a house and get settled in.

'What you mean is,' said Gwenda, 'do all the work!'

But she liked the idea of finding a home and having it all ready, cosy and lived in, for when Giles came back.

They had been married just three months and she loved him very much.

After sending for breakfast in bed, Gwenda got up and arranged her plans. She spent a day seeing Plymouth which she enjoyed and on the following day she hired a comfortable Daimler car and chauffeur and set off on her journey through England.

The weather was good and she enjoyed her tour very much. She saw several possible residences in Devonshire but nothing that she felt was exactly right. There was no hurry. She would go on looking. She learned to read between the lines of the house agents' enthusiastic descriptions and saved herself a certain number of fruitless errands.

It was on a Tuesday evening about a week later that the car came gently down the curving hill road into Dillmouth and on the outskirts of that still charming seaside resort, passed a For Sale board where, through the trees, a glimpse of a small white Victorian villa could be seen.

Immediately Gwenda felt a throb of appreciation – almost of recognition. This was *her* house! Already she was sure of it. She could picture the garden, the long windows – she was sure that the house was just what she wanted.

It was late in the day, so she put up at the Royal Clarence Hotel and went to the house agents whose name she had noted on the board the following morning.

Presently, armed with an order to view, she was standing in the old-fashioned long drawing-room with its two french windows giving on to a flagged terrace in front of which a kind of rockery interspersed with flowering shrubs fell sharply to a stretch of lawn below. Through the trees at the bottom of the garden the sea could be seen.

This is *my* house, thought Gwenda. It's *home*. I feel already as though I know every bit of it.

The door opened and a tall melancholy woman with a cold in the head entered, sniffing. 'Mrs Hengrave? I have an order from Messrs Galbraith and Penderley. I'm afraid it's rather early in the day –'

Mrs Hengrave, blowing her nose, said sadly that that didn't matter at all. The tour of the house began.

Yes, it was just right. Not too large. A bit old-fashioned, but she and Giles could put in another bathroom or two. The kitchen could be modernized. It already had an Aga, fortunately. With a new sink and up-to-date equipment –

Through all Gwenda's plans and preoccupations, the voice of Mrs Hengrave droned thinly on recounting the details of the late Major Hengrave's last illness. Half of Gwenda attended to making the requisite noises of condolence, sympathy and understanding. Mrs Hengrave's people all lived in Kent – anxious she should come and settle near them . . . the Major had been very fond of Dillmouth, secretary for many years of the Golf Club, but she herself . . .

'Yes . . . Of course . . . Dreadful for you . . . Most natural . . . Yes, nursing homes *are* like that . . . Of course . . . You must be . . .'

And the other half of Gwenda raced along in thought: Linen cupboard here, I expect . . . Yes. Double room – nice view of sea – Giles will like that. Quite a useful little room here – Giles might have it as a dressing room . . . Bathroom – I expect the bath has a mahogany surround – Oh yes, it *has*! How lovely – and standing in the middle of the floor! I shan't change *that* – it's a period piece!

Such an enormous bath!

One could have apples on the surround. And sail boats – and painted ducks. You could pretend you were in the sea . . . I know: we'll make that dark back spare room into a couple of really up-to-date green and chromium bathrooms – the pipes ought to be all right over the kitchen – and keep this just as it is . . .

'Pleurisy,' said Mrs Hengrave. 'Turning to double pneumonia on the third day –'

'Terrible,' said Gwenda. 'Isn't there another bedroom at the end of this passage?'

There was – and it was just the sort of room she had imagined it would be – almost round, with a big bow window. She'd have to do it up, of course. It was in quite good condition, but why were people like Mrs Hengrave so fond of that mustard-cum-biscuit shade of wall paint?

They retraced their steps along the corridor. Gwenda murmured, conscientiously, 'Six, no seven bedrooms, counting the little one and the attic.'

The boards creaked faintly under her feet. Already she felt that it was she and not Mrs Hengrave who lived here! Mrs Hengrave was an interloper – a woman who did up rooms in mustard-cum-biscuit colour and liked a frieze of wisteria in her drawing-room. Gwenda glanced down at the typewritten paper in her hand on which the details of the property and the price asked were given.

In the course of a few days Gwenda had become fairly conversant with house values. The sum asked was not large – of course the house needed a certain amount of modernization – but even then ... And she noted the words 'Open to offer'. Mrs Hengrave must be very anxious to go to Kent and live near 'her people' ...

They were starting down the stairs when quite suddenly Gwenda felt a wave of irrational terror sweep over her. It was a sickening sensation, and it passed almost as quickly as it came. Yet it left behind it a new idea.

'The house isn't – haunted, is it?' demanded Gwenda.

Mrs Hengrave, a step below, and having just got to the moment in her narrative when Major Hengrave was sinking fast, looked up in an affronted manner.

'Not that I am aware of, Mrs Reed. Why – has anyone – been saying something of the kind?'

'You've never felt or seen anything yourself? Nobody's *died* here?'

Rather an unfortunate question, she thought, a split second of a moment too late, because presumably Major Hengrave –

'My husband died in the St Monica's Nursing Home,' said Mrs Hengrave stiffly.

'Oh, of course. You told me so.'

Mrs Hengrave continued in the same rather glacial manner: 'In a house which was presumably built about a hundred years ago, there would normally be deaths during that period. Miss Elworthy from whom my dear husband acquired this house seven years ago, was in excellent health, and indeed planning to go abroad and do missionary work, and she did not mention any recent demises in her family.'

Gwenda hastened to soothe the melancholy Mrs Hengrave down. They were now once more in the drawing-room. It was a peaceful and charming room, with exactly the kind of atmosphere that Gwenda coveted. Her momentary panic just now seemed quite incomprehensible. What *had* come over her? There was nothing wrong with the house.

Asking Mrs Hengrave if she could take a look at the garden, she went out through the french windows on to the terrace.

There should be steps here, thought Gwenda, going down to the lawn.

But instead there was a vast uprising of forsythia which at this particular place seemed to have got above itself and effectually shut out all view of the sea.

Gwenda nodded to herself. She would alter all that.

Following Mrs Hengrave, she went along the terrace and down some steps at the far side on to the lawn. She noted that the rockery was neglected and overgrown, and that most of the flowering shrubs needed pruning.

Mrs Hengrave murmured apologetically that the garden had been rather neglected. Only able to afford a man twice a week. And quite often *he* never turned up.

They inspected the small but adequate kitchen garden and returned to the house. Gwenda explained that she had other houses to see, and that though she liked Hillside (what a commonplace name!) very much, she could not decide immediately.

Mrs Hengrave parted from her with a somewhat wistful look and a last long lingering sniff.

Gwenda returned to the agents, made a firm offer subject to surveyor's report and spent the rest of the morning walking round Dillmouth. It was a charming and old-fashioned little seaside town. At the far, 'modern' end, there were a couple of new-looking hotels and some raw-looking bungalows, but the geographical formation of the coast with the hills behind had saved Dillmouth from undue expansion.

After lunch Gwenda received a telephone call from the agents saying that Mrs Hengrave accepted her offer. With a mischievous smile on her lips Gwenda made her way to the post office and despatched a cable to Giles.

HAVE BOUGHT A HOUSE. LOVE. GWENDA.

'That'll tickle him up,' said Gwenda to herself. 'Show him that the grass doesn't grow under *my* feet!'

CHAPTER 2

Wallpaper

A month had passed and Gwenda had moved into Hillside. Giles's aunt's furniture had come out of store and was arranged round the house. It was good quality old-fashioned stuff. One or two over-large wardrobes Gwenda had sold, but the rest fitted in nicely and was in harmony with the house. There were small gay papier mâché tables in the drawing-room, inlaid with mother-of-pearl and painted with castles and roses. There was a prim little work-table with a gathered sack underneath of pure silk, there was a rosewood bureau and a mahogany sofa table.

The so-called easy chairs Gwenda had relegated to various bedrooms and had bought two large squashy wells of comfort for herself and Giles to stand each side of the fireplace. The large chesterfield sofa was placed near the windows. For curtains Gwenda had chosen old-fashioned chintz of pale egg-shell blue with prim urns of roses and yellow birds on them. The room, she now considered, was exactly right.

She was hardly settled yet, since she had workmen in the house still. They should have been out by now, but Gwenda rightly estimated that until she herself came into residence, they would not go.

The kitchen alterations were finished, the new bathrooms nearly so. For further decorating Gwenda was going to wait a while. She wanted time to savour her new home and decide on the exact colour schemes she wanted for the bedrooms. The house was really in very good order and there was no need to do everything at once.

In the kitchen a Mrs Cocker was now installed, a lady of condescending graciousness, inclined to repulse Gwenda's over-democratic friendliness, but who, once Gwenda had been satisfactorily put in her place, was willing to unbend.

On this particular morning, Mrs Cocker deposited a breakfast tray on Gwenda's knees, as she sat up in bed.

'When there's no gentleman in the house,' Mrs Cocker affirmed, 'a lady prefers her breakfast in bed.' And Gwenda had bowed to this supposedly English enactment.

'Scrambled this morning,' Mrs Cocker observed, referring to the eggs. 'You said something about finnan haddock, but you wouldn't like it in the bedroom. It leaves a smell. I'm giving it to you for your supper, creamed on toast.'

'Oh, thank you, Mrs Cocker.'

196

Mrs Cocker smiled graciously and prepared to withdraw.

Gwenda was not occupying the big double bedroom. That could wait until Giles returned. She had chosen instead the end room, the one with the rounded walls and the bow window. She felt thoroughly at home in it and happy.

Looking round her now, she exclaimed impulsively: 'I do like this room.'

Mrs Cocker looked round indulgently.

'It is quaite a naice room, madam, though small. By the bars on the window I should say it had been the nursery at one time.'

'I never thought of that. Perhaps it has.'

'Ah, well,' said Mrs Cocker, with implication in her voice, and withdrew.

'Once we have a gentleman in the house,' she seemed to be saying, 'who knows? A nursery *may* be needed.'

Gwenda blushed. She looked round the room. A nursery? Yes, it would be a nice nursery. She began furnishing it in her mind. A big dolls' house there against the wall. And low cupboards with toys in them. A fire burning cheerfully in the grate and a tall guard round it with things airing on the rail. But not this hideous mustard wall. No, she would have a gay wallpaper. Something bright and cheerful. Little bunches of poppies alternating with bunches of cornflowers ... Yes, that would be lovely. She'd try and find a wallpaper like that. She felt sure she had seen one somewhere.

One didn't need much furniture in the room. There were two built-in cupboards, but one of them, a corner one, was locked and the key lost. Indeed the whole thing had been painted over, so that it could not have been opened for many years. She must get the men to open it up before they left. As it was, she hadn't got room for all her clothes.

She felt more at home every day in Hillside. Hearing a throat being ponderously cleared and a short dry cough through the open window, she hurried over her breakfast. Foster, the temperamental jobbing gardener, who was not always reliable in his promises, must be here today as he had said he would be.

Gwenda bathed, dressed, put on a tweed skirt and a sweater and hurried out into the garden. Foster was at work outside the drawing-room window. Gwenda's first action had been to get a path made down through the rockery at this point. Foster had been recalcitrant, pointing out that the forsythia would have to go and the weigela, and them there lilacs, but Gwenda had been adamant, and he was now almost enthusiastic about his task.

He greeted her with a chuckle.

'Looks like you're going back to old times, miss.' (He persisted in calling Gwenda 'miss'.)

'Old times? How?'

197

Foster tapped with his spade.

'I come on the old steps – see, that's where they went – just as you want 'em now. Then someone planted them over and covered them up.'

'It was very stupid of them,' said Gwenda. 'You want a vista down to the lawn and the sea from the drawing-room window.'

Foster was somewhat hazy about a vista – but he gave a cautious and grudging assent.

'I don't say, mind you, that it won't be an improvement . . . Gives you a view – and them shrubs made it dark in the drawing-room. Still they was growing a treat – never seen a healthier lot of forsythia. Lilacs isn't much, but them wiglers costs money – and mind you – they're too old to replant.'

'Oh, I know. But this is much, much nicer.'

'Well,' Foster scratched his head. 'Maybe it is.'

'It's *right*,' said Gwenda, nodding her head. She asked suddenly, 'Who lived here before the Hengraves? They weren't here very long, were they?'

'Matter of six years or so. Didn't belong. Afore them? The Miss Elworthys. Very churchy folk. Low church. Missions to the heathen. Once had a black clergyman staying here, they did. Four of 'em there was, and their brother – but he didn't get much of a look-in with all those women. Before them – now let me see, it was Mrs Findeyson – ah! she was the real gentry, she was. She belonged. Was living here afore I was born.'

'Did she die here?' asked Gwenda.

'Died out in Egypt or some such place. But they brought her home. She's buried up to churchyard. She planted that magnolia and those labiurnams. And those pittispores. Fond of shrubs, she was.'

Foster continued: 'Weren't none of those new houses built up along the hill then. Countrified, it was. No cinema then. And none of them new shops. Or that there parade on the front!' His tone held the disapproval of the aged for all innovations. 'Changes,' he said with a snort. 'Nothing but changes.'

'I suppose things are bound to change,' said Gwenda. 'And after all there are lots of improvements nowadays, aren't there?'

'So they say. I ain't noticed them. Changes!' He gestured towards the macrocarpa hedge on the left through which the gleam of a building showed. 'Used to be the cottage hospital, that used,' he said. 'Nice place and handy. Then they goes and builds a great place near to a mile out of town. Twenty minutes' walk if you want to get there on a visiting day – or threepence on the bus.' He gestured once more towards the hedge . . . 'It's a girls' school now. Moved in ten years ago. Changes all the time. People takes a house nowadays and lives in it ten or twelve years and then off they goes. Restless. What's the good of that? You can't do any proper planting unless you can look well ahead.'

Gwenda looked affectionately at the magnolia.

'Like Mrs Findeyson,' she said.

'Ah. She was the proper kind. Come here as a bride, she did. Brought up her children and married them, buried her husband, had her grandchildren down in the summers, and took off in the end when she was nigh on eighty.'

Foster's tone held warm approval.

Gwenda went back into the house smiling a little.

She interviewed the workmen, and then returned to the drawing-room where she sat down at the desk and wrote some letters. Amongst the correspondence that remained to be answered was a letter from some cousins of Giles who lived in London. Any time she wanted to come to London they begged her to come and stay with them at their house in Chelsea.

Raymond West was a well-known (rather than popular) novelist and his wife Joan, Gwenda knew, was a painter. It would be fun to go and stay with them, though probably they would think she was a most terrible Philistine. Neither Giles nor I are a bit highbrow, reflected Gwenda.

A sonorous gong boomed pontifically from the hall. Surrounded by a great deal of carved and tortured black wood, the gong had been one of Giles's aunt's prized possessions. Mrs Cocker herself appeared to derive distinct pleasure from sounding it and always gave full measure. Gwenda put her hands to her ears and got up.

She walked quickly across the drawing-room to the wall by the far window and then brought herself up short with an exclamation of annoyance. It was the third time she'd done that. She always seemed to expect to be able to walk through solid wall into the dining-room next door.

She went back across the room and out into the front hall and then round the angle of the drawing-room wall and so along to the dining-room. It was a long way round, and it would be annoying in winter, for the front hall was draughty and the only central heating was in the drawing-room and dining-room and two bedrooms upstairs.

I don't see, thought Gwenda to herself as she sat down at the charming Sheraton dining table which she had just bought at vast expense in lieu of Aunt Lavender's massive square mahogany one, I don't see why I shouldn't have a doorway made through from the drawing-room to the dining-room. I'll talk to Mr Sims about it when he comes this afternoon.

Mr Sims was the builder and decorator, a persuasive middle-aged man with a husky voice and a little notebook which he always held at the ready, to jot down any expensive idea that might occur to his patrons.

Mr Sims, when consulted, was keenly appreciative.

'Simplest thing in the world, Mrs Reed – and a great improvement, if I may say so.'

'Would it be very expensive?' Gwenda was by now a little doubtful of Mr Sims's assents and enthusiasms. There had been a little unpleasantness over various extras not included in Mr Sims's original estimate.

'A mere trifle,' said Mr Sims, his husky voice indulgent and reassuring. Gwenda looked more doubtful than ever. It was Mr Sims's trifles that she had learnt to distrust. His straightforward estimates were studiously moderate.

'I'll tell you what, Mrs Reed,' said Mr Sims coaxingly, 'I'll get Taylor to have a look when he's finished with the dressing-room this afternoon, and then I can give you an exact idea. Depends what the wall's like.'

Gwenda assented. She wrote to Joan West thanking her for her invitation, but saying that she would not be leaving Dillmouth at present since she wanted to keep an eye on the workmen. Then she went out for a walk along the front and enjoyed the sea breeze. She came back into the drawing-room, and Taylor, Mr Sims's leading workman, straightened up from the corner and greeted her with a grin.

'Won't be no difficulty about this, Mrs Reed,' he said. 'Been a door here before, there has. Somebody as didn't want it has just had it plastered over.'

Gwenda was agreeably surprised. How extraordinary, she thought, that I've always seemed to feel there was a door there. She remembered the confident way she had walked to it at lunch-time. And remembering it, quite suddenly, she felt a tiny shiver of uneasiness. When you came to think of it, it was really rather odd . . . Why should she have felt so sure that there was a door there? There was no sign of it on the outside wall. How had she guessed – known – that there was a door just there? Of course it would be convenient to have a door through to the dining-room, but why had she always gone so unerringly to that one particular spot? Anywhere on the dividing wall would have done equally well, but she had always gone automatically, thinking of other things, to the one place where a door had actually been.

I hope, thought Gwenda uneasily, that I'm not *clairvoyant* or anything . . .

There had never been anything in the least psychic about her. She wasn't that kind of person. Or was she? That path outside from the terrace down through the shrubbery to the lawn. Had she in some way known it was there when she was so insistent on having it made in that particular place?

Perhaps I *am* a bit psychic, thought Gwenda uneasily. Or is it something to do with the house?

Why had she asked Mrs Hengrave that day if the house was haunted?

It wasn't haunted! It was a darling house! There couldn't be anything wrong with the house. Why, Mrs Hengrave had seemed quite surprised by the idea.

Or had there been a trace of reserve, of wariness, in her manner?

Good Heavens, I'm beginning to imagine things, thought Gwenda.

She brought her mind back with an effort to her discussion with Taylor.

'There's one other thing,' she added. 'One of the cupboards in my room upstairs is stuck. I want to get it opened.'

The man came up with her and examined the door.

'It's been painted over more than once,' he said. 'I'll get the men to get it open for you tomorrow if that will do.'

Gwenda acquiesced and Taylor went away.

That evening Gwenda felt jumpy and nervous. Sitting in the drawing-room and trying to read, she was aware of every creak of the furniture. Once or twice she looked over her shoulder and shivered. She told herself repeatedly that there was nothing in the incident of the door and the path. They were just coincidences. In any case they were the result of plain common sense.

Without admitting it to herself, she felt nervous of going up to bed. When she finally got up and turned off the lights and opened the door into the hall, she found herself dreading to go up the stairs. She almost ran up them in her haste, hurried along the passage and opened the door of her room. Once inside she at once felt her fears calmed and appeased. She looked round the room affectionately. She felt safe in here, safe and happy. Yes, now she was here, she was safe. (Safe from what, you idiot? she asked herself.) She looked at her pyjamas spread out on the bed and her bedroom slippers below them.

Really, Gwenda, you might be six years old! You ought to have bunny shoes, with rabbits on them.

She got into bed with a sense of relief and was soon asleep.

The next morning she had various matters to see to in the town. When she came back it was lunch-time.

'The men have got the cupboard open in your bedroom, madam,' said Mrs Cocker as she brought in the delicately fried sole, the mashed potatoes and the creamed carrots.

'Oh good,' said Gwenda.

She was hungry and enjoyed her lunch. After having coffee in the drawing-room, she went upstairs to her bedroom. Crossing the room she pulled open the door of the corner cupboard.

Then she uttered a sudden frightened little cry and stood staring.

The inside of the cupboard revealed the original papering of the wall, which elsewhere had been done over in the yellowish wall paint. The room had once been gaily papered in a floral design, a design of little bunches of scarlet poppies alternating with bunches of blue cornflowers ...

II

Gwenda stood there staring a long time, then she went shakily over to the bed and sat down on it.

Here she was in a house she had never been in before, in a country she had never visited – and only two days ago she had lain in bed imagining a paper for this very room – and the paper she had imagined corresponded exactly with the paper that had once hung on the walls.

Wild fragments of explanation whirled round in her head. Dunne, *Experiment with Time* – seeing forward instead of back ...

She could explain the garden path and the connecting door as coincidence – but there couldn't be coincidence about this. You couldn't conceivably imagine a wallpaper of such a distinctive design and then find one exactly as you had imagined it ... No, there was some explanation that eluded her and that – yes, frightened her. Every now and then she was seeing, not forward, but back – back to some former state of the house. Any moment she might see something more – something she didn't want to see ... The house frightened her ... But was it the house or *herself*? She didn't want to be one of those people who *saw* things ...

She drew a long breath, put on her hat and coat and slipped quickly out of the house. At the post office she sent the following telegram:

WEST, 19 ADDWAY SQUARE CHELSEA LONDON. MAY I CHANGE MY MIND AND COME TO YOU TOMORROW GWENDA.

She sent it reply paid.

CHAPTER 3

'Cover her face . . .'

Raymond West and his wife did all they could to make young Giles's wife feel welcome. It was not their fault that Gwenda found them secretly rather alarming. Raymond, with his odd appearance, rather like a pouncing raven, his sweep of hair and his sudden crescendos of quite incomprehensible conversation, left Gwenda round-eyed and nervous. Both he and Joan seemed to talk a language of their own. Gwenda had never been plunged in a highbrow atmosphere before and practically all its terms were strange.

'We've planned to take you to a show or two,' said Raymond whilst Gwenda was drinking gin and rather wishing she could have had a cup of tea after her journey.

Gwenda brightened up immediately.

'The Ballet tonight at Sadler's Wells, and tomorrow we've got a birthday party on for my quite incredible Aunt Jane – *The Duchess of Malfi* with Gielgud, and on Friday you simply must see *They Walked without Feet*. Translated from the Russian – absolutely the most significant piece of drama for the last twenty years. It's at the little Witmore Theatre.'

Gwenda expressed herself grateful for these plans for her entertainment. After all, when Giles came home, they would go together to the musical shows and all that. She flinched slightly at the prospect of *They Walked without Feet*, but supposed she might enjoy it – only the point about 'significant' plays was that you usually didn't.

'You'll adore my Aunt Jane,' said Raymond. 'She's what I should describe as a perfect Period Piece. Victorian to the core. All her dressing-tables have their legs swathed in chintz. She lives in a village, the kind of village where nothing ever happens, exactly like a stagnant pond.'

'Something did happen there once,' his wife said drily.

'A mere drama of passion – crude – no subtlety to it.'

'You enjoyed it frightfully at the time,' Joan reminded him with a slight twinkle.

'I sometimes enjoy playing village cricket,' said Raymond, with dignity.

'Anyway, Aunt Jane distinguished herself over that murder.'

'Oh, she's no fool. She adores problems.'

'Problems?' said Gwenda, her mind flying to arithmetic.

Raymond waved a hand.

'Any kind of problem. Why the grocer's wife took her umbrella to the church social on a fine evening. Why a gill of picked shrimps was found where it was. What happened to the Vicar's surplice. All grist to my Aunt Jane's mill. So if you've any problem in your life, put it to her, Gwenda. She'll tell you the answer.'

He laughed and Gwenda laughed too, but not very heartily. She was introduced to Aunt Jane, otherwise Miss Marple, on the following day. Miss Marple was an attractive old lady, tall and thin, with pink cheeks and blue eyes, and a gentle, rather fussy manner. Her blue eyes often had a little twinkle in them.

After an early dinner at which they drank Aunt Jane's health, they all went off to His Majesty's Theatre. Two extra men, an elderly artist and a young barrister were in the party. The elderly artist devoted himself to Gwenda and the young barrister divided his attentions between Joan and Miss Marple whose remarks he seemed to enjoy very much. At the theatre, however, this arrangement was reversed. Gwenda sat in the middle of the row between Raymond and the barrister.

The lights went down and the play began.

It was superbly acted and Gwenda enjoyed it very much. She had not seen very many first-rate theatrical productions.

The play drew to a close, came to that supreme moment of horror. The actor's voice came over the footlights filled with the tragedy of a warped and perverted mentality.

'*Cover her face. Mine eyes dazzle, she died young* . . .'

Gwenda screamed.

She sprang up from her seat, pushed blindly past the others out into the aisle, through the exit and up the stairs and so to the street. She did not stop, even then, but half walked, half ran, in a blind panic up the Haymarket.

It was not until she had reached Piccadilly that she noticed a free taxi cruising along, hailed it and, getting in, gave the address of the Chelsea house. With fumbling fingers she got out money, paid the taxi and went up the steps. The servant who let her in glanced at her in surprise.

'You've come back early, miss. Didn't you feel well?'

'I – no, yes – I – I felt faint.'

'Would you like anything, miss? Some brandy?'

'No, nothing. I'll go straight up to bed.'

She ran up the stairs to avoid further questions.

She pulled off her clothes, left them on the floor in a heap and got into bed. She lay there shivering, her heart pounding, her eyes staring at the ceiling.

She did not hear the sound of fresh arrivals downstairs, but after about five minutes the door opened and Miss Marple came in. She had two hot-water bottles tucked under her arm and a cup in her hand.

Gwenda sat up in bed, trying to stop herself shivering.

'Oh, Miss Marple, I'm frightfully sorry. I don't know what – it was awful of me. Are they very annoyed with me?'

'Now don't worry, my dear child,' said Miss Marple. 'Just tuck yourself up warmly with these hot-water bottles.'

'I don't really need a hot-water bottle.'

'Oh yes, you do. That's right. And now drink this cup of tea . . .'

It was hot and strong and far too full of sugar, but Gwenda drank it obediently. The shivering was less acute now.

'Just lie down now and go to sleep,' said Miss Marple. 'You've had a shock, you know. We'll talk about it in the morning. Don't worry about anything. Just go to sleep.'

She drew the covers up, smiled, patted Gwenda and went out.

Downstairs Raymond was saying irritably to Joan: 'What on earth was the matter with the girl? Did she feel ill, or what?'

'My dear Raymond, I don't know, she just screamed! I suppose the play was a bit too *macabre* for her.'

'Well, of course Webster *is* a bit grisly. But I shouldn't have thought –' He broke off as Miss Marple came into the room. 'Is she all right?'

'Yes, I think so. She'd had a bad shock, you know.'

'Shock? Just seeing a Jacobean drama?'

'I think there must be a little more to it than that,' said Miss Marple thoughtfully.

Gwenda's breakfast was sent up to her. She drank some coffee and nibbled a little piece of toast. When she got up and came downstairs, Joan had gone to her studio, Raymond was shut up in his workroom and only Miss Marple was sitting by the window, which had a view over the river; she was busily engaged in knitting.

She looked up with a placid smile as Gwenda entered.

'Good morning, my dear. You're feeling better, I hope.'

'Oh yes, I'm quite all right. How I could make such an utter *idiot* of myself last night, I don't know. Are they – are they very mad with me?'

'Oh no, my dear. They quite understand.'

'Understand what?'

Miss Marple glanced up over her knitting.

'That you had a bad shock last night.' She added gently: 'Hadn't you better tell me all about it?'

Gwenda walked restlessly up and down.

'I think I'd better go and see a psychiatrist or someone.'

'There are excellent mental specialists in London, of course. But are you sure it is necessary?'

'Well – I think I'm going mad . . . I *must* be going mad.'

An elderly parlourmaid entered the room with a telegram on a salver which she handed to Gwenda.

'The boy wants to know if there's an answer, ma'am?'

Gwenda tore it open. It had been retelegraphed on from Dillmouth. She stared at it for a moment or two uncomprehendingly, then screwed it into a ball.

'There's no answer,' she said mechanically.

The maid left the room.

'Not bad news, I hope, dear?'

'It's Giles – my husband. He's flying home. He'll be here in a week.'

Her voice was bewildered and miserable. Miss Marple gave a gentle little cough.

'Well – surely – that is very nice, isn't it?'

'Is it? When I'm not sure if I'm mad or not? If I'm mad I ought never to have married Giles. And the house and everything. I can't go back there. Oh, I don't know what to do.'

Miss Marple patted the sofa invitingly.

'Now suppose you sit down here, dear, and just tell me all about it.'

It was with a sense of relief that Gwenda accepted the invitation. She poured out the whole story, starting with her first view of Hillside and going on to the incidents that had first puzzled her and then worried her.

'And so I got rather frightened,' she ended. 'And I thought I'd come up to London – get away from it all. Only, you see, I couldn't get away from it. It followed me. Last night –' she shut her eyes and gulped reminiscently.

'Last night?' prompted Miss Marple.

'I dare say you won't believe this,' said Gwenda, speaking very fast. 'You'll think I'm hysterical or queer or something. It happened quite suddenly, right at the end. I'd enjoyed the play. I'd never thought once of the house. And then it came – out of the blue – when he said those words –'

She repeated in a low quivering voice: '*Cover her face, mine eyes dazzle, she died young.*

'I was back there – on the stairs, looking down on the hall through the banisters, and I saw her lying there. Sprawled out – dead. Her hair all golden and her face all – all *blue*! She was dead, strangled, and someone was saying those words in that same horrible gloating way – and I saw his hands – grey, wrinkled – not hands – monkey's paws . . . It was horrible, I tell you. She was dead . . .'

Miss Marple asked gently: 'Who was dead?'

The answer came back quick and mechanical.

'Helen . . .'

206

CHAPTER 4

Helen?

For a moment Gwenda stared at Miss Marple, then she pushed back the hair from her forehead.

'Why did I say that?' she said. 'Why did I say Helen? I don't know any Helen!'

She dropped her hands with a gesture of despair.

'You see,' she said, 'I'm mad! I imagine things! I go about seeing things that aren't there. First it was only wallpapers – but now it's dead bodies. So I'm getting worse.'

'Now don't rush to conclusions, my dear –'

'Or else it's the *house*. The house is haunted – or bewitched or something . . . I see things that have happened there – or else I see things that are going to happen there – and that would be worse. Perhaps a woman called Helen is going to be murdered there . . . Only I don't see if it's the *house* that's haunted why I should see these awful things when I am away from it. So I think really that it must be me that's going queer. And I'd better go and see a psychiatrist *at once* – this morning.'

'Well, of course, Gwenda dear, you can always do that when you've exhausted every other line of approach, but I always think myself that it's better to examine the simplest and most commonplace explanations first. Let me get the facts quite clear. There were three definite incidents that upset you. A path in the garden that had been planted over but that you felt was there, a door that had been bricked up, and a wallpaper which you imagined correctly and in detail without having seen it? Am I right?'

'Yes.'

'Well, the easiest, the most natural explanation would be that you *had* seen them before.'

'In another life, you mean?'

'Well no, dear. I meant in *this* life. I mean that they might be actual *memories*.'

'But I've never been in England until a month ago, Miss Marple.'

'You are quite sure of that, my dear?'

'Of course I'm sure. I've lived near Christchurch in New Zealand all my life.'

'Were you born there?'

'No, I was born in India. My father was a British Army officer. My mother died a year or two after I was born and he sent me back to her people in New Zealand to bring up. Then he himself died a few years later.'

'You don't remember coming from India to New Zealand?'

'Not really. I do remember, frightfully vaguely, being on a boat. A round window thing – a porthole, I suppose. And a man in white uniform with a red face and blue eyes, and a mark on his chin – a scar, I suppose. He used to toss me up in the air and I remember being half frightened and half loving it. But it's all very fragmentary.'

'Do you remember a nurse – or an ayah?'

'Not an ayah – Nannie. I remember Nannie because she stayed for some time – until I was five years old. She cut ducks out of paper. Yes, she was on the boat. She scolded me when I cried because the Captain kissed me and I didn't like his beard.'

'Now that's very interesting, dear, because you see you are mixing up two different voyages. In one, the Captain had a beard and in the other he had a red face and a scar on his chin.'

'Yes,' Gwenda considered, 'I suppose I must be.'

'It seems possible to me,' said Miss Marple, 'that when your mother died, your father brought you to *England* with him first, and that you actually lived at this house, Hillside. You've told me, you know, that the house felt like home to you as soon as you got inside it. And that room you chose to sleep in, it was probably your nursery –'

'It *was* a nursery. There were bars on the windows.'

'You see? It had this pretty gay paper of cornflowers and poppies. Children remember their nursery walls very well. I've always remembered the mauve irises on my nursery walls and yet I believe it was repapered when I was only three.'

'And that's why I thought at once of the toys, the dolls' house and the toy cupboards?'

'Yes. And the bathroom. The bath with the mahogany surround. You told me that you thought of sailing ducks in it as soon as you saw it.'

Gwenda said thoughtfully. 'It's true that I seemed to know right away just where everything was – the kitchen and the linen cupboard. And that I kept thinking there was a door through from the drawing-room to the dining-room. But surely it's quite impossible that I should come to England and actually buy the identical house I'd lived in long ago?'

'It's not *impossible*, my dear. It's just a very remarkable coincidence – and remarkable coincidences do happen. Your husband wanted a house on the south coast, you were looking for one, and you passed a house that stirred memories, and attracted you. It was the right size and a reasonable price and so you bought it. No, it's not too wildly improbable. Had the house been merely what is called (perhaps rightly) a haunted house, you would have reacted differently, I think. But you had no feeling of violence or repulsion except, so you have told me, at one very definite moment, and that was when you were just starting to come down the staircase and looking down into the hall.'

Some of the scared expression came back into Gwenda's eyes.

She said: 'You mean – that – that Helen – that *that's* true too?'

Miss Marple said very gently: 'Well, I think so, my dear ... I think we must face the position that if the other things are memories, *that* is a memory too ...'

'That I really saw someone killed – strangled – and lying there dead?'

'I don't suppose you knew consciously that she was strangled, that was suggested by the play last night and fits in with your adult recognition of what a blue convulsed face must mean. I think a very young child, creeping down the stairs, would realize violence and death and evil and associate them with a certain series of words – for I think there's no doubt that the murderer actually *said* those words. It would be a very severe shock to a child. Children are odd little creatures. If they are badly frightened, especially by something they don't understand, they don't talk about it. They bottle it up. Seemingly, perhaps, they forget it. But the memory is still there deep down.'

Gwenda drew a deep breath.

'And you think that's what happened to me? But why don't I remember it all *now*?'

'One can't remember to order. And often when one tries to, the memory goes further away. But I think there are one or two indications that that is what did happen. For instance when you told me just now about your experience in the theatre last night you used a very revealing turn of words. You said you seemed to be looking "*through* the banisters" – but normally, you know, one doesn't look down into a hall *through* the banisters but *over* them. Only a child would look *through*.'

'That's clever of you,' said Gwenda appreciatively.

'These little things are very significant.'

'But who was Helen?' asked Gwenda in a bewildered way.

'Tell me, my dear, are you still quite sure it was Helen?'

'Yes ... It's frightfully odd, because I don't know who "Helen" is – but at the same time I do know – I mean I know that it was "Helen" lying there ... How am I going to find out more?'

'Well, I think the obvious thing to do is to find out definitely if you ever were in England as a child, or if you could have been. Your relatives –'

Gwenda interrupted. 'Aunt Alison. She would know, I'm sure.'

'Then I should write to her by air mail. Tell her circumstances have arisen which make it imperative for you to know if you have ever been in England. You would probably get an answer by air mail by the time your husband arrives.'

'Oh, thank you, Miss Marple. You've been frightfully kind. And I do hope what you've suggested is true. Because if so, well, it's quite all right. I mean, it won't be anything supernatural.'

Miss Marple smiled.

'I hope it turns out as we think. I am going to stay with some old friends of mine in the North of England the day after tomorrow. I shall be passing back through London in about ten days. If you and your husband are here then, or if you have received an answer to your letter, I should be *very* curious to know the result.'

'*Of course*, dear Miss Marple! Anyway, I want you to meet Giles. He's a perfect pet. And we'll have a good pow-wow about the whole thing.'

Gwenda's spirits were fully restored by now.

Miss Marple, however, looked thoughtful.

CHAPTER 5

Murder in Retrospect

It was some ten days later that Miss Marple entered a small hotel in Mayfair, and was given an enthusiastic reception by young Mr and Mrs Reed.

'This is my husband, Miss Marple. Giles, I can't tell you how kind Miss Marple was to me.'

'I'm delighted to meet you, Miss Marple. I hear Gwenda nearly panicked herself into a lunatic asylum.'

Miss Marple's gentle blue eyes summed up Giles Reed favourably. A very likeable young man, tall and fair with a disarming way of blinking every now and then out of a natural shyness. She noted his determined chin and the set of his jaw.

'We'll have tea in the little waiting-room, the dark one,' said Gwenda. 'Nobody ever comes there. And then we can show Miss Marple Aunt Alison's letter.

'Yes,' she added, as Miss Marple looked up sharply. 'It's come, and it's almost exactly what you thought.'

Tea over, the air mail letter was spread out and read.

Dearest Gwenda, (Miss Danby had written)

I was much disturbed to hear you had had some worrying experience. To tell you the truth, it had really entirely escaped my memory that you had actually resided for a short time in England as a young child.

Your mother, my sister Megan, met your father, Major Halliday, when she was on a visit to some friends of ours at that time stationed in India. They were married and you were born there. About two years after your birth your mother died. It was a great shock to us and we wrote to your father with whom we had corresponded, but whom actually we had never seen, begging him to entrust you to our care, as we would be only too glad to have you, and it might be difficult for an Army man stranded with a young child. Your father, however, refused, and told us he was resigning from the Army and taking you back with him to England. He said he hoped we would at some time come over and visit him there.

I understand that on the voyage home, your father met a young woman, became engaged to her, and married her as soon as he got to England. The marriage was not, I gather, a happy one, and I understand they parted about a year later. It was then that your father wrote to us and asked if we were still willing to give you a home. I need hardly tell you, my

211

dear, how happy we were to do so. You were sent out to us in the charge of an English nurse, and at the same time your father settled the bulk of his estate upon you and suggested that you might legally adopt our name. This, I may say, seemed a little curious to us, but we felt that it was kindly meant – and intended to make you more one of the family – we did not, however, adopt that suggestion. About a year later your father died in a nursing home. I surmise that he had already received bad news about his health at the time when he sent you out to us.

I'm afraid I cannot tell you where you lived whilst with your father in England. His letter naturally had the address on it at the time but that is now eighteen years ago and I'm afraid one doesn't remember such details. It was in the South of England, I know – and I fancy Dillmouth is correct. I had a vague idea it was Dartmouth, but the two names are not unlike. I believe your stepmother married again, but I have no recollection of her name, nor even of her unmarried name, though your father had mentioned it in the original letter telling of his remarriage. We were, I think, a little resentful of his marrying again so soon, but of course one knows that on board ship the influence of propinquity is very great – and he may also have thought that it would be a good thing on your account.

It seemed stupid of me not to have mentioned to you that you had been in England even if you didn't remember the fact, but, as I say, the whole thing had faded from my mind. Your mother's death in India and your subsequently coming to live with us always seemed the important points.

I hope this is all cleared up now?

I do trust Giles will soon be able to join you. It is hard for you both being parted at this early stage.

All my news in my next letter, as I am sending this off hurriedly in answer to your wire.

Your loving aunt,
Alison Danby.

PS. You do not say what your worrying experience was?

'You see,' said Gwenda. 'It's almost exactly as you suggested.'

Miss Marple smoothed out the flimsy sheet.

'Yes – yes, indeed. The common-sense explanation. I've found, you know, that that is so often right.'

'Well, I'm very grateful to you, Miss Marple,' said Giles. 'Poor Gwenda was thoroughly upset, and I must say I'd have been rather worried myself to think that Gwenda was clairvoyant or psychic or something.'

'It might be a disturbing quality in a wife,' said Gwenda. 'Unless you've always led a thoroughly blameless life.'

'Which I have,' said Giles.

'And the house? What do you feel about the house?' said Miss Marple.

'Oh, that's all right. We're going down tomorrow. Giles is dying to see it.'

'I don't know whether you realize it, Miss Marple,' said Giles, 'but what it amounts to is, that we've got a first-class murder mystery on our hands. Actually on our very doorstep – or more accurately in our front hall.'

'I *had* thought of that, yes,' said Miss Marple slowly.

'And Giles simply loves detective stories,' said Gwenda.

'Well, I mean, it *is* a detective story. Body in the hall of a beautiful strangled woman. Nothing known of her but her Christian name. Of course I know it's nearly twenty years ago. There can't be any clues after all this time, but one can at least cast about, and try to pick up some of the threads. Oh! I dare say one won't succeed in solving the riddle –'

'I think you might,' said Miss Marple. 'Even after eighteen years. Yes, I think you might.'

'But at any rate it won't do any harm to have a real good try?'

Giles paused, his face beaming.

Miss Marple moved uneasily, her face was grave – almost troubled.

'But it might do a great deal of harm,' she said. 'I would advise you both – oh yes, I really would advise it very strongly – to leave the whole thing alone.'

'Leave it alone? Our very own murder mystery – if it *was* murder!'

'It was murder, I think. And that's just why I should leave it alone. Murder isn't – it really isn't – a thing to tamper with light-heartedly.'

Giles said: 'But, Miss Marple, if everybody felt like that –'

She interrupted him.

'Oh, I know. There are times when it is one's *duty* – an innocent person accused – suspicion resting on various other people – a dangerous criminal at large who may strike again. But you must realize that this murder is very much in the *past*. Presumably it wasn't known for murder – if so, you would have heard fast enough from your old gardener or someone down there – a murder, however long ago, is always news. No, the body must have been disposed of somehow, and the whole thing never suspected. Are you sure – are you really sure, that you are wise to dig it all up again?'

'Miss Marple,' cried Gwenda, 'you sound really concerned?'

'I am, my dear. You are two very nice and charming young people (if you will allow me to say so). You are newly married and happy together. Don't, I beg of you, start to uncover things that may – well, that may – how shall I put it? – that may *upset* and *distress* you.'

Gwenda stared at her. 'You're thinking of something special – of something – what is it you're hinting at?'

'Not hinting, dear. Just advising you (because I've lived a long time and know how very upsetting human nature can be) to let well alone. That's *my* advice: *let well alone.*'

'But it isn't letting well alone.' Giles's voice held a different note, a sterner note. 'Hillside is our house, Gwenda's and mine, and someone was murdered in that house, or so we believe. I'm not going to stand for murder in my house and do nothing about it, even if it *is* eighteen years ago!'

Miss Marple sighed. 'I'm sorry,' she said. 'I imagine that most young men of spirit would feel like that. I even sympathize and almost admire you for it. But I wish – oh, I do wish – that you wouldn't do it.'

II

On the following day, news went round the village of St Mary Mead that Miss Marple was at home again. She was seen in the High Street at eleven o'clock. She called at the Vicarage at ten minutes to twelve. That afternoon three of the gossipy ladies of the village called upon her and obtained her impressions of the gay Metropolis and, this tribute to politeness over, themselves plunged into details of an approaching battle over the fancywork stall at the Fête and the position of the tea tent.

Later that evening Miss Marple could be seen as usual in her garden, but for once her activities were more concentrated on the depredations of weeds than on the activities of her neighbours. She was *distraite* at her frugal evening meal, and hardly appeared to listen to her little maid Evelyn's spirited account of the goings-on of the local chemist. The next day she was still *distraite*, and one or two people, including the Vicar's wife, remarked upon it. That evening Miss Marple said that she did not feel very well and took to her bed. The following morning she sent for Dr Haydock.

Dr Haydock had been Miss Marple's physician, friend and ally for many years. He listened to her account of her symptoms, gave her an examination, then sat back in his chair and waggled his stethoscope at her.

'For a woman of your age,' he said, 'and in spite of that misleading frail appearance, you're in remarkably good fettle.'

'I'm sure my general health is sound,' said Miss Marple. 'But I confess I do feel a little overtired – a little run down.'

'You've been gallivanting about. Late nights in London.'

'That, of course. I do find London a little tiring nowadays. And the air – so used up. Not like fresh seaside air.'

'The air of St Mary Mead is nice and fresh.'

'But often damp and rather muggy. Not, you know, exactly *bracing*.'

Dr Haydock eyed her with a dawning of interest.

214

'I'll send you round a tonic,' he said obligingly.

'Thank you, Doctor. Easton's syrup is always very helpful.'

'There's no need for you to do my prescribing for me, woman.'

'I wondered if, perhaps, a change of air –?'

Miss Marple looked questioningly at him with guileless blue eyes.

'You've just been away for three weeks.'

'I know. But to London which, as you say, is enervating. And then up North – a manufacturing district. Not like bracing sea air.'

Dr Haydock packed up his bag. Then he turned round, grinning.

'Let's hear why you sent for me,' he said. 'Just tell me what it's to be and I'll repeat it after you. You want my professional opinion that what you need is sea air –'

'I knew you'd understand,' said Miss Marple gratefully.

'Excellent thing, sea air. You'd better go to Eastbourne right away, or your health may suffer seriously.'

'Eastbourne, I think, is rather cold. The downs, you know.'

'Bournemouth, then, or the Isle of Wight.'

Miss Marple twinkled at him.

'I always think a small place is much pleasanter.'

Dr Haydock sat down again.

'My curiosity is roused. What small seaside town are you suggesting?'

'Well, I *had* thought of Dillmouth.'

'Pretty little place. Rather dull. Why Dillmouth?'

For a moment or two Miss Marple was silent. The worried look had returned to her eyes. She said: 'Supposing that one day, by accident, you turned up a fact that seemed to indicate that many years ago – nineteen or twenty – a murder had occurred. That fact was known to you alone, nothing of the kind had ever been suspected or reported. What would you do about it?'

'Murder in retrospect in fact?'

'Just exactly that.'

Haydock reflected for a moment.

'There had been no miscarriage of justice? Nobody had suffered as a result of this crime?'

'As far as one can see, no.'

'Hm. Murder in retrospect. Sleeping murder. Well, I'll tell you. I'd let sleeping murder lie – that's what I'd do. Messing about with murder is dangerous. It could be *very* dangerous.'

'That's what I'm afraid of.'

'People say a murderer always repeats his crimes. That's not true. There's a type who commits a crime, manages to get away with it, and is darned careful never to stick his neck out again. I won't say they live happily ever after – I don't believe that's true – there are many kinds of retribution. But outwardly at least all goes well. Perhaps that was so in the case of Madeleine Smith or again in the case of Lizzie Borden. It was not proven in the case of Madeleine Smith and Lizzie was acquitted – but many people believe both of those women were guilty. I could name you others. They never repeated their crimes – one crime gave them what they wanted and they were content. But suppose some danger had menaced them? I take it your killer, whoever he or she is, was one of that kind. He committed a crime and got away with it and nobody suspected. But supposing somebody goes poking about, digging into things, turning up stones and exploring avenues and finally, perhaps, hitting the target? What's your killer going to do about it? Just stay there smiling while the hunt comes nearer and nearer? No, if there's no principle involved, I'd say let it alone.' He repeated his former phrase: 'Let sleeping murder lie.'

He added firmly: 'And those are my orders to *you*. *Let the whole thing alone*.'

'But it's not I who am involved. It's two very delightful children. Let me tell you!'

She told him the story and Haydock listened.

'Extraordinary,' he said when she had finished. 'Extraordinary coincidence. Extraordinary business altogether. I suppose you see what the implications are?'

'Oh, of course. But I don't think it's occurred to *them* yet.'

'It will mean a good deal of unhappiness and they'll wish they'd never meddled with the thing. Skeletons should be kept in their cupboards. Still, you know, I can quite see young Giles's point of view. Dash it all, I couldn't leave the thing alone myself. Even now, I'm curious . . .'

He broke off and directed a stern glance at Miss Marple.

'So that's what you're doing with your excuses to get to Dillmouth. Mixing yourself up in something that's no concern of yours.'

'Not at all, Dr Haydock. But I'm worried about those two. They're very young and inexperienced and much too trusting and credulous. I feel I ought to be there to look after them.'

'So that's why you're going. To look after them! Can't you *ever* leave murder alone, woman? Even murder in retrospect?'

Miss Marple gave a small prim smile.

'But you do think, don't you, that a few weeks at Dillmouth would be beneficial to my health?'

'More likely to be the end of you,' said Dr Haydock. 'But you won't listen to me!'

216

On her way to call upon her friends, Colonel and Mrs Bantry, Miss Marple met Colonel Bantry coming along the drive, his gun in his hand and his spaniel at his heels. He welcomed her cordially.

'Glad to see you back again. How's London?'

Miss Marple said that London was very well. Her nephew had taken her to several plays.

'Highbrow ones, I bet. Only care for a musical comedy myself.'

Miss Marple said that she had been to a Russian play that was very interesting, though perhaps a little too long.

'Russians!' said Colonel Bantry explosively. He had once been given a novel by Dostoievsky to read in a nursing home.

He added that Miss Marple would find Dolly in the garden.

Mrs Bantry was almost always to be found in the garden. Gardening was her passion. Her favourite literature was bulb catalogues and her conversation dealt with primulas, bulbs, flowering shrubs and alpine novelties. Miss Marple's first view of her was a substantial posterior clad in faded tweed.

At the sound of approaching steps, Mrs Bantry reassumed an erect position with a few creaks and winces, her hobby had made her rheumaticky, wiped her hot brow with an earth-stained hand and welcomed her friend.

'Heard you were back, Jane,' she said. 'Aren't my new delphiniums doing well? Have you seen these new little gentians? I've had a bit of trouble with them, but I think they're all set now. What we need is rain. It's been terribly dry.' She added, 'Esther told me you were ill in bed.' Esther was Mrs Bantry's cook and liaison officer with the village. 'I'm glad to see it's not true.'

'Just a little overtired,' said Miss Marple. 'Dr Haydock thinks I need some sea air. I'm rather run down.'

'Oh, but you couldn't go away *now*,' said Mrs Bantry. 'This is absolutely the best time of the year in the garden. Your border must be just coming into flower.'

'Dr Haydock thinks it would be advisable.'

'Well, Haydock's not such a fool as some doctors,' admitted Mrs Bantry grudgingly.

'I was wondering, Dolly, about that cook of yours.'

'Which cook? Do you want a cook? You don't mean that woman who drank, do you?'

'No, no, no. I mean the one who made such delicious pastry. With a husband who was the butler.'

217

'Oh, you mean the Mock Turtle,' said Mrs Bantry with immediate recognition. 'Woman with a deep mournful voice who always sounded as though she was going to burst into tears. She *was* a good cook. Husband was a fat, rather lazy man. Arthur always said he watered the whisky. I don't know. Pity there's always one of a couple that's unsatisfactory. They got left a legacy by some former employer and they went off and opened a boarding-house on the south coast.'

'That's just what I thought. Wasn't it at Dillmouth?'

'That's right. 14 Sea Parade, Dillmouth.'

'I was thinking that as Dr Haydock has suggested the seaside I might go to – was their name Saunders?'

'Yes. That's an excellent idea, Jane. You couldn't do better. Mrs Saunders will look after you well, and as it's out of the season they'll be glad to get you and won't charge very much. With good cooking and sea air you'll soon pick up.'

'Thank you, Dolly,' said Miss Marple, 'I expect I shall.'

CHAPTER 6

Exercise in Detection

'Where do you think the body was? About here?' asked Giles.

He and Gwenda were standing in the front hall of Hillside. They had arrived back the night before, and Giles was now in full cry. He was as pleased as a small boy with his new toy.

'Just about,' said Gwenda. She retreated up the stairs and peered down critically. 'Yes – I think that's about it.'

'Crouch down,' said Giles. 'You're only about three years old, you know.'

Gwenda crouched obligingly.

'You couldn't actually see the man who said the words?'

'I can't remember seeing him. He must have been just a bit further back – yes, there. I could only see his paws.'

'*Paws*.' Giles frowned.

'They *were* paws. Grey paws – not human.'

'But look here, Gwenda. This isn't a kind of Murder in the Rue Morgue. A man doesn't have paws.'

'Well, *he* had paws.'

Giles looked doubtfully at her.

'You must have imagined that bit afterwards.'

Gwenda said slowly, 'Don't you think I may have imagined the whole thing? You know, Giles, I've been thinking. It seems to me far more probable that the whole thing was a *dream*. It might have been. It was the sort of dream a child might have, and be terribly frightened, and go on remembering about. Don't you think really that's the proper explanation? Because nobody in Dillmouth seems to have the faintest idea that there was ever a murder, or a sudden death, or a disappearance or *anything* odd about this house.'

Giles looked like a different kind of little boy – a little boy who has had his nice new toy taken away from him.

'I suppose it might have been a nightmare,' he admitted grudgingly. Then his face cleared suddenly.

'No,' he said. 'I don't believe it. You could have dreamt about monkeys' paws and someone dead – but I'm damned if you could have dreamt that quotation from *The Duchess of Malfi*.'

'I could have heard someone say it and then dreamt about it afterwards.'

'I don't think any child could do that. Not unless you heard it in conditions of great stress – and if that was the case we're back again where

219

we were – hold on, I've got it. It was the *paws* you dreamt. You saw the body and heard the words and you were scared stiff and then you had a nightmare about it, and there were waving monkeys' paws too – probably you were frightened of monkeys.'

Gwenda looked slightly dubious – she said slowly: 'I suppose that *might* be it . . .'

'I wish you could remember a bit more . . . Come down here in the hall. Shut your eyes. Think . . . Doesn't anything more come back to you?'

'No, it doesn't, Giles . . . The more I think, the further it all goes away . . . I mean, I'm beginning to doubt now if I ever really saw anything at all. Perhaps the other night I just had a brainstorm in the theatre.'

'No. There *was* something. Miss Marple thinks so, too. What about "Helen"? Surely you must remember *something* about Helen?'

'I don't remember anything at all. It's just a *name*.'

'It mightn't even be the right name.'

'Yes, it was. It *was* Helen.'

Gwenda looked obstinate and convinced.

'Then if you're so sure it was Helen, you must know something about her,' said Giles reasonably. 'Did you know her well? Was she living here? Or just staying here?'

'I tell you I don't *know*.' Gwenda was beginning to look strained and nervy.

Giles tried another tack.

'Who else can you remember? Your father?'

'No. I mean, I can't tell. There was always his photograph, you see. Aunt Alison used to say: "That's your Daddy." I don't remember him *here*, in this house . . .'

'And no servants – nurses – anything like that?'

'No – no. The more I try to remember, the more it's all a blank. The things I know are all underneath – like walking to that door automatically. I didn't *remember* a door there. Perhaps if you wouldn't worry me so much, Giles, things would come back more. Anyway, trying to find out about it all is hopeless. It's so long ago.'

'Of course it's not hopeless – even old Miss Marple admitted that.'

'She didn't help us with any ideas of how to set about it,' said Gwenda. 'And yet I feel, from the glint in her eye, that she had a few. I wonder how *she* would have gone about it.'

'I don't suppose she would be likely to think of ways that we wouldn't,' said Giles positively. 'We must stop speculating, Gwenda, and set about things in a systematic way. We've made a beginning – I've looked through the Parish registers of deaths. There's no "Helen" of the right age amongst them. In fact there doesn't seem to be a Helen at all in the period I covered – Ellen Pugg, ninety-four, was the nearest. Now we must think of the next profitable approach. If your father, and presumably your stepmother, lived in this house, they must either have bought it or rented it.'

'According to Foster, the gardener, some people called Elworthy had it before the Hengraves and before them Mrs Findeyson. Nobody else.'

'Your father might have bought it and lived in it for a very short time – and then sold it again. But I think that it's much more likely that he rented it – probably rented it furnished. If so, our best bet is to go round the house agents.'

Going round the house agents was not a prolonged labour. There were only two house agents in Dillmouth. Messrs Wilkinson were a comparatively new arrival. They had only opened their premises eleven years ago. They dealt mostly with the small bungalows and new houses at the far end of the town. The other agents, Messrs Galbraith and Penderley, were the ones from whom Gwenda had bought the house. Calling upon them, Giles plunged into his story. He and his wife were delighted with Hillside and with Dillmouth generally. Mrs Reed had only just discovered that she had actually lived in Dillmouth as a small child. She had some very faint memories of the place, and had an idea that Hillside was actually the house in which she had lived but could not be quite certain about it. Had they any record of the house being let to a Major Halliday? It would be about eighteen or nineteen years ago . . .

Mr Penderley stretched out apologetic hands.

'I'm afraid it's not possible to tell you, Mr Reed. Our records do not go back that far – not, that is, of furnished or short-period lets. Very sorry I can't help you, Mr Reed. As a matter of fact if our old head clerk, Mr Narracott, had still been alive – he died last winter – he might have been able to assist you. A most remarkable memory, really quite remarkable. He had been with the firm for nearly thirty years.'

'There's no one else who would possibly remember?'

'Our staff is all on the comparatively young side. Of course there is old Mr Galbraith himself. He retired some years ago.'

'Perhaps I could ask him?' said Gwenda.

'Well, I hardly know about that . . .' Mr Penderley was dubious. 'He had a stroke last year. His faculties are sadly impaired. He's over eighty, you know.'

'Does he live in Dillmouth?'

'Oh yes. At Calcutta Lodge. A very nice little property on the Seaton road. But I really don't think –'

'It's rather a forlorn hope,' said Giles to Gwenda. 'But you never know. I don't think we'll write. We'll go there together and exert our personality.'

Calcutta Lodge was surrounded by a neat trim garden, and the sitting-room into which they were shown was also neat if slightly overcrowded. It smelt of beeswax and Ronuk. Its brasses shone. Its windows were heavily festooned.

A thin middle-aged woman with suspicious eyes came into the room.

Giles explained himself quickly, and the expression of one who expects to have a vacuum cleaner pushed at her left Miss Galbraith's face.

'I'm sorry, but I really don't think I can help you,' she said. 'It's so long ago, isn't it?'

'One does sometimes remember things,' said Gwenda.

'Of course I shouldn't know anything myself. I never had any connection with the business. A Major Halliday, you said? No, I never remember coming across anyone in Dillmouth of that name.'

'Your father might remember, perhaps,' said Gwenda.

'Father?' Miss Galbraith shook her head. 'He doesn't take much notice nowadays, and his memory's very shaky.'

Gwenda's eyes were resting thoughtfully on a Benares brass table and they shifted to a procession of ebony elephants marching along the mantelpiece.

'I thought he might remember, perhaps,' she said, 'because my father had just come from India. Your house is called Calcutta Lodge?'

She paused interrogatively.

'Yes,' said Miss Galbraith. 'Father was out in Calcutta for a time. In business there. Then the war came and in 1920 he came into the firm here, but would have liked to go back, he always says. But my mother didn't fancy foreign parts – and of course you can't say the climate's really healthy. Well, I don't know – perhaps you'd like to see my father. I don't know that it's one of his good days –'

She led them into a small black study. Here, propped up in a big shabby leather chair sat an old gentleman with a white walrus moustache. His face was pulled slightly sideways. He eyed Gwenda with distinct approval as his daughter made the introductions.

'Memory's not what it used to be,' he said in a rather indistinct voice. 'Halliday, you say? No, I don't remember the name. Knew a boy at school in Yorkshire – but that's seventy-odd years ago.'

'He rented Hillside, we think,' said Giles.

'Hillside? Was it called Hillside then?' Mr Galbraith's one movable eyelid snapped shut and open. 'Findeyson lived there. Fine woman.'

'My father might have rented it furnished . . . He'd just come from India.'

'India? India, d'you say? Remember a fellow – Army man. Knew that old rascal Mohammed Hassan who cheated me over some carpets. Had a young wife – and a baby – little girl.'

'That was me,' said Gwenda firmly.

'In – deed – you don't say so! Well, well, time flies. Now what *was* his name? Wanted a place furnished – yes – Mrs Findeyson had been ordered to Egypt or some such place for the winter – all tomfoolery. Now what was his name?'

'Halliday,' said Gwenda.

'That's right, my dear – Halliday. Major Halliday. Nice fellow. Very pretty wife – quite young – fair-haired, wanted to be near her people or something like that. Yes, very pretty.'

'Who were her people?'

'No idea at all. No idea. You don't look like her.'

Gwenda nearly said, 'She was only my stepmother,' but refrained from complicating the issue. She said, 'What did she look like?'

Unexpectedly Mr Galbraith replied : 'Looked worried. That's what she looked, worried. Yes, very nice fellow, that Major chap. Interested to hear I'd been out in Calcutta. Not like these chaps that have never been out of England. Narrow – that's what they are. Now *I've* seen the world. What was his name, that Army chap – wanted a furnished house?'

He was like a very old gramaphone, repeating a worn record.

'St Catherine's. That's it. Took St Catherine's – six guineas a week – while Mrs Findeyson was in Egypt. Died there, poor soul. House was put up for auction – who bought it now? Elworthys – that is – pack of women – sisters. Changed the name – said St Catherine's was Popish. Very down on anything Popish – Used to send out tracts. Plain women, all of 'em – Took an interest in niggers – Sent 'em out trousers and bibles. Very strong on converting the heathen.'

He signed suddenly and leant back.

'Long time ago,' he said fretfully. 'Can't remember names. Chap from India – nice chap . . . I'm tired, Gladys. I'd like my tea.'

Giles and Gwenda thanked him, thanked his daughter, and came away.

'So that's proved,' said Gwenda. 'My father and I were at Hillside. What do we do next?'

'I've been an idiot,' said Giles. 'Somerset House.'

'What's Somerset House?' asked Gwenda.

'It's a record office where you can look up marriages. I'm going there to look up your father's marriage. According to your aunt, your father was married to his second wife immediately on arriving in England. Don't you see, Gwenda – it ought to have occurred to us before – it's perfectly possible that "Helen" may have been a relation of your stepmother's – a young sister, perhaps. Anyway, once we knew what her surname was, we may be able to get on to someone who knows about the general set-up at Hillside. Remember the old boy said they wanted a house in Dillmouth to be near Mrs Halliday's people. If her people live near here we may get something.'

'Giles,' said Gwenda. 'I think you're wonderful.'

III

Giles did not, after all, find it necessary to go to London. Though his energetic nature always made him prone to rush hither and thither and try to do everything himself, he admitted that a purely routine enquiry could be delegated.

He put through a trunk call to his office.

'Got it,' he exclaimed enthusiastically, when the expected reply arrived.

From the covering letter he extracted a certified copy of a marriage certificate.

'Here we are, Gwenda. Friday, Aug. 7th Kensington Registry Office. Kelvin James Halliday to Helen Spenlove Kennedy.'

Gwenda cried out sharply!

'*Helen?*'

They looked at each other.

Giles said slowly: 'But – but – it can't be *her*. I mean – they separated, and she married again – and went away.'

'We don't know,' said Gwenda, 'that she went away . . .'

She looked again at the plainly written name: *Helen Spenlove Kennedy. Helen . . .*

CHAPTER 7

Dr Kennedy

A few days later Gwenda, walking along the Esplanade in a sharp wind, stopped suddenly beside one of the glass shelters which a thoughtful Corporation had provided for the use of its visitors.

'Miss Marple?' she exclaimed in lively surprise.

For indeed Miss Marple it was, nicely wrapped up in a thick fleecy coat and well wound round with scarves.

'Quite a surprise to you, I'm sure, to find me here,' said Miss Marple briskly. 'But my doctor ordered me away to the seaside for a little change, and your description of Dillmouth sounded so attractive that I decided to come here – especially as the cook and butler of a friend of mine take in boarders.'

'But why didn't you come and see us?' demanded Gwenda.

'Old people can be rather a nuisance, my dear. Newly married young couples should be left to themselves.' She smiled at Gwenda's protest. 'I'm sure you'd have made me very welcome. And how are you both? And are you progressing with your mystery?'

'We're hot on the trail,' Gwenda said, sitting beside her.

She detailed their various investigations up to date.

'And now,' she ended, 'we've put an advertisement in lots of papers – local ones and *The Times* and the other big dailies. We've just said will anyone with any knowledge of Helen Spenlove Halliday, née Kennedy, communicate etc. I should think, don't you, that we're bound to get *some* answers.'

'I should think so, my dear – yes, I should think so.'

Miss Marple's tone was placid as ever, but her eyes looked troubled. They flashed a quick appraising glance at the girl sitting beside her. That tone of determined heartiness did not ring quite true. Gwenda, Miss Marple thought, looked worried. What Dr Haydock had called 'the implications' were, perhaps, beginning to occur to her. Yes, but now it was too late to go back ...

Miss Marple said gently and apologetically, 'I have really become most interested in all this. My life, you know, has so *few* excitements. I hope you won't think me *very* inquisitive if I ask you to let me know how you progress?'

'Of course we'll let you know,' said Gwenda warmly. 'You shall be in on everything. Why, but for you, I should be urging doctors to shut me up in a

225

loony bin. Tell me your address here, and then you must come and have a drink – I mean, have tea with us, and see the house. You've got to see the scene of the crime, haven't you?'

She laughed, but there was a slightly nervy edge to her laugh.

When she had gone on her way Miss Marple shook her head very gently and frowned.

II

Giles and Gwenda scanned the mail eagerly every day, but at first their hopes were disappointed. All they got was two letters from private enquiry agents who pronounced themselves willing and skilled to undertake investigations on their behalf.

'Time enough for them later,' said Giles. 'And if we do have to employ some agency, it will be a thoroughly first-class firm, not one that touts through the mail. But I don't really see what they could do that we aren't doing.'

His optimism (or self-esteem) was justified a few days later. A letter arrived, written in one of those clear and yet somewhat illegible handwritings that stamp the professional man.

Galls Hill
Woodleigh Bolton.

Dear Sir,

In answer to your advertisement in *The Times*, Helen Spenlove Kennedy is my sister. I have lost touch with her for many years and should be glad to have news of her.

Yours faithfully,
James Kennedy, MD

'Woodleigh Bolton,' said Giles. 'That's not too far away. Woodleigh Camp is where they go for picnics. Up on the moorland. About thirty miles from here. We'll write and ask Dr Kennedy if we may come and see him, or if he would prefer to come to us.'

A reply was received that Dr Kennedy would be prepared to receive them on the following Wednesday; and on that day they set off.

Woodleigh Bolton was a straggling village set along the side of a hill. Galls Hill was the highest house just at the top of the rise, with a view over Woodleigh Camp and the moors towards the sea.

'Rather a bleak spot,' said Gwenda shivering.

The house itself was bleak and obviously Dr Kennedy scorned such modern innovations as central heating. The woman who opened the door was dark and rather forbidding. She led them across the rather bare hall, and into a study where Dr Kennedy rose to receive them. It was a long, rather high room, lined with well-filled bookshelves.

Dr Kennedy was a grey-haired elderly man with shrewd eyes under tufted brows. His gaze went sharply from one to the other of them.

'Mr and Mrs Reed? Sit here, Mrs Reed, it's probably the most comfortable chair. Now, what's all this about?'

Giles went fluently into their prearranged story.

He and his wife had been recently married in New Zealand. They had come to England, where his wife had lived for a short time as a child, and she was trying to trace old family friends and connections.

Dr Kennedy remained stiff and unbending. He was polite but obviously irritated by Colonial insistence on sentimental family ties.

'And you think my sister – my half-sister – and possibly myself – are connections of yours?' he asked Gwenda, civilly, but with slight hostility.

'She was my stepmother,' said Gwenda. 'My father's second wife. I can't really remember her properly, of course. I was so small. My maiden name was Halliday.'

He stared at her – and then suddenly a smile illuminated his face. He became a different person, no longer aloof.

'Good Lord,' he said. 'Don't tell me that you're Gwennie!'

Gwenda nodded eagerly. The pet name, long forgotten, sounded in her ears with reassuring familiarity.

'Yes,' she said. 'I'm Gwennie.'

'God bless my soul. Grown up and married. How time flies! It must be – what – fifteen years – no, of course, much longer than that. You don't remember me, I suppose?'

Gwenda shook her head.

'I don't even remember my father. I mean, it's all a vague kind of blur.'

'Of course – Halliday's first wife came from New Zealand – I remember his telling me so. A fine country, I should think.'

'It's the loveliest country in the world – but I'm quite fond of England, too.'

'On a visit – or settling down here?' He rang the bell. 'We must have tea.'

When the tall woman came, he said, 'Tea, please – and – er – hot buttered toast, or – or cake, or something.'

The respectable housekeeper looked venomous, but said, 'Yes, sir,' and went out.

'I don't usually go in for tea,' said Dr Kennedy vaguely. 'But we must celebrate.'

'It's very nice of you,' said Gwenda. 'No, we're not on a visit. We've bought a house.' She paused and added, 'Hillside.'

Dr Kennedy said vaguely, 'Oh yes. In Dillmouth. You wrote from there.'

'It's the most extraordinary coincidence,' said Gwenda. 'Isn't it, Giles?'

'I should say so,' said Giles. 'Really quite staggering.'

'It was for sale, you see,' said Gwenda, and added in face of Dr Kennedy's apparent non-comprehension, 'It's the same house where we used to live long ago.'

Dr Kennedy frowned. 'Hillside? But surely – Oh yes, I did hear they'd changed the name. Used to be St Something or other – if I'm thinking of the right house – on the Leahampton road, coming down into the town, on the right-hand side?'

'Yes.'

'That's the one. Funny how names go out of your head. Wait a minute. St Catherine's – that's what it used to be called.'

'And I did live there, didn't I?' Gwenda said.

'Yes, of course you did.' He stared at her, amused. 'Why did you want to come back there? You can't remember much about it, surely?'

'No. But somehow – it felt like home.'

'It felt like home,' the doctor repeated. There was no expression in the words, but Giles wondered what he was thinking about.

'So you see,' said Gwenda, 'I hoped you'd tell me about it all – about my father and Helen and –' she ended lamely – 'and everything . . .'

He looked at her reflectively.

'I suppose they didn't know very much – out in New Zealand. Why should they? Well, there isn't much to tell. Helen – my sister – was coming back from India on the same boat with your father. He was a widower with a small daughter. Helen was sorry for him or fell in love with him. He was lonely, or fell in love with her. Difficult to know just the way things happen. They were married in London on arrival, and came down to Dillmouth to me. I was in practice there, then. Kelvin Halliday seemed a nice chap, rather nervy and run down – but they seemed happy enough together – then.'

He was silent for a moment before he said, 'However, in less than a year, she ran away with someone else. You probably know that?'

'Who did she run away with?' asked Gwenda.

He bent his shrewd eyes upon her.

'She didn't tell me,' he said. 'I wasn't in her confidence. I'd seen – couldn't help seeing – that there was friction between her and Kelvin. I didn't know why. I was always a strait-laced sort of fellow – a believer in marital fidelity. Helen wouldn't have wanted me to know what was going on. I'd heard rumours – one does – but there was no mention of any particular name. They often had guests staying with them who came from London, or from other parts of England. I imagined it was one of them.'

'There wasn't a divorce, then?'

'Helen didn't want a divorce. Kelvin told me that. That's why I imagined, perhaps wrongly, that it was a case of some married man. Someone whose wife was an RC perhaps.'

'And my father?'

'He didn't want a divorce, either.'

Dr Kennedy spoke rather shortly.

'Tell me about my father,' said Gwenda. 'Why did he decide suddenly to send me out to New Zealand?'

Kennedy paused a moment before saying, 'I gather your people out there had been pressing him. After the break-up of his second marriage, he probably thought it was the best thing.'

'Why didn't he take me out there himself?'

Dr Kennedy looked along the mantelpiece searching vaguely for a pipe cleaner.

'Oh, I don't know . . . He was in rather poor health.'

'What was the matter with him? What did he die of?'

The door opened and the scornful housekeeper appeared with a laden tray.

There was buttered toast and some jam, but no cake. With a vague gesture Dr Kennedy motioned Gwenda to pour out. She did so. When the cups were filled and handed round and Gwenda had taken a piece of toast, Dr Kennedy said with rather forced cheerfulness: 'Tell me what you've done to the house? I don't suppose I'd recognize it now – after you two have finished with it.'

'We're having a little fun with bathrooms,' admitted Giles.

Gwenda, her eyes on the doctor, said: 'What did my father die of?'

'I couldn't really tell, my dear. As I say, he was in rather poor health for a while, and he finally went into a Sanatorium – somewhere on the east coast. He died about two years later.'

'Where was this Sanatorium exactly?'

'I'm sorry. I can't remember now. As I say, I have an impression it was on the east coast.'

There was definite evasion now in his manner. Giles and Gwenda looked at each other for a brief second.

Giles said, 'At least, sir, you can tell us where he's buried? Gwenda is – naturally – very anxious to visit his grave.'

Dr Kennedy bent over the fireplace, scraping in the bowl of his pipe with a penknife.

'Do you know,' he said, rather indistinctly, 'I don't really think I should dwell too much on the past. All this ancestor worship – it's a mistake. The future is what matters. Here you are, you two, young and healthy with the world in front of you. Think forward. No use going about putting flowers on the grave of someone whom, for all practical purposes, you hardly knew.'

Gwenda said mutinously: 'I should like to see my father's grave.'

'I'm afraid I can't help you.' Dr Kennedy's tones were pleasant but cold. 'It's a long time ago, and my memory isn't what it was. I lost touch with your father after he left Dillmouth. I think he wrote to me once from the Sanatorium and, as I say, I have an impression it was on the east coast – but I couldn't really be sure even of that. And I've no idea at all of where he is buried.'

'How very odd,' said Giles.

'Not really. The link between us, you see, was Helen. I was always very fond of Helen. She's my half-sister and very many years younger than I am, but I tried to bring her up as well as I could. The right schools and all that. But there's no gainsaying that Helen – well, that she never had a stable character. There was trouble when she was quite young with a very undesirable young man. I got her out of that safely. Then she elected to go out to India and marry Walter Fane. Well, that was all right, nice lad, son of Dillmouth's leading solicitor, but frankly, dull as ditchwater. He'd always adored her, but she never looked at him. Still, she changed her mind and went out to India to marry him. When she saw him again, it was all off. She wired to me for money for her passage home. I sent it. On the way back, she met Kelvin. They were married before I knew about it. I've felt, shall we say, apologetic for that sister of mine. It explains why Kelvin and I didn't keep up the relationship after she went away.' He added suddenly: 'Where's Helen now? Can you tell me? I'd like to get in touch with her.'

'But we don't know,' said Gwenda. 'We don't know at all.'

'Oh! I thought from your advertisement –' He looked at them with sudden curiosity. 'Tell me, why did you advertise?'

Gwenda said: 'We wanted to get in touch –' and stopped.

'With someone you can hardly remember?' Dr Kennedy looked puzzled.

Gwenda said quickly: 'I thought – if I could get in touch with her – she'd tell me – about my father.'

'Yes – yes – I see. Sorry I can't be of much use. Memory not what it was. And it's a long time ago.'

230

'At least,' said Giles, 'you know what kind of a Sanatorium it was? Tubercular?'

Dr Kennedy's face again looked suddenly wooden: 'Yes – yes, I rather believe it was.'

'Then we ought to be able to trace that *quite* easily,' said Giles. 'Thank you very much, sir, for all you've told us.'

He got up and Gwenda followed suit.

'Thank you very much,' she said. 'And do come and see us at Hillside.'

They went out of the room and Gwenda, glancing back over her shoulder, had a final view of Dr Kennedy standing by the mantelpiece, pulling his grizzled moustache and looking troubled.

'He knows something he won't tell us,' said Gwenda, as they got into the car. 'There's *something* – oh, Giles! I wish – I wish now that we'd never started . . .'

They looked at each other, and in each mind, unacknowledged to the other, the same fear sprang.

'Miss Marple was right,' said Gwenda. 'We should have left the past alone.'

'We needn't go any further,' said Giles uncertainly. 'I think perhaps, Gwenda darling, we'd better not.'

Gwenda shook her head.

'No, Giles, we can't stop now. We should always be wondering and imagining. No, we've got to go on . . . Dr Kennedy wouldn't tell us because he wanted to be kind – but that sort of business is no good. We'll have to go on and find out what really happened. Even if – even if – it was my father who . . .' But she couldn't go on.

CHAPTER 8

Kelvin Halliday's Delusion

They were in the garden on the following morning when Mrs Cocker came out and said: 'Excuse me, sir. There's a Doctor Kennedy on the telephone.'

Leaving Gwenda in consultation with old Foster, Giles went into the house and picked up the telephone receiver.

'Giles Reed here.'

'This is Dr Kennedy. I've been thinking over our conversation yesterday, Mr Reed. There are certain facts which I think perhaps you and your wife ought to know. Will you be at home if I come over this afternoon?'

'Certainly I shall. What time?'

'Three o'clock?'

'Suits us.'

In the garden old Foster said to Gwenda, 'Is that Dr Kennedy as used to live over at West Cliff?'

'I expect so. Did you know him?'

''e was allus reckoned to be best doctor here – not but what Dr Lazenby wasn't more popular. Always had a word and a laugh to jolly you along, Dr Lazenby did. Dr Kennedy was always short and a bit dry, like – but he knew his job.'

'When did he give up his practice?'

'Long time ago now. Must be fifteen years or so. His health broke down, so they say.'

Giles came out of the window and answered Gwenda's unspoken question.

'He's coming over this afternoon.'

'Oh.' She turned once more to Foster. 'Did you know Dr Kennedy's sister at all?'

'Sister? Not as I remember. She was only a bit of a lass. Went away to school, and then abroad, though I heard she come back here for a bit after she married. But I believe she run off with some chap – always wild she was, they said. Don't know as I ever laid eyes on her myself. I was in a job over to Plymouth for a while, you know.'

Gwenda said to Giles as they walked to the end of the terrace, 'Why is he coming?'

'We'll know at three o'clock.'

Dr Kennedy arrived punctually. Looking round the drawing-room he said: 'Seems odd to be here again.'

Then he came to the point without preamble.

'I take it that you two are quite determined to track down the Sanatorium where Kelvin Halliday died and learn all the details you can about his illness and death?'

'Definitely,' said Gwenda.

'Well, you can manage that quite easily, of course. So I've come to the conclusion that it will be less shock to you to hear the facts from me. I'm sorry to have to tell you, for it won't do you or anybody else a bit of good, and it will probably cause *you*, Gwennie, a good deal of pain. But there it is. Your father wasn't suffering from tuberculosis and the Sanatorium in question was a mental home.'

'A mental home? Was he out of his mind, then?'

Gwenda's face had gone very white.

'He was never certified. And in my opinion he was not insane in the general meaning of the term. He had had a very severe nervous breakdown and suffered from certain delusional obsessions. He went into the nursing home of his own will and volition and could, of course, have left it at any time he wanted to. His condition did not improve, however, and he died there.'

'Delusional obsessions?' Giles repeated the words questioningly. 'What kind of delusions?'

Dr Kennedy said drily, 'He was under the impression that he had strangled his wife.'

Gwenda gave a stifled cry. Giles stretched out a hand quickly and took her cold hand in his.

Giles said, 'And – and had he?'

'Eh?' Dr Kennedy stared at him. 'No, of course he hadn't. No question of such a thing.'

'But – but how do you know?' Gwenda's voice came uncertainly.

'My dear child! There was never any question of such a thing. Helen left him for another man. He'd been in a very unbalanced condition for some time; nervous dreams, sick fancies. The final shock sent him over the edge. I'm not a psychiatrist myself. They have their explanations for such matters. If a man would rather his wife was dead than unfaithful, he can manage to make himself believe that she is dead – even that he has killed her.'

Warily, Giles and Gwenda exchanged a warning glance.

Giles said quietly, 'So you are quite sure that there was no question of his having actually done what he said he had done?'

'Oh, quite sure. I had two letters from Helen. The first one from France about a week after she went away and one about six months later. Oh no, the whole thing was a delusion pure and simple.'

Gwenda drew a deep breath.

'Please,' she said 'Will you tell me all about it?'

'I'll tell you everything I can, my dear. To begin with, Kelvin had been in a rather peculiar neurotic state for some time. He came to me about it. Said he had had various disquieting dreams. These dreams, he said, were always the same, and they ended in the same way – with his throttling Helen. I tried to get at the root of the trouble – there must, I think, have been some conflict in early childhood. His father and mother, apparently, were not a happy couple ... Well, I won't go into all that. That's only interesting to a medical man. I actually suggested that Kelvin should consult a psychiatrist, there are several first-class chaps – but he wouldn't hear of it – thought that kind of thing was all nonsense.

'I had an idea that he and Helen weren't getting along too well, but he never spoke about that, and I didn't like to ask questions. The whole thing came to a head when he walked into my house one evening – it was a Friday, I remember, I'd just come back from the hospital and found him waiting for me in the consulting room; he'd been there about a quarter of an hour. As soon as I came in, he looked up and said, *I've killed Helen.*'

'For a moment I didn't know what to think. He was so cool and matter of fact. I said, 'You mean – you've had another dream?' He said, 'It isn't a dream this time. It's true. She's lying there strangled. I strangled her.'

'Then he said – quite coolly and reasonably: "You'd better come back with me to the house. Then you can ring up the police from there." I didn't know what to think. I got out the car again, and we drove along here. The house was quiet and dark. We went up to the bedroom –'

Gwenda broke in, *'The bedroom?'* Her voice held pure astonishment.

Dr Kennedy looked faintly surprised.

'Yes, yes, that's where it all happened. Well, of course when we go up there – there was nothing at all! No dead woman lying across the bed. Nothing disturbed – the coverlets not even rumpled. The whole thing had been an hallucination.'

'But what did my father say?'

'Oh, he persisted in his story, of course. He really believed it, you see. I persuaded him to let me give him a sedative and I put him to bed in the dressing-room. Then I had a good look round. I found a note that Helen had left crumpled up in the wastepaper basket in the drawing-room. It was quite clear. She had written something like this: "This is Goodbye. I'm sorry – but our marriage has been a mistake from the beginning. I'm going away with the only man I've ever loved. Forgive me if you can. Helen."

'Evidently Kelvin had come in, read her note, gone upstairs, had a kind of emotional brainstorm and had then come over to me persuaded that he had killed Helen.

'Then I questioned the housemaid. It was her evening out and she had come in late. I took her into Helen's room and she went through Helen's clothes, etc. It was all quite clear. Helen had packed a suitcase and a bag and had taken them away with her. I searched the house, but there was no trace of anything unusual – certainly no sign of a strangled woman.

'I had a very difficult time with Kelvin in the morning, but he realized at last that it was a delusion – or at least he said he did, and he consented to go into a nursing home for treatment.

'A week later I got, as I say, a letter from Helen. It was posted from Biarritz, but she said she was going on to Spain. I was to tell Kelvin that she did not want a divorce. He had better forget her as soon as possible.

'I showed the letter to Kelvin. He said very little. He was going ahead with his plans. He wired out to his first wife's people in New Zealand asking them to take the child. He settled up his affairs and he then entered a very good private mental home and consented to have appropriate treatment. The treatment, however, did nothing to help him. He died there two years later. I can give you the address of the place. It's in Norfolk. The present Superintendent was a young doctor there at the time, and will probably be able to give you full details of your father's case.'

Gwenda said: 'And you got another letter from your sister – after that again?'

'Oh yes. About six months later. She wrote from Florence – gave an address post restante as "Miss Kennedy". She said she realized that perhaps it was unfair to Kelvin not to have a divorce – though she herself did not want one. If he wanted a divorce and I would let her know, she would see that he had the necessary evidence. I took the letter to Kelvin. He said at once that he did not want a divorce. I wrote to her and told her so. Since then I have never heard any more. I don't know where she is living, or indeed if she is alive or dead. That is why I was attracted by your advertisement and hoped that I should get news of her.'

He added gently: 'I'm very sorry about this, Gwennie. But you had to know. I only wish you could have left well alone . . .'

CHAPTER 9

Unknown Factor?

When Giles came back from seeing Dr Kennedy off, he found Gwenda sitting where he had left her. There was a bright red patch on each of her cheeks, and her eyes looked feverish. When she spoke her voice was harsh and brittle.

'What's the old catchphrase? Death or madness either way? That's what this is – death or madness.'

'Gwenda – darling.' Giles went to her – put his arm round her. Her body felt hard and stiff.

'Why didn't we leave it all alone? Why didn't we? It was my own father who strangled her. And it was my own father's voice I heard saying those words. No wonder it all came back – no wonder I was frightened. My own father.'

'Wait, Gwenda – wait. We don't really know –'

'Of course we know! He told Dr Kennedy he had strangled his wife, didn't he?'

'But Kennedy is quite positive he didn't –'

'Because he didn't find a body. But there *was* a body – and I *saw* it.'

'You saw it in the hall – not the bedroom.'

'What difference does that make?'

'Well, it's queer, isn't it? Why should Halliday say he strangled his wife in the bedroom if he actually strangled her in the hall?'

'Oh, I don't know. That's just a minor detail.'

'I'm not so sure. Pull your socks up, darling. There are some very funny points about the whole set-up. We'll take it, if you like, that your father *did* strangle Helen. In the hall. What happened next?'

'He went off to Dr Kennedy.'

'And told him he had strangled his wife in the bedroom, brought him back with him and there was no body in the hall – *or* in the bedroom. Dash it all, there can't be a murder *without* a body. What had he done with the body?'

'Perhaps there was one and Dr Kennedy helped him and hushed it all up – only of course he couldn't tell *us* that.'

Giles shook his head.

'No, Gwenda – I don't see Kennedy acting that way. He's a hard-headed, shrewd, unemotional Scotsman. You're suggesting that he'd be willing to put himself in jeopardy as an accessory after the fact. I don't believe he

236

would. He'd do his best for Halliday by giving evidence as to his mental state – that, yes. But why should he stick his neck out to hush the whole thing up? Kelvin Halliday wasn't any relation to him, nor a close friend. It was his own sister who had been killed and he was clearly fond of her – even if he did show slight Victorian disapproval of her gay ways. It's not, even, as though *you* were his sister's child. No, Kennedy wouldn't connive at concealing murder. If he did, there's only one possible way he could have set about it, and that would be deliberately to give a death certificate that she had died of heart failure or something. I suppose he *might* have got away with that – but we know definitely that he *didn't* do that. Because there's no record of her death in the Parish registers, and if he *had* done it, he would have told us that his sister had died. So go on from there and explain, if you can, what happened to the body.'

'Perhaps my father buried it somewhere – in the garden?'

'And *then* went to Kennedy and told him he'd murdered his wife? Why? Why not rely on the story that she'd "left him"?'

Gwenda pushed back her hair from her forehead. She was less stiff and rigid now, and the patches of sharp colour were fading.

'I don't know,' she admitted. 'It does seem a bit screwy now you've put it that way. Do you think Dr Kennedy was telling us the truth?'

'Oh yes – I'm pretty sure of it. From his point of view it's a perfectly reasonable story. Dreams, hallucinations – finally a major hallucination. He'd got no doubt that it was a hallucination because, as we've just said, you can't have a murder without a body. That's where we're in a different position from him. We know that there was a body.'

He paused and went on: 'From his point of view, everything fits in. Missing clothes and suitcase, the farewell note. And later, two letters from his sister.'

Gwenda stirred.

'Those letters. How do we explain those?'

'We don't – but we've got to. If we assume that Kennedy was telling us the truth (and as I say, I'm pretty sure that he was), we've got to explain those letters.'

'I suppose they really were in his sister's handwriting? He recognized it?'

'You know, Gwenda, I don't believe that point would arise. It's not like a signature on a doubtful cheque. If those letters were given in a reasonably close imitation of his sister's writing, it wouldn't occur to him to doubt them. He's already got the preconceived idea that she's gone away with someone. The letter just confirmed that belief. If he had never heard from her at all – why, then he *might* have got suspicious. All the same, there are certain curious points about those letters that wouldn't strike him, perhaps, but do strike me. They're strangely anonymous. No address except a poste restante. No indication of who the man in the case was. A clearly stated determination to make a clean break with all old ties. What I mean is, they're exactly the kind of letters a *murderer* would devise if he wanted to allay any suspicions on the part of his victim's family. It's the old Crippen touch again. To get the letters posted from abroad would be easy.'

'You think my father –'

'*No* – that's just it – I *don't*. Take a man who's deliberately decided to get rid of his wife. He spreads rumours about her possible unfaithfulness. He stages her departure – note left behind, clothes packed and taken. Letters will be received from her at carefully spaced intervals from somewhere abroad. Actually he has murdered her quietly and put her, say, under the cellar floor. That's one pattern of murder – and it's often been done. But what that type of murderer *doesn't* do is to rush to his brother-in-law and say he's murdered his wife and hadn't they better go to the the police? On the other hand, if your father was the emotional type of killer, and was terribly in love with his wife and strangled her in a fit of frenzied jealousy – Othello fashion – (and that fits in with the words you heard) he certainly doesn't pack clothes and arrange for letters to come, before he rushes off to broadcast his crime to a man who isn't the type likely to hush it up. It's all wrong, Gwenda. The whole pattern is wrong.'

'Then what are you trying to get at, Giles?'

'I don't know ... It's just that throughout it all, there seems to be an unknown factor – call him X. Someone who hasn't appeared as yet. But one gets glimpses of his technique.'

'X?' said Gwenda wonderingly. Then her eyes darkened. 'You're making that up, Giles. To comfort me.'

'I swear I'm not. Don't you see yourself that you can't make a satisfactory outline to fit all the facts? We know that Helen Halliday was strangled because you saw –'

He stopped.

'Good Lord! I've been a fool. I see it now. It covers everything. You're right. And Kennedy's right, too. Listen, Gwenda. Helen's preparing to go away with a lover – who that is we don't know.'

'X?'

Giles brushed her interpolation aside impatiently.

'She's written her note to her husband – but at that moment he comes in, reads what she's writing and goes haywire. He crumples up the note, slings it into the waste-basket, and goes for her. She's terrified, rushes out into the hall – he catches up with her, throttles her – she goes limp and he drops her. And then, standing a little way from her, he quotes those words from *The*

Duchess of Malfi just as the child upstairs has reached the banisters and is peering down.'

'And after that?'

'The point is, *that she isn't dead*. He may have thought she was dead – but she's merely semi-suffocated. Perhaps her lover comes round – after the frantic husband has started for the doctor's house on the other side of the town, or perhaps she regains consciousness by herself. Anyway, as soon as she has come to, she beats it. Beats it quickly. And that explains everything. Kelvin's belief that he has killed her. The disappearance of the clothes; packed and taken away earlier in the day. And the subsequent letters *which are perfectly genuine*. There you are – that explains everything.'

Gwenda said slowly, 'It doesn't explain why Kelvin said he had strangled her in the bedroom.'

'He was so het up, he couldn't remember where it had all happened.'

Gwenda said: 'I'd like to believe you. I want to believe . . . But I go on feeling sure – quite sure – that when I looked down she was dead – quite dead.'

'But how could you possibly tell? A child of barely three.'

She looked at him queerly.

'I think one can tell – better than if one was older. It's like dogs – they know death and throw back their heads and howl. I think children – know death . . .'

'That's nonsense – that's fantastic.'

The ring of the front-door bell interrupted him. He said, 'Who's that, I wonder?'

Gwenda looked dismayed.

'I quite forgot. It's Miss Marple. I asked her to tea today. Don't let's say anything about all this to her.'

II

Gwenda was afraid that tea might prove a difficult meal – but Miss Marple fortunately seemed not to notice that her hostess talked a little too fast and too feverishly, and that her gaiety was somewhat forced. Miss Marple herself was gently garrulous – she was enjoying her stay in Dillmouth so much and – wasn't it exciting? – some friends of friends of hers had written to friends of theirs in Dillmouth, and as a result she had received some very pleasant invitations from the local residents.

'One feels so much less of an outsider, if you know what I mean, my dear, if one gets to know some of the people who have been established here for years. For instance, I am going to tea with Mrs Fane – she is the widow of the senior partner in the best firm of solicitors here. Quite an old-fashioned family firm. Her son is carrying it on now.'

The gentle gossiping voice went on. Her landlady was so kind – and made her so comfortable – 'and really delicious cooking. She was for some years with my old friend Mrs Bantry – although she does not come from this part of the world herself – her aunt lived here for many years and she and her husband used to come here for holidays – so she knows a great deal of the local gossip. Do you find your gardener satisfactory, by the way? I hear that he is considered locally as rather a *scrimshanker* – more talk than work.'

'Talk and tea is his speciality,' said Giles. 'He has about five cups of tea a day. But he works splendidly when we are looking.'

'Come out and see the garden,' said Gwenda.

They showed her the house and the garden, and Miss Marple made the proper comments. If Gwenda had feared her shrewd observation of something amiss, then Gwenda was wrong. For Miss Marple showed no cognizance of anything unusual.

Yet, strangely enough, it was Gwenda who acted in an unpredictable manner. She interrupted Miss Marple in the midst of a little anecdote about a child and a seashell to say breathlessly to Giles:

'I don't care – I'm going to tell her . . .'

Miss Marple turned her head attentively. Giles started to speak, then stopped. Finally he said, 'Well, it's your funeral, Gwenda.'

And so Gwenda poured it all out. Their call on Dr Kennedy and his subsequent call on them and what he had told them.

'That was what you meant in London, wasn't it?' Gwenda asked breathlessly. 'You thought, then, that – that my father might be involved?'

Miss Marple said gently, 'It occurred to me as a possibility – yes. "Helen" might very well be a young stepmother – and in a case of – er – strangling, it is so often a husband who is involved.'

Miss Marple spoke as one who observes natural phenomena without surprise or emotion.

'I do see why you urged us to leave it alone,' said Gwenda. 'Oh, and I wish now we had. But one can't go back.'

'No,' said Miss Marple, 'one can't go back.'

'And now you'd better listen to Giles. He's been making objections and suggestions.'

'All I say is,' said Giles, 'that it doesn't fit.'

And lucidly, clearly, he went over the points as he had previously outlined them to Gwenda.

Then he particularized his final theory.

240

'If you'll only convince Gwenda that that's the only way it could have been.'

Miss Marple's eyes went from him to Gwenda and back again.

'It is a perfectly reasonable hypothesis,' she said. 'But there is always, as you yourself pointed out, Mr Reed, the possibility of X.'

'X!' said Gwenda.

'The unknown factor,' said Miss Marple. 'Someone, shall we say, who hasn't appeared yet – but whose presence, behind the obvious facts, can be deduced.'

'We're going to the Sanatorium in Norfolk where my father died,' said Gwenda. 'Perhaps we'll find out something there.'

CHAPTER 10

A Case History

Saltmarsh House was set pleasantly about six miles inland from the coast. It had a good train service to London from the five-miles-distant town of South Benham.

Giles and Gwenda were shown into a large airy sitting-room with cretonne covers patterned with flowers. A very charming-looking old lady with white hair came into the room holding a glass of milk. She nodded to them and sat down near the fireplace. Her eyes rested thoughtfully on Gwenda and presently she leaned forward towards her and spoke in what was almost a whisper.

'*Is it your poor child, my dear?*'

Gwenda looked slightly taken aback. She said doubtfully: 'No – no. It isn't.'

'Ah, I wondered.' The old lady nodded her head and sipped her milk. Then she said conversationally, 'Half past ten – that's the time. It's always at half past ten. Most remarkable.' She lowered her voice and leaned forward again.

'Behind the fireplace,' she breathed. 'But don't say I told you.'

At this moment, a white uniformed maid came into the room and requested Giles and Gwenda to follow her.

They were shown into Dr Penrose's study, and Dr Penrose rose to greet them.

Dr Penrose, Gwenda could not help thinking, looked a little mad himself. He looked, for instance, much madder than the nice old lady in the drawing-room – but perhaps psychiatrists always looked a little mad.

'I had your letter, and Dr Kennedy's,' said Dr Penrose. 'And I've been looking up your father's case history, Mrs Reed. I remembered his case quite well, of course, but I wanted to refresh my memory so that I should be in a position to tell you everything you wanted to know. I understand that you have only recently become aware of the facts?'

Gwenda explained that she had been brought up in New Zealand by her mother's relations and that all she had known about her father was that he had died in a nursing home in England.

Dr Penrose nodded. 'Quite so. Your father's case, Mrs Reed, presented certain rather peculiar features.'

'Such as?' Giles asked.

'Well, the obsession – or delusion – was very strong. Major Halliday,

242

though clearly in a very nervous state, was most emphatic and categorical in his assertion that he had strangled his second wife in a fit of jealous rage. A great many of the usual signs in these cases were absent, and I don't mind telling you frankly, Mrs Reed, that had it not been for Dr Kennedy's assurance that Mrs Halliday was actually alive, I should have been prepared, at that time, to take your father's assertion at its face value.'

'You formed the impression that he had actually killed her?' Giles asked.

'I said "at that time". Later, I had cause to revise my opinion, as Major Halliday's character and mental make-up became more familiar to me. Your father, Mrs Reed, was most definitely *not* a paranoiac type. He had no delusions of persecution, no impulses of violence. He was a gentle, kindly, and well-controlled individual. He was neither what the world calls mad, nor was he dangerous to others. But he did have this obstinate fixation about Mrs Halliday's death and to account for its origin I am quite convinced we have to go back a long way – to some childish experience. But I admit that all methods of analysis failed to give us the right clue. Breaking down a patient's resistance to analysis is sometimes a very long business. It may take several years. In your father's case, the time was insufficient.'

He paused, and then, looking up sharply, said: 'You know, I presume, that Major Halliday committed suicide.'

'Oh *no*!' cried Gwenda.

'I'm sorry, Mrs Reed. I thought you knew that. You are entitled, perhaps, to attach some blame to us on that account. I admit that proper vigilance would have prevented it. But frankly I saw no sign of Major Halliday's being a suicidal type. He showed no tendency to melancholia – no brooding or despondency. He complained of sleeplessness and my colleague allowed him a certain amount of sleeping tablets. whilst pretending to take them, he actually kept them until he had accumulated a sufficient amount and –'

He spread out his hands.

'Was he so dreadfully unhappy?'

'No. I do not think so. It was more, I should judge, a guilt complex, a desire for a penalty to be exacted. He had insisted at first, you know, on calling in the police, and though persuaded out of that, and assured that he had actually committed no crime at all, he obstinately refused to be wholly convinced. Yet it was proved to him over and over again, and he had to admit, that he had no recollection of committing the actual act.' Dr Penrose ruffled over the papers in front of him. 'His account of the evening in question never varied. He came into the house, he said, and it was dark. The servants were out. He went into the dining-room, as he usually did, poured himself out a drink and drank it, then went through the connecting door

243

into the drawing-room. After that he remembered nothing – nothing at all, until he was standing in his bedroom looking down at his wife who was dead – strangled. He knew he had done it –'

Giles interrupted. 'Excuse me, Dr Penrose, but *why* did he know he had done it?'

'There was no doubt in his mind. For some months past he had found himself entertaining wild and melodramatic suspicions. He told me, for instance, that he had been convinced his wife was administering drugs to him. He had, of course, lived in India, and the practice of wives driving their husbands insane by datura poisoning often comes up there in the native courts. He had suffered fairly often from hallucinations, with confusion of time and place. He denied strenuously that he suspected his wife of infidelity, but nevertheless I think that that was the motivating power. It seems that what actually occurred was that he went into the drawing-room, read the note his wife left saying she was leaving him, and that his way of eluding this fact was to prefer to "kill" her. Hence the hallucination.'

'You mean he cared for her very much?' asked Gwenda.

'Obviously, Mrs Reed.'

'And he never – recognized – that it was a hallucination?'

'He had to acknowledge that it *must* be – but his inner belief remained unshaken. The obsession was too strong to yield to reason. If we could have uncovered the underlying childish fixation –'

Gwenda interrupted. She was uninterested in childish fixations.

'But *you're* quite sure, you say, that he – that he didn't do it?'

'Oh, if that is what is worrying you, Mrs Reed, you can put it right out of your head. Kelvin Halliday, however jealous he may have been of his wife, was emphatically not a killer.'

Dr Penrose coughed and picked up a small shabby black book.

'If you would like this, Mrs Reed, you are the proper person to have it. It contains various jottings set down by your father during the time he was here. When we turned over his effects to his executor (actually a firm of solicitors), Dr McGuire, who was then Superintendent, retained this as part of the case history. Your father's case, you know, appears in Dr McGuire's book – only under initials, of course. Mr K.H. If you would like this diary –'

Gwenda stretched out her hand eagerly.

'Thank you,' she said. 'I should like it very much.'

In the train on the way back to London, Gwenda took out the shabby little black book and began to read.

She opened it at random.

Kelvin Halliday had written:

I suppose these doctor wallahs know their business . . . It all sounds such poppycock. Was I in love with my mother? Did I hate my father? I don't believe a word of it . . . I can't help feeling this is a simple police case – criminal court – not a crazy loony-bin matter. And yet – some of these people here – so natural, so reasonable – just like everyone else – except when you suddenly come across the kink. Very well, then, it seems that I, too, have a kink . . .

I've written to James . . . urged him to communicate with Helen . . . Let her come and see me in the flesh if she's alive . . . He says he doesn't know where she is . . . that's because he knows that she's dead and that I killed her . . . he's a good fellow, but I'm not deceived . . . Helen is dead . . .

When did I begin to suspect her? A long time ago . . . Soon after we came to Dillmouth . . . Her manner changed . . . She was concealing something . . . I used to watch her . . . Yes, and she used to watch me . . .

Did she give me drugs in my food? Those queer awful nightmares. Not ordinary dreams . . . living nightmares . . . I know it was drugs . . . Only she could have done that . . . Why? . . . There's some man . . . Some man she was afraid of . . .

Let me be honest. I suspected, didn't I, that she had a lover? There was someone – I know there was someone – she said as much to me on the boat . . . Someone she loved and couldn't marry . . . It was the same for both of us . . . I couldn't forget Megan . . . How like Megan little Gwennie looks sometimes. Helen played with Gwennie so sweetly on the boat . . . Helen . . . You are so lovely, Helen . . .

Is Helen alive? Or did I put my hands round her throat and choke the life out of her? I went through the dining-room door and I saw the note – propped up on the desk, and then – and then – all black – just blackness. But there's no doubt about it . . . I killed her . . . Thank God Gwennie's all right in New Zealand. They're good people. They'll love her for Megan's sake. Megan – Megan, how I wish you were here . . .

It's the best way . . . No scandal . . . The best way for the child. I can't go on. Not year after year. I must take the short way out. Gwennie will never know anything about all this. She'll never know her father was a murderer . . .

Tears blinded Gwenda's eyes. She looked across at Giles, sitting opposite her. But Giles's eyes were riveted on the opposite corner.

Aware of Gwenda's scrutiny, he motioned faintly with his head.

Their fellow passenger was reading an evening paper. On the outside of it, clearly presented to their view was a melodramatic caption: WHO WERE THE MEN IN HER LIFE?

Slowly, Gwenda nodded her head. She looked down at the diary.

There was someone – I know there was someone . . .

CHAPTER 11

The Men in Her Life

Miss Marple crossed Sea Parade and walked along Fore Street, turning up the hill by the Arcade. The shops here were the old-fashioned ones. A wool and art needlework shop, a confectioner, a Victorian-looking Ladies' Outfitter and Draper and others of the same kind.

Miss Marple looked in at the window of the art needlework shop. Two young assistants were engaged with customers, but an elderly woman at the back of the shop was free.

Miss Marple pushed open the door and went in. She seated herself at the counter and the assistant, a pleasant woman with grey hair, asked, 'What can I do for you, madam?'

Miss Marple wanted some pale blue wool to knit a baby's jacket. The proceedings were leisurely and unhurried. Patterns were discussed, Miss Marple looked through various children's knitting books and in the course of it discussed her great-nephews and nieces. Neither she nor the assistant displayed impatience. The assistant had attended to customers such as Miss Marple for many years. She preferred these gentle, gossipy, rambling old ladies to the impatient, rather impolite young mothers who didn't know what they wanted and had an eye for the cheap and showy.

'Yes,' said Miss Marple. 'I think that will be very nice indeed. And I always find Storkleg so reliable. It really doesn't shrink. I think I'll take an extra two ounces.'

The assistant remarked that the wind was very cold today, as she wrapped up the parcel.

'Yes, indeed, I noticed it as I was coming along the front. Dillmouth has changed a good deal. I have not been here for, let me see, nearly nineteen years.'

'Indeed, madam? Then you will find a lot of changes. The Superb wasn't built then, I suppose, nor the Southview Hotel?'

'Oh no, it was quite a small place. I was staying with friends . . . A house called St Catherine's – perhaps you know it? On the Leahampton road.'

But the assistant had only been in Dillmouth a matter of ten years.

Miss Marple thanked her, took the parcel, and went into the draper's next door. Here, again, she selected an elderly assistant. The conversation ran much on the same lines, to an accompaniment of summer vests. This time, the assistant responded promptly.

'That would be Mrs Findeyson's house.'

'Yes – yes. Though the friends I knew had it furnished. A Major Halliday and his wife and a baby girl.'

'Oh yes, madam. They had it for about a year, I think.'

'Yes. He was home from India. They had a very good cook – she gave me a wonderful recipe for baked apple pudding – and also, I think, for gingerbread. I often wonder what became of her.'

'I expect you mean Edith Pagett, madam. She's still in Dillmouth. She's in service now – at Windrush Lodge.'

'Then there were some other people – the Fanes. A lawyer, I think he was!'

'Old Mr Fane died some years ago – young Mr Fane, Mr Walter Fane, lives with his mother. Mr Walter Fane never married. He's the senior partner now.'

'Indeed? I had an idea Mr Walter Fane had gone out to India – tea-planting or something.'

'I believe he did, madam. As a young man. But he came home and went into the firm after about a year or two. They do all the best business round here – they're very highly thought of. A very nice quiet gentleman, Mr Walter Fane. Everybody likes him.'

'Why, of course,' exclaimed Miss Marple. 'He was engaged to Miss Kennedy, wasn't he? And then she broke it off and married Major Halliday.'

'That's right, madam. She went out to India to marry Mr Fane, but it seems as she changed her mind and married the other gentleman instead.'

A faintly disapproving note had entered the assistant's voice.

Miss Marple leaned forward and lowered her voice.

'I was always so sorry for poor Major Halliday (I knew his mother) and his little girl. I understand his second wife left him. Ran away with someone. A rather flighty type, I'm afraid.'

'Regular flibbertigibbet, she was. And her brother the doctor, such a nice man. Did my rheumatic knee a world of good.'

'Whom did she run away with? I never heard.'

'That I couldn't tell you, madam. Some said it was one of the summer visitors. But I know Major Halliday was quite broken up. He left the place and I believe his health gave way. Your change, madam.'

Miss Marple accepted her change and her parcel.

'Thank you so much,' she said. 'I wonder if – Edith Pagett, did you say – still has that nice recipe for gingerbread? I lost it – or rather my careless maid lost it – and I'm so fond of good gingerbread.'

'I expect so, madam. As a matter of fact her sister lives next door here, married to Mr Mountford, the confectioner. Edith usually comes there on her days out and I'm sure Mrs Mountford would give her a message.'

'That's a very good idea. Thank you *so much* for all the trouble you've taken.'

'A pleasure, madam, I assure you.'

Miss Marple went out into the street.

'A nice old-fashioned firm,' she said to herself. 'And those vests are really very nice, so it isn't as though I had wasted any money.' She glanced at the pale blue enamel watch that she wore pinned to one side of her dress. 'Just five minutes to go before meeting those two young things at the Ginger Cat. I hope they didn't find things too upsetting at the Sanatorium.'

II

Giles and Gwenda sat together at a corner table at the Ginger Cat. The little black notebook lay on the table between them.

Miss Marple came in from the street and joined them.

'What will you have, Miss Marple? Coffee?'

'Yes, thank you – no, not cakes, just a scone and butter.'

Giles gave the order, and Gwenda pushed the little black book across to Miss Marple.

'First you must read that,' she said, 'and then we can talk. It's what my father – what he wrote himself when he was at the nursing home. Oh, but first of all, just tell Miss Marple exactly what Dr Penrose said, Giles.'

Giles did so. Then Miss Marple opened the little black book and the waitress brought three cups of weak coffee, and a scone and butter, and a plate of cakes. Giles and Gwenda did not talk. They watched Miss Marple as she read.

Finally she closed the book and laid it down. Her expression was difficult to read. There was, Gwenda thought, anger in it. Her lips were pressed tightly together, and her eyes shone very brightly, unusually so, considering her age.

'Yes, indeed,' she said. 'Yes, indeed!'

Gwenda said: 'You advised us once – do you remember? – not to go on. I can see why you did. But we did go on – and this is where we've got to. Only now, it seems as though we'd got to another place where one could – if one liked – stop . . . Do you think we ought to stop? Or not?'

Miss Marple shook her head slowly. She seemed worried, perplexed.

'I don't know,' she said. 'I really don't know. It might be better to do so, much better to do so. Because after this lapse of time there is nothing that you can do – nothing, I mean, of a constructive nature.'

'You mean that after this lapse of time, there is nothing we can find out?' asked Giles.

'Oh no,' said Miss Marple. 'I didn't mean that *at all*. Nineteen years is not such a long time. There are people who would remember things, who could answer questions – quite a lot of people. Servants for instance. There must have been at least *two* servants in the house at the time, *and* a nurse, and probably a gardener. It will only take time and a little trouble to find and talk to these people. As a matter of fact, I've found *one* of them already. The cook. No, it wasn't that. It was more the question of what practical *good* you can accomplish, and I'd be inclined to say to that – None. And yet . . .'

She stopped: 'There *is* a yet . . . I'm a little slow in thinking things out, but I have a feeling that there is something – something, perhaps, not very tangible – that would be worth taking risks for – even that one *should* take risks for – but I find it difficult to say just what that is . . .'

Giles began: 'It seems to me –' and stopped.

Miss Marple turned to him gratefully.

'Gentlemen,' she said, 'always seem to be able to tabulate things so clearly. I'm sure you have thought things out.'

'I've been thinking things out,' said Giles. 'And it seems to me that there are just two conclusions one can come to. One is the same as I suggested before. Helen Halliday wasn't dead when Gwennie saw her lying in the hall. She came to, and went away with her lover, whoever he was. That would still fit the facts as we know them. It would square with Kelvin Halliday's rooted belief that he had killed his wife, and it would square with the missing suitcase and clothes and with the note that Dr Kennedy found. But it leaves certain points unaccounted for. It doesn't explain why Kelvin was convinced he strangled his wife in the *bedroom*. And it doesn't cover the one, to my mind, really staggering question – *where is Helen Halliday now?* Because it seems to me against all reason that Helen should never have been heard of or from again. Grant that the two letters she wrote are genuine, what happened *after* that? Why did she never write again? She was on affectionate terms with her brother, he's obviously deeply attached to her and always has been. He might disapprove of her conduct, but that doesn't mean that he expected never to hear from her again. And if you ask me, that point has obviously been worrying Kennedy himself. Let's say he accepted at the time absolutely the story he's told us. His sister's going off and Kelvin's breakdown. But he didn't expect never to hear from his sister again. I think, as the years went on, and he didn't hear, and Kelvin Halliday persisted in his delusion and finally committed suicide, that a terrible doubt began to creep up in his mind. Supposing that Kelvin's story was *true*? That he actually *had* killed Helen? There's no word from her – and surely if she

250

had died somewhere abroad, word would have come to him? I think that explains his eagerness when he saw our advertisement. He hoped that it might lead to some account of where she was or what she has been doing. I'm sure it's absolutely unnatural for someone to disappear as – as *completely* as Helen seems to have done. That, in itself, is highly suspicious.'

'I agree with you,' said Miss Marple. 'But the alternative, Mr Reed?'

Giles said slowly, 'I've been thinking out the alternative. It's pretty fantastic, you know, and even rather frightening. Because it involves – how can I put it – a kind of *malevolence* . . .'

'Yes,' said Gwenda. 'Malevolence is just right. Even, I think, something that isn't quite sane . . .' She shivered.

'That *is* indicated, I think,' said Miss Marple. 'You know, there's a great deal of – well, *queerness* about – more than people imagine. I have seen some of it . . .'

Her face was thoughtful.

'There can't be, you see, any *normal* explanation,' said Giles. 'I'm taking now the fantastic hypothesis that Kelvin Halliday *didn't* kill his wife, but genuinely *thought* he had done so. That's what Dr Penrose, who seems a decent sort of bloke, obviously wants to think. His first impression of Halliday was that here was a man who had killed his wife and wanted to give himself up to the police. Then he had to take Kennedy's word for it that that wasn't so, so he had perforce to believe that Halliday was a victim of a complex or a fixation of whatever the jargon is – but he didn't really *like* that solution. He's had a good experience of the type and Halliday didn't square with it. However, on knowing Halliday better he became quite genuinely sure that Halliday was not the type of man who would strangle a woman under any provocation. So he accepted the fixation theory, but with misgivings. And that really means that only one theory will fit the case – Halliday was induced to believe that he had killed his wife, *by someone else*. In other words, we've come to X.

'Going over the facts very carefully, I'd say that that hypothesis is at least *possible*. According to his own account, Halliday came into the house that evening, went into the dining-room, took a drink *as he usually did* – and then went into the next room, saw a note on the desk and had a blackout –'

Giles paused and Miss Marple nodded her head in approval. He went on:

'Say it wasn't a blackout – that it was just simply dope – knock-out drops in the whisky. The next step is quite clear, isn't it? X had strangled Helen in the hall, but afterwards he took her upstairs and arranged her artistically as a *crime passionel* on the bed, and that's where Kelvin is when he comes to; and the poor devil, who may have been suffering from jealousy where she's concerned, *thinks that he's done it*. What does he do next? Goes off to find his

251

brother-in-law – on the other side of the town and on foot. And this gives X time to do his next trick. Pack and remove a suitcase of clothes and also remove the body – though what he did with the body,' Giles ended vexedly, 'beats me completely.'

'It surprises me you should say that, Mr Reed,' said Miss Marple. 'I should say that that problem would present few difficulties. But do please go on.'

"WHO WERE THE MEN IN HER LIFE?" quoted Giles. 'I saw that in a newspaper as we came back in the train. It set me wondering, because that's really the crux of the matter, isn't it? If there *is* an X, as we believe, all we know about him is that he must have been crazy about her – literally crazy about her.'

'And so he hated my father,' said Gwenda. 'And he wanted him to suffer.'

'So that's where we come up against it,' said Giles. 'We know what kind of a girl Helen was –' he hesitated.

'Man mad,' supplied Gwenda.

Miss Marple looked up suddenly as though to speak, and then stopped.

'– and that she was beautiful. But we've no clue to what other men there were in her life besides her husband. There may have been any number.'

Miss Marple shook her head.

'Hardly that. She was quite young, you know. But you are not quite accurate, Mr Reed. We do know something about what you have termed "the men in her life". There was the man she was going out to marry –'

'Ah yes – the lawyer chap? What was his name?'

'Walter Fane,' said Miss Marple.

'Yes. But you can't count him. He was out in Malaya or India or somewhere.'

'But was he? He didn't remain a tea-planter, you know,' Miss Marple pointed out. 'He came back here and went into the firm, and is now the senior partner.'

Gwenda exclaimed: 'Perhaps he followed her back here?'

'He may have done. We don't know.'

Giles was looking curiously at the old lady.

'How did you find all this out?'

Miss Marple smiled apologetically.

'I've been gossiping a little. In shops – and waiting for buses. Old ladies are supposed to be inquisitive. Yes, one can pick up quite a lot of local news.'

'Walter Fane,' said Giles thoughtfully. 'Helen turned him down. That may have rankled quite a lot. Did he ever marry?'

'No,' said Miss Marple. 'He lives with his mother. I'm going to tea there at the end of the week.'

'There's someone else we know about, too,' said Gwenda suddenly. 'You remember there was somebody she got engaged to, or entangled with, when she left school – someone undesirable, Dr Kennedy said. I wonder just *why* he was undesirable . . .'

'That's two men,' said Giles. 'Either of them may have had a grudge, may have brooded . . . Perhaps the first young man may have had some unsatisfactory mental history.'

'Dr Kennedy could tell us that,' said Gwenda. 'Only it's going to be a little difficult asking him. I mean, it's all very well for me to go along and ask for news of my stepmother whom I barely remember. But it's going to take a bit of explaining if I want to know about her early love-affairs. It seems rather excessive interest in a stepmother you hardly knew.'

'There are probably other ways of finding out,' said Miss Marple. 'Oh yes, I think with time and patience, we can gather the information we want.'

'Anyway, we've got two possibilities,' said Giles.

'We might, I think, infer a third,' said Miss Marple. 'It would be, of course, a pure hypothesis, but justified, I think, by the turn of events.'

Gwenda and Giles looked at her in slight surprise.

'It is just an inference,' said Miss Marple, turning a little pink. 'Helen Kennedy went out to India to marry young Fane. Admittedly she was not wildly in love with him, but she must have been fond of him, and quite prepared to spend her life with him. Yet as soon as she gets there, she breaks off the engagement and wires her brother to send her money to get home. Now why?'

'Changed her mind, I suppose,' said Giles.

Both Miss Marple and Gwenda looked at him in mild contempt.

'Of course she changed her mind,' said Gwenda. 'We know that. What Miss Marple means is – why?'

'I suppose girls do change their minds,' said Giles vaguely.

'*Under certain circumstances,*' said Miss Marple.

Her words held all the pointed innuendo that elderly ladies are able to achieve with the minimum of actual statement.

'Something he did –' Giles was suggesting vaguely, when Gwenda chipped in sharply.

'Of course,' she said. 'Another man!'

She and Miss Marple looked at each other with the assurance of those admitted to a freemasonary from which men were excluded.

Gwenda added with certainty: 'On the boat! Going out!'

'Propinquity,' said Miss Marple.

'Moonlight on the boat deck,' said Gwenda. 'All that sort of thing. Only – it must have been serious – not just a flirtation.'

253

'Oh yes,' said Miss Marple, 'I think it was serious.'

'If so, why didn't she marry the chap?' demanded Giles.

'Perhaps he didn't really care for her,' Gwenda said slowly. Then shook her head. 'No, I think in that case she would still have married Walter Fane. Oh, of course, I'm being stupid. Married man.'

She looked triumphantly at Miss Marple.

'Exactly,' said Miss Marple. 'That's how I should reconstruct it. They fell in love, probably desperately in love. But if he was a married man – with children, perhaps – and probably an honourable type – well, that would be the end of it.'

'Only she couldn't go on and marry Walter Fane,' said Gwenda. 'So she wired her brother and went home. Yes, that all fits. And on the boat home, she met my father . . .'

She paused, thinking it out.

'Not wildly in love,' she said. 'But attracted . . . and then there was me. They were both unhappy . . . and they consoled each other. My father told her about my mother, and perhaps she told him about the other man . . . Yes – of course –' She flicked over the pages of the diary. '*I knew there was someone – she said as much to me on the boat – someone she loved and couldn't marry.* Yes – that's it. Helen and my father felt they were alike – and there was me to be looked after, and she thought she could make him happy – and she even thought, perhaps, that she'd be quite happy herself in the end.'

She stopped, nodded violently at Miss Marple, and said brightly: 'That's it.'

Giles was looking exasperated.

'Really, Gwenda, you make a whole lot of things up and pretend that they actually happened.'

'They did happen. They must have happened. And that gives us a third person for X.'

'You mean –?'

'The married man. We don't know what he was like. He mayn't have been nice at all. He may have been a little mad. He may have followed her here –'

'You've just placed him as going out to India.'

'Well, people can come back from India, can't they? Walter Fane did. It was nearly a year later. I don't say this man *did* come back, but I say he's a possibility. You keep harping on who the men were in her life. Well, we've got three of them. Walter Fane, and some young man whose name we don't know, and a married man –'

'Whom we don't know exists,' finished Giles.

'We'll find out,' said Gwenda. 'Won't we, Miss Marple?'

'With time and patience,' said Miss Marple, 'we may find out a great deal. Now for my contribution. As a result of a very fortunate little conversation in the draper's today, I have discovered that Edith Pagett who was cook at St Catherine's at the time we are interested in, is still in Dillmouth. Her sister is married to a confectioner here. I think it would be quite natural, Gwenda, for you to want to see her. She may be able to tell us a good deal.'

'That's wonderful,' said Gwenda. 'I've thought of something else,' she added. 'I'm going to make a new will. Don't look so grave, Giles, I shall still leave my money to you. But I shall get Walter Fane to do it for me.'

'Gwenda,' said Giles. 'Do be careful.'

'Making a will,' said Gwenda, 'is a most natural thing to do. And the line of approach I've thought up is quite good. Anyway, I want to see him. I want to see what he's like, and if I think that possibly –'

She left the sentence unfinished.

'What surprises me,' said Giles, 'is that no one else answered that advertisement of ours – this Edith Pagett, for example –'

Miss Marple shook her head.

'People take a long time to make up their minds about a thing like that in these country districts,' she said. 'They're suspicious. They like to think things over.'

255

CHAPTER 12

Lily Kimble

Lily Kimble spread a couple of old newspapers on the kitchen table in readiness for draining the chipped potatoes which were hissing in the pan. Humming tunelessly a popular melody of the day she leaned forward aimlessly studying the newsprint spread out before her.

Then suddenly she stopped humming and called: 'Jim – Jim. Listen here, will you?'

Jim Kimble, an elderly man of few words, was washing at the scullery sink. To answer his wife, he used his favourite monosyllable.

'Ar?' said Jim Kimble.

'It's a piece in the paper. Will anyone with any knowledge of Helen Spenlove Halliday, née Kennedy, communicate with Messrs Reed and Hardy, Southampton Row! Seems to me they might be meaning Mrs Halliday as I was in service with at St Catherine's. Took it from Mrs Findeyson, they did, she and 'er 'usband. *Her* name was Helen right enough – Yes, and she was sister to Dr Kennedy, him as always said I ought to have had my adenoids out.'

There was a momentary pause as Mrs Kimble adjusted the frying chips with an expert touch. Jim Kimble was snorting into the roller towel as he dried his face.

'Course, it's an old paper, this,' resumed Mrs Kimble. She studied its date. 'Nigh on a week or more old. Wonder what it's all about? Think as there's any money in it, Jim?'

Mr Kimble said, 'Ar,' noncommittally.

'Might be a will or something,' speculated his wife. 'Powerful lot of time ago.'

'Ar.'

'Eighteen years or more, I shouldn't wonder . . . Wonder what they're raking it all up for now? You don't think it could be *police*, do you, Jim?'

'Whatever?' asked Mr Kimble.

'Well, you know what I always thought,' said Mrs Kimble mysteriously. 'Told you at the time, I did, when we was walking out. Pretending that she'd gone off with a feller. That's what they say, husbands, when they do their wives in. Depend upon it, it was murder. That's what I said to you and what I said to Edie, but Edie she wouldn't have it at any price. Never no imagination, Edie hadn't. Those clothes she was supposed to have took away with her – well, they weren't right, if you know what I mean. There

256

was a suitcase gone and a bag, and enough clothes to fill 'em, but they wasn't right, those clothes. And that's when I said to Edie, "Depend up it," I said, "the master's murdered her and put her in the cellar." Only not really the cellar, because that Layonee, the Swiss nurse, she saw something. Out of the window. Come to the cinema along of me, she did, though she wasn't supposed to leave the nursery – but there, I said, the child never wakes up – good as gold she was, always, in her bed at night. "And madam never comes up to the nursery in the evening," I says. "Nobody will know if you slip out with me." So she did. And when we got in there was ever such a schemozzle going on. Doctor was there and the master ill and sleeping in the dressing-room, and the doctor looking after him, and it was then he asked me about the clothes, and it seemed all right at the time. I thought she'd gone off all right with that fellow she was so keen on – and him a married man, too – and Edie said she did hope and pray we wouldn't be mixed up in any divorce case. What was his name now? I can't remember. Began with an M – or was it an R? Bless us, your memory does go.'

Mr Kimble came in from the scullery and ignoring all matters of lesser moment demanded if his supper was ready.

'I'll just drain the chips . . . Wait, I'll get another paper. Better keep this one. 'Twouldn't be likely to be police – not after all this time. Maybe it's lawyers – and money in it. It doesn't *say* something to your advantage . . . but it might be all the same . . . Wish I knew who I could ask about it. It says write to some address in London – but I'm not sure I'd like to do a thing like that . . . not to a lot of people in London . . . What do you say, Jim?'

'Ar,' said Mr Kimble, hungrily eyeing the fish and chips.

The discussion was postponed.

257

CHAPTER 13

Walter Fane

Gwenda looked across the broad mahogany desk at Mr Walter Fane.

She saw a rather tired-looking man of about fifty, with a gentle, nondescript face. The sort of man, Gwenda thought, that you would find it a little difficult to recollect if you had just met him casually . . . A man who, in modern phrase, lacked personality. His voice, when he spoke, was slow and careful and pleasant. Probably, Gwenda decided, a very sound lawyer.

She stole a glance round the office – the office of the senior partner of the firm. It suited Walter Fane, she decided. It was definitely old-fashioned, the furniture was shabby, but was made of good solid Victorian material. There were deed boxes piled up against the walls – boxes with respectable County names on them. Sir John Vavasour-Trench. Lady Jessup. Arthur ffoulkes, Esq. Deceased.

The big sash windows, the panes of which were rather dirty, looked into a square backyard flanked by the solid walls of a seventeenth-century adjoining house. There was nothing smart or up to date anywhere, but there was nothing sordid either. It was superficially an untidy office with its piled-up boxes, and its littered desk, and its row of law books leaning crookedly on a shelf – but it was actually the office of someone who knew exactly where to lay his hand upon anything he wanted.

The scratching of Walter Fane's pen ceased. He smiled his slow, pleasant smile.

'I think that's all quite clear, Mrs Reed,' he said. 'A very simple will. When would you like to come in and sign it?'

Gwenda said whenever he liked. There was no particular hurry.

'We've got a house down here, you know,' she said. 'Hillside.'

Walter Fane said, glancing down at his notes, 'Yes, you gave me the address . . .'

There was no change in the even tenor of his voice.

'It's a very nice house,' said Gwenda. 'We love it.'

'Indeed?' Walter Fane smiled. 'Is it on the sea?'

'No,' said Gwenda. 'I believe the name has been changed. It used to be St Catherine's.'

Mr Fane took off his pince-nez. He polished them with a silk handkerchief, looking down at the desk.

'Oh yes,' he said. 'On the Leahampton road?'

He looked up and Gwenda thought how different people who habitually

258

wear glasses look without them. His eyes, a very pale grey, seemed strangely weak and unfocussed.

It makes his whole face look, thought Gwenda, as though he isn't really there.

Walter Fane put on the pince-nez again. He said in his precise lawyer's voice, 'I think you said you did make a will on the occasion of your marriage?'

'Yes. But I'd left things in it to various relatives in New Zealand who have died since, so I thought it would be simpler really to make a new one altogether – especially as we mean to live permanently in this country.'

Walter Fane nodded.

'Yes, quite a sound view to take. Well, I think this is all quite clear, Mrs Reed. Perhaps if you come in the day after tomorrow? Will eleven o'clock suit you?'

'Yes, that will be quite all right.'

Gwenda rose to her feet and Walter Fane rose also.

Gwenda said, with exactly the little rush she had rehearsed beforehand, 'I – I asked specially for you, because I think – I mean I believe – that you once knew my – my mother.'

'Indeed?' Walter Fane put a little additional social warmth into his manner. 'What was her name?'

'Halliday. Megan Halliday. I think – I've been told – that you were once engaged to her?'

A clock on the wall ticked. One, two, one two, one two.

Gwenda suddenly felt her heart beating a little faster. What a very *quiet* face Walter Fane had. You might see a house like that – a house with all the blinds pulled down. That would mean a house with a dead body in it. (What idiotic thoughts you do have, Gwenda!)

Walter Fane, his voice unchanged, unruffled, said 'No, I never knew your mother, Mrs Reed. But I was once engaged, for a short period, to Helen Kennedy who afterwards married Major Halliday as his second wife.'

'Oh, I see. How stupid of me. I've got it all wrong. It was Helen – my stepmother. Of course it's all long before I remember. I was only a child when my father's second marriage broke up. But I heard someone say that you'd once been engaged to Mrs Halliday in India – and I thought of course it was my own mother – because of India, I mean ... My father met her in India.'

'Helen Kennedy came out to India to marry me,' said Walter Fane. 'Then she changed her mind. On the boat going home she met your father.'

It was a plain unemotional statement of fact. Gwenda still had the impression of a house with the blinds down.

259

'I'm so sorry,' she said. 'Have I put my foot in it?'

Walter Fane smiled – his slow, pleasant smile. The blinds were up.

'It's nineteen or twenty years ago, Mrs Reed,' he said. 'One's youthful troubles and follies don't mean much after that space of time. So you are Halliday's baby daughter. You know, don't you, that your father and Helen actually lived here in Dillmouth for a while?'

'Oh yes,' said Gwenda, 'that's really why we came here. I didn't remember it properly, of course, but when we had to decide where we'd live in England, I came to Dillmouth first of all, to see what it was really like, and I thought it was such an attractive place that I decided that we'd park ourselves right here and nowhere else. And wasn't it luck? We've actually got the same house that my people lived in long ago.'

'I remember the house,' said Walter Fane. Again he gave that slow, pleasant smile. 'You may not remember me, Mrs Reed, but I rather imagine I used to give you piggybacks once.'

Gwenda laughed.

'Did you really? Then you're quite an old friend, aren't you? I can't pretend I remember you – but then I was only about two and a half or three, I suppose . . . Were you back on leave from India or something like that?'

'No, I'd chucked India for good. I went out to try tea-planting – but the life didn't suit me. I was cut out to follow in my father's footsteps and be a prosy unadventurous country solicitor. I'd passed all my law exams earlier, so I simply came back and went straight into the firm.' He paused and said, 'I've been here ever since.'

Again there was a pause and he repeated in a lower voice, 'Yes – ever since . . .'

But eighteen years, thought Gwenda, isn't really such a long time as all that . . .

Then, with a change of manner, he shook hands with her and said, 'Since we seem to be old friends, you really must bring your husband to tea with my mother one day. I'll get her to write to you. In the meanwhile, eleven o'clock on Thursday?'

Gwenda went out of the office and down the stairs. There was a cobweb in the angle of the stairway. In the middle of the web was a pale, rather nondescript spider. It didn't look, Gwenda thought, like a real spider. Not the fat juicy kind of spider who caught flies and ate them. It was more like a ghost of a spider. Rather like Walter Fane, in fact.

Giles met his wife on the seafront.

'Well?' he asked.

'He was here in Dillmouth at the time,' said Gwenda. 'Back from India, I mean. Because he gave me piggybacks. But he couldn't have murdered anyone – not possibly. He's much too quiet and gentle. Very nice, really, but the kind of person you never really notice. You know, they come to parties, but you never notice when they leave. I should think he was frightfully upright and all that, and devoted to his mother, and with a lot of virtues. But from a woman's point of view, terribly *dull*. I can see why he didn't cut any ice with Helen. You know, a nice safe person to marry – but you don't really want to.'

'Poor devil,' said Giles. 'And I suppose he was just crazy about her.'

'Oh, I don't know ... I shouldn't think so, really. Anyway, I'm sure he wouldn't be our malevolent murderer. He's not my idea of a murderer at all.'

'You don't really know a lot about murderers, though, do you, my sweet?'

'What do you mean?'

'Well – I was thinking about quiet Lizzie Borden – only the jury said she didn't do it. And Wallace, a quiet man whom the jury insisted did kill his wife, though the sentence was quashed on appeal. And Armstrong who everybody said for years was such a kind unassuming fellow. I don't believe murderers are ever a special type.'

'I really can't believe that Walter Fane –'

Gwenda stopped.

'What is it?'

'Nothing.'

But she was remembering Walter Fane polishing his eyeglasses and the queer blind stare of his eyes when she had first mentioned St Catherine's.

'Perhaps,' she said uncertainly, 'he *was* crazy about her ...'

CHAPTER 14

Edith Pagett

Mrs Mountford's back parlour was a comfortable room. It had a round table covered with a cloth, and some old-fashioned armchairs and a stern-looking but unexpectedly well-sprung sofa against the wall. There were china dogs and other ornaments on the mantelpiece, and a framed coloured representation of the Princess Elizabeth and Margaret Rose. On another wall was the King in Naval uniform, and a photograph of Mr Mountford in a group of other bakers and confectioners. There was a picture made with shells and a watercolour of a very green sea at Capri. There were a great many other things, none of them with any pretensions to beauty or the higher life; but the net result was a happy, cheerful room where people sat round and enjoyed themselves whenever there was time to do so.

Mrs Mountford, née Pagett, was short and round and dark-haired with a few grey streaks in the dark. Her sister, Edith Pagett, was tall and dark and thin. There was hardly any grey in her hair though she was at a guess round about fifty.

'Fancy now,' Edith Pagett was saying. 'Little Miss Gwennie. You must excuse me, m'am, speaking like that, but it does take one back. You used to come into my kitchen, as pretty as could be. "Winnies," you used to say. "Winnies." And what you meant was raisins – though why you called them winnies is more than I can say. But raisins was what you meant and raisins it was I used to give you, sultanas, that is, on account of the stones.'

Gwenda stared hard at the upright figure and the red cheeks and black eyes, trying to remember – to remember – but nothing came. Memory was an inconvenient thing.

'I wish I could remember –' she began.

'It's not likely that you would. Just a tiny little mite, that's all you were. Nowadays nobody seems to want to go in a house where there's children. I can't see it, myself. Children give life to a house, that's what I feel. Though nursery meals are always liable to cause a bit of trouble. But if you know what I mean, m'am, that's the nurse's fault, not the child's. Nurses are nearly always difficult – trays and waiting upon and one thing and another. Do you remember Layonee at all, Miss Gwennie? Excuse me, Mrs Reed, I should say.'

'Léonie? Was she my nurse?'

'Swiss girl, she was. Didn't speak English very well, and very sensitive in her feelings. Used to cry a lot if Lily said something to upset her. Lily was house-parlourmaid. Lily Abbott. A young girl and pert in her ways and a bit flighty. Many a game Lily used to have with you, Miss Gwennie. Play peep-bo through the stairs.'

Gwenda gave a quick uncontrollable shiver.

The stairs . . .

Then she said suddenly, 'I remember Lily. She put a bow on the cat.'

'There now, fancy you remembering that! On your birthday it was, and Lily she was all for it, Thomas must have a bow on. Took one off the chocolate box, and Thomas was mad about it. Ran off into the garden and rubbed through the bushes until he got it off. Cats don't like tricks being played on them.'

'A black and white cat.'

'That's right. Poor old Tommy. Caught mice something beautiful. A real proper mouser.' Edith Pagett paused and coughed primly. 'Excuse me running on like this, m'am. But talking brings the old days back. You wanted to ask me something?'

'I like hearing you talk about the old days,' said Gwenda. 'That's just what I want to hear about. You see, I was brought up by relations in New Zealand and of course they could never tell me anything about – about my father, and my stepmother. She – she was nice, wasn't she?'

'Very fond of you, she was. On yes, she used to take you down to the beach and play with you in the garden. She was quite young herself, you understand. Nothing but a girl, really. I often used to think she enjoyed the games as much as you did. You see she'd been an only child, in a manner of speaking. Dr Kennedy, her brother, was years and years older and always shut up with his books. When she wasn't away at school, she had to play by herself . . .'

Miss Marple, sitting back against the wall, asked gently, 'You've lived in Dillmouth all your life, haven't you?'

'Oh yes, madam. Father had the farm up behind the hill – Rylands it was always called. He'd no sons, and Mother couldn't carry on after he died, so she sold it and bought the little fancy shop at the end of the High Street. Yes, I've lived here all my life.'

'And I suppose you know all about everyone in Dillmouth?'

'Well, of course it used to be a small place, then. Though there used always to be a lot of summer visitors as long as I can remember. But nice quiet people who came here every year, not these trippers and charabancs we have nowadays. Good families they were, who'd come back to the same rooms year after year.'

'I suppose,' said Giles, 'that you knew Helen Kennedy before she was Mrs Halliday?'

'Well, I knew *of* her, so to speak, and I may have seen her about. But I didn't know her proper until I went into service there.'

'And you liked her,' said Miss Marple.

Edith Pagett turned towards her.

'Yes, madam, I did,' she said. There was a trace of defiance in her manner. 'No matter what anybody says. She was as nice as could be to me always. I'd never have believed she'd do what she did do. Took my breath away, it did. Although, mind you, there *had* been talk –'

She stopped rather abruptly and gave a quick apologetic glance at Gwenda.

Gwenda spoke impulsively.

'I want to know,' she said. 'Please don't think I shall mind anything you say. She wasn't my own mother –'

'That's true enough, m'am.'

'And you see, we are very anxious to – to find her. She went away from here – and she seems to have been quite lost sight of. We don't know where she is living now, or even if she is alive. And there are reasons –'

She hesitated and Giles said quickly, 'Legal reasons. We don't know whether to presume death or – or what.'

'Oh, I quite understand, sir. My cousin's husband was missing – after Ypres it was – and there was a lot of trouble about presuming death and that. Real vexing it was for her. Naturally, sir, if there is anything I can tell you that will help in any way – it isn't as if you were strangers. Miss Gwenda and her "winnies". So funny you used to say it.'

'That's very kind of you,' said Giles. 'So, if you don't mind, I'll just fire away. Mrs Halliday left home quite suddenly, I understand?'

'Yes, sir, it was a great shock to all of us – and especially to the Major, poor man. He collapsed completely.'

'I'm going to ask you right out – have you any idea who the man was she went away with?'

Edith Pagett shook her head.

'That's what Dr Kennedy asked me – and I couldn't tell him. Lily couldn't either. And of course that Layonee, being a foreigner, didn't know a thing about it.'

'You didn't *know*,' said Giles. 'But could you make a guess? Now that it's all so long ago, it wouldn't matter – even if the guess is all wrong. You must, surely, have had some suspicion.'

'Well, we had our suspicions ... but mind you, it wasn't more than suspicions. And as far as I'm concerned, I never saw anything at all. But Lily who, as I told you, was a sharp kind of girl, Lily had her ideas – had had them for a long time. "Mark my words," she used to say. "That chap's sweet

264

on her. Only got to see him looking at her as she pours out the tea. And does his wife look daggers!" '

'I see. And who was the – er – chap?'

'Now I'm afraid, sir, I just don't remember his name. Not after all these years. A Captain – Esdale – no, that wasn't it – Emery – no. I have a kind of feeling it began with an E. Or it might have been H. Rather an unusual kind of name. But I've never even thought of it for sixteen years. He and his wife were staying at the Royal Clarence.'

'Summer visitors?'

'Yes, but I think that he – or maybe both of them – had known Mrs Halliday before. They came to the house quite often. Anyway, according to Lily he was sweet on Mrs Halliday.'

'And his wife didn't like it.'

'No, sir . . . But mind you, I never believed for a moment that there was anything wrong about it. And I still don't know what to think.'

Gwenda asked, 'Were they still here – at the Royal Clarence – when – when Helen – my stepmother went away?'

'As far as I recollect they went away just about the same time, a day earlier or a day later – anyway, it was close enough to make people talk. But I never heard anything definite. It was all kept very quiet if it *was* so. Quite a nine days' wonder Mrs Halliday going off like that, so sudden. But people did say she'd always been flighty – not that I ever saw anything of the kind myself. I wouldn't have been willing to go to Norfolk with them if I'd thought that.'

For a moment three people stared at her intently. Then Giles said 'Norfolk? Were they going to Norfolk?'

'Yes, sir. They'd bought a house there. Mrs Halliday told me about three weeks before – before all this happened. She asked me if I'd come with them when they moved, and I said I would. After all, I'd never been away from Dillmouth, and I thought perhaps I'd like a change – seeing as I liked the family.'

'I never heard they had bought a house in Norfolk,' said Giles.

'Well, it's funny you should say that, sir, because Mrs Halliday seemed to want it kept very quiet. She asked me not to speak about it to anyone at all – so of course I didn't. But she'd been wanting to go away from Dillmouth for some time. She'd been pressing Major Halliday to go, but he liked it at Dillmouth. I even believe he wrote to Mrs Findeyson whom St Catherine's belonged to, asking if she'd consider selling it. But Mrs Halliday was dead against it. She seemed to have turned right against Dillmouth. It's almost as though she was afraid to stop there.'

The words came out quite naturally, yet at the sound of them the three people listening again stiffened to attention.

Giles said, 'You don't think she wanted to go to Norfolk to be near this – the man whose name you can't remember?'

Edith Pagett looked distressed.

'Oh indeed, sir, I wouldn't like to think *that*. And I don't think it, not for a moment. Besides I don't think that – I remember now – they came from up North somewhere, that lady and gentleman did. Northumberland, I think it was. Anyway, they liked coming south for a holiday because it was so mild down here.'

Gwenda said: 'She was afraid of something, wasn't she? Or of someone? My stepmother, I mean.'

'I do remember – now that you say that –'

'Yes?'

'Lily came into the kitchen one day. She'd been dusting the stairs, and she said, "Ructions!" she said. She had a very common way of talking sometimes, Lily had, so you must excuse me.

'So I asked her what she meant and she said that the missus had come in from the garden with the master into the drawing-room and the door to the hall being open, Lily heard what they said.

' "*I'm afraid of you*," that's what Mrs Halliday had said.

' "And she sounded scared too," Lily said. "*I've been afraid of you for a long time. You're mad. You're not normal. Go away and leave me alone. You* must *leave me alone. I'm frightened. I think, underneath, I've always been frightened of you ...*"

'Something of that kind – of course I can't say now to the exact words. But Lily, she took it very seriously, and that's why, after it all happened, she –'

Edith Pagett stopped dead. A curious frightened look came over her face.

'I didn't mean, I'm sure –' she began. 'Excuse me, madam, my tongue runs away with me.'

Giles said gently: 'Please tell us, Edith. It's really important, you see, that we should know. It's all a long time ago now, but we've got to *know*.'

'I couldn't say, I'm sure,' said Edith helplessly.

Miss Marple asked: 'What was it Lily didn't believe – or did believe?'

Edith Pagett said apologetically: 'Lily was always one to get ideas in her head. I never took no notice of them. She was always one for going to the pictures and she got a lot of silly melodramatic ideas that way. She was out at the pictures the night it happened – and what's more she took Layonee with her – and very wrong *that* was, and I told her so. "Oh, that's all right," she said. "It's not leaving the child alone in the house. You're down in the kitchen and the master and the missus will be in later and anyway that child never wakes once she's off to sleep." But it was wrong, and I told her so,

266

though of course I never knew about Layonee going till afterwards. If I had, I'd have run up to see she – you, I mean, Miss Gwenda – were quite all right. You can't hear a thing from the kitchen when the baize door's shut.'

Edith Pagett paused and then went on: 'I was doing some ironing. The evening passed ever so quick and the first thing I knew Dr Kennedy came out in the kitchen and asked me where Lily was and I said it was her night off but she'd be in any minute now and sure enough she came in that very minute and he took her upstairs to the mistress's room. Wanted to know if she'd taken any clothes away with her, and what. So Lily looked about and told him and then she come down to me. All agog she was. "She's hooked it," she said. "Gone off with someone. The master's all in. Had a stroke or something. Apparently it's been a terrible shock to him. More fool he. He ought to have seen it coming." "You shouldn't speak like that," I said. "How do you know she's gone off with anybody? Maybe she had a telegram from a sick relation." "Sick relation my foot," Lily says (always a common way of speaking, as I said). "She left a note." "Who's she gone off with?" I said. "Who do you think?" Lily said. "Not likely to be Mr Sobersides Fane, for all his sheep's eyes and the way he follows her round like a dog." So I said, "You think it's Captain – whatever his name was." And she said, "He's my bet. Unless it's our mystery man in the flashy car." (That's just a silly joke we had.) And I said, "I don't believe it. Not Mrs Halliday. She wouldn't do a thing like that." And Lily says, "Well, it seems she's done it."

'All this was at first, you understand. But later on, up in our bedroom, Lily woke me up. "Look here," she says. "It's all wrong." "What's wrong?" I said. And she said, "Those clothes." "Whatever are you talking about?" I said. "Listen, Edie," she said. "I went through her clothes because the doctor asked me to. And there's a suitcase gone and enough to fill it – but they're the *wrong* things." "What do you mean?" I said. And Lily said, "She took an evening dress, her grey and silver – but she didn't take her evening belt and brassière, nor the slip that goes with it, and she took her gold brocade evening shoes, not the silver strap ones. And she took her green tweed – which she never wears until late on in the autumn, but she didn't take that fancy pullover and she took her lace blouses that she only wears with a town suit. Oh and her undies, too, they were a job lot. You mark my words, Edie," Lily said. "She's not gone away at all. The master's done her in."

'Well, that made me wide awake. I sat right up and asked her what on earth she was talking about.

' "Just like it was in the *News of the World* last week," Lily says. "The master found she'd been carrying on and he killed her and put her down in the cellar and buried her under the floor. *You'd* never hear anything because it's under the front hall. That's what he's done, and then he packed a suitcase to make it look as though she'd gone away. But that's where she is – under the cellar floor. *She never left this house alive.*" I gave her a piece of my mind then, saying such awful things. But I'll admit I slipped down to the cellar the next morning. But there, it was all just as usual and nothing disturbed and no digging been done – and I went and told Lily she'd just been making a fool of herself, but she stuck to it as the master had done her in. "Remember," she says, "she was scared to death of him. I heard her telling him so." "And that's just where you're wrong, my girl," I said, "because it wasn't the master at all. Just after you'd told me, that day, I looked out of the window and there was the master coming down the hill with his golf-clubs, so it couldn't have been him who was with the mistress in the drawing-room. It was someone else." '

The words echoed lingeringly in the comfortable common-place sitting-room.

Giles said softly under his breath, '*It was someone else ...*'

268

CHAPTER 15

An Address

The Royal Clarence was the oldest hotel in the town. It had a mellow bow-fronted façade and an old-world atmosphere. It still catered for the type of family who came for a month to the seaside.

Miss Narracott who presided behind the reception desk was a full-bosomed lady of forty-seven with an old-fashioned style of hairdressing.

She unbent to Giles whom her accurate eyes summed up as 'one of our nice people'. And Giles, who had a ready tongue and a persuasive way with him when he liked, spun a very good tale. He had a bet on with his wife – about her godmother – and whether she had stayed at the Royal Clarence eighteen years ago. His wife had said that they could never settle the dispute because of course all the old registers would be thrown away by this time, but he had said Nonsense. An establishment like the Royal Clarence would keep its registers. They must go back for a hundred years.

'Well, not quite that, Mr Reed. But we do keep all our old Visitors' Books as we prefer to call them. Very interesting names in them, too. Why, the King stayed here once when he was Prince of Wales, and Princess Adlemar of Holstein-Rotz used to come every winter with her lady-in-waiting. And we've had some very famous novelists, too, and Mr Dovey, the portrait-painter.'

Giles responded in suitable fashion with interest and respect and in due course the sacred volume for the year in question was brought out and exhibited to him.

Having first had various illustrious names pointed out to him, he turned the pages to the month of August.

Yes, here surely was the entry he was seeking.

Major and Mrs Setoun Erskine, Anstell Manor, Daith, Northumberland, July 27th – August 17th.

'If I may copy this out?'

'Of course, Mr Reed. Paper and ink – Oh, you have your pen. Excuse me, I must just go back to the outer office.'

She left him with the open book, and Giles set to work.

On his return to Hillside he found Gwenda in the garden, bending over the herbaceous border.

She straightened herself and gave him a quick glance of interrogation.

'Any luck?'

'Yes, I think this must be it.'

Gwenda said softly, reading the words: 'Anstell Manor, Daith, Northumberland. Yes, Edith Pagett said Northumberland. I wonder if they're still living there –'

'We'll have to go and see.'

'Yes – yes, it would be better to go – when?'

'As soon as possible. Tomorrow? We'll take the car and drive up. It will show you a little more of England.'

'Suppose they're dead – or gone away and somebody else is living there?' Giles shrugged his shoulders.

'Then we come back and go on with our other leads. I've written to Kennedy, by the way, and asked him if he'll send me those letters Helen wrote after she went away – if he's still got them – *and* a specimen of her handwriting.'

'I wish,' said Gwenda, 'that we could get in touch with the other servant – with Lily – the one who put the bow on Thomas –'

'Funny your suddenly remembering that, Gwenda.'

'Yes, wasn't it? I remember Tommy, too. He was black with white patches and he had three lovely kittens.'

'What? Thomas?'

'Well, he was called Thomas – but actually he turned out to be Thomasina. You know what cats are. But about Lily – I wonder what's become of her? Edith Pagett seems to have lost sight of her entirely. She didn't come from round here – and after the break-up at St Catherine's she took a place in Torquay. She wrote once or twice but that was all. Edith said she'd heard she'd got married but she didn't know who to. If we could get hold of her we might learn a lot more.'

'And from Léonie, the Swiss girl.'

'Perhaps – but she was a foreigner and wouldn't catch on to much of what went on. You know, I don't remember her at all. No, it's Lily I feel would be useful. Lily was the sharp one ... I know, Giles, let's put in another advertisement – an advertisement for her – Lily Abbott, her name was.'

'Yes,' said Giles, 'We might try that. And we'll definitely go north tomorrow and see what we can find out about the Erskines.'

CHAPTER 16

Mother's Son

'Down, Henry,' said Mrs Fane to an asthmatic spaniel whose liquid eyes burned with greed. 'Another scone, Miss Marple, while they're hot?'

'Thank you. Such delicious scones. You have an excellent cook.'

'Louisa is not bad, really. Forgetful, like all of them. And no variety in her puddings. Tell me, how is Dorothy Yarde's sciatica nowadays? She used to be a martyr to it. Largely nerves, I suspect.'

Miss Marple hastened to oblige with details of their mutual acquaintance's ailments. It was fortunate, she thought, that amongst her many friends and relations, scattered over England, she had managed to find a woman who knew Mrs Fane and who had written explaining that a Miss Marple was at present in Dillmouth and would dear Eleanor be very kind and ask her to something.

Eleanor Fane was a tall, commanding woman with a steely grey eye, crisp white hair, and a baby pink and white complexion which masked the fact that there was no baby-like softness whatever about her.

They discussed Dorothy's ailments or imagined ailments and went on to Miss Marple's health, the air of Dillmouth, and the general poor condition of most of the younger generation.

'Not made to eat their crusts as children,' Mrs Fane pronounced. 'None of that allowed in *my* nursery.'

'You have more than one son?' asked Miss Marple.

'Three. The eldest, Gerald, is in Singapore, in the Far East Bank. Robert is in the Army.' Mrs Fane sniffed. 'Married a Roman Catholic,' she said with significance. 'You know what *that* means! All the children brought up as Catholics. What Robert's father would have said, I don't know. My husband was very low church. I hardly ever hear from Robert nowadays. He takes exception to some of the things I have said to him purely for his own good. I believe in being sincere and saying exactly what one thinks. His marriage was, in my opinion, a great misfortune. He may *pretend* to be happy, poor boy – but I can't feel that it is at all satisfactory.'

'Your youngest son is not married, I believe?'

Mrs Fane beamed.

'No, Walter lives at home. He is slightly delicate – always was from a child – and I have always had to look after his health very carefully. (He will be in presently.) I can't tell you what a thoughtful and devoted son he is. I am really a very lucky woman to have such a son.'

271

'And he has never thought of marrying?' enquired Miss Marple.

'Walter always says he really cannot be bothered with the modern young woman. They don't appeal to him. He and I have so much in common that I'm afraid he doesn't go out as much as he should. He reads Thackeray to me in the evenings, and we usually have a game of picquet. Walter is a real home bird.'

'How very nice,' said Miss Marple. 'Has he always been in the firm? Somebody told me that you had a son who was out in Ceylon, as a tea-planter, but perhaps they got it wrong.'

A slight frown came over Mrs Fane's face. She urged walnut cake upon her guest and explained.

'That was as a very young man. One of those youthful impulses. A boy always longs to see the world. Actually, there was a girl at the bottom of it. Girls can be *so* unsettling.'

'Oh yes, indeed. My own nephew, I remember –'

Mrs Fane swept on, ignoring Miss Marple's nephew. She held the floor and was enjoying the opportunity to reminisce to this sympathetic friend of dear Dorothy's.

'A *most* unsuitable girl – as seems always to be the way. Oh, I don't mean an *actress* or anything like that. The local doctor's sister – more like his daughter, really, years younger – and the poor man with no idea how to bring her up. Men are so helpless, aren't they? She ran quite wild, entangled herself first with a young man in the office – a mere clerk – and a very unsatisfactory character, too. They had to get rid of him. Repeated confidential information. Anyway, this girl, Helen Kennedy, was, I suppose, very pretty. *I* didn't think so. I always thought her hair was touched up. But Walter, poor boy, fell very much in love with her. As I say, quite unsuitable, no money and no prospects, and not the kind of girl one wanted as a daughter-in-law. Still, what can a mother do? Walter proposed to her and she refused him, and then he got this silly idea into his head of going out to India and being a tea-planter. My husband said, "Let him go," though of course he was very disappointed. He had been looking forward to having Walter with him in the firm and Walter had passed all his law exams and everything. Still, there it was. Really, the havoc these young women cause!'

'Oh, I know. My nephew –'

Once again Mrs Fane swept over Miss Marple's nephew.

'So the dear boy went out to Assam or was it Bangalore – really I can't remember after all these years. And I felt most upset because I knew his health wouldn't stand it. And he hadn't been out there a year (doing very well, too. Walter does everything well) than – would you believe it? – this impudent chit of a girl changes her mind and writes out that she'd like to marry him after all.'

'Dear, dear.' Miss Marple shook her head.

'Gets together her trousseau, books her passage – and what do you think the next move is?'

'I can't imagine.' Miss Marple leaned forward in rapt attention.

'Has a love-affair with a married man, if you please. On the boat going out. A married man with three children, I believe. Anyway there is Walter on the quay to meet her and the first thing she does is to say she can't marry him after all. Don't you call that a wicked thing to do?'

'Oh, I do indeed. It might have completely destroyed your son's faith in human nature.'

'It should have shown her to him in her true colours. But there, that type of woman gets away with anything.'

'He didn't –' Miss Marple hesitated – *'resent* her action? Some men would have been terribly angry.'

'Walter has always had wonderful self-control. However upset and annoyed Walter may be over anything, he never shows it.'

Miss Marple peered at her speculatively. Hesitantly, she put out a feeler.

'That is because it goes really deep, perhaps? One is really astonished sometimes, with children. A sudden outburst from some child that one has thought didn't care at all. A sensitive nature that can't express itself until it's driven absolutely beyond endurance.'

'Ah, it's very curious you should say that, Miss Marple. I remember so well. Gerald and Robert, you know, both hot-tempered and always apt to *fight*. Quite natural, of course, for healthy boys –'

'Oh, quite natural.'

'And dear Walter, always so quiet and patient. And then, one day, Robert got hold of his model aeroplane – he'd built it up himself with days of work – so patient and clever with his fingers – and Robert, who was a dear high-spirited boy but careless, smashed it. And when I came into the schoolroom there was Robert down on the floor and Walter attacking him with the poker, he'd practically knocked him out – and I simply had all I could do to drag Walter off him. He kept repeating, "He did it on purpose – he did it on purpose. I'm going to kill him." You know, I was quite frightened. Boys feel things so intensely, do they not?'

'Yes, indeed,' said Miss Marple. Her eyes were thoughtful.

She reverted to the former topic.

'And so the engagement was finally broken off. What happened to the girl?'

'She came home. Had another love-affair on the way back, and this time

273

married the man. A widower with one child. A man who has just lost his wife is always a fair target – helpless, poor fellow. She married him and they settled down here in a house the other side of the town – St Catherine's – next door to the hospital. It didn't last, of course – she left him within the year. Went off with some man or other.'

'Dear, dear!' Miss Marple shook her head. 'What a lucky escape your son had!'

'That's what I always tell him.'

'And did he give up tea-planting because his health wouldn't stand it?' A slight frown appeared on Mrs Fane's brow.

'The life wasn't really congenial to him,' she said. 'He came home about six months after the girl did.'

'It must have been rather awkward,' ventured Miss Marple. 'If the young woman was actually living here. In the same town –'

'Walter was wonderful,' said Walter's mother. 'He behaved exactly as though nothing had happened. I should have thought myself (indeed I said so at the time) that it would be advisable to make a clean break – after all, meetings could only be awkward for both parties. But Walter insisted on going out of his way to be friendly. He used to call at the house in the most informal fashion, and play with the child – Rather curious, by the way, the child's come back here. She's grown up now, with a husband. Came into Walter's office to make her will the other day. Reed, that's her name now. Reed.'

'Mr and Mrs Reed! I know them. Such a nice unaffected young couple. Fancy that now – and she is actually the child –'

'The first wife's child. The first wife died out in India. Poor Major – I've forgotten his name – Hallway – something like that – was completely broken up when that minx left him. Why the worst women should always attract the best men is something hard to fathom!'

'And the young man who was originally entangled with her? A clerk, I think you said, in your son's office. What happened to him?'

'Did very well for himself. He runs a lot of those Coach Tours. Daffodil Coaches. Afflick's Daffodil Coaches. Painted bright yellow. It's a vulgar world nowadays.'

'Afflick?' said Miss Marple.

'Jackie Afflick. A nasty pushing fellow. Always determined to get on, I imagine. Probably why he took up with Helen Kennedy in the first place. Doctor's daughter and all that – thought it would better his social position.'

'And this Helen has never come back again to Dillmouth?'

'No. Good riddance. Probably gone completely to the bad by now. I was sorry for Dr Kennedy. Not his fault. His father's second wife was a fluffy

274

little thing, years younger than he was. Helen inherited her wild blood from her, I expect. I've always thought –'

Mrs Fane broke off.

'Here is Walter.' Her mother's ear had distinguished certain well-known sounds in the hall. The door opened and Walter Fane came in.

'This is Miss Marple, my son. Ring the bell, son, and we'll have some fresh tea.'

'Don't bother, Mother. I had a cup.'

'Of course we will have fresh tea – and some scones, Beatrice,' she added to the parlourmaid who had appeared to take the teapot.

'Yes, madam.'

With a slow, likeable smile Walter Fane said: 'My mother spoils me, I'm afraid.'

Miss Marple studied him as she made a polite rejoinder.

A gentle quiet-looking person, slightly diffident and apologetic in manner – colourless. A very nondescript personality. The devoted type of young man whom women ignore and only marry because the man they love does not return their affection. Walter, who is Always There. Poor Walter, his mother's darling ... Little Walter Fane who had attacked his older brother with a poker and had tried to kill him ...

Miss Marple wondered.

CHAPTER 17

Richard Erskine

Anstell Manor had a bleak aspect. It was a white house, set against a background of bleak hills. A winding drive led up through dense shrubbery.

Giles said to Gwenda, 'Why have we come? What can we possibly say?'

'We've got it worked out.'

'Yes – so far as that goes. It's lucky that Miss Marple's cousin's aunt's brother-in-law or whatever it was lives near hear . . . But it's a far step from a social call to asking your host about his bygone love-affairs.'

'And such a long time ago. Perhaps – perhaps he doesn't even remember her.'

'Perhaps he doesn't. And perhaps there never was a love-affair.'

'Giles, are we making unutterable fools of ourselves?'

'I don't know . . . Sometimes I feel that. I don't see why we're concerning ourselves with all this. What does it matter now?'

'So long after . . . Yes, I know . . . Miss Marple and Dr Kennedy both said, "Leave it alone." Why don't we, Giles? What makes us go on? Is it *her*?'

'Her?'

'Helen, Is that why I remember? Is my childish memory the only link she's got with life – with truth? Is it Helen who's using me – and you – so that the truth will be known?'

'You mean, because she died a violent death –?'

'Yes. They say – books say – that sometimes they can't rest . . .'

'I think you're being fanciful, Gwenda.'

'Perhaps I am. Anyway, we can – choose. This is only a social call. There's no need for it to be anything more – unless we want it to be –'

Giles shook his head.

'We shall go on. We can't help ourselves.'

'Yes – you're right. All the same, Giles, I think I'm rather frightened –'

II

'Looking for a house, are you?' said Major Erskine.

He offered Gwenda a plate of sandwiches. Gwenda took one, looking up at him. Richard Erskine was a small man, five foot nine or so. His hair was grey and he had tired, rather thoughtful eyes. His voice was low and pleasant with a slight drawl. There was nothing remarkable about him, but he was, Gwenda thought, definitely attractive ... He was actually not nearly as good-looking as Walter Fane, but whereas most women would pass Fane without a second glance, they would not pass Erskine. Fane was nondescript. Erskine, in spite of his quietness, had personality. He talked of ordinary things in an ordinary manner, but there was *something* – that something that women are quick to recognize and to which they react in a purely female way. Almost unconsciously Gwenda adjusted her skirt, tweaked at a side curl, retouched her lips. Nineteen years ago Helen Kennedy could have fallen in love with this man. Gwenda was quite sure of that.

She looked up to find her hostess's eyes full upon her, and involuntarily she flushed. Mrs Erskine was talking to Giles, but she was watching Gwenda and her glance was both appraising and suspicious. Janet Erskine was a tall woman, her voice was deep – almost as deep as a man's. Her build was athletic, she wore a well-cut tweed with big pockets. She looked older than her husband, but, Gwenda decided, well might not be so. There was a certain haggardness about her face. An unhappy, hungry woman, thought Gwenda.

I bet she gives him Hell, she said to herself.

Aloud she continued the conversation.

'House-hunting is terribly discouraging,' she said. 'House agents' descriptions are always glowing – and then, when you actually get there, the place is quite unspeakable.'

'You're thinking of settling down in this neighbourhood?'

'Well – this is one of the neighbourhoods we thought of. Really because it's near Hadrian's Wall. Giles has always been fascinated by Hadrian's Wall. You see – it sounds rather odd, I expect, to you – but almost anywhere in England is the same to us. My own home is in New Zealand and I haven't any ties here. And Giles was taken in by different aunts for different holidays and so hasn't any particular ties either. The one thing we don't want is to be too near London. We want the real country.'

Erskine smiled.

'You'll certainly find it real country all round here. It's completely isolated. Our neighbours are few and far between.'

Gwenda thought she detected an undercurrent of bleakness in the pleasant voice. She had a sudden glimpse of a lonely life – of short dark winter days with the wind whistling in the chimneys – the curtains drawn – shut in – shut in with that woman with the hungry, unhappy eyes – and neighbours few and far between.

Then the vision faded. It was summer again, with the french windows open to the garden – with the scent of roses and the sounds of summer drifting in.

She said: 'This is an old house, isn't it?'

Erskine nodded.

'Queen Anne. My people have lived here for nearly three hundred years.'

'It's a lovely house. You must be very proud of it.'

'It's rather a shabby house now. Taxation makes it difficult to keep anything up properly. However, now the children are out in the world, the worst strain is over.'

'How many children have you?'

'Two boys. One's in the Army. The other's just come down from Oxford. He's going into a publishing firm.'

His glance went to the mantelpiece and Gwenda's eyes followed his. There was a photograph there of two boys – presumably about eighteen and nineteen, taken a few years ago, she judged. There was pride and affection in his expression.

'They're good lads,' he said, 'though I say it myself.'

'They look awfully nice,' said Gwenda.

'Yes,' said Erskine. 'I think it's worth it – really. Making sacrifices for one's children, I mean,' he added in answer to Gwenda's enquiring look.

'I suppose – often – one has to give up a good deal,' said Gwenda.

'A great deal sometimes . . .'

Again she caught a dark undercurrent, but Mrs Erskine broke in, saying in her deep authoritative voice, 'And you are really looking for a house in this part of the world? I'm afraid I don't know of anything at all suitable round here.'

And wouldn't tell me if you did, thought Gwenda, with a faint spurt of mischief. That foolish old woman is actually jealous, she thought. Jealous because I'm talking to her husband and because I'm young and attractive!

'It depends how much of a hurry you're in,' said Erskine.

'No hurry at all really,' said Giles cheerfully. 'We want to be sure of finding something we really like. At the moment we've got a house in Dillmouth – on the south coast.'

Major Erskine turned away from the tea-table. He went to get a cigarette box from a table by the window.

'Dillmouth,' said Mrs Erskine. Her voice was expressionless. Her eyes watched the back of her husband's head.

'Pretty little place,' said Giles. 'Do you know it at all?'

There was a moment's silence, then Mrs Erskine said in that same expressionless voice, 'We spent a few weeks there one summer – many, many years ago. We didn't care for it – found it too relaxing.'

'Yes,' said Gwenda. 'That's just what we find. Giles and I feel we'd prefer more bracing air.'

Erskine came back with the cigarettes. He offered the box to Gwenda.

'You'll find it bracing enough round here,' he said. There was a certain grimness in his voice.

Gwenda looked up at him as he lighted her cigarette for her.

'Do you remember Dillmouth at all well?' she asked artlessly.

His lips twitched in what she guessed to be a sudden spasm of pain. In a noncommittal voice he answered, 'Quite well, I think. We stayed – let me see – at the Royal George – no, Royal Clarence Hotel.'

'Oh yes, that's the nice old-fashioned one. Our house is quite near there. Hillside it's called, but it used to be called St – St – Mary's, was it, Giles?'

'St Catherine's,' said Giles.

This time there was no mistaking the reaction. Erskine turned sharply away, Mrs Erskine's cup chattered on her saucer.

'Perhaps,' she said abruptly, 'you would like to see the garden.'

'Oh yes, please.'

They went out through the french windows. It was a well-kept, well-stocked garden, with a long border and flagged walks. The care of it was principally Major Erskine's, so Gwenda gathered. Talking to her about roses, about herbaceous plants, Erskine's dark, sad face lit up. Gardening was clearly his enthusiasm.

When they finally took their leave, and were driving away in the car, Giles asked hesitantly, 'Did you – did you drop it?'

Gwenda nodded.

'By the second clump of delphiniums.' She looked down at her finger and twisted the wedding ring on it absently.

'And supposing you never find it again?'

'Well, it's not my real engagement ring. I wouldn't risk *that*.'

'I'm glad to hear it.'

'I'm very sentimental about that ring. Do you remember what you said when you put it on my finger? A green emerald because I was an intriguing green-eyed little cat.'

'I dare say,' said Giles dispassionately, 'that our peculiar form of endearments might sound odd to someone of, say, Miss Marple's generation.'

'I wonder what she's doing now, the dear old thing. Sitting in the sun on the front?'

'Up to something – if I know her! Poking here, or prying there, or asking a few questions. I hope she doesn't ask too many one of these days.'

'It's quite a natural thing to do – for an old lady, I mean. It's not as

279

noticeable as though we did it.'

Giles's face sobered again.

'That's why I don't like –' He broke off. 'It's you having to do it that I mind. I can't bear the feeling that I sit at home and send you out to do the dirty work.'

Gwenda ran a finger down his worried cheek.

'I know, darling, I know. But you must admit, it's tricky. It's impertinent to catechize a man about his past love-affairs – but it's the kind of impertinence a woman can just get away with – if she's clever. And I mean to be clever.'

'I know you're clever. But if Erskine is the man we are looking for –'

Gwenda said meditatively: 'I don't think he is.'

'You mean we're barking up the wrong tree?'

'Not entirely. I think he was in love with Helen all right. But he's *nice*, Giles, awfully nice. Not the strangling kind at all.'

'You haven't an awful lot of experience of the strangling kind, have you, Gwenda?'

'No. But I've got my woman's instinct.'

'I dare say that's what a strangler's victims often say. No, Gwenda, joking apart, do be careful, won't you?'

'Of course. I feel so sorry for the poor man – that dragon of a wife. I bet he's had a miserable life.'

'She's an odd woman . . . Rather alarming somehow.'

'Yes, quite sinister. Did you see how she watched me all the time?'

'I hope the plan will go off all right.'

III

The plan was put into execution the following morning.

Giles, feeling, as he put it, rather like a shady detective in a divorce suit, took up his position at a point of vantage overlooking the front gate of Anstell Manor. About half past eleven he reported to Gwenda that all had gone well. Mrs Erskine had left in a small Austin car, clearly bound for the market town three miles away. The coast was clear.

Gwenda drove up to the front door and rang the bell. She asked for Mrs Erskine and was told she was out. She then asked for Major Erskine. Major Erskine was in the garden. He straightened up from operations on a flowerbed as Gwenda approached.

'I'm so sorry to bother you,' said Gwenda. 'But I think I must have dropped a ring somewhere out here yesterday. I know I had it when we

280

came out from tea. It's rather loose, but I couldn't bear to lose it because it's my engagement ring.'

The hunt was soon under way. Gwenda retraced her steps of yesterday, tried to recollect where she had stood and what flowers she had touched. Presently the ring came to light near a large clump of delphiniums. Gwenda was profuse in her relief.

'And now can I get you a drink, Mrs Reed? Beer? A glass of sherry? Or would you prefer coffee, or something like that?

'I don't want anything – no, really. Just a cigarette – thanks.'

She sat down on a bench and Erskine sat down beside her.

They smoked for a few minutes in silence. Gwenda's heart was beating rather fast. No two ways about it. She had to take the plunge.

'I want to ask you something,' she said 'Perhaps you'll think it terribly impertinent of me. But I want to know dreadfully – and you're probably the only person who could tell me. I believe you were once in love with my stepmother.'

He turned an astonished face towards her.

'With your stepmother?'

'Yes. Helen Kennedy. Helen Halliday as she became afterwards.'

'I see.' The man beside her was very quiet. His eyes looked out across the sunlit lawn unseeingly. The cigarette between his fingers smouldered. Quiet as he was, Gwenda sensed a turmoil within that taut figure, the arm of which touched her own.

As though answering some question he had put to himself, Erskine said: 'Letters, I suppose.'

Gwenda did not answer.

'I never wrote her many – two, perhaps three. She said she had destroyed them – but women never do destroy letters, do they? And so they came into *your* hands. And you want to know.'

'I want to know more about her. I was – very fond of her. Although I was such a small child when – she went away.'

'She went away?'

'Didn't you know?'

His eyes, candid and surprised, met hers.

'I've no news of her,' he said, 'since – since that summer in Dillmouth.'

'Then you don't know where she is now?'

'How should I? It's years ago – years. All finished and done with. Forgotten.'

He smiled rather bitterly.

'No, perhaps not forgotten ... You're very perceptive, Mrs Reed. But tell me about her. She's not – dead, is she?'

A small cold wind sprang up suddenly, chilled their necks and passed.

'I don't know if she is dead or not,' said Gwenda. 'I don't know anything about her. I thought perhaps *you* might know?'

She went on as he shook his head: 'You see, she went away from Dillmouth that summer. Quite suddenly one evening. Without telling anyone. And she never came back.'

'And you thought I might have heard from her?'

'Yes.'

He shook his head.

'No. Never a word. But surely her brother – doctor chap – lives in Dillmouth. He must know. Or is he dead too?'

'No, he's alive. But he doesn't know either. You see – they all thought she went away – with somebody.'

He turned his head to look at her. Deep sorrowful eyes.

'They thought she went away with *me*?'

'Well, it was a possibility.'

'Was it a possibility? I don't think so. It was never that. Or were we fools – conscientious fools who passed up our chance of happiness?'

Gwenda did not speak. Again Erskine turned his head and looked at her.

'Perhaps you'd better hear about it. There isn't really very much to hear. But I wouldn't like you to misjudge Helen. We met on a boat going out to India. One of the children had been ill, and my wife was following on the next boat. Helen was going to marry a man in the Woods and Forests or something of that kind. She didn't love him. He was just an old friend, nice and kind, and she wanted to get away from home where she wasn't happy. We fell in love.'

He paused.

'Always a bald kind of statement. But it wasn't – I want to make that quite clear – just the usual shipboard love-affair. It was serious. We were both – well – shattered by it. And there wasn't anything to be done. I couldn't let Janet and the children down. Helen saw it the same way as I did. If it had been only Janet – but there were the boys. It was all hopeless. We agreed to say goodbye and try and forget.'

He laughed, a short mirthless laugh.

'Forget? I never forgot – not for one moment. Life was just a living Hell. I couldn't stop thinking about Helen . . .'

'Well, she didn't marry the chap she had been going out to marry. At the last moment, she just couldn't face it. She went home to England and on the way home she met this other man – your father, I suppose. She wrote to me a couple of months later telling me what she had done. He was very unhappy over the loss of his wife, she said, and there was a child. She thought that she could make him happy and that it was the best thing to do. She wrote from Dillmouth. About eight months later my father died and I came into this place. I sent in my papers and came back to England. We wanted a few weeks' holiday until we could get into this house. My wife suggested Dillmouth. Some friend had mentioned it as a pretty place and quiet. She didn't know, of course, about Helen. Can you imagine the temptation? To see her again. To see what this man she had married was like.'

There was a short silence, then Erskine said:

'We came and stayed at the Royal Clarence. It was a mistake. Seeing Helen again was Hell . . . She seemed happy enough, on the whole – I didn't know whether she cared still, or whether she didn't . . . Perhaps she'd got over it. My wife, I think, suspected something . . . She's – she's a very jealous woman – always has been.'

He added brusquely, 'That's all there is to it. We left Dillmouth –'

'On August 17th,' said Gwenda.

'Was that the date? Probably. I can't remember exactly.'

'It was a Saturday,' said Gwenda.

'Yes, you're right. I remember Janet said it might be a crowded day to travel north – but I don't think it was . . .'

'Please try and remember, Major Erskine. When was the last time you saw my stepmother – Helen?'

He smiled, a gentle, tired smile.

'I don't need to try very hard. I saw her the evening before we left. On the beach. I'd strolled down there after dinner – and she was there. There was no one else about. I walked up with her to her house. We went through the garden –'

'What time?'

'I don't know . . . Nine o'clock, I suppose.'

'And you said goodbye?'

'And we said goodbye.' Again he laughed. 'Oh, not the kind of goodbye you're thinking of. It was very brusque and curt. Helen said: "Please go away now. Go quickly. I'd rather not –" She stopped then – and I – I just went.'

'Back to the hotel?'

'Yes, yes, eventually. I walked a long way first – right out into the country.'

Gwenda said, 'It's difficult with dates – after so many years. But I think that that was the night she went away – and didn't come back.'

'I see. And as I and my wife left the next day, people gossiped and said she'd gone away with me. Charming minds people have.'

'Anyway,' said Gwenda bluntly, 'she didn't go away with you?'

'Good Lord, no, there was never any question of such a thing.'

'Then why do you think,' asked Gwenda, 'that she went away?'

Erskine frowned. His manner changed, became interested.

'I see,' he said. 'That is a bit of a problem. She didn't – er – leave any explanation?'

Gwenda considered. Then she voiced her own belief.

'I don't think she left any word at all. Do you think she went away with someone else?'

'No, of course she didn't.'

'You seem rather sure about that.'

'I am sure.'

'Then why did she go?'

'If she went off – suddenly – like that – I can only see one possible reason. She was running *away* from me.'

'From you?'

'Yes. She was afraid, perhaps, that I'd try to see her again – that I'd pester her. She must have seen that I was still – crazy about her . . . Yes, that must have been it.'

'It doesn't explain,' said Gwenda, 'why she never came back. Tell me, did Helen say anything to you about my father? That she was worried about him? Or – or afraid of him? Anything like that?'

'Afraid of him? Why? Oh I see, you thought he might have been jealous. Was he a jealous man?'

'I don't know. He died when I was a child.'

'Oh, I see. No – looking back – he always seemed normal and pleasant. He was fond of Helen, proud of her – I don't think more. No, I was the one who was jealous of *him.*'

'They seemed to you reasonably happy together?'

'Yes, they did. I was glad – and yet, at the same time, it hurt, to see it . . . No, Helen never discussed him with me. As I tell you, we were hardly ever alone, never confidential together. But now that you have mentioned it, I do remember thinking that Helen was worried . . .'

'Worried?'

'Yes. I thought perhaps it was because of my wife –' He broke off. 'But it was more than that.'

He looked again sharply at Gwenda.

'Was she afraid of her husband? Was he jealous of other men where she was concerned?'

'You seem to think not.'

'Jealousy is a very queer thing. It can hide itself sometimes so that you'd never suspect it.' He gave a short quick shiver. 'But it can be frightening –

284

very frightening . . .'

'Another thing I would like to know –' Gwenda broke off.

A car had come up the drive. Major Erskine said, 'Ah, my wife has come back from shopping.'

In a moment, as it were, he became a different person. His tone was easy yet formal, his face expressionless. A slight tremor betrayed that he was nervous.

Mrs Erskine came striding round the corner of the house.

Her husband went towards her.

'Mrs Reed dropped one of her rings in the garden yesterday,' he said.

Mrs Erskine said abruptly: 'Indeed?'

'Good morning,' said Gwenda. 'Yes, luckily I have found it.'

'That's very fortunate.'

'Oh, it is. I should have hated to lose it. Well, I must be going.'

Mrs Erskine said nothing. Major Erskine said: 'I'll see you to your car.'

He started to follow Gwenda along the terrace. His wife's voice came sharply.

'Richard. If Mrs Reed will excuse you, there is a very important call –'

Gwenda said hastily, 'Oh, that's quite all right. Please don't bother.'

She ran quickly along the terrace and round the side of the house to the drive.

Then she stopped. Mrs Erskine had drawn up her car in such a way that Gwenda doubted whether she could get her own car past and down the drive. She hesitated, then slowly retraced her steps to the terrace.

Just short of the french windows she stopped dead. Mrs Erskine's voice, deep and resonant, came distinctly to her ears.

'I don't care what you say. You arranged it – arranged it yesterday. You fixed it up with that girl to come here whilst I was in Daith. You're always the same – any pretty girl. I won't stand it, I tell you. I won't stand it.'

Erskine's voice cut in – quiet, almost despairing.

'Sometimes, Janet, I really think you're insane.'

'I'm not the one who's insane. It's *you*! You can't leave women alone.'

'You know that's not true, Janet.'

'It *is* true! Even long ago – in the place where this girl comes from – Dillmouth. Do you dare tell me that you weren't in love with that yellow-haired Halliday woman?'

'Can you never forget anything? Why must you go on harping on these things? You simply work yourself up and –'

'It's you! You break my heart . . . I won't stand it, I tell you! I won't stand it! Planning assignations! Laughing at me behind my back! You don't care for me – you've never cared for me. I'll kill myself! I'll throw myself over a

285

cliff – I wish I were dead –'

'Janet – Janet – for God's sake . . .'

The deep voice had broken. The sound of passionate sobbing floated out into the summer air.

On tip-toe Gwenda crept away and round into the drive again. She cogitated for a moment, then rang the front-door bell.

'I wonder,' she said, 'if there is anyone who – er – could move this car. I don't think I can get out.'

The servant went into the house. Presently a man came round from what had been the stable yard. He touched his cap to Gwenda, got into the Austin and drove it into the yard. Gwenda got into her car and drove rapidly back to the hotel where Giles was waiting for her.

'What a time you've been,' he greeted her. 'Get anything?'

'Yes. I know all about it now. It's really rather pathetic. He was terribly in love with Helen.'

She narrated the events of the morning.

'I really think,' she ended, 'that Mrs Erskine is a bit insane. She sounded quite mad. I see now what he meant by jealousy. It must be awful to feel like that. Anyway, we know now that Erskine wasn't the man who went away with Helen, and that he knows nothing about her death. She was alive that evening when he left her.'

'Yes,' said Giles. 'At least – that's what he says.'

Gwenda looked indignant.

'That,' repeated Giles firmly, 'is what he *says*.'

CHAPTER 18

Bindweed

Miss Marple bent down on the terrace outside the french window and dealt with some insidious bindweed. It was only a minor victory, since beneath the surface the bindweed remained in possession as always. But at least the delphiniums knew a temporary deliverance.

Mrs Cocker appeared in the drawing-room window.

'Excuse me, madam, but Dr Kennedy has called. He is anxious to know how long Mr and Mrs Reed will be away, and I told him I couldn't take it upon myself to say exactly, but that you might know. Shall I ask him to come out here?'

'Oh. Oh, yes please, Mrs Cocker.'

Mrs Cocker reappeared shortly afterwards with Dr Kennedy.

Rather flutteringly, Miss Marple introduced herself.

'– and I arranged with dear Gwenda that I would come round and do a little weeding while she was away. I think, you know, that my young friends are being imposed upon by their jobbing gardener. Foster. He comes twice a week, drinks a great many cups of tea, does a lot of talking, and not – so far as I can see – very much work.'

'Yes,' said Dr Kennedy rather absently. 'Yes. They're all alike – all alike.'

Miss Marple looked at him appraisingly. He was an older man than she had thought from the Reeds' description of him. Prematurely old, she guessed. He looked, too, both worried and unhappy. He stood there, his fingers caressing the long, pugnacious line of his jaw.

'They've gone away,' he said. 'Do you know for how long?'

'Oh, not for long. They have gone to visit some friends in the North of England. Young people seem to me so restless, always dashing about here and there.'

'Yes,' said Dr Kennedy. 'Yes – that's true enough.'

He paused and then said rather diffidently, 'Young Giles Reed wrote and asked me for some papers – er – letters, if I could find them –'

He hesitated, and Miss Marple said quietly, 'Your sister's letters?'

He shot her a quick, shrewd glance.

'So – you're in their confidence, are you? A relation?'

'Only a friend,' said Miss Marple. 'I have advised them to the best of my capacity. But people seldom take advice . . . A pity, perhaps, but there it is . . .'

287

'What was your advice?' he asked curiously.

'To let sleeping murder lie,' said Miss Marple firmly.

Dr Kennedy sat down heavily on an uncomfortable rustic seat.

'That's not badly put,' he said. 'I'm fond of Gwennie. She was a nice small child. I should judge that she's grown up to be a nice young woman. I'm afraid that she's heading for trouble.'

'There are so many kinds of trouble,' said Miss Marple.

'Eh? Yes – yes – true enough.'

He sighed. Then he said, 'Giles Reed wrote and asked me if I could let him have my sister's letters, written after she left me – and also some authentic specimen of her handwriting.' He shot a keen glance at her. 'You see what that means?'

Miss Marple nodded. 'I think so.'

'They're harking back to the idea that Kelvin Halliday, when he said he had strangled his wife, was speaking neither more nor less than the truth. They believe that the letters my sister Helen wrote after she went away weren't written by her at all – that they were forgeries. They believe that she never left his house alive.'

Miss Marple said gently, 'And you are not, by now, so very sure yourself?'

'I was at the time.' Kennedy still stared ahead of him. 'It seemed absolutely clear. Pure hallucination on Kelvin's part. There was no body, a suitcase and clothes were taken – what else could I think?'

'And your sister had been – recently – rather – ahem –' Miss Marple coughed delicately – 'interested in – in a certain gentleman?'

Dr Kennedy looked at her. There was deep pain in his eyes.

'I loved my sister,' he said, 'but I have to admit that, with Helen, there was always some man in the offing. There are women who are made that way – they can't help it.'

'It all seemed clear to you at the time,' said Miss Marple. 'But it does not seem so clear now. Why?'

'Because,' said Kennedy with frankness, 'it seems incredible to me that, if Helen is still alive, she has not communicated with me all these years. In the same way, if she is dead, it is equally strange that I have not been notified of the fact. Well –'

He got up. he took a packet from his pocket.

'Here is the best I can do. The first letter I received from Helen I must have destroyed. I can find no trace of it. But I did keep the second one – the one that gave the poste restante address. And here, for comparison, is the only bit of Helen's handwriting I've been able to find. It's a list of bulbs, etc., for planting. A copy that she had kept of some order. The handwriting

288

of the order and the letter look alike to me, but then I'm no expert. I'll leave them here for Giles and Gwenda when they return. It's probably not worth forwarding.'

'Oh no, I believe they expect to return tomorrow – or the next day.'

The doctor nodded. He stood, looking along the terrace, his eyes still absent. He said suddenly, 'You know what's worrying me? If Kelvin Halliday did kill his wife, he must have concealed the body or got rid of it in some way – and that means (I don't know what else it can mean) that his story to me was a cleverly made-up tale – that he'd already hidden a suitcase full of clothes to give colour to the idea that Helen had gone away – that he'd even arranged for letters to arrive from abroad . . . It means, in fact, that it was a cold-blooded premeditated murder. Little Gwennie was a nice child. It would be bad enough for her to have a father who's a paranoiac, but it's ten times worse to have a father who's a deliberate murderer.'

He swung round to the open window. Miss Marple arrested his departure by a swift question.

'Who was your sister afraid of, Dr Kennedy?'

He turned back to her and stared.

'Afraid of? No one, as far as I know.'

'I only wondered . . . Pray excuse me if I am asking indiscreet questions – but there was a young man, wasn't there? – I mean, some entanglement – when she was very young. Somebody called *Afflick*, I believe.'

'Oh, that. Silly business most girls go through. An undesirable young fellow, shifty – and of course not her class, not her class at all. He got into trouble here afterwards.'

'I just wondered if he could have been – revengeful.'

Dr Kennedy smiled rather sceptically.

'Oh, I don't think it went deep. Anyway, as I say, he got into trouble here, and left the place for good.'

'What sort of trouble?'

'Oh, nothing criminal. Just indiscretions. Blabbed about his employer's affairs.'

'And his employer was Mr Walter Fane?'

Dr Kennedy looked a little surprised.

'Yes – yes – now you say so, I remember, he did work in Fane and Watchman's. Not articled. Just an ordinary clerk.'

Just an ordinary clerk? Miss Marple wondered, as she stooped again to the bindweed, after Dr Kennedy had gone . . .

CHAPTER 19

Mr Kimble Speaks

'I dunno, I'm sure,' said Mrs Kimble.

Her husband, driven into speech by what was neither more nor less than an outrage, became vocal.

He shoved his cup forward.

'What you thinking of, Lily?' he demanded. '*No sugar!*'

Mrs Kimble hastily remedied the outrage, and then proceeded to elaborate on her own theme.

'Thinking about this advert, I am,' she said. 'Lily Abbott, it says, plain as plain. And "formerly house-parlourmaid at St Catherine's Dillmouth." That's me, all right.'

'Ar,' agreed Mr Kimble.

'After all these years – you must agree it's odd, Jim.'

'Ar,' said Mr Kimble.

'Well, what am I going to do, Jim?'

'Leave it be.'

'Suppose there's money in it?'

There was a gurgling sound as Mr Kimble drained his teacup to fortify himself for the mental effort of embarking on a long speech. He pushed his cup along and prefaced his remarks with a laconic: 'More.' Then he got under way.

'You went on a lot at one time about what 'appened at St Catherine's. I didn't take much account of it – reckoned as it was mostly foolishness – women's chatter. Maybe it wasn't. Maybe something did 'appen. If so it's police business and you don't want to be mixed up in it. All over and done with, ain't it? You leave well alone, my girl.'

'All very well to say that. It may be money as has been left me in a will. Maybe Mrs Halliday's alive all the time and now she's dead and left me something in 'er will.'

'Left you something in 'er will? What for? Ar!' said Mr Kimble, reverting to his favourite monosyllable to express scorn.

'Even if it's police . . . You know, Jim, there's a big reward sometimes for anyone as can give information to catch a murderer.'

'And what could you give? All you know you make up yourself in your head!'

'That's what you say. But I've been thinking –'

'Ar,' said Mr Kimble disgustedly.

290

'Well, I have. Ever since I saw that first piece in the paper. Maybe I got things a bit wrong. That Layonee, she was a bit stupid like all foreigners, couldn't understand proper what you said to her – and her English was something awful. If she didn't mean what I thought she meant . . . I've been trying to remember the name of that man . . . Now if it was him she saw . . . Remember that picture I told you about? *Secret Lover.* Ever so exciting. They tracked him down in the end through his car. Fifty thousand dollars he paid the garage man to forget he filled up with petrol that night. Dunno what that is in pounds . . . And the other one was there, too, and the husband crazy with jealousy. All mad about her, they were. And in the end –'

Mr Kimble pushed back his chair with a grating sound. He rose to his feet with slow and ponderous authority. Preparatory to leaving the kitchen, he delivered an ultimatum – the ultimatum of a man who, though usually inarticulate, had a certain shrewdness.

'You leave the whole thing alone, my girl,' he said. 'Or else, likely as not, you'll be sorry.'

He went into the scullery, put on his boots (Lily was particular about her kitchen floor) and went out.

Lily sat on at the table, her sharp foolish little brain working things out. Of course she couldn't exactly go against what her husband said, but all the same . . . Jim was so hidebound, so stick-in-the-mud. She wished there was somebody else she could ask. Someone who would know all about rewards and the police and what it all meant. Pity to turn up a chance of good money.

That wireless set . . . the home perm . . . that cherry-coloured coat in Russell's (ever so smart) . . . even, maybe, a whole Jacobean suite for the sitting-room . . .

Eager, greedy, shortsighted, she went on dreaming . . . What exactly *had* Layonee said all those years ago?

Then an idea came to her. She got up and fetched the bottle of ink, the pen, and a pad of writing paper.

'Know what I'll do,' she said to herself. 'I'll write to the doctor, Mrs Halliday's brother. He'll tell me what I ought to do – if he's alive still, that is. Anyway, it's on my conscience I never told him about Layonee – or about that car.'

There was silence for some time apart from the laborious scratching of Lily's pen. It was very seldom that she wrote a letter and she found the composition of it a considerable effort.

However it was done at last and she put it into an envelope and sealed it up.

But she felt less satisfied that she had expected. Ten to one the doctor was dead or had gone away from Dillmouth.

Was there anyone else?

What was the name, now, of that fellow?

If she could only remember *that* . . .

292

CHAPTER 20

The Girl Helen

Giles and Gwenda had just finished breakfast on the morning after their return from Northumberland when Miss Marple was announced. She came rather apologetically.

'I'm afraid this is a very early call. Not a thing I am in the habit of doing. But there was something I wanted to explain.'

'We're delighted to see you,' said Giles, pulling out a chair for her. 'Do have a cup of coffee.'

'Oh no, no, thank you – nothing at all. I have breakfasted *most* adequately. Now let me explain. I came in whilst you were away, as you kindly said I might, to do a little weeding –'

'Angelic of you,' said Gwenda.

'And it really did strike me that two days a week is not quite enough for this garden. In any case I think Foster is taking advantage of you. Too much tea and too much talk. I found out that he couldn't manage another day himself, so I took it upon myself to engage another man just for one day a week – Wednesdays – today, in fact.'

Giles looked at her curiously. He was a little surprised. It might be kindly meant, but Miss Marple's action savoured, very faintly, of interference. And interference was unlike her.

He said slowly: 'Foster's far too old, I know, for really hard work.'

'I'm afraid, Mr Reed, that Manning is even older. Seventy-five, he tells me. But you see, I thought employing him, just for a few odd days, might be quite an advantageous move, because he used, many years ago, to be employed at Dr Kennedy's. The name of the young man Helen got engaged to was Afflick, by the way.'

'Miss Marple,' said Giles, 'I maligned you in thought. You are a genius. You know I've got those specimens of Helen's handwriting from Kennedy?'

'I know. I was here when he brought them.'

'I'm posting them off today. I got the address of a good handwriting expert last week.'

'Let's go into the garden and see Manning,' said Gwenda.

Manning was a bent, crabbed-looking old man with a rheumy and slightly cunning eye. The pace at which he was raking a path accelerated noticeably as his employers drew near.

'Morning, sir. Morning, m'am. The lady said as how you could do with a little extra help of a Wednesday. I'll be pleased. Shameful neglected, this place looks.'

'I'm afraid the garden's been allowed to run down for some years.'

'It has that. Remember it, I do, in Mrs Findeyson's time. A picture it were, then. Very fond of her garden she was, Mrs Findeyson.'

Giles leaned easily against a roller. Gwenda snipped off some rose heads. Miss Marple, retreating a little up stage, bent to the bindweed. Old Manning leant on his rake. All was set for a leisurely morning discussion of old times and gardening in the good old days.

'I suppose you know most of the gardens round here,' said Giles encouragingly.

'Ar, I know this place moderate well, I do. And the fancies people went in for. Mrs Yule, up at Niagra, she had a yew hedge used to be clipped like a squirrel. Silly, I thought it. Peacocks is one thing and squirrels is another. Then Colonel Lampard, he was a great man for begonias – lovely beds of begonias he used to have. Bedding out now, that's going out of fashion. I wouldn't like to tell you how often I've had to fill up beds in the front lawns and turf 'em over in the last six years. Seems people ain't got no eye for geraniums and a nice bit of lobelia edging no more.'

'You worked at Dr Kennedy's, didn't you?'

'Ar. Long time ago, that were. Must have been 1920 and on. He's moved now – given up. Young Dr Brent's up at Crosby Lodge now. Funny ideas, he has – little white tablets and so on. Vittapins he calls 'em.'

'I suppose you remember Miss Helen Kennedy, the doctor's sister.'

'Ar, I remember Miss Helen right enough. Pretty-maid, she was, with her long yellow hair. The doctor set a lot of store by her. Come back and lived in this very house here, she did, after she was married. Army gentleman from India.'

'Yes,' said Gwenda. 'We know.'

'Ar. I did 'ear – Saturday night it was – as you and your 'usband was some kind of relations. Pretty as a picter, Miss Helen was, when she first come back from school. Full of fun, too. Wanting to go everywhere – dances and tennis and all that. 'Ad to mark the tennis court, I 'ad – hadn't been used for nigh twenty years, I'd say. And the shrubs overgrowing it cruel. 'Ad to cut 'em back, I did. *And* get a lot of whitewash and mark out the lines. Lot of work it made – and in the end hardly played on. Funny thing I always thought that was.'

'What was a funny thing?' asked Giles.

'Business with the tennis court. Someone come along one night – and cut it to ribbons. Just to ribbons it was. Spite, as you might say. That was what it was – nasty bit of spite.'

'But who would do a thing like that?'

294

'That's what the doctor wanted to know. Proper put out about it he was – and I don't blame him. Just paid for it, he had. But none of us could tell who'd done it. We never did know. And he said he wasn't going to get another – quite right, too, for if it's spite one time, it would be spite again. But Miss Helen, she was rare and put out. She didn't have no luck, Miss Helen didn't. First that net – and then her bad foot.'

'A bad foot?' asked Gwenda.

'Yes – fell over a scraper or some such and cut it. Not much more than a graze, it seemed, but it wouldn't heal. Fair worried about it, the doctor was. He was dressing it and treating it, but it didn't get well. I remember him saying "I can't understand it – there must have been something spectic – or some word like that – on that scraper. And anyway," he says, "what was the scraper doing out in the middle of the drive?" Because that's where it was when Miss Helen fell over it, walking home on a dark night. The poor maid, there she was, missing going to dances and sitting about with her foot up. Seemed as though there was nothing but bad luck for her.'

The moment had come, Giles thought. He asked casually, 'Do you remember somebody called Afflick?'

'Ar. You mean Jackie Afflick? As was in Fane and Watchman's office?'

'Yes. Wasn't he a friend of Miss Helen's?'

'That were just a bit of nonsense. Doctor put a stop to it and quite right too. He wasn't any class, Jackie Afflick. And he was the kind that's too sharp by half. Cut themselves in the end, that kind do. But he weren't here long. Got himself into hot water. Good riddance. Us don't want the likes of he in Dillmouth. Go and be smart somewhere else, that's what he were welcome to do.'

Gwenda said: 'Was he here when that tennis net was cut up?'

'Ar. I see what you're thinking. But he wouldn't do a senseless thing like that. He were smart, Jackie Afflick were. Whoever did that it was just spite.'

'Was there anybody who had a down on Miss Helen? Who would be likely to feel spiteful?'

Old Manning chuckled softly.

'Some of the young ladies might have felt spiteful all right. Not a patch on Miss Helen to look at, most of 'em weren't. No, I'd say that was done just in foolishness. Some tramp with a grudge.'

'Was Helen very upset about Jackie Afflick?' asked Gwenda.

'Don't think as Miss Helen cared much about any of the young fellows. Just liked to enjoy herself, that's all. Very devoted some of them were – young Mr Walter Fane, for one. Used to follow her round like a dog.'

'But she didn't care for him at all?'

295

'Not Miss Helen. Just laughed – that's all she did. Went abroad to foreign parts, he did. But he come back later. Top one in the firm he is now. Never married. I don't blame him. Women causes a lot of trouble in a man's life.'

'Are you married?' asked Gwenda.

'Buried two, I have,' said old Manning. 'Ar, well, I can't complain. Smoke me pipe in peace where I likes now.'

In the ensuing silence, he picked up his rake again.

Giles and Gwenda walked back up the path towards the house and Miss Marple desisting from her attack on bindweed joined them.

'Miss Marple,' said Gwenda. 'You don't look well. Is there anything –'

'It's nothing, my dear.' The old lady paused for a moment before saying with a strange kind of insistence, 'You know, I don't like that bit about the tennis net. Cutting it to ribbons. Even then –'

She stopped. Giles looked at her curiously.

'I don't quite understand –' he began.

'Don't you? It seems so horribly plain to me. But perhaps it's better that you shouldn't understand. And anyway – perhaps I am wrong. Now do tell me how you got on in Northumberland.'

They gave her an account of their activities, and Miss Marple listened attentively.

'It's really all very sad,' said Gwenda. 'Quite tragic, in fact.'

'Yes, indeed. Poor thing – poor thing.'

'That's what I felt. How that man must suffer –'

'He? Oh yes. Yes, of course.'

'But you meant –'

'Well, yes – I was thinking of *her* – of the wife. Probably very deeply in love with him, and he married her because she was suitable, or because he was sorry for her, or for one of those quite kindly and sensible reasons that men often have, and which are actually so terribly unfair.'

> 'I know a hundred ways of love,
> And each one makes the loved one rue,'

quoted Giles softly.

Miss Marple turned to him.

'Yes, that is so true. Jealousy, you know, is usually not an affair of *causes*. It is much more – how shall I say? – fundamental than that. Based on the knowledge that one's love is not returned. And so one goes on waiting, watching, expecting . . . that the loved one will turn to someone else. Which, again, invariably happens. So this Mrs Erskine has made life a hell for her husband, and he, without being able to help it, has made life a hell for her. But I think she has suffered most. And yet, you know, I dare say he is really quite fond of her.'

'He can't be,' cried Gwenda.

'Oh, my dear, you are very young. He has never left his wife, and that means something, you know.'

'Because of the children. Because it was his duty.'

'The children, perhaps,' said Miss Marple. 'But I must confess that gentlemen do not seem to me to have a great regard for duty in so far as their wives are concerned – public service is another matter.'

Giles laughed.

'What a wonderful cynic you are, Miss Marple.'

'Oh dear, Mr Reed, I do hope not *that*. One always has *hope* for human nature.'

'I still don't feel it can have been Walter Fane,' said Gwenda thoughtfully. 'And I'm sure it wasn't Major Erskine. In fact I *know* it wasn't.'

'One's feelings are not always reliable guides,' said Miss Marple. 'The most unlikely people do things – quite a sensation there was in my own little village when the Treasurer of the Christmas Club was found to have put every penny of the funds on a horse. He disapproved of horse-racing and indeed any kind of betting or gambling. His father had been a Turf Agent and had treated his mother very badly – so, intellectually speaking, he was quite sincere. But he chanced one day to be motoring near Newmarket and saw some horses training. And then it all came over him – blood does tell.'

'The antecedents of both Walter Fane and Richard Erskine seem above suspicion,' said Giles gravely but with a slight amused twist to his mouth. 'But then murder is by way of being an amateur crime.'

'The important thing is,' said Miss Marple, 'that they were *there*. On the spot. Walter Fane was here in Dillmouth. Major Erskine, by his own account, must actually have been with Helen Halliday very shortly before her death – *and* he did not return to his hotel for some time that night.'

'But he was quite frank about it. He –'

Gwenda broke off. Miss Marple was looking at her very hard.

'I only want to emphasize,' said Miss Marple, 'the importance of being *on the spot*.' She looked from one to the other of them.

Then she said, 'I think you will have no trouble in finding out J. J. Afflick's address. As proprietor of the Daffodil Coaches, it should be easy enough.'

Giles nodded. 'I'll get on to it. Probably in the telephone directory.' He paused. 'You think we should go and see him?'

Miss Marple waited for a moment or two, then she said: 'If you do – you must be very careful. Remember what that old gardener just said – Jackie Afflick is smart. Please – *please* be careful . . .'

CHAPTER 21

J. J. Afflick

J. J. Afflick, Daffodil Coaches, Devon & Dorset Tours, etc. had two numbers listed in the telephone book. An office address in Exeter and a private address on the outskirts of that town.

An appointment was made for the following day.

Just as Giles and Gwenda were leaving in the car, Mrs Cocker ran out and gesticulated. Giles put on the brake and stopped.

'It's Dr Kennedy on the telephone, sir.'

Giles got out and ran back. He picked up the receiver.

'Giles Reed here.'

'Morning. I've just received rather an odd letter. From a woman called Lily Kimble. I've been racking my brains to remember who she is. Thought of a patient first – that put me off the scent. But I rather fancy she must be a girl who was in service once at your house. House-parlourmaid at the time we know of. I'm almost sure her name was Lily, though I don't recollect her last name.'

'There *was* a Lily. Gwenda remembers her. She tied a bow on the cat.'

'Gwennie must have a very remarkable memory.'

'Oh, she has.'

'Well, I'd like to have a word with you about this letter – not over the phone. Will you be in if I come over?'

'We're just on our way to Exeter. We could drop in on you, if you prefer, sir. It's all on our way.'

'Good. That'll do splendidly.'

'I don't like to talk too much about all this over the phone,' explained the doctor when they arrived. 'I always have an idea the local exchanges listen in. Here's the woman's letter.'

He spread the letter on the table. It was written on cheap lined paper in an uneducated hand.

Dear sir (Lily Kimble had written)

I'd be grateful if you could give me advise about the enclosed wot i cut out of paper. I been thinking and i talked it over with mr Kimble, but i don't know wots best to do about it. Do you think as it means money or a reward becos i could do with the money im sure but woodnt want the police or anything like that, i often hav been thinking about that nite wen mrs Halliday went away and i don't think sir she ever did becos the

299

clothes was wrong. i thort at first the master done it but now im not so sure becos of the car i saw out of the window. A posh car it was and i seen it before but i woodnt like to do anything without asking you first if it was all rite and not police becos i never hav been mixed up with police and mr Kimble woodnt like it. I could come and see you sir if i may next thursday as its market day and mr Kimble will be out. id be very grateful if you could.

yours respectfully,

Lily Kimble.

'It was addressed to my old house in Dillmouth,' said Kennedy, 'and forwarded on to me here. The cutting is your advertisement.'

'It's wonderful,' said Gwenda. 'This Lily – you see – she *doesn't* think it was my father who did it!'

She spoke with jubilation. Dr Kennedy looked at her with tired, kindly eyes.

'Good for you, Gwennie,' he said gently. 'I hope you're right. Now this is what I think we'd better do. I'll answer her letter and tell her to come here on Thursday. The train connection is quite good. By changing at Dillmouth Junction she can get here shortly after 4.30. If you two will come over that afternoon, we can tackle her all together.'

'Splendid,' said Giles. He glanced at his watch. 'Come on, Gwenda, we must hurry. We've got an appointment,' he explained. 'With Mr Afflick of the Daffodil Coaches, and, so he told us, he's a busy man.'

'Afflick?' Kennedy frowned. 'Of course! Devon Tours in Daffodil Coaches, horrible great butter-coloured brutes. But the name seemed familiar in some other way.'

'Helen,' said Gwenda.

'My goodness – not that chap?'

'Yes.'

'But he was a miserable little rat. So he's come up in the world?'

'Will you tell me something, sir?' said Giles. 'You broke up some funny business between him and Helen. Was that simply because of his – well, social position?'

Dr Kennedy gave him a dry glance.

'I'm old-fashioned, young man. In the modern gospel, one man is as good as another. That holds morally, no doubt. But I'm a believer in the fact that there is a state of life into which you are born – and I believe you're happiest staying in it. Besides,' he added, 'I thought the fellow was a wrong 'un. As he proved to be.'

'What did he do exactly?'

'That I can't remember now. It was a case, as far as I can recall, of his trying to cash in on some information obtained through his employment with Fane. Some confidential matter relating to one of their clients.'

'Was he – sore about his dismissal?'

Kennedy gave him a sharp glance and said briefly: 'Yes.'

'And there wasn't any other reason at all for your disliking his friendship with your sister? You didn't think he was – well – odd in any way.'

'Since you have brought the matter up, I will answer you frankly. It seemed to me, especially after his dismissal from his employment, that Jackie Afflick displayed certain signs of an unbalanced temperament. Incipient persecution mania, in fact. But that does not seem to have been borne out by his subsequent rise in life.'

'Who dismissed him? Walter Fane?'

'I have no idea if Walter Fane was concerned. He was dismissed by the firm.'

'And he complained that he had been victimized?'

Kennedy nodded.

'I see . . . Well, we must drive like the wind. Till Thursday, sir.'

II

The house was newly built. It was of Snowcrete, heavily curved, with a big expanse of window. They were shown in through an opulent hall to a study, half of which was taken up by a big chromium-plated desk.

Gwenda murmured nervously to Giles, 'Really, I don't know what we should have done without Miss Marple. We lean upon her at every turn. First her friends in Northumberland and now her Vicar's wife's Boys' Club Annual Outing.'

Giles raised an admonitory hand as the door opened and J. J. Afflick surged into the room.

He was a stout man of middle age, dressed in a rather violently checked suit. His eyes were dark and shrewd, his face rubicund and good-natured. He looked like the popular idea of a successful bookmaker.

'Mr Reed? Good morning. Pleased to meet you.'

Giles introduced Gwenda. She felt her hand taken in a rather over-zealous grip.

'And what can I do for you, Mr Reed?'

Afflick sat down behind his huge desk. He offered cigarettes from an onyx box.

Giles entered upon the subject of the Boys' Club Outing. Old friends of

301

his ran the show. He was anxious to arrange for a couple of days' touring in Devon.

Afflick replied promptly in a businesslike manner – quoting prices and making suggestions. But there was a faintly puzzled look on his face.

Finally he said: 'Well, that's all clear enough, Mr Reed, and I'll send you a line to confirm it. But this is strictly office business. I understood from my clerk that you wanted a private appointment at my private address.'

'We did, Mr Afflick. There were actually two matters on which I wanted to see you. We've disposed of one. The other is a purely private matter. My wife here is very anxious to get in touch with her stepmother whom she has not seen for many years, and we wondered if you could possibly help us.'

'Well, if you tell me the lady's name – I gather that I'm acquainted with her?'

'You were acquainted with her at one time. Her name is Helen Halliday and before her marriage she was Miss Helen Kennedy.'

Afflick sat quite still. He screwed up his eyes and tilted his chair slowly backwards.

'Helen Halliday – I don't recall . . . Helen Kennedy . . .'

'Formerly of Dillmouth,' said Gwenda.

The legs of Afflick's chair came down sharply.

'Got it,' he said. 'Of course.' His round rubicund face beamed with pleasure. 'Little Helen Kennedy! Yes, I remember her. But it's a long time ago. Must be twenty years.'

'Eighteen.'

'Is it really? Time flies, as the saying goes. But I'm afraid you're going to be disappointed, Mrs Reed. I haven't seen anything of Helen since that time. Never heard of her, even.'

'Oh dear,' said Gwenda. 'That's very disappointing. We did so hope you could help.'

'What's the trouble?' His eyes flickered quickly from one face to another. 'Quarrel? Left home? Matter of money?'

Gwenda said: 'She went away – suddenly – from Dillmouth – eighteen years ago with – with someone.'

Jackie Afflick said amusedly: 'And you thought she might have gone away with me? Now why?'

Gwenda spoke boldly: 'Because we heard that you – and she – had once – been – well, fond of each other.'

'Me and Helen? Oh, but there was nothing in that. Just a boy and girl affair. Neither of us took it seriously.' He added drily, 'We weren't encouraged to do so.'

'You must think us dreadfully impertinent,' began Gwenda, but he

302

interrupted her.

'What's the odds? I'm not sensitive. You want to find a certain person and you think I may be able to help. Ask me anything you please – I've nought to conceal.' He looked at her thoughtfully. 'So you're Halliday's daughter?'

'Yes. Did you know my father?'

He shook his head.

'I dropped in to see Helen once when I was over at Dillmouth on business. I'd heard she was married and living there. She was civil enough –' he paused – 'but she didn't ask me to stay to dinner. No, I didn't meet your father.'

Had there, Gwenda wondered, been a trace of rancour in that 'She didn't ask me to stay to dinner'?

'Did she – if you remember – seem happy?'

Afflick shrugged his shoulders.

'Happy enough. But there, it's a long time ago. I'd have remembered if she'd looked unhappy.'

He added with what seemed a perfectly natural curiosity: 'Do you mean to say you've never heard anything of her since Dillmouth eighteen years ago?'

'Nothing.'

'No – letters?'

'There were two letters,' said Giles. 'But we have some reason to think that she didn't write them.'

'You think she didn't write them?' Afflick seemed faintly amused. 'Sounds like a mystery on the flicks.'

'That's rather what it seems like to us.'

'What about her brother, the doctor chap, doesn't he know where she is?'

'No.'

'I see. Regular mystery, isn't it? Why not advertise?'

'We have.'

Afflick said casually: 'Looks as though she's dead. You mightn't have heard.'

Gwenda shivered.

'Cold, Mrs Reed?'

'No. I was thinking of Helen dead. I don't like to think of her dead.'

'You're right there. I don't like to think of it myself. Stunning looks she had.'

Gwenda said impulsively: 'You knew her. You knew her well. I've only got a child's memory of her. What was she like? What did people feel about her? What did *you* feel?'

He looked at her for a moment or two.

303

'I'll be honest with you, Mrs Reed. Believe it or not, as you like. I was sorry for the kid.'

'Sorry?' She turned a puzzled stare on him.

'Just that. There she was – just home from school. Longing for a bit of fun like any girl might, and there was that stiff middle-aged brother of hers with his ideas about what a girl could do and couldn't do. No fun at all, that kid hadn't. Well, I took her about a bit – showed her a bit of life. I wasn't really keen on her and she wasn't really keen on me. She just liked the fun of being a daredevil. Then of course they found out we were meeting and he put a stop to it. Don't blame him, really. Cut above me, she was. We weren't engaged or anything of that kind. I meant to marry some time – but not till I was a good bit older. And I meant to get on and to find a wife who'd help me get on. Helen hadn't any money, and it wouldn't have been a suitable match in any way. We were just good friends with a bit of flirtation thrown in.'

'But you must have been angry with the doctor –'

Gwenda paused and Afflick said: 'I was riled, I admit. You don't fancy being told you're not good enough. But there, it's no good being thin-skinned.'

'And then,' said Giles, 'you lost your job.'

Afflick's face was not quite so pleasant.

'Fired, I was. Out of Fane and Watchman's. And I've a very good idea who was responsible for that.'

'Oh?' Giles made his tone interrogative, but Afflick shook his head.

'I'm not saying anything. I've my own ideas. I was framed – that's all – and I've a very fair idea of who did it. *And* why!' The colour suffused his cheeks. 'Dirty work,' he said. 'Spying on a man – laying traps for him – lying about him. Oh, I've had my enemies all right. But I've never let them get me down. I've always given as good as I got. *And* I don't forget.'

He stopped. Suddenly his manner changed back again. He was genial once more.

'So I can't help you, I'm afraid. A little bit of fun between me and Helen – that was all. It didn't go deep.'

Gwenda stared at him. It was a clear enough story – but was it true? she wondered. Something jarred – it came to the surface of her mind what that something was.

'All the same,' she said, 'you looked her up when you came to Dillmouth later.'

He laughed.

'You've got me there, Mrs Reed. Yes, I did. Wanted to show her perhaps that I wasn't down and out just because a long-faced lawyer had pushed me out of his office. I had a nice business and I was driving a posh car and I'd

304

done very well for myself.'

'You came to see her more than once, didn't you?'

He hesitated a moment.

'Twice – perhaps three times. Just dropped in.' He nodded with sudden finality. 'Sorry I can't help you.'

Giles got up.

'We must apologize for taking up so much of your time.'

'That's all right. Quite a change to talk about old times.'

The door opened and a woman looked in and apologized swiftly.

'Oh, I'm so sorry – I didn't know you had anyone –'

'Come in, my dear, come in. Meet my wife. This is Mr and Mrs Reed.'

Mrs Afflick shook hands. She was a tall, thin, depressed-looking woman, dressed in rather unexpectedly well-cut clothes.

'Been talking over old times, we have,' said Mr Afflick. 'Old times before I met you, Dorothy.'

He turned to them.

'Met my wife on a cruise,' he said. 'She doesn't come from this part of the world. Cousin of Lord Polterham's, she is.'

He spoke with pride – the thin woman flushed.

'They're very nice, these cruises,' said Giles.

'Very educational,' said Afflick. 'Now, I didn't have any education to speak of.'

'I always tell my husband we must go on one of those Hellenic cruises,' said Mrs Afflick.

'No time. I'm a busy man.'

'And we mustn't keep you,' said Giles. 'Goodbye and thank you. You'll let me know about the quotation for the outing?'

Afflick escorted them to the door. Gwenda glanced back over her shoulder. Mrs Afflick was standing in the doorway of the study. Her face, fastened on her husband's back, was curiously and rather unpleasantly apprehensive.

Giles and Gwenda said goodbye again and went towards their car.

'Bother, I've left my scarf,' said Gwenda.

'You're always leaving something,' said Giles.

'Don't look martyred. I'll get it.'

She ran back into the house. Through the open door of the study she heard Afflick say loudly: 'What do you want to come butting in for? Never any sense.'

'I'm sorry, Jackie. I didn't know. Who are those people and why have they upset you so?'

'They haven't upset me. I –' He stopped as he saw Gwenda standing in

305

the doorway.

'Oh, Mr Afflick, did I leave a scarf?'

'Scarf? No, Mrs Reed. It's not here.'

'Stupid of me. It must be in the car.'

She went out again.

Giles had turned the car. Drawn up by the kerb was a large yellow limousine resplendent with chromium.

'Some car,' said Giles.

' "A posh car",' said Gwenda. 'Do you remember, Giles? Edith Pagett when she was telling us what Lily said? Lily had put her money on Captain Erskine, not "our mystery man in the flashy car". Don't you see, the mystery man in the flashy car was Jackie Afflick?'

'Yes,' said Giles. 'And in her letter to the doctor Lily mentioned a "posh car".'

They looked at each other.

'He was there – "on the spot", as Miss Marple would say – on that night. Oh Giles, I can hardly wait until Thursday to hear what Lily Kimble says.'

'Suppose she gets cold feet and doesn't turn up after all?'

'Oh, she'll come. Giles, if that flashy car was there that night –'

'Think it was a yellow peril like this?'

'Admiring my bus?' Mr Afflick's genial voice made them jump. He was leaning over the neatly clipped hedge behind them. 'Little Buttercup, that's what I call her. I've always liked a nice bit of bodywork. Hits you in the eye, doesn't she?'

'She certainly does,' said Giles.

'Fond of flowers, I am,' said Mr Afflick. 'Daffodils, buttercups, calceolarias – they're all my fancy. Here's your scarf, Mrs Reed. It had slipped down behind the table. Goodbye. Pleased to have met you.'

'Do you think he heard us calling his car a yellow peril?' asked Gwenda as they drove away.

'Oh, I don't think so. He seemed quite amiable, didn't he?'

Giles looked slightly uneasy.

'Ye-es – but I don't think that means much . . . Giles, that wife of his – she's frightened of him, I saw her face.'

'What? That jovial pleasant chap?'

'Perhaps he isn't so jovial and pleasant underneath . . . Giles, I don't think I like Mr Afflick . . . I wonder how long he'd been there behind us listening to what we were saying . . . Just what did we say?'

'Nothing much,' said Giles.

But he still looked uneasy.

CHAPTER 22

Lily Keeps An Appointment

'Well, I'm damned,' exclaimed Giles.

He had just torn open a letter that had arrived by the after-lunch post and was staring in complete astonishment at its contents.

'What's the matter?'

'It's the report of the handwriting experts.'

Gwenda said eagerly: 'And she *didn't* write that letter from abroad?'

'That's just it, Gwenda. *She did.*'

They stared at each other.

Gwenda said incredulously: 'Then those letters *weren't* a fake. They were *genuine*. Helen *did* go away from the house that night. And she *did* write from abroad. And she wasn't strangled at all?'

Giles said slowly: 'It seems so. But it really is very upsetting. I don't understand it. Just as everything seems to be pointing the other way.'

'Perhaps the experts are wrong?'

'I suppose they might be. But they seem quite confident. Gwenda, I really don't understand a single thing about all this. Have we been making the most colossal idiots of ourselves?'

'All based on my silly behaviour at the theatre? I tell you what, Giles, let's call round on Miss Marple. We'll have time before we get to Dr Kennedy's at four-thirty.'

Miss Marple, however, reacted rather differently from the way they had expected. She said it was very nice indeed.

'But darling Miss Marple,' said Gwenda, 'what do you mean by that?'

'I mean, my dear, that somebody hasn't been as clever as they might have been.'

'But how – in what way?'

'Slipped up,' said Miss Marple, nodding her head with satisfaction.

'But how?'

'Well, dear Mr Reed, surely you can see how it narrows the field.'

'Accepting the fact that Helen actually wrote the letters – do you mean that she might still have been murdered?'

'I mean that it seemed very important to someone that the letters should actually be in Helen's handwriting.'

'I see ... At least I think I see. There must be certain possible circumstances in which Helen could have been induced to write those particular letters ... That would narrow things down. But what circumstances exactly?'

'Oh, come now, Mr Reed. You're not really thinking. It's perfectly simple, really.'

Giles looked annoyed and mutinous.

'It's not obvious to me, I can assure you.'

'If you'd just reflect a little –'

'Come on, Giles,' said Gwenda. 'We'll be late.'

They left Miss Marple smiling to herself.

'That old woman annoys me sometimes,' said Giles. 'I don't know now what the hell she was driving at.'

They reached Dr Kennedy's house in good time.

The doctor himself opened the door to them.

'I've let my housekeeper go out for the afternoon,' he explained. 'It seemed to be better.'

He led the way into the sitting-room where a tea-tray with cups and saucers, bread and butter and cakes was ready.

'Cup of tea's a good move, isn't it?' he asked rather uncertainly of Gwenda. 'Put this Mrs Kimble at her ease and all that.'

'You're absolutely right,' said Gwenda.

'Now what about you two? Shall I introduce you straight away? Or will it put her off?'

Gwenda said slowly: 'Country people are very suspicious. I believe it would be better if you received her alone.'

'I think so too,' said Giles.

Dr Kennedy said, 'If you were to wait in the room next door, and if this communicating door were slightly ajar, you would be able to hear what went on. Under the circumstances of the case, I think that you would be justified.'

'I suppose it's eavesdropping, but I really don't care,' said Gwenda.

Dr Kennedy smiled faintly and said: 'I don't think any ethical principle is involved. I do not propose, in any case, to give a promise of secrecy – though I am willing to give my advice if I am asked for it.'

He glanced at his watch.

'The train is due at Woodleigh Road at four-thirty-five. It should arrive in a few minutes now. Then it will take her about five minutes to walk up the hill.'

He walked restlessly up and down the room. His face was lined and haggard.

'I don't understand,' he said. 'I don't understand in the least what it all means. If Helen never left that house, if her letters to me were forgeries.'

Gwenda moved sharply – but Giles shook her head at her. The doctor went on: 'If Kelvin, poor fellow, didn't kill her, then what on earth did happen?'

'Somebody else killed her,' said Gwenda.

'But my dear child, if somebody else killed her, why on earth should Kelvin insist that he had done so?'

'Because he thought he had. He found her there on the bed and he thought he had done it. That could happen, couldn't it?'

Dr Kennedy rubbed his nose irritably.

'How should I know? I'm not a psychiatrist. Shock? Nervous condition already? Yes, I suppose it's possible. But who would want to kill Helen?'

'We think one of three people,' said Gwenda.

'Three people? What three people? Nobody could have any possible reason for killing Helen – unless they were completely off their heads. She'd no enemies. Everybody liked her.'

He went to the desk drawer and fumbled through its contents.

He held out a faded snapshot. It showed a tall schoolgirl in a gym tunic, her hair tied back, her face radiant. Kennedy, a younger, happy-looking Kennedy, stood beside her, holding a terrier puppy.

'I've been thinking a lot about her lately,' he said indistinctly. 'For many years I hadn't thought about her at all – almost managed to forget . . . Now I think about her all the time. That's *your* doing.'

His words sounded almost accusing.

'I think it's *her* doing,' said Gwenda.

He wheeled round on her sharply.

'What do you mean?'

'Just that. I can't explain. But it's not really us. It's Helen herself.'

The faint melancholy scream of an engine came to their ears. Dr Kennedy stepped out of the window and they followed him. A trail of smoke showed itself retreating slowly along the valley.

'There goes the train,' said Kennedy.

'Coming into the station?'

'No, leaving it,' He paused. 'She'll be here any minute now.'

But the minutes passed and Lily Kimble did not come.

II

Lily Kimble got out of the train at Dillmouth Junction and walked across the bridge to the siding where the little local train was waiting. There were few passengers – a half-dozen at most. It was a slack time of day and in any case it was market day at Helchester.

Presently the train started – puffing its way importantly along a winding

309

valley. There were three stops before the terminus at Lonsbury Bay: Newton Langford, Matchings Halt (for Woodleigh Camp) and Woodleigh Bolton.

Lily Kimble looked out of the window with eyes that did not see the lush countryside, but saw instead a Jacobean suite upholstered in jade green . . .

She was the only person to alight at the tiny station of Matchings Halt. She gave up her ticket and went out through the booking office. A little way along the road a signpost with 'To Woodleigh Camp' indicated a footpath leading up a steep hill.

Lily Kimble took the footpath and walked briskly uphill. The path skirted the side of a wood, on the other side the hill rose steeply covered with heather and gorse.

Someone stepped out from the trees and Lily Kimble jumped.

'My, you did give me a start,' she exclaimed. 'I wasn't expecting to meet you here.'

'Gave you a surprise, did I? I've got another surprise for you.'

It was very lonely in among the trees. There was no one to hear a cry or a struggle. Actually there was no cry and the struggle was very soon over.

A wood-pigeon, disturbed, flew out of the wood . . .

III

'What can have become of the woman?' demanded Dr Kennedy irritably.

The hands of the clock pointed to ten minutes to five.

'Could she have lost her way coming from the station?'

'I gave her explicit directions. In any case its quite simple. Turn to the left when she got out of the station and then take the first road to the right. As I say, it's only a few minutes' walk.'

'Perhaps she's changed her mind,' said Giles.

'It looks like it.'

'Or missed the train,' suggested Gwenda.

Kennedy said slowly, 'No, I think it's more likely that she decided not to come after all. Perhaps her husband stepped in. All these country people are quite incalculable.'

He walked up and down the room.

Then he went to the telephone and asked for a number.

'Hullo? Is that the station? This is Dr Kennedy speaking. I was expecting someone by the four-thirty-five. Middle-aged country woman. Did anyone ask to be directed to me? Or – what do you say?'

The others were near enough to hear the soft lazy accent of Woodleigh

310

Bolton's one porter.

'Don't think as there could be anyone for you, Doctor. Weren't no strangers on the four-thirty-five. Mr Narracotts from Meadows, and Johnnie Lawes, and old Benson's daughter. Weren't no other passengers at all.'

'So she changed her mind,' said Dr Kennedy. 'Well, I can offer *you* tea. The kettle's on. I'll go out and make it.'

He returned with the teapot and they sat down.

'It's only a temporary check,' he said more cheerfully. 'We've got her address. We'll go over and see her, perhaps.'

The telephone rang and the doctor got up to answer.

'Dr Kennedy?'

'Speaking.'

'This is Inspector Last, Longford police station. Were you expecting a woman called Lily Kimble – Mrs Lily Kimble – to call upon you this afternoon?'

'I was. Why? Has there been an accident?'

'Not what you'd call an accident exactly. She's dead. We found a letter from you on the body. That's why I rang you up. Can you make it convenient to come along to Longford police station as soon as possible?'

'I'll come at once.'

IV

'Now let's get this quite clear,' Inspector Last was saying.

He looked from Kennedy to Giles and Gwenda who had accompanied the doctor. Gwenda was very pale and held her hands tightly clasped together. 'You were expecting this woman by the train that leaves Dillmouth Junction at four-five? And gets to Woodleigh Bolton at four-thirty-five?'

Dr Kennedy nodded.

Inspector Last looked down at the letter he had taken from the dead woman's body. It was quite clear.

Dear Mrs Kimble (Dr Kennedy had written)

I shall be glad to advise you to the best of my power. As you will see from the heading of this letter I no longer live in Dillmouth. If you will take the train leaving Coombeleigh at 3.30, change at Dillmouth Junction, and come by the Lonsbury Bay train to Woodleigh Bolton, my house is only a few minutes' walk. Turn to the left as you come out of the station, then take the first road on the right. My house is at the end of it on

311

the right. The name is on the gate.

Yours truly,

James Kennedy.

'There was no question of her coming by an earlier train?'

'An earlier train?' Dr Kennedy looked astonished.

'Because that's what she did. She left Coombeleigh, not at three-thirty but at one-thirty – caught the two-five from Dillmouth Junction and got out, not at Woodleigh Bolton, but at Matchings Halt, the station before it.'

'But that's extraordinary!'

'Was she consulting you professionally, Doctor?'

'No. I retired from practice some years ago.'

'That's what I thought. You knew her well?'

Kennedy shook his head.

'I hadn't seen her for nearly twenty years.'

'But you – er – recognized her just now?'

Gwenda shivered, but dead bodies did not affect a doctor and Kennedy replied thoughtfully: 'Under the circumstances it is hard to say if I recognized her or not. She was strangled, I presume?'

'She was strangled. The body was found in a copse a short way along the track leading from Matchings Halt to Woodleigh Camp. It was found by a hiker coming down from the Camp at about ten minutes to four. Our police surgeon puts the time of death at between two-fifteen and three o'clock. Presumably she was killed shortly after she left the station. No other passenger got out at Matchings Halt. She was the only person to get out of the train there.

'Now why did she get out at Matchings Halt? Did she mistake the station? I hardly think so. In any case she was two hours early for her appointment with you, and had not come by the train you suggested, although she had your letter with her.

'Now just what was her business with you, Doctor?'

Dr Kennedy felt in his pocket and brought out Lily's letter.

'I brought this with me. The enclosed cutting and the insertion put in the local paper by Mr and Mrs Reed here.'

Inspector Last read Lily Kimble's letter and the enclosure. Then he looked from Dr Kennedy to Giles and Gwenda.

'Can I have the story behind all this? It goes back a long way, I gather?'

'Eighteen years,' said Gwenda.

Piecemeal, with additions, and parentheses, the story came out. Inspector Last was a good listener. He let the three people in front of him tell things in their own way. Kennedy was dry, and factual, Gwenda was slightly incoherent, but her narrative had imaginative power. Giles gave,

312

perhaps, the most valuable contribution. He was clear and to the point, with less reserve than Kennedy, and with more coherence than Gwenda. It took a long time.

Then Inspector Last sighed and summed up.

'Mrs Halliday was Dr Kennedy's sister and your stepmother, Mrs Reed. She disappeared from the house you are at present living in eighteen years ago. Lily Kimble (whose maiden name was Abbot) was a servant (house-parlourmaid) in the house at the time. For some reason Lily Kimble inclines (after the passage of years) to the theory that there was foul play. At the time it was assumed that Mrs Halliday had gone away with a man (identity unknown). Major Halliday died in a mental establishment fifteen years ago still under the delusion that he had strangled his wife – if it was a delusion –'

He paused.

'These are all interesting but somewhat unrelated facts. The crucial point seems to be, is Mrs Halliday alive or dead? If dead, when did she die? And what did Lily Kimble know?'

'It seems, on the face of it, that she must have known something rather important. So important that she was killed in order to prevent her talking about it.'

Gwenda cried, 'But how could anyone possibly know she was going to talk about it – except us?'

Inspector Last turned his thoughtful eyes on her.

'It is a significant point, Mrs Reed, that she took the two-five instead of the four-five train from Dillmouth Junction. There must be some reason for that. Also, she got out at the station before Woodleigh Bolton. Why? It seems possible to me that, *after* writing to the doctor, she wrote to *someone else*, suggesting a rendezvous at Woodleigh Camp, perhaps, and that she proposed after that rendezvous, if it was unsatisfactory, to go on to Dr Kennedy and ask his advice. It is possible that she had suspicions of some definite person, and she may have written to that person hinting at her knowledge and suggesting a rendezvous.'

'Blackmail,' said Giles bluntly.

'I don't suppose she thought of it that way,' said Inspector Last. 'She was just greedy and hopeful – and a little muddled about what she could get out of it all. We'll see. Maybe the husband can tell us more.'

v

'Warned her, I did,' said Mr Kimble heavily. ' "Don't have nought to do with it," them were my words. Went behind my back, she did. Thought as

313

she knew best. That were Lily all over. Too smart by half.'

Questioning revealed that Mr Kimble had little to contribute.

Lily had been in service at St Catherine's before he met her and started walking out with her. Fond of the pictures, she was, and told him that likely as not, she'd been in a house where there'd been a murder.

'Didn't pay much account, I didn't. All imagination, I thought. Never content with plain fact, Lily wasn't. Long rigmarole she told me, about the master doing in the missus and maybe putting the body in the cellar – and something about a French girl what had looked out of the window and seen something or somebody. "Don't you pay no attention to foreigners, my girl," I said. "One and all they're liars. Not like us." And when she run on about it, I didn't listen because, mark you, she was working it all up out of nothing. Liked a bit of crime, Lily did. Used to take the *Sunday News* what was running a series about Famous Murderers. Full of it, she was, and if she liked to think she'd been in a house where there was a murder, well, thinking don't hurt nobody. But when she was on at me about answering this advertisement – "You leave it alone," I says to her. "It's no good stirring up trouble." And if she'd done as I told her, she'd be alive today.'

He thought for a moment or two.

'Ar,' he said. 'She'd be alive right now. Too smart by half, that was Lily.'

CHAPTER 23

Which Of Them?

Giles and Gwenda had not gone with Inspector Last and Dr Kennedy to interview Mr Kimble. They arrived home about seven o'clock. Gwenda looked white and ill. Dr Kennedy had said to Giles: 'Give her some brandy and make her eat something, then get her to bed. She's had a bad shock.'

'It's so awful, Giles,' Gwenda kept saying. 'So awful. That silly woman, making an appointment with the murderer, and going along so confidently – to be killed. Like a sheep to the slaughter.'

'Well, don't think about it, darling. After all, we did know there was someone – a killer.'

'No, we didn't. Not a killer *now*. I mean, it was *then* – eighteen years ago. It wasn't, somehow, quite real . . . It might all have been a mistake.'

'Well, this proves that it wasn't a mistake. You were right all the time, Gwenda.'

Giles was glad to find Miss Marple at Hillside. She and Mrs Cocker between them fussed over Gwenda who refused brandy because she said it always reminded her of Channel steamers, but accepted some hot whisky and lemon, and then, coaxed by Mrs Cocker, sat down and ate an omelette.

Giles would have talked determinedly of other things, but Miss Marple, with what Giles admitted to be superior tactics, discussed the crime in a gentle aloof manner.

'Very dreadful, my dear,' she said. 'And of course a great shock, but interesting, one must admit. And of course I am so old that death doesn't shock me as much as it does you – only something lingering and painful like cancer really distresses me. The really vital thing is that this proves definitely and beyond any possible doubt that poor young Helen Halliday was killed. We've thought so all along and now we *know*.'

'And according to you we ought to know where the body is,' said Giles. 'The cellar, I suppose.'

'No, no, Mr Reed. You remember Edith Pagett said she went down there on the morning after because she was disturbed by what Lily had said, and she found no signs of anything of the kind – and there would be signs, you know, if somebody was really looking for them.'

'Then what happened to it? Taken away in a car and thrown over a cliff into the sea?'

'No. Come now, my dears, what struck you first of all when you came here – struck you, Gwenda, I should say. The fact that from the drawing-room window, you had no view down to the sea. Where you felt, very properly, that steps should lead down to the lawn – there was instead a plantation of shrubs. The steps, you found subsequently, had been there originally, but had at some time been transferred to the end of the terrace. Why were they moved?'

Gwenda stared at her with dawning comprehension.

'You mean that *that's* where –'

'There must have been a reason for making the change, and there doesn't really seem to be a sensible one. It is, frankly, a stupid place to have steps down to the lawn. But that end of the terrace is a very quiet place – it's not overlooked from the house except by one window – the window of the nursery, on the first floor. Don't you see, that if you want to bury a body the earth will be disturbed and there must be a *reason* for its being disturbed. The reason was that it had been decided to move the steps from in front of the drawing-room to the end of the terrace. I've learnt already from Dr Kennedy that Helen Halliday and her husband were very keen on the garden, and did a lot of work in it. The daily gardener they employed used merely to carry out their orders, and if he arrived to find that this change was in progress and some of the flags had already been moved, he would only have thought that the Hallidays had started on the work when he wasn't there. The body, of course, could have been buried at either place, but we can be quite certain, I think, that it is actually buried at the end of the terrace and not in front of the drawing-room window.'

'Why can we be sure?' asked Gwenda.

'Because of what poor Lily Kimble said in her letter – that she changed her mind about the body being in the cellar because of what Léonie saw when she looked out of the window. That makes it very clear, doesn't it? The Swiss girl looked out of the nursery window at some time during the night and saw the grave being dug. Perhaps she actually saw who it was digging it.'

'And never said anything to the police?'

'My dear, there was no question at the time of a *crime* having occurred. Mrs Halliday had run away with a lover – that was all that Léonie would grasp. She probably couldn't speak much English anyway. She did mention to Lily, perhaps not at the time, but later, a curious thing she had observed from her window that night, and that stimulated Lily's belief in a crime having occurred. But I've no doubt that Edith Pagett told Lily off for talking nonsense, and the Swiss girl would accept her point of view and would certainly not wish to be mixed up with the police. Foreigners always seem to be particularly nervous about the police when they are in a strange country. So she went back to Switzerland and very likely never thought

316

of it again.'

Giles said: 'If she's alive now – if she can be traced –'

Miss Marple nodded her head. 'Perhaps.'

Giles demanded: 'How can we set about it?'

Miss Marple said: 'The police will be able to do that much better than you can.'

'Inspector Last is coming over here tomorrow morning.'

'Then I think I should tell him – about the steps.'

'And about what I saw – or think I saw – in the hall?' asked Gwenda nervously.

'Yes, dear. You've been very wise to say nothing of that until now. Very wise. But I think the time has come.'

Giles said slowly: 'She was strangled in the hall, and then the murderer carried her upstairs and put her on the bed. Kelvin Halliday came in, passed out with doped whisky, and in his turn was carried upstairs to the bedroom. He came to, and thought he had killed her. The murderer must have been watching somewhere near at hand. When Kelvin went off to Dr Kennedy's, the murderer took away the body, probably hid it in the shrubbery at the end of the terrace and waited until everybody had gone to bed and was presumably asleep, before he dug the grave and buried the body. That means he must have been here, hanging about the house, pretty well all that night?'

Miss Marple nodded.

'He had to be – *on the spot*. I remember your saying that that was important. We've got to see which of our three suspects fits in best with the requirements. We'll take Erskine first. Now he definitely was on the spot. By his own admission he walked up here with Helen Kennedy from the beach at round about nine o'clock. He said goodbye to her. But did he say goodbye to her? Let's say instead that he strangled her.'

'But it was all over between them,' cried Gwenda. 'Long ago. He said himself that he was hardly ever alone with Helen.'

'But don't you see, Gwenda, that the way we must look at it now, we can't depend on anything anyone *says*.'

'Now I'm so glad to hear you say that,' said Miss Marple. 'Because I've been a little worried, you know, by the way you two have seemed willing to accept, as actual fact, all the things that people have told you. I'm afraid I have a sadly distrustful nature, but, especially in a matter of *murder*, I make it a rule to take nothing that is told to me as true, unless it is *checked*. For instance, it does seem quite certain that Lily Kimble mentioned the clothes packed and taken away in a suitcase were not the ones Helen Halliday would herself have taken, because not only did Edith Pagett tell us that Lily said so

317

to her, but Lily herself mentioned the fact in her letter to Dr Kennedy. So that is one *fact*. Dr Kennedy told us that Kelvin Halliday believed that his wife was secretly drugging him, and Kelvin Halliday in his diary confirms that – so there is another fact – and a very curious fact it is, don't you think? However, we will not go into that now.

'But I would like to point out that a great many of the assumptions you have made have been based upon what has been told you – possibly told you very plausibly.'

Giles stared hard at her.

Gwenda, her colour restored, sipped coffee, and leaned across the table.

Giles said: 'Let's check up now on what three people have said to us. Take Erskine first. He says –'

'You've got a down on him,' said Gwenda. 'It's waste of time going on about him, because now he's definitely out of it. He couldn't have killed Lily Kimble.'

Giles went on imperturbably: 'He says that he met Helen on the boat going out to India and they fell in love, but that he couldn't bring himself to leave his wife and children, and that they agreed they must say goodbye. Suppose it wasn't quite like that. Suppose he fell desperately in love with Helen, and that it was *she* who wouldn't run off with him. Supposing he threatened that if she married anyone else he would kill her.'

'Most improbable,' said Gwenda.

'Things like that do happen. Remember what you overheard his wife say to him. You put it all down to jealousy, but it may have been true. Perhaps she *has* had a terrible time with him where women are concerned – he may be a little bit of a sex maniac.'

'I don't believe it.'

'No, because he's attractive to women. I think, myself, that there is something a little queer about Erskine. However, let's go on with my case against him. Helen breaks off her engagement to Fane and comes home and marries your father and settles down here. And then suddenly, Erskine turns up. He comes down ostensibly on a summer holiday with his wife. That's an odd thing to do, really. He admits he came here to see Helen again. Now let's take it that *Erskine* was the man in the drawing-room with her that day when Lily overheard her say she was afraid of him. "*I'm afraid of you – I've always been afraid of you – I think you're mad.*"

'And, because she's afraid, she makes plans to go and live in Norfolk, but she's very secretive about it. No one is to know. No one is to know, that is, until the Erskines have left Dillmouth. So far that fits. Now we come to the fatal night. What the Hallidays were doing earlier that evening we don't know –'

Miss Marple coughed.

'As a matter of fact, I saw Edith Pagett again. She remembers that there was early supper that night – seven o'clock – because Major Halliday was going to some meeting – Golf Club, she thinks it was, or some Parish meeting. Mrs Halliday went out after supper.'

'Right. Helen meets Erskine, by appointment, perhaps, on the beach. He is leaving the following day. Perhaps he refuses to go. He urges Helen to go away with him. She comes back here and he comes with her. Finally, in a fit of frenzy he strangles her. The next bit is as we have already agreed. He's slightly mad, he wants Kelvin Halliday to believe it is *he* who has killed her. Later, Erskine buries the body. You remember, he told Gwenda that he didn't go back to the hotel until very late because he was walking about Dillmouth.'

'One wonders,' said Miss Marple, 'what his wife was doing?'

'Probably frenzied with jealousy,' said Gwenda. 'And gave him hell when he did get in.'

'That's my reconstruction,' said Giles. 'And it's possible.'

'But he couldn't have killed Lily Kimble,' said Gwenda, 'because he lives in Northumberland. So thinking about him is just waste of time. Let's take Walter Fane.'

'Right. Walter Fane is the repressed type. He seems gentle and mild and easily pushed around. But Miss Marple has brought us one valuable bit of testimony. Walter Fane was once in such a rage that he nearly killed his brother. Admittedly he was a child at the time, but it was startling because he had always seemed of such a gentle forgiving nature. Anyway, Walter Fane falls in love with Helen Halliday. Not merely in love, he's crazy about her. She won't have him and he goes off to India. Later she writes him that she will come out and marry him. She starts. Then comes the second blow. She arrives and promptly jilts him. She has "met someone on the boat". She goes home and marries Kelvin Halliday. Possibly Walter Fane thinks that Kelvin Halliday was the original cause of her turning him down. He broods, nurses a crazy jealous hate and comes home. He behaves in a most forgiving, friendly manner, is often at this house, has become apparently a tame cat around the house, the faithful Dobbin. But perhaps Helen realizes that this isn't true. She gets a glimpse of what is going on below the surface. Perhaps, long ago, she sensed something disturbing in quiet young Walter Fane. She says to him, "I think I've always been afraid of you." She makes plans, secretly, to go right away from Dillmouth and live in Norfolk. Why? Because she's afraid of Walter Fane.

'Now we come again to the fatal evening. Here, we're not on very sure ground. We don't know what Walter Fane was doing that night, and I don't see any probability of ever finding out. But he fulfils Miss Marple's requirement of being "on the spot" to the extent of living in a house that is only two or three minutes' walk away. He may have said he was going to bed early with a headache, or shut himself into his study with work to do – something of that kind. He could have done all the things we've decided the murderer did do, and I think that he's the most likely of the three to have made mistakes in packing a suitcase. He wouldn't know enough about what women wear to do it properly.'

'It was queer,' said Gwenda. 'In his office that day I had an odd sort of feeling that he was like a house with its blinds pulled down ... and I even had a fanciful idea that – that there was someone dead in the house.'

She looked at Miss Marple.

'Does that seem very silly to you?' she asked.

'No, my dear. I think that perhaps you were right.'

'And now,' said Gwenda, 'we come to Afflick. Afflick's Tours. Jackie Afflick who was always too smart by half. The first thing against him is that Dr Kennedy believed he had incipient persecution mania. That is – he was never really normal. He's told us about himself and Helen – but we'll agree now that that was all a pack of lies. He didn't just think she was a cute kid – he was madly, passionately in love with her. But she wasn't in love with him. She was just amusing herself. She was man mad, as Miss Marple says.'

'No, dear. *I* didn't say that. Nothing of the kind.'

'Well, a nymphomanic if you prefer the term. Anyway, she had an affair with Jackie Afflick and then wanted to drop him. He didn't want to be dropped. Her brother got her out of her scrape, but Jackie Afflick never forgave or forgot. He lost his job – according to him through being framed by Walter Fane. That shows definite signs of persecution mania.'

'Yes,' agreed Giles. 'But on the other hand, if it was true, it's another point against Fane – quite a valuable point.'

Gwenda went on.

'Helen goes abroad, and he leaves Dillmouth. But he never forgets her, and when she returns to Dillmouth, married, he comes over and visits her. He said first of all, he came *once*, but later on, he admits that he came more than once. And, oh Giles, don't you remember? Edith Pagett used a phrase about "our mystery man in a flashy car". You see, he came often enough to make the servants talk. But Helen took pains not to ask him to a meal – not to let him meet Kelvin. Perhaps she was afraid of him. Perhaps –'

Giles interrupted.

'This might cut both ways. Supposing Helen was in love with him – the first man she ever was in love with, and supposing she went on being in love with him. Perhaps they had an affair together and she didn't let anyone

320

know about it. But perhaps he wanted her to go away with him, and by that time she was tired of him, and wouldn't go, and so – and so – he killed her. And all the rest of it. Lily said in her letter to Dr Kennedy there was a posh car standing outside that night. It was Jackie Afflick's car. Jackie Afflick was "on the spot", too.

'It's an assumption,' said Giles. 'But it seems to me a reasonable one. But there are Helen's letters to be worked into our reconstruction. I've been puzzling my brains to think of the "circumstances", as Miss Marple put it, under which she could have been induced to write those letters. It seems to me that to explain them, we've got to admit that she actually *had* a lover, and that she was expecting to go away with him. We'll test our three possibles again. Erskine first. Say that he still wasn't prepared to leave his wife or break up his home, but that Helen had agreed to leave Kelvin Halliday and go somewhere where Erskine could come and be with her from time to time. The first thing would be to disarm Mrs Erskine's suspicions, so Helen writes a couple of letters to reach her brother in due course which will look as though she has gone abroad with someone. That fits in very well with her being so mysterious about who the man in question is.'

'But if she was going to leave her husband for him, why did he kill her?' asked Gwenda.

'Perhaps because she suddenly changed her mind. Decided that she did really care for her husband after all. He just saw red and strangled her. Then, he took the clothes and suitcase and used the letters. That's a perfectly good explanation covering everything.'

'The same might apply to Walter Fane. I should imagine that scandal might be absolutely disastrous to a country solicitor. Helen might have agreed to go somewhere nearby where Fane could visit her but pretend that she had gone abroad with someone else. Letters all prepared and then, as you suggested, she changed her mind. Walter went mad and killed her.'

'What about Jackie Afflick?'

'It's more difficult to find a reason for the letters with him. I shouldn't imagine that scandal would affect him. Perhaps Helen was afraid, not of him, but of my father – and so thought it would be better to pretend she'd gone abroad – or perhaps Afflick's wife had the money at that time, and he wanted her money to invest in his business. Oh yes, there are lots of possibilities for the letters.'

'Which one do you fancy, Miss Marple?' asked Gwenda. 'I don't really think Walter Fane – but then –'

Mrs Cocker had just come in to clear away the coffee cups.

'There now, madam,' she said. 'I quite forgot. All this about a poor woman being murdered and you and Mr Reed mixed up in it, not at all the right thing for you, madam, *just now*. Mr Fane was here this afternoon, asking for you. He waited quite half an hour. Seemed to think you were expecting him.'

'How strange,' said Gwenda. 'What time?'

'It must have been about four o'clock or just after. And then, after that, there was another gentleman, came in a great big yellow car. He was positive you were expecting him. Wouldn't take no for an answer. Waited twenty minutes. I wondered if you'd had some idea of a tea-party and forgotten it.'

'No,' said Gwenda. 'How odd.'

'Let's ring up Fane now,' said Giles. 'He won't have gone to bed.'

He suited the action to the word.

'Hullo, is that Fane speaking? Giles Reed here. I hear you came round to see us this afternoon – What? – No – no, I'm sure of it – no, how very odd. Yes, I wonder, too.'

He laid down the receiver.

'Here's an odd thing. He was rung up in his office this morning. A message left would he come round and see us this afternoon. It was very important.'

Giles and Gwenda stared at each other. Then Gwenda said, 'Ring up Afflick.'

Again Giles went to the telephone, found the number and rang through. It took a little longer, but presently he got the connection.

'Mr Afflick? Giles Reed, I –'

Here he was obviously interrupted by a flow of speech from the other end.

At last he was able to say:

'But we didn't – no, I assure you – nothing of the kind – Yes – yes, I know you're a busy man. I wouldn't have dreamed of – Yes, but look here, who was it rang you – a man? – No, I tell you it wasn't me. No – no, I see. Well, I agree, it's quite extraordinary.'

He replaced the receiver and came back to the table.

'Well, there it is,' he said. 'Somebody, a man who said he was me, rang up Afflick and asked him to come over here. It was urgent – big sum of money involved.'

They looked at each other.

'It could have been either of them,' said Gwenda. 'Don't you see, Giles? Either of them *could have killed Lily and come on here as an alibi.*'

'Hardly an alibi, dear,' put in Miss Marple.

'I don't mean quite an alibi, but an excuse for being away from their office. What I mean is, one of them is speaking the truth and one is lying. One of them rang up the other and asked him to come here – to throw suspicion on him – but we don't know which. It's a clear issue now between the two of them. Fane or Afflick. I say – Jackie Afflick.'

'I think Walter Fane,' said Giles.

They both looked at Miss Marple.

She shook her head.

'There's another possibility,' she said.

'Of course. Erskine.'

Giles fairly ran across to the telephone.

'What are you going to do?' asked Gwenda.

'Put through a trunk call to Northumberland.'

'Oh Giles – you can't really think –'

'We've got to *know*. If he's there – he can't have killed Lily Kimble this afternoon. No private aeroplanes or silly stuff like that.'

They waited in silence until the telephone bell ran.

Giles picked up the receiver.

'You were asking for a personal call to Major Erskine. Go ahead, please. Major Erskine is waiting.'

Clearing his throat nervously, Giles said, 'Er – Erskine? Giles Reed here – Reed, yes.'

He cast a sudden agonized glance at Gwenda which said as plainly as possible, 'What the hell do I say now?'

Gwenda got up and took the receiver from him.

'Major Erskine? This is Mrs Reed here. We've heard of – of a house. Linscott Brake. Is – is it – do you know anything about it? It's somewhere near you, I believe.'

Erskine's voice said: 'Linscott Brake? No, I don't think I've ever heard of it. What's the postal town?'

'It's terribly blurred,' said Gwenda. 'You know those awful typescripts agents send out. But it says fifteen miles from Daith so we thought –'

'I'm sorry. I haven't heard of it. Who lives there?'

'Oh, it's empty. But never mind, actually we've – we've practically settled on a house. I'm so sorry to have bothered you. I expect you were busy.'

'No, not at all. At least only busy domestically. My wife's away. And our cook had to go off to her mother, so I've been dealing with domestic routine. I'm afraid I'm not much of a hand at it. Better in the garden.'

'I'd always rather do gardening than housework. I hope your wife isn't ill?'

'Oh no, she was called away to a sister. She'll be back tomorrow.'

'Well, good night, and so sorry to have bothered you.'

She put down the receiver.

323

'Erskine is out of it,' she said triumphantly. 'His wife's away and he's doing all the chores. So that leaves it between the two others. Doesn't it, Miss Marple?'

Miss Marple was looking grave.

'I don't think, my dears,' she said, 'that you have given quite enough thought to the matter. Oh dear – I am really very worried. If only I knew exactly what to do ...'

CHAPTER 24

The Monkey's Paws

Gwenda leaned her elbows on the table and cupped her chin in her hands while her eyes roamed dispassionately over the remains of a hasty lunch. Presently she must deal with them, carry them out to the scullery, wash up, put things away, see what there would be, later, for supper.

But there was no wild hurry. She felt she needed a little time to take things in. Everything had been happening too fast.

The events of the morning, when she reviewed them, seemed to be chaotic and impossible. Everything had happened too quickly and too improbably.

Inspector Last had appeared early – at half past nine. With him had come Detective Inspector Primer from headquarters and the Chief Constable of the County. The latter had not stayed long. It was Inspector Primer who was now in charge of the case of Lily Kimble deceased and all the ramifications arising therefrom.

It was Inspector Primer, a man with a deceptively mild manner and a gentle apologetic voice, who had asked her if it would inconvenience her very much if his men did some digging in the garden.

From the tone of his voice, it might have been a case of giving his men some healthful exercise, rather than of seeking for a dead body which had been buried for eighteen years.

Giles had spoken up then. He had said: 'I think, perhaps, we could help you with a suggestion or two.'

And he told the Inspector about the shifting of the steps leading down to the lawn, and took the Inspector out on to the terrace.

The Inspector had looked up at the barred window on the first floor at the corner of the house and had said: 'That would be the nursery, I presume.'

And Giles said that it would.

Then the Inspector and Giles had come back into the house, and two men with spades had gone out into the garden, and Giles, before the Inspector could get down to questions, had said:

'I think, Inspector, you had better hear something that my wife has so far not mentioned to anyone except myself – and – er – one other person.'

The gentle, rather compelling gaze of Inspector Primer came to rest on Gwenda. It was faintly speculative. He was asking himself, Gwenda thought: 'Is this a woman who can be depended upon, or is she the kind who imagines things?'

So strongly did she feel this, that she started in a defensive way: 'I may have imagined it. Perhaps I did. But it seems awfully real.'

Inspector Primer said softly and soothingly:

'Well, Mrs Reed, let's hear about it.'

And Gwenda had explained. How the house had seemed familiar to her when she first saw it. How she had subsequently learned that she had, in fact, lived there as a child. How she had remembered the nursery wallpaper, and the connecting door, and the feeling she had had that there ought to be steps down to the lawn.

Inspector Primer nodded. He did not say that Gwenda's childish recollections were not particularly interesting, but Gwenda wondered whether he were thinking it.

Then she nerved herself to the final statement. How she had suddenly remembered, when sitting in a theatre, looking through the banisters at Hillside and seeing a dead woman in the hall.

'With a blue face, strangled, and golden hair – and it was Helen – But it was so stupid, I didn't know at all who Helen *was*.'

'We think that –' Giles began, but Inspector Primer, with unexpected authority, held up a restraining hand.

'Please let Mrs Reed tell me in her own words.'

And Gwenda had stumbled on, her face flushed, with Inspector Primer gently helping her out, using a dexterity that Gwenda did not appreciate as the highly technical performance it was.

'Webster?' he said thoughtfully. 'Hm, *Duchess of Malfi*. Monkey's paws?'

'But that was probably a nightmare,' said Giles.

'Please, Mr Reed.'

'It may all have been a nightmare,' said Gwenda.

'No, I don't think it was,' said Inspector Primer. 'It would be very hard to explain Lily Kimble's death, unless we assume that there *was* a woman murdered in this house.'

That seemed so reasonable and almost comforting, that Gwenda hurried on.

'And it wasn't my father who murdered her. It wasn't, really. Even Dr Penrose says he wasn't the right type, and that he couldn't have murdered anybody. And Dr Kennedy was quite sure he hadn't done it, but only thought he had. So you see it was someone who wanted it to *seem* as though my father had done it, and we think we know who – at least it's one of two people –'

'Gwenda,' said Giles. 'We can't really –'

'I wonder, Mr Reed,' said the Inspector, 'if you would mind going out

326

into the garden and seeing how my men are getting on. Tell them I sent you.'

He closed the french windows after Giles and latched them and came back to Gwenda.

'Now just tell me all your ideas, Mrs Reed. Never mind if they are rather incoherent.'

And Gwenda had poured out all her and Giles's speculations and reasonings, and the steps they had taken to find out all they could about the three men who might have figured in Helen Halliday's life, and the final conclusions they had come to – and how both Walter Fane and J. J. Afflick had been rung up, as though by Giles, and had been summoned to Hillside the preceding afternoon.

'But you do see, don't you, Inspector – that one of them might be lying?'

And in a gentle, rather tired voice, the Inspector said: 'That's one of the principal difficulties in my kind of work. So many people may be lying. And so many people usually are . . . Though not always for the reasons that you'd think. And some people don't even know they're lying.'

'Do you think I'm like that?' Gwenda asked apprehensively.

And the Inspector had smiled and said: 'I think you're a very truthful witness, Mrs Reed.'

'And you think I'm right about who murdered her?'

The Inspector sighed and said: 'It's not a question of thinking – not with us. It's a question of checking up. Where everybody was, what account everybody gives of their movements. We know accurately enough, to within ten minutes or so, when Lily Kimble was killed. Between two-twenty and two-forty-five. Anyone could have killed her and then come on here yesterday afternoon. I don't see, myself, any reason for those telephone calls. It doesn't give either of the people you mention an alibi for the time of the murder.'

'But you will find out, won't you, what they were doing at the time? Between two-twenty and two-forty-five. You will ask them.'

Inspector Primer smiled.

'We shall ask all the questions necessary, Mrs Reed, you may be sure of that. All in good time. There's no good in rushing things. You've got to see your way ahead.'

Gwenda had a sudden vision of patience and quite unsensational work. Unhurried, remorseless . . .

She said: 'I see . . . yes. Because you're professional. And Giles and I are just amateurs. We might make a lucky hit – but we wouldn't really know how to follow it up.'

'Something of the kind, Mrs Reed.'

327

The Inspector smiled again. He got up and unfastened the french windows. Then, just as he was about to step through them, he stopped. Rather, Gwenda thought, like a pointing dog.

'Excuse me, Mrs Reed. That lady wouldn't be a Miss Jane Marple, would she?'

Gwenda had come to stand beside him. At the bottom of the garden Miss Marple was still waging a losing war with bindweed.

'Yes, that's Miss Marple. She's awfully kind in helping us with the garden.'

'Miss Marple,' said the Inspector. '*I see.*'

And as Gwenda looked at him enquiringly and said, 'She's rather a dear,' he replied:

'She's a very celebrated lady, is Miss Marple. Got the Chief Constables of at least three counties in her pocket. She's not got my Chief yet, but I dare say that will come. So Miss Marple's got her finger in this pie.'

'She's made an awful lot of helpful suggestions,' said Gwenda.

'I bet she has,' said the Inspector. 'Was it her suggestion where to look for the deceased Mrs Halliday?'

'She said that Giles and I ought to know quite well where to look,' said Gwenda. 'And it did seem stupid of us not to have thought of it before.'

The Inspector gave a soft little laugh, and went down to stand by Miss Marple. He said: 'I don't think we've been introduced, Miss Marple. But you were pointed out to me once by Colonel Melrose.'

Miss Marple stood up, flushed and grasping a handful of clinging green.

'Oh yes. Dear Colonel Melrose. He has always been *most* kind. Ever since –'

'Ever since a churchwarden was shot in the Vicar's study. Quite a while ago. But you've had other successes since then. A little poison pen trouble down near Lymstock.'

'You seem to know quite a lot about me, Inspector –'

'Primer, my name is. And you've been busy here, I expect.'

'Well, I try to do what I can in the garden. Sadly neglected. This bindweed, for instance, such nasty stuff. Its roots,' said Miss Marple, looking very earnestly at the Inspector, 'go down underground a long way. A very long way – they run along underneath the soil.'

'I think you're right about that,' said the Inspector. 'A long way down. A long way back . . . this murder, I mean. Eighteen years.'

'And perhaps before that,' said Miss Marple. 'Running underground . . . And terribly harmful, Inspector, squeezing the life out of the pretty growing flowers . . .'

One of the police constables came along the path. He was perspiring and

328

had a smudge of earth on his forehead.

'We've come to – something, sir. Looks as though it's her all right.'

II

And it was then, Gwenda reflected, that the nightmarish quality of the day had begun. Giles coming in, his face rather pale, saying: 'It's – she's there all right, Gwenda.'

Then one of the constables had telephoned and the police surgeon, a short, bustling man, had arrived.

And it was then that Mrs Cocker, the calm and imperturbable Mrs Cocker, had gone out into the garden – not led, as might have been expected, by ghoulish curiosity, but solely in the quest of culinary herbs for the dish she was preparing for lunch. And Mrs Cocker, whose reaction to the news of a murder on the preceding day had been shocked censure and an anxiety for the effect upon Gwenda's health (for Mrs Cocker had made up her mind that the nursery upstairs was to be tenanted after the due number of months), had walked straight in upon the gruesome discovery, and had been immediately 'taken queer' to an alarming extent.

'Too horrible, madam. Bones is a thing I never could abide. Not skeleton bones, as one might say. And here in the garden, just by the mint and all. And my heart's beating at such a rate – palpitations – I can hardly get my breath. And if I might make so bold, just a thimbleful of brandy . . .'

Alarmed by Mrs Cocker's gasps and her ashy colour, Gwenda had rushed to the sideboard, poured out some brandy and brought it to Mrs Cocker to sip.

And Mrs Cocker had said: 'That's just what I needed, madam –' when, quite suddenly, her voice had failed, and she had looked so alarming, that Gwenda had screamed for Giles, and Giles had yelled to the police surgeon.

'And it's fortunate I was on the spot,' the latter said afterwards. 'It was touch and go anyway. Without a doctor, that woman would have died then and there.'

And then Inspector Primer had taken the brandy decanter, and then he and the doctor had gone into a huddle over it, and Inspector Primer had asked Gwenda when she and Giles had last had any brandy out of it.

Gwenda said she thought not for some days. They'd been away – up North, and the last few times they'd had a drink, they'd had gin. 'But I nearly had some brandy yesterday,' said Gwenda. 'Only it makes me think of Channel steamers, so Giles opened a new bottle of whisky.'

'That was very lucky for you, Mrs Reed. If you'd drunk brandy

329

yesterday, I doubt if you would be alive today.'

'Giles nearly drank some – but in the end he had whisky with me.'
Gwenda shivered.

Even now, alone in the house, with the police gone and Giles gone with them after a hasty lunch scratched up out of tins (since Mrs Cocker had been removed to hospital), Gwenda could hardly believe in the morning turmoil of events.

One thing stood out clearly: the presence in the house yesterday of Jackie Afflick and Walter Fane. Either of them could have tampered with the brandy, and what was the purpose of the telephone calls unless it was to afford one or other of them the opportunity to poison the brandy decanter? Gwenda and Giles had been getting too near the truth. Or had a third person come in from outside, through the open dining-room window perhaps, whilst she and Giles had been sitting in Dr Kennedy's house waiting for Lily Kimble to keep her appointment? A third person who had engineered the telephone calls to steer suspicion on the other two?

But a third person, Gwenda thought, didn't make sense. For a third person, surely, would have telephoned to only *one* of the two men. A third person would have wanted one suspect, not two. And anyway, who could the third person be? Erskine had definitely been in Northumberland. No, either Walter Fane had telephoned to Afflick and had pretended to be telephoned to himself. Or else Afflick had telephoned Fane, and had made the same pretence of receiving a summons. One of those two, and the police, who were cleverer and had more resources than she and Giles had, would find out which. And in the meantime both of those men would be watched. They wouldn't be able to – to try again.

Again Gwenda shivered. It took a little getting used to – the knowledge that someone had tried to kill you. 'Dangerous,' Miss Marple had said long ago. But she and Giles had not really taken the idea of danger seriously. Even after Lily Kimble had been killed, it still hadn't occurred to her that anyone would try and kill her and Giles. Just because she and Giles were getting too near the truth of what had happened eighteen years ago. Working out what must have happened then – and who had made it happen.

Walter Fane and Jackie Afflick . . .

Which?

Gwenda closed her eyes, seeing them afresh in the light of her new knowledge.

Quiet Walter Fane, sitting in his office – the pale spider in the centre of its web. So quiet, so harmless-looking. A house with its blinds down. Someone dead in the house. Someone dead eighteen years ago – but still there. How sinister the quiet Walter Fane seemed now. Walter Fane who had once flung himself murderously upon his brother. Walter Fane whom Helen had scornfully refused to marry, once here at home, and once again in India. A double rebuff. A double ignominy. Walter Fane, so quiet, so unemotional, who could express himself, perhaps, only in sudden murderous violence – as, possibly, quiet Lizzie Borden had once done . . .

Gwenda opened her eyes. She had convinced herself, hadn't she, that Walter Fane was the man?

One might, perhaps, just consider Afflick. With her eyes open, not shut.

His loud check suit, his domineering manner – just the opposite to Walter Fane – nothing repressed or quiet about Afflick. But possibly he had put that manner on because of an inferiority complex. It worked that way, experts said. If you weren't sure of yourself, you had to boast and assert yourself, and be overbearing. Turned down by Helen because he wasn't good enough for her. The sore festering, not forgotten. Determination to get on in the world. Persecution. Everyone against him. Discharged from his employment by a faked charge made up by an 'enemy'. Surely that did show that Afflick wasn't normal. And what a feeling of power a man like that would get out of killing. That good-natured, jovial face of his, it was a cruel face really. He was a cruel man – and his thin pale wife knew it and was afraid of him. Lily Kimble had threatened him and Lily Kimble had died. Gwenda and Giles had interfered – then Gwenda and Giles must die, too, and he would involve Walter Fane who had sacked him long ago. That fitted in very nicely.

Gwenda shook herself, came out of her imaginings, and returned to practicality. Giles would be home and want his tea. She must clear away and wash up lunch.

She fetched a tray and took the things out to the kitchen. Everything in the kitchen was exquisitely neat. Mrs Cocker was really a treasure.

By the side of the sink was a pair of surgical rubber gloves. Mrs Cocker always wore a pair for washing up. Her niece, who worked in a hospital, got them at a reduced price.

Gwenda fitted them on over her hands and began to wash up the dishes. She might as well keep her hands nice.

She washed the plates and put them in the rack, washed and dried the other things and put everything neatly away.

Then, still lost in thought, she went upstairs. She might as well, she thought, wash out those stockings and a jumper or two. She'd keep the gloves on.

These things were in the forefront of her mind. But somewhere, underneath them, something was nagging at her.

Walter Fane or Jackie Afflick, she had said. One or the other of them.

331

And she had made out quite a good case against either of them. Perhaps that was what really worried her. Because, strictly speaking, it would be much more satisfactory if you could only make out a good case against *one* of them. One ought to be sure, by now, *which*. And Gwenda wasn't sure.

If only there was someone else ... But there couldn't be anyone else. Because Richard Erskine was out of it. Richard Erskine had been in Northumberland when Lily Kimble was killed and when the brandy in the decanter had been tampered with. Yes, Richard Erskine was right out of it.

She was glad of that, because she liked Richard Erskine. Richard Erskine was attractive, very attractive. How sad for him to be married to the megalith of a woman with her suspicious eyes and deep bass voice. Just like a man's voice ...

Like a man's voice ...

The idea flashed through her mind with a queer misgiving.

A man's voice ... Could it have been Mrs Erskine, not her husband, who had replied to Giles on the telephone last night?

No – no, surely not. No, of course not. She and Giles would have known. And anyway, to begin with, Mrs Erskine could have had no idea of who was ringing up. No, of course it was Erskine speaking, and his wife, as he said, was away.

His wife was away ...

Surely – no, that was impossible ... Could it have been *Mrs* Erskine? Mrs Erskine, driven insane by jealousy? Mrs Erskine to whom Lily Kimble had written? Was it a *woman* Léonie had seen in the garden that night when she looked out of the window?

There was a sudden bang in the hall below. Somebody had come in through the front door.

Gwenda came out from the bathroom on to the landing and looked over the banisters. She was relieved to see it was Dr Kennedy. She called down:

'I'm here.'

Her hands were held out in front of her – wet, glistening, a queer pinkish grey – they reminded her of something ...

Kennedy looked up, shading his eyes.

'Is that you, Gwennie? I can't see your face ... My eyes are dazzled –'

And then Gwenda screamed ...

Looking at those smooth monkey's paws and hearing that voice in the hall –

'It was you,' she gasped. 'You killed her ... killed Helen ... I – know now. It was you ... all along ... You ...'

He came up the stairs towards her. Slowly. Looking up at her.

'Why couldn't you leave me alone?' he said. 'Why did you have to meddle? Why did you have to bring – Her – back? Just when I'd begun to forget – to forget. You brought her back again – Helen – my Helen. Bringing it all up again. I had to kill Lily – now I'll have to kill you. Like I killed Helen . . . Yes, like I killed Helen . . .'

He was close upon her now – his hands out towards her – reaching, she knew, for her throat. That kind, quizzical face – that nice, ordinary, elderly face – the same still, but for the eyes – the eyes were not sane . . .

Gwenda retreated before him, slowly, the scream frozen in her throat. She had screamed once. She could not scream again. And if she did scream no one would hear.

Because there was no one in the house – not Giles, and not Mrs Cocker, not even Miss Marple in the garden. Nobody. And the house next door was too far away to hear if she screamed. And anyway, she couldn't scream . . . Because she was too frightened to scream. Frightened of those horrible reaching hands . . .

She could back away to the nursery door and then – and then – those hands would fasten round her throat . . .

A pitiful little stifled whimper came from between her lips.

And then, suddenly, Dr Kennedy stopped and reeled back as a jet of soapy water struck him between the eyes. He gasped and blinked and his hands went to his face.

'So fortunate,' said Miss Marple's voice, rather breathless, for she had run violently up the back stairs, 'that I was just syringing the greenfly off your roses.'

333

CHAPTER 25

Postscript at Torquay

'But, of course, dear Gwenda, I should never have dreamed of going away and leaving you alone in the house,' said Miss Marple. 'I knew there was a very dangerous person at large, and I was keeping an unobtrusive watch from the garden.'

'Did you know it was – him – all along?' asked Gwenda.

They were all three, Miss Marple, Gwenda and Giles, sitting on the terrace of the Imperial Hotel at Torquay.

'A change of scene,' Miss Marple had said, and Giles had agreed, would be the best thing for Gwenda. So Inspector Primer had concurred and they had driven to Torquay forthwith.

Miss Marple said in answer to Gwenda's question, 'Well, he did seem indicated, my dear. Although unfortunately there was nothing in the way of evidence to go upon. Just indications, nothing more.'

Looking at her curiously, Giles said, 'But I can't see any indications even.'

'Oh dear, Giles, think. He was *on the spot*, to begin with.'

'On the spot?'

'But certainly. When Kelvin Halliday came to him that night he *had just come back from the hospital*. And the hospital, at that time, as several people told us, was actually next door to Hillside, or St Catherine's as it was then called. So that, as you see, puts him in *the right place at the right time*. And then there were a hundred and one little significant facts. Helen Halliday told Richard Erskine she had gone out to marry Walter Fane because *she wasn't happy at home*. Not happy, that is, living with her brother. Yet her brother was by all accounts devoted to her. So why wasn't she happy? Mr Afflick told you that "he was sorry for the poor kid". I think that he was absolutely truthful when he said that. He *was* sorry for her. Why did she have to go and meet young Afflick in that clandestine way? Admittedly she was not wildly in love with him. Was it because she couldn't meet young men in the ordinary normal way? Her brother was "strict" and "old-fashioned". It is vaguely reminiscent, is it not, of Mr Barrett of Wimpole Street?'

Gwenda shivered.

'He was mad,' she said. 'Mad.'

'Yes,' said Miss Marple. 'He wasn't normal. He adored his half-sister, and that affection became possessive and unwholesome. That kind of thing happens oftener than you'd think. Fathers who don't want their daughters to marry – or even to meet young men. Like Mr Barrett. I thought of that when I heard about the tennis net.'

'The tennis net?'

'Yes, that seemed to me very significant. Think of that girl, young Helen, coming home from school, and eager for all a young girl wants out of life, anxious to meet young men – to flirt with them –'

'A little sex-crazy.'

'*No*,' said Miss Marple with emphasis. '*That* is one of the wickedest things about this crime. Dr Kennedy didn't only kill her physically. If you think back carefully, you'll see that the only evidence for Helen Kennedy's having been man mad or practically – what is the word you used, dear? oh yes, a nymphomaniac – came actually from *Dr Kennedy* himself. I think, myself, that she was a perfectly normal young girl who wanted to have fun and a good time and flirt a little and finally settle down with the man of her choice – no more than that. And see what steps her brother took. First he was strict and old-fashioned about allowing her liberty. Then, when she wanted to give tennis parties – a most normal and harmless desire – he pretended to agree and then one night secretly cut the tennis net to ribbons – a very significant and sadistic action. Then, since she could still go out to play tennis or to dances, he took advantage of a grazed foot which he treated, to infect it so that it wouldn't heal. Oh yes, I think he did that . . . in fact, I'm sure of it.

'Mind you. I don't think Helen realized any of all this. She knew her brother had a deep affection for her and I don't think she knew *why* she felt uneasy and unhappy at home. But she did feel like that and at last she decided to go out to India and marry young Fane simply in order to get away. To get away from *what*? She didn't know. She was too young and guileless to know. So she went off to India and on the way she met Richard Erskine and fell in love with him. There again, she behaved not like a sex-crazy girl, but like a decent and honourable girl. She didn't urge him to leave his wife. She urged him not to do so. But when she saw Walter Fane she knew that she couldn't marry him, and because she didn't know what else to do, she wired her brother for money to go home.

'On the way home she met your father – and another way of escape showed itself. This time it was one with good prospect of happiness.

'She didn't marry your father under false pretences, Gwenda. He was recovering from the death of a dearly loved wife. She was getting over an unhappy love-affair. They could both help each other. I think it is significant that she and Kelvin Halliday were married in London and then went down to Dillmouth to break the news to Dr Kennedy. She must have

335

had some instinct that that would be a wiser thing to do than to go down and be married in Dillmouth, which ordinarily would have been the normal thing to do. I still think she didn't know what she was up against – but she was uneasy, and she felt safer in presenting her brother with the marriage as a *fait accompli.*

'Kelvin Halliday was very friendly to Kennedy and liked him. Kennedy seems to have gone out of his way to appear pleased about the marriage. The couple took a furnished house there.

'And now we come to that very significant fact – the suggestion that Kelvin was being drugged by his wife. There are only two possible explanations of that – because there are only two people who could have had the opportunity of doing such a thing. Either Helen Halliday *was* drugging her husband, and if so, why? Or else the drugs were being administered by Dr Kennedy. Kennedy was Halliday's physician as is clear by Halliday's consulting him. He had confidence in Kennedy's medical knowledge – and the suggestion that his wife was drugging him was very cleverly put to him by Kennedy.'

'But could any drug make a man have the hallucination that he was strangling his wife?' asked Giles. 'I mean there isn't any drug, is there, that has that *particular* effect?'

'My dear Giles, you've fallen into the trap again – the trap of believing *what is said to you.* There is only Dr Kennedy's word for it that Halliday ever had *that* hallucination. He himself never says so in his diary. He had hallucinations, yes, but he does not mention their nature. But I dare say Kennedy talked to him about men who had strangled their wives after passing through a phase such as Kelvin Halliday was experiencing.'

'Dr Kennedy was really wicked,' said Gwenda.

'I think,' said Miss Marple, 'that he'd definitely passed the borderline between sanity and madness by that time. And Helen, poor girl, began to realize it. It was to her brother she must have been speaking that day when she was overheard by Lily. "I think I've always been afraid of you." That was one of the things she said. And that always was very significant. And so she determined to leave Dillmouth. She persuaded her husband to buy a house in Norfolk, she persuaded him not tell anyone about it. The secrecy about it was very illuminating. She was clearly very afraid of *someone* knowing about it – but that did not fit in with the Walter Fane theory or the Jackie Afflick theory – and certainly not with Richard Erskine's being concerned. No, it pointed to somewhere much nearer home.

'And in the end, Kelvin Halliday, whom doubtless the secrecy irked and who felt it to be pointless, told his brother-in-law.

'And in so doing, sealed his own fate and that of his wife. For Kennedy

336

was not going to let Helen go and live happily with her husband. I think perhaps his idea was simply to break down Halliday's health with drugs. But at the revelation that his victim and Helen were going to escape him, he became completely unhinged. From the hospital he went through into the garden of St Catherine's and he took with him a pair of surgical gloves. He caught Helen in the hall, and he strangled her. Nobody saw him, there was no one there to see him, or so he thought, and so, racked with love and frenzy, he quoted those tragic lines that were so apposite.'

Miss Marple sighed and clucked her tongue.

'I was stupid – very stupid. We were all stupid. We should have seen at once. Those lines from *The Duchess of Malfi* were really the clue to the whole thing. They are said, are they not, by a *brother* who has just contrived his sister's death to avenge her marriage to the man she loved. Yes, we were stupid –'

'And then?' asked Giles.

'And then he went through with the whole devilish plan. The body carried upstairs. The clothes packed in a suitcase. A note, written and thrown in the wastepaper basket to convince Halliday later.'

'But I should have thought,' said Gwenda, 'that it would have been better from his point of view for my father actually to have been convicted of the murder.'

Miss Marple shook her head.

'Oh no, he couldn't risk that. He had a lot of shrewd Scottish common sense, you know. He had a wholesome respect for the police. The police take a lot of convincing before they believe a man guilty of murder. The police might have asked a lot of awkward questions and made a lot of awkward enquiries as to times and places. No, his plan was simpler and, I think, more devilish. He only had Halliday to convince. First, that he had killed his wife. Secondly that he was mad. He persuaded Halliday to go into a mental home, but I don't think he really wanted to convince him that it was all a delusion. Your father accepted that theory, Gwennie, mainly, I should imagine, for your sake. He continued to believe that he had killed Helen. He died believing that.'

'Wicked,' said Gwenda. 'Wicked – wicked – wicked.'

'Yes,' said Miss Marple. 'There isn't really any other word. And I think, Gwenda, that that is why your childish impression of what you saw remained so strong. It was real evil that was in the air that night.'

'But the letters,' said Giles. 'Helen's letters? They *were* in her hand-writing, so they couldn't be forgeries.'

'Of course they were forgeries! But that is where he overreached himself. He was so anxious, you see, to stop you and Giles making investigations. He

337

could probably imitate Helen's handwriting quite nicely – but it wouldn't fool an expert. So the sample of Helen's handwriting he sent you with the letter wasn't her handwriting either. He wrote it himself. So naturally it tallied.'

'Goodness,' said Giles. 'I never thought of that.'

'No,' said Miss Marple. '*You believed what he said*. It really is very dangerous to believe people. *I* never have for years.'

'And the brandy?'

'He did that the day he came to Hillside with Helen's letter and talked to me in the garden. He was waiting in the house while Mrs Cocker came out and told me he was there. It would only take a minute.'

'Good Lord,' said Giles, 'And he urged me to take Gwenda home and *give her brandy* after we were at the police station when Lily Kimble was killed. How did he arrange to meet her earlier?'

'That was very simple. The original letter he sent her asked her to meet him at Woodleigh Camp and come to Matchings Halt by the two-five train from Dillmouth Junction. He came out of the copse of trees, probably, and accosted her as she was going up the lane – and strangled her. Then he simply substituted the letter you all saw for the letter she had with her (and which he had asked her to bring because of the directions in it) and went home to prepare for you and play out the little comedy of waiting for Lily.'

'And Lily really was threatening him? Her letter didn't sound as though she was. Her letter sounded as though she suspected Afflick.'

'Perhaps she did. But Léonie, the Swiss girl, had talked to Lily, and Léonie was the one danger to Kennedy. Because she looked out of the nursery window and saw him digging in the garden. In the morning he talked to her, told her bluntly that Major Halliday had killed his wife – that Major Halliday was insane, and that he, Kennedy, was hushing up the matter for the child's sake. If, however, Léonie felt she ought to go to the police, she must do so, but it would be very unpleasant for her – and so on.

'Léonie took immediate fright at the mention of the police. She adored you and had implicit faith in what *M. le docteur* thought best. Kennedy paid her a handsome sum of money and hustled her back to Switzerland. But before she went, she hinted something to Lily as to your father's having killed his wife and that she had seen the body buried. That fitted in with Lily's ideas at the time. She took it for granted that it was Kelvin Halliday Léonie had seen digging the grave.'

'But Kennedy didn't know that, of course,' said Gwenda.

'Of course not. When he got Lily's letter the words in it that frightened him were that Léonie had told Lily what she had seen *out of the window* and the mention of the car outside.'

'The car? Jackie Afflick's car?'

'Another misunderstanding. Lily remembered, or thought she remembered, a car like Jackie Afflick's being outside in the road. Already her imagination had got to work on the Mystery Man who came over to see Mrs Halliday. With the hospital next door, no doubt a good many cars did park along this road. But you must remember that the *doctor's* car was actually standing outside the hospital that night – he probably leaped to the conclusion that she meant *his* car. The adjective posh was meaningless to him.'

'I see,' said Giles. 'Yes, to a guilty conscience that letter of Lily's might look like blackmail. But how do you know all about Léonie?'

Her lips pursed close together, Miss Marple said: 'He went – right over the edge, you know. As soon as the men Inspector Primer had left rushed in and seized him, he went over the whole crime again and again – everything he'd done. Léonie died, it seems, very shortly after her return to Switzerland. Overdose of some sleeping tablets . . . Oh no, he wasn't taking any chances.'

'Like trying to poison me with the brandy.'

'You were very dangerous to him, you and Giles. Fortunately you never told him about your memory of seeing Helen dead in the hall. He never knew there had been an eye-witness.'

'Those telephone calls to Fane and Afflick.' said Giles. 'Did he put those through?'

'Yes. If there was an enquiry as to who could have tampered with the brandy, either of them would make an admirable suspect, and if Jackie Afflick drove over in his car alone, it might tie him in with Lily Kimble's murder. Fane would most likely have an alibi.'

'And he seemed fond of me.' said Gwenda. 'Little Gwennie.'

'He had to play his part,' said Miss Marple. 'Imagine what it meant to him. After eighteen years, you and Giles come along, asking questions, burrowing into the past, disturbing a murder that had seemed dead but was only sleeping . . . Murder in retrospect . . . A horribly dangerous thing to do, my dears. I have been sadly worried.'

'Poor Mrs Cocker,' said Gwenda. 'She had a terribly near escape. I'm glad she's going to be all right. Do you think she'll come back to us, Giles? After all this?'

'She will if there's a nursery,' said Giles gravely, and Gwenda blushed, and Miss Marple smiled a little and looked out across Torbay.

'How very odd it was that it should happen the way it did,' mused Gwenda. 'My having those rubber gloves on, and looking at them, and then his coming into the hall and saying those words that sounded so like the others. "Face" . . . and then: "Eyes dazzled" –'

She shuddered.

'Cover her face . . . Mine eyes dazzle . . . she died young . . . that might have been me . . . if Miss Marple hadn't been there.'

She paused and said softly, 'Poor Helen . . . Poor lovely Helen, who died young . . . You know, Giles, she isn't there any more – in the house – in the hall. I could feel that yesterday before we left. There's just the house. And the house is fond of us. We can go back if we like . . .'

At Bertram's Hotel

In the heart of the West End, there are many quiet pockets, unknown to almost all but taxi drivers who traverse them with expert knowledge, and arrive triumphantly thereby at Park Lane, Berkeley Square or South Audley Street.

If you turn off on an unpretentious street from the Park, and turn left and right once or twice, you will find yourself in a quiet street with Bertram's Hotel on the right hand side. Bertram's Hotel has been there a long time. During the war, houses were demolished on the right of it, and a little farther down on the left of it, but Bertram's itself remained unscathed. Naturally it could not escape being, as house agents would say, scratched, bruised and marked, but by the expenditure of only a reasonable amount of money it was restored to its original condition. By 1955 it looked precisely as it had looked in 1939 – dignified, unostentatious, and quietly expensive.

Such was Bertram's, patronized over a long stretch of years by the higher *échelons* of the clergy, dowager ladies of the aristocracy up from the country, girls on their way home for the holidays from expensive finishing schools. ('So few places where a girl can stay alone in London but of course it is *quite* all right at Bertram's. We have stayed there for *years*.')

There had, of course, been many other hotels on the model of Bertram's. Some still existed, but nearly all had felt the wind of change. They had had necessarily to modernize themselves, to cater for a different clientele. Bertram's, too, had had to change, but it had been done so cleverly that it was not at all apparent at the first casual glance.

Outside the steps that led up to the big swing doors stood what at first sight appeared to be no less than a Field-Marshal. Gold braid and medal ribbons adorned a broad and manly chest. His deportment was perfect. He received you with tender concern as you emerged with rheumatic difficulty from a taxi or a car, guided you carefully up the steps and piloted you through the silently swinging doorway.

Inside, if this was the first time you had visited Bertram's, you felt, almost with alarm, that you had re-entered a vanished world. Time had gone back. You were in Edwardian England once more.

There was, of course, central heating, but it was not apparent. As there had always been, in the big central lounge, there were two magnificent coal fires; beside them big brass coal scuttles shone in the way they used to shine when Edwardian housemaids polished them, and they were filled with exactly the right sized lumps of coal. There was a general appearance of rich red velvet and plushy cosiness. The armchairs were not of this time and age. They were well above the level of the floor, so that rheumatic old ladies had not to struggle in an undignified manner in order to get to their feet. The seats of the chairs did not, as in so many modern high-priced arm-chairs, stop half-way between the thigh and the knee, thereby inflicting agony on those suffering from arthritis and sciatica; and they were not all of a pattern. There were straight backs and reclining backs, different widths to accommodate the slender and the obese. People of almost any dimension could find a comfortable chair at Bertram's.

Since it was now the tea hour, the lounge hall was full. Not that the lounge hall was the only place where you could have tea. There was a drawing-room (chintz), a smoking-room (by some hidden influence reserved for gentlemen only), where the vast chairs were of fine leather, two writing-rooms, where you could take a special friend and have a cosy little gossip in a quiet corner – and even write a letter as well if you wanted to. Besides these amenities of the Edwardian age, there were other retreats, not in any way publicized, but known to those who wanted them. There was a double bar, with two bar attendants, an American barman to make the Americans feel at home and to provide them with bourbon, rye, and every kind of cocktail, and an English one to deal with sherries and Pimm's No. 1, and to talk knowledgeably about the runners at Ascot and Newbury to the middle-aged men who stayed at Bertram's for the more serious race meetings. There was also, tucked down a passage, in a secretive way, a television-room for those who asked for it.

But the big entrance lounge was the favourite place for the afternoon tea drinking. The elderly ladies enjoyed seeing who came in and out, recognizing old friends, and commenting unfavourably on how these had aged. There were also American visitors fascinated by seeing the titled English really getting down to their traditional afternoon tea. For afternoon tea was quite a feature of Bertram's.

It was nothing less than splendid. Presiding over the ritual was Henry, a large and magnificent figure, a ripe fifty, avuncular, sympathetic, and with the courtly manners of that long vanished species: the perfect butler. Slim youths performed the actual work under Henry's austere direction. There were large crested silver trays, and Georgian silver teapots. The china, if not actually Rockingham and Davenport, looked like it. The Blind Earl services were particular favourites. The tea was the best Indian, Ceylon, Darjeeling, Lapsang, etc. As for eatables, you could ask for anything you liked – and get it!

On this particular day, November the 17th, Lady Selina Hazy, sixty-five, up from Leicestershire, was eating delicious well-buttered muffins with all an elderly lady's relish.

Her absorption with muffins, however, was not so great that she failed to look up sharply every time the inner pair of swing doors opened to admit a newcomer.

So it was that she smiled and nodded to welcome Colonel Luscombe – erect, soldierly, race glasses hanging round his neck. Like the old autocrat that she was, she beckoned imperiously and in a minute or two, Luscombe came over to her.

'Hello, Selina, what brings you up to Town?'

'Dentist,' said Lady Selina, rather indistinctly, owing to muffin. 'And I thought as I *was* up, I might as well go and see that man in Harley Street about my arthritis. You know who I mean.'

Although Harley Street contained several hundreds of fashionable practitioners for all and every ailment, Luscombe did know whom she meant.

'Do you any good?'

'I rather think he did,' said Lady Selina grudgingly. 'Extraordinary fellow. Took me by the neck when I wasn't expecting it, and wrung it like a chicken.' She moved her neck gingerly.

'Hurt you?'

'It must have done, twisting it like that, but really I hadn't time to know.' She continued to move her neck gingerly. 'Feels all right. Can look over my right shoulder for the first time in years.'

She put this to a practical test and exclaimed,

'Why I do believe that's old Jane Marple. Thought she was dead years ago. Looks a hundred.'

Colonel Luscombe threw a glance in the direction of Jane Marple thus resurrected, but without much interest: Bertram's always had a sprinkling of what he called fluffy old pussies.

Lady Selina was continuing.

'Only place in London you can still get muffins. Real muffins. Do you know when I went to America last year they had something *called* muffins on the breakfast menu. Not real muffins at all. Kind of teacake with raisins in them. I mean, why call them muffins?'

She pushed in the last buttery morsel and looked round vaguely. Henry materialized immediately. Not quickly or hurriedly. It seemed that, just suddenly, he was there.

'Anything further I can get you, my lady? Cake of any kind?'

'Cake?' Lady Selina thought about it, was doubtful.

'We are serving very good seed cake, my lady. I can recommend it.'

'Seed cake? I haven't eaten cake for *years*. It is *real* seed cake?'

'Oh, yes, my lady. The cook has had the recipe for years. You'll enjoy it, I'm sure.'

Henry gave a glance at one of his retinue, and the lad departed in search of seed cake.

'I suppose you've been at Newbury, Derek?'

'Yes. Darned cold, I didn't wait for the last two races. Disastrous day. That filly of Harry's was no good at all.'

'Didn't think she would be. What about Swanhilda?'

'Finished fourth.' Luscombe rose. 'Got to see about my room.'

He walked across the lounge to the reception desk. As he went he noted the tables and their occupants. Astonishing number of people having tea here. Quite like old days. Tea as a meal had rather gone out of fashion since the war. But evidently not at Bertram's. Who *were* all these people? Two Canons and the Dean of Chislehampton. Yes, and another pair of gaitered legs over in the corner, a Bishop, no less! Mere Vicars were scarce. 'Have to be at least a Canon to afford Bertram's,' he thought. The rank and file of the clergy certainly couldn't, poor devils. As far as that went, he wondered how on earth people like old Selina Hazy could. She'd only got twopence or so a year to bless herself with. And there was old Lady Berry, and Mrs Posselthwaite from Somerset, and Sybil Kerr – all poor as church mice.

Still thinking about this he arrived at the desk and was pleasantly greeted by Miss Gorringe the receptionist. Miss Gorringe was an old friend. She knew every one of the clientele and, like Royalty, never forgot a face. She looked frumpy but respectable. Frizzled yellowish hair (old-fashioned tongs, it suggested), black silk dress, a high bosom on which reposed a large gold locket and a cameo brooch.

'Number fourteen,' said Miss Gorringe. 'I think you had fourteen last time, Colonel Luscombe, and liked it. It's quiet.'

'How you always manage to remember these things, I can't imagine, Miss Gorringe.'

'We like to make our old friends comfortable.'

'Takes me back a long way, coming in here. Nothing seems to have changed.'

He broke off as Mr Humfries came out from an inner sanctum to greet him.

Mr Humfries was often taken by the uninitiated to be Mr Bertram in person. Who the actual Mr Bertram was, or indeed, if there ever *had* been a Mr Bertram was now lost in the mists of antiquity. Bertram's had existed since about 1840, but nobody had taken any interest in tracing its past history. It was just there, solid, in fact. When addressed as Mr Bertram, Mr Humfries never corrected the impression. If they wanted him to be Mr Bertram he would be Mr Bertram. Colonel Luscombe knew his name, though he didn't know if Humfries was the manager or the owner. He rather fancied the latter.

Mr Humfries was a man of about fifty. He had very good manners, and the presence of a Junior Minister. He could, at any moment, be all things to all people. He could talk racing shop, cricket, foreign politics, tell anecdotes of Royalty, give Motor Show information, knew the most interesting plays on at present – advise on places Americans ought really to see in England however short their stay. He had knowledgeable information about where it would suit persons of all incomes and tastes to dine. With all this, he did not make himself too cheap. He was not on tap all the time. Miss Gorringe had all the same facts at her fingertips and could retail them efficiently. At brief intervals Mr Humfries, like the sun, made his appearance above the horizon and flattered someone by his personal attention.

This time it was Colonel Luscombe who was so honoured. They exchanged a few racing platitudes, but Colonel Luscombe was absorbed by his problem. And here was the man who could give him the answer.

'Tell me, Humfries, how do all these old dears manage to come and stay here?'

'Oh you've been wondering about that?' Mr Humfries seemed amused. 'Well, the answer's simple. They couldn't afford it. Unless –'

He paused.

'Unless you make special prices for them? Is that it?'

'More or less. They don't know, usually, that they *are* special prices, or if they do realize it, they think it's because they're old customers.'

'And it isn't just that?'

'Well, Colonel Luscombe, I *am* running a hotel. I couldn't afford actually to lose money.'

'But how can that pay you?'

'It's a question of atmosphere ... Strangers coming to this country (Americans, in particular, because they are the ones who have the money) have their own rather queer ideas of what England is like. I'm not talking, you understand, of the rich business tycoons who are always crossing the Atlantic. They usually go to the Savoy or the Dorchester. They want modern décor, American food, all the things that will make them feel at home. But there are a lot of people who come abroad at rare intervals and who expect this country to be – well, I won't go back as far as Dickens, but they've read *Cranford* and Henry James, and they don't want to find this country just the same as their own! So they go back home afterwards and say: "There's a wonderful place in London; Bertram's Hotel, it's called. It's just like stepping back a hundred years. It just *is* old England! And the people who stay there! People you'd never come across anywhere else. Wonderful old Duchesses. They serve all the old English dishes, there's a marvellous old-fashioned beef steak pudding! You've never tasted anything like it; and great sirloins of beef and saddles of mutton, and an old-fashioned English tea and a wonderful English breakfast. And of course all the usual things as well. And it's wonderfully comfortable. *And* warm. Great log fires."

Mr Humfries ceased his impersonation and permitted himself something nearly approaching a grin.

'I see,' said Luscombe thoughtfully. 'These people; decayed aristocrats, impoverished members of the old County families, they are all so much *mise en scène?*'

Mr Humfries nodded agreement.

'I really wonder no one else thought of it. Of course I found Bertram's ready made, so to speak. All it needed was some rather expensive restoration. All the people who come here think it's something that they've discovered for themselves, that no one else knows about.'

'I suppose,' said Luscombe, 'that the restoration *was* quite expensive?'

'Oh yes. The place has got to *look* Edwardian, but it's got to have the modern comforts that we take for granted in these days. Our old dears – if you will forgive me referring to them as that – have got to feel that nothing has changed since the turn of the century, and our travelling clients have got to feel they can have period surroundings, and still have what they are used to having at home, and can't really live without!'

'Bit difficult sometimes?' suggested Luscombe.

'Not really. Take central heating for instance. Americans require – need, I should say – at least ten degrees Fahrenheit higher than English people do. We actually have two quite different sets of bedrooms. The English we put in one lot, the Americans in the other. The rooms all look alike, but they are full of actual differences – electric razors, and showers as well as tubs in some of the bathrooms, and if you want an American breakfast, it's there – cereals and iced orange juice and all – or if you prefer you can have the English breakfast.'

'Eggs and bacon?'

'As you say – but a good deal more than that if you want it. Kippers, kidneys and bacon, cold grouse, York ham. Oxford marmalade.'

'I must remember all that tomorrow morning. Don't get that sort of thing any more at home.'

Humfries smiled.

'Most gentlemen only ask for eggs and bacon. They've – well, they've got out of the way of thinking about the things there used to be.'

'Yes, yes . . . I remember when I was a child . . Sideboards groaning with hot dishes. Yes, it was a luxurious way of life.'

'We endeavour to give people anything they ask for.'

'Including seed cake and muffins – yes, I see. To each according to his need – I see . . . Quite Marxian.'

'I beg your pardon?'

'Just a thought, Humfries. Extremes meet.'

Colonel Luscombe turned away, taking the key Miss Gorringe offered him. A page-boy sprang to attention and conducted him to the lift. He saw in passing that Lady Selina Hazy was now sitting with her friend Jane Something or other.

'And I suppose you're still living at that dear St Mary Mead?' Lady Selina was asking. 'Such a sweet unspoilt village. I often think about it. Just the same as ever, I suppose?'

'Well, not quite.' Miss Marple reflected on certain aspects of her place of residence. The new Building Estate. The additions to the Village Hall, the altered appearance of the High Street with its up-to-date shop fronts – She sighed. 'One has to accept change, I suppose.'

'Progress,' said Lady Selina vaguely. 'Though it often seems to me that it isn't progress. All these smart plumbing fixtures they have nowadays. Every shade of colour and superb what they call "finish" – but do any of them really *pull*? Or *push*, when they're that kind. Every time you go to a friend's house, you find some kind of a notice in the Loo – "Press sharply and release," "Pull to the *left*," "Release *quickly*." But in the old days, one just pulled up a handle *any* kind of way, and cataracts of water came *at once* – There's the dear Bishop of Medmenham,' Lady Selina broke off to say, as a handsome, elderly cleric passed by. 'Practically quite blind, I believe. But such a splendid *militant* priest.'

A little clerical talk was indulged in, interspersed by Lady Selina's recognition of various friends and acquaintances, many of whom were not the people she thought they were. She and Miss Marple talked a little of 'old days,' though Miss Marple's upbringing, of course, had been quite different from Lady Selina's, and their reminiscences were mainly confined to the few years when Lady Selina, a recent widow of severely straitened means, had taken a small house in the village of St Mary Mead during the time her second son had been stationed at an airfield nearby.

'Do you always stay here when you come up, Jane? Odd I haven't seen you here before.'

'Oh no, indeed. I couldn't afford to, and anyway, I hardly ever leave home these days. No, it was a very kind niece of mine who thought it would be a treat for me to have a short visit to London. Joan is a very kind girl – at least perhaps hardly a girl.' Miss Marple reflected with a qualm that Joan must now be close on fifty. 'She is a painter, you know. Quite a well-known painter. Joan West. She had an exhibition not long ago.'

Lady Selina had little interest in painters, or indeed in anything artistic. She regarded writers, artists and musicians as a species of clever performing animal; she was prepared to feel indulgent towards them, but to wonder privately why they wanted to do what they did.

'This modern stuff, I suppose,' she said, her eyes wandering. 'There's Cicely Longhurst – dyed her hair again, I see.'

'I'm afraid dear Joan *is* rather modern.'

Here Miss Marple was quite wrong. Joan West had been modern about twenty years ago, but was now regarded by the young *arriviste* artists as completely old-fashioned.

Casting a brief glance at Cicely Longhurst's hair, Miss Marple relapsed into a pleasant remembrance of how kind Joan had been. Joan had actually said to her husband, 'I wish we could do something for poor old Aunt Jane. She never gets away from home. Do you think she'd like to go to Bournemouth for a week or two?'

'Good idea,' said Raymond West. His last book was doing very well indeed, and he felt in a generous mood.

'She enjoyed her trip to the West Indies, I think, though it was a pity she had to get mixed up in a murder case. Quite the wrong thing at her age.'

'That sort of thing seems to happen to her.'

Raymond was very fond of his old aunt and was constantly devising treats for her, and sending her books that he thought might interest her. He was surprised when she often politely declined the treats, and though she always said the books were 'so interesting' he sometimes suspected that she had not read them. But then, of course, her eyes were failing.

In this last he was wrong. Miss Marple had remarkable eyesight for her age, and was at that moment taking in everything that was going on round her with keen interest and pleasure.

To Joan's proffer of a week or two at one of Bournemouth's best hotels, she had hesitated, murmured, 'It's very, very kind of you, my dear, but I really don't think –'

'But it's *good* for you, Aunt Jane. Good to get away from home sometimes. It gives you new ideas, and new things to think about.'

'Oh yes, you are quite right there, and I *would* like a little visit somewhere for a change. Not, perhaps, Bournemouth.'

Joan was slightly surprised. She had thought Bournemouth would have been Aunt Jane's Mecca.

'Eastbourne? Or Torquay?'

'What I would really like –' Miss Marple hesitated.

'Yes?'

'I dare say you will think it rather silly of me.'

'No, I'm sure I shan't.' (Where *did* the old dear want to go?)

'I would really like to go to Bertram's Hotel – in London.'

'Bertram's Hotel?' The name was vaguely familiar.

Words came from Miss Marple in a rush.

'I stayed there once – when I was fourteen. With my uncle and aunt, Uncle Thomas, that was, he was Canon of Ely. And I've never forgotten it.

If I could stay there – a week would be quite enough – two weeks might be too expensive.'

'Oh, that's all right. Of course you shall go. I ought to have thought that you might want to go to London – the shops and everything. We'll fix it up – if Bertram's Hotel still exists. So many hotels have vanished, sometimes bombed in the war and sometimes just given up.'

'No, I happen to know Bertram's Hotel is still going. I had a letter from there – from my Americam friend Amy McAllister of Boston. She and her husband were staying there.'

'Good, then I'll go ahead and fix it up.' She added gently, I'm afraid you may find it's changed a good deal from the days when you knew it. So don't be disappointed.'

But Bertram's Hotel had not changed. It was just as it had always been. Quite miraculously so, in Miss Marple's opinion. In fact, she wondered . . .

It really seemed too good to be true. She knew quite well, with her usual clear-eyed common sense, that what she wanted was simply to refurbish her memories of the past in their old original colours. Much of her life had, perforce, to be spent recalling past pleasures. If you could find someone to remember them with, that was indeed happiness. Nowadays that was not easy to do; she had outlived most of her contemporaries. But she still sat and remembered. In a queer way, it made her come to life again – Jane Marple, that pink and white eager young girl . . . Such a silly girl in many ways . . . now who was that very unsuitable young man whose name – oh dear, she couldn't even remember it now! How wise her mother had been to nip that friendship so firmly in the bud. She had come across him years later – and really he was quite dreadful! At the time she had cried herself to sleep for at least a week!

Nowadays, of course – she considered nowadays . . . These poor young things. Some of them had mothers, but never mothers who seemed to be any good – mothers who were quite incapable of protecting their daughters from silly affairs, illegitimate babies, and early and unfortunate marriages. It was all very sad.

Her friend's voice interrupted these meditations.

'Well, I never. It is – yes, it is – Bess Sedgwick over there! Of all the unlikely places –'

Miss Marple had been listening with only half an ear to Lady Selina's comments on her surroundings. She and Miss Marple moved in entirely different circles, so that Miss Marple had been unable to exchange scandalous tit-bits about the various friends or acquaintances that Lady Selina recognized or thought she recognized.

But Bess Sedgwick was different. Bess Sedgwick was a name that almost everyone in England knew. For over thirty years now, Bess Sedgwick had been reported by the Press as doing this or that outrageous or extraordinary thing. For a good part of the war she had been a member of the French Resistance, and was said to have six notches on her gun representing dead Germans. She had flown solo across the Atlantic years ago, had ridden on horseback across Europe and fetched up at Lake Van. She had driven racing cars, had once saved two children from a burning house, had several marriages to her credit and discredit and was said to be the second best-dressed woman in Europe. It was also said that she had successfully smuggled herself aboard a nuclear submarine on its test voyage.

It was therefore with the most intense interest that Miss Marple sat up and indulged in a frankly avid stare.

Whatever she had expected of Bertram's Hotel, it was not to find Bess Sedgwick there. An expensive night club, or a lorry driver's pull up – either of those would be quite in keeping with Bess Sedgwick's wide range of interests. But this highly respectable and old world hostelry seemed strangely alien.

Still there she was – no doubt of it. Hardly a month passed without Bess Sedgwick's face appearing in the fashion magazines or the popular press. Here she was in the flesh, smoking a cigarette in a quick impatient manner and looking in a surprised way at the large tea tray in front of her as though she had never seen one before. She had ordered – Miss Marple screwed up her eyes and peered – it was rather far away – yes, *doughnuts*. Very interesting.

As she watched, Bess Sedgwick stubbed out her cigarette in her saucer, lifted a doughnut and took an immense bite. Rich red real strawberry jam gushed out over her chin. Bess threw back her head and laughed, one of the loudest and gayest sounds to have been heard in the lounge of Bertram's Hotel for some time.

Henry was immediately beside her, a small delicate napkin proffered. She took it, scrubbed her chin with the vigour of a schoolboy, exclaiming: 'That's what I call a *real* doughnut. Gorgeous.'

She dropped the napkin on the tray and stood up. As usual every eye was on her. She was used to that. Perhaps she liked it, perhaps she no longer noticed it. She was worth looking at – a striking woman rather than a beautiful one. The palest of platinum hair fell sleek and smooth to her shoulders. The bones of her head and face were exquisite. Her nose was faintly aquiline, her eyes deep set and a real grey in colour. She had the wide mouth of a natural comedian. Her dress was of such simplicity that it puzzled most men. It looked like the coarsest kind of sacking, had no ornamentation of any kind, and no apparent fastening or seams. But women knew better. Even the provincial old dears in Bertram's knew, quite certainly, that it had cost the earth!

Striding across the lounge towards the lift, she passed quite close to Lady Selina and Miss Marple, and she nodded to the former.

'Hello, Lady Selina. Haven't seen you since Crufts. How are the Borzois?'

'What on earth are you doing here, Bess?'

'Just staying here. I've just driven up from Land's End. Four hours and three quarters. Not bad.'

'You'll kill yourself one of these days. Or someone else.'

'Oh I hope not.'

'But why are you staying *here*?'

Bess Sedgwick threw a swift glance round. She seemed to see the point and acknowledge it with an ironic smile.

'Someone told me I ought to try it. I think they're right. I've just had the most marvellous doughnut.'

'My dear, they have *real* muffins too.'

'Muffins,' said Lady Sedgwick thoughtfully. 'Yes . . .' She seemed to concede the point. 'Muffins!'

She nodded and went on towards the lift.

'Extraordinary girl,' said Lady Selina. To her, like to Miss Marple, every woman under sixty was a girl. 'Known her ever since she was a child. Nobody could do anything with her. Ran away with an Irish groom when she was sixteen. They managed to get her back in time – or perhaps not in time. Anyway they bought him off and got her safely married to old Coniston – thirty years older than she was, awful old rip, quite dotty about her. *That* didn't last long. She went off with Johnnie Sedgwick. That *might* have stuck if he hadn't broken his neck steeplechasing. After that she married Ridgway Becker, the American yacht owner. He discovered her three years ago and I hear she's taken up with some Racing Motor Driver – a Pole or something. I don't know whether she's actually married or not. After the American divorce she went back to calling herself Sedgwick. She goes about with *the* most extraordinary people. They *say* she takes drugs . . . I don't know, I'm sure.'

'One wonders if she is happy,' said Miss Marple.

Lady Selina, who had clearly never wondered anything of the kind, looked rather startled.

'She's got packets of money, I suppose,' she said doubtfully. 'Alimony and all that. Of course that isn't everything . . .'

'No, indeed.'

'And she's usually got a man – or several men – in tow.'

'Yes?'

'Of course when some women get to that age, that's all they want . . . But somehow –'

She paused.

'No,' said Miss Marple. '*I* don't think so either.'

There were people who would have smiled in gentle derision at the pronouncement on the part of an old-fashioned old lady who could hardly be expected to be an authority on nymphomania, and indeed it was not a word that Miss Marple would have used – her own phrase would have been 'always too fond of men.' But Lady Selina accepted her opinion as a confirmation of her own.

'There have been a lot of men in her life,' she pointed out.

'Oh yes, but I should say, wouldn't you, that men were an adventure to her, not a need?'

And would any woman, Miss Marple wondered, come to Bertram's Hotel for an assignation with a man? Bertram's was very definitely not that sort of place. But possibly that could be, to some of Bess Sedgwick's disposition, the very reason for choosing it.

She sighed, looked up at the handsome grandfather clock decorously ticking in the corner, and rose with the careful effort of the rheumatic to her feet. She walked slowly towards the lift. Lady Selina cast a glance around her and pounced upon an elderly gentleman of military appearance who was reading the *Spectator*.

'How nice to see you again. Er – it is General Arlington, isn't it?'

But with great courtesy the old gentleman declined being General Arlington. Lady Selina apologized, but was not unduly discomposed. She combined short sight with optimism and since the thing she enjoyed most was meeting old friends and acquaintances, she was always making this kind of mistake. Many other people did the same, since the lights were pleasantly dim and heavily shaded. But nobody ever took offence – usually indeed it seemed to give them pleasure.

Miss Marple smiled to herself as she waited for the lift to come down. So like Selina! Always convinced that she knew everybody. She herself could not compete. Her solitary achievement in that line had been the handsome and well-gaitered Bishop of Westchester whom she had addressed affectionately as 'dear Robbie' and who had responded with equal affection and with memories of himself as a child in a Hampshire vicarage calling out lustily 'Be a crocodile now, Aunty Janie. Be a crocodile and eat me.'

The lift came down, the uniformed middle-aged man threw open the door. Rather to Miss Marple's surprise the alighting passenger was Bess Sedgwick whom she had seen go up only a minute or two before.

357

And then, one foot poised, Bess Sedgwick stopped dead, with a suddenness that surprised Miss Marple and made her own forward step falter. Bess Sedgwick was staring over Miss Marple's shoulder with such concentration that the old lady turned her own head.

The commissionaire had just pushed open the two swing doors of the entrance and was holding them to let two women pass through into the lounge. One of them was a fussy looking middle-aged lady wearing a rather unfortunate flowered violet hat, the other was a tall, simply but smartly dressed, girl of perhaps seventeen or eighteen with long straight flaxen hair.

Bess Sedgwick pulled herself together, wheeled round abruptly and re-entered the lift. As Miss Marple followed her in, she turned to her and apologized.

'I'm so sorry. I nearly ran into you.' She had a warm friendly voice. 'I just remembered I'd forgotten something – which sounds nonsense but isn't really.'

'Second floor?' said the operator. Miss Marple smiled and nodded in acknowledgement of the apology, got out and walked slowly along to her room, pleasurably turning over sundry little unimportant problems in her mind as was so often her custom.

For instance what Lady Sedgwick had said wasn't true. She had only just gone up to her room, and it must have been then that she 'remembered she had forgotten something' (if there had been any truth in that statement at all) and had come down to find it. Or had she perhaps come down to meet someone or look for someone? But if so, what she had seen as the lift door opened had startled and upset her, and she had immediately swung into the lift again and gone up so as *not* to meet whoever it was she had seen.

It must have been the two newcomers. The middle-aged woman and the girl. Mother and daughter? No, Miss Marple thought, *not* mother and daughter.

Even at Bertram's, thought Miss Marple, happily, interesting things could happen . . .

CHAPTER 3

'Er – is Colonel Luscombe –?'

The woman in the violet hat was at the desk. Miss Gorringe smiled in a welcoming manner and a page, who had been standing at the ready, was immediately dispatched but had no need to fulfil his errand, as Colonel Luscombe himself entered the lounge at that moment and came quickly across to the desk.

'How do you do, Mrs Carpenter.' He shook hands politely, then turned to the girl. 'My dear Elvira.' He took both hands affectionately in his. 'Well, well, this *is* nice. Splendid – splendid. Come and let's sit down.' He led them to chairs, established them. 'Well, well,' he repeated, 'this is nice.'

The effort he made was somewhat palpable as was his lack of ease. He could hardly go on saying how nice this was. The two ladies were not very helpful. Elvira smiled very sweetly. Mrs Carpenter gave a meaningless little laugh, and smoothed her gloves.

'A good journey, eh?'

'Yes, thank you,' said Elvira.

'No fog. Nothing like that?'

'Oh no.'

'Our flight was five minutes ahead of time,' said Mrs Carpenter.

'Yes, yes. Good, very good.' He took a pull upon himself. 'I hope this place will be all right for you?'

'Oh, I'm sure it's *very* nice,' said Mrs Carpenter warmly, glancing round her. 'Very comfortable.'

'Rather old-fashioned, I'm afraid,' said the Colonel apologetically. 'Rather a lot of old fogies. No – er – dancing, anything like that.'

'No, I suppose not,' agreed Elvira.

She glanced round in an expressionless manner. It certainly seemed impossible to connect Bertram's with dancing.

'Lot of old fogies here, I'm afraid,' said Colonel Luscombe, repeating himself. 'Ought, perhaps, to have taken you somewhere more modern. Not very well up in these things, you see.'

'This is very nice,' said Elvira politely.

'It's only for a couple of nights,' went on Colonel Luscombe. 'I thought we'd go to a show this evening. A musical –' he said the word rather doubtfully, as though not sure he was using the right term. '*Let Down Your Hair Girls*. I hope that will be all right?'

'How delightful,' exclaimed Mrs Carpenter. 'That will be a treat, won't it, Elvira?'

'Lovely,' said Elvira, tonelessly.

'And then supper afterwards? At the Savoy?'

Fresh exclamations from Mrs Carpenter. Colonel Luscombe, stealing a glance at Elvira, cheered up a little. He thought that Elvira was pleased, though quite determined to express nothing more than polite approval in front of Mrs Carpenter. 'And I don't blame her,' he said to himself.

He said to Mrs Carpenter:

'Perhaps you'd like to see your rooms – see they're all right and all that –'

'Oh, I'm sure they will be.'

'Well, if there's anything you don't like about them, we'll make them change it. They know me here very well.'

Miss Gorringe, in charge at the desk, was pleasantly welcoming. Nos 28 and 29 on the second floor with an adjoining bathroom.

'I'll go up and get things unpacked,' said Mrs Carpenter. 'Perhaps, Elvira, you and Colonel Luscombe would like to have a little gossip.'

Tact, thought Colonel Luscombe. A bit obvious, perhaps, but anyway it would get rid of her for a bit. Though what he was going to gossip about to Elvira, he really didn't know. A very nice-mannered girl, but he wasn't used to girls. His wife had died in childbirth and the baby, a boy, had been brought up by his wife's family whilst an elder sister had come to keep house for him. His son had married and gone to live in Kenya, and his grandchildren were eleven, five and two and a half and had been entertained on their last visit by football and space science talk, electric trains, and a ride on his foot. Easy! But young girls!

He asked Elvira if she would like a drink. He was about to propose a bitter lemon, ginger ale, or orangeade, but Elvira forestalled him.

'Thank you. I should like a gin and vermouth.'

Colonel Luscombe looked at her doubtfully. He supposed girls of – what was she? sixteen? seventeen? – did drink gin and vermouth. But he reassured himself that Elvira knew, so to speak, correct Greenwich social time. He ordered a gin and vermouth and a dry sherry.

He cleared his throat and asked:

'How was Italy?'

'Very nice, thank you.'

'And that place you were at, the Contessa what's-her-name? Not too grim?'

'She is rather strict. But I didn't let that worry me.'

He looked at her, not quite sure whether the reply was not slightly ambiguous.

He said, stammering a little, but with a more natural manner than he had been able to manage before:

'I'm afraid we don't know each other as well as we ought to, seeing I'm your guardian as well as your godfather. Difficult for me, you know – difficult for a man who's an old buffer like me – to know what a girl wants – at least – I mean to know what a girl ought to have. Schools and then after school – what they used to call finishing in my day. But now, I suppose it's all more serious. Careers eh? Jobs? All that? We'll have to have a talk about all that sometime. Anything in particular you want to do?'

'I suppose I shall take a secretarial course,' said Elvira without enthusiasm.

'Oh. You want to be a secretary?'

'Not particularly –'

'Oh – well, then –'

'It's just what you start with,' Elvira explained.

Colonel Luscombe had an odd feeling of being relegated to his place.

'These cousins of mine, the Melfords. You think you'll like living with them? If not –'

'Oh I think so. I like Nancy quite well. And Cousin Mildred is rather a dear.'

'That's all right then?'

'Quite, for the present.'

Luscombe did not know what to say to that. Whilst he was considering what next to say, Elvira spoke. Her words were simple and direct.

'Have I any money?'

Again he took his time before answering, studying her thoughtfully. Then he said:

'Yes. You've got quite a lot of money. That is to say, you will have when you are twenty-one.'

'Who has got it now?'

He smiled. 'It's held in trust for you; a certain amount is deducted each year from the income to pay for your maintenance and education.'

'And you are the trustee?'

'One of them. There are three.'

'What happens if I die?'

'Come, come, Elvira, you're not going to die. What nonsense!'

'I hope not – but one never knows, does one? An airliner crashed only last week and everyone was killed.'

'Well, it's not going to happen to you,' said Luscombe firmly.

'You can't really know that,' said Elvira. 'I was just wondering who would get my money if I died?'

'I haven't the least idea,' said the Colonel irritably. 'Why do you ask?'

'It might be interesting,' said Elvira thoughtfully. 'I wondered if it would be worth anyone's while to kill me.'

'Really, Elvira! This is a most unprofitable conversation. I can't understand why your mind dwells on such things.'

'Oh. Just ideas. One wants to know what the facts really are.'

'You're not thinking of the *Mafia* – or something like that?'

'Oh no. That would be silly. Who would get my money if I was married?'

'Your husband, I suppose. But really –'

'Are you sure of that?'

'No, I'm not in the least sure. It depends on the wording of the Trust. But you're not married, so why worry?'

Elvira did not reply. She seemed lost in thought. Finally she came out of her trance and asked:

'Do you ever see my mother?'

'Sometimes. Not very often.'

'Where is she now?'

'Oh – abroad.'

'Where abroad?'

'France – Portugal. I don't really know.'

'Does she ever want to see me?'

Her limpid gaze met his. He didn't know what to reply. Was this a moment for truth? Or for vagueness? Or for a good thumping lie? What could you say to a girl who asked a question of such simplicity, when the answer was of great complexity? He said unhappily:

'I don't know.'

Her eyes searched him gravely. Luscombe felt thoroughly ill at ease. He was making a mess of this. The girl must wonder – clearly was wondering. Any girl would.

He said, 'You mustn't think – I mean it's difficult to explain. Your mother is, well, rather different from –' Elvira was nodding energetically.

'I know. I'm always reading about her in the papers. She's something rather special, isn't she? In fact, she's rather a wonderful person.'

'Yes,' agreed the Colonel. 'That's exactly right. She's a wonderful person.' He paused and then went on. 'But a wonderful person is very often –' He stopped and started again – 'it's not always a happy thing to have a wonderful person for a mother. You can take that from me because it's the truth.'

'You don't like speaking the truth very much, do you? But I think what you've just said *is* the truth.'

They both sat staring towards the big brass bound swing doors that led to the world outside.

Suddenly the doors were pushed open with violence – a violence quite unusual in Bertram's Hotel – and a young man strode in and went straight across to the desk. He wore a black leather jacket. His vitality was such that Bertram's Hotel took on the atmosphere of a museum by way of contrast. The people were the dust encrusted relics of a past age. He bent towards Miss Gorringe and asked:

'Is Lady Sedgwick staying here?'

Miss Gorringe on this occasion had no welcoming smile. Her eyes were flinty. She said:

'Yes.' Then, with definite unwillingness, she stretched out her hand towards the telephone. 'Do you want to –?'

'No,' said the young man. 'I just wanted to leave a note for her.'

He produced it from a pocket of his leather coat and slid it across the mahogany counter.

'I only wanted to be sure this was the right hotel.'

There might have been some slight incredulity in his voice as he looked round him, then turned back towards the entrance. His eyes passed indifferently over the people sitting round him. They passed over Luscombe and Elvira in the same way, and Luscombe felt a sudden unsuspected anger. 'Dammit all,' he thought to himself, 'Elvira's a pretty girl. When I was a young chap I'd have noticed a pretty girl, especially among all these fossils.' But the young man seemed to have no interested eyes to spare for pretty girls. He turned back to the desk and asked, raising his voice slightly as though to call Miss Gorringe's attention:

'What's the telephone number here? 1129 isn't it?'

'No,' said Miss Gorringe, '3925.'

'Regent?'

'No. Mayfair.'

He nodded. Then swiftly he strode across to the door and passed out, swinging the doors to behind him with something of the same explosive quality he had shown on entering.

Everybody seemed to draw a deep breath; to find difficulty in resuming their interrupted conversations.

'Well,' said Colonel Luscombe, rather inadequately, as if at a loss for words 'Well, really! These young fellows nowadays . . .'

Elvira was smiling.

'You recognized him, didn't you?' she said. 'You know who he is?' She spoke in a slightly awed voice. She proceeded to enlighten him. 'Ladislaus Malinowski.'

'Oh, that chap.' The name was indeed faintly familiar to Colonel Luscombe. 'Racing driver.'

'Yes. He was world champion two years running. He had a bad crash a year ago. Broke lots of things. But I believe he's driving again now.' She raised her head to listen. 'That's a racing car he's driving now.'

The roar of the engine had penetrated through to Bertram's Hotel from the street outside. Colonel Luscombe perceived that Ladislaus Malinowski was one of Elvira's heroes. 'Well,' he thought to himself, 'better that than one of those pop singers or crooners or long-haired Beatles or whatever they call themselves.' Luscombe was old-fashioned in his views of young men.

The swing doors opened again. Both Elvira and Colonel Luscombe looked at them expectantly but Bertram's Hotel had reverted to normal. It was merely a white-haired elderly cleric who came in. He stood for a moment looking round him with a slightly puzzled air as of one who fails to understand where he was or how he had come there. Such an experience was no novelty to Canon Pennyfather. It came to him in trains when he did not remember where he had come from, where he was going, or why! It came to him when he was walking along the street, it came to him when he found himself sitting on a committee. It had come to him before now when he was in his cathedral stall, and did not know whether he had already preached his sermon or was about to do so.

'I believe I know that old boy,' said Luscombe, peering at him. 'Who is he now? Stays here fairly often, I believe. Abercombie? Archdeacon Abercrombie – no, it's not Abercrombie, though he's rather like Abercrombie.'

Elvira glanced round at Canon Pennyfather without interest. Compared with a racing driver he had no appeal at all. She was not interested in ecclesiastics of any kind although, since being in Italy, she admitted to a mild admiration for Cardinals whom she considered as at any rate properly picturesque.

Canon Pennyfather's face cleared and he nodded his head appreciatively. He had recognized where he was. In Bertram's Hotel, of course; where he was going to spend the night on his way to – now where was he on his way to? Chadminster? No, no, he had just *come* from Chadminster. He was going to – of course – to the Congress at Lucerne. He stepped forward, beaming, to the reception desk and was greeted warmly by Miss Gorringe.

'So glad to see you, Canon Pennyfather. How well you are looking.'

'Thank you – thank you – I had a severe cold last week but I've got over it now. You have a room for me. I *did* write?'

Miss Gorringe reassured him.

'Oh yes, Canon Pennyfather, we got your letter. We've reserved No. 19 for you, the room you had last time.'

'Thank you – thank you. For – let me see – I shall want it for four days. Actually I am going to Lucerne and I shall be away for one night, but please keep the room. I shall leave most of my things here and only take a small bag to Switzerland. There won't be any difficulty over that?'

Again Miss Gorringe reassured him.

'Everything's going to be quite all right. You explained very clearly in your letter.'

Other people might not have used the word 'clearly'. 'Fully' would have been better, since he had certainly written at length.

All anxieties set at rest, Canon Pennyfather breathed a sigh of relief and was conveyed, together with his baggage, to Room 19.

In Room 28 Mrs Carpenter had removed her crown of violets from her head and was carefully adjusting her nightdress on the pillow of her bed. She looked up as Elvira entered.

'Ah, there you are, my dear. Would you like me to help you with your unpacking'

'No, thank you,' said Elvira politely. 'I shan't unpack very much, you know.'

'Which of the bedrooms would you like to have? The bathroom is between them. I told them to put your luggage in the far one. I thought this room might be a little noisy.'

'That was very kind of you,' said Elvira in her expressionless voice.

'You're sure you wouldn't like me to help you?'

'No, thanks, really I wouldn't. I think I might perhaps have a bath.'

'Yes, I think that's a very good idea. Would you like to have the first bath? I'd rather finish putting my things away.'

Elvira nodded. She went into the adjoining bathroom, shut the door behind her and pushed the bolts across. She went into her own room, opened her suitcase and flung a few things on the bed. Then she undressed, put on a dressing-gown, went into the bathroom and turned the taps on. She went back into her own room and sat down on the bed by the telephone. She listened a moment or two in case of interruption, then lifted the receiver.

'This is Room 29. Can you give me Regent 1129 please?'

CHAPTER 4

Within the confines of Scotland Yard a conference was in progress. It was by way of being an informal conference. Six or seven men were sitting easily around a table and each of those six men was a man of some importance in his own line. The subject that occupied the attention of these guardians of the law was a subject that had grown terrifically in importance during the last two or three years. It concerned a branch of crime whose success had been overwhelmingly disquieting. Robbery on a big scale was increasing. Bank hold-ups, snatches of payrolls, thefts of consignments of jewels sent through the mail, train robberies. Hardly a month passed but some daring and stupendous coup was attempted and brought off successfully.

Sir Ronald Graves, Assistant Commissioner of Scotland Yard, was presiding at the head of the table. According to his usual custom he did more listening than talking. No formal reports were being presented on this occasion. All that belonged to the ordinary routine of C.I.D. work. This was a high level consultation, a general pooling of ideas between men looking at affairs from slightly different points of view. Sir Ronald Graves' eyes went slowly round his little group, then he nodded his head to a man at the end of the table.

'Well, Father,' he said, 'let's hear a few homely wisecracks from you.'

The man addressed as 'Father' was Chief-Inspector Fred Davy. His retirement lay not long ahead and he appeared to be even more elderly than he was. Hence his nickname of 'Father'. He had a comfortable spreading presence, and such a benign and kindly manner that many criminals had been disagreeably surprised to find him a less genial and gullible man that he had seemed to be.

'Yes, Father, let's hear your views,' said another Chief-Inspector.

'It's big,' said Chief-Inspector Davy with a deep sigh. 'Yes, it's big. Maybe it's growing.'

'When you say big, do you mean numerically?'

'Yes, I do.'

Another man, Comstock, with a sharp, foxy face and alert eyes, broke in to say:

'Would you say that was an advantage to them?'

'Yes and no,' said Father. 'It *could* be a disaster. But so far, devil take it, they've got it all well under control.'

Superintendent Andrews, a fair, slight, dreamy-looking man said, thoughtfully:

'I've always thought there's a lot more to size than people realize. Take a little one-man business. If that's well run and if it's the right size, it's a sure and certain winner. Branch out, make it bigger, increase personnel, and perhaps you'll get it suddenly to the *wrong* size and down the hill it goes. The same way with a great big chain of stores. An empire in industry. If that's *big* enough it will succeed. If it's *not* big enough it just won't manage it. Everything has got its right size. When it is its right size and well run it's the tops.'

'How big do you think this show is?' Sir Ronald barked.

'Bigger than we thought at first,' said Comstock.

A tough looking man, Inspector McNeill, said:

'It's growing, I'd say. Father's right. Growing all the time.'

'That may be a good thing,' said Davy. 'It may grow a bit *too* fast, and then it'll get out of hand.'

'The question is, Sir Ronald,' said McNeill, 'who we pull in and when?'

'There's a round dozen or so we could pull in,' said Comstock. 'The Harris lot are mixed up in it, we know that. There's a nice little pocket down Luton way. There's a garage at Epsom, there's a pub near Maidenhead, and there's a farm on the Great North Road.'

'Any of them worth pulling in?'

'I don't think so. Small fry all of them. Links. Just links here and there in the chain. A spot where cars are converted, and turned over quickly; a respectable pub where messages get passed; a second-hand clothes shop where appearance can be altered, a theatrical costumier in the East End, also very useful. They're paid, these people. Quite well paid but they don't really *know* anything!'

The dreamy Superintendent Andrews said again:

'We're up against some good brains. We haven't got near them yet. We know some of their affiliations and that's all. As I say, the Harris crowd are in it and Marks is in on the financial end. The foreign contacts are in touch with Weber but he's only an agent. We've nothing actually *on* any of these people. We know that they all have ways of maintaining contact with each other, and with the different branches of the concern, but we don't know exactly how they do it. We watch them and follow them, and they know we're watching them. *Somewhere* there's a great central exchange. What we want to get at is the planners.'

Comstock said:

'It's like a giant network. I agree that there must be an operational headquarters somewhere. A place where each operation is planned and detailed and dovetailed completely. Somewhere, someone plots it all, and produces a working blueprint of Operation Mailbag or Operation Payroll. Those are the people we're out to get.'

'Possibly they are not even in this country,' said Father quietly.

'No, I dare say that's true. Perhaps they're in an igloo somewhere, or in a tent in Morocco or in a chalet in Switzerland.'

'I don't believe in these master-minds,' said McNeill, shaking his head: 'they sound all right in a story. There's got to *be* a head, of course, but I don't believe in a Master Criminal. I'd say there was a very clever little Board of Directors behind this. Centrally planned, with a Chairman. They've got on to something good, and they're improving their technique all the time. All the same —'

'Yes?' said Sir Ronald encouragingly.

'Even in a right tight little team, there are probably expendables. What I call the Russian Sledge principle. From time to time, if they think we might be getting hot on the scent, they throw off one of them, the one they think they can best afford.'

'Would they dare to do that? Wouldn't it be rather risky?'

'I'd say it could be done in such a way that whoever it was wouldn't even know he *had* been pushed off the sledge. He'd just think he'd fallen off. He'd keep quiet because he'd think it was worth his while to keep quiet. So it would be, of course. They've got plenty of money to play with, and they can afford to be generous. Family looked after, if he's got one, whilst he's in prison. Possibly an escape engineered.'

'There's been too much of that,' said Comstock.

'I think, you know,' said Sir Ronald, 'that it's not much good going over and over our speculations again. We always say much the same thing.'

McNeill laughed.

'What is it you really wanted us for, sir?'

'Well —' Sir Ronald thought a moment, 'we're all agreed on the main things,' he said slowly. 'We're agreed on our main policy, on what we're trying to do. I think it *might* be profitable to have a look around for some of the small things, the things that don't matter much, that are just a bit out of the usual run. It's hard to explain what I mean, but like that business some years ago in the Culver case. An ink stain. Do you remember? An ink stain round a mouse-hole. Now why on earth should a man empty a bottle of ink into a mouse-hole? It didn't seem important. It was hard to get at the answer. But when we did hit on the answer, it led somewhere. That's — roughly — the sort of thing I was thinking about. Odd things. Don't mind saying if you come across something that strikes you as a bit out of the usual. Petty if you like, but irritating, because it doesn't quite fit in. I see Father's nodding his head.'

'Couldn't agree with you more,' said Chief-Inspector Davy. 'Come on, boys, try to come up with something. Even if it's only a man wearing a funny hat.'

There was no immediate response. Everyone looked a little uncertain and doubtful.

'Come on,' said Father, 'I'll stick my neck out first. It's just a funny story, really, but you might as well have it for what's it's worth. The London and Metropolitan Bank hold up. Carmolly Street Branch. Remember it? A whole list of car numbers and car colours and makes. We appealed to people to come forward and they responded – how they responded! About a hundred and fifty pieces of misleading information! Got it sorted out in the end to about seven cars that had been seen in the neighbourhood, any one of which *might* have been concerned in the robbery.'

'Yes,' said Sir Ronald, 'go on.'

'There were one or two we couldn't get tags on. Looked as though the numbers might have been changed. Nothing out of the way in that. It's often done. Most of them got tracked down in the end. I'll just bring up one instance. Morris Oxford, black saloon, number CMG 265, reported by a probation officer. He said it was being driven by Mr Justice Ludgrove.'

He looked round. They were listening to him, but without any manifest interest.

'I know,' he said, 'wrong as usual. Mr Justice Ludgrove is a rather noticeable old boy, ugly as sin for one thing. Well, it wasn't Mr Justice Ludgrove because at that exact time he was actually in Court. He *has* got a Morris Oxford, but its number isn't CMG 256.' He looked round. 'All right. All right. So there's no point in it, you'll say. But do you know what the number *was*? CMG 265. Near enough, eh? Just the sort of mistake one does make when you're trying to remember a car number.'

'I'm sorry,' said Sir Ronald, 'I don't quite see –'

'No,' said Chief-Inspector Davy, 'there's nothing *to* see really, is there? Only – it was very like the actual car number, wasn't it? 265 – 256 CMG. Really rather a coincidence that there should be a Morris Oxford car of the right colour with the number just one digit wrong, and with a man in it closely resembling the owner of the car.'

'Do you mean –?'

'Just one little digit difference. Today's "deliberate mistake". It almost seems like that.'

'Sorry, Davy. I still don't get it.'

'Oh, I don't suppose there's anything *to* get. There's a Morris Oxford car, CMG 265, proceeding along the street two and half minutes after the bank snatch. In it, the probation officer recognizes Mr Justice Ludgrove.'

'Are you suggesting it really *was* Mr Justice Ludgrove? Come now, Davy.'

'No, I'm not suggesting that it was Mr Justice Ludgrove and that he was mixed up in a bank robbery. He was staying at Bertram's Hotel in Pond Street, and he was at the Law Courts at that exact time. All proved up to the hilt. I'm saying the car number and make and the identification by a probation officer who knows old Ludgrove quite well by sight is the kind of coincidence that *ought* to mean something. Apparently it doesn't. Too bad.'

Comstock stirred uneasily.

'There was another case like that in connection with the Jewellery business at Brighton. Some old Admiral or other. I've forgotten his name now. Some woman identified him most positively as having been on the scene.'

'And he wasn't?'

'No, he'd been in London that night. Went up for some Naval dinner or other, I think.'

'Staying at his club?'

'No, he was staying at a hotel – I believe it was that one you mentioned just now, Father, Bertram's, isn't it? Quiet place. A lot of old service geezers go there, I believe.'

'Bertram's Hotel,' said Chief-Inspector Davy, thoughtfully.

Miss Marple awoke early because she always woke early. She was appreciative of her bed. Most comfortable.

She pattered across to the window and pulled the curtains, admitting a little pallid London daylight. As yet, however, she did not try to dispense with the electronic light. A very nice bedroom they had given her, again quite in the tradition of Bertram's. A rose-flowered wallpaper, a large well-polished mahogany chest of drawers – a dressing-table to correspond. Two upright chairs, one easy chair of a reasonable height from the ground. A connecting door led to a bathroom which was modern but which had a tiled wallpaper of roses and so avoided any suggestion of over-frigid hygiene.

Miss Marple got back into bed, plumped her pillows up, glanced at her clock, half-past seven, picked up the small devotional book that always accompanied her, and read as usual the page and a half allotted to the day. Then she picked up her knitting and began to knit, slowly at first, since her fingers were stiff and rheumatic when she first awoke, but very soon her pace grew faster, and her fingers lost their painful stiffness.

'Another day,' said Miss Marple to herself, greeting the fact with her usual gentle pleasure. Another day – and who knew what it might bring forth?

She relaxed, and abandoning her knitting, let thoughts pass in an idle stream through her head . . . Selina Hazy . . . what a pretty cottage she had had in St Mary Mead's – and now someone had put on that ugly green roof . . . Muffins . . . very wasteful in butter . . . but very good . . . And fancy serving old-fashioned seed cake! She had never expected, not for a moment, that things would be as much like they used to be . . . because, after all, Time didn't stand still . . . And to have made it stand still in this way must really have cost a lot of money . . . Not a bit of plastic in the place! . . . It must pay them, she supposed. The out-of-date returns in due course as the picturesque . . . Look how people wanted old-fashioned roses now, and scorned hybrid teas! . . . None of this place seemed real at all . . . Well, why should it? . . . It was fifty – no, nearer sixty years since she had stayed here. And it didn't seem real to her because she was now acclimatized in this present year of Our Lord – Really, the whole thing opened up a very interesting set of problems . . . The atmosphere and the *people* . . . Miss Marple's fingers pushed her knitting farther away from her.

'Pockets,' she said aloud . . . 'Pockets, I suppose . . . And quite difficult to find . . .'

Would that account for that curious feeling of uneasiness she had had last night? That feeling that something was wrong ...

All those elderly people – really very much like those she remembered when she had stayed here fifty years ago. They had been natural then – but they weren't very natural now. Elderly people nowadays weren't like elderly people then – they had that worried harried look of domestic anxieties with which they are too tired to cope, or they rushed around to committees and tried to appear bustling and competent, or they dyed their hair gentian blue, or wore wigs, and their hands were not the hands she remembered, tapering, delicate hands – they were harsh from washing up and detergents ...

And so – well, so these people didn't look real. But the point was that they *were* real. Selina Hazy was real. And that rather handsome old military man in the corner was real – she had met him once, although she did not recall his name – and the Bishop (dear Robbie!) was dead.

Miss Marple glanced at her little clock. It was eight-thirty. Time for her breakfast.

She examined the instructions given by the hotel – splendid big print so that it wasn't necessary to put one's spectacles on.

Meals could be ordered through the telephone by asking for Room Service, or you could press the bell labelled Chambermaid.

Miss Marple did the latter. Talking to Room Service always flustered her.

The result was excellent. In no time at all there was a tap on the door and a highly satisfactory chambermaid appeared. A real chambermaid looking unreal, wearing a striped lavender print dress and actually a *cap*, a freshly laundered cap. A smiling, rosy, positively *countrified* face. (Where did they *find* these people?)

Miss Marple ordered her breakfast. Tea, poached eggs, fresh rolls. So adept was the chambermaid that she did not even mention cereals or orange juice.

Five minutes later breakfast came. A comfortable tray with a big pot-bellied teapot, creamy-looking milk, a silver hot water jug. Two beautifully poached eggs on toast, poached the proper way, not little round hard bullets shaped in tin cups, a good-sized round of butter stamped with a thistle. Marmalade, honey and strawberry jam. Delicious-looking rolls, not the hard kind with papery interiors – they *smelt* of fresh bread (the most delicious smell in the world!). There was also an apple, a pear and a banana.

Miss Marple inserted a knife gingerly but with confidence. She was not disappointed. Rich deep yellow yolk oozed out, thick and creamy. *Proper* eggs!

Everything's piping hot. A *real* breakfast. She could have cooked it herself but she hadn't had to! It was brought to her as if – no, not as though she were a queen – as though she were a middle-aged lady staying in a good but not unduly expensive hotel. In fact – back to 1909. Miss Marple expressed appreciation to the chambermaid who replied smiling,

'Oh, yes, Madam, the Chef is very particular about his breakfasts.'

Miss Marple studied her appraisingly. Bertram's Hotel could certainly produce marvels. A *real* housemaid. She pinched her left arm surreptitiously.

'Have you been here long?' she asked.

'Just over three years, Madam.'

'And before that?'

'I was in a hotel at Eastbourne. Very modern and up-to-date – but I prefer an old-fashioned place like this.'

Miss Marple took a sip of tea. She found herself humming in a vague way – words fitting themselves to a long forgotten song.

'Oh where have you been all my life . . .'

The chambermaid was looking slightly startled.

'I was just remembering an old song,' twittered Miss Marple apologetically. 'Very popular at one time.'

Again she sang softly. 'Oh where have you been all my life . . .'

'Perhaps you know it?' she asked.

'Well –' The chambermaid looked rather apologetic.

'Too long ago for you,' said Miss Marple. 'Ah well, one gets to remembering things – in a place like this.'

'Yes, Madam, a lot of the ladies who stay here feel like that, I think.'

'It's partly why they come, I expect,' said Miss Marple.

The chambermaid went out. She was obviously used to old ladies who twittered and reminisced.

Miss Marple finished her breakfast, and got up in a pleasant leisurely fashion. She had a plan ready made for a delightful morning of shopping. Not too much – to over-tire herself. Oxford Street today, perhaps. And tomorrow Knightsbridge. She planned ahead happily.

It was about ten o'clock when she emerged from her room fully equipped: hat, gloves, umbrella – just in case, though it looked fine – handbag – her smartest shopping bag –

The door next but one on the corridor opened sharply and someone looked out. It was Bess Sedgwick. She withdrew back into the room and closed the door sharply.

Miss Marple wondered as she went down the stairs. She preferred the stairs to the lift first thing in the morning. It limbered her up. Her steps grew slower and slower . . . she stopped.

As Colonel Luscombe strode along the passage from his room, a door at the top of the stairs opened sharply and Lady Sedgwick spoke to him.

'There you are at last! I've been on the look-out for you – waiting to pounce. Where can we go and talk? That is to say without falling over some old pussy every second.'

'Well, really, Bess, I'm not quite sure – I think on the mezzanine floor there's a sort of writing-room.'

'You'd better come in here. Quick now, before the chambermaid gets peculiar ideas about us.'

Rather unwillingly, Colonel Luscombe stepped across the threshold and had the door shut firmly behind him.

'I'd no idea you would be staying here, Bess, I hadn't the faintest idea of it.'

'I don't suppose you had.'

'I mean – I would never have brought Elvira here. I *have* got Elvira here, you know?'

'Yes, I saw her with you last night.'

'But I really didn't know that you were here. It seemed such an unlikely place for you.'

'I don't see why,' said Bess Sedgwick, coldy. 'It's far and away the most comfortable hotel in London. Why shouldn't I stay here?'

'You must understand that I hadn't any idea of . . . I mean –'

She looked at him and laughed. She was dressed ready to go out in a well cut dark suit and a shirt of bright emerald green. She looked gay and very much alive. Beside her, Colonel Luscombe looked rather old and faded.

'Darling Derek, don't look so worried. I'm not accusing you of trying to stage a mother and daughter sentimental meeting. It's just one of those things that happen; where people meet each other in unsuspected places. But you *must* get Elvira out of here, Derek. You must get her out of it at once – today.'

'Oh, she's going. I mean, I only brought her here just for a couple of nights. Do a show – that sort of thing. She's going down to Melford's tomorrow.'

'Poor girl, that'll be boring for her.'

Luscombe looked at her with concern. 'Do you think she will be very bored?'

Bess took pity on him.

'Probably not after duress in Italy. She might even think it wildly thrilling.'

Luscombe took his courage in both hands.

'Look here, Bess, I was startled to find you here, but don't you think it – well, you know, it might be *meant* in a way. I mean that it might be an opportunity – I don't think you really know how – well, how the girl might feel.'

'What are you trying to say, Derek?'

'Well, you *are* her mother, you know.'

'Of course I'm her mother. She's my daughter. And what good has that fact ever been to either of us, or ever will be?'

'You can't be sure. I think – I think she feels it.'

'What gives you that idea?' said Bess Sedgwick sharply.

'Something she said yesterday. She asked where you were, what you were doing.'

Bess Sedgwick walked across the room to the window. She stood there a moment tapping on the pane.

'You're so nice, Derek,' she said. 'You have such nice ideas. But they don't work, my poor angel. That's what you've got to say to yourself. They don't work and they might be dangerous.'

'Oh come now, Bess. Dangerous?'

'Yes, yes, yes. Dangerous. *I'm* dangerous. I've always been dangerous.'

'When I think of some of the things you've done,' said Colonel Luscombe.

'That's my own business,' said Bess Sedgwick. 'Running into danger has become a kind of habit with me. No, I wouldn't say habit. More an addiction. Like a drug. Like that nice little dollop of heroin addicts have to have every so often to make life seem bright coloured and worth living. Well, that's all right. That's my funeral – or not – as the case may be. I've never taken drugs – never needed them – Danger has been my drug. But people who live as I do can be a source of harm to others. Now don't be an obstinate old fool, Derek. You keep that girl well away from me. I can do her no good. Only harm. If possible, don't even let her know I was staying in the same hotel. Ring up the Melfords and take her down there *today*. Make some excuse about a sudden emergency –'

Colonel Luscombe hesitated, pulling his moustaches.

'I think you're making a mistake, Bess.' He sighed. 'She asked where you were. I told her you were abroad.'

'Well, I shall be in another twelve hours, so that all fits very nicely.'

She came up to him, kissed him on the point of his chin, turned him smartly around as though they were about to play Blind Man's Buff, opened the door, gave him a gentle little propelling shove out of it. As the door shut behind him, Colonel Luscombe noticed an old lady turning the corner from

375

the stairs. She was muttering to herself as she looked into her handbag. 'Dear, dear me. I suppose I must have left it in my room. Oh dear.'

She passed Colonel Luscombe without paying much attention to him apparently, but as he went on down the stairs Miss Marple paused by her room door and directed a piercing glance after him. Then she looked towards Bess Sedgwick's door. 'So that's who she was waiting for,' said Miss Marple to herself. 'I wonder why?'

III

Canon Pennyfather, fortified by breakfast, wandered across the lounge, remembered to leave his key at the desk, pushed his way through the swinging doors, and was neatly inserted into a taxi by the Irish commissionaire who existed for this purpose.

'Where to, sir?'

'Oh dear,' said Canon Pennyfather in sudden dismay. 'Now let me see – where *was* I going?'

The traffic in Pond Street was held up for some minutes whilst Canon Pennyfather and the commissionaire debated this knotty point.

Finally Canon Pennyfather had a brainwave and the taxi was directed to go to the British Museum.

The commissionaire was left on the pavement with a broad grin on his face, and since no other exits seemed to be taking place, he strolled a little way along the façade of the hotel whistling an old tune in a muted manner.

One of the windows on the ground floor of Bertram's was flung up – but the commissionaire did not even turn his head until a voice spoke unexpectedly through the open window.

'So this is where you've landed up, Micky. What on earth brought you to this place?'

He swung round, startled – and stared.

Lady Sedgwick thrust her head through the open window.

'Don't you know me?' she demanded.

A sudden gleam of recognition came across the man's face.

'Why, if it isn't little Bessie now! Fancy that! After all these years. Little Bessie.'

'Nobody but you ever called me Bessie. It's a revolting name. What have you been doing all these years?'

'This and that,' said Micky with some reserve. 'I've not been in the news like you have. I've read of your doings in the paper time and again.'

Bess Sedgwick laughed. 'Anyway, I've worn better than you have,' she

376

said. 'You drink too much. You always did.'

'You've worn well because you've always been in the money.'

'Money wouldn't have done you any good. You'd have drunk even more and gone to the dogs completely. Oh yes, you would! What brought you *here*? That's what I want to know. How did you ever get taken on at this place?'

'I wanted a job, I had these –' his hand flicked over the row of medals.

'Yes, I see.' She was thoughtful. 'All genuine too, aren't they?'

'Sure they're genuine. Why shouldn't they be?'

'Oh I believe you. You always had courage. You've always been a good fighter. Yes, the army suited you. I'm sure of that.'

'The army's all right in time of war, but it's no good in peace time.'

'So you took to this stuff. I hadn't the last idea –' she stopped.

'You hadn't the least idea what, Bessie?'

'Nothing. It's queer seeing you again after all these years.'

'*I* haven't forgotten,' said the man. 'I've never forgotten you, little Bessie. Ah! A lovely girl you were! A lovely slip of a girl.'

'A damn' fool of a girl, that's what I was,' said Lady Sedgwick.

'That's true now. You hadn't much sense. If you had, you wouldn't have taken up with me. What hands you had for a horse. Do you remember that mare – what was her name now? – Molly O'Flynn. Ah, she was a wicked devil, that one was.'

'You were the only one that could ride her,' said Lady Sedgwick.

'She'd have had me off if she could! When she found she couldn't, she gave in. Ah, she was a beauty, now. But talking of sitting a horse, there wasn't one lady in those parts better than you. A lovely seat you had, lovely hands. Never any fear in you, not for a minute! And it's been the same ever since, so I judge. Aeroplanes, racing cars.'

Bess Sedgwick laughed.

'I must get on with my letters.'

She drew back from the window.

Micky leaned over the railing. 'I've not forgotten, Ballygowlan,' he said with meaning. 'Sometimes I've thought of writing to you –'

Bess Sedgwick's voice came out harshly.

'And what do you mean by that, Mick Gorman?'

'I was just saying as I haven't forgotten – anything. I was just – reminding you like.'

Bess Sedgwick's voice still held its harsh note.

'If you mean what I think you mean, I'll give you a piece of advice. Any trouble from you, and I'd shoot you as easily as I'd shoot a rat. I've shot men before –'

'In foreign parts, maybe –'

'Foreign parts or here – it's all the same to me.'

'Ah, good Lord, now, and I believe you would do just that!' His voice held admiration. 'In Ballygowlan –'

'In Ballygowlan,' she cut in, 'they paid you to keep your mouth shut and paid you well. You took the money. You'll get no more from me so don't think it.'

'It would be a nice romantic story for the Sunday papers . . .'

'You heard what I said.'

'Ah,' he laughed, 'I'm not serious, I was just joking. I'd never do anything to hurt my little Bessie. I'll keep my mouth shut.'

'Mind you do,' said Lady Sedgwick.

She shut down the window. Staring down at the desk in front of her she looked at her unfinished letter on the blotting paper. She picked it up, looked at it, crumpled it into a ball and slung it into the waste-paper basket. Then abruptly she got up from her seat and walked out of the room. She did not even cast a glance around her before she went.

The smaller writing-rooms at Bertram's often had an appearance of being empty even when they were not. Two well-appointed desks stood in the windows, there was a table on the right that held a few magazines, on the left were two very high-backed arm-chairs turned towards the fire. These were favourite spots in the afternoon for elderly military or naval gentlemen to ensconce themselves and fall happily asleep until tea-time. Anyone coming in to write a letter did not usually even notice them. The chairs were not so much in demand during the morning.

As it happened, however, they were on this particular morning both occupied. An old lady was in one and a young girl in the other. The young girl rose to her feet. She stood a moment looking uncertainly towards the door through which Lady Sedgwick had passed out, then she moved slowly towards it. Elvira Blake's face was deadly pale.

It was another five minutes before the old lady moved. Then Miss Marple decided that the little rest which she always took after dressing and coming downstairs had lasted quite long enough. It was time to go out and enjoy the pleasures of London. She might walk as far as Piccadilly, and take a No. 9 bus to High Street, Kensington, or she might walk along to Bond Street and take a 25 bus to Marshall & Snelgrove's, or she might take a 25 the other way which as far as she remembered would land her up at the Army & Navy Stores. Passing through the swing doors she was still savouring these delights in her mind. The Irish commissionaire, back on duty, made up her mind for her.

'You'll be wanting a taxi, Ma'am,' he said with firmness.

'I don't think I do,' said Miss Marple. 'I think there's a 25 bus I could take quite near here – or a 2 from Park Lane.'

'You'll not be wanting a bus,' said the commissionaire firmly. 'It's very dangerous springing on a bus when you're getting on in life. The way they start and stop and go on again. Jerk you off your feet, they do. No heart at all, these fellows, nowadays. I'll whistle you along a taxi and you'll go to wherever you want to like a queen.'

Miss Marple considered and fell.

'Very well then,' she said, 'perhaps I *had* better have a taxi.'

The commissionaire had no need even to whistle. He merely clicked his thumb and a taxi appeared like magic. Miss Marple was helped into it with every possible care and decided on the spur of the moment to go to Robinson & Cleaver's and look at their splendid offer of real linen sheets. She sat happily in her taxi feeling indeed as the commissionaire had promised her, just like a queen. Her mind was filled with pleasurable anticipation of linen sheets, linen pillow cases and proper glass-and-kitchen-cloths without pictures of bananas, figs or performing dogs and other pictorial distractions to annoy you when you were washing up.

Lady Sedgwick came up to the Reception desk.

'Mr Humfries in his office?'

'Yes, Lady Sedgwick.' Miss Gorringe looked startled.

Lady Sedgwick passed behind the desk, tapped on the door and went in without waiting for any response.

Mr Humfries looked up startled.

'What –'

'Who engaged the man Michael Gorman?'

Mr Humfries spluttered a little.

'Parfitt left – he had a car accident a month ago. We had to replace him quickly. This man seemed all right. References O.K. – ex-Army – quite good record – Not very bright perhaps – but that's all the better sometimes – you don't know anything against him, do you?'

'Enough not to want him here.'

'If you insist,' Humfries said slowly, 'we'll give him his notice –'

'No,' said Lady Sedgwick slowly. 'No – it's too late for that – Never mind.'

CHAPTER 6

'Elvira.'

'Hallo, Bridget.'

The Hon. Elvira Blake pushed her way through the front door of 180 Onslow Square, which her friend Bridget had rushed down to open for her, having been watching through the window.

'Let's go upstairs,' said Elvira.

'Yes, we'd better. Otherwise we'll get entangled by Mummy.'

The two girls rushed up the stairs, thereby circumventing Bridget's mother, who came out on to the landing from her own bedroom just too late.

'You really are lucky not to have a mother,' said Bridget, rather breathlessly as she took her friend into her bedroom and shut the door firmly. 'I mean, Mummy's quite a pet and all that, but the *questions* she asks! Morning, noon and night. When are you going, and who have you met? And are they cousins of somebody else of the same name in Yorkshire? I mean, the *futility* of it all.'

'I suppose they have nothing else to think about,' said Elvira vaguely. 'Look here, Bridget, there's something terribly important I've got to do, and you've got to help me.'

'Well, I will if I can. What is it – a man?'

'No, it isn't, as a matter of fact.' Bridget looked disappointed. 'I've got to get away to Ireland for twenty-four hours or perhaps longer, and you've got to cover up for me.'

'To Ireland? Why?'

'I can't tell you all about it now. There's no time. I've got to meet my guardian, Colonel Luscombe, at Prunier's for lunch at half-past one.'

'What have you done with the Carpenter?'

'Gave her the slip in Debenham's.'

Bridget giggled.

'And after lunch they're taking me down to the Melfords. I'm going to live with them until I'm twenty-one.'

'How ghastly!'

'I expect I shall manage. Cousin Mildred is fearfully easy to deceive. It's arranged I'm to come up for classes and things. There's a place called World of Today. They take you to lectures and to Museums and to Picture Galleries and the House of Lords, and all that. The whole point is that nobody will know whether you're where you ought to be or not! We'll manage lots of things.'

'I expect we will.' Bridget giggled. 'We managed in Italy, didn't we? Old Macaroni thought she was so strict. Little did she know what we got up to

380

when we tried.'

Both girls laughed in the pleasant consciousness of successful wickedness.

'Still, it did need a lot of planning,' said Elvira.

'And some splendid lying,' said Bridget. 'Have you heard from Guido?'

'Oh yes, he wrote me a long letter signed Ginevra as though he was a girl friend. But I do wish you'd stop talking so much, Bridget. We've got a lot to do and only about an hour and a half to do it in. Now first of all just *listen*. I'm coming up tomorrow for an appointment with the dentist. That's easy, I can put it off by telephone – or you can from here. Then, about midday, you can ring up the Melfords pretending to be your mother and explain that the dentist wants to see me again the next day and so I'm staying over with you here.'

'That ought to go down all right. They'll say how very kind and gush. But supposing you're *not* back the next day?'

'Then you'll have to do some more ringing up.'

Bridget looked doubtful.

'We'll have lots of time to think up something before then,' said Elvira impatiently. 'What's worrying me now is *money*. You haven't got any, I suppose?' Elvira spoke without much hope.

'Only about two pounds.'

'That's no good. I've got to buy my air ticket. I've looked up the flights. It only takes about two hours. A lot depends upon how long it takes me when I get there.'

'Can't you tell me what you're going to do?'

'No, I can't. But it's terribly, terribly important.'

Elvira's voice was so different that Bridget looked at her in some surprise.

'Is anything really the matter, Elvira?'

'Yes, it is.'

'Is it something nobody's got to know about?'

'Yes, that's the sort of thing. It's frightfully, frightfully secret. I've got to find out if something is really true or not. It's a bore about the money. What's maddening is that I'm really quite rich. My guardian told me so. But all they give me is a measly dress allowance. And that seems to go as soon as I get it.'

'Wouldn't your guardian – Colonel Thingummybob – lend you some money?'

'That wouldn't do at all. He'd ask a lot of questions and want to know what I wanted it for.'

'Oh, dear, I suppose he would. I can't think why everybody wants to ask so many questions. Do you know that if somebody rings me up, Mummy has to ask *who it is*? When it really is *no* business of hers!'

Elvira agreed, but her mind was on another tack.

'Have you ever pawned anything, Bridget?'

'Never. I don't think I'd know how to.'

'It's quite easy, I believe,' said Elvira. 'You go to the sort of jeweller who has three balls over the door, isn't that right?'

'I don't think I've got anything that would be any good taking to a pawnbroker,' said Bridget.

'Hasn't your mother got some jewellery somewhere?'

'I don't think we'd better ask her to help.'

'No, perhaps not – But we could pinch something perhaps.'

'Oh, I don't think we could do that,' said Bridget, shocked.

'No? Well, perhaps you're right. But I bet she wouldn't notice. We could get it back before she missed it. *I* know. We'll go to Mr Bollard.'

'Who's Mr Bollard?'

'Oh, he's a sort of family jeweller. I take my watch there always to have it mended. He's known me ever since I was six. Come on, Bridget, we'll go there right away. We'll just have time.'

'We'd better go out the back way,' said Bridget, 'and then Mummy won't ask us where we're going.'

Outside the old established business of Bollard and Whitley in Bond Street the two girls made their final arrangements.

'Are you sure you understand, Bridget?'

'I think so,' said Bridget in a far from happy voice.

'First,' said Elvira, 'we synchronize our watches.'

Bridget brightened up a little. This familiar literary phrase had a heartening effect. They solemnly synchronized their watches, Bridget adjusting hers by one minute.

'Zero hour will be twenty-five past exactly,' said Elvira.

'That will give me plenty of time. Perhaps even more than I need, but it's better that way about.'

'But supposing –' began Bridget.

'Supposing what?' asked Elvira.

'Well, I mean, supposing I *really* got run over?'

'Of course you won't get run over,' said Elvira. 'You know how nippy you are on your feet, and all London traffic is used to pulling up suddenly. It'll be all right.'

Bridget looked far from convinced.

'You won't let me down, Bridget, will you?'

'All right,' said Bridget, 'I won't let you down.'

'Good,' said Elvira.

382

Bridget crossed to the other side of Bond Street and Elvira pushed open the doors of Messrs Bollard and Whitley, old established jewellers and watchmakers. Inside there was a beautiful and hushed atmosphere. A frock-coated nobleman came forward and asked Elvira what he could do for her.

'Could I see Mr Bollard?'

'Mr Bollard. What name shall I say?'

'Miss Elvira Blake.'

The nobleman disappeared and Elvira drifted to a counter where, below plate glass, brooches, rings and bracelets showed off their jewelled proportions against suitable shades of velvet. In a very few moments Mr Bollard made his appearance. He was the senior partner of the firm, an elderly man of sixty odd. He greeted Elvira with warm friendliness.

'Ah, Miss Blake, so you are in London. It's a great pleasure to see you. Now what can I do for you?'

Elvira produced a dainty little evening wrist-watch.

'This watch doesn't go properly,' said Elvira. 'Could you do something to it?'

'Oh yes, of course. There's no difficulty about *that*.' Mr Bollard took it from her. 'What address shall I send it to?'

Elvira gave the address.

'And there's another thing,' she said. 'My guardian – Colonel Luscombe you know –'

'Yes, yes, of course.'

'He asked me what I'd like for a Christmas present,' said Elvira. 'He suggested I should come in here and look at some different things. He said would I like him to come with me, and I said I'd rather come along first – because I always think it's rather embarrassing, don't you? I mean, prices and all that.'

'Well, that's certainly one aspect,' said Mr Bollard, beaming in an avuncular manner. 'Now what had you in mind, Miss Blake? A brooch, bracelet – a ring?'

'I think really brooches are more useful,' said Elvira. 'But I wonder – could I look at a *lot* of things?' She looked up at him appealingly. He smiled sympathetically.

'Of course, of course. No pleasure at all if one has to make up one's mind too quickly, is it?'

The next five minutes were spent very agreeably. Nothing was too much trouble for Mr Bollard. He fetched things from one case and another, brooches and bracelets piled up on the piece of velvet spread in front of Elvira. Occasionally she turned aside to look at herself in a mirror, trying the effect of a brooch or a pendant. Finally, rather uncertainly, a pretty little bangle, a small diamond wrist-watch and two brooches were laid aside.

'We'll make a note of these,' said Mr Bollard, 'and then when Colonel Luscombe is in London next, perhaps he'll come in and see what he decides himself he'd like to give you.'

'I think that way will be very nice,' said Elvira. 'Then he'll feel more that he's chosen my present himself, won't he?' Her limpid blue gaze was raised to the jeweller's face. That same blue gaze had registered a moment earlier that the time was now exactly twenty-five minutes past the hour.

Outside there was the squealing of brakes and a girl's loud scream. Inevitably the eyes of everyone in the shop turned towards the windows of the shop giving on Bond Street. The movement of Elvira's hand on the counter in front of her and then to the pocket of her neat tailor-made coat and skirt was so rapid and unobtrusive as to be almost unnoticeable, even if anybody had been looking.

'Tcha, tcha,' said Mr Bollard, turning back from where he had been peering out into the street. 'Very nearly an accident. Silly girl! Rushing across the road like that.'

Elvira was already moving towards the door. She looked at her wrist-watch and uttered an exclamation.

'Oh dear, I've been far too long in here. I shall miss my train back to the country. Thank you *so* much, Mr Bollard, and you won't forget which the four things are, will you?'

In another minute, she was out of the door. Turning rapidly to the left and then to the left again, she stopped in the arcade of a shoe shop until Bridget, rather breathless, rejoined her.

'Oh,' said Bridget, 'I was terrified. I thought I was going to be killed. And I've torn a hole in my stocking, too.'

'Never mind,' said Elvira and walked her friend rapidly along the street and round yet another corner to the right. 'Come on.'

'Is it – was it – all right?'

Elvira's hand slipped into her pocket and out again showing the diamond and sapphire bracelet in her palm.

'Oh, Elvira, how you dared!'

'Now, Bridget, you've got to get along to that pawnshop we marked down. Go in and see how much you can get for this. Ask for a hundred.'

'Do you think – supposing they say – I mean – I mean, it might be on a list of stolen things –'

'Don't be silly. How could it be on a list so soon? They haven't even noticed it's gone yet.'

'But Elvira, when they *do* notice it's gone, they'll think – perhaps they'll know – that you must have taken it.'

'They *might* think so – if they discover it soon.'

'Well, then they'll go to the police and –'

She stopped as Elvira shook her head slowly, her pale yellow hair swinging to and fro and a faint enigmatic smile curving up the corners of her mouth.

'They won't go to the police, Bridget. Certainly not if they think *I* took it.'

'Why – you mean –?'

'As I told you, I'm going to have a lot of money when I'm twenty-one. I shall be able to buy lots of jewels from them. *They* won't make a scandal. Go on and get the money quick. Then go to Aer Lingus and book the ticket – I must take a taxi to Prunier's. I'm already ten minutes late. I'll be with you tomorrow morning by half-past ten.'

'Oh, Elvira, I wish you wouldn't take such frightful risks,' moaned Bridget.

But Elvira had hailed a taxi.

II

Miss Marple had a very enjoyable time at Robinson & Cleaver's. Besides purchasing expensive but delicious sheets – she loved linen sheets with their texture and their coolness – she also indulged in a purchase of good quality red-bordered glass-cloths. Really the difficulty in getting proper glass-cloths nowadays! Instead, you were offered things that might as well have been ornamental table-cloths, decorated with radishes or lobsters or the *Tour Eiffel* or Trafalgar Square, or else littered with lemons and oranges. Having given her address in St Mary Mead, Miss Marple found a convenient bus which took her to the Army & Navy Stores.

The Army & Navy Stores had been a haunt of Miss Marple's aunt in days long gone. It was not, of course, quite the same nowadays. Miss Marple cast her thoughts back to Aunt Helen seeking out her own special man in the grocery department, settling herself comfortably in a chair, wearing a bonnet and what she always called her 'black poplin' mantle. Then there would ensue a long hour with nobody in a hurry and Aunt Helen thinking of every conceivable grocery that could be purchased and stored up for future use. Christmas was provided for, and there was even a far-off look towards Easter. The young Jane had fidgeted somewhat, and had been told to go and look at the glass department by way of amusement.

Having finished her purchases, Aunt Helen would then proceed to lengthy inquiries about her chosen shop-assistant's mother, wife, second boy and crippled sister-in-law. Having had a thoroughly pleasant morning, Aunt Helen would say in the playful manner of those times, 'And how would a little girl feel about some luncheon?' Whereupon they went up in the lift to the fourth floor and had luncheon which always finished with a strawberry ice. After that, they bought half a pound of coffee chocolate creams and went to a matinée in a four wheeler.

Of course, the Army & Navy Stores had had a good many face lifts since those days. In fact, it was now quite unrecognizable from the old times. It was gayer and much brighter. Miss Marple, though throwing a kindly and indulgent smile at the past, did not object to the amenities of the present. There was still a restaurant, and there she repaired to order her lunch.

As she was looking carefully down the menu and deciding what to have, she looked across the room and her eyebrows went up a little. How extraordinary coincidence was! Here was a woman she had never seen till the day before, though she had seen plenty of newspaper photographs of her – at race meetings, in Bermuda, or standing by her own plane or car. Yesterday, for the first time, she had seen her in the flesh. And now, as was so often the case, there was the coincidence of running into her again in a most unlikely place. For somehow she did not connect lunch at the Army & Navy Stores with Bess Sedgwick. She would not have been surprised to see Bess Sedgwick emerging from a den in Soho, or stepping out of Covent Garden Opera House in evening dress with a diamond tiara on her head. But somehow, not in the Army & Navy Stores which in Miss Marple's mind was, and always would be, connected with the armed forces, their wives, daughters, aunts and grandmothers. Still, there Bess Sedgwick was, looking as usual very smart, in her dark suit and her emerald shirt, lunching at a table with a man. A young man with a lean hawklike face, wearing a black leather jacket. They were leaning forward talking earnestly together, forking in mouthfuls of food as though they were quite unaware what they were eating.

An assignation, perhaps? Yes, probably an assignation. The man must be fifteen or twenty years younger than she was – but Bess Sedgwick was a magnetically attractive woman.

Miss Marple looked at the young man consideringly and decided that he was what she called a 'handsome fellow'. She also decided that she didn't like him very much. 'Just like Harry Russell,' said Miss Marple to herself, dredging up a prototype as usual from the past. 'Never up to any good. Never did any woman who had anything to do with him any good either.

'She wouldn't take advice from me,' thought Miss Marple, 'but I could give her some.' However, other people's love affairs were no concern of hers, and Bess Sedgwick, by all accounts, could take care of herself very well when it came to love affairs.

Miss Marple sighed, ate her lunch, and meditated a visit to the stationery department.

Curiosity, or what she preferred herself to call 'taking an interest' in other people's affairs, was undoubtedly one of Miss Marple's characteristics.

Deliberately leaving her gloves on the table, she rose and crossed the floor to the cash desk, taking a route that passed close to Lady Sedgwick's table. Having paid her bill she 'discovered' the absence of her gloves and returned to get them – unfortunately dropping her handbag on the return route. It came open and spilled various oddments. A waitress rushed to assist her in picking them up, and Miss Marple was forced to show a great shakiness and dropped coppers and keys a second time.

She did not get very much by these subterfuges but they were not entirely in vain – and it was interesting that neither of the two objects of her curiosity spared as much as a glance for the dithery old lady who kept dropping things.

As Miss Marple waited for the lift down she memorized such scraps as she had heard.

'What about the weather forecast?'

'O.K. No fog.'

'All set for Lucerne?'

'Yes. Plane leaves 9.40.'

That was all she had got the first time. On the way back it had lasted a little longer.

Bess Sedgwick had been speaking angrily.

'What possessed you to come to Bertram's yesterday – you shouldn't have come near the place.'

'It's all right. I asked if you were staying there and everyone knows we're close friends –'

'That's not the point. Bertram's is all right for me – Not for you. You stick out like a sore thumb. Everyone stares at you.'

'Let them!'

'You really are an idiot. Why – why? What reasons did you have? You had a reason – I know you . . .'

'Calm down, Bess.'

'You're such a liar!'

That was all she had been able to hear. She found it interesting.

387

On the evening of 19th November Canon Pennyfather had finished an early dinner at the Athenaeum, he had nodded to one or two friends, had had a pleasant acrimonious discussion on some crucial point of the dating of the Dead Sea scrolls and now, glancing at his watch, saw that it was time to leave to catch his plane to Lucerne. As he passed through the hall he was greeted by one more friend: Dr Whittaker of the S.O.A.S., who said cheerfully:

'How are you, Pennyfather? Haven't seen you for a long time. How did you get on at the Congress? Any points of interest come up?'

'I am sure there will be.'

'Just come back from it, haven't you?'

'No, no, I am on my way there. I'm catching a plane this evening.'

'Oh I see.' Whittaker looked slightly puzzled. 'Somehow or other I thought the Congress was today.'

'No, no. Tomorrow, the 19th.'

Canon Pennyfather passed out through the door while his friend, looking after him, was just saying:

'But my dear chap, *today* is the 19th, isn't it?'

Canon Pennyfather, however, had gone beyond earshot. He picked up a taxi in Pall Mall, and was driven to the air terminal in Kensington. There was quite a fair crowd this evening. Presenting himself at the desk it at last came to his turn. He managed to produce ticket and passport and other necessities for the journey. The girl behind the desk, about to stamp these credentials, paused abruptly.

'I beg your pardon, sir, this seems to be the wrong ticket.'

'The wrong ticket? No, no, that is quite right. Flight one hundred and – well, I can't really read without my glasses – one hundred and something to Lucerne.'

'It's the date, sir. This is dated Wednesday the 18th.'

'No, no, surely. At least – I mean – today is Wednesday the 18th.'

'I'm sorry, sir. Today is the 19th.'

'The 19th!' The Canon was dismayed. He fished out a small diary, turning the pages eagerly. In the end he had to be convinced. Today *was* the 19th. The plane he had meant to catch had gone yesterday.

'Then that means – that means – dear me, it means the Congress at Lucerne has taken place *today.*'

He stared in deep dismay across the counter; but there were many others travelling; the Canon and his perplexities were elbowed aside. He stood sadly, holding the useless ticket in his hand. His mind ranged over various possibilities. Perhaps his ticket could be changed? But that would be no use

– no indeed – what time was it now? Going on for 9 o'clock? The conference had actually taken place; starting at 10 o'clock this morning. Of course, that was what Whittaker had meant at the Athenaeum. He thought Canon Pennyfather had already *been* to the Congress.

'Oh dear, oh dear,' said Canon Pennyfather, to himself. 'What a muddle I have made of it all!' He wandered sadly and silently into the Cromwell Road, not at its best a very cheerful place.

He walked slowly along the street carrying his bag and revolving perplexities in his mind. When at last he had worked out to his satisfaction the various reasons for which he had made a mistake in the day, he shook his head sadly.

'Now, I suppose,' he said to himself, 'I suppose – let me see, it's after nine o'clock, yes, I suppose I had better have something to eat.'

It was curious, he thought, that he did not feel hungry.

Wandering disconsolately along the Cromwell Road he finally settled upon a small restaurant which served Indian curries. It seemed to him that though he was not quite as hungry as he ought to be, he had better keep his spirits up by having a meal, and after that he must find a hotel and – but no, there was no need to do *that*. He had a hotel! Of course. He was staying at Bertram's; and has reserved his room for four days. What a piece of luck! What a splendid piece of luck! So his room was there, waiting for him. He had only to ask for his key at the desk and – here another reminiscence assailed him. Something heavy in his pocket?

He dipped his hand in and brought out one of those large and solid keys with which hotels try and discourage their vaguer guests from taking them away in their pockets. It had not prevented the Canon from doing so!

'No. 19,' said the Canon, in happy recognition. 'That's right. It's very fortunate that I haven't got to go and find a room in a hotel. They say they're very crowded just now. Yes, Edmunds was saying so at the Athenaeum this evening. He had a terrible job finding a room.'

Somewhat pleased with himself and the care he had taken over his travelling arrangements by booking a hotel beforehand, the Canon abandoned his curry, remembered to pay for it, and strode out once more into the Cromwell Road.

It seemed a little tame to go home just like this when he ought to have been dining in Lucerne and talking about all sorts of interesting and fascinating problems. His eye was caught by a cinema. *Walls of Jericho*. It seemed an eminently suitable title. It would be interesting to see if biblical accuracy had been preserved.

He bought himself a seat and stumbled into the darkness. He enjoyed the film, though it seemed to him to have no relationship to the biblical story whatsoever. Even Joshua seemed to have been left out. The walls of Jericho seemed to be a symbolical way of referring to a certain lady's marriage vows. When they had tumbled down several times, the beautiful star met the dour and uncouth hero whom she had secretly loved all along and between them they proposed to build up the walls in a way that would stand the test of time better. It was not a film destined particularly to appeal to an elderly clergyman; but Canon Pennyfather enjoyed it very much. It was not the sort of film he often saw and he felt it was enlarging his knowledge of life. The film ended, the lights went up, the National Anthem was played and Canon Pennyfather stumbled out into the lights of London, slightly consoled for the sad events of earlier in the evening.

It was a fine night and he walked home to Bertram's Hotel after first getting into a bus which took him in the opposite direction. It was midnight when he got in and Bertram's Hotel at midnight usually preserved a decorous appearance of everyone having gone to bed. The lift was on a higher floor so the Canon walked up the stairs. He came to his room, inserted the key in the lock, threw the door open and entered!

Good gracious, was he seeing things? But who – how – he saw the upraised arm too late . . .

Stars exploded in a kind of Guy Fawkes' display within his head . . .

The Irish Mail rushed through the night. Or, more correctly, through the darkness of the early morning hours.

At intervals the diesel engine gave its weird banshee warning cry. It was travelling at well over eighty miles an hour. It was on time.

Then, with some suddenness, the pace slackened as the brakes came on. The wheels screamed as they gripped the metals. Slower . . . slower . . . The guard put his head out of the window noting the red signal ahead as the train came to a final halt. Some the passengers woke up. Most did not.

One elderly lady, alarmed by the suddenness of the deceleration, opened the door and looked out along the corridor. A little way along one of the doors to the line was open. An elderly cleric with a thatch of thick white hair was climbing up from the permanent way. She presumed he had previously climbed down to the line to investigate. The morning air was distinctly chilly. Someone at the end of the corridor said: 'Only a signal.' The elderly lady withdrew into her compartment and tried to go to sleep again.

Farther up the line, a man waving a lantern was running towards the train from a signal box. The fireman climbed down from the engine. The guard who had descended from the train came along to join him. The man with the lantern arrived, rather short of breath and spoke in a series of gasps.

'Bad crash ahead . . . Goods train derailed . . .'

The engine driver looked out of his cab, then climbed down also to join the others.

At the rear of the train, six men who had just climbed up the embankment boarded the train through a door left open for them in the last coach. Six passengers from different coaches met them. With well rehearsed speed, they proceeded to take charge of the postal van, isolating it from the rest of the train. Two men in Balaclava helmets at front and rear of the compartment stood on guard, coshes in hand.

A man in railway uniform went forward along the corridor of the stationary train, uttering explanations to such as demanded them.

'Block on the line ahead. Ten minutes' delay, maybe, not much more . . .' It sounded friendly and reassuring.

By the engine, the driver and the fireman lay neatly gagged and trussed up. The man with the lantern called out:

'Everything O.K. here.'

The guard lay by the embankment, similarly gagged and tied.

The expert cracksmen in the postal van had done their work. Two more neatly trussed bodies lay on the floor. The special mailbags sailed out to where other men on the embankment awaited them.

In their compartments, passengers grumbled to each other that the railways were not what they used to be.

Then, as they settled themselves to sleep again, there came through the darkness the roar of an exhaust.

'Goodness,' murmured a woman. 'Is that a jet plane?'

'Racing car, I should say.'

The roar died away . . .

On the Bedhampton Motorway, nine miles away, a steady stream of night lorries was grinding its way north. A big white racing car flashed past them.

Ten minutes later, it turned off the motorway.

The garage on the corner of the B road bore the sign CLOSED. But the big doors swung open and the white car was driven straight in, the doors closing again behind it. Three men worked at lightning speed. A fresh set of number-plates were attached. The driver changed his coat and cap. He had worn white sheepskin before. Now he wore black leather. He drove out again. Three minutes after his departure, an old Morris Oxford, driven by a clergyman, chugged out on to the road and proceeded to take a route through various turning and twisting country lanes.

A station wagon, driven along a country road, slowed up as it came upon an old Morris Oxford stationary by the hedge, with an elderly man standing over it.

The driver of the station wagon put out a head.

'Having trouble? Can I help?'

'Very good of you. It's my lights.'

The two drivers approached each other – listened. 'All clear.'

Various expensive American-style cases were transferred from the Morris Oxford to the station wagon.

A mile or two farther on, the station wagon turned off on what looked like a rough track but which presently turned out to be the back way to a large and opulent mansion. In what had been a stableyard, a big white Mercedes car was standing. The driver of the station wagon opened its boot with a key, transferred the cases to the boot, and drove away again in the station wagon.

In a nearby farmyard a cock crowed noisily.

Elvira Blake looked up at the sky, noted that it was a fine morning and went into a telephone box. She dialled Bridget's number in Onslow Square. Satisfied by the response, she said:

'Hallo? Bridget?'

'Oh Elvira, is that you?' Bridget's voice sounded agitated.

'Yes. Has everthing been all right?'

'Oh no. It's been *awful*. Your cousin, Mrs Melford, rang up Mummy yesterday afternoon.'

'What, about me?'

'Yes. I thought I'd done it so well when I rang her up at lunch-time. But it seems she got worried about your teeth. Thought there might be something really wrong with them. Abscesses or something. So she rang up the dentist herself and found, of course, that you'd never been there at all. So then she rang up Mummy and unfortunately Mummy was right there by the telephone. So I couldn't get there first. And naturally Mummy said *she* didn't know anything about it, and that you certainly weren't staying *here*. I didn't know *what* to do.'

'What *did* you do?'

'Pretended I knew nothing about it. I did say that I thought you'd said something about going to see some friends at Wimbledon.'

'Why Wimbledon?'

'It was the first place came into my head.'

Elvira sighed. 'Oh well, I suppose I'll have to cook up something. An old governess, perhaps, who lives at Wimbledon. All this fussing does make things so *complicated*. I hope Cousin Mildred doesn't make a real fool of herself and ring up the police or something like that.'

'Are you going down there now?'

'Not till this evening. I've got a lot to do first.'

'You got to Ireland. Was it – all right?'

'I found out what I wanted to know.'

'You sound – sort of grim.'

'I'm feeling grim.'

'Can't I help you, Elvira? Do anything?'

'Nobody can help me really . . . It's a thing I have to do myself. I hoped something wasn't true, but it *is* true. I don't know quite what to do about it.'

'Are you in danger, Elvira?'

'Don't be melodramatic, Bridget. I'll have to be careful, that's all. I'll have to be very careful.'

'Then you *are* in danger.'

Elvira said after a moment's pause, 'I expect I'm just imagining things, that's all.'

'Elvira, what are you going to do about that bracelet?'

'Oh, that's all right. I've arranged to get some money from someone, so I can go and – what's the word – redeem it. Then just take it back to Bollards.'

'D'you think they'll be all right about it? – No, Mummy, its just the laundry. They say we never sent that sheet. Yes, Mummy, yes, I'll tell the manageress. All right then.'

At the other end of the line Elvira grinned and put down the receiver. She opened her purse, sorted through her money, counted out the coins she needed and arranged them in front of her and proceeded to put through a call. When she got the number she wanted she put in the necessary coins, pressed Button A and spoke in a small rather breathless voice.

'Hallo, Cousin Mildred. Yes, it's me . . . I'm terribly sorry . . . Yes, I know . . . well I was going to . . . yes it was dear old Maddy, you know our old Mademoiselle . . . yes I wrote a postcard, then I forgot to post it. It's still in my pocket now . . . well, you see she was ill and there was no one to look after her and so I just stopped to see she was all right. Yes, I *was* going to Bridget's but this changed things . . . I don't understand about the message you got. Someone must have jumbled it up . . . Yes, I'll explain it all to you when I get back . . . yes, this afternoon. No, I shall just wait and see the nurse who's coming to look after old Maddy – well, not really a nurse. You know one of those – er – practical aid nurses or something like that. No, she would hate to go to hospital . . . But I *am* sorry, Cousin Mildred, I really am very, very sorry.' She put down, the receiver and sighed in an exasperated manner. 'If only,' she murmered to herself, 'one didn't have to tell so many lies to everybody.'

She came out of the telephone box, noting as she did so the big newspaper placards – BIG TRAIN ROBBERY, IRISH MAIL ATTACKED BY BANDITS.

II

Mr Bollard was serving a customer when the shop door opened. He looked up to see the Honourable Elvira Blake entering.

'No,' she said to an assistant who came forward to her. 'I'd rather wait until Mr Bollard is free.'

Presently Mr Bollard's customer's business was concluded and Elvira moved into the vacant place.

'Good morning, Mr Bollard,' she said.

'I'm afraid your watch isn't done quite so soon as this, Miss Elvira,' said

Mr Bollard.

'Oh, it's not the watch,' said Elvira. 'I've come to apologize. A dreadful thing happened.' She opened her bag and took out a small box. From it she extracted the sapphire and diamond bracelet. 'You will remember when I came in with my watch to be repaired that I was looking at things for a Christmas present and there was an accident outside in the street. Somebody was run over I think, or nearly run over. I suppose I must have had the bracelet in my hand and put it into the pocket of my suit without thinking, although I only found it this morning. So I rushed along *at once* to bring it back. I'm so terribly sorry, Mr Bollard, I don't know how I came to do such an idiotic thing.'

'Why, that's quite all right, Miss Elvira,' said Mr Bollard, slowly.

'I suppose you thought someone had stolen it,' said Elvira.

Her limpid blue eyes met him.

'We *had* discovered its loss,' said Mr Bollard. 'Thank you very much, Miss Elvira, for bringing it back so promptly.'

'I felt simply awful about it when I found it,' said Elvira. 'Well, thank you very much, Mr Bollard, for being so nice about it.'

'A lot of strange mistakes do occur,' said Mr Bollard. He smiled at her in an avuncular manner. 'We won't think of it any more. But don't do it again, though.' He laughed with the air of one making a genial little joke.

'Oh no,' said Elvira, 'I shall be terribly careful in future.'

She smiled at him, turned and left the shop.

'Now I wonder,' said Mr Bollard to himself, 'I really do wonder . . .'

One of his partners, who had been standing near, moved nearer to him.

'So she *did* take it?' he said.

'Yes. She took it all right,' said Mr Bollard.

'But she brought it back,' his partner pointed out.

'She brought it back,' agreed Mr Bollard. 'I didn't actually expect that.'

'You mean you didn't expect her to bring it back?'

'No, not if it was she who'd taken it.'

'Do you think her story is true?' his partner inquired curiously. 'I mean, that she slipped it into her pocket by accident?'

'I suppose it's possible,' said Bollard, thoughtfully.

'Or it *could* be kleptomania, I suppose.'

'Or it could be kleptomania,' agreed Bollard. 'It's more likely that she took it on purpose . . . But if so, why did she bring it back so soon? It's curious –'

'Just as well we didn't notify the police. I admit *I* wanted to.'

'I know, I know. You haven't got as much experience as I have. In this case, it was defintely better not.' He added softly to himself, 'The thing's

395

interesting, though. Quite interesting. I wonder how old she is? Seventeen or eighteen I suppose. She might have got herself in a jam of some kind.'

'I thought you said she was rolling in money.'

'You may be an heiress and rolling in money,' said Bollard, 'but at seventeen you can't always get your hands on it. The funny thing is, you know, they keep heiresses much shorter of cash than they keep the more impecunious. It's not always a good idea. Well, I don't suppose we shall ever know the truth of it.'

He put the bracelet back in its place in the display case and shut down the lid.

The offices of Egerton, Forbes & Wilborough were in Bloomsbury, in one of those imposing and dignified squares which have as yet not felt the wind of change. Their brass plate was suitably worn down to illegibility. The firm had been going for over a hundred years and a good proportion of the landed gentry of England were their clients. There was no Forbes in the firm any more and no Wilboroughs. Instead there were Atkinsons, father and son, and a Welsh Lloyd and a Scottish McAllister. There was, however, still an Egerton, descendant of the original Egerton. This particular Egerton was a man of fifty-two and he was adviser to several families which had in their day been advised by his grandfather, his uncle, and his father.

At this moment he was sitting behind a large mahogany desk in his handsome room on the first floor, speaking kindly but firmly to a dejected looking client. Richard Egerton was a handsome man, tall, dark with a touch of grey at the temples and very shrewd grey eyes. His advice was always good advice, but he seldom minced his words.

'Quite frankly you haven't got a leg to stand upon, Freddie,' he was saying. 'Not with those letters you've written.'

'You don't think –' Freddie murmured dejectedly.

'No, I don't,' said Egerton. 'The only hope is to settle out of court. It might even be held that you've rendered yourself liable to criminal prosecution.'

'Oh, look here, Richard, that's carrying things a bit far.'

There was a small discreet buzz on Egerton's desk. He picked up the telephone receiver with a frown.

'I thought I said I wasn't to be disturbed.'

There was a murmur at the other end. Egerton said, 'Oh. Yes – Yes, I see. Ask her to wait, will you.'

He replaced the receiver and turned once more to his unhappy looking client.

'Look here, Freddie,' he said, 'I know the law and you don't. You're in a nasty jam. I'll do my best to get you out of it, but it's going to cost you a bit. I doubt if they'd settle for less than twelve thousand.'

'Twelve thousand!' The unfortunate Freddie was aghast. 'Oh, I say! I haven't got it, Richard.'

'Well, you'll have to raise it then. There are always ways and means. If she'll settle for twelve thousand, you'll be lucky, and if you fight the case it'll cost you a lot more.'

'You lawyers!' said Freddie. 'Sharks, all of you!'

He rose to his feet. 'Well,' he said, 'do your bloody best for me, Richard old boy.'

He took his departure, shaking his head sadly. Richard Egerton put Freddie and his affairs out of his mind, and thought about his next client. He said softly to himself, 'The Honourable Elvira Blake. I wonder what she's like . . .' He lifted his receiver. 'Lord Frederick's gone. Send up Miss Blake, will you.'

As he waited he made little calculations on his desk pad. How many years since –? She must be fifteen – seventeen – perhaps even more than that. Time went so fast. 'Coniston's daughter,' he thought, 'and Bess's daughter. I wonder which of them she takes after?'

The door opened, the clerk announced Miss Elvira Blake and the girl walked into the room. Egerton rose from his chair and came towards her. In appearance, he thought, she did not resemble either of her parents. Tall, slim, very fair, Bess's colouring but none of Bess's vitality, with an old-fashioned air about her; though that was difficult to be sure of, since the fashion in dress happened at the moment to be ruffles and baby bodices.

'Well, well,' he said, as he shook hands with her. 'This is a surprise. Last time I saw you, you were eleven years old. Come and sit here.' He pulled forward a chair and she sat down.

'I suppose,' said Elvira, a little uncertainly, 'that I ought to have written first. Written and made an appointment. Something like that, but I really made up my mind very suddenly and it seemed an opportunity, since I was in London.'

'And what are you doing in London?'

'Having my teeth seen to.'

'Beastly things, teeth,' said Egerton. 'Give us trouble from the cradle to the grave. But I am grateful for the teeth, if it gives me an opportunity of seeing you. Let me see now; you've been in Italy, haven't you, finishing your education there at one of these places all girls go to nowadays?'

'Yes,' said Elvira, 'the Contessa Martinelli. But I've left there now for good. I'm living with the Melfords in Kent until I make up my mind if there's anything I'd like to do.'

'Well, I hope you'll find something satisfactory. You're not thinking of a university or anything like that?'

'No,' said Elvira, 'I don't think I'd be clever enough for that.' She paused before saying, 'I suppose *you'd* have to agree to anything if I did want to do it?'

Egerton's keen eyes focused sharply.

'I am one of your guardians, and a trustee under your father's will, yes,' he said. 'Therefore, you have a perfect right to approach me at any time.'

Elvira said, 'Thank you,' politely. Egerton asked:

398

'Is there anything worrying you?'

'No. Not really. But you see, I don't *know* anything. Nobody's ever told me things. One doesn't always like to ask.'

He looked at her attentively.

'You mean things about yourself?'

'Yes,' said Elvira. 'It's kind of you to understand. Uncle Derek –' she hesitated.

'Derek Luscombe, you mean?'

'Yes. I've always called him uncle.'

'I see.'

'He's very kind,' said Elvira, 'but he's not the sort of person who ever tells you anything. He just arranges things, and looks a little worried in case they mightn't be what I'd like. Of course he listens to a lot of people – women, I mean – who tell him things. Like Contessa Martinelli. He arranges for me to go to schools or to finishing places.'

'And they haven't been where you wanted to go?'

'No, I didn't mean that. They've been quite all right. I mean they've been more or less where everyone else goes.'

'I see.'

'But I don't know anything about *myself*, I mean what money I've got, and how much, and what I could do with it if I wanted.'

'In fact,' said Egerton, with his attractive smile, 'you want to talk business. Is that it? Well, I think you're quite right. Let's see. How old are you? Sixteen – seventeen?'

'I'm nearly twenty.'

'Oh dear. I'd no idea.'

'You see,' explained Elvira, 'I feel all the time that I'm being shielded and sheltered. It's nice in a way, but it can get very irritating.'

'It's an attitude that's gone out of date,' agreed Egerton, 'but I can quite see that it would appeal to Derek Luscombe.'

'He's a dear,' said Elvira, 'but very difficult, somehow, to talk to seriously.'

'Yes, I can see that that might be so. Well, how much *do* you know about yourself, Elvira? About your family circumstances?'

'I know that my father died when I was five and that my mother had run away from him with someone when I was about two, I don't remember her at all. I barely remember my father. He was very old and had his leg up on a chair. He used to swear. I was rather scared of him. After he died I lived first with an aunt or a cousin or something of my father's, until *she* died, and then I lived with Uncle Derek and his sister. But then she died and I went to Italy. Uncle Derek has arranged for me, now, to live with the Melfords who are his cousins and very kind and nice and have two daughters about my age.'

'You're happy there?'

'I don't know yet. I've barely got there. They're all very dull. I really wanted to know how much money I've got.'

'So it's financial information you really want?'

'Yes,' said Elvira. 'I've got *some* money. Is it a lot?'

Egerton was serious now.

'Yes,' he said. 'You've got a lot of money. Your father was a very rich man. You were his only child. When he died, the title and the estate went to a cousin. He didn't like the cousin, so he left all his personal property, which was considerable, to his daughter – to you, Elvira. You're a very rich woman, or will be, when you are twenty-one.'

'You mean I am not rich *now*?'

'Yes,' said Egerton, 'you're rich now, but the money is not yours to dispose of until you are twenty-one or marry. Until that time it is in the hands of your Trustees. Luscombe, myself and another.' He smiled at her. 'We haven't embezzled it or anything like that. It's still there. In fact, we've increased your capital considerably by investments.'

'How much will I have?'

'At the age of twenty-one or upon your marriage, you will come into a sum which at a rough estimate would amount to six or seven hundred thousand pounds.'

'That *is* a lot,' said Elvira, impressed.

'Yes, it is a lot. Probably it is because it is such a lot that nobody has ever talked to you about it much.'

He watched her as she reflected upon this. Quite an interesting girl, he thought. Looked an unbelievably milk-and-water Miss, but she was more than that. A good deal more. He said, with a faintly ironic smile:

'Does that satisfy you?'

She gave him a sudden smile.

'It ought to, oughtn't it?'

'Rather better than winning the pools,' he suggested.

She nodded, but her mind was elsewhere. Then she came out abruptly with a question.

'Who gets it if I die?'

'As things stand now, it would go to your next of kin.'

'I mean – I couldn't make a will now, could I? Not until I was twenty-one. That's what someone told me.'

'They were quite right.'

'That's really rather annoying. If I was married and died I suppose my

400

husband would get the money?'

'Yes.'

'And if I wasn't married my mother would be my next of kin and get it. I really seem to have very few relations – I don't even know my mother. What is she like?'

'She's a very remarkable woman,' said Egerton shortly. 'Everybody would agree to that.'

'Didn't she ever *want* to see me?'

'She may have done . . . I think it's very possible that she did. But having made in – certain ways – rather a mess of her own life, she may have thought that it was better for you that you should be brought up quite apart from her.'

'Do you actually *know* that she thinks that?'

'No. I don't really know anything about it.'

Elvira got up.

'Thank you,' she said. 'It's very kind of you to tell me all this.'

'I think perhaps you ought to have been told more about things before,' said Egerton.

'It's humiliating *not* to know things,' said Elvira. 'Uncle Derek, of course, thinks I'm just a *child*.'

'Well, he's not a very young man himself. He and I, you know, are well advanced in years. You must make allowances for us when we look at things from the point of view of our advanced age.'

Elvira stood looking at him for a moment or two.

'But *you* don't think I'm really a child, do you?' she said shrewdly, and added, 'I expect you know rather more about girls than Uncle Derek does. He just lived with his sister.' Then she stretched out her hand and said, very prettily, 'Thank you so much. I hope I haven't interrupted some important work you had to do,' and went out.

Egerton stood looking at the door that had closed behind her. He pursed up his lips, whistled a moment, shook his head and sat down again, picked up a pen and tapped thoughtfully on his desk. He drew some papers towards him, then thrust them back and picked up his telephone.

'Miss Cordell, get me Colonel Luscombe, will you? Try his club first. And then the Shropshire address.'

He put back the receiver. Again he drew his papers towards him and started reading them but his mind was not on what he was doing. Presently his buzzer went.

'Colonel Luscombe is on the wire now, Mr Egerton.'

'Right. Put him through. Hallo, Derek. Richard Egerton here. How are you? I've just been having a visit from someone you know. A visit from your ward.'

'From Elvira?' Derek Luscombe sounded very surprised.

'Yes.'

'But why – what on earth – what did she come to you for? Not in any trouble?'

'No, I wouldn't say so. On the contrary, she seemed rather – well, pleased with herself. She wanted to know all about her financial position.'

'You didn't tell her, I hope?' said Colonel Luscombe, in alarm.

'Why not? What's the point of secrecy?'

'Well, I can't help feeling it's a little unwise for a girl to know that she is going to come into such a large amount of money.'

'Somebody else will tell her that, if we don't. She's go to be prepared, you know. Money is a responsibility.'

'Yes, but she's so much of a child still.'

'Are you sure of that?'

'What do you mean? Of course she's a child.'

'I wouldn't describe her as such. Who's the boy friend?'

'I beg your parden.'

'I said who's the boy friend? There *is* a boy friend in the offing, isn't there?'

'No, indeed. Nothing of the sort. What on earth makes you think that?'

'Nothing that she actually said. But I've got some experience you know. I think you'll find there *is* a boy friend.'

'Well, I can assure you you're quite wrong. I mean, she's been most carefully brought up, she's been at very strict schools, she's been in a very select finishing establishment in Italy. I should know if there was anything of that kind going on. I dare say she's met one or two pleasant young fellows and all that, but I'm sure there's been nothing of the kind you suggest.'

'Well, my diagnosis is a boy friend – and probably an undesirable one.'

'But why, Richard. Why? What do *you* know about young girls?'

'Quite a lot,' said Egerton dryly. 'I've had three clients in the last year, two of whom were made wards of court and the third one managed to bully her parents into agreeing to an almost certainly disastrous marriage. Girls don't get looked after the way they used to be. Conditions are such that it's very difficult to look after them at all –'

'But I assure you Elivra has been most carefully looked after.'

'The ingenuity of the young female of the species is beyond anything you could conjecture! You keep an eye on her, Derek. Make a few inquiries as to what she's been up to.'

'Nonsense. She's just a sweet simple girl.'

'What you don't know about sweet simple girls would fill an album! Her

402

mother ran away and caused a scandal – remember? – when she was younger than Elvira is today. As for old Coniston, he was one of the worst rips in England.'

'You upset me, Richard. You upset me very much.'

'You might as well be warned. What I didn't quite like was one of her other questions. Why is she so anxious to know who'd inherit her money if she dies?'

'It's queer your saying that, because she asked me that same question.'

'Did she now? Why should her mind run on early death? She asked me about her mother, by the way.'

Colonel Luscombe's voice sounded worried as he said: 'I wish Bess would get in touch with the girl.'

'Have you been talking to her on the subject – to Bess, I mean?'

'Well, yes ... Yes I did. I ran across her by chance. We were staying in the same hotel, as a matter of fact. I urged Bess to make some arrangements to see the girl.'

'What did she say?' asked Egerton curiously.

'Refused point blank. She more or less said that she wasn't a safe person for the girl to know.'

'Looked at from one point of view I don't suppose she is,' said Egerton. 'She's mixed up with that racing fellow, isn't she?'

'I've heard rumours.'

'Yes, I've heard them too. I don't know if there's much in it really. There might be, I suppose. That could be why she feels as she does. Bess's friends are strong meat from time to time! But what a woman she is, eh Derek? What a woman.'

'Always been her own worst enemy,' said Derek Luscombe, gruffly.

'A really nice conventional remark,' said Egerton. 'Well, sorry I bothered you, Derek, but keep a look out for undesirables in the background. Don't say you haven't been warned.'

He replaced the receiver and drew the pages on his desk towards him once more. This time he was able to put his whole attention on what he was doing.

Mrs McCrae, Canon Pennyfather's housekeeper, had ordered a Dover sole for the evening of his return. The advantages attached to a good Dover sole were manifold. It need not be introduced to the grill or frying pan until the Canon was safely in the house. It could be kept until the next day if necessary. Canon Pennyfather was fond of Dover sole; and, if a telephone call or telegram arrived saying that the Canon would after all be elsewhere on this particular evening, Mrs McCrae was fond of a good Dover sole herself. All therefore was in good trim for the Canon's return. The Dover sole would be followed by pancakes. The sole sat on the kitchen table, the batter for the pancakes was ready in a bowl. All was in readiness. The brass shone, the silver sparkled, not a minuscule of dust showed anywhere. There was only one thing lacking. The Canon himself.

The Canon was scheduled to return on the train arriving at 6.30 from London.

At 7 o'clock he had not returned. No doubt the train was late. At 7.30 he still had not returned. Mrs McCrae gave a sign of vexation. She suspected that this was going to be another of these things. Eight o'clock came and no Canon. Mrs McCrae gave a long, exasperated sigh. Soon, no doubt, she would get a telephone call, though it was quite within the bounds of possibility that there would not be even a telephone call. He might have written to her. No doubt he had written, but he had probably omitted to post the letter.

'Dear, dear!' said Mrs McCrae.

At 9 o'clock she made herself three pancakes with the pancake batter. The sole she put carefully away in the Frigidaire. 'I wonder where the good man's got to now,' she said to herself. She knew by experience that he might be anywhere. The odds were that he would discover his mistake in time to telegraph her or telephone her before she retired to bed. 'I shall sit up until 11 o'clock but no longer,' said Mrs McCrae. Ten-thirty was her bed-time, an extension to eleven she considered her duty, but if at eleven there was nothing, no word from the Canon, then Mrs McCrae would duly lock up the house and betake herself to bed.

It cannot be said that she was worried. This sort of thing had happened before. There was nothing to be done but wait for news of some kind. The possibilities were numerous. Canon Pennyfather might have got on the wrong train and failed to discover his mistake until he was at Land's End or John o'Groats, or he might still be in London having made some mistake in the date, and was therefore convinced he was not returning until tomorrow. He might have met a friend or friends at this foreign conference he was going to and been induced to stay out there perhaps over the weekend. He would have meant to let her know but had entirely forgotten to do so. So, as has been already said, she was not worried. The day after tomorrow his old friend, Archdeacon Simmons, was coming to stay. That was the sort of thing the Canon *did* remember, so no doubt he himself or a telegram from him would arrive tomorrow and at latest he would be home on the day after, or there would be a letter.

The morning of the day after, however, arrived without a word from him. For the first time Mrs McCrae began to be uneasy. Between 9 a.m. and 1 p.m. she eyed the telephone in a doubtful manner. Mrs McCrae had her own fixed views about the telephone. She used it and recognized its convenience but she was not fond of the telephone. Some of her household shopping was done by telephone, though she much preferred to do it in person owing to a fixed belief that if you did not see what you were being given, a shopkeeper was sure to try and cheat you. Still, telephones were useful for domestic matters. She occasionally, though rarely, telephoned her friends or relations in the near neighbourhood. To make a call of any distance, or a London call, upset her severely. It was a shameful waste of money. Nevertheless, she began to meditate facing that problem.

Finally, when yet another day dawned without any news of him, she decided to act. She knew where the Canon was staying in London. Bertram's Hotel. A nice old-fashioned place. It might be as well, perhaps, if she rang up and made certain inquiries. They would probably know where the Canon was. It was not an ordinary hotel. She would ask to be put through to Miss Gorringe. Miss Gorringe was always efficient and thoughtful. The Canon might, of course, return by the twelve-thirty. If so he would be here any minute now.

But the minutes passed and there was no Canon. Mrs McCrae took a deep breath, nerved herself and asked for a call to London. She waited, biting her lips and holding the receiver clamped firmly to her ear.

'Bertram's Hotel, at your service,' said a voice.

'I would like, if you please, to speak to Miss Gorringe,' said Mrs McCrae.

'Just a moment. What name shall I say?'

'It's Canon Pennyfather's housekeeper. Mrs McCrae.'

'Just a moment please.'

Presently the calm and efficient voice of Miss Gorringe came through.

'Miss Gorringe here. Did you say Canon Pennyfather's housekeeper?'

'That's right. Mrs McCrae.'

'Oh yes. Of course. What can I do for you, Mrs McCrae?'

'Is Canon Pennyfather staying at the hotel still?'

'I'm glad you've rung up,' said Miss Gorringe. 'We have been rather worried as to what exactly to do.'

'Do you mean something's happened to Canon Pennyfather? Has he had an accident?'

'No, no, nothing of that kind. But we expected him back from Lucerne on Friday or Saturday.'

'Eh – that'd be right.'

'But he didn't arrive. Well, of course that wasn't really surprising. He had booked his room on – booked it, that is, until yesterday. He didn't come back yesterday or send any word and his things are still here. The major part of his baggage. We hadn't been quite sure what to do about it. Of course,' Miss Gorringe went on hastily, 'we know the Canon is, well – somewhat forgetful sometimes.'

'You may well say that!'

'It makes it a little difficult for us. We are so fully booked up. His room is actually booked for another guest.' She added: 'You have no idea where he is?'

With bitterness Mrs McCrae said:

'The man might be anywhere!' She pulled herself together. 'Well, thank you, Miss Gorringe.'

'Anything I can do –' Miss Gorringe suggested helpfully.

'I daresay I'll hear soon enough,' said Mrs McCrae. She thanked Mrs Gorringe again and rang off.

She sat by the telephone, looking upset. She did not fear for the Canon's personal safety. If he had had an accident she would by now have been notified. She felt sure of that. On the whole the Canon was not what one could call accident prone. He was what Mrs McCrae called to herself 'one of the scatty ones', and the scatty ones seemed always to be looked after by a special providence. Whilst taking no care or thought, they could still survive even a Panda crossing. No, she did not visualize Canon Pennyfather as lying groaning in a hospital. He was *somewhere*, no doubt innocently and happily prattling with some friend or other. Maybe he was abroad still. The difficulty was that Archdeacon Simmons was arriving this evening and Archdeacon Simmons would expect to find a host to receive him. She couldn't put Archdeacon Simmons off because she didn't know where he was. It was all very difficult, but it had, like most difficulties, its bright spot. Its bright spot was Archdeacon Simmons. Archdeacon Simmons would know what to do. She would place the matter in his hands.

Archdeacon Simmons was a complete contrast to her employer. He knew where he was going, and what he was doing, and was always cheerfully sure of knowing the right thing to be done and doing it. A confident cleric. Archdeacon Simmons, when he arrived, to be met by Mrs McCrae's explanations, apologies and perturbation, was a tower of strength. He, too, was not alarmed.

'Now don't you worry, Mrs McCrae,' he said in his genial fashion, as he sat down to the meal she had prepared for his arrival. 'We'll hunt the absent-minded fellow down. Ever heard that story about Chesterton? G. K. Chesterton, you know, the writer. Wired to his wife when he'd gone on a lecture tour "Am at Crewe Station. Where ought I to be?" '

He laughed. Mrs McCrae smiled dutifully. She did not think it was very funny because it was so exactly the sort of thing that Canon Pennyfather might have done.

'Ah,' said Archdeacon Simmons, with appreciation, 'one of your excellent veal cutlets! You're a marvellous cook, Mrs McCrae. I hope my old friend appreciates you.'

Veal cutlets having been succeeded by some small castle puddings with a blackberry sauce which Mrs McCrae had remembered was one of the Archdeacon's favourite sweets, the good man applied himself in earnest to the tracking down of his missing friend. He addressed himself to the telephone with vigour and a complete disregard for expense, which made Mrs McCrae purse her lips anxiously, although not really disapproving, because definitely her master had got to be tracked down.

Having first dutifully tried the Canon's sister who took little notice of her brother's goings and comings and as usual had not the faintest idea where he was or might be, the Archdeacon spread his net farther afield. He addressed himself once more to Bertram's Hotel and got details as precisely as possible. The Canon had definitely left there on the early evening of the 19th. He had with him a small B.E.A. handbag, but his other luggage had remained behind in his room, which he had duly retained. He had mentioned that he was going to a conference of some kind at Lucerne. He had not gone direct to the airport from the hotel. The commissionaire, who knew him well by sight, had put him into a taxi and had directed it as told by the Canon, to the Athenaeum Club. That was the last time that anyone at Bertram's Hotel had seen Canon Pennyfather. Oh yes, a small detail – he had omitted to leave his key behind but had taken it with him. It was not the first time that that had happened.

Archdeacon Simmons paused for a few minutes' consideration before the next call. He could ring up the air station in London. That would no doubt take some time. There might be a short cut. He rang up Dr Weissgarten, a learned Hebrew scholar who was almost certain to have been at the conference.

Dr Weissgarten was at his home. As soon as he heard who was speaking to him he launched out into a torrent of verbiage consisting mostly of

407

disparaging criticism of two papers that had been read at the conference in Lucerne.

'Most unsound, that fellow Hogarov,' he said, 'most unsound. How he gets away with it I don't know! Fellow isn't a scholar at all. Do you know what he actually said?'

The Archdeacon sighed and had to be firm with him. Otherwise there was a good chance that the rest of the evening would be spent in listening to criticism of fellow scholars at the Lucerne Conference. With some reluctance Dr Weissgarten was pinned down to more personal matters.

'Pennyfather?' he said, 'Pennyfather? He ought to have been there. Can't think why he wasn't there. Said he was going. Told me so only a week before when I saw him in the Athenaeum.'

'You mean he wasn't at the conference at all?'

'That's what I've just said. He *ought* to have been there.'

'Do you know *why* he wasn't there? Did he send an excuse?'

'How should I know? He certainly talked about being there. Yes, now I remember. He was expected. Several people remarked on his absence. Thought he might have had a chill or something. Very treacherous weather.' He was about to revert to his criticisms of his fellow scholars but Archdeacon Simmons rang off.

He had got a fact but it was a fact that for the first time awoke in him an uneasy feeling. Canon Pennyfather had not been at the Lucerne Conference. He had meant to go to that conference. It seemed very extraordinary to the Archdeacon that he had not been there. He might, of course, have taken the wrong plane, though on the whole B.E.A. were pretty careful of you and shepherded you away from such possibilities. Could Canon Pennyfather have forgotten the actual day that he was going to the conference? It was always possible, he supposed. But if so where had he gone instead?

He addressed himself now to the air terminal. It involved a great deal of patient waiting and being transferred from department to department. In the end he got a definite fact. Canon Pennyfather had booked as a passenger on the 21.40 plane to Lucerne on the 18th but he had not been on the plane.

'We're getting on,' said Archdeacon Simmons to Mrs McCrae, who was hovering in the background. 'Now, let me see. Who shall I try next?'

'All this telephoning will cost a fearful lot of money,' said Mrs McCrae.

'I'm afraid so. I'm afraid so,' said Archdeacon Simmons. 'But we've got to get on his track, you know. He's not a very young man.'

'Oh, sir, you don't think there's anything could really have happened to him?'

'Well, I hope not . . . I don't think so, because I think you'd have heard if

408

so. He – er – always had his name and address on him, didn't he?'

'Oh yes, sir, he had cards on him. He'd have letters too, and all sorts of things in his wallet.'

'Well, I don't think he's in a hospital then,' said the Archdeacon. 'Let me see. When he left the hotel he took a taxi to the Athenaeum. I'll ring them up next.'

Here he got some definite information. Canon Pennyfather, who was well known there, had dined there at seven thirty on the evening of the 19th. It was then that the Archdeacon was struck by something he had overlooked until then. The aeroplane ticket had been for the 18th but the Canon had left Bertram's Hotel by taxi to the Athenaeum, having mentioned he was going to the Lucerne Conference, on the 19th. Light began to break. 'Silly old ass,' thought Archdeacon Simmons to himself, but careful not to say it aloud in front of Mrs McCrae. 'Got his dates wrong. The conference was on the 19th. I'm sure of it. He must have thought that he was leaving on the 18th. He was only one day wrong.'

He went over the next bit carefully. The Canon would have gone to the Athenaeum, he would have dined, he would have gone on to Kensington Air Station. There, no doubt, it would have been pointed out to him that his ticket was for the day before and he would then have realized that the conference he was going to attend was now over.

'That's what happened,' said Archdeacon Simmons, 'depend upon it.' He explained it to Mrs McCrae, who agreed that it was likely enough. 'Then what would he do?'

'Go back to his hotel,' said Mrs McCrae.

'He wouldn't have come straight down here – gone straight to the station, I mean.'

'Not if his luggage was at the hotel. At any rate, he would have called there for his luggage.'

'True enough,' said Simmons. 'All right. We'll think of it like this. He left the airport with his little bag and he went back to the hotel, or started for the hotel at all events. He might have had dinner perhaps – no, he'd dined at the Athenaeum. All right, he went back to the hotel. *But* he never arrived there.' He paused a moment or two and then said doubtfully, 'Or did he? Nobody seems to have seen him there. So what happened to him on the way?'

'He could have met someone,' said Mrs McCrae, doubtfully.

'Yes. Of course that's perfectly possible. Some old friend he hadn't seen for a long time . . . He could have gone off with a friend to the friend's hotel or the friend's house, but he wouldn't have stayed there three days, would he? He couldn't have forgotten for three whole days that his luggage was at

409

the hotel. He'd have rung up about it, he'd have called for it, or in a supreme fit of absent-mindedness he might have come straight home. Three days' silence. That's what's so inexplicable.'

'If he had an accident –'

'Yes, Mrs McCrae, of course that's possible. We can try the hospitals. You say he had plenty of papers on him to identify him? Hm – I think there's only one thing for it.'

Mrs McCrae looked at him apprehensively.

'I think, you know,' said the Archdeacon gently, 'that we've got to go to the police.'

Miss Marple had found no difficulty in enjoying her stay in London. She did a lot of the things that she had not had the time to do in her hitherto brief visits to the capital. It has to be regretfully noted that she did not avail herself of the wide cultural activities that would have been possible to her. She visited no picture galleries and no museums. The idea of patronizing a dress show of any kind would not even have occurred to her. What she did visit were the glass and china departments of the large stores, and the household linen departments, and she also availed herself of some marked down lines in furnishing fabrics. Having spent what she considered a reasonable sum upon these household investments, she indulged in various excursions of her own. She went to places and shops she remembered from her young days, sometimes merely with the curiosity of seeing whether they were still there. It was not a pursuit that she had ever had time for before, and she enjoyed it very much. After a nice little nap after lunch, she would go out, and, avoiding the attentions of the commissionaire if possible, because he was so firmly imbued with the idea that a lady of her age and frailty should always go in a taxi, she walked towards a bus stop, or tube station. She had bought a small guide to buses and their routes – and an Underground Transport Map; and she would plan her excursion carefully. One afternoon she could be seen walking happily and nostalgically round Evelyn Gardens or Onslow Square murmuring softly, 'Yes, that was Mrs Van Dylan's house. Of course it looks *quite* different now. They seem to have remodelled it. Dear me, I see it's got four bells. Four flats, I suppose. Such a nice old-fashioned square this always was.'

Rather shamefacedly she paid a visit to Madame Tussaud's, a well-remembered delight of her childhood. In Westbourne Grove she looked in vain for Bradley's. Aunt Helen had always gone to Bradley's about her sealskin jacket.

Window shopping in the general sense did not interest Miss Marple, but she had a splendid time rounding up knitting patterns, new varieties of knitting wool, and such-like delights. She made a special expedition to Richmond to see the house that had been occupied by Great-Uncle Thomas, the retired admiral. The handsome terrace was still there but here again each house seemed to be turned into flats. Much more painful was the house in Lowndes Square where a distant cousin, Lady Merridew, had lived in some style. Here a vast skyscraper building of modernistic design appeared to have arisen. Miss Marple shook her head sadly and said firmly to herself, 'There must *be* progress I suppose. If Cousin Ethel knew, she'd turn in her grave, I'm sure.'

It was on one particularly mild and pleasant afternoon that Miss Marple embarked on a bus that took her over Battersea Bridge. She was going to combine the double pleasure of taking a sentimental look at Princes Terrace Mansions where an old governess of hers had once lived, and visiting Battersea Park. The first part of her quest was abortive. Miss Ledbury's former home had vanished without trace and had been replaced by a great deal of gleaming concrete. Miss Marple turned into Battersea Park. She had always been a good walker but had to admit that nowadays her walking powers were not what they were. Half a mile was quite enough to tire her. She could manage, she thought, to cross the Park and go out over Chelsea Bridge and find herself once more on a convenient bus route, but her steps grew gradually slower and slower, and she was pleased to come upon a tea enclosure situated on the edge of the lake.

Teas were still being served there in spite of the autumn chill. There were not many people today, a certain amount of mothers and prams, and a few pairs of young lovers. Miss Marple collected a tray with tea and two sponge cakes. She carried her tray carefully to a table and sat down. The tea was just what she needed. Hot, strong and very reviving. Revived, she looked round her, and, her eyes stopping suddenly at a particular table, she sat up very straight in her chair. Really, a very strange coincidence, very strange indeed! First the Army & Navy Stores and now here. Very unusual places those particular two people chose! But no! She was wrong. Miss Marple took a second and stronger pair of glasses from her bag. Yes, she had been mistaken. There was a certain similarity, of course. That long straight blonde hair; but this was not Bess Sedgwick. It was someone years younger. Of course! It was the daughter! The young girl who had come into Bertram's with Lady Selina Hazy's friend, Colonel Luscombe. But the man was the same man who had been lunching with Lady Sedgwick in the Army & Navy Stores. No doubt about it, the same handsome, hawklike look, the same leanness, the same predatory toughness and – yes, the same strong, virile attraction.

'Bad!' said Miss Marple. 'Bad all through! Cruel! Unscrupulous. I don't *like* seeing this. First the mother, now the daughter. What does it mean?'

It meant no good. Miss Marple was sure of that. Miss Marple seldom gave anyone the benefit of the doubt; she invariably thought the worst, and nine times out of ten, so she insisted, she was right in so doing. Both these meetings, she was sure, were more or less secret meetings. She observed now the way these two bent forward over the table until their heads nearly touched; and the earnestness with which they talked. The girl's face – Miss Marple took off her spectacles, rubbed the lenses carefully, then put them on again. Yes, this girl was in love. Desperately in love, as only the young can be in love. But what were her guardians about to let her run about London and have these clandestine assignments in Battersea Park? A nicely brought up, well-behaved girl like that. *Too* nicely brought up, no doubt! Her people probably believed her to be in some quite other spot. She had to tell lies.

On the way out Miss Marple passed the table where they were sitting, slowing down as much as she could without its being too obvious. Unfortunately, their voices were so low that she could not hear what they said. The man was speaking, the girl was listening, half pleased, half afraid. 'Planning to run away together, perhaps?' thought Miss Marple. 'She's still under age.'

Miss Marple passed through the small gate in the fence that led to the side-walk of the park. There were cars parked along there and presently she stopped beside one particular car. Miss Marple was not particularly knowledgeable over cars but such cars as this one did not come her way very often, so she had noted and remembered it. She had acquired a little information about cars of this style from an enthusiastic great-nephew. It was a racing car. Some foreign make – she couldn't remember the name now. Not only that, she had seen this car, or one exactly like it, seen it only yesterday in a side street close to Bertram's Hotel. She had noticed it not only because of its size and its powerful and unusual appearance but because the number had awakened some vague memory, some trace of association in her memory. FAN 2266. It had made her think of her cousin Fanny Godfrey. Poor Fanny who stuttered, who had said 'I have got t-t-t-wo s-s-s-potz . . .'

She walked along and looked at the number of this car. Yes, she was quite right. FAN 2266. It was the same car. Miss Marple, her footsteps growing more painful every moment, arrived deep in thought at the other side of Chelsea Bridge and by then was so exhausted that she hailed the first taxi she saw with decision. She was worried by the feeling that there was something she ought to do about things. But what things and what to do about them? It was all so indefinite. She fixed her eyes absently on some newsboards.

'Sensational developments in train robbery,' they ran. 'Engine driver's story,' said another one. Really! Miss Marple thought to herself, every day there seemed to be a bank hold-up or a train robbery or a wage pay snatch.

Crime seemed to have got above itself.

413

Vaguely reminiscent of a large bumble bee, Chief-Inspector Fred Davy wandered around the confines of the Criminal Investigation Department, humming to himself. It was a well-known idiosyncrasy of his, and caused no particular notice except to give rise to the remark that 'Father was on the prowl again.'

His prowling led him at last to the room where Inspector Campbell was sitting behind a desk with a bored expression. Inspector Campbell was an ambitious young man and he found much of his occupation tedious in the extreme. Nevertheless, he coped with the duties appointed to him and achieved a very fair measure of success in so doing. The powers that be approved of him, thought he should do well and doled out from time to time a few words of encouraging commendation.

'Good morning, sir,' said Inspector Campbell, respectfully, when Father entered his domain. Naturally he called Chief-Inspector Davy 'Father' behind his back as everyone else did; but he was not yet of sufficient seniority to do such a thing to his face.

'Anything I can do for you, sir?' he inquired.

'La, la, boom, boom,' hummed the Chief-Inspector, slightly off key. 'Why must they call me Mary when my name's Miss Gibbs?' After this rather unexpected resurrection of a by-gone musical comedy, he drew up a chair and sat down.

'Busy?' he asked.

'Moderately so.'

'Got some disappearance case or other on, haven't you, to do with some hotel or other. What's the name of it now? Bertram's. Is that it?'

'Yes, that's right, sir. Bertram's Hotel.'

'Contravening the licensing hours? Call girls?'

'Oh no, sir,' said Inspector Campbell, slightly shocked at hearing Bertram's Hotel being referred to in such a connection. 'Very nice, quiet, old-fashioned place.'

'Is it now?' said Father. 'Yes, is it now? Well, that's interesting, really.'

Inspector Campbell wondered why it was interesting. He did not like to ask, as tempers in the upper hierarchy were notoriously short since the mail train robbery, which had been a spectacular success for the criminals. He looked at Father's large, heavy, bovine face and wondered, as he had once or twice wondered before, how Chief-Inspector Davy had reached his present rank and why he was so highly thought of in the department. 'All right in his day, I suppose,' thought Inspector Campbell, 'but there are plenty of go-ahead chaps about who could do with some promotion, once the deadwood is cleared away.' But the deadwood had begun another song, partly hummed, with an occasional word or two here and there.

'*Tell me, gentle stranger, are there any more at home like you?*' intoned Father and then in a sudden falsetto, '*A few, kind sir, and nicer girls you never knew.* No, let's see, I've got the sexes mixed up. *Floradora*. That was a good show, too.'

'I believe I've heard of it, sir,' said Inspector Campbell.

'Your mother sang you to sleep in the cradle with it, I expect,' said Chief-Inspector Davy. 'Now then, what's been going on at Bertram's Hotel? Who has disappeared and how and why?'

'A Canon Pennyfather, sir. Elderly clergyman.'

'Dull case, eh?'

Inspector Campbell smiled.

'Yes, sir, it *is* rather dull in a way.'

'What did he look like?'

'Canon Pennyfather?'

'Yes – you've got a description, I suppose?'

'Of course.' Campbell shuffled papers and read: 'Height 5 ft 8. Large thatch of white hair – stoops ...'

'And he disappeared from Bertram's Hotel – when?'

'About a week ago – November 19th.'

'And they've just reported it. Took their time about it, didn't they?'

'Well, I think there was a general idea that he'd turn up.'

'Any idea what's behind it?' asked Father. 'Has a decent God-fearing man suddenly gone off with one of the church-wardens' wives? Or does he do a bit of secret drinking, or has he embezzled church funds? Or is he the sort of absent-minded old chap who goes in for this sort of thing?'

'Well, from all I can hear, sir, I should say the latter. He's done it before.'

'What – disappeared from a respectable West End hotel?'

'No, not exactly that, but he's not always returned home when he was expected. Occasionally he's turned up to stay with friends on a day when they haven't asked him, or not turned up on the date when they *had* asked him. That sort of thing.'

'Yes,' said Father. 'Yes. Well that sounds very nice and natural and according to plan, doesn't it? When exactly did you say he disappeared?'

'Thursday. November 19th. He was supposed to be attending a congress at –' He bent down and studied some papers on his desk. '– oh yes, Lucerne. Society of Biblical Historical Studies. That's the English translation of it. I think it's actually a German society.'

'And it was held at Lucerne? The old boy – I suppose he *is* an old boy?'

'Sixty-three, sir, I understand.'

415

'The old boy didn't turn up, is that it?'

Inspector Campbell drew his papers towards him and gave Father the ascertainable facts in so far as they had been ascertained.

'Doesn't sound as if he'd gone off with a choirboy,' observed Chief-Inspector Davy.

'I expect he'll turn up all right,' said Campbell, 'but we're looking into it, of course. Are you – er – particularly interested in the case, sir?' He could hardly restrain his curiosity on this point.

'No,' said Davy thoughtfully. 'No, I'm not interested in the *case*. I don't see anything to be interested about in it.'

There was a pause, a pause which clearly contained the words, 'Well, then?' with a question mark after it from Inspector Campbell, which he was too well trained to utter in audible tones.

'What I'm *really* interested in,' said Father, 'is the date. And Bertram's Hotel, of course.'

'It's always been very well conducted, sir. No trouble there.'

'That's very nice, I'm sure,' said Father. He added thoughtfully, 'I'd rather like to have a look at the place.'

'Of course, sir,' said Inspector Campbell. 'Any time you like. I was thinking of going round there myself.'

'I might as well come along with you,' said Father. 'Not to butt in, nothing like that. But I'd just rather like to have a look at the place, and this disappearing Archdeacon of yours, or whatever he is, makes rather a good excuse. No need to call me "sir" when you're there – you throw your weight about. I'll just be your stooge.'

Inspector Campbell became interested.

'Do you think there's something that might tie in there, sir, something that might tie in with something else?'

'There's no reason to believe so, so far,' said Father. 'But you know how it is. One gets – I don't know what to call them – whims, do you think? Bertram's Hotel, somehow, sounds almost too good to be true.'

He resumed his impersonation of a bumble bee with a rendering of 'Let's All Go Down the Strand.'

The two detective officers went off together, Campbell looking smart in a lounge suit (he had an excellent figure), and Chief-Inspector Davy carrying with him a tweedy air of being up from the country. They fitted in quite well. Only the astute eye of Miss Gorringe, as she raised it from her ledgers, singled out and appreciated them for what they were. Since she had reported the disappearance of Canon Pennyfather herself and had already had a word with a lesser personage in the police force, she had been expecting something of this kind.

416

A faint murmur to the earnest-looking girl assistant whom she kept handy in the background, enabled the latter to come forward and deal with any ordinary inquiries or services while Miss Gorringe gently shifted herself a little farther along the counter and looked up at the two men. Inspector Campbell laid down his card on the desk in front of her and she nodded. Looking past him to the large tweed-coated figure behind him, she noted that he had turned slightly sideways, and was observing the lounge and its occupants with an apparently naïve pleasure at beholding such a well bred, upper-class world in action.

'Would you like to come into the office?' said Miss Gorringe. 'We can talk better there perhaps.'

'Yes, I think that would be best.'

'Nice place you've got here,' said the large, fat, bovine-looking man, turning his head back towards her. 'Comfortable,' he added, looking approvingly at the large fire. 'Good old-fashioned comfort.'

Miss Gorringe smiled with an air of pleasure.

'Yes, indeed. We pride ourselves on making our visitors comfortable,' she said. She turned to her assistant. 'Will you carry on, Alice? There is the ledger. Lady Jocelyn will be arriving quite soon. She is sure to want to change her room as soon as she sees it but you must explain to her we are really full up. If necessary, you can show her number 340 on the third floor and offer her that instead. It's not a very pleasant room and I'm sure she will be content with her present one as soon as she sees that.'

'Yes, Miss Gorringe. I'll do just that, Miss Gorringe.'

'And remind Colonel Mortimer that his field glasses are here. He asked me to keep them for him this morning. Don't let him go off without them.'

'No, Miss Gorringe.'

These duties accomplished, Miss Gorringe looked at the two men, came out from behind the desk and walked along to a plain mahogany door with no legend on it. Miss Gorringe opened it and they went into a small, rather sad-looking office. All three sat down.

'The missing man is Canon Pennyfather, I understand,' said Inspector Campbell. He looked at his notes. 'I've got Sergeant Wadell's report. Perhaps you'll tell me in your own words just what occurred.'

'I don't think that Canon Pennyfather has really disappeared in the sense in which one would usually use that word,' said Miss Gorringe. 'I think, you know, that he's just met someone somewhere, some old friend or something like that, and has perhaps gone off with him to some scholarly meeting or reunion or something of that kind, on the Continent – he is so very vague.'

'You've known him for a long time?'

'Oh yes, he's been coming here to stay for – let me see – oh five or six years

417

at least, I should think.'

'You've been here some time yourself, ma'am,' said Chief Inspector Davy, suddenly putting in a word.

'I have been here, let me think, fourteen years,' said Miss Gorringe.

'It's a nice place,' repeated Davy again. 'And Canon Pennyfather usually stayed here when he was in London? Is that right?'

'Yes. He always came to us. He wrote well beforehand to retain his room. He was much less vague on paper than he was in real life. He asked for a room from the 17th to the 21st. During that time he expected to be away for one or two nights, and he explained that he wished to keep his room on while he was away. He quite often did that.'

'When did you begin to get worried about him?' asked Campbell.

'Well, I didn't really. Of course it was awkward. You see, his room was let on from the 23rd and when I realized – I didn't at first – that he hadn't come back from Lugano –'

'I've got Lucerne here in my notes,' said Campbell.

'Yes, yes, I think it *was* Lucerne. Some Archaeological Congress or other. Anyway, when I realized he hadn't come back here and that his baggage was still here waiting in his room, it made things rather awkward. You see, we are very booked up at this time of year and I had someone else coming into his room. The Honourable Mrs Saunders, who lives at Lyme Regis. She always has that room. And then his housekeeper rang up. She was worried.'

'The housekeeper's name is Mrs McCrae, so I understand from Archdeacon Simmons. Do you know her?'

'Not personally, no, but I have spoken to her on the telephone once or twice. She is, I think, a very reliable woman and has been with Canon Pennyfather for some years. She was worried naturally. I believe she and Archdeacon Simmons got in touch with near friends and relations but they knew nothing of Canon Pennyfather's movements. And since he was expecting the Archdeacon to stay with him it certainly seemed very odd – in fact it still does – that the Canon should not have returned home.'

'Is this Canon usually as absent-minded as that? asked Father.

Miss Gorringe ignored him. This large man, presumably the accompanying sergeant, seemed to her to be pushing himself forward a little too much.

'And now I understand,' continued Miss Gorringe, in an annoyed voice, 'and now I understand from Archdeacon Simmons that the Canon never even went to this conference in Lucerne.'

'Did he send any message to say he wouldn't go?'

'I don't think so – not from here. No telegram or anything like that. I really know nothing about Lucerne – I am really only concerned with *our*

418

side of the matter. It has got into the evening papers, I see – the fact that he is missing, I mean. They haven't mentioned he was staying *here*. I hope they won't. We don't want the Press here, our visitors wouldn't like that at all. If you can keep them off us, Inspector Campbell, we should be very grateful. I mean it's not as if he had disappeared from *here*.'

'His luggage is still here?'

'Yes. In the baggage-room. If he didn't go to Lucerne, have you considered the possibility of his being run over? Something like that?'

'Nothing like that has happened to him.'

'It really does seem very, very curious,' said Miss Gorringe, a faint flicker of interest appearing in her manner, to replace the annoyance. 'I mean, it does make one wonder where he *could* have gone and why?'

Father looked at her comprehendingly.

'Of course,' he said. 'You've only been thinking of it from the hotel angle. Very natural.'

'I understand,' said Inspector Campbell, referring once more to his notes, 'that Canon Pennyfather left here about six-thirty on the evening of Thursday the 19th. He had with him a small overnight bag and he left here in a taxi, directing the commissionaire to tell the driver to drive to the Athenaeum Club.'

Miss Gorringe nodded her head.

'Yes, he dined at the Athenaeum Club – Archdeacon Simmons told me that *that* was the place he was last seen.'

There was a firmness in Miss Gorringe's voice as she transferred the responsibility of seeing the Canon last from Bertram's Hotel to the Athenaeum Club.

'Well, it's nice to get the facts straight,' said Father in a gentle rumbling voice. 'We've got 'em straight now. He went off with his little blue B.O.A.C. bag or whatever he'd got with him – it *was* a blue B.O.A.C. bag, yes? He went off and he didn't come back, and that's that.'

'So you see, really I cannot help you,' said Miss Gorringe, showing a disposition to rise to her feet and get back to work.

'It doesn't *seem* as if you could help us,' said Father, 'but someone else might be able to,' he added.

'Someone else?'

'Why, yes,' said Father. 'One of the staff perhaps.'

'I don't think anyone knows *anything*; or they would certainly have reported it to me.'

'Well, perhaps they might. Perhaps they mightn't. What I mean is, they'd have told you if they'd distinctly *known* anything. But I was thinking more of something he might have *said*.'

'What sort of thing?' said Miss Gorringe, looking perplexed.

'Oh, just some chance word that might give one a clue. Something like "I'm going to see an old friend tonight that I haven't seen since we met in Arizona." Something like that. Or "I'm going to stay next week with a niece of mine for her daughter's confirmation." With absent-minded people, you know, clues like that are a great help. They show what was in the person's mind. It may be that after his dinner at the Athenaeum, he gets into a taxi and thinks "Now where am I going?" and having got – say – the confirmation in his mind – thinks he's going off there.'

'Well, I see what you mean,' said Miss Gorringe doubtfully. 'It seems a little unlikely.'

'Oh, one never knows one's luck,' said Father cheerfully. 'Then there are the various guests here. I suppose Canon Pennyfather knew some of them since he came here fairly often.'

'Oh yes,' said Miss Gorringe, 'Let me see now. I've seen him talking to – yes, Lady Selina Hazy. Then there was the Bishop of Norwich. They're old friends, I believe. They were at Oxford together. And Mrs Jameson and her daughters. They come from the same part of the world. Oh yes, quite a lot of people.'

'You see,' said Father, 'he might have talked to one of *them*. He might have just mentioned some little thing that would give us a clue. Is there anyone staying here now that the Canon knew fairly well?'

Miss Gorringe frowned in thought.

'Well, I think General Radley is here still. And there's an old lady who came up from the country – who used to stay here as a girl, so she told me. Let me see, I can't remember her name at the moment, but I can find it for you. Oh yes, Miss Marple, that's her name. I believe she knew him.'

'Well, we could make a start with those two. And there'd be a chambermaid, I suppose.'

'Oh yes,' said Miss Gorringe. 'But she has been interviewed already by Sergeant Wadell.'

'I know. But not perhaps from this angle. What about the waiter who attended on his table. Or the head waiter?'

'There's Henry, of course,' said Miss Gorringe.

'Who's Henry?' asked Father.

Miss Gorringe looked almost shocked. It was to her impossible that anyone should not know Henry.

'Henry has been here for more years than I can say,' she said. 'You must have noticed him serving teas as you came in.'

'Kind of personality,' said Davy. 'I remember noticing him.'

'I don't know what we should do without Henry,' said Miss Gorringe with feeling. 'He really is wonderful. He sets the tone of the place, you know.'

'Perhaps he might like to serve tea to me,' said Chief-Inspector Davy. 'Muffins, I saw he'd got there. I'd like a good muffin again.'

'Certainly if you like,' said Miss Gorringe, rather coldly. 'Shall I order two teas to be served to you in the lounge?' she added, turning to Inspector Campbell.

'That would –' the inspector began, when suddenly the door opened and Mr Humfries appeared in his Olympian manner.

He looked slightly taken aback, then looked inquiringly at Miss Gorringe. Miss Gorringe explained.

'These are two gentlemen from Scotland Yard, Mr Humfries,' she said.

'Detective-Inspector Campbell,' said Campbell.

'Oh yes. Yes, of course,' said Mr Humfries. 'The matter of Canon Pennyfather, I suppose? Most extraordinary business. I hope nothing's happened to him, poor old chap.'

'So do I,' said Miss Gorringe. 'Such a dear old man.'

'One of the old school,' said Mr Humfries approvingly.

'You seem to have quite a lot of the old school here,' observed Chief-Inspector Davy.

'I suppose we do, I suppose we do,' said Mr Humfries. 'Yes, in many ways we are quite a survival.'

'We have our regulars you know,' said Miss Gorringe. She spoke proudly. 'The same people come back year after year. We have a lot of Americans. People from Boston, and Washington. Very quiet, nice people.'

'They like our English atmosphere,' said Mr Humfries, showing his very white teeth in a smile.

Father looked at him thoughtfully. Inspector Campbell said,

'You're quite sure that no message came here from the Canon? I mean it might have been taken by someone who forgot to write it down or pass it on.'

'Telephone messages are always taken down *most* carefully,' said Miss Gorringe with ice in her voice. 'I cannot conceive it possible that a message would not have been passed on to me or to the appropriate person on duty.'

She glared at him.

Inspector Campbell looked momentarily taken aback.

'We've really answered all these questions before, you know,' said Mr Humfries, also with a touch of ice in his voice. 'We gave all the information at our disposal to your sergeant – I can't remember his name for the moment.'

Father stirred a little and said, in a kind of homely way,

'Well you see, things have begun to look rather more serious. It looks like a bit more than absent mindedness. That's why, I think, it would be a good thing if we could have a word or two with those two people you mentioned – General Radley and Miss Marple.'

'You want me to – to arrange an interview with them?' Mr Humfries looked rather unhappy. 'General Radley's very deaf.'

'I don't think it will be necessary to make it too formal,' said Chief-Inspector Davy. 'We don't want to worry people. You can leave it quite safely to us. Just point out those two you mentioned. There is just a chance, you know, that Canon Pennyfather *might* have mentioned some plan of his, or some person he was going to meet at Lucerne or who was going with him to Lucerne. Anyway, it's worth trying.'

Mr Humfries looked somewhat relieved.

'Nothing more we can do for you?' he asked. 'I'm sure you understand that we wish to help you in every way, only you do understand how we feel about any press publicity.'

'Quite,' said Inspector Campbell.

'And I'll just have a word with the chambermaid,' said Father.

'Certainly, if you like. I doubt very much whether she can tell you anything.'

'Probably not. But there might be some detail – some remark the Canon made about a letter or an appointment. One never knows.'

Mr Humfries glanced at his watch.

'She'll be on duty at six,' he said, 'Second floor. Perhaps, in the meantime, you'd care for tea?'

'Suits me,' said Father promptly.

They left the office together.

Miss Gorringe said, 'General Radley will be in the smoking-room. The first room down the passage on the left. He'll be in front of the fire there with *The Times*. I think,' she added discreetly, 'he might be asleep. You're sure you don't want me to –'

'No, no, I'll see to it,' said Father. 'And what about the other one – the old lady?'

'She's sitting over there, by the fireplace,' said Miss Gorringe.

'The one with white fluffy hair and the knitting?' said Father, taking a look. 'Might almost be on the stage, mightn't she? Everybody's universal great-aunt.'

'Great-aunts aren't much like that nowadays,' said Miss Gorringe, 'nor grandmothers nor great-grandmothers, if it comes to that. We had the Marchioness of Barlowe in yesterday. She's a great-grandmother. Honestly, I didn't know her when she came in. Just back from Paris. Her face a mask of pink and white and her hair platinum blonde and I suppose an entirely false figure, but it looked wonderful.'

'Ah,' said Father, 'I prefer the old-fashioned kind myself. Well, thank you, ma'am.' He turned to Campbell. 'I'll look after it, shall I, sir? I know you've got an important appointment.'

'That's right,' said Campbell, taking his cue. 'I don't suppose anything much will come of it, but it's worth trying.'

Mr Humfries disappeared into his inner sanctum, saying as he did so:

'Miss Gorringe – just a moment, please.'

Miss Gorringe followed him in and shut the door behind her.

Humfries was walking up and down. He demanded sharply:

'What do they want to see Rose for? Wadell asked all the necessary questions.'

'I suppose it's just routine,' said Miss Gorringe, doubtfully.

'You'd better have a word with her first.'

Miss Gorringe looked a little startled.

'But surely Inspector Campbell –'

'Oh, I'm not worried about Campbell. It's the other one. Do you know who he is?'

'I don't think he gave his name. Sergeant of some kind, I suppose. He looks rather a yokel.'

'Yokel, my foot,' said Mr Humfries, abandoning his elegance. 'That's Chief-Inspector Davy, an old fox if there ever was one. They think a lot of him at the Yard. I'd like to know what *he's* doing here, nosing about and playing the genial hick. I don't like it at all.'

'You can't think –'

'I don't know what to think. But I tell you I don't like it. Did he ask to see anyone else besides Rose?'

'I think he's going to have a word with Henry.'

Mr Humfries laughed. Miss Gorringe laughed too.

'We needn't worry about Henry.'

'No, indeed.'

'And the visitors who knew Canon Pennyfather?'

Mr Humfries laughed again.

'I wish him joy of old Radley. He'll have to shout the place down and then he won't get anything worth having. He's welcome to Radley and that funny old hen, Miss Marple. All the same, I don't much like his poking his nose in . . .'

423

'You know,' said Chief-Inspector Davy thoughtfully, 'I don't much like that chap Humfries.'

'Think there's something wrong with him?' asked Campbell.

'Well –' Father sounded apologetic, 'you know the sort of feeling one gets. Smarmy sort of chap. I wonder if he's the owner or only the manager.'

'I could ask him.' Campbell took a step back towards the desk.

'No, don't ask him,' said Father. 'Just find out – quietly.'

Campbell looked at him curiously.

'What's on your mind, sir?'

'Nothing in particular,' said Father. 'I just think I'd like to have a good deal more information about this place. I'd like to know who is behind it, what its financial status is. All that sort of thing.'

Campbell shook his head.

'I should have said if there was one place in London that was absolutely above suspicion –'

'I know, I know,' said Father. 'And what a useful thing it is to have that reputation!'

Campbell shook his head and left. Father went down the passage to the smoking-room. General Radley was just waking up. *The Times* had slipped from his knees and disintegrated slightly. Father picked it up and reassembled the sheets and handed it to him.

'Thank ye, sir. Very kind,' said General Radley gruffly.

'General Radley?'

'Yes.'

'You'll excuse me,' said Father, raising his voice, 'but I want to speak to you about Canon Pennyfather.'

'Eh – what's that?' The General approached a hand to his ear.

'Canon Pennyfather,' bellowed Father.

'My father? Dead years ago.'

'Canon *Penny*father.'

'Oh. What about him? Saw him the other day. He was staying here.'

'There was an address he was going to give me. Said he'd leave it with you.'

That was rather more difficult to get over but he succeeded in the end.

'Never gave me any address. Must have mixed me up with somebody else. Muddle-headed old fool. Always was. Scholarly sort of chap, you know. They're always absent-minded.'

Father persevered for a little longer but soon decided that conversation with General Radley was practically impossible and almost certainly unprofitable. He went and sat down in the lounge at a table adjacent to that of Miss Jane Marple.

'Tea, sir?'

Father looked up. He was impressed, as everyone was impressed, by Henry's personality. Though such a large and portly man he had appeared, as it were, like some vast travesty of Ariel who could materialize and vanish at will. Father ordered tea.

'Did I see you've got muffins here?' he asked.

Henry smiled benignly.

'Yes, sir. Very good indeed our muffins are, if I may say so. Everyone enjoys them. Shall I order you muffins, sir? Indian or China tea?'

'Indian,' said Father. 'Or Ceylon if you've got it.'

'Certainly we have Ceylon, sir.'

Henry made the faintest gesture with a finger and the pale young man who was his minion departed in search of Ceylon tea and muffins. Henry moved graciously elsewhere.

'You're *Someone*, you are,' thought Father. 'I wonder where they got hold of you and what they pay you. A packet, I bet, *and* you'd be worth it.' He watched Henry bending in a fatherly manner over an elderly lady. He wondered what Henry thought, if he thought anything, about Father. Father considered that he fitted into Bertram's Hotel reasonably well. He might have been a prosperous gentleman farmer or he might have been a peer of the realm with a resemblance to a bookmaker. Father knew two peers who were very like that. On the whole, he thought, he passed muster, but he also thought it possible that he had not deceived Henry. 'Yes, you're *Someone* you are,' Father thought again.

Tea came and the muffins. Father bit deeply. Butter ran down his chin. He wiped it off with a large handkerchief. He drank two cups of tea with plenty of sugar. Then he leaned forward and spoke to the lady sitting in the chair next to him.

'Excuse me,' he said, 'but aren't you Miss Jane Marple?'

Miss Marple transferred her gaze from her knitting to Chief Detective-Inspector Davy.

'Yes,' she said, 'I am Miss Marple.'

'I hope you don't mind my speaking to you. As a matter of fact I am a police officer.'

'Indeed? Nothing seriously wrong here, I hope?'

Father hastened to reassure her in his best paternal fashion.

'Now, don't you worry, Miss Marple,' he said. 'It's not the sort of thing you mean at all. No burglary or anything like that. Just a little difficulty about an absent-minded clergyman, that's all. I think he's a friend of yours.

Canon Pennyfather.'

'Oh, Canon Pennyfather. He was here only the other day. Yes, I've known him slightly for many years. As you say, he *is* very absent-minded.' She added, with some interest, 'What has he done now?'

'Well, as you might say in a manner of speaking, he's lost himself.'

'Oh dear,' said Miss Marple. 'Where ought he to be?'

'Back at home in his Cathedral Close,' said Father, 'but he isn't.'

'He told *me*,' said Miss Marple, 'he was going to a conference at Lucerne. Something to do with the Dead Sea scrolls, I believe. He's a great Hebrew and Aramaic scholar, you know.'

'Yes,' said Father. 'You're quite right. That's where he – well, that's where he was supposed to be going.'

'Do you mean he didn't turn up there?'

'No,' said Father, 'he didn't turn up.'

'Oh, well,' said Miss Marple, 'I expect he got his dates wrong.'

'Very likely, very likely.'

'I'm afraid,' said Miss Marple, 'that that's not the first time that that's happened. I went to have tea with him in Chadminster once. He was actually absent from home. His housekeeper told me then how very absent-minded he was.'

'He didn't say anything to you when he was staying here that might give us a clue, I suppose?' asked Father, speaking in an easy and confidential way. 'You know the sort of thing I mean, any old friend he'd met or any plans he'd made apart from this Lucerne Conference?'

'Oh no. He just mentioned the Lucerne Conference. I think he said it was on the 19th. Is that right?'

'That was the date of the Lucerne Conference, yes.'

'I didn't notice the date particularly. I mean –' like most old ladies, Miss Marple here became slightly involved – 'I *thought* he said the 19th and he *might* have said the 19th, but at the same time he might have *meant* the 19th and it might really have been the *20th*. I mean, he may have thought the 20th *was* the 19th or he may have thought the 19th was the 20th.'

'Well –' said Father, slightly dazed.

'I'm putting it badly,' said Miss Marple, 'but I mean people like Canon Pennyfather, if they say they're going somewhere on a Thursday, one is quite prepared to find that they didn't mean Thursday, it may be Wednesday or Friday they really mean. Usually they find out in time but sometimes they just don't. I thought at the time that something like that must have happened.'

Father looked slightly puzzled.

'You speak as though you knew already, Miss Marple, that Canon

426

Pennyfather hadn't gone to Lucerne.'

'I knew he wasn't in Lucerne on *Thursday*,' said Miss Marple. 'He was here all day – or most of the day. That's why I thought, of course, that though he may have said Thursday to me, it was really Friday he meant. He certainly left here on Thursday evening carrying his B.E.A. bag.'

'Quite so.'

'I took it he was going off to the airport then,' said Miss Marple. 'That's why I was so surprised to see he was back again.'

'I beg your pardon, what do you mean by "back again"?'

'Well, that he was back here again, I mean.'

'Now, let's get this quite clear,' said Father, careful to speak in an agreeable and reminiscent voice, and not as though it was really important. 'You saw the old idio – you saw the Canon, that is to say, leave as you thought for the airport with his overnight bag, fairly early in the evening. Is that right?'

'Yes. About half-past six, I would say, or quarter to seven.'

'But you say he came *back*.'

'Perhaps he missed the plane. That would account for it.'

'*When* did he come back?'

'Well, I don't really know. I didn't see him come back.'

'Oh,' said Father, taken aback. 'I thought you said you *did* see him.'

'Oh, I did see him *later*,' said Miss Marple, 'I meant I didn't see him actually come into the hotel.'

'You saw him later? When?'

Miss Marple thought.

'Let me see. It was about 3 a.m. I couldn't sleep very well. Something woke me. Some sound. There are so many queer noises in London. I looked at my little clock, it was ten minutes past three. For some reason – I'm not quite sure what – I felt uneasy. Footsteps, perhaps, outside my door. Living in the country, if one hears footsteps in the middle of the night it makes one nervous. So I just opened my door and looked out. There was Canon Pennyfather leaving his room – it's next door to mine – and going off down the stairs wearing his overcoat.'

'He came out of his room wearing his overcoat and went down the stairs at 3 a.m. in the morning?'

'Yes,' said Miss Marple and added: 'I thought it odd at the time.'

Father looked at her for some moments.

'Miss Marple,' he said, 'why haven't you told anyone this before?'

'Nobody asked me,' said Miss Marple simply.

CHAPTER 15

Father drew a deep breath.

'No,' he said. 'No, I suppose nobody would ask you. It's as simple as that.'

He relapsed into silence again.

'You think something has happened to him, don't you?' asked Miss Marple.

'It's over a week now,' said Father. 'He didn't have a stroke and fall down in the street. He's not in a hospital as a result of an accident. So where *is* he? His disappearance has been reported in the Press, but nobody's come forward with any information yet.'

'They may not have seen it. *I* didn't.'

'It looks – it really looks –' Father was following out his own line of thought – 'as though he *meant* to disappear. Leaving this place like that in the middle of the night. You're quite sure about it, aren't you?' he demanded sharply. 'You didn't dream it?'

'I am absolutely sure,' said Miss Marple with finality.

Father heaved himself to his feet.

'I'd better go and see that chambermaid,' he said.

Father found Rose Sheldon on duty and ran an approving eye over her pleasant person.

'I'm sorry to bother you,' he said. 'I know you've seen our sergeant already. But it's about that missing gentleman, Canon Pennyfather.'

'Oh yes, sir, a very nice gentleman. He often stays here.'

'Absent-minded,' said Father.

Rose Sheldon permitted a discreet smile to appear on her respectful mask of a face.

'Now let me see.' Father pretended to consult some notes. 'The last time you saw Canon Pennyfather – was –'

'On the Thursday morning, sir. Thursday the 19th. He told me that he would not be back that night and possibly not the next either. He was going, I think, to Geneva. Somewhere in Switzerland, anyway. He gave me two shirts he wanted washed and I said they would be ready for him on the morning of the following day.'

'And that's the last you saw of him, eh?'

'Yes, sir. You see, I'm not on duty in the afternoons. I come back again at 6 o'clock. By then he must have left, or at any rate he was downstairs. Not in his room. He had left two suitcases behind.'

'That's right,' said Father. The contents of the suitcases had been examined, but had given no useful lead. He went on: 'Did you call him the next morning?'

'Call him? No, sir, he was away.'

'What did you do ordinarily – take him early tea? Breakfast?'

'Early tea, sir. He breakfasted downstairs always.'

'So you didn't go into his room at all the next day?'

'Oh yes, sir.' Rose sounded shocked. 'I went into his rooms as usual. I took his shirts in for one thing. And of course I dusted the room. We dust all the rooms every day.'

'Had the bed been slept in?'

She stared at him. 'The bed, sir? Oh no.'

'Was it rumpled – creased in any way?'

She shook her head.

'What about the bathroom?'

'There was a damp hand towel, sir, that had been used, I presume that would be the evening before. He may have washed his hands last thing before going off.'

'And there was nothing to show that he had come back into the room – perhaps quite late – after midnight?'

She stared at him with an air of bewilderment. Father opened his mouth, then shut it again. Either she knew nothing about the Canon's return or she was a highly accomplished actress.

'What about his clothes – suits. Were they packed up in his suitcases?'

'No, sir, they were hanging up in the cupboards. He was keeping his room on, you see, sir.'

'Who did pack them up?'

'Miss Gorringe gave orders, sir. When the room was wanted for the new lady coming in.'

A straightforward coherent account. But if that old lady was correct in stating that she saw Canon Pennyfather leaving his room at 3 a.m. on Friday morning, then he must have come back to that room sometime. Nobody had seen him enter the hotel. Had he, for some reason, deliberately avoided being seen? He had left no traces in the room. He hadn't even lain down on the bed. Had Miss Marple dreamed the whole thing? At her age it was possible enough. An idea struck him.

'What about the airport bag?'

'I beg your pardon, sir?'

'A small bag, dark blue – a B.E.A. or B.O.A.C. bag – you must have seen it?'

'Oh that – yes, sir. But of course he'd take that with him abroad.'

'But he didn't go abroad. He never went to Switzerland after all. So he must have left it behind. Or else he came back and left it here with his other luggage.'

'Yes – yes – I think – I'm not quite sure – I believe he did.'

Quite unsolicited, the thought raced into Father's mind: *They didn't brief you on that, did they?*

Rose Sheldon had been calm and competent up till now. But that question had rattled her. She hadn't known the right answer to it. *But she ought to have known.*

The Canon had taken his bag to the airport, had been turned away from the airport. If he had come back to Bertram's, the bag would have been with him. *But Miss Marple had made no mention of it when she had described the Canon leaving his room and going down the stairs.*

Presumably it was left in the bedroom, but it had not been put in the baggage-room with the suitcases. Why not? *Because the Canon was supposed to have gone to Switzerland?*

He thanked Rose genially and went downstairs again.

Canon Pennyfather! Something of an enigma, Canon Pennyfather. Talked a lot about going to Switzerland, muddled up things so that he didn't go to Switzerland, came back to his hotel so secretly that nobody saw him, left it again in the early hours of the morning. (To go where? To do what?)

Could absent-mindedness account for all this?

If not, then what was Canon Pennyfather up to? And more important, where was he?

From the staircase, Father cast a jaundiced eye over the occupants of the lounge, and wondered whether *anyone* was what they seemed to be. He had got to that stage! Elderly people, middle-aged people (nobody very young) nice old-fashioned people, nearly all well-to-do, all highly respectable. Service people, lawyers, clergymen; American husband and wife near the door, a French family near the fireplace. Nobody flashy, nobody out of place; most of them enjoying an old-fashioned English afternoon tea. Could there really be anything seriously wrong with a place that served old-fashioned afternoon teas?

The Frenchman made a remark to his wife that fitted in appositely enough.

'*Le Five-o'-clock,*' he was saying. '*C'est bien Anglais ça, n'est ce pas?*' He looked round him with approval.

'Le-Five-o'-clock,' thought Davy as he passed through the swing doors to the street. 'That chap doesn't know that "le Five-o'clock" is as dead as the Dodo!'

Outside, various vast American wardrobe cases and suitcases were being loaded on to a taxi. It seemed that Mr and Mrs Elmer Cabot were on their way to the Hotel Vendôme, Paris.

Beside him on the kerb, Mrs Elmer Cabot was expressing her views to her husband.

'The Pendleburys were quite right about this place, Elmer. It just *is* old England. So beautifully Edwardian. I just feel Edward the Seventh could walk right in any moment and sit down there for his afternoon tea. I mean to come back here next year – I really do.'

'If we've got a million dollars or so to spare,' said her husband dryly.

'Now, Elmer, it wasn't as bad as all *that*.'

The baggage was loaded, the tall commissionaire helped them in, murmuring 'Thank you, sir' as Mr Cabot made the expected gesture. The taxi drove off. The commissionaire transferred his attention to Father.

'Taxi, sir?'

Father looked up at him.

Over six feet. Good-looking chap. A bit run to seed. Ex-Army. Lot of medals – genuine, probably. A bit shifty? Drinks too much.

Aloud he said: 'Ex-Army man?'

'Yes, sir. Irish Guards.'

'Military Medal, I see. Where did you get that?'

'Burma.'

'What's your name?'

'Michael Gorman. Sergeant.'

'Good job here?'

'It's a peaceful spot.'

'Wouldn't you prefer the Hilton?'

'I would not. I like it here. Nice people come here, and quite a lot of racing gentlemen – for Ascot and Newbury. I've had good tips from them now and again.'

'Ah, so you're an Irishman and gambler, is that it?'

'Och! Now, what would life be without a gamble?'

'Peaceful and dull,' said Chief-Inspector Davy, 'Like mine.'

'Indeed, sir?'

'Can you guess what my profession is?' asked Father.

The Irishman grinned.

'No offence to you, sir, but if I may guess I'd say you were a cop.'

'Right first time,' said Chief-Inspector Davy. 'You remember Canon Pennyfather?'

'Canon Pennyfather now, I don't seem to mind the name –'

'Elderly clergyman.'

Michael Gorman laughed.

'Ah now, clergyman are as thick as peas in a pod in there.'

431

'This one disappeared from here.'

'Oh, *that* one!' The commissionaire seemed slightly taken aback.

'Did you know him?'

'I wouldn't remember him if it hadn't been for people asking me questions about him. All I know is, I put him into a taxi and he went to the Athenaeum Club. That's the last I saw of him. Somebody told me he'd gone to Switzerland, but I hear he never got there. Lost himself, it seems.'

'You didn't see him later that day?'

'Later – No, indeed.'

'What time do you go off duty?'

'Eleven-thirty.'

Chief-Inspector Davy nodded, refused a taxi and moved slowly away along Pond Street. A car roared past him close to the kerb, and pulled up outside Bertram's Hotel, with a scream of brakes. Chief-Inspector Davy turned his head soberly and noted the number plate. FAN 2266. There was something reminiscent about that number, though he couldn't for the moment place it.

Slowly he retraced his steps. He had barely reached the entrance before the driver of the car, who had gone through the doors a moment or two before, came out again. He and the car matched each other. It was a racing model, white with long gleaming lines. The young man had the same eager greyhound look with a handsome face and a body with not a superfluous inch of flesh on it.

The commissionaire held the car door open, the young man jumped in, tossed a coin to the commissionaire and drove off with a burst of powerful engine.

'You know who *he* is?' said Michael Gorman to Father.

'A dangerous driver, anyway.'

'Ladislaus Malinowski. Won the Grand Prix two years ago – world champion he was. Had a bad smash last year. They say he's all right again now.'

'Don't tell me *he's* staying at Bertram's. Highly unsuitable.'

Michael Gorman grinned.

'He's not staying here, no. But a friend of his is –' He winked.

A porter in a striped apron came out with more American luxury travel equipment.

Father stood absent-mindedly watching them being ensconced in a Daimler Hire Car whilst he tried to remember what he knew about Ladislaus Malinowski. A reckless fellow – said to be tied up with some well-known woman – what was her name now? Still staring at a small wardrobe case, he was just turning away when he changed his mind and re-entered the hotel again.

He went to the desk and asked Miss Gorringe for the hotel register. Miss Gorringe was busy with departing Americans, and pushed the book along the counter towards him. He turned the pages. Lady Selina Hazy, Little Cottage, Merryfield, Hants. Mr and Mrs Hennessey King, Elderberries, Essex. Sir John Woodstock, 5 Beaumont Crescent, Cheltenham. Lady Sedgwick, Hurstings House, Northumberland. Mr and Mrs Elmer Cabot, Connecticut. General Radley, 14, The Green, Chichester. Mr and Mrs Woolmer Pickington, Marble Head, Connecticut. La Comtesse de Beauville, Les Sapins, St Germain en Laye. Miss Jane Marple, St Mary Mead, Much Benham. Colonel Luscombe, Little Green, Suffolk. Mrs Carpenter, The Hon. Elvira Blake. Canon Pennyfather, The Close, Chadminster. Mrs Holding, Mr Holding, Miss Audrey Holding, The Manor House, Carmanton. Mr and Mrs Ryesville, Valley Forge, Pennsylvania. The Duke of Barnstable, Doone Castle, N. Devon ... A cross section of the kind of people who stayed at Bertram's Hotel. They formed, he thought, a kind of pattern ...

As he shut the book, a name on an earlier page caught his eye. Sir William Ludgrove.

Mr Justice Ludgrove who had been recognized by a probation officer near the scene of a bank robbery. Mr Justice Ludgrove – Canon Pennyfather – both patrons of Bertram's Hotel ...

'I hope you enjoyed your tea, sir?' It was Henry, standing at his elbow. He spoke courteously, and with the slight anxiety of the perfect host.

'The best tea I've had for years,' said Chief-Inspector Davy.

He remembered he hadn't paid for it. He attempted to do so; but Henry raised a deprecating hand.

'Oh no, sir. I was given to understand that your tea was on the house. Mr Humfries' orders.'

Henry moved away. Father was left uncertain whether he ought to have offered Henry a tip or not. It was galling to think that Henry knew the answer to that social problem much better than he did!

As he moved away along the street, he stopped suddenly. He took out his note-book and put down a name and an address – no time to lose. He went into a telephone box. He was going to stick out his neck. Come hell or high water, he was going all out on a hunch.

It was the wardrobe that worried Canon Pennyfather. It worried him before he was quite awake. Then he forgot it and he fell asleep again. But when his eyes opened once more, there the wardrobe still was in the wrong place. He was lying on his left side facing the window and the wardrobe ought to have been there between him and the window on the left wall. But it wasn't. It was on the right. It worried him. It worried him so much that it made him feel tired. He was conscious of his head aching badly, and on top of that, to have the wardrobe in the wrong place. At this point once more his eyes closed.

There was rather more light in the room the next time he woke. It was not daylight yet. Only the faint light of dawn. 'Dear me,' said Canon Pennyfather to himself, suddenly solving the problem of the wardrobe. 'How stupid I am! Of course, I'm not at home.'

He moved gingerly. No, this wasn't his own bed. He was away from home. He was – where was he? Oh, of course. He'd gone to London, hadn't he? He was in Bertram's Hotel and – but no, he *wasn't* in Bertram's Hotel. In Bertram's Hotel his bed was facing the window. So that was wrong, too.

'Dear me, where can I be?' said Canon Pennyfather.

Then he remembered that he was going to Lucerne. 'Of course,' he said to himself, 'I'm in Lucerne.' He began thinking about the paper he was going to read. He didn't think about it long. Thinking about his paper seemed to make his head ache so he went to sleep again.

The next time he woke his head was a great deal clearer. Also there was a good deal more light in the room. He was not at home, he was not at Bertram's Hotel and he was fairly sure that he was not in Lucerne. This wasn't a hotel bedroom at all. He studied it fairly closely. It was an entirely strange room with very little furniture in it. A kind of cupboard (what he'd taken for the wardrobe) and a window with flowered curtains through which the light came. A chair and a table and a chest of drawers. Really, that was about all.

'Dear me,' said Canon Pennyfather, 'this is *most* odd. Where am I?'

He was thinking of getting up to investigate but when he sat up in bed his headache began again so he lay down.

'I must have been ill,' decided Canon Pennyfather. 'Yes, definitely I must have been ill.' He thought a minute or two and then said to himself, 'As a matter of fact, I think perhaps I'm still ill. Influenza, perhaps?' Influenza, people often said, came on very suddenly. Perhaps – perhaps it had come on at dinner at the Athenaeum. Yes that was right. He remembered that he had dined at the Athenaeum.

There were sounds of moving about in the house. Perhaps they'd taken him to a nursing home. But no, he didn't think this was a nursing home. With the increased light it showed itself as a rather shabby and ill-furnished small bedroom. Sounds of movement went on. From downstairs a voice called out, 'Goodbye, ducks. Sausage and mash this evening.'

Canon Pennyfather considered this. Sausage and mash. The words had a faintly agreeable quality.

'I believe,' he said to himself, 'I'm *hungry*.'

The door opened. A middle-aged woman came in, went across to the curtains, pulled back a little and turned towards the bed.

'Ah, you're awake now,' she said. 'And how are you feeling?'

'Really,' said Canon Pennyfather, rather feebly, 'I'm not quite sure.'

'Ah, I expect not. You've been quite bad, you know. Something hit you a nasty crack, so the doctor said. These motorists! Not even stopped after they'd knocked you down.'

'Have I had an accident?' said Canon Pennyfather. 'A motor accident?'

'That's right,' said the woman. 'Found you by the side of the road when we come home. Thought you was drunk at first.' She chuckled pleasantly at the reminiscence. 'Then my husband said he'd better take a look. It may have been an accident, he said. There wasn't no smell of drink or anything. No blood or anything neither. Anyway, there you was, out like a log. So my husband said, "we can't leave him here lying like that" and he carried you in here. See?'

'Ah,' said Canon Pennyfather, faintly, somewhat overcome by all these revelations. 'A good Samaritan.'

'And he saw you were a cleryman so my husband said, "it's all quite respectable." Then he said he'd better not call the police because being a clergyman and all that you mightn't like it. That's if you was drunk, in spite of there being no smell of drink. So then we hit upon getting Dr Stokes to come and have a look at you. We still call him Dr Stokes although he's been struck off. A very nice man he is, embittered a bit, of course, by being struck off. It was only his kind heart really, helping a lot of girls who were no better than they should be. Anyway, he's a good enough doctor and we got him to come and take a look at you. He says you've come to no real harm, says it's mild concussion. All we'd got to do was to keep you lying flat and quiet in a dark room. "Mind you," he said, "I'm not giving an opinion or anything like that. This is unofficial. I've no right to prescribe or to say anything. By rights I dare say you ought to report it to the police, but if you don't want to, why should you?" Give the poor old geezer a chance, that's what he said. Excuse me if I'm speaking disrespectful. He's a rough and ready speaker, the doctor is. Now what about a drop of soup or some hot bread and milk?'

'Either,' said Canon Pennyfather faintly, 'would be very welcome.'

He relapsed on to his pillows. An accident? So *that* was it. An accident, and he couldn't remember a thing about it! A few minutes later the good woman returned bearing a tray with a steaming bowl on it.

'You'll feel better after this,' she said. 'I'd like to have put a drop of whisky or a drop of brandy in it but the doctor said you wasn't to have nothing like that.'

'Certainly not,' said Canon Pennyfather, 'not with concussion. No. It would have been unadvisable.'

'I'll put another pillow behind your back, shall I, ducks? There, is that all right?'

Canon Pennyfather was a little startled by being addressed as 'ducks'. He told himself that it was kindly meant.

'Upsydaisy,' said the woman, 'there we are.'

'Yes, but where are we?' said Canon Pennyfather. 'I mean, where am I? Where is this place?'

'Milton St John,' said the woman. 'Didn't you know?'

'Milton St John?' said Canon Pennyfather. He shook his head. 'I never heard the name before.'

'Oh well, it's not much of a place. Only a village.'

'You have been very kind,' said Canon Pennyfather. 'May I ask your name?'

'Mrs Wheeling. Emma Wheeling.'

'You are most kind,' said Canon Pennyfather again. 'But this accident now. I simply cannot remember –'

'You put yourself outside that, luv, and you'll feel better and up to remembering things.'

'Milton St John,' said Canon Pennyfather to himself, in a tone of wonder. 'The name means nothing to me *at all*. How very extraordinary!'

Sir Ronald Graves drew a cat upon his blotting pad. He looked at the large portly figure of Chief-Inspector Davy sitting opposite him and drew a bulldog.

'Ladislaus Malinowski?' he said. 'Could be. Got any evidence?'

'No. He'd fit the bill, would he?'

'A daredevil. No nerves. Won the World Championship. Bad crash about a year ago. Bad reputation with women. Sources of income doubtful. Spends money here and abroad freely. Always going to and fro to the Continent. Have you got some idea that he's the man behind these organized robberies and hold-ups?'

'I don't think he's the planner. But I think he's in with them.'

'Why?'

'For one thing, he runs a Mercedes-Otto car. Racing model. A car answering to that description was seen near Bedhampton on the morning of the mail robbery. Different number plates – but we're used to that. And it's the same stunt – unlike, but not too unlike. FAN 2299 instead of 2266. There aren't so many Mercedes-Otto models of that type about. Lady Sedgwick has one and young Lord Merrivale.'

'You don't think Malinowski runs the show?'

'No – I think there are better brains than his at the top. But he's in it. I've looked back over the files. Take the hold-up at the Midland and West London. Three vans happened – just happened – to block a certain street. A Mercedes-Otto that was on the scene got clear away owing to that block.'

'It was stopped later.'

'Yes. And given a clean bill of health. Especially as the people who'd reported it weren't sure of the correct number. It was reported as FAM 3366 – Malinowski's registration number is FAN 2266 – It's all the same picture.'

'And you persist in tying it up with Bertram's Hotel. They dug up some stuff about Bertram's for you –'

Father tapped his pocket.

'Got it here. Properly registered company. Balance – paid up capital – directors – etcetera, etcetera, etcetera. Doesn't mean a thing! These financial shows are all the same – just a lot of snakes swallowing each other! Companies, and holding companies – makes your brain reel!'

'Come now, Father. That's just a way they have in the City. Has to do with taxation –'

'What I want is the real dope. If you'll give me a chit, sir, I'd like to go and see some top brass.'

The A.C. stared at him.

437

'And what exactly do you mean by top brass?'

Father mentioned a name.

The A.C. looked upset. 'I don't know about that. I hardly think we dare approach *him*.'

'It might be very helpful.'

There was a pause. The two men looked at each other. Father looked bovine, placid, and patient. The A.C. gave in.

'You're a stubborn old devil, Fred,' he said. 'Have it your own way. Go and worry the top brains behind the international financiers of Europe.'

'*He'll* know,' said Chief-Inspector Davy. 'He'll *know*. And if he doesn't, he can find out by pressing one buzzer on his desk or making one telephone call.'

'I don't know that he'll be pleased.'

'Probably not,' said Father, 'but it won't take much of his time. I've got to have authority behind me, though.'

'You're really serious about this place, Bertram's, aren't you? But what have you got to go on? It's well run, has a good respectable clientele – no trouble with the licensing laws.'

'I know – I know. No drinks, no drugs, no gambling, no accommodation for criminals. All pure as the driven snow. No beatniks, no thugs, no juvenile delinquents. Just sober Victorian-Edwardian old ladies, county families, visiting travellers from Boston and the more respectable parts of the U.S.A. All the same, a respectable Canon of the church is seen to leave it at 3 a.m. in the morning in a somewhat surreptitious manner –'

'Who saw that?'

'An old lady.'

'How did she manage to see him. Why wasn't she in bed and asleep?'

'Old ladies are like that, sir.'

'You're not talking of – what's his name – Canon Pennyfather?'

'That's right, sir. His disappearance was reported and Campbell has been looking into it.'

'Funny coincidence – his name's just come up in connection with the mail robbery at Bedhampton.'

'Indeed? In what way, sir?'

'Another old lady – or middle-aged anyway. When the train was stopped by that signal that had been tampered with, a good many people woke up and looked out into the corridor. This woman, who lives in Chadminster and knows Canon Pennyfather by sight, says she saw him entering the train by one of the doors. She thought he'd got out to see what was wrong and was getting in again. We were going to follow it up because of his disappearance being reported –'

438

'Let's see – the train was stopped at 5.30 a.m. Canon Pennyfather left Bertram's Hotel not long after 3 a.m. Yes, it could be done. If he were driven there – say – in a racing car . . .'

'So we're back again to Ladislaus Malinowski!'

The A.C. looked at his blotting pad doodles. 'What a bulldog you are, Fred,' he said.

Half an hour later Chief-Inspector Davy was entering a quiet and rather shabby office.

The large man behind the desk rose and put forward a hand.

'Chief-Inspector Davy? Do sit down,' he said. 'Do you care for a cigar?'

Chief-Inspector Davy shook his head.

'I must apologize,' he said, in his deep countryman's voice, 'for wasting your valuable time.'

Mr Robinson smiled. He was a fat man and very well dressed. He had a yellow face, his eyes were dark and sad looking and his mouth was large and generous. He frequently smiled to display over-large teeth. 'The better to eat you with,' thought Chief-Inspector Davy irrelevantly. His English was perfect and without accent but he was not an Englishman. Father wondered, as many others had wondered before him, what nationality Mr Robinson really was.

'Well, what can I do for you?'

'I'd like to know,' said Chief-Inspector Davy, 'who owns Bertram's Hotel.'

The expression on Mr Robinson's face did not change. He showed no surprise at hearing the name nor did he show recognition. He said thoughtfully:

'You want to know who owns Bertram's Hotel. That, I think, is in Pond Street, off Piccadilly.'

'Quite right, sir.'

'I have occasionally stayed there myself. A quiet place. Well run.'

'Yes,' said Father, 'particularly well run.'

'And you want to know who owns it? Surely that is easy to ascertain?'

There was a faint irony behind his smile.

'Through the usual channels, you mean? Oh yes,' Father took a small piece of paper from his pocket and read out three or four names and addresses.

'I see,' said Mr Robinson, 'someone has taken quite a lot of trouble. Interesting. And you come to me?'

'If anyone knows, you would, sir.'

'Actually I do not know. But it is true that I have ways of obtaining information. One has –' he shrugged his very large, fat shoulders – 'one

439

has contacts.'

'Yes, sir,' said Father with an impassive face.

Mr Robinson looked at him, then he picked up the telephone on his desk.

'Sonia? Get me Carlos.' He waited a minute or two then spoke again. 'Carlos?' He spoke rapidly half a dozen sentences in a foreign language. It was not a language that Father could even recognize.

Father could converse in good British French. He had a smattering of Italian and he could make a guess at plain travellers' German. He knew the sounds of Spanish, Russian and Arabic, though he could not understand them. This language was none of those. At a faint guess he hazarded it might be Turkish or Persian or Armenian, but even of that he was by no means sure. Mr Robinson replaced the receiver.

'I do not think,' he said genially, 'that we shall have long to wait. I am interested, you know. Very much interested. I have occasionally wondered myself –'

Father looked inquiring.

'About Bertram's Hotel,' said Mr Robinson. 'Financially, you know. One wonders how it can pay. However, it has never been any of my business. And one appreciates –' He shrugged his shoulders, '– a comfortable hostelry with an unusually talented personnel and staff ... Yes, I have wondered.' He looked at Father. 'You know how and why?'

'Not yet,' said Father, 'but I mean to.'

'There are several possibilities,' said Mr Robinson, thoughtfully. 'It is like music, you know. Only so many notes to the octave, yet one can combine them in – what is it – several million different ways? A musician told me once that you do not get the same tune twice. Most interesting.'

There was a slight buzz on his desk and he picked up the receiver once more.

'Yes? Yes, you have been very prompt. I am pleased. I see. Oh! Amsterdam yes ... Ah ... Thank you ... Yes. You will spell that? Good.'

He wrote rapidly on a pad at his elbow.

'I hope this will be useful to you,' he said, as he tore off the sheet and passed it across the table to Father, who read the name out aloud. 'Wilhelm Hoffman.'

'Nationality Swiss,' said Mr Robinson. 'Though not, I would say, born in Switzerland. Has a good deal of influence in Banking circles and though keeping strictly on the right side of the law, he has been behind a great many – questionable deals. He operates solely on the Continent, not in this country.'

'Oh.'

'But he has a brother,' said Mr Robinson. 'Robert Hoffman. Living in

London – a diamond merchant – most respectable business – His wife is Dutch – He also has offices in Amsterdam – Your people may know about him. As I say, he deals mainly in diamonds, but he is a very rich man, and he owns a lot of property, not usually in his own name. Yes, he is behind quite a lot of enterprises. He and his brother are the real owners of Bertram's Hotel.'

'Thank you, sir,' Chief-Inspector Davy rose to his feet. 'I needn't tell you that I'm much obliged to you. It's wonderful,' he added, allowing himself to show more enthusiasm that was normal.

'That I should know?' inquired Mr Robinson, giving one of his larger smiles. 'But this is one of my specialities. Information. I like to know. That is why you came to me, is it not?'

'Well,' said Chief-Inspector Davy, 'we do know about you. The Home Office. The Special Branch and all the rest of it.' He added almost naïvely, 'It took a bit of nerve on my part to approach you.'

Again Mr Robinson smiled.

'I find you an interesting personality, Chief-Inspector Davy,' he said. 'I wish you success in whatever you are undertaking.'

'Thank you, sir. I think I shall need it. By the way, these two brothers, would you say they were violent men?'

'Certainly not,' said Mr Robinson. 'It would be quite against their policy. The brothers Hoffman do not apply violence in business matters. They have other methods that serve them better. Year by year, I would say, they get steadily richer, or so my information from Swiss Banking circles tells me.'

'It's a useful place, Switzerland,' said Chief-Inspector Davy.

'Yes, indeed. What we should all do without it I do not know! So much rectitude. Such a fine business sense! Yes, we business men must all be very grateful to Switzerland. I myself,' he added, 'have also a high opinion of Amsterdam.' He looked hard at Davy, then smiled again, and the Chief-Inspector left.

When he got back to headquarters again, he found a note awaiting him.

Canon Pennyfather has turned up – safe if not sound. Apparently was knocked down by a car at Milton St John and has concussion.

Canon Pennyfather looked at Chief-Inspector Davy and Inspector Campbell, and Chief-Inspector Davy and Inspector Campbell looked at him. Canon Pennyfather was at home again. Sitting in the big arm-chair in his library, a pillow behind his head and his feet up on a pouffe, with a rug over his knees to emphasize his invalid status.

'I'm afraid,' he was saying politely, 'that I simply cannot remember anything at all.'

'You can't remember the accident when the car hit you?'

'I'm really afraid not.'

'Then how did you know a car did hit you?' demanded Inspector Campbell acutely.

'The woman there, Mrs – Mrs – was her name Wheeling? – told me about it.'

'And how did she know?'

Canon Pennyfather looked puzzled.

'Dear me, you are quite right. She couldn't have known, could she? I suppose she thought it was what must have happened.'

'And you really cannot remember *anything*? How did you come to be in Milton St John?'

'I've no idea,' said Canon Pennyfather. 'Even the name is quite unfamiliar to me.'

Inspector Campbell's exasperation was mounting, but Chief-Inspector Davy said in his soothing, homely voice:

'Just tell us again the last thing you do remember, sir.'

Canon Pennyfather turned to him with relief. The inspector's dry scepticism had made him uncomfortable.

'I was going to Lucerne to a congress. I took a taxi to the airport – at least to Kensington Air Station.'

'Yes. And then?'

'That's all. I can't remember any more. The next thing I remember is the wardrobe.'

'What wardrobe?' demanded Inspector Campbell.

'It was in the wrong place.'

Inspector Campbell was tempted to go into this question of a wardrobe in the wrong place. Chief-Inspector Davy cut in.

'Do you remember arriving at the air station, sir?'

'I suppose so,' said Canon Pennyfather, with the air of one who has a great deal of doubt on the matter.

'And you duly flew to Lucerne.'

442

'Did I? I don't remember anything about it if so.'

'Do you remember arriving back at Bertram's Hotel that night?'

'No.'

'You do remember Bertram's Hotel?'

'Of course. I was staying there. Very comfortable. I kept my room on.'

'Do you remember travelling in a train?'

'A train? No, I can't recall a train.'

'There was a hold-up. The train was robbed. Surely, Canon Pennyfather, you can remember *that*.'

'I ought to, oughtn't I?' said Canon Pennyfather. 'But somehow –' he spoke apologetically, '– I don't.' He looked from one to the other of the officers with a bland gentle smile.

'Then your story is that you remember nothing after going in a taxi to the air station until you woke up in the Wheelings' cottage at Milton St John.'

'There is nothing unusual in that,' the Canon assured him. 'It happens quite often in cases of concussion.'

'What did you think had happened to you when you woke up?'

'I had such a headache I really couldn't think. Then of course I began to wonder where I was and Mrs Wheeling explained and brought me some excellent soup. She called me "love" and "dearie" and "ducks",' said the Canon with slight distaste, 'but she was very kind. Very kind indeed.'

'She ought to have reported the accident to the police. Then you would have been taken to hospital and properly looked after,' said Campbell.

'She looked after me very well,' the Canon protested, with spirit, 'and I understand that with concussion there is very little you *can* do except keep the patient quiet.'

'If you should remember anything more, Canon Pennyfather –'

The Canon interrupted him.

'Four whole days I seem to have lost out of my life,' he said. 'Very curious. Really very curious indeed. I wonder so much where I was and what I was doing. The doctor tells me it may all come back to me. On the other hand it may not. Possibly I shall never know what happened to me during those days.' His eyelids flickered. 'You'll excuse me. I think I am rather tired.'

'That's quite enough now,' said Mrs McCrae, who had been hovering by the door, ready to intervene if she thought it necessary. She advanced upon them. 'Doctor says he wasn't to be worried,' she said firmly.

The policemen rose and moved towards the door. Mrs McCrae shepherded them out into the hall rather in the manner of a conscientious sheep-dog. The Canon murmured something and Chief-Inspector Davy, who was the last to pass through the door, wheeled round at once.

443

'What was that?' he asked, but the Canon's eyes were now closed.

'What did you think he said?' said Campbell as they left the house after refusing Mrs McCrae's lukewarm offer of refreshment.

Father said thoughtfully:

'I thought he said "the walls of Jericho".'

'What could he mean by that?'

'It sounds biblical,' said Father.

'Do you think we'll ever know,' asked Campbell, 'how that old boy got from the Cromwell Road to Milton St John?'

'It doesn't seem as if we shall get much help from him,' agreed Davy.

'That woman who says she saw him on the train after the hold-up. Can she possibly be right? Can he be mixed up in some way with these robberies? It seems impossible. He's such a thoroughly respectable old boy. Can't very well suspect a Canon of Chadminster Cathedral of being mixed up with a train robbery, can one?'

'No,' said Father thoughtfully, 'no. No more than one can imagine Mr Justice Ludgrove being mixed up with a bank hold-up.'

Inspector Campbell looked at his superior officer curiously.

The expedition to Chadminster concluded with a short and unprofitable interview with Dr Stokes.

Dr Stokes was aggressive, uncooperative and rude.

'I've known the Wheelings quite a while. They're by way of being neighbours of mine. They'd picked some old chap off the road. Didn't know whether he was dead drunk, or ill. Asked me in to have a look. I told them he wasn't drunk – that it was concussion –'

'And you treated him after that.'

'Not at all. I didn't treat him, or prescribe for him or attend him. I'm not a doctor – I was once, but I'm not now – I told them what they ought to do was ring up the police. Whether they did or not I don't know. Not my business. They're a bit dumb, both of them – but kindly folk.'

'You didn't think of ringing up the police yourself?'

'No, I did not. I'm not a doctor. Nothing to do with me. As a human being I told them not to pour whisky down his throat and keep him quiet and flat until the police came.'

He glared at them and, reluctantly, they had to leave it at that.

Mr Hoffman was a big solid-looking man. He gave the appearance of being carved out of wood – preferably teak.

His face was so expressionless as to give rise to surmise – could such a man be capable of thinking – of feeling emotion? It seemed impossible.

His manner was highly correct.

He rose, bowed, and held out a wedge-like hand.

'Chief-Inspector Davy? It is some years since I had the pleasure – you may not even remember –'

'Oh yes I do, Mr Hoffman. The Aaronberg Diamond Case. You were a witness for the Crown – a most excellent witness, let me say. The defence was quite unable to shake you.'

'I am not easily shaken,' said Mr Hoffman gravely.

He did not look a man who would easily be shaken.

'What can I do for you?' he went on. 'No trouble, I hope – I always want to agree well with the police. I have the greatest admiration for your superb police force.'

'Oh! There is no trouble. It is just that we wanted you to confirm a little information.'

'I shall be delighted to help you in any way I can. As I say, I have the highest opinion of your London Police Force. You have such a splendid class of men. So full of integrity, so fair, so just.'

'You'll make me embarrassed,' said Father.

'I am at your service. What is it that you want to know?'

'I was just going to ask you to give me a little dope about Bertram's Hotel.'

Mr Hoffman's face did not change. It was possible that his entire attitude became for a moment or two even more static than it had been before – that was all.

'Bertram's Hotel?' he said. His voice was inquiring, slightly puzzled. It might have been that he had never heard of Bertram's Hotel or that he could not quite remember whether he knew Bertram's Hotel or not.

'You have a connection with it, have you not, Mr Hoffman?'

Mr Hoffman moved his shoulders.

'There are so many things,' he said. 'One cannot remember them all. So much business – so much – it keeps me very busy.'

'You have your fingers in a lot of pies, I know that.'

'Yes,' Mr Hoffman smiled a wooden smile. 'I pull out many plums, that is what you think? And so you believe I have a connection with this – Bertram's Hotel?'

'I shouldn't have said a connection. As a matter of fact, you own it, don't you?' said Father genially.

This time, Mr Hoffman definitely did stiffen.

'Now who told you *that*, I wonder?' he said softly.

'Well, it's true, isn't it?' said Chief-Inspector Davy, cheerfully. 'Very nice place to own, I should say. In fact, you must be quite proud of it.'

'Oh yes,' said Hoffman. 'For the moment – I could not quite remember – you see –' he smiled deprecatingly, '– I own quite a lot of property in London. It is a good investment – property. If something comes on the market in what I think is a good position, and there is a chance of snapping it up cheap, I invest.'

'And was Bertram's Hotel going cheap?'

'As a running concern, it had gone down the hill,' said Mr Hoffman, shaking his head.

'Well, it's on its feet now,' said Father. 'I was in there just the other day. I was very much struck with the atmosphere there. Nice old-fashioned clientele, comfortable, old-fashioned premises, nothing rackety about it, a lot of luxury without looking luxurious.'

'I know very little about it personally,' explained Mr Hoffman. 'It is just one of my investments – but I believe it is doing well.'

'Yes, you seem to have a first-class fellow running it. What is his name? Humfries? Yes, Humfries.'

'An excellent man,' said Mr Hoffman. 'I leave everything to him. I look at the balance sheet once a year to see that all is well.'

'The place was thick with titles,' said Father. 'Rich travelling Americans too.' He shook his head thoughtfully. 'Wonderful combination.'

'You say you were in there the other day?' Mr Hoffman inquired. 'Not – not officially, I hope?'

'Nothing serious. Just trying to clear up a little mystery.'

'A mystery? In Bertram's Hotel?'

'So it seems. The case of the Disappearing Clergyman, you might label it.'

'That is a joke,' Mr Hoffman said. 'That is your Sherlock Holmes language.'

'This cleryman walked out of the place one evening and was never seen again.'

'Peculiar,' said Mr Hoffman, 'but such things happen. I remember many, many years ago now, a great sensation. Colonel – now let me think of his name – Colonel Fergusson I think, one of the equerries of Queen Mary. He walked out of his club one night and he, too, was never seen again.'

'Of course,' said Father, with a sigh, 'a lot of these disappearances are voluntary.'

'You know more about that than I do, my dear Chief-Inspector,' said Mr Hoffman. He added, 'I hope they gave you every assistance at Bertram's Hotel?'

'They couldn't have been nicer,' Father assured him. 'That Miss Gorringe, she has been with you some time, I believe?'

'Possibly. I really know so very little about it. I take no *personal* interest, you understand. In fact –' he smiled disarmingly, 'I was surprised that you even knew it belonged to me.'

It was not quite a question; but once more there was a slight uneasiness in his eyes. Father noted it without seeming to.

'The ramifications that go on in the City are like a gigantic jigsaw,' he said. 'It would make my head ache if I had to deal with that side of things. I gather that a company – Mayfair Holding Trust or some name like that – is the registered owner. They're owned by another company and so on and so on. The real truth of the matter is that it belongs to *you*. Simple as that. I'm right, aren't I?'

'I and my fellow directors are what I dare say you'd call behind it, yes,' admitted Mr Hoffman rather reluctantly.

'Your fellow directors. And who might they be? Yourself and, I believe, a brother of yours?'

'My brother Wilhelm is associated with me in this venture. You must understand that Bertram's is only a part of a chain of various hotels, offices, clubs and other London properties.'

'Any other directors?'

'Lord Pomfret, Abel Isaacstein.' Hoffman's voice was suddenly edged. 'Do you really need to know all these things? Just because you are looking into the Case of the Disappearing Clergyman?'

Father shook his head and looked apologetic.

'I suppose it's really curiosity. Looking for my disappearing clergyman was what took me to Bertram's, but then I got – well, interested if you understand what I mean. One thing leads to another sometimes, doesn't it?'

'I suppose that could be so, yes. And now?' he smiled, 'Your curiosity is satisfied?'

'Nothing like coming to the horse's mouth when you want information, is there?' said Father, genially. He rose to his feet. 'There's only one thing I'd really like to know – and I don't suppose you'll tell me that.'

'Yes, Chief-Inspector?' Hoffman's voice was wary.

'Where do Bertram's get hold of their staff? Wonderful! That fellow what's-his-name – Henry. The one that looks like an Archduke or an Archbishop, I'm not sure which. Anyway, he serves you tea and muffins –

most wonderful muffins! An unforgettable experience.'

'You like muffins with much butter, yes?' Mr Hoffman's eyes rested for a moment on the rotundity of Father's figure with disapprobation.

'I expect you can see I do,' said Father. 'Well, I mustn't be keeping you. I expect you're pretty busy talking over take-over bids, or something like that.'

'Ah. It amuses you to pretend to be ignorant of all these things. No, I am not busy. I do not let business absorb me too much. My tastes are simple. I live simply, with leisure, with growing of roses, and my family to whom I am much devoted.'

'Sounds ideal,' said Father. 'Wish I could live like that.'

Mr Hoffman smiled and rose ponderously to shake hands with him.

'I hope you will find your disappearing clergyman very soon.'

'Oh! That's all right. I'm sorry I didn't make myself clear. He's found – disappointing case, really. Had a car accident and got concussion – simple as that.'

Father went to the door, then turned and asked:

'By the way, is Lady Sedgwick a director of your company?'

'Lady Sedgwick?' Hoffman took a moment or two. 'No. Why should she be?'

'Oh well, one hears things – Just a shareholder?'

'I – yes.'

'Well, goodbye, Mr Hoffman. Thanks very much.'

Father went back to the Yard and straight to the A.C.

'The two Hoffman brothers are the ones behind Bertram's Hotel – financially.'

'What? Those scoundrels?' demanded Sir Ronald.

'Yes.'

'They've kept it very dark.'

'Yes – and Robert Hoffman didn't half like our finding it out. It was a shock to him.'

'What did he say?'

'Oh, we kept it all very formal and polite. He tried, not too obviously, to learn how I had found out about it.'

'And you didn't oblige him with that information, I suppose.'

'I certainly did not.'

'What excuse did you give for going to see him?'

'I didn't give any,' said Father.

'Didn't he think that a bit odd?'

'I expect he did. On the whole I thought that was a good way to play it, sir.'

448

'If the Hoffmans are behind all this, it accounts for a lot. They're never concerned in anything crooked themselves – oh no! *They* don't organize crime – they finance it though!

'Wilhelm deals with the banking side from Switzerland. He was behind those foreign currency rackets just after the war – we knew it – but we couldn't prove it. Those two brothers control a great deal of money and they use it for backing all kinds of enterprises – some legitimate – some not. But they're careful – they know every trick of the trade. Robert's diamond broking is straightforward enough – but it makes a suggestive picture – diamonds – banking interests, and property – clubs, cultural foundations, office buildings, restaurants, hotels – all apparently owned by somebody else.'

'Do you think Hoffman is the planner of these organized robberies?'

'No, I think those two deal only with finance. No, you'll have to look elsewhere for your planner. Somewhere there's a first-class brain at work.'

The fog had come down over London suddenly that evening. Chief-Inspector Davy pulled up his coat collar and turned into Pond Street. Walking slowly, like a man who was thinking of something else, he did not look particularly purposeful but anyone who knew him well would realise that his mind was wholly alert. He was prowling as a cat prowls before the moment comes for it to pounce on its prey.

Pond Street was quiet tonight. There were few cars about. The fog had been patchy to begin with, had almost cleared, then had deepened again. The noise of the traffic from Park Lane was muted to the level of a suburban side road. Most of the buses had given up. Only from time to time individual cars went on their way with determined optimism. Chief-Inspector Davy turned up a cul-de-sac, went to the end of it and came back again. He turned again, aimlessly as it seemed, first one way, then the other, but he was not aimless. Actually his cat prowl was taking him in a circle round one particular building. Bertram's Hotel. He was appraising carefully just what lay to the east of it, to the west of it, to the north of it and to the south of it. He examined the cars that were parked by the pavement, he examined the cars that were in the cul-de-sac. He examined a mews with special care. One car in particular interested him and he stopped. He pursed his lips and said softly, 'So you're here again, you beauty.' He checked the number and nodded to himself. 'FAN 2266 tonight, are you?' He bent down and ran his fingers over the number plate delicately, then nodded approval. 'Good job they made of it,' he said under his breath.

He went on, came out at the other end of the mews, turned right and right again and came out in Pond Street once more, fifty yards from the entrance of Bertram's Hotel. Once again he paused, admiring the handsome lines of yet another racing car.

'You're a beauty too,' said Chief-Inspector Davy. 'Your number plate's the same as the last time I saw you. I rather fancy your number plate always *is* the same. And that should mean –' he broke off '– or should it?' he muttered. He looked up towards what could have been the sky. 'Fog's getting thicker,' he said to himself.

Outside the door to Bertram's, the Irish commissionaire was standing swinging his arms backwards and forwards with some violence to keep himself warm. Chief-Inspector Davy said good evening to him.

'Good evening, sir. Nasty night.'

'Yes, I shouldn't think anyone would want to go out tonight who hadn't got to.'

The swing doors were pushed open and a middle-aged lady came out and paused uncertainly on the step.

'Want a taxi, ma'am?'

'Oh dear. I meant to walk.'

'I wouldn't if I were you, ma'am. It's very nasty, this fog. Even in a taxi it won't be too easy.'

'Do you think you could find me a taxi?' asked the lady doubtfully.

'I'll do my best. You go inside now and keep warm, and I'll come in and tell you if I've got one.' His voice changed, modulated to a persuasive tone. 'Unless you *have* to, ma'am, I wouldn't go out tonight at all.'

'Oh dear. Perhaps you're right. But I'm expected at some friends in Chelsea. I don't know. It might be very difficult getting back here. What do you think?'

Michael Gorman took charge.

'If I were you, ma'am,' he said firmly. 'I'd go in and telephone to your friends. It's not nice for a lady like you to be out on a foggy night like this.'

'Well – really – yes, well, perhaps you're right.'

She went back in again.

'I have to look after them,' said Micky Gorman turning in an explanatory manner to Father. 'That kind would get her bag snatched, she would. Going out this time of night in a fog and wandering about Chelsea or West Kensington or wherever she's trying to go.'

'I suppose you've had a good deal of experience of dealing with elderly ladies?' said Davy.

'Ah yes, indeed. This place is a home from home to them, bless their ageing hearts. How about you, sir. Were you wanting a taxi?'

'Don't suppose you could get me one if I did,' said Father. 'There don't seem to be many about in this. And I don't blame them.'

'Ah, no, I might lay my hand on one for you. There's a place round the corner where there's usually a taxi driver got his cab parked, having a warm up and a drop of something to keep the cold out.'

'A taxi's no good to me,' said Father with a sigh.

He jerked his thumb towards Bertram's Hotel.

'I've got to go inside. I've got a job to do.'

'Indeed now? Would it be still the missing Canon?'

'Not exactly. He's been found.'

'Found?' The man stared at him. 'Found where?'

'Wandering about with concussion after an accident.'

'Ah, that's just what one might expect of him. Crossed the road without looking, I expect.'

'That seems to be the idea,' said Father.

He nodded, and pushed through the doors into the hotel. There were not

451

very many people in the lounge this evening. He saw Miss Marple sitting in a chair near the fire and Miss Marple saw him. She made, however, no sign of recognition. He went towards the desk. Miss Gorringe, as usual, was behind her books. She was, he thought, faintly discomposed to see him. It was a very slight reaction, but he noted the fact.

'You remember me, Miss Gorringe,' he said. 'I came here the other day.'

'Yes, of course I remember you, Chief-Inspector. Is there anything more you want to know? Do you want to see Mr Humfries?'

'No thank you. I don't think that'll be necessary. I'd just like one more look at your register if I may.'

'Of course.' She pushed it along to him.

He opened it and looked slowly down the pages. To Miss Gorringe he gave the appearance of a man looking for one particular entry. In actuality this was not the case. Father had an accomplishment which he had learnt early in life and had developed into a highly skilled art. He could remember names and addresses with a perfect and photographic memory. That memory would remain with him for twenty-four or even forty-eight hours. He shook his head as he shut the book and returned it to her.

'Canon Pennyfather hasn't been in, I suppose?' he said in a light voice.

'Canon Pennyfather?'

'You know he's turned up again?'

'No indeed. Nobody has told *me*. Where?'

'Some place in the country. Car accident it seems. Wasn't reported to us. Some good Samaritan just picked him up and looked after him.'

'Oh! I am pleased. Yes, I really am very pleased. I was worried about him.'

'So were his friends,' said Father. 'Actually I was looking to see if one of them might be staying here now. Archdeacon – Archdeacon – I can't remember his name now, but I'd know it if I saw it.'

'Tomlinson?' said Miss Gorringe helpfully. 'He is due next week. From Salisbury.'

'No, not Tomlinson. Well, it doesn't matter.' He turned away.

It was quiet in the lounge tonight.

An ascetic-looking middle-aged man was reading through a badly typed thesis, occasionally writing a comment in the margin in such small crabbed handwriting as to be almost illegible. Every time he did this, he smiled in vinegary satisfaction.

There were one or two married couples of long standing who had little need to talk to each other. Occasionally two or three people were gathered together in the name of the weather conditions, discussing anxiously how they or their families were going to get where they wanted to be.

'– I rang up and begged Susan not to come by car . . . it means the M1 and always so dangerous in fog –'

'They say it's clearer in the Midlands . . .'

Chief-Inspector Davy noted them as he passed. Without haste, and with no seeming purpose, he arrived at his objective.

Miss Marple was sitting near the fire and observing his approach.

'So you're still here, Miss Marple. I'm glad.'

'I go tomorrow,' said Miss Marple.

That fact had, somehow, been implicit in her attitude. She had sat, not relaxed, but upright, as one sits in an airport lounge, or a railway waiting-room. Her luggage, he was sure, would be packed, only toilet things and night wear to be added.

'It is the end of my fortnight's holiday,' she explained.

'You've enjoyed it, I hope?'

Miss Marple did not answer at once.

'In a way – yes . . .' She stopped.

'And in another way, no?'

'It's difficult to explain what I mean –'

'Aren't you, perhaps, a little too near the fire? Rather hot, here. Wouldn't you like to move – into that corner perhaps?'

Miss Marple looked at the corner indicated, then she looked at Chief-Inspector Davy.

'I think you are quite right,' she said.

He gave her a hand up, carried her handbag and her book for her and established her in the quiet corner he had indicated.

'All right?'

'Quite all right.'

'You know why I suggested it?'

'You thought – very kindly – that it was too hot for me by the fire. Besides,' she added, 'our conversation cannot be overheard here.'

'Have you got something you want to tell me, Miss Marple?'

'Now why should you think that?'

'You looked as though you had,' said Davy.

'I'm sorry I showed it so plainly,' said Miss Marple. 'I didn't mean to.'

'Well, what about it?'

'I don't know if I ought to do so. I would like you to believe, Inspector, that I am not really fond of interfering. I am against interference. Though often well meant, it can cause a great deal of harm.'

'It's like that, is it? I see. Yes, it's quite a problem for you.'

'Sometimes one sees people doing things that seem to one unwise – even dangerous. But has one any right to interfere? Usually not, I think.'

453

'Is this Canon Pennyfather you're talking about?'

'Canon Pennyfather?' Miss Marple sounded very surprised. 'Oh no. Oh dear me no, nothing whatever to do with him. It concerns – a girl.'

'A girl, indeed? And you thought I could help?'

'I don't know,' said Miss Marple. 'I simply don't know. But I'm worried, very worried.'

Father did not press her. He sat there looking large and comfortable and rather stupid. He let her take her time. She had been willing to do her best to help him, and he was quite prepared to do anything he could to help her. He was not, perhaps, particularly interested. On the other hand, one never knew.

'One reads in the papers,' said Miss Marple in a low clear voice, 'accounts of proceedings in court; of young people, children or girls "in need of care and protection." It's just a sort of legal phrase, I suppose, but it could mean something real.'

'This girl you mentioned, you feel she is in need of care and protection?'

'Yes. Yes I do.'

'Alone in the world?'

'Oh no,' said Miss Marple. 'Very much not so, if I may put it that way. She is to all outward appearances very heavily protected and very well cared for.'

'Sounds interesting,' said Father.

'She was staying in this hotel,' said Miss Marple, 'with a Mrs Carpenter, I think. I looked in the register to see the name. The girl's name is Elvira Blake.'

Father looked up with a quick air of interest.

'She was a lovely girl. Very young, very much, as I say, sheltered and protected. Her guardian was a Colonel Luscombe, a very nice man. Quite charming. Elderly of course, and I am afraid terribly innocent.'

'The guardian or the girl?'

'I meant the guardian,' said Miss Marple. 'I don't know about the girl. But I do think she is in danger. I came across her quite by chance in Battersea Park. She was sitting at a refreshment place there with a young man.'

'Oh, that's it, is it?' said Father. 'Undesirable, I suppose. Beatnik – spiv – thug –'

'A very handsome man,' said Miss Marple. 'Not so very young. Thirty-odd, the kind of man that I should say is very attractive to women, but his face is a bad face. Cruel, hawklike, predatory.'

'He mayn't be as bad as he looks,' said Father soothingly.

'If anything he is worse than he looks,' said Miss Marple. 'I am convinced of it. He drives a large racing car.'

Father looked up quickly.

'Racing car?'

'Yes. Once or twice I've seen it standing near this hotel.'

'You don't remember the number, do you?'

'Yes, indeed I do. FAN 2266. I had a cousin who stuttered,' Miss Marple explained. 'That's how I remember it.'

Father looked puzzled.

'Do you know who he is?' demanded Miss Marple.

'As a matter of fact I do,' said Father slowly. 'Half French, half Polish. Very well-known racing driver, he was world champion three years ago. His name is Ladislaus Malinowski. You're quite right in some of your views about him. He has a bad reputation where women are concerned. That is to say, he is not a suitable friend for a young girl. But it's not easy to do anything about that sort of thing. I suppose she is meeting him on the sly, is that it?'

'Almost certainly,' said Miss Marple.

'Did you approach her guardian?'

'I don't know him,' said Miss Marple. 'I've only just been introduced to him once by a mutual friend. I don't like the idea of going to him in a tale-bearing way. I wondered if perhaps in some way *you* could do something about it.'

'I can try,' said Father. 'But the way, I thought you might like to know that your friend, Canon Pennyfather, has turned up all right.'

'Indeed!' Miss Marple looked animated. 'Where?'

'A place called Milton St John.'

'How very odd. What was he doing there? Did he know?'

'*Apparently* –' Chief-Inspector Davy stressed the word, '– he had had an accident.'

'What kind of an accident?'

'Knocked down by a car – concussed – or else, of course, he might have been conked on the head.'

'Oh! I see.' Miss Marple considered the point. 'Doesn't he know himself?'

'He *says* –' again the Chief-Inspector stressed the word, '– that he does not know anything.'

'Very remarkable.'

'Isn't it? The last thing he remembers is driving in a taxi to Kensington Air Station.'

Miss Marple shook her head perplexedly.

'I know it does happen that way in concussion,' she murmured. 'Didn't he say anything – useful?'

'He murmured something about the Walls of Jericho.'

'Joshua?' hazarded Miss Marple, 'or Archaeology – excavations? – or I remember, long ago, a play – by Mr Sutro, I think.'

'And all this week north of the Thames, Gaumont Cinemas – *The Walls of Jericho*, featuring Olga Radbourne and Bart Levinne,' said Father.

Miss Marple looked at him suspiciously.

'He could have gone to that film in the Cromwell Road. He could have come out about eleven and come back here – though if so, someone ought to have seen him – it would be well before midnight –'

'Took the wrong bus,' Miss Marple suggested. 'Something like that –'

'Say he got back here *after* midnight,' Father said, '– he could have walked up to his room without anyone seeing him – But if so, what happened then – and why did he go out again three hours later?'

Miss Marple groped for a word.

'The only idea that occurs to me is – oh!'

She jumped as a report sounded from the street outside.

'Car backfiring,' said Father soothingly.

'I'm sorry to be so jumpy – I am nervous tonight – that feeling one has –'

'That something's going to happen? I don't think you need worry.'

'I have never liked fog.'

'I wanted to tell you,' said Chief-Inspector Davy, 'that you've given me a lot of help. The things you've noticed here – just little things – they've added up.'

'So there *was* something wrong with this place?'

'There was and is everything wrong with it.'

Miss Marple sighed.

'It seemed wonderful at first – unchanged you know – like stepping back into the past – to the part of the past that one had loved and enjoyed.'

She paused.

'But of course, it wasn't really like that. I learned (what I suppose I really knew already) that one can never go back, that one should not ever try to go back – that the essence of life is going forward. Life is really a One Way Street, isn't it?'

'Something of the sort,' agreed Father.

'I remember,' said Miss Marple, diverging from her main topic in a characteristic way, 'I remember being in Paris with my mother and my grandmother, and we went to have tea at the Elysée Hotel. And my grandmother looked round, and she said suddenly, "Clara, I do believe I am the only woman here in a *bonnet*!" And she was, too! When she got home she packed up all her bonnets, and her headed mantles too – and sent them off –'

'To the Jumble Sale?' inquired Father, sympathetically.

'Oh no. Nobody would have wanted them at a jumble sale. She sent them to a theatrical Repertory Company. They appreciated them very much. But let me see –' Miss Marple recovered her direction. '– Where was I?'

'Summing up this place.'

'Yes. It seemed all right – but it wasn't. It was mixed up – real people and people who weren't real. One couldn't always tell them apart.'

'What do you mean by not real?'

'There were retired military men, but there were also what seemed to be military men but who had never been in the army. And clergymen who weren't clergymen. And admirals and sea captains who've never been in the navy. My friend, Selina Hazy – it amused me at first how she was always so anxious to recognize people she knew (quite natural, of course) and how often she was mistaken and they weren't the people she thought they were. But it happened too often. And so – I began to wonder. Even Rose, the chambermaid – so nice – but I began to think that perhaps *she* wasn't real, either.'

'If it interests you to know, she's an ex-actress. A good one. Gets a better salary here than she ever drew on the stage.'

'But – why?'

'Mainly, as part of the décor. Perhaps there's more than that to it.'

'I'm glad to be leaving here,' said Miss Marple. She gave a little shiver. 'Before anything happens.'

Chief-Inspector Davy looked at her curiously.

'What do you expect to happen?' he asked.

'Evil of some kind,' said Miss Marple.

'Evil is rather a big word –'

'You think it is too melodramatic? But I have some experience – seem to have been – so often – in contact with murder.'

'Murder?' Chief-Inspector Davy shook his head. 'I'm not suspecting murder. Just a nice cosy round-up of some remarkably clever criminals –'

'That's not the same thing. Murder – the wish to do murder – is something quite different. It – how shall I say? – it defies God.'

He looked at her and shook his head gently and reassuringly.

'There won't be any murders,' he said.

A sharp report, louder than the former one, came from outside. It was followed by a scream and another report.

Chief-Inspector Davy was on his feet, moving with a speed surprising in such a bulky man. In a few seconds he was through the swing doors and out in the street.

The screaming – a woman's – was piercing the mist with a note of terror. Chief-Inspector Davy raced down Pond Street in the direction of the screams. He could dimly visualize a woman's figure backed against a railing. In a dozen strides he had reached her. She wore a long pale fur coat, and her shining blonde hair hung down each side of her face. He thought for a moment that he knew who she was, then he realized that this was only a slip of a girl. Sprawled on the pavement at her feet was the body of a man in uniform. Chief-Inspector Davy recognized him. It was Michael Gorman.

As Davy came up to the girl, she clutched at him, shivering all over, stammering out broken phrases.

'Someone tried to kill me . . . Someone . . . they shot at me . . . If it hadn't been for *him* –' she pointed down at the motionless figure at her feet. 'He pushed me back and got in front of me – and then the second shot came . . . and he fell . . . He saved my life. I think he's hurt – badly hurt . . .'

Chief-Inspector Davy went down on one knee. His torch came out. The tall Irish commissionaire had fallen like a soldier. The left hand side of his tunic showed a wet patch that was growing wetter as the blood oozed out into the cloth. Davy rolled up an eyelid, touched a wrist. He rose to his feet again.

'He's had it all right,' he said.

The girl gave a sharp cry. 'Do you mean he's *dead*? Oh no, no! He can't be *dead*.'

'Who was it shot at you?'

'I don't know . . . I'd left my car just round the corner and was feeling my way along by the railings – I was going to Bertram's Hotel. And then suddenly there was a shot – and a bullet went past my cheek and then – he – the porter from Bertram's – came running down the street towards me, and shoved me behind him, and then another shot came . . . I think – I think whoever it was must have been hiding in that area there.'

Chief-Inspector Davy looked where she pointed. At this end of Bertram's Hotel there was an old-fashioned area below the level of the street, with a gate and some steps down to it. Since it gave only on some store-rooms it was not much used. But a man could have hidden there easily enough.

'You didn't see him?'

'Not properly. He rushed past me like a shadow. It was all thick fog.'

Davy nodded.

The girl began to sob hysterically.

'But who could possibly want to kill me? Why should anyone want to kill me? That's the second time. I don't understand . . . why . . .'

One arm round the girl, Chief-Inspector Davy fumbled in his pocket with the other hand.

The shrill notes of a police whistle penetrated the mist.

III

In the lounge of Bertram's Hotel, Miss Gorringe had looked up sharply from the desk.

One or two of the visitors had looked up also. The older and deafer did not look up.

Henry, about to lower a glass of old brandy to a table, stopped poised with it still in his hand.

Miss Marple sat forward, clutching the arms of her chair. A retired admiral said derisively:

'Accident! Cars collided in the fog, I expect.'

The swing doors from the street were pushed open. Through them came what seemed like an outsize policeman, looking a good deal larger than life.

He was supporting a girl in a pale fur coat. She seemed hardly able to walk. The policeman looked round for help with some embarrassment.

Miss Gorringe came out from behind the desk, prepared to cope. But at that moment the lift came down. A tall figure emerged, and the girl shook herself free from the policeman's support, and ran frantically across the lounge.

'Mother,' she cried. 'Oh *Mother, Mother . . .*' and threw herself, sobbing, into Bess Sedgwick's arms.

Chief-Inspector Davy settled himself back in his chair and looked at the two women sitting opposite him. It was past midnight. Police officials had come and gone. There had been doctors, fingerprint men, an ambulance to remove the body; and now everything had narrowed to this one room dedicated for the purposes of the law by Bertram's Hotel. Chief-Inspector Davy sat one side of the table. Bess Sedgwick and Elvira sat the other side. Against the wall a policeman sat unobtrusively writing. Detective-sergeant Wadell sat near the door.

Father looked thoughtfully at the two women facing him. Mother and daughter. There was, he noted, a strong superficial likeness between them. He could understand how for one moment in the fog he had taken Elvira Blake for Bess Sedgwick. But now, looking at them, he was more struck by the points of difference than the points of resemblance. They were not really alike save in colouring, yet the impression persisted that here he had a positive and a negative version of the same personality. Everything about Bess Sedgwick was positive. Her vitality, her energy, her magnetic attraction. He admired Lady Sedgwick. He always had admired her. He had admired her courage and had always been excited over her exploits; had said, reading his Sunday papers: 'She'll never get away with *that*,' and invariably she had got away with it! He had not thought it possible that she would reach journey's end and she had reached journey's end. He admired particularly the indestructible quality of her. She had had one air crash, several car crashes, had been thrown badly twice from her horse, but at the end of it here she was. Vibrant, alive, a personality one could not ignore for a moment. He took off his hat to her mentally. Some day, of course, she would come a cropper. You could only bear a charmed life for so long. His eyes went from mother to daughter. He wondered. He wondered very much.

In Elvira Blake, he thought, everything had been driven inward. Bess Sedgwick had got through life by imposing her will on it. Elvira, he guessed, had a different way of getting through life. She submitted, he thought. She obeyed. She smiled in compliance and behind that, he thought, she slipped away through your fingers. 'Sly,' he said to himself, appraising that fact. 'That's the only way she can manage, I expect. She can never brazen things out or impose herself. That's why, I expect, the people who've looked after her have never had the least idea of what she might be up to.'

He wondered what she had been doing slipping along the street to Bertrams's Hotel on a late foggy evening. He was going to ask her presently.

He thought it highly probable that the answer he would get would not be the true one. 'That's the way,' he thought, 'that the poor child defends herself.' Had she come here to meet her mother or to find her mother? It was perfectly possible, but he didn't think so. Not for a moment. Instead he thought of the big sports car tucked away round the corner – the car with the number plate FAN 2266. Ladislaus Malinowski must be somewhere in the neighbourhood since his car was there.

'Well,' said Father, addressing Elvira in his most kindly and fatherlike manner, 'well, and how are you feeling now?'

'I'm quite all right,' said Elvira.

'Good. I'd like you to answer a few questions if you feel up to it; because, you see, time is usually the essence of these things. You were shot at twice and a man was killed. We want as many clues as we can get to the person who killed him.'

'I'll tell you everything I can, but it all came so suddenly. And you can't *see* anything in a fog. I've no idea myself who it could have been – or even what he looked like. That's what was so frightening.'

'You said this was the second time somebody had tried to kill you. Does that mean there was an attempt on your life before?'

'Did I say that? I can't remember.' Her eyes moved uneasily. 'I don't think I said that.'

'Oh, but you did, you know,' said Father.

'I expect I was just being – hysterical.'

'No,' said Father, 'I don't think you were. I think you meant just what you said.'

'I might have been imagining things,' said Elvira. Her eyes shifted again.

Bess Sedgwick moved. She said quietly:

'You'd better tell him, Elvira.'

Elvira shot a quick, uneasy look at her mother.

'You needn't worry,' said Father, reassuringly. 'We know quite well in the police force that girls don't tell their mothers or their guardians everything. We don't take those things too seriously, but we've got to *know* about them, because, you see, it all helps.'

Bess Sedgwick said:

'Was it in Italy?'

'Yes,' said Elvira.

Father said: 'That's where you've been at school, isn't it, or a finishing place or whatever they call it nowadays?'

'Yes. I was at Contessa Martinelli's. There were about eighteen or twenty of us.'

'And you thought that somebody tried to kill you. How was that?'

'Well, a big box of chocolates and sweets and things came for me. There was a card with it written in Italian in a flowery hand. The sort of thing they say, you know, "To the bellissima Signorina." Something like that. And my friends and I – well – we laughed about it a bit, and wondered who'd sent it.'

'Did it come by post?'

'No. No, it couldn't have come by post. It was just there in my room. Someone must have put it there.'

'I see. Bribed one of the servants, I suppose. I am to take it that you didn't let the Contessa whoever-it-was in on this?'

A faint smile appeared on Elvira's face. 'No. No. We certainly didn't. Anyway we opened the box and they were lovely chocolates. Different kinds, you know, but there were some violet creams. That's the sort of chocolate that has a crystallized violet on top. My favourite. So of course I ate one or two of those first. And then afterwards, in the night, I felt terribly ill. I didn't think it was the chocolates, I just thought it was something perhaps that I'd eaten at dinner.'

'Anybody else ill?'

'No. Only me. Well, I was very sick and all that, but I felt all right by the end of the next day. Then a day or two later I ate another of the same chocolates, and the same thing happened. So I talked to Bridget about it. Bridget was my special friend. And we looked at the chocolates, and we found that the violet creams had got a sort of hole in the bottom that had been filled up again, so we thought that someone had put some poison in and they'd only put it in the violet creams so that I would be the one who ate them.'

'Nobody else was ill?'

'No.'

'So presumably nobody else ate the violet creams?'

'No. I don't think they could have. You see, it was my present and they knew I liked the violet ones, so they'd leave them for me.'

'The chap took a risk, whoever he was,' said Father. 'The whole place might have been poisoned.'

'It's absurd,' said Lady Sedgwick sharply. 'Utterly absurd! I never heard of anything so crude.'

Chief-Inspector Davy made a slight gesture with his hand. 'Please,' he said, then he went on to Elvira: 'Now I find that very interesting, Miss Blake. And you still didn't tell the Contessa?'

'Oh no, we didn't. She'd have made a terrible fuss.'

'What did you do with the chocolates?'

'We threw them away,' said Elvira. 'They were lovely chocolates,' she added, with a tone of slight grief.

'You didn't try and find out who sent them?'

Elvira looked embarrassed.

'Well, you see, I thought it might have been Guido.'

'Yes?' said Chief-Inspector Davy, cheerfully. 'And who is Guido?'

'Oh, Guido . . .' Elvira paused. She looked at her mother.

'Don't be stupid,' said Bess Sedgwick. 'Tell Chief-Inspector Davy about Guido, whoever he is. Every girl of your age has a Guido in her life. You met him out there, I suppose?'

'Yes. When we were taken to the opera. He spoke to me there. He was nice. Very attractive. I used to see him sometimes when we went to classes. He used to pass me notes.'

'And I suppose,' said Bess Sedgwick, 'that you told a lot of lies, and made plans with some friends and you managed to get out and meet him? Is that it?'

Elvira looked relieved by this short cut to confession. 'Sometimes Guido managed to –'

'What was Guido's other name?'

'I don't know,' said Elvira. 'He never told me.'

Chief-Inspector Davy smiled at her.

'You mean you're not going to tell? Never mind. I dare say we'll be able to find out quite all right without your help, if it should really matter. But why should you think that this young man, who was presumably fond of you, should want to kill you?'

'Oh, because he used to threaten things like that. I mean, we used to have rows now and then. He'd bring some of his friends with him, and I'd pretend to like them better than him, and then he'd get very, very wild and angry. He said I'd better be careful what I did. I couldn't give him up just like that! That if I wasn't faithful to him he'd kill me! I just thought he was being melodramatic and theatrical.' Elvira smiled suddenly and unexpectedly. 'But it was all rather fun. I didn't think it was *real* or *serious*.'

'Well,' said Chief-Inspector Davy, 'I don't think it *does* seem very likely that a young man such as you describe would really poison chocolates and send them to you.'

'Well, I don't think so really either,' said Elvira, 'but it must have been him because I can't see that there's anyone else. It worried me. And then, when I came back here, I got a note –' She stopped.

'What sort of a note?'

'It just came in an envelope and was printed. It said "*Be on your guard. Somebody wants to kill you.*"'

Chief-Inspector Davy's eyebrows went up.

'Indeed? Very curious. Yes, very curious. And it worried you. You were frightened?'

'Yes. I began to – to wonder who could possibly want me out of the way. That's why I tried to find out if I was really very rich.'

'Go on.'

'And the other day in London something else happened. I was in the tube and there were a lot of people on the platform. I thought someone tried to push me on to the line.'

'My dear child!' said Bess Sedgwick. 'Don't romance.'

Again Father made that slight gesture of his hand.

'Yes,' said Elvira apologetically. 'I expect I *have* been imagining it all but – I don't know – I mean, after what happened this evening it seems, doesn't it, as though it might all be true?' She turned suddenly to Bess Sedgwick, speaking with urgency, '*Mother*! You *might* know. *Does* anyone want to kill me? *Could* there be anyone? Have I got an enemy?'

'Of course you've not got an enemy,' said Bess Sedgwick, impatiently. 'Don't be an idiot. Nobody wants to kill you. Why should they?'

'Then who shot at me tonight?'

'In that fog,' said Bess Sedgwick, 'you might have been mistaken for someone else. That's possible, don't you think?' she said, turning to Father.

'Yes, I think it might be quite possible,' said Chief-Inspector Davy.

Bess Sedgwick was looking at him very intently. He almost fancied the motion of her lips saying 'later'.

'Well,' he said cheerfully, 'we'd better get down to some more facts now. Where had you come from tonight? What were you doing walking along Pond Street on such a foggy evening?'

'I came up for an Art class at the Tate this morning. Then I went to lunch with my friend Bridget. She lives in Onslow Square. We went to a film and when we came out, there was this fog – quite thick and getting worse, and I thought perhaps I'd better not drive home.'

'You drive a car, do you?'

'Yes. I took my driving test last summer. Only, I'm not a very good driver and I hate driving in fog. So Bridget's mother said I could stay the night, so I rang up Cousin Mildred – that's where I live in Kent –'

Father nodded.

'– and I said I was going to stay up over-night. She said that was very wise.'

'And what happened next?' asked Father.

'And then the fog seemed lighter suddenly. You know how patchy fogs are. So I said I would drive down to Kent after all. I said goodbye to Bridget and started off. But then it began to come down again. I didn't like it very much. I ran into a very thick patch of it and I lost my way and I didn't know where I was. Then after a bit I realized I was at Hyde Park Corner and I thought "I really *can't* go down to Kent in this." At first, I thought I'd go back to Bridget's but then I remembered how I'd lost my way already. And then I realized that I was quite close to this nice hotel where Uncle Derek took me when I came back from Italy and I thought, "I'll go there and I'm sure they can find me a room." That was fairly easy, I found a place to leave the car and then I walked back up the street towards the hotel.'

'Did you meet anyone or did you hear anyone walking near you?'

'It's funny you saying that, because I did think I heard someone walking behind me. Of course, there must be lots of people walking about in London. Only in a fog like this, it gives you a nervous feeling. I waited and listened but I didn't hear any footsteps and I thought I'd imagined them. I was quite close to the hotel by then.'

'And then?'

'And then quite suddenly there was a shot. As I told you, it seemed to go right past my ear. The commissionaire man who stands outside the hotel came running down towards me and he pushed me behind him and then – then – the other shot came . . . He – he fell down and I screamed.' She was shaking now. Her mother spoke to her.

'Steady, girl,' said Bess in a low, firm voice. 'Steady now.' It was the voice Bess Sedgwick used for her horses and it was quite as efficacious when used on her daughter. Elvira blinked at her, drew herself up a little, and became calm again.

'Good girl,' said Bess.

'And then *you* came,' said Elvira to Father. 'You blew your whistle, you told the policeman to take me into the hotel. And as soon as I got in, I saw – I saw Mother.' She turned and looked at Bess Sedgwick.

'And that brings us more or less up to date,' said Father. He shifted his bulk a little in the chair.

'Do you know a man called Ladislaus Malinowski?' he asked. His tone was even, casual, without any direct inflection. He did not look at the girl, but he was aware, since his ears were functioning at full attention, of a quick little gasp she gave. His eyes were not on the daughter but on the mother.

'No,' said Elvira, having waited just a shade too long to say it. 'No, I don't.'

'Oh,' said Father. 'I thought you might. I thought he might have been here this evening.'

'Oh? Why should he be here?'

'Well, his car is here,' said Father. 'That's why I thought he might be.'

'I don't know him,' said Elvira.

'My mistake,' said Father. 'You do, of course?' he turned his head

465

towards Bess Sedgwick.

'Naturally,' said Bess Sedgwick. 'Known him for many years.' She added, smiling slightly. 'He's a madman, you know. Drives like an angel or a devil – he'll break his neck one of these days. Had a bad smash eighteen months ago.'

'Yes, I remember reading about it,' said Father. 'Not racing again yet, is he?'

'No, not yet. Perhaps he never will.'

'Do you think I could go to bed now?' asked Elvira, plaintively. 'I'm – really terribly tired.'

'Of course. You must be,' said Father. 'You've told us all you can remember?'

'Oh. Yes.'

'I'll go up with you,' said Bess.

Mother and daughter went out together.

'*She* knows him all right,' said Father.

'Do you really think so?' asked Sergeant Wadell.

'I know it. She had tea with him in Battersea Park only a day or two ago.'

'How did you find that out?'

'Old lady told me – distressed. Didn't think he was a nice friend for a young girl. He isn't of course.'

'Especially if he and the mother –' Waddell broke off delicately. 'It's pretty general gossip –'

'Yes. May be true, may not. Probably *is*.'

'In that case which one is he really after?'

Father ignored that point. He said:

'I want him picked up. I want him badly. His car's here – just round the corner.'

'Do you think he might be actually staying in this hotel?'

'Don't think so. It wouldn't fit into the picture. He's not supposed to be here. *If* he came here, he came to meet the girl. She definitely came to meet him, I'd say.'

The door opened and Bess Sedgwick reappeared.

'I came back,' she said, 'because I wanted to speak to you.'

She looked from him to the other two men.

'I wonder if I could speak to you alone? I've given you all the information I have, such as it is; but I would like a word or two with you in private.'

'I don't see any reason why not,' said Chief-Inspector Davy. He motioned with his head, and the young detective-constable took his note-book and went out. Wadell went with him. 'Well?' said Chief-Inspector Davy.

Lady Sedgwick sat down again opposite him.

'That silly story about poisoned chocolates,' she said. 'It's nonsense. Absolutely ridiculous. I don't believe anything of the kind ever happened.'

'You don't, eh?'

'Do you?'

Father shook his head doubtfully. 'You think your daughter cooked it up?'

'Yes. But why?'

'Well, if you don't know why,' said Chief-Inspector Davy, 'how should I know? She's your daughter. Presumably you know her better than I do.'

'I don't know her at all,' said Bess Sedgwick bitterly. 'I've not seen her or had anything to do with her since she was two years old, when I ran away from my husband.'

'Oh yes. I know all that. I find it curious. You see, Lady Sedgwick, courts usually give the mother, even if she is a guilty party in a divorce, custody of a young child if she asks for it. Presumably then you didn't ask for it? You didn't want it.'

'I thought it – better not.'

'Why?'

'I didn't think it was – safe for her.'

'On moral grounds?'

'No. Not on moral grounds. Plenty of adultery nowadays. Children have to learn about it, have to grow up with it. No. It's just that *I* am not really a safe person to be with. The life I'd lead wouldn't be a safe life. You can't help the way you're born. I was born to live dangerously. I'm not law-abiding or conventional. I thought it would be better for Elvira, happier, to have a proper English conventional bringing-up. Shielded, looked after ...'

'But minus a mother's love?'

'I thought if she learned to love me it might bring sorrow to her. Oh, you mayn't believe me, but that's what I felt.'

'I see. Do you still think you were right?'

'No,' said Bess. 'I don't. I think now I may have been entirely wrong.'

'*Does* your daughter know Ladislaus Malinowski?'

'I'm sure she doesn't. She said so. You heard her.'

'I heard her, yes.'

'Well, then?'

'She was afraid, you know, when she was sitting here. In our profession we get to know fear when we meet up with it. She was afraid – why? Chocolates or no chocolates, her life *has* been attempted. That tube story may be true enough –'

'It was ridiculous. Like a thriller –'

467

'Perhaps. But that sort of thing does happen, Lady Sedgwick. Oftener than you'd think. Can you give me any idea who might want to kill your daughter?'

'Nobody – nobody at all!'

She spoke vehemently.

Chief-Inspector Davy sighed and shook his head.

Chief-Inspector Davy waited patiently until Mrs Melford had finished talking. It had been a singularly unprofitable interview. Cousin Mildred had been incoherent, unbelieving and generally feather-headed. Or that was Father's private view. Accounts of Elvira's sweet manners, nice nature, troubles with her teeth, odd excuses told through the telephone, had led on to serious doubts whether Elvira's friend Bridget was really a suitable friend for her. All these matters had been presented to the Chief-Inspector in a kind of general hasty pudding. Mrs Melford knew nothing, had heard nothing, had seen nothing and had apparently deduced very little.

A short telephone call to Elvira's guardian, Colonel Luscombe, had been even more unproductive, though fortunately less wordy. 'More Chinese monkeys,' he muttered to his sergeant as he put down the receiver. 'See no evil, hear no evil, speak no evil.'

'The trouble is that everyone who's had anything to do with this girl has been far too nice – if you get my meaning. Too many nice people who don't know anything about evil. Not like my old lady.'

'The Bertram's Hotel one?'

'Yes, that's the one. She's had a long life of experience in noticing evil, fancying evil, suspecting evil and going forth to do battle with evil. Let's see what we can get out of girl friend Bridget.'

The difficulties in this interview were represented first, last, and most of the time by Bridget's mamma. To talk to Bridget without the assistance of her mother took all Chief-Inspector Davy's adroitness and cajolery. He was, it must be admitted, ably seconded by Bridget. After a certain amount of stereotyped questions and answers and expressions of horror on the part of Bridget's mother at hearing of Elvira's narrow escape from death, Bridget said, 'You know it's time for that committee meeting, Mum. You said it was very important.'

'Oh dear, dear,' said Bridget's mother.

'You know they'll get into a frightful mess without you, Mummy.'

'Oh they will, they certainly will. But perhaps I ought –'

'Now that's quite all right, Madam,' said Chief-Inspector Davy, putting on his kindly old father look. 'You don't want to worry. Just you get off. I've finished all the important things. You've told me really everything I wanted to know. I've just one or two routine inquiries about people in Italy which I think your daughter, Miss Bridget, might be able to help me with.'

'Well, if you think you can manage, Bridget –'

'Oh, I can manage, Mummy,' said Bridget.

Finally, with a great deal of fuss, Bridget's mother went off to her committee.

'Oh, dear,' said Bridget, sighing, as she came back after closing the front door. 'Really! I do think mothers are *difficult.*'

'So they tell me,' said Chief-Inspector Davy. 'A lot of young ladies I come across have a lot of trouble with their mothers.'

'I'd have thought you'd put it the other way round,' said Bridget.

'Oh I do, I do,' said Davy. 'But that's not how the young ladies see it. Now you can tell me a little more.'

'I couldn't really speak frankly in front of Mummy,' explained Bridget. 'But I do feel, of course, that it is really important that you should know as much as possible about all this. I do know Elvira was terribly worried about something and afraid. She wouldn't exactly admit she was in danger, but she was.'

'I thought that might have been so. Of course I didn't like to ask you too much in front of your mother.'

'Oh no,' said Bridget, 'We don't want *Mummy* to hear about it. She gets in such a frightful state about things and she'd go and *tell* everyone. I mean, if Elvira doesn't want things like this to be known ...'

'First of all,' said Chief-Inspector Davy, 'I want to know about a box of chocolates in Italy. I gather there was some idea that a box was sent to her which might have been poisoned.'

Bridget's eyes opened wide. 'Poisoned,' she said. 'Oh no. I don't think so. At least ...'

'There was something?'

'Oh yes. A box of chocolates came and Elvira did eat a lot of them and she was rather sick that night. Quite ill.'

'But she didn't suspect poison?'

'No. At least – oh yes, she did say that someone was trying to poison one of us and we looked at the chocolates to see, you know, if anything had been injected into them.'

'And had it?'

'No, it hadn't,' said Bridget. 'At least, not as far as we could see.'

'But perhaps your friend, Miss Elvira, might still have thought so?'

'Well, she might – but she didn't *say* any more.'

'But you think she was afraid of someone?'

'I didn't think so at the time or notice anything. It was only here, later.'

'What about this man, Guido?'

Bridget giggled.

'He had a terrific crush on Elvira,' she said.

'And you and your friend used to meet him places?'

'Well, I don't mind telling *you*,' said Bridget. 'After all you're the police.

470

It isn't important to you, that sort of thing and I expect you understand. Countess Martinelli was frightfully strict – or thought she was. And of course we had all sorts of dodges and things. We all stood in with each other. You know.'

'And told the right lies, I suppose?'

'Well, I'm afraid so,' said Bridget. 'But what can one do when anyone is so suspicious?'

'So you did meet Guido and all that. And used he to threaten Elvira?'

'Oh, not seriously, I don't think.'

'Then perhaps there was someone else she used to meet?'

'Oh – that – well, I don't know.'

'Please tell me, Miss Bridget. It might be – vital, you know.'

'Yes. Yes I can see that. Well there was *someone*. I don't know who it was, but there was someone else – she really minded about. She was deadly serious. I mean it was a really *important* thing.'

'She used to meet him?'

'I think so. I mean she'd *say* she was meeting Guido but it wasn't Guido. It was this other man.'

'Any idea who it was?'

'No.' Bridget sounded a little uncertain.

'It wouldn't be a racing motorist called Ladislaus Malinowski?'

Bridget gaped at him.

'So you *know*?'

'Am I right?'

'Yes – I think so. She's got a photograph of him torn out of a paper. She kept it under her stockings.'

'That might have been just a pin-up hero, mightn't it?'

'Well it *might*, of course, but I don't think it was.'

'Did she meet him here in this country, do you know?'

'I don't know. You see I don't know really what she's been doing since she came back from Italy.'

'She came up to London to the dentist,' Davy prompted her. 'Or so she said. Instead she came to you. She rang up Mrs Melford with some story about an old governess.'

A faint giggle came from Bridget.

'That wasn't true, was it?' said the Chief-Inspector, smiling. 'Where did she really go?'

Bridget hesitated and then said, 'She went to Ireland.'

'She went to Ireland, did she? Why?'

'She wouldn't tell me. She said there was something she had to find out.'

'Do you know where she went in Ireland?'

'Not exactly. She mentioned a name. Bally something. Ballygowlan, I think it was.'

'I see. You're sure she went to Ireland?'

'I saw her off at Kensington Airport. She went by Aer Lingus.'

'She came back when?'

'The following day.'

'Also by air?'

'Yes.'

'You're quite sure, are you, that she came back by air?'

'Well – I suppose she did!'

'Had she taken a return ticket?'

'No. No, she didn't. I remember.'

'She might have come back another way, mightn't she?'

'Yes, I suppose so.'

'She might have come back for instance by the Irish Mail?'

'She didn't say she had.'

'But she didn't *say* she'd come by air, did she?'

'No,' Bridget agreed. 'But why should she come back by boat and train instead of by air?'

'Well, if she had found out what she wanted to know and had had nowhere to stay, she might think it would be easier to come back by the Night Mail.'

'Why, I suppose she *might*.'

Davy smiled faintly.

'I don't suppose you young ladies,' he said, 'think of going anywhere except in terms of flying, do you, nowadays?'

'I suppose we don't really,' agreed Bridget.

'Anyway, she came back to England. Then what happened? Did she come to you or ring you up?'

'She rang up.'

'What time of day?'

'Oh, in the morning sometime. Yes, it must have been about eleven or twelve o'clock, I think.'

'And she said, what?'

'Well, she just asked if everything was all right.'

'And was it?'

'No, it wasn't, because, you see, Mrs Melford had rung up and Mummy had answered the phone and things had been very difficult and I hadn't known what to say. So Elvira said she would not come to Onslow Square, but that she'd ring up her cousin Mildred and try to fix up some story or other.'

472

'And that's all that you can remember?'

'That's all,' said Bridget, making certain reservations. She thought of Mr Bollard and the bracelet. That was certainly a thing she was not going to tell Chief-Inspector Davy. Father knew quite well that something was being kept from him. He could only hope that it was not something pertinent to his inquiry. He asked again:

'You think your friend was really frightened of someone or something?'

'Yes I do.'

'Did she mention it to you or did you mention it to her?'

'Oh, I asked her outright. At first she said no and then she admitted that she *was* frightened. And I know she was,' went on Bridget violently. 'She was in danger. She was quite sure of it. But I don't know why or how or anything about it.'

'Your surety on this point relates to that particular morning, does it, the morning she had come back from Ireland?'

'Yes. Yes, that's when I was so sure about it.'

'On the morning when she *might* have come back on the Irish Mail?'

'I don't think it's very likely that she did. Why don't you ask her?'

'I probably shall do in the end. But I don't want to call attention to that point. Not at the moment. It might just possibly make things more dangerous for her.'

Bridget opened round eyes.

'What do you mean?'

'You may not remember it, Miss Bridget, but that was the night, or rather the early morning, of the Irish Mail robbery.'

'Do you mean that Elvira was in *that* and never told me a thing about it?'

'I agree it's unlikely,' said Father. 'But it just occurred to me that she might have seen something or someone, or some incident might have occurred connected with the Irish Mail. She might have seen someone she knew, for instance, and that might have put her in danger.'

'Oh!' said Bridget. She thought it over. 'You mean – someone she knew was mixed up in the robbery.'

Chief-Inspector Davy got up.

'I think that's all,' he said. 'Sure there's nothing more you can tell me? Nowhere where your friend went that day? Or the day before?'

Again visions of Mr Bollard and the Bond Street shop rose before Bridget's eyes.

'No,' she said.

'I think there is something you haven't told me,' said Chief-Inspector Davy.

Bridget grasped thankfully at a straw.

473

'Oh, I forgot,' she said. 'Yes. I mean she did go to some lawyers. Lawyers who were trustees, to find out something.'

'Oh, she went to some lawyers who were her trustees. I don't suppose you know their name?'

'Their name was Egerton – Forbes Egerton and Something,' said Bridget. 'Lots of names. I think that's more or less right.'

'I see. And she wanted to find out something, did she?'

'She wanted to know how much money she'd got,' said Bridget.

Inspector Davy's eyebrows rose.

'Indeed!' he said. 'Interesting. Why didn't she know herself?'

'Oh, because people never told her anything about money,' said Bridget. 'They seem to think it's bad for you to know actually how much money you have.'

'And she wanted to know badly, did she?'

'Yes,' said Bridget. 'I think she thought it was important.'

'Well, thank you,' said Chief-Inspector Davy. 'You've helped me a good deal.'

Richard Egerton looked again at the official card in front of him, then up into the Chief-Inspector's face.

'Curious business,' he said.

'Yes, sir,' said Chief Inspector Davy, 'a very curious business.'

'Bertram's Hotel,' said Egerton, 'in the fog. Yes it was a bad fog last night. I suppose you get a lot of that sort of thing in fogs, don't you? Snatch and grab – handbags – that sort of thing?'

'It wasn't quite like that,' said Father. 'Nobody attempted to snatch anything from Miss Blake.'

'Where did the shot come from?'

'Owing to the fog we can't be sure. She wasn't sure herself. But we think – it seems the best idea – that the man may have been standing in the area.'

'He shot at her twice, you say?'

'Yes. The first shot missed. The commissionaire rushed along from where he was standing outside the hotel door and shoved her behind him just before the second shot.'

'So that he got hit instead, eh?'

'Yes.'

'Quite a brave chap.'

'Yes. He was brave,' said the Chief-Inspector. 'His military record was very good. An Irishman.'

'What's his name?'

'Gorman. Michael Gorman.'

'Michael Gorman.' Egerton frowned for a minute. 'No,' he said. 'For a moment I thought the name meant something.'

'It's a very common name, of course. Anyway, he saved the girl's life.'

'And why exactly have you come to me, Chief-Inspector?'

'I hoped for a little information. We always like full information, you know, about the victim of a murderous assault.'

'Oh, naturally, naturally. But really, I've only seen Elvira twice since she was a child.'

'You saw her when she came to call upon you about a week ago, didn't you?'

'Yes, that's quite right. What exactly do you want to know? If it's anything about her personality, who her friends were or about boy friends, or lovers' quarrels – all that sort of thing – you'd do better to go to one of the women. There's a Mrs Carpenter who brought her back from Italy, I believe, and there's Mrs Melford with whom she lives in Kent.'

'I've seen Mrs Melford.'

'Oh.'

'No good. Absolutely no good at all, sir. And I don't so much want to know about the girl personally – after all, I've seen her for myself and I've heard what she can tell me – or rather what she's willing to tell me –'

At a quick movement of Egerton's eyebrows he saw that the other had appreciated the point of the word 'willing'.

'I've been told that she was worried, upset, afraid about something, and convinced that her life was in danger. Was that your impression when she came to see you?'

'No,' said Egerton, slowly, 'no, I wouldn't go as far as that; though she did say one or two things that struck me as curious.'

'Such as?'

'Well, she wanted to know who would benefit if she were to die suddenly.'

'Ah,' said Chief-Inspector Davy, 'so she had that possibility in her mind, did she? That she might die suddenly. Interesting.'

'She'd got something in her head but I didn't know what it was. She also wanted to know how much money she had – or would have when she was twenty-one. That, perhaps, is more understandable.'

'It's a lot of money I believe.'

'It's a very large fortune, Chief-Inspector.'

'Why do you think she wanted to know?'

'About the money?'

'Yes, and about who would inherit it.'

'I don't know,' said Egerton. 'I don't know at all. She also brought up the subject of marriage –'

'Did you form the impression that there was a man in the case?'

'I've no evidence – but – yes, I did think just that. I felt sure there was a boy friend somewhere in the offing. There usually is! Luscombe – that's Colonel Luscombe, her guardian, doesn't seem to know anything about a boy friend. But then dear old Derek Luscombe wouldn't. He was quite upset when I suggested that there was such a thing in the background and probably an unsuitable one at that.'

'He is unsuitable,' said Chief-Inspector Davy.

'Oh. Then you know who he is?'

'I can have a very good guess at it. Ladislaus Malinowski.'

'The racing motorist? Really! A handsome dare-devil. Women fall for him easily. I wonder how he came across Elvira. I don't see very well where their orbits would meet except – yes, I believe he was in Rome a couple of months ago. Possibly she met him there.'

'Very possibly. Or could she have met him through her mother?'

'What, through Bess? I wouldn't say that was at all likely.'

Davy coughed.

'Lady Sedgwick and Malinowski are said to be close friends, sir.'

'Oh yes, yes, I know that's the gossip. May be true, may not. They are close friends – thrown together constantly by their way of life. Bess has had her affairs, of course; though, mind you, she's not the nymphomaniac type. People are ready enough to say that about a woman, but it's not true in Bess's case. Anyway, as far as I know, Bess and her daughter are practically not even acquainted with each other.'

'That's what Lady Sedgwick told me. And you agree?'

Egerton nodded.

'What other relatives has Miss Blake got?'

'For all intents and purposes, none. Her mother's two brothers were killed in the war – and she was old Coniston's only child. Mrs Melford, though the girl calls her "Cousin Mildred", is actually a cousin of Colonel Luscombe's. Luscombe's done his best for the girl in his conscientious old-fashioned way – but it's difficult . . . for a man.'

'Miss Blake brought up the subject of marriage, you say? There's no possibility, I suppose, that she may actually already *be* married –'

'She's well under age – she'd have to have the assent of her guardian and trustees.'

'Technically, yes. But they don't always wait for that,' said Father.

'I know. Most regrettable. One has to go through all the machinery of making them Wards of Court, and all the rest of it. And even that has its difficulties.'

'And once they're married, they're married,' said Father. 'I suppose, if she *were* married, and died suddenly, her husband would inherit?'

'This idea of marriage is most unlikely. She has been most carefully looked after and . . .' He stopped, reacting to Chief-Inspector Davy's cynical smile.

However carefully Elvira had been looked after, she seemed to have succeeded in making the acquaintance of the highly unsuitable Ladislaus Malinowski.

He said dubiously, 'Her mother bolted, it's true.'

'Her mother bolted, yes – that's what she would do – but Miss Blake's a different type. She's just as set on getting her own way, but she'd go about it differently.'

'You don't really think –'

'I don't think anything – *yet*,' said Chief-Inspector Davy.

Ladislaus Malinowski looked from one to the other of the two police officers and flung back his head and laughed.

'It is very amusing!' he said. 'You look solemn as owls. It is ridiculous that you should ask me to come here and wish to ask me questions. You have nothing against me, nothing.'

'We think you may be able to assist us in our inquiries, Mr Malinowski.' Chief-Inspector Davy spoke with official smoothness. 'You own a car, Mercedes-Otto, registration number FAN 2266.'

'Is there any reason why I should not own such a car?'

'No reason at all, sir. There's just a little uncertainty as to the correct number. Your car was on a motor road, M7, and the registration plate on that occasion was a different one.'

'Nonsense. It must have been some other car.'

'There aren't so many of that make. We have checked up on those there are.'

'You believe everything, I suppose, that your traffic police tell you! It is laughable! Where was all this?'

'The place where the police stopped you and asked to see your licence is not very far from Bedhampton. It was on the night of the Irish Mail robbery.'

'You really do amuse me,' said Ladislaus Malinowski.

'You have a revolver?'

'Certainly, I have a revolver and an automatic pistol. I have proper licences for them.'

'Quite so. They are both still in your possession?'

'Certainly.'

'I have already warned you, Mr Malinowski.'

'The famous policeman's warning! Anything you say will be taken down and used against you at your trial.'

'That's not quite the wording,' said Father mildly. 'Used, yes. Against, no. You don't want to qualify that statement of yours?'

'No, I do not.'

'And you are sure you don't want your solicitors here?'

'I do not like solicitors.'

'Some people don't. Where are those firearms now?'

'I think you know very well where they are, Chief-Inspector. The small pistol is in the pocket of my car, the Mercedes-Otto whose registered number is, as I have said, FAN 2266. The revolver is in a drawer in my flat.'

'You're quite right about the one in the drawer in your flat,' said Father,

478

'but the other – the pistol – is not in your car.'

'Yes, it is. It is in the left-hand pocket.'

Father shook his head. 'It may have been once. It isn't now. Is this it, Mr Malinowski?'

He passed a small automatic pistol across the table. Ladislaus Malinowski, with an air of great surprise, picked it up.

'Ah-ha, yes. This is it. So it was *you* who took it from my car?'

'No,' said Father, 'we didn't take it from your car. It was not in your car. We found it somewhere else.'

'Where did you find it?'

'We found it,' said Father, 'in an area in Pond Street which – as you no doubt know – is a street near Park Lane. It could have been dropped by a man walking down that street – or running perhaps.'

Ladislaus Malinowski shrugged his shoulders. 'That is nothing to do with me – I did not put it there. It was in my car a day or two ago. One does not continually look to see if a thing is still where one has put it. One assumes it will be.'

'Do you know, Mr Malinowski, that this is the pistol which was used to shoot Michael Gorman on the night of November 26th?'

'Michael Gorman? I do not know a Michael Gorman.'

'The commissionaire from Bertram's Hotel.'

'Ah yes, the one who was shot. I read about it. And you say *my* pistol shot him? Nonsense!'

'It's not nonsense. The ballistic experts have examined it. You know enough of firearms to be aware that their evidence is reliable.'

'You are trying to frame me. I know what you police do!'

'I think you know the police of this country better than that, Mr Malinowski.'

'Are you suggesting that I shot Michael Gorman?'

'So far we are only asking for a statement. No charge has been made.'

'But that is what you think – that I shot that ridiculous dressed-up military figure. Why should I? I didn't owe him money, I had no grudge against him.'

'It was a young lady who was shot at. Gorman ran to protect her and received the second bullet in his chest.'

'A young lady?'

'A young lady whom I think you know. Miss Elvira Blake.'

'Do you say someone tried to shoot Elvira with *my* pistol?'

He sounded incredulous.

'It could be that you had had a disagreement.'

'You mean that I quarrelled with Elvira and shot her? What madness!

479

Why should I shoot the girl I am going to marry?'

'Is that part of your statement? That you are going to marry Miss Elvira Blake?'

Just for a moment or two Ladislaus hesitated. Then he said, shrugging his shoulders:

'She is still very young. It remains to be discussed.'

'Perhaps she had promised to marry you, and then – she changed her mind. There was *someone* she was afraid of. Was it you, Mr Malinowski?'

'Why should *I* want her to die? Either I am in love with her and want to marry her or if I do not want to marry her I need not marry her. It is as simple as that. So why should I kill her?'

'There aren't many people close enough to her to want to kill her.' Davy waited a moment and then said, almost casually: 'There's her mother, of course.'

'What!' Malinowski sprang up. *'Bess?* Bess kill her own daughter? You are mad! Why should Bess kill Elvira?'

'Possibly because, as next of kin, she might inherit an enormous fortune.'

'Bess? You mean Bess would kill for money? She has plenty of money from her American husband. Enough, anyway.'

'Enough is not the same as a great fortune,' said Father. 'People do murder for a large fortune, mothers have been known to kill their children and children have killed their mothers.'

'I tell you, you are mad!'

'You say that you may be going to marry Miss Blake. Perhaps you have already married her? If so, then *you* would be the one to inherit a vast fortune.'

'What more crazy, stupid things can you say! No, I am not married to Elvira. She is a pretty girl. I like her, and she is in love with me. Yes, I admit it. I met her in Italy. We had fun – but that is all. No more, do you understand?'

'Indeed? Just now, Mr Malinowski, you said quite definitely that she was the girl you were going to marry.'

'Oh that.'

'Yes – that. Was it true?'

'I said it because – it sounded more respectable that way. You are so – prudish in this country –'

'That seems to me an unlikely explanation.'

'You do not understand anything at all. The mother and I – we are lovers – I did not wish to say so – I suggest instead that the daughter and I – we are engaged to be married. That sounds very English and proper.'

'It sounds to me even more far-fetched. You're rather badly in need of money, aren't you, Mr Malinowski?'

'My dear Chief-Inspector, I am always in need of money. It is very sad.'

'And yet a few months ago I understand you were flinging money about in a very carefree way.'

'Ah. I had had a lucky flutter. I am a gambler. I admit it.'

'I find that quite easy to believe. Where did you have this "flutter"?'

'That I do not tell. You can hardly expect it.'

'I don't expect it.'

'Is that all you have to ask me?'

'For the moment, yes. You have identified the pistol as yours. That will be very helpful.'

'I don't understand – I can't conceive –' he broke off and stretched out his hand. 'Give it me please.'

'I'm afraid we'll have to keep it for the present, so I'll write you out a receipt for it.'

He did so and handed it to Malinowski.

The latter went out slamming the door.

'Temperamental chap,' said Father.

'You didn't press him on the matter of the false number plate and Bedhampton?'

'No. I wanted him rattled. But not too badly rattled. We'll give him one thing to worry about at a time – And he *is* worried.'

'The Old Man wanted to see you, sir, as soon as you were through.'

Chief-Inspector Davy nodded and made his way to Sir Ronald's room.

'Ah! Father. Making progress?'

'Yes. Getting along nicely – quite a lot of fish in the net. Small fry mostly. But we're closing in on the big fellows. Everything's in train –'

'Good show, Fred,' said the A.C.

Miss Marple got out of her train at Paddington and saw the burly figure of Chief-Inspector Davy standing on the platform waiting for her.

He said, 'Very good of you, Miss Marple,' put his hand under her elbow and piloted her through the barrier to where a car was waiting. The driver opened the door, Miss Marple got in, Chief-Inspector Davy followed her and the car drove off.

'Where are you taking me, Chief-Inspector Davy?'

'To Bertram's Hotel.'

'Dear me, Bertram's Hotel again. Why?'

'The official reply is: because the police think you can assist them in their inquiries.'

'That sounds familiar, but surely rather sinister? So often the prelude to an arrest, is it not?'

'I am not going to arrest you, Miss Marple.' Father smiled. 'You have an alibi.'

Miss Marple digested this in silence. Then she said, 'I see.'

They drove to Bertram's Hotel in silence. Miss Gorringe looked up from the desk as they entered, but Chief-Inspector Davy piloted Miss Marple to the lift.

'Second floor.'

The lift ascended, stopped, and Father led the way along the corridor. As he opened the door of No. 18 Miss Marple said:

'This is the same I had when I was staying here before.'

'Yes,' said Father.

Miss Marple sat down in the arm-chair.

'A very comfortable room,' she observed, looking round with a slight sigh.

'They certainly know what comfort is here,' Father agreed.

'You look tired, Chief-Inspector,' said Miss Marple unexpectedly.

'I've had to get around a bit. As a matter of fact I've just got back from Ireland.'

'Indeed. From Ballygowlan?'

'Now how the devil did *you* know about Ballygowlan? I'm sorry – I beg your pardon.'

Miss Marple smiled forgiveness.

'I suppose Michael Gorman happened to tell you he came from there – was that it?'

'No, not exactly,' said Miss Marple.

'Then how, if you'll excuse me asking you, *did* you know?'

'Oh dear,' said Miss Marple, 'it's really very embarrassing. It was just something I – happened to overhear.'

'Oh, I see.'

'I wasn't eavesdropping. It was in a public room – at least technically a public room. Quite frankly, I enjoy listening to people talking. One does. Especially when one is old and doesn't get about very much. I mean, if people are talking near you, you listen.'

'Well, that seems to me quite natural,' said Father.

'Up to a point, yes,' said Miss Marple. 'If people do not choose to lower their voices, one must assume that they are prepared to be overheard. But of course matters may develop. The situation sometimes arises when you realize that though it *is* a public room, other people talking do not realize that there is anyone else in it. And then one has to decide what to do about it. Get up and cough, or just stay quiet and hope they won't realize you've been there. Either way is embarrassing.'

Chief-Inspector Davy glanced at his watch.

'Look here,' he said, 'I want to hear more about this – but I've got Canon Pennyfather arriving at any moment. I must go and collect him. You don't mind?'

Miss Marple said she didn't mind. Chief-Inspector Davy left the room.

II

Canon Pennyfather came through the swing doors into the hall of Bertram's Hotel. He frowned slightly, wondering what it was that seemed a little different about Bertram's today. Perhaps it had been painted or done up in some way? He shook his head. That was not it, but there was *something*. It did not occur to him that it was the difference between a six foot commissionaire with blue eyes and dark hair and a five foot seven commissionaire with sloping shoulders, freckles and a sandy thatch of hair bulging out under his commissionaire's cap. He just knew something was different. In his usual vague way he wandered up to the desk. Miss Gorringe was there and greeted him.

'Canon Pennyfather. How nice to see you. Have you come to fetch your baggage? It's all ready for you. If you'd only let us know we could have sent it to you to any address you like.'

'Thank you,' said Canon Pennyfather, 'thank you very much. You're always most kind, Miss Gorringe. But as I had to come up to London anyway today I thought I might as well call for it.'

'We were so worried about you,' said Miss Gorringe. 'Being missing, you

483

know. Nobody able to find you. You had a car accident, I hear?'

'Yes,' said Canon Pennyfather. 'Yes. People drive much too fast nowadays. Most dangerous. Not that I can remember much about it. It affected my head. Concussion, the doctor says. Oh well, as one is getting on in life, one's memory –' he shook his head sadly. 'And how are you, Miss Gorringe?'

'Oh, I'm very well,' said Miss Gorringe.

At that moment it struck Canon Pennyfather that Miss Gorringe also was different. He peered at her, trying to analyse where the difference lay. Her hair? That was the same as usual. Perhaps even a little frizzier. Black dress, large locket, cameo brooch. All there as usual. But there was a difference. Was she perhaps a little thinner? Or was it – yes, surely, she looked *worried*. It was not often that Canon Pennyfather noticed whether people looked worried, he was not the kind of man who noticed emotion in the faces of others, but it struck him today, perhaps because Miss Gorringe had so invariably presented exactly the same countenance to guests for so many years.

'You've not been ill, I hope?' he asked solicitously. 'You look a little thinner.'

'Well, we've had a good deal of worry, Canon Pennyfather.'

'Indeed. Indeed. I'm sorry to hear it. Not due to my disappearance, I hope?'

'Oh no,' said Miss Gorringe. 'We were worried, of course, about that, but as soon as we heard that you were all right –' She broke off and said, 'No. No – it's this – well, perhaps you haven't read about it in the papers. Gorman, our outside porter, got killed.'

'Oh yes,' said Canon Pennyfather. 'I remember now. I did see it mentioned in the paper – that you had had a murder here.'

Miss Gorringe shuddered at this blunt mention of the word murder. The shudder went all up her black dress.

'Terrible,' she said, 'terrible. Such a thing has *never* happened at Bertram's. I mean, we're not the sort of hotel where murders happen.'

'No, no, indeed,' said Canon Pennyfather quickly. 'I'm sure you're not. I mean it would never have occurred to me that anything like that could happen *here*.'

'Of course it wasn't *inside* the hotel,' said Miss Gorringe, cheering up a little as this aspect of the affair struck her. 'It was outside in the street.'

'So really nothing to do with you at all,' said the Canon, helpfully.

That apparently was not quite the right thing to say.

'But it was connected with Bertram's. We had to have the police here questioning people, since it was our commissionaire who was shot.'

'So that's a new man you have outside. D'you know, I thought somehow things looked a little strange.'

'Yes, I don't know that he's very satisfactory. I mean, not quite the style we're used to here. But of course we had to get someone quickly.'

'I remember all about it now,' said Canon Pennyfather, assembling some rather dim memories of what he had read in the paper a week ago. 'But I thought it was a *girl* who was shot.'

'You mean Lady Sedgwick's daughter? I expect you remember seeing her here with her guardian, Colonel Luscombe. Apparently she was attacked by someone in the fog. I expect they wanted to snatch her bag. Anyway they fired a shot at her and then Gorman, who of course had been a soldier and was a man with a lot of presence of mind, rushed down, got in front of her and got shot himself, poor fellow.'

'Very sad, very sad,' said the Canon, shaking his head.

'It makes everything terribly difficult,' complained Miss Gorringe. 'I mean, the police constantly in and out. I suppose that's to be expected, but we don't *like* it here, though I must say Chief-Inspector Davy and Sergeant Wadell are very respectable-looking. Plain clothes, and very good style, not the sort with boots and mackintoshes like one sees on films. Almost like one of *us*.'

'Er – yes,' said Canon Pennyfather.

'Did you have to go to hospital?' inquired Miss Gorringe.

'No,' said the Canon, 'some very nice people, really good Samaritans – a market gardener, I believe – picked me up and his wife nursed me back to health. I'm most grateful, most grateful. It is refreshing to find that there is still human kindness in the world. Don't you think so?'

Miss Gorringe said she thought it was very refreshing. 'After all one reads about the increase in crime,' she added, 'all those dreadful young men and girls holding up banks and robbing trains and ambushing people.' She looked up and said, 'There's Chief-Inspector Davy coming down the stairs now. I think he wants to speak to you.'

'I don't know why he should want to speak to me,' said Canon Pennyfather, puzzled. 'He's already been to see me, you know,' he said, 'at Chadminster. He was very disappointed, I think, that I couldn't tell him anything useful.'

'You couldn't?'

The Canon shook his head sorrowfully.

'I couldn't remember. The accident took place somewhere near a place called Bedhampton and really I don't understand *what* I can have been doing there. The Chief-Inspector kept asking me why I was there and I couldn't tell him. Very odd, isn't it? He seemed to think I'd been driving a car from somewhere near a railway station to a vicarage.'

'That sounds very possible,' said Miss Gorringe.

'It doesn't seem possible at all,' said Canon Pennyfather. 'I mean, why should I be driving about in a part of the world that I don't really know?'

Chief-Inspector Davy had come up to them.

'So here you are, Canon Pennyfather,' he said. 'Feeling quite yourself again?'

'Oh, I feel quite well now,' said the Canon, 'but rather inclined to have headaches still. And I've been told not to do too much. But I still don't seem to remember what I ought to remember and the doctor says it may never come back.'

'Oh well,' said Chief-Inspector Davy, 'we mustn't give up hope.' He led the Canon away from the desk. 'There's a little experiment I want you to try,' he said. 'You don't mind helping me, do you?'

III

When Chief-Inspector Davy opened the door of Number 18, Miss Marple was still sitting in the arm-chair by the window.

'A good many people in the street today,' she observed. 'More than usual.'

'Oh well – this is a way through to Berkeley Square and Shepherd Market.'

'I didn't mean only passers-by. Men doing things – road repairs, a telephone repair van – meat trolley – a couple of private cars –'

'And what – may I ask – do you deduce from that?'

'I didn't say that I deduced anything.'

Father gave her a look. Then he said:

'I want you to help me.'

'Of course. That is why I am here. What do you want me to do?'

'I want you to do exactly what you did on the night of November 19th. You were asleep – you woke up – possibly awakened by some unusual noise. You switched on the light, looked at the time, got out of bed, opened the door and looked out. Can you repeat those actions?'

'Certainly,' said Miss Marple. She got up and went across to the bed.

'Just a moment.'

Chief-Inspector Davy went and tapped on the connecting walls of the next room.

'You'll have to do that louder,' said Miss Marple. 'This place is very well built.'

486

The Chief-Inspector redoubled the force of his knuckles.

'I told Canon Pennyfather to count ten,' he said, looking at his watch. 'Now then, off you go.'

Miss Marple touched the electric lamp, looked at an imaginary clock, got up, walked to the door, opened it and looked out. To her right, just leaving his room, walking to the top of the stairs, was Canon Pennyfather. He arrived at the top of the stairs and started down them. Miss Marple gave a slight catch of her breath. She turned back.

'Well?' said Chief-Inspector Davy.

'The man I saw that night can't have been Canon Pennyfather,' said Miss Marple. 'Not if that's Canon Pennyfather now.'

'I thought you said –'

'I know. He looked like Canon Pennyfather. His hair and his clothes and everything. But he didn't walk the same way. I think – I think he must have been a younger man. I'm sorry, very sorry, to have misled you, but it wasn't Canon Pennyfather that I saw that night. I'm quite sure of it.'

'You really are quite sure this time, Miss Marple?'

'Yes,' said Miss Marple. 'I'm sorry,' she added again, 'to have misled you.'

'You were very nearly right. Canon Pennyfather did come back to the hotel that night. Nobody saw him come in – but that wasn't remarkable. He came in after midnight. He came up the stairs, he opened the door of his room next door and he went in. What he saw or what happened next we don't know, because he can't or won't tell us. If there was only some way we could jog his memory . . .'

'There's that German word of course,' said Miss Marple, thoughtfully.

'What German word?'

'Dear me, I've forgotten it now, but –'

There was a knock at the door.

'May I come in?' said Canon Pennyfather. He entered. 'Was it satisfactory?'

'Most satisfactory,' said Father. 'I was just telling Miss Marple – you know Miss Marple?'

'Oh yes,' said Canon Pennyfather, really slightly uncertain as to whether he did or not.

'I was just telling Miss Marple how we have traced your movements. You came back to the hotel that night after midnight. You came upstairs and you opened the door of your room and went in –' He paused.

Miss Marple gave an exclamation.

'I remember now, she said, 'what the German word is. *Doppelganger!*'

Canon Pennyfather uttered an exclamation. 'But of course,' he said, 'of *course*! How could I have forgotten? You're quite right, you know. After that film, *The Walls of Jericho*, I came back here and I came upstairs and I opened my room and I saw – extraordinary, I distinctly saw *myself* sitting in a chair facing me. As you say, dear lady, a *doppelganger*. How very remarkable! And then – let me see –' He raised his eyes, trying to think.

'And then,' said Father, 'startled out of their lives to see you, when they thought you were safely in Lucerne, somebody hit you on the head.'

Canon Pennyfather had been sent on his way in a taxi to the British Museum. Miss Marple had been ensconced in the lounge by the Chief-Inspector. Would she mind waiting for him there for about ten minutes? Miss Marple had not minded. She welcomed the opportunity to sit and look around her and think.

Bertram's Hotel. So many memories ... The past fused itself with the present. A French phrase came back to her. *Plus ça change, plus c'est la même chose.* She reversed the wording. *Plus c'est la même chose, plus ça change.* Both true, she thought.

She felt sad – for Bertram's Hotel and for herself. She wondered what Chief-Inspector Davy wanted of her next. She sensed in him the excitement of purpose. He was a man whose plans were at last coming to fruition. It was Chief-Inspector Davy's D-Day.

The life of Bertram's went on as usual. No, Miss Marple decided, *not* as usual. There was a difference, though she could not have defined where the difference lay. An underlying uneasiness, perhaps?

'All set?' he inquired genially.

'Where are you taking me now?'

'We're going to pay a call on Lady Sedgwick.'

'Is she staying here?'

'Yes. With her daughter.'

Miss Marple rose to her feet. She cast a glance round her and murmured: 'Poor Bertram's.'

'What do you mean – poor Bertram's?'

'I think you know quite well what I mean.'

'Well – looking at it from your point of view, perhaps I do.'

'It is always sad when a work of art has to be destroyed.'

'You call this place a work of art?'

'Certainly I do. So do you.'

'I see what you mean,' admitted Father.

'It is like when you get ground elder really badly in a border. There's nothing else you can do about it – except dig the whole thing up.'

'I don't know much about gardens. But change the metaphor to dry rot and I'd agree.'

They went up in the lift and along a passage to where Lady Sedgwick and her daughter had a corner suite.

Chief-Inspector Davy knocked on the door, a voice said, Come in, and he entered with Miss Marple behind him.

Bess Sedgwick was sitting in a high-backed chair near the window. She had a book on her knee which she was not reading.

'So it's you again, Chief-Inspector.' Her eyes went past him towards Miss Marple, and she looked slightly surprised.

'This is Miss Marple,' explained Chief-Inspector Davy. 'Miss Marple – Lady Sedgwick.'

'I've met you before,' said Bess Sedgwick. 'You were with Selina Hazy the other day, weren't you? Do sit down,' she added. Then she turned towards Chief-Inspector Davy again. 'Have you any news of the man who shot at Elvira?'

'Not actually what you'd call *news*.'

'I doubt if you ever will have. In a fog like that, predatory creatures come out and prowl around looking for women walking alone.'

'True up to a point,' said Father. 'How is your daughter?'

'Oh, Elvira is quite all right again.'

'You've got her here with you?'

'Yes. I rang up Colonel Luscombe – her guardian. He was delighted that I was willing to take charge.' She gave a sudden laugh. 'Dear old boy. He's always been urging a mother-and-daughter reunion act!'

'He may be right at that,' said Father.

'Oh no, he isn't. Just at the moment, yes, I think it is the best thing.' She turned her head to look out of the window and spoke in a changed voice. 'I hear you've arrested a friend of mine – Ladislaus Malinowski. On what charge?'

'Not *arrested*,' Chief-Inspector Davy corrected her. 'He's just assisting us with our inquiries.'

'I've sent my solicitor to look after him.'

'Very wise,' said Father approvingly. 'Anyone who's having a little difficulty with the police is very wise to have a solicitor. Otherwise they may so easily say the wrong thing.'

'Even if completely innocent?'

'Possibly it's even more necessary in that case,' said Father.

'You're quite a cynic, aren't you? What are you questioning him about, may I ask? Or mayn't I?'

'For one thing we'd like to know just exactly what his movements were on the night when Michael Gorman died.'

Bess Sedgwick sat up sharply in her chair.

'Have you got some ridiculous idea that *Ladislaus* fired those shots at Elvira? They didn't even know each other.'

'He could have done it. His car was just round the corner.'

'Rubbish,' said Lady Sedgwick robustly.

'How much did that shooting business the other night upset you,

490

Lady Sedgwick?'

She looked faintly surprised.

'Naturally I was upset when my daughter had a narrow escape of her life. What do you expect?'

'I didn't mean that. I mean how much did the death of Michael Gorman upset you?'

'I was very sorry about it. He was a brave man.'

'Is that all?'

'What more would you expect me to say?'

'You knew him, didn't you?'

'Of course. He worked here.'

'You knew him a little better than that, though, didn't you?'

'What do you mean?'

'Come, Lady Sedgwick. He was your husband, wasn't he?'

She did not answer for a moment or two, though she displayed no signs of agitation or surprise.

'You know a good deal, don't you, Chief-Inspector?' She sighed and sat back in her chair. 'I hadn't seen him for – let me see – a great many years. Twenty – more than twenty. And then I looked out of the window one day, and suddenly recognized Micky.'

'And he recognized you?'

'Quite surprising that we did recognize each other,' said Bess Sedgwick. 'We were only together for about a week. Then my family caught up with us, paid Micky off, and took me home in disgrace.'

She sighed.

'I was very young when I ran away with him. I knew very little. Just a fool of a girl with a head full of romantic notions. He was a hero to me, mainly because of the way he rode a horse. He didn't know what fear was. And he was handsome and gay with an Irishman's tongue! I suppose really *I* ran away with *him*! I doubt if he'd have thought of it himself! But I was wild and headstrong and madly in love!' She shook her head. 'It didn't last long . . . The first twenty-four hours were enough to disillusion me. He drank and he was coarse and brutal. When my family turned up and took me back with them, I was thankful. I never wanted to see him or hear of him again.'

'Did your family know that you were married to him?'

'No.'

'You didn't tell them?'

'I didn't think I *was* married.'

'How did that come about?'

'We were married in Ballygowlan, but when my people turned up, Micky came to me and told me the marriage had been a fake. He and his friends had

491

cooked it up between them, he said. By that time it seemed to me quite a natural thing for him to have done. Whether he wanted the money that was being offered him, or whether he was afraid he'd committed a breach of the law by marrying me when I wasn't of age, I don't know. Anyway, I didn't doubt for a moment that what he said was true – not then.'

'And later?'

She seemed lost in her thoughts. 'It wasn't until – oh, quite a number of years afterwards, when I knew a little more of life, and of legal matters, but it suddenly occurred to me that probably I was married to Micky Gorman after all!'

'In actual fact, then, when you married Lord Coniston, you committed bigamy.'

'And when I married Johnnie Sedgwick, and again when I married my American husband, Ridgway Becker.' She looked at Chief-Inspector Davy and laughed with what seemed like genuine amusement.

'So much bigamy,' she said. 'It really does seem very ridiculous.'

'Did you never think of getting a divorce?'

She shrugged her shoulders. 'It all seemed like a silly dream. Why rake it up? I told Johnnie, of course.' Her voice softened and mellowed as she said his name.

'And what did he say?'

'He didn't care. Neither Johnnie nor I were ever very law-abiding.'

'Bigamy carries certain penalties, Lady Sedgwick.'

She looked at him and laughed.

'Who was ever going to worry about something that had happened in Ireland years ago? The whole thing was over and done with. Micky had taken his money and gone off. Oh don't you understand? It seemed just a silly little incident. An incident I wanted to forget. I put it aside with the things – the very many things – that don't matter in life.'

'And then,' said Father, in a tranquil voice, 'one day in November, Michael Gorman turned up again and blackmailed you?'

'Nonsense! Who said he blackmailed me?'

Slowly Father's eyes went round to the old lady sitting quietly, very upright in her chair.

'You.' Bess Sedgwick stared at Miss Marple. 'What can *you* know about it?'

Her voice was more curious than accusing.

'The arm-chairs in this hotel have very high backs,' said Miss Marple. 'Very comfortable they are. I was sitting in one in front of the fire in the writing-room. Just resting before I went out one morning. You came in to write a letter. I suppose you didn't realize there was anyone else in the room.

492

And so – I heard your conversation with this man Gorman.'

'You listened?'

'Naturally,' said Miss Marple. 'Why not? It was a public room. When you threw up the window and called to the man outside, I had no idea that it was going to be a private conversation.'

Bess stared at her for a moment, then she nodded her head slowly.

'Fair enough,' she said. 'Yes, I see. But all the same you misunderstood what you heard. Micky didn't blackmail me. He might have thought of it – but I warned him off before he could try!' Her lips curled up again in that wide generous smile that made her face so attractive. 'I frightened him off.'

'Yes,' agreed Miss Marple. 'I think you probably did. You threatened to shoot him. You handled it – if you won't think it impertinent of me to say so – very well indeed.'

Bess Sedgwick's eyebrows rose in some amusement.

'But I wasn't the only person to hear you,' Miss Marple went on.

'Good gracious! Was the whole hotel listening?'

'The other arm-chair was also occupied.'

'By whom?'

Miss Marple closed her lips. She looked at Chief-Inspector Davy, and it was almost a pleading glance. 'If it *must* be done, *you* do it,' the glance said, 'but I can't . . .'

'Your daughter was in the other chair,' said Chief-Inspector Davy.

'Oh no!' The cry came out sharply. 'Oh *no*. Not Elvira! I see – yes, I see. She must have thought –'.

'She thought seriously enough of what she had overheard to go to Ireland and search for the truth. It wasn't difficult to discover.'

Again Bess Sedgwick said softly: 'Oh no . . .' And then: 'Poor child . . . Even now, she's never asked me a thing. She's kept it all to herself. Bottled it up inside herself. If she'd only told me I could have explained it all to her – showed her how it didn't matter.'

'She mightn't have agreed with you there,' said Chief-Inspector Davy. 'It's a funny thing, you know,' he went on, in a reminiscent, almost gossipy manner, looking like an old farmer discussing his stock and his land, 'I've learnt after a great many years' trial and error – I've learned to distrust a pattern when it's simple. Simple patterns are often too good to be true. The pattern of this murder the other night was like that. Girl says someone shot at her and missed. The commissionaire came running to save her, and copped it with a second bullet. That may be all true enough. That may be the way the girl saw it. But actually behind the appearances, things might be rather different.

'You said pretty vehemently just now, Lady Sedgwick, that there could

493

be no reason for Ladislaus Malinowski to attempt your daughter's life. Well, I'll agree with you. I don't think there was. He's the sort of young man who might have a row with a woman, pull out a knife and stick it into her. But I don't think he'd hide in an area, and wait cold-bloodedly to shoot her. But supposing he wanted to shoot *someone else*. Screams and shots – but what actually has happened is that *Michael Gorman* is dead. Suppose that was actually what was *meant* to happen. Malinowski plans it very carefully. He chooses a foggy night, hides in the area and waits until your daughter comes up the street. He knows she's coming because he has managed to arrange it that way. He fires a shot. It's not meant to hit the girl. He's careful not to let the bullet go anywhere near her, but *she* thinks it's aimed at her all right. She screams. The porter from the hotel, hearing the shot and the scream, comes rushing down the street *and then Malinowski shoots the person he's come to shoot. Michael Gorman.*'

'I don't believe a word of it! Why on earth should Ladislaus want to shoot Micky Gorman?'

'A little matter of blackmail, perhaps,' said Father.

'Do you mean that Micky was blackmailing *Ladislaus*? What about?'

'Perhaps,' said Father, 'about the things that go on at Bertram's Hotel. Michael Gorman might have found out quite a lot about that.'

'Things that go on at Bertram's Hotel? What *do* you mean?'

'It's been a good racket,' said Father. 'Well planned, beautifully executed. But nothing lasts for ever. Miss Marple here asked me the other day what was wrong with this place. Well, I'll answer that question now. Bertram's Hotel is to all intents and purposes the headquarters of one of the best and biggest crime syndicates that's been known for years.'

CHAPTER 27

There was silence for about a minute and a half. Then Miss Marple spoke.

'How *very* interesting,' she said conversationally.

Bess Sedgwick turned on her. 'You don't seem surprised, Miss Marple.'

'I'm not. Not really. There were so many curious things that didn't seem quite to fit in. It was all too good to be true – if you know what I mean. What they call in theatrical circles, a beautiful performance. But it *was* a performance – not real.

'And there were a lot of little things, people claiming a friend or an acquaintance – and turning out to be wrong.'

'These things happen,' said Chief-Inspector Davy, 'but they happened too often. Is that right, Miss Marple?'

'Yes,' agreed Miss Marple. 'People like Selina Hazy do make that kind of mistake. But there were so many other people doing it too. One couldn't help *noticing* it.'

'She notices a lot,' said Chief-Inspector Davy, speaking to Bess Sedgwick as though Miss Marple was his pet performing dog.

Bess Sedgwick turned on him sharply.

'What did you mean when you said this place was the headquarters of a Crime Syndicate? I should have said that Bertram's Hotel was the most respectable place in the world.'

'Naturally,' said Father. 'It would have to be. A lot of money, time, and thought has been spent on making it just what it is. The genuine and the phony are mixed up very cleverly. You've got a superb actor manager running the show in Henry. You've got that chap, Humfries, wonderfully plausible. He hasn't got a record in this country but he's been mixed up in some rather curious hotel dealings abroad. There are some very good character actors playing various parts here. I'll admit, if you like, that I can't help feeling a good deal of admiration for the whole set-up. It has cost this country a mint of money. It's given the C.I.D. and the provincial police forces constant headaches. Every time we seemed to be getting somewhere, and put our finger on some particular incident – it turned out to be the kind of incident that had nothing to do with anything else. But we've gone on working on it, a piece there, a piece here. A garage where stacks of number plates were kept, transferable at a moment's notice to certain cars. A firm of furniture vans, a butcher's van, a grocer's van, even one or two phony postal vans. A racing driver with a racing car covering incredible distances in incredibly few minutes, and at the other end of the scale an old clergyman jogging along in his old Morris Oxford. A cottage with a market gardener in it who lends first aid if necessary and who is in touch with a useful doctor. I needn't go into it all. The ramifications seem unending. That's one half of it. The foreign visitors who come to Bertram's are the other half. Mostly from America, or from the Dominions. Rich people above suspicion, coming here with a good lot of luxury luggage, leaving here with a good lot of luxury luggage which looks the same but isn't. Rich tourists arriving in France and not worried unduly by the Customs because the Customs don't worry tourists when they're bringing money into the country. Not the same tourists too many times. The pitcher mustn't go to the well too often. None of it's going to be easy to prove or to tie up, but it will all tie up in the end. We've made a beginning. The Cabots, for instance –'

'What about the Cabots?' asked Bess sharply.

'You remember them? Very nice Americans. Very nice indeed. They stayed here last year and they've been here again this year. They wouldn't have come a third time. Nobody ever comes here more than twice on the same racket. Yes, we arrested them when they arrived at Calais. Very well-made job, that wardrobe case they had with them. It had over three hundred thousand pounds neatly stashed. Proceeds of the Bedhampton train robbery. Of course, that's only a drop in the ocean.

'Bertram's Hotel, let me tell you, is the headquarters of the whole thing! Half the staff are in on it. Some of the guests are in on it. Some of the guests are who they say they are – some are not. The real Cabots, for instance, are in Yucatan just now. Then there was the identification racket. Take Mr Justice Ludgrove. A familiar face, bulbous nose and a wart. Quite easy to impersonate. Canon Pennyfather. A mild country clergyman, with a great white thatch of hair and notable absent-minded behaviour. His mannerisms, his way of peering over his spectacles – all very easily imitated by a good character actor.'

'But what was the use of all that?' asked Bess.

'Are you really asking me? Isn't it obvious? Mr Justice Ludgrove is seen near the scene of a bank hold-up. Someone recognizes him, mentions it. We go into it. It's all a mistake. He was somewhere else at the time. But it wasn't for a while that we realized that these were all what is sometimes called "deliberate mistakes". Nobody's bothered about the man who had looked so like him. And doesn't look particularly like him really. He takes off his make-up and stops acting his part. The whole thing brings about confusion. At one time we had a High Court judge, an Archdeacon, an Admiral, a Major-General, all seen near the scene of a crime.

'After the Bedhampton train robbery at least four vehicles were concerned before the loot arrived in London. A racing car driven by Malinowski took part in it, a false Metal Box lorry, an old-fashioned Daimler with an admiral in it, and an old clergyman with a thatch of white hair in a Morris Oxford. The whole thing was a splendid operation, beautifully planned.

'And then one day the gang had a bit of bad luck. That muddle-headed old ecclesiastic, Canon Pennyfather, went off to catch his plane on the wrong day, they turned him away from the air station, he wandered out into Cromwell Road, went to a film, arrived back here after midnight, came up to his room, of which he had the key in his pocket, opened the door, and walked in to get the shock of his life when he saw what appeared to be *himself* sitting in a chair facing him! The last thing the gang expected was to see the real Canon Pennyfather, supposed to be safely in Lucerne, walk in! His double was just getting ready to start off to play his part at Bedhampton when in walked the real man. They didn't know what to do but there was a quick reflex action from one member of the party. Humfries, I suspect. He hit the old man on the head, and he went down unconscious. Somebody, I think, was angry over that. Very angry. However, they examined the old boy, decided he was only knocked out, and would probably come round later and they went on with their plans. The false Canon Pennyfather left his room, went out of the hotel and drove to the scene of activities where he was to play his part in the relay race. What they did with the real Canon Pennyfather I don't know. I can only guess. I presume he too was moved later that night, driven down in a car, taken to the market gardener's cottage which was at a spot not too far from where the train was to be held up and where a doctor could attend to him. Then, if reports came through about Canon Pennyfather having been seen in the neighbourhood, it would all fit in. It must have been an anxious moment for all concerned until he regained consciousness and they found that at least three days had been knocked out of his remembrance.'

'Would they have killed him otherwise?' said Miss Marple.

'No,' said Father. 'I don't think they would have killed him. Someone wouldn't have let that happen. It had seemed very clear all along that whoever ran this show had an objection to murder.'

'It sounds fantastic,' said Bess Sedgwick. 'Utterly fantastic! And I don't believe you have any evidence whatever to link Ladislaus Malinowski with this rigmarole.'

'I've got plenty of evidence against Ladislaus Malinowski,' said Father. 'He's careless, you know. He hung around here when he shouldn't have. On the first occasion he came to establish connection with your daughter. They had a code arranged.'

'Nonsense. She told you herself that she didn't know him.'

'She may have told me that but it wasn't true. She's in love with him. She wants the fellow to marry her.'

'I don't believe it!'

'You're not in a position to know,' Chief-Inspector Davy pointed out. 'Malinowski isn't the sort of person who tells all his secrets and your daughter you don't know at all. You admitted as much. You were angry, weren't you, when you found out Malinowski had come to Bertram's Hotel.'

'Why should I be angry?'

'*Because you're the brains of the show*,' said Father. 'You and Henry. The financial side was run by the Hoffman brothers. They made all the arrangements with the continental banks and accounts and that sort of thing, but the boss of the syndicate, the brains that run it, and plan it, are your brains, Lady Sedgwick.'

Bess looked at him and laughed. 'I never heard anything so ridiculous!' she said.

'Oh no, it's not ridiculous at all. You've got brains, courage and daring. You've tried most things; you thought you'd turn your hand to crime. Plenty of excitement in it, plenty of risk. It wasn't the money that attracted you, I'd say, it was the fun of the whole thing. But you wouldn't stand for murder, or for undue violence. There were no killings, no brutal assaults, only nice quiet scientific taps on the head if necessary. You're a very interesting woman, you know. One of the few really interesting great criminals.'

There was silence for some few minutes. Then Bess Sedgwick rose to her feet.

'I think you must be mad.' She put her hand out to the telephone.

'Going to ring up your solicitor? Quite the right thing to do before you say too much.'

With a sharp gesture she slammed the receiver back on the hook.

'On second thoughts I hate solicitors . . . All right. Have it your own way. Yes, I ran this show. You're quite correct when you say it was fun. I loved every minute of it. It was fun scooping money from banks, trains and post offices and so-called security vans! It was fun planning and deciding; glorious fun and I'm glad I had it. The pitcher goes to the well once too often? That's what you said just now, wasn't it? I suppose it's true. Well, I've had a good run for my money! But you're wrong about Ladislaus Malinowski shooting Michael Gorman! He didn't. *I did*.' She laughed a sudden high, excited laugh. 'Never mind what it was he did, what he threatened . . . I told him I'd shoot him – Miss Marple heard me – and I *did* shoot him. I did very much what you suggested Ladislaus did. I hid in that area. When Elvira passed, I fired one shot wild, and when she screamed and Micky came running down the street, I'd got him where I wanted him, and I

498

let him have it! I've got keys to all the hotel entrances, of course. I just slipped in through the area door and up to my room. It never occurred to me you'd trace the pistol to Ladislaus – or would even suspect him. I'd pinched it from his car without his knowing. But not, I can assure you, with any idea of throwing suspicion on *him*.'

She swept round on Miss Marple. 'You're a witness to what I've said, remember. *I killed Gorman.*'

'Or perhaps you are saying so because you're in love with Malinowski,' suggested Davy.

'I'm not.' Her retort came sharply. 'I'm his good friend, that's all. Oh yes, we've been lovers in a casual kind of way, but I'm not in love with him. In all my life, I've only loved one person – John Sedgwick.' Her voice changed and softened as she pronounced the name.

'But Ladislaus is my friend. I don't want him railroaded for something he didn't do. *I killed Michael Gorman.* I've said so, and Miss Marple has heard me ... And now, dear Chief-Inspector Davy –' Her voice rose excitedly, and her laughter rang out – '*Catch me if you can.*'

With a sweep of her arm, she smashed the window with the heavy telephone set, and before Father could get to his feet, she was out of the window and edging her way rapidly along the narrow parapet. With surprising quickness in spite of his bulk, Davy had moved to the other window and flung up the sash. At the same time he blew the whistle he had taken from his pocket.

Miss Marple, getting to her feet with rather more difficulty a moment or two later, joined him. Together they stared out along the façade of Bertram's Hotel.

'She'll fall. She's climbing up a drainpipe,' Miss Marple exclaimed. 'But why *up*?'

'Going to the roof. It's her only chance and she knows it. Good God, look at her. Climbs like a cat. She looks like a fly on the side of the wall. The risks she's taking!'

Miss Marple murmured, her eyes half closing, 'She'll fall. She can't do it ...'

The woman they were watching disappeared from sight. Father drew back a little into the room.

Miss Marple asked:

'Don't you want to go and –'

Father shook his head. 'What good am I with my bulk? I've got my men posted ready for something like this. They know what to do. In a few minutes we shall know ... I wouldn't put it past her to beat the lot of them! She's a woman in a thousand, you know.' He sighed. 'One of the wild ones.

Oh, we've some of them in every generation. You can't tame them, you can't bring them into the community and make them live in law and order. They go their own way. If they're saints they go and tend lepers or something, or get themselves martyred in jungles. If they're bad lots they commit the atrocities that you don't like hearing about: and sometimes – they're just wild! They'd have been all right, I suppose, born in another age when it was everyone's hand for himself, everyone fighting to keep life in their veins. Hazards at every turn, danger all round them, and they themselves perforce dangerous to others. That world would have suited them; they'd have been at home in it. This one doesn't.'

'Did you know what she was going to do?'

'Not really. That's one of her gifts. The unexpected. She must have thought this out, you know. She knew what was coming. So she sat looking at us – keeping the ball rolling – and thinking. Thinking and planning hard. I expect – ah –' He broke off as there came the sudden roar of a car's exhaust, the screaming of wheels, and the sound of a big racing engine. He leaned out. 'She's made it, she's got to her car.'

There was more screaming as the car came round the corner on two wheels, a great roar, and the beautiful white monster came tearing up the street.

'She'll kill someone,' said Father, 'she'll kill a lot of people . . . even if she doesn't kill herself.'

'I wonder,' said Miss Marple.

'She's a good driver, of course. A damn good driver. Whoof, that was a near one!'

They heard the roar of the car racing away with the horn blaring, heard it grow fainter. Heard cries, shouts, the sound of brakes, cars hooting and pulling up and finally a great scream of tyres and a roaring exhaust and –

'She's crashed,' said Father.

He stood there very quietly waiting with the patience that was characteristic of his whole big patient form. Miss Marple stood silent beside him. Then, like a relay race, word came down along the street. A man on the pavement opposite looked up at Chief-Inspector Davy and made rapid signs with his hands.

'She's had it,' said Father heavily. 'Dead! Went about ninety miles an hour into the park railings. No other casualties bar a few slight collisions. Magnificent driving. Yes, she's dead.' He turned back into the room and said heavily, 'Well, she told her story first. You heard her.'

'Yes,' said Miss Marple. 'I heard her.' There was a pause. 'It wasn't true, of course,' said Miss Marple quietly.

Father looked at her. 'You didn't believe her, eh?'

'Did you?'

'No,' said Father. 'No, it wasn't the right story. She thought it out so that it would meet the case exactly, but it wasn't true. She didn't shoot Michael Gorman. D'you happen to know who did?'

'Of course I know,' said Miss Marple. 'The girl.'

'Ah! When did you begin to think that?'

'I always wondered,' said Miss Marple.

'So did I,' said Father. 'She was full of fear that night. And the lies she told were poor lies. But I couldn't see a motive at first.'

'That puzzled me,' said Miss Marple. 'She had found out her mother's marriage was bigamous, but would a girl do murder for that? Not nowadays! I suppose there was a money side to it?'

'Yes, it was money,' said Chief-Inspector Davy. 'Her father left her a colossal fortune. When she found out that her mother was married to Michael Gorman she realized that the marriage to Coniston hadn't been legal. She thought that meant that the money wouldn't come to her because, though she was his daughter, she wasn't legitimate. She was wrong, you know. We had a case something like that before. Depends on the terms of a will. Coniston left it quite clearly to her, naming her by name. She'd get it all right, but she didn't know that. And she wasn't going to let go of the cash.'

'Why did she need it so badly?'

Chief-Inspector Davy said grimly. 'To buy Ladislaus Malinowski. He would have married her for her money. He wouldn't have married her without it. She wasn't a fool, that girl. She knew that. But she wanted him on any terms. She was desperately in love with him.'

'I know,' said Miss Marple. She explained: 'I saw her face that day in Battersea Park . . .'

'She knew that with the money she'd get him, and without the money she'd lose him,' said Father. 'And so she planned a cold-blooded murder. She didn't hide in the area, of course. There was nobody in the area. She just stood by the railings and fired a shot and screamed, and when Michael Gorman came racing down the street from the hotel, she shot him at close quarters. Then she went on screaming. She was a cool hand. She'd no idea of incriminating young Ladislaus. She pinched his pistol because it was the only way she could get hold of one easily; and she never dreamed that he would be suspected of the crime, or that he would be anywhere in the neighbourhood that night. She thought it would be put down to some thug taking advantage of the fog. Yes, she was a cool hand. But she was afraid that night – afterwards! And her mother was afraid for her . . .'

'And now – what will you do?'

'I know she did it,' said Father, 'But I've no evidence. Maybe she'll have

501

beginner's luck ... Even the law seems to go on the principle now of allowing a dog to have one bite – translated into human terms. An experienced counsel could make great play with the sob stuff – so young a girl, unfortunate upbringing – and she's beautiful, you know.'

'Yes,' said Miss Marple. 'The children of Lucifer are often beautiful – And as we know, they flourish like the green bay tree.'

'But as I tell you, it probably won't even come to that – there's no evidence – take yourself – you'll be called as a witness – a witness to what her mother said – to her mother's confession of the crime.'

'I know,' said Miss Marple. 'She impressed it on me, didn't she? She chose death for herself, at the price of her daughter going free. She forced it on me as a dying request ...'

The connecting door to the bedroom opened. Elvira Blake came through. She was wearing a straight shift dress of pale blue. Her fair hair fell down each side of her face. She looked like one of the angels in an early primitive Italian painting. She looked from one to the other of them. She said:

'I heard a car and a crash and people shouting ... Has there been an accident?'

'I'm sorry to tell you, Miss Blake,' said Chief-Inspector Davy formally, 'that your mother is dead.'

Elvira gave a little gasp. 'Oh no,' she said. It was a faint uncertain protest.

'Before she made her escape,' said Chief-Inspector Davy, 'because it *was* an escape – she confessed to the murder of Michael Gorman.'

'You mean – she said – that it was *she* –'

'Yes,' said Father. 'That is what she *said*. Have you anything to add?'

Elvira looked for a long time at him. Very faintly she shook her head.

'No,' she said, 'I haven't anything to add.'

Then she turned and went out of the room.

'Well,' said Miss Marple. 'Are you going to let her get away with it?'

There was a pause, then Father brought down his fist with a crash on the table.

'No,' he roared – 'No, by God I'm not!'

Miss Marple nodded her head slowly and gravely.

'May God have mercy on her soul,' she said.

The Murder at the Vicarage

CHAPTER 1

It is difficult to know quite where to begin this story, but I have fixed my choice on a certain Wednesday at luncheon at the Vicarage. The conversation, though in the main irrelevant to the matter in hand, yet contained one or two suggestive incidents which influenced later developments.

I had just finished carving some boiled beef (remarkably tough by the way) and on resuming my seat I remarked, in a spirit most unbecoming to my cloth, that anyone who murdered Colonel Protheroe would be doing the world at large a service.

My young nephew, Dennis, said instantly:

'That'll be remembered against you when the old boy is found bathed in blood. Mary will give evidence, won't you, Mary? And describe how you brandished the carving knife in a vindictive manner.'

Mary, who is in service at the Vicarage as a stepping-stone to better things and higher wages, merely said in a loud, businesslike voice, 'Greens', and thrust a cracked dish at him in a truculent manner.

My wife said in a sympathetic voice: 'Has he been *very* trying?'

I did not reply at once, for Mary, setting the greens on the table with a bang, proceeded to thrust a dish of singularly moist and unpleasant dumplings under my nose. I said, 'No, thank you,' and she deposited the dish with a clatter on the table and left the room.

'It is a pity that I am such a shocking housekeeper,' said my wife, with a tinge of genuine regret in her voice.

I was inclined to agree with her. My wife's name is Griselda – a highly suitable name for a parson's wife. But there the suitability ends. She is not in the least meek.

I have always been of the opinion that a clergyman should be unmarried. Why I should have urged Griselda to marry me at the end of twenty-four hours' acquaintance is a mystery to me. Marriage, I have always held, is a serious affair, to be entered into only after long deliberation and forethought, and suitability of tastes and inclinations is the most important consideration.

Griselda is nearly twenty years younger than myself. She is most distractingly pretty and quite incapable of taking anything seriously. She is incompetent in every way, and extremely trying to live with. She treats the parish as a kind of huge joke arranged for her amusement. I have endeavoured to form her mind and failed. I am more than ever convinced that celibacy is desirable for clergy. I have frequently hinted as much to Griselda, but she has only laughed.

'My dear,' I said, 'if you would only exercise a little care –'

'I do sometimes,' said Griselda. 'But, on the whole, I think things go worse when I'm trying. I'm evidently *not* a housekeeper by nature. I find it better to leave things to Mary and just make up my mind to be uncomfortable and have nasty things to eat.'

'And what about your husband, my dear?' I said reproachfully, and proceeding to follow the example of the devil in quoting Scripture for his own ends I added: 'She looketh to the ways of her household . . .'

'Think how lucky you are not to be torn to pieces by lions,' said Griselda, quickly interrupting. 'Or burnt at the stake. Bad food and lots of dust and dead wasps is really nothing to make a fuss about. Tell me more about Colonel Protheroe. At any rate the early Christians were lucky enough not to have churchwardens.'

'Pompous old brute,' said Dennis. 'No wonder his first wife ran away from him.'

'I don't see what else she could do,' said my wife.

'Griselda,' I said sharply. 'I will not have you speaking in that way.'

'Darling,' said my wife affectionately. 'Tell me about him. What was the trouble? Was it Mr Hawes's becking and nodding and crossing himself every other minute?'

Hawes is our new curate. He has been with us just over three weeks. He has High Church views and fasts on Fridays. Colonel Protheroe is a great opposer of ritual in any form.

'Not this time. He did touch on it in passing. No, the whole trouble arose out of Mrs Price Ridley's wretched pound note.'

Mrs Price Ridley is a devout member of my congregation. Attending early service on the anniversary of her son's death, she put a pound note in the offertory bag. Later, reading the amount of the collection posted up, she was pained to observe that one ten-shilling note was the highest item mentioned.

She complained to me about it, and I pointed out, very reasonably, that she must have made a mistake.

'We're none of us so young as we were,' I said, trying to turn it off tactfully. 'And we must pay the penalty of advancing years.'

Strangely enough, my words only seemed to incense her further. She said that things had a very odd look and that she was surprised I didn't think so also. And she flounced away and, I gather, took her troubles to Colonel Protheroe. Protheroe is the kind of man who enjoys making a fuss on every conceivable occasion. He made a fuss. It is a pity he made it on a Wednesday. I teach in the Church Day School on Wednesday mornings, a proceeding that causes me acute nervousness and leaves me unsettled for the rest of the day.

'Well, I suppose he must have some fun,' said my wife, with the air of trying to sum up the position impartially. 'Nobody flutters round him and calls him the dear vicar, and embroiders awful slippers for him, and gives him bed-socks for Christmas. Both his wife and his daughter are fed up to the teeth with him. I suppose it makes him happy to feel important somewhere.'

'He needn't be offensive about it,' I said with some heat. 'I don't think he quite realized the implications of what he was saying. He wants to go over all the Church accounts – in case of defalcations – that was the word he used. Defalcations! Does he suspect me of embezzling the Church funds?'

'Nobody would suspect you of anything, darling,' said Griselda. 'You're so transparently above suspicion that really it would be a marvellous opportunity. I wish you'd embezzle the S.P.G. funds. I hate missionaries – I always have.'

I would have reproved her for that sentiment, but Mary entered at that moment with a partially cooked rice pudding. I made a mild protest, but Griselda said that the Japanese always ate half-cooked rice and had marvellous brains in consequence.

'I dare say,' she said, 'that if you had a rice pudding like this every day till Sunday, you'd preach the most marvellous sermon.'

'Heaven forbid,' I said with a shudder.

'Protheroe's coming over tomorrow evening and we're going over the accounts together,' I went on. 'I must finish preparing my talk for the C.E.M.S. today. Looking up a reference, I became so engrossed in Canon Shirley's *Reality* that I haven't got on as well as I should. What are you doing this afternoon, Griselda?'

'My duty,' said Griselda. 'My duty as the Vicaress. Tea and scandal at four-thirty.'

'Who is coming?'

Griselda ticked them off on her fingers with a glow of virtue on her face.

'Mrs Price Ridley, Miss Wetherby, Miss Hartnell, and that terrible Miss Marple.'

'I rather like Miss Marple,' I said. 'She has, at least, a sense of humour.'

'She's the worst cat in the village,' said Griselda. 'And she always knows every single thing that happens – and draws the worst inferences from it.'

Griselda, as I have said, is much younger than I am. At my time of life, one knows that the worst is usually true.

'Well, don't expect *me* in for tea, Griselda,' said Dennis.

'Beast!' said Griselda.

'Yes, but look here, the Protheroes really *did* ask me for tennis today.'

'Beast!' said Griselda again.

509

Dennis beat a prudent retreat and Griselda and I went together into my study.

'I wonder who we shall have for tea,' said Griselda, seating herself on my writing-table. 'Dr Stone and Miss Cram, I suppose, and perhaps Mrs Lestrange. By the way, I called on her yesterday, but she was out. Yes, I'm sure we shall have Mrs Lestrange for tea. It's so mysterious, isn't it, her arriving like this and taking a house down here, and hardly ever going outside it? Makes one think of detective stories. You know – *"Who was she, the mysterious woman with the pale, beautiful face? What was her past history? Nobody knew. There was something faintly sinister about her."* I believe Dr Haydock knows something about her.'

'You read too many detective stories, Griselda,' I observed mildly.

'What about you?' she retorted. 'I was looking everywhere for *The Stain on the Stairs* the other day when you were in here writing a sermon. And at last I came in to ask you if you'd seen it anywhere, and what did I find?'

I had the grace to blush.

'I picked it up at random. A chance sentence caught my eye and . . .'

'I know those chance sentences,' said Griselda. She quoted impressively, *"And then a very curious thing happened – Griselda rose, crossed the room and kissed her elderly husband affectionately."* ' She suited the action to the word.

'Is that a very curious thing?' I inquired.

'Of course it is,' said Griselda. 'Do you realize, Len, that I might have married a Cabinet Minister, a Baronet, a rich Company Promoter, three subalterns and a ne'er-do-well with attractive manners, and that instead I chose you? Didn't it astonish you very much?'

'At the time it did,' I replied. 'I have often wondered why you did it.'

Griselda laughed.

'It made me feel so powerful,' she murmured. 'The others thought me simply wonderful and of course it would have been very nice for *them* to have *me*. But I'm everything you most dislike and disapprove of, and yet you couldn't withstand me! My vanity couldn't hold out against that. It's so much nicer to be a secret and delightful sin to anybody than to be a feather in their cap. I make you frightfully uncomfortable and stir you up the wrong way the whole time, and yet you adore me madly. You adore me madly, don't you?'

'Naturally I am very fond of you, my dear.'

'Oh! Len, you adore me. Do you remember that day when I stayed up in town and sent you a wire you never got because the postmistress's sister was having twins and she forgot to send it round? The state you got into and you telephoned Scotland Yard and made the most frightful fuss.'

There are things one hates being reminded of. I had really been strangely

510

foolish on the occasion in question. I said:

'If you don't mind, dear, I want to get on with the C.E.M.S.'

Griselda gave a sigh of intense irritation, ruffled my hair up on end, smoothed it down again, said:

'You don't deserve me. You really don't. I'll have an affair with the artist. I will – really and truly. And then think of the scandal in the parish.'

'There's a good deal already,' I said mildly.

Griselda laughed, blew me a kiss, and departed through the window.

Griselda is a very irritating woman. On leaving the luncheon table, I had felt myself to be in a good mood for preparing a really forceful address for the Church of England Men's Society. Now I felt restless and disturbed.

Just when I was really settling down to it, Lettice Protheroe drifted in.

I use the word drifted advisedly. I have read novels in which young people are described as bursting with energy – *joie de vivre*, the magnificent vitality of youth . . . Personally, all the young people I come across have the air of animal wraiths.

Lettice was particularly wraith-like this afternoon. She is a pretty girl, very tall and fair and completely vague. She drifted through the French window, absently pulled off the yellow beret she was wearing and murmured vaguely with a kind of far-away surprise: 'Oh! it's you.'

There is a path from Old Hall through the woods which comes out by our garden gate, so that most people coming from there come in at that gate and up to the study window instead of going a long way round by the road and coming to the front door. I was not surprised at Lettice coming in this way, but I did a little resent her attitude.

If you come to a Vicarage, you ought to be prepared to find a Vicar.

She came in and collapsed in a crumpled heap in one of my big armchairs. She plucked aimlessly at her hair, staring at the ceiling.

'Is Dennis anywhere about?'

'I haven't seen him since lunch. I understood he was going to play tennis at your place.'

'Oh!' said Lettice. 'I hope he isn't. He won't find anybody there.'

'He said you asked him.'

'I believe I did. Only that was Friday. And today's Tuesday.'

'It's Wednesday,' I said.

'Oh, how dreadful!' said Lettice. 'That means that I've forgotten to go to lunch with some people for the third time.'

Fortunately it didn't seem to worry her much.

'Is Griselda anywhere about?'

'I expect you'll find her in the studio in the garden – sitting to Lawrence Redding.'

'There's been quite a shemozzle about him,' said Lettice. 'With father, you know. Father's dreadful.'

'What was the she – whatever it was about?' I inquired.

'About his painting me. Father found out about it. Why shouldn't I be painted in my bathing dress? If I go on a beach in it, why shouldn't I be painted in it?'

Lettice paused and then went on.

'It's really absurd – father forbidding a young man the house. Of course, Lawrence and I simply shriek about it. I shall come and be done here in your studio.'

'No, my dear,' I said. 'Not if your father forbids it.'

'Oh! dear,' said Lettice, sighing. 'How tiresome everyone is. I feel shattered. Definitely. If only I had some money I'd go away, but without it I can't. If only father would be decent and die, I should be all right.'

'You must not say things like that, Lettice.'

'Well, if he doesn't want me to want him to die, he shouldn't be so horrible over money. I don't wonder mother left him. Do you know, for years I believed she was dead. What sort of a young man did she run away with? Was he nice?'

'It was before your father came to live here.'

'I wonder what's become of her. I expect Anne will have an affair with someone soon. Anne hates me – she's quite decent to me, but she hates me. She's getting old and she's doesn't like it. That's the age you break out, you know.'

I wondered if Lettice was going to spend the entire afternoon in my study.

'You haven't seen my gramophone records, have you?' she asked.

'No.'

'How tiresome. I know I've left them somewhere. And I've lost the dog. And my wrist watch is somewhere, only it doesn't much matter because it won't go. Oh! dear, I am so sleepy. I can't think why, because I didn't get up till eleven. But life's very shattering, don't you think? Oh! dear, I must go. I'm going to see Dr Stone's barrow at three o'clock.'

I glanced at the clock and remarked that it was now five-and-twenty to four.

'Oh! Is it? How dreadful. I wonder if they've waited or if they've gone without me. I suppose I'd better go down and do something about it.'

She got up and drifted out again, murmuring over her shoulder:

'You'll tell Dennis, won't you?'

I said 'Yes' mechanically, only realizing too late that I had no idea what it was I was to tell Dennis. But I reflected that in all probability it did not matter. I fell to cogitating on the subject of Dr Stone, a well-known archaeologist who had recently come to stay at the Blue Boar, whilst he superintended the excavation of a barrow situated on Colonel Protheroe's property. There had already been several disputes between him and the Colonel. I was amused at his appointment to take Lettice to see the operations.

It occurred to me that Lettice Protheroe was something of a minx. I wondered how she would get on with the archaeologist's secretary, Miss Cram. Miss Cram is a healthy young woman of twenty-five, noisy in manner, with a high colour, fine animal spirits and a mouth that always seems to have more than its full share of teeth.

Village opinion is divided as to whether she is no better than she should be, or else a woman of iron virtue who purposes to become Mrs Stone at an early opportunity. She is in every way a great contrast to Lettice.

I could imagine that the state of things at Old Hall might not be too happy. Colonel Protheroe had married again some five years previously. The second Mrs Protheroe was a remarkably handsome woman in a rather unusual style. I had always guessed that the relations between her and her stepdaughter were not too happy.

I had one more interruption. This time, it was my curate, Hawes. He wanted to know the details of my interview with Protheroe. I told him that the colonel had deplored his 'Romish tendencies' but that the real purpose of his visit had been on quite another matter. At the same time, I entered a protest of my own, and told him plainly that he must conform to my ruling. On the whole, he took my remarks very well.

I felt rather remorseful when he had gone for not liking him better. These irrational likes and dislikes that one takes to people are, I am sure, very unChristian.

With a sigh, I realized that the hands of the clock on my writing-table pointed to a quarter to five, a sign that it was really half-past four, and I made my way to the drawing-room.

Four of my parishioners were assembled there with teacups. Griselda sat behind the tea table trying to look natural in her environment, but only succeeded in looking more out of place than usual.

I shook hands all round and sat down between Miss Marple and Miss Wetherby.

Miss Marple is a white-haired old lady with a gentle, appealing manner – Miss Wetherby is a mixture of vinegar and gush. Of the two Miss Marple is much the more dangerous.

'We were just talking,' said Griselda in a honeysweet voice, 'about Dr Stone and Miss Cram.'

A ribald rhyme concocted by Dennis shot through my head.

'Miss Cram doesn't give a damn.'

I had a sudden yearning to say it out loud and observe the effect, but fortunately I refrained. Miss Wetherby said tersely:

'No nice girl would do it,' and shut her thin lips disapprovingly.

'Do what?' I inquired.

'Be a secretary to an unmarried man,' said Miss Wetherby in a horrified tone.

'Oh! my dear,' said Miss Marple. '*I* think married ones are the worst. Remember poor Mollie Carter.'

'Married men living apart from their wives are, of course, notorious,' said Miss Wetherby.

'And even some of the ones living with their wives,' murmured Miss Marple. 'I remember . . .'

I interrupted these unsavoury reminiscences.

'But surely,' I said, 'in these days a girl can take a post in just the same way as a man does.'

'To come away to the country? And stay at the same hotel?' said Mrs Price Ridley in a severe voice.

Miss Wetherby murmured to Miss Marple in a low voice:

'And all the bedrooms on the same floor . . .'

Miss Hartnell, who is weather-beaten and jolly and much dreaded by the poor, observed in a loud, hearty voice:

'The poor man will be caught before he knows where he is. He's as innocent as a babe unborn, you can see that.'

Curious what turns of phrase we employ. None of the ladies present would have dreamed of alluding to an actual baby till it was safely in the cradle, visible to all.

'Disgusting, I call it,' continued Miss Hartnell, with her usual tactlessness. 'The man must be at least twenty-five years older than she is.'

Three female voices rose at once making disconnected remarks about the Choir Boys' Outing, the regrettable incident at the last Mothers' Meeting, and the draughts in the church. Miss Marple twinkled at Griselda.

'Don't you think,' said my wife, 'that Miss Cram may just like having an interesting job? And that she considers Dr Stone just as an employer?'

There was a silence. Evidently none of the four ladies agreed. Miss Marple broke the silence by patting Griselda on the arm.

'My dear,' she said, 'you are very young. The young have such innocent minds.'

Griselda said indignantly that she hadn't got at all an innocent mind.

'Naturally,' said Miss Marple, unheeding of the protest, 'you think the best of everyone.'

'Do you really think she wants to marry that bald-headed dull man?'

'I understand he is quite well off,' said Miss Marple. 'Rather a violent temper, I'm afraid. He had quite a serious quarrel with Colonel Protheroe the other day.'

Everyone leaned forward interestedly.

'Colonel Protheroe accused him of being an ignoramus.'

'How like Colonel Protheroe, and how absurd,' said Mrs Price Ridley.

'Very like Colonel Protheroe, but I don't know about it being absurd,' said Miss Marple, 'You remember the woman who came down here and said she represented Welfare, and after taking subscriptions she was never heard of again and proved to having nothing whatever to do with Welfare. One is so inclined to be trusting and take people at their own valuation.'

I should never have dreamed of describing Miss Marple as trusting.

'There's been some fuss about that young artist, Mr Redding, hasn't there?' asked Miss Wetherby.

Miss Marple nodded.

'Colonel Protheroe turned him out of the house. It appears he was painting Lettice in her bathing dress.'

'I always *thought* there was something between them,' said Mrs Price Ridley. 'That young fellow is always mouching off up there. Pity the girl hasn't got a mother. A stepmother is never the same thing.'

'I dare say Mrs Protheroe does her best,' said Miss Hartnell.

'Girls are so sly,' deplored Mrs Price Ridley.

'Quite a romance, isn't it?' said the softer-hearted Miss Wetherby. 'He's a very good-looking young fellow.'

'But loose,' said Miss Hartnell. 'Bound to be. An artist! Paris! Models! The Altogether!'

'Painting her in her bathing dress,' said Mrs Price Ridley. 'Not quite nice.'

'He's painting me too,' said Griselda.

'But not in your bathing dress, dear,' said Miss Marple.

'It might be worse,' said Griselda solemnly.

'Naughty girl,' said Miss Hartnell, taking the joke broadmindedly. Everybody else looked slightly shocked.

'Did dear Lettice tell you of the trouble?' asked Miss Marple of me.

'Tell me?'

'Yes. I saw her pass through the garden and go round to the study window.'

Miss Marple always sees everything. Gardening is as good as a smoke screen, and the habit of observing birds through powerful glasses can always be turned to account.

'She mentioned it, yes,' I admitted.

'Mr Hawes looked worried,' said Miss Marple. 'I hope he hasn't been working too hard.'

'Oh!' cried Miss Wetherby excitedly. 'I quite forgot. I knew I had some news for you. I saw Dr Haydock coming out of Mrs Lestrange's cottage.'

Everyone looked at each other.

'Perhaps she's ill,' suggested Mrs Price Ridley.

'It must have been very sudden, if so,' said Miss Hartnell. 'For I saw her walking round her garden at three o'clock this afternoon, and she seemed in perfect health.'

'She and Dr Haydock must be old acquaintances,' said Mrs Price Ridley. 'He's been very quiet about it.'

'It's curious,' said Miss Wetherby, 'that he's never *mentioned* it.'

'As a matter of fact –' said Griselda in a low, mysterious voice, and stopped. Everyone leaned forward excitely.

'I happen to *know*,' said Griselda impressively. 'Her husband was a missionary. Terrible story. *He was eaten*, you know. Actually eaten. And she was forced to become the chief's head wife. Dr Haydock was with an expedition and rescued her.'

For a moment excitement was rife, then Miss Marple said reproachfully, but with a smile: 'Naughty girl!'

She tapped Griselda reprovingly on the arm.

'Very unwise thing to do my dear. If you make up these things, people are quite likely to believe them. And sometimes that leads to complications.'

A distinct frost had come over the assembly. Two of the ladies rose to take their departure.

'I wonder if there *is* anything between young Lawrence Redding and Lettice Protheroe,' said Miss Wetherby. 'It certainly looks like it. What do you think, Miss Marple?'

Miss Marple seemed thoughtful.

'I shouldn't have said so myself. Not *Lettice*. *Quite* another person I should have said.'

'But Colonel Protheroe must have thought . . .'

'He has always struck me as rather a stupid man,' said Miss Marple. 'The kind of man who gets the wrong idea into his head and is obstinate about it. Do you remember Joe Bucknell who used to keep the Blue Boar? Such a to-do about his daughter carrying on with young Bailey. And all the time it was that minx of a wife of his.'

She was looking full at Griselda as she spoke, and I suddenly felt a wild surge of anger.

'Don't you think, Miss Marple,' I said, 'that we're all inclined to let our tongues run away with us too much. Charity thinketh no evil, you know. Inestimable harm may be done by foolish wagging of tongues in ill-natured gossip.'

'Dear Vicar,' said Miss Marple, 'You are so unworldly. I'm afraid that observing human nature for as long as I have done, one gets not to expect

517

very much from it. I dare say the idle tittle-tattle is very wrong and unkind, but it so often true, isn't it?'

That last Parthian shot went home.

518

CHAPTER 3

'Nasty old cat,' said Griselda, as soon as the door was closed.

She made a face in the direction of the departing visitors and then looked at me and laughed.

'Len, do you really suspect me of having an affair with Lawrence Redding?'

'My dear, of course not.'

'But you thought Miss Marple was hinting at it. And you rose to my defence simply beautifully. Like – like an angry tiger.'

A momentary uneasiness assailed me. A clergyman of the Church of England ought never to put himself in the position of being described as an angry tiger.

'I felt the occasion could not pass without a protest,' I said. 'But Griselda, I wish you would be a little more careful in what you say.'

'Do you mean the cannibal story?' she asked. 'Or the suggestion that Lawrence was painting me in the nude! If they only knew that he was painting me in a thick cloak with a very high fur collar – the sort of thing that you could go quite purely to see the Pope in – not a bit of sinful flesh showing anywhere! In fact, it's all marvellously pure. Lawrence never even attempts to make love to me – I can't think why.'

'Surely knowing that you're a married woman –'

'Don't pretend to come out of the ark, Len. You know very well that an attractive young woman with an elderly husband is a kind of gift from heaven to a young man. There must be some other reason – it's not that I'm unattractive – I'm not.'

'Surely you don't want him to make love to you?'

'N-n-o,' said Griselda, with more hesitation than I thought becoming.

'If he's in love with Lettice Protheroe –'

'Miss Marple didn't seem to think he was.'

'Miss Marple may be mistaken.'

'She never is. That kind of old cat is always right.' She paused a minute and then said, with a quick sidelong glance at me: 'You do believe me, don't you? I mean, that there's nothing between Lawrence and me.'

'My dear Griselda,' I said, surprised. 'Of course.'

My wife came across and kissed me.

'I wish you weren't so terribly easy to deceive, Len. You'd believe me whatever I said.'

'I should hope so. But, my dear, I do beg you to guard your tongue and be careful of what you say. These women are singularly deficient in humour, remember, and take everything seriously.'

'What they need,' said Griselda, 'is a little immorality in their lives. Then they wouldn't be so busy looking for it in other people's.'

And on this she left the room, and glancing at my watch I hurried out to pay some visits that ought to have been made earlier in the day.

That Wednesday evening service was sparsely attended as usual, but when I came out through the church, after disrobing in the vestry, it was empty save for a woman who stood staring up at one of our windows. We have some rather fine old stained glass, and indeed the church itself is well worth looking at. She turned at my footsteps, and I saw that it was Mrs Lestrange.

We both hesitated a moment, and then I said:

'I hope you like our little church.'

'I've been admiring the screen,' she said.

Her voice was pleasant, low, yet very distinct, with a clearcut enunciation. She added:

'I'm so sorry to have missed your wife yesterday.'

We talked a few minutes longer about the church. She was evidently a cultured woman who knew something of Church history and architecture. We left the building together and walked down the road, since one way to the Vicarage led past her house. As we arrived at the gate, she said pleasantly:

'Come in, won't you? And tell me what you think of what I have done.'

I accepted the invitation. Little Gates had formerly belonged to an Anglo-Indian colonel, and I could not help feeling relieved by the disappearance of the brass tables and Burmese idols. It was furnished now very simply, but in exquisite taste. There was a sense of harmony and rest about it.

Yet I wondered more and more what had brought such a woman as Mrs Lestrange to St Mary Mead. She was so very clearly a woman of the world that it seemed a strange taste to bury herself in a country village.

In clear light of her drawing-room I had an opportunity of observing her closely for the first time.

She was a very tall woman. Her hair was gold with a tinge of red in it. Her eyebrows and eyelashes were dark, whether by art or by nature I could not decide. If she was, as I thought, made up, it was done very artistically. There was something Sphinxlike about her face when it was in repose and she had the most curious eyes I have ever seen – they were almost golden in shade.

Her clothes were perfect and she had all the ease of manner of a well-bred woman, and yet there was something about her that was incongruous and baffling. You felt that she was a mystery. The word Griselda had used

520

occurred to me – *sinister*. Absurd, of course, and yet – was it so absurd? The thought sprang unbidden into my mind: 'This woman would stick at nothing.'

Our talk was on most normal lines – pictures, books, old churches. Yet somehow I got very strongly the impression that there was something else – something of quite a different nature that Mrs Lestrange wanted to say to me.

I caught her eye on me once or twice, looking at me with a curious hesitancy, as though she were unable to make up her mind. She kept the talk, I noticed, strictly to impersonal subjects. She made no mention of a husband or relations.

But all the time there was that strange urgent appeal in her glance. It seemed to say: 'Shall I tell you? I want to. Can't you help me?'

Yet in the end it died away – or perhaps it had all been my fancy. I had the feeling that I was being dismissed. I rose and took my leave. As I went out of the room, I glanced back and saw her staring after me with a puzzled, doubtful expression. On an impulse I came back:

'If there is anything I can do –'

She said doubtfully: 'It's very kind of you –'

We were both silent. Then she said:

'I wish I knew. It's difficult. No, I don't think anyone can help me. But thank you for offering to do so.'

That seemed final, so I went. But as I did so, I wondered. We are not used to mysteries in St Mary Mead.

So much is this the case that as I emerged from the gate I was pounced upon. Miss Hartnell is very good at pouncing in a heavy and cumbrous way.

'*I* saw you!' she exclaimed with ponderous humour. 'And I *was* so excited. Now you can tell us all about it.'

'About what?'

'The mysterious lady! Is she a widow or has she a husband somewhere?'

'I really couldn't say. She didn't tell me.'

'How very peculiar. One would think she would be certain to mention something casually. It almost looks, doesn't it, as though she had a reason for not speaking?'

'I really don't see that.'

'Ah! But as dear Miss Marple says, you are so unworldly, dear vicar. Tell me, has she known Dr Haydock long?'

'She didn't mention him, so I don't know.'

'Really? But what did you talk about then?'

'Pictures, music, books,' I said truthfully.

Miss Hartnell, whose only topics of conversation are the purely personal, looked suspicious and unbelieving. Taking advantage of a momentary hestitation on her part as to how to proceed next, I bade her good-night and walked rapidly away.

I called in at a house farther down the village and returned to the Vicarage by the garden gate, passing, as I did so, the danger point of Miss Marple's garden. However, I did not see how it was humanly possible for the news of my visit to Mrs Lestrange to have yet reached her ears, so I felt reasonably safe.

As I latched the gate, it occurred to me that I would just step down to the shed in the garden which young Lawrence Redding was using as a studio, and see for myself how Griselda's portrait was progressing.

I append a rough sketch here which will be useful in the light of after happenings, only sketching in such details as are necessary.

I had no idea there was anyone in the studio. There had been no voices from within to warn me, and I suppose that my own footsteps made no noise upon the grass.

I opened the door and then stopped awkwardly on the threshold. For there were two people in the studio, and the man's arms were round the woman and he was kissing her passionately.

The two people were the artist, Lawrence Redding, and Mrs Protheroe.

I backed out precipitately and beat a retreat to my study. There I sat down in a chair, took out my pipe, and thought things over. The discovery had come as a great shock to me. Especially since my conversation with Lettice that afternoon, I had felt fairly certain that there was some kind of understanding growing up between her and the young man. Moreover, I was convinced that she herself thought so. I felt positive that she had no idea of the artist's feelings for her stepmother.

A nasty tangle. I paid a grudging tribute to Miss Marple. She had not been deceived but had evidently suspected the true state of things with a fair amount of accuracy. I had entirely misread her meaning glance at Griselda.

I had never dreamt of considering Mrs Protheroe in the matter. There has always been rather a suggestion of Caesar's wife about Mrs Protheroe – a quiet, self-contained woman whom one would not suspect of any great depths of feeling.

I had got to this point in my meditations when a tap on my study window aroused me. I got up and went to it. Mrs Protheroe was standing outside. I opened the window and she came in, not waiting for an invitation on my part. She crossed the room in a breathless sort of way and dropped down on the sofa.

I had the feeling that I had never really seen her before. The quiet self-contained woman that I knew had vanished. In her place was a

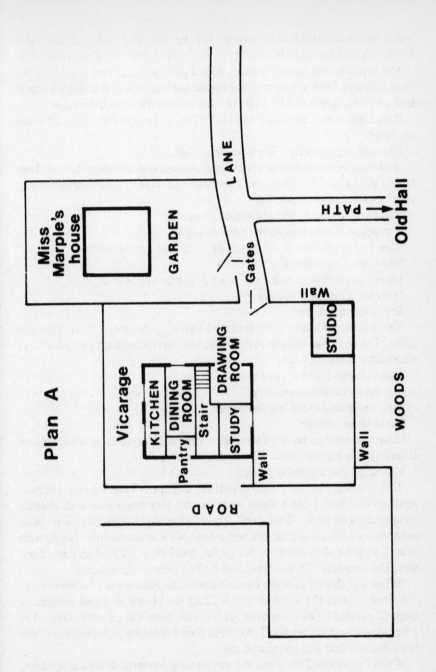

Plan A

quick-breathing, desperate creature. For the first time I realized that Anne Protheroe was beautiful.

She was a brown-haired woman with a pale face and very deep set grey eyes. She was flushed now and her breast heaved. It was as though a statue had suddenly come to life. I blinked my eyes at the transformation.

'I thought it best to come,' she said. 'You – you saw just now?' I bowed my head.

She said very quietly: 'We love each other . . .'

And even in the middle of her evident distress and agitation she could not keep a little smile from her lips. The smile of a woman who sees something very beautiful and wonderful.

I still said nothing, and she added presently:

'I suppose to you that seems very wrong?'

'Can you expect me to say anything else, Mrs Protheroe?'

'No – no, I suppose not.'

I went on, trying to make my voice as gentle as possible:

'You are a married woman –'

She interrupted me.

'Oh! I know – I know. Do you think I haven't gone over all that again and again? I'm not a bad woman really – I'm not. And things aren't – aren't – as you might think they are.'

I said gravely: 'I'm glad of that.'

She asked rather timorously:

'Are you going to tell my husband?'

I said rather dryly:

'There seems to be a general idea that a clergyman is incapable of behaving like a gentleman. That is not true.'

She threw me a grateful glance.

'I'm so unhappy. Oh! I'm so dreadfully unhappy. I can't go on. I simply can't go on. And I don't know what to do.' Her voice rose with slightly hysterical note in it. 'You don't know what my life is like. I've been miserable with Lucius from the beginning. No woman could be happy with him. I wish he were dead . . . It's awful, but I do . . . I'm desperate. I tell you, I'm desperate.' She started and looked over at the window.

'What was that? I thought I heard someone? Perhaps it's Lawrence.'

I went over to the window which I had not closed as I had thought. I stepped out and looked down the garden, but there was no one in sight. Yet I was almost convinced that I, too, had heard someone. Or perhaps it was her certainty that had convinced me.

When I re-entered the room she was leaning forward, drooping her head down. She looked the picture of despair. She said again:

'I don't know what to do. I don't know what to do.'

I came and sat down beside her. I said the things I thought it was my duty to say, and tried to say them with the necessary conviction, uneasily conscious all the time that that same morning I had given voice to the sentiment that a world without Colonel Protheroe in it would be improved for the better.

Above all, I begged her to do nothing rash. To leave her home and her husband was a very serious step.

I don't suppose I convinced her. I have lived long enough in the world to know that arguing with anyone in love is next door to useless, but I do think my words brought to her some measure of comfort.

When she rose to go, she thanked me, and promised to think over what I had said.

Nevertheless, when she had gone, I felt very uneasy. I felt that hitherto I had misjudged Anne Protheroe's character. She impressed me now as a very desperate woman, the kind of woman who would stick at nothing once her emotions were aroused. And she was desperately, wildly, madly in love with Lawrence Redding, a man several years younger than herself. I didn't like it.

I had entirely forgotten that we had asked Lawrence Redding to dinner that night. When Griselda burst in and scolded me, pointing out that it lacked two minutes to dinner time, I was quite taken aback.

'I hope everthing will be all right,' Griselda called up the stairs after me. 'I've thought over what you said at lunch, and I've really thought of some quite good things to eat.'

I may say, in passing, that our evening meal amply bore out Griselda's assertion that things went much worse when she tried than when she didn't. The menu was ambitious in conception, and Mary seemed to have taken a perverse pleasure in seeing how best she could alternate undercooking and overcooking. Some oysters which Griselda had ordered, and which would seem to be beyond the reach of incompetence, we were, unfortunately, not able to sample as we had nothing in the house to open them with – an omission which was discovered only when the moment for eating them arrived.

I have rather doubted whether Lawrence Redding would put in an appearance. He might very easily have sent an excuse.

However, he arrived punctually enough, and the four of us went in to dinner.

Lawrence Redding has an undeniably attractive personality. He is, I suppose, about thirty years of age. He has dark hair, but his eyes are of a brilliant, almost startling blue. He is the kind of young man who does everything well. He is good at games, an excellent shot, a good amateur actor, and can tell a first-rate story. He is capable of making any party go. He has, I think, Irish blood in his veins. He is not, at all, one's idea of the typical artist. Yet I believe he is a clever painter in the modern style. I know very little of painting myself.

It was only natural that on this particular evening he should appear a shade *distrait*. On the whole, he carried off things very well. I don't think Griselda or Dennis noticed anything wrong. Probably I should not have noticed anything myself if I had not known beforehand.

Griselda and Dennis were particularly gay – full of jokes about Dr Stone and Miss Cram – the Local Scandal! It suddenly came home to me with something of a pang that Dennis is nearer Griselda's age than I am. He calls me Uncle Len, but her Griselda. It gave me, somehow, a lonely feeling.

I must, I think, have been upset by Mrs Protheroe. I'm not usually given to such unprofitable reflections.

Griselda and Dennis went rather far now and then, but I hadn't the heart to check them. I have always thought it a pity that the mere presence of a clergyman should have a dampening effect.

Lawrence took a gay part in the conversation. Nevertheless I was aware of his eyes continually straying to where I sat, and I was not surprised when after dinner he manoeuvred to get me into the study.

As soon as we were alone his manner changed.

'You've surprised our secret, sir,' he said. 'What are you going to do about it?'

I could speak far more plainly to Redding than I could to Mrs Protheroe, and I did so. He took it very well.

'Of course,' he said, when I had finished, 'you're bound to say all this. You're a parson. I don't mean that in any way offensively. As a matter of fact I think you're probably right. But this isn't the usual sort of thing between Anne and me.'

I told him that people had been saying that particular phrase since the dawn of time, and a queer little smile creased his lips.

'You mean everyone thinks their case is unique? Perhaps so. But one thing you must believe.'

He assured me that so far – 'there was nothing wrong in it.' Anne, he said, was one of the truest and most loyal women that ever lived. What was going to happen he didn't know.

'If this were only a book,' he said gloomily, 'the old man would die – and a good riddance to everybody.'

I reproved him.

'Oh! I didn't mean I was going to stick him in the back with a knife, though I'd offer my best thanks to anyone else who did so. There's not a soul in the world who's got a good word to say for him. I rather wonder the first Mrs Protheroe didn't do him in. I met her once, years ago, and she looked quite capable of it. One of those calm dangerous women. He goes blustering along, stirring up trouble everywhere, mean as the devil, and with a particularly nasty temper. You don't know what Anne has had to stand from him. If I had a penny in the world I'd take her away without any more ado.'

Then I spoke to him very earnestly. I begged him to leave St Mary Mead. By remaining there, he could only bring greater unhappiness on Anne Protheroe than was already her lot. People would talk, the matter would get to Colonel Protheroe's ears – and things would be made infinitely worse for her.

Lawrence protested.

'Nobody knows a thing about it except you, padre.'

'My dear young man, you underestimate the detective instinct of village life. In St Mary Mead everyone knows your most intimate affairs. There is

527

no detective in England equal to a spinster lady of uncertain age with plenty of time on her hands.'

He said easily that that was all right. Everyone thought it was Lettice.

'Has it occurred to you,' I asked, 'that possibly Lettice might think so herself?'

He seemed quite surprised by the idea. Lettice, he said, didn't care a hang about him. He was sure of that.

'She's a queer sort of girl,' he said. 'Always seems in a kind of dream, and yet underneath I believe she's really rather practical. I believe all that vague stuff is a pose. Lettice knows jolly well what she's doing. And there's a funny vindictive streak in her. The queer thing is that she hates Anne. Simply loathes her. And yet Anne's been a perfect angel to her always.'

I did not, of course, take his word for this last. To infatuated young men, their *inamorata* always behaves like an angel. Still, to the best of my observation, Anne had always behaved to her stepdaughter with kindness and fairness. I had been surprised myself that afternoon at the bitterness of Lettice's tone.

We had to leave the conversation there, because Griselda and Dennis burst in upon us and said I was not to make Lawrence behave like an old fogy.

'Oh dear!' said Griselda, throwing herself into an arm-chair. 'How I would like a thrill of some kind. A murder – or even a burglary.'

'I don't suppose there's anyone much worth burgling,' said Lawrence, trying to enter into her mood. 'Unless we stole Miss Hartnell's false teeth.'

'They do click horribly,' said Griselda. 'But you're wrong about there being no one worth while. There's some marvellous old silver at Old Hall. Trencher salts and a Charles II Tazza – all kinds of things like that. Worth thousands of pounds, I believe.'

'The old man would probably shoot you with an army revolver,' said Dennis. 'Just the sort of thing he'd enjoy doing.'

'Oh, we'd get in first and hold him up!' said Griselda. 'Who's got a revolver?'

'I've got a Mauser pistol,' said Lawrence.

'Have you? How exciting. Why do you have it?'

'Souvenir of the war,' said Lawrence briefly.

'Old Protheroe was showing the silver to Stone today,' volunteered Dennis. 'Old Stone was pretending to be no end interested in it.'

'I thought they'd quarrelled about the barrow,' said Griselda.

'Oh, they've made that up!' said Dennis. 'I can't think what people want to grub about in barrows for, anyway.'

'The man Stone puzzles me,' sand Lawrence. 'I think he must be very absent-minded. You'd swear sometimes he knew nothing about his own subject.'

'That's love,' said Dennis. 'Sweet Gladys Cram, you are no sham. Your teeth are white and fill me with delight. Come, fly with me, my bride to be. And at the Blue Boar, on the bedroom floor –'

'That's enough, Dennis,' I said.

'Well,' said Lawrence Redding, 'I must be off. Thank you very much, Mrs Clement, for a very pleasant evening.'

Griselda and Dennis saw him off. Dennis returned to the study alone. Something had happened to ruffle the boy. He wandered about the room aimlessly, frowning and kicking the furniture.

Our furniture is so shabby already that it can hardly be damaged further, but I felt impelled to utter a mild protest.

'Sorry,' said Dennis.

He was silent for a moment and then burst out:

'What an absolutely rotten thing gossip is!'

I was a little surprised. 'What's the matter?' I asked.

'I don't know whether I ought to tell you.'

I was more and more surprised.

'It's such an absolutely rotten thing,' Dennis said again. 'Going round and saying things. Not even saying them. Hinting them. No, I'm damned – sorry – if I'll tell you! It's too absolutely rotten.'

I looked at him curiously, but I did not press him further. I wondered very much, though. It is very unlike Dennis to take anything to heart.

Griselda came in at that moment.

'Miss Wetherby's just rung up,' she said. 'Mrs Lestrange went out at a quarter past eight and hasn't come in yet. Nobody knows where she's gone.'

'Why should they know?'

'But it isn't to Dr Haydock's. Miss Wetherby does know that, because she telephoned to Miss Hartnell who lives next door to him and who would have been sure to see her.'

'It is a mystery to me,' I said, 'how anyone ever gets any nourishment in this place. They must eat their meals standing up by the window so as to be sure of not missing anything.'

'And that's not all,' said Griselda, bubbling with pleasure. 'They've found out about the Blue Boar. Dr Stone and Miss Cram have got rooms next door to each other, BUT' – she waved an impressive forefinger – '*no communicating door!*'

'That,' I said, 'must be very disappointing to everybody.'

At which Griselda laughed.

Thursday started badly. Two of the ladies of my parish elected to quarrel about the church decorations. I was called in to adjudicate between two middle-aged ladies, each of whom was literally trembling with rage. If it had not been so painful, it would have been quite an interesting physical phenomenon.

Then I had to reprove two of our choir boys for persistent sweet sucking during the hours of divine service, and I had an uneasy feeling that I was not doing the job as wholeheartedly as I should have done.

Then our organist, who is distinctly 'touchy', had taken offence and had to be smoothed down.

And four of my poorer parishioners declared open rebellion against Miss Hartnell, who came to me bursting with rage about it.

I was just going home when I met Colonel Protheroe. He was in high good-humour, having sentenced three poachers, in his capacity as magistrate.

'Firmness,' he shouted in his stentorian voice. He is slightly deaf and raises his voice accordingly as deaf people often do. 'That's what's needed nowadays – firmness! Make an example. That rogue Archer came out yesterday and is vowing vengeance against me, I hear. Impudent scoundrel. Threatened men live long, as the saying goes. I'll show him what his vengeance is worth next time I catch him taking my pheasants. Lax! We're too lax nowadays! I believe in showing a man up for what he is. You're always being asked to consider a man's wife and children. Damned nonsense. Fiddlesticks. Why should a man escape the consequences of his acts just because he whines about his wife and children? It's all the same to me – no matter what a man is – doctor, lawyer, clergyman, poacher, drunken wastrel – if you catch him on the wrong side of the law, let the law punish him. You agree with me, I'm sure.'

'You forget,' I said. 'My calling obliges me to respect one quality above all others – the quality of mercy.'

'Well, I'm a just man. No one can deny that.'

I did not speak, and he said sharply:

'Why don't you answer? A penny for your thoughts, man.'

I hesitated, then I decided to speak.

'I was thinking,' I said, 'that when my time comes, I should be sorry if the only plea I had to offer was that of justice. Because it might mean that only justice would be meted out to me . . .'

'Pah! What we need is a little militant Christianity. I've always done my duty, I hope. Well, no more of that. I'll be along this evening, as I said. We'll make it a quarter past six instead of six, if you don't mind. I've got to see a man in the village.'

'That will suit me quite well.'

He flourished his stick and strode away. Turning, I ran into Hawes. I thought he looked distinctly ill this morning. I had meant to upbraid him mildly for various matters in his province which had been muddled or shelved, but seeing his white strained face, I felt that the man was ill.

I said as much, and he denied it, but not very vehemently. Finally he confessed that he was not feeling too fit, and appeared ready to accept my advice of going home to bed.

I had a hurried lunch and went out to do some visits. Griselda had gone to London by the cheap Thursday train.

I came in about a quarter to four with the intention of sketching the outline of my Sunday sermon, but Mary told me that Mr Redding was waiting for me in the study.

I found him pacing up and down with a worried face. He looked white and haggard.

He turned abruptly at my entrance.

'Look here, sir. I've been thinking over what you said yesterday. I've had a sleepless night thinking about it. You're right. I've got to cut and run.'

'My dear boy,' I said.

'You were right in what you said about Anne. I'll only bring trouble on her by staying here. She's – she's too good for anything else. I see I've got to go. I've made things hard enough for her as it is, heaven help me.'

'I think you have made the only decision possible,' I said. 'I know that it is a hard one, but believe me, it will be for the best in the end.'

I could see that he thought that that was the kind of thing easily said by someone who didn't know what he was talking about.

'You'll look after Anne? She needs a friend.'

'You can rest assured that I will do everything in my power.'

'Thank you, sir.' He wrung my hand. 'You're a good sort, Padre. I shall see her to say goodbye this evening, and I shall probably pack up and go tomorrow. No good prolonging the agony. Thanks for letting me have the shed to paint in. I'm sorry not to have finished Mrs Clement's portrait.'

'Don't worry about that, my dear boy. Goodbye, and God bless you.'

When he had gone I tried to settle down to my sermon, but with very poor success. I kept thinking of Lawrence and Anne Protheroe.

I had rather an unpalatable cup of tea, cold and black, and at half-past five the telephone rang. I was informed that Mr Abbott of Lower Farm was dying and would I please come at once.

I rang up Old Hall immediately, for Lower Farm was nearly two miles away and I could not possibly get back by six-fifteen. I have never succeeded in learning to ride a bicycle.

I was told, however, that Colonel Protheroe had just started out in the car, so I departed, leaving word with Mary that I had been called away, but would try to be back by six-thirty or soon after.

It was nearer seven than half-past six when I approached the Vicarage gate on my return. Before I reached it, it swung open and Lawrence Redding came out. He stopped dead on seeing me, and I was immediately struck by his appearance. He looked like a man who was on the point of going mad. His eyes stared in a peculiar manner, he was deathly white, and he was shaking and twitching all over.

I wondered for a moment whether he could have been drinking, but repudiated the idea immediately.

'Hallo,' I said, 'have you been to see me again? Sorry I was out. Come back now. I've got to see Protheroe about some accounts – but I dare say we shan't be long.'

'Protheroe,' he said. He began to laugh. 'Protheroe? You're going to see Protheroe? Oh, you'll see Protheroe all right! Oh, my God – yes!'

I stared. Instinctively I stretched out a hand towards him. He drew sharply aside.

'No,' he almost cried out. 'I've got to get away – to think. I've got to think. I must think.'

He broke into a run and vanished rapidly down the road towards the village, leaving me staring after him, my first idea of drunkenness recurring.

Finally I shook my head, and went on to the Vicarage. The front door is always left open, but nevertheless I rang the bell. Mary came, wiping her hands on her apron.

'So you're back at last,' she observed.

'Is Colonel Protheroe here?' I asked.

'In the study. Been here since a quarter past six.'

'And Mr Redding's been here?'

'Come a few minutes ago. Asked for you. I told him you'd be back at any minute and that Colonel Protheroe was waiting in the study, and he said he'd wait too, and went there. He's there now.'

'No, he isn't,' I said. 'I've just met him going down the road.'

'Well, I didn't hear him leave. He can't have stayed more than a couple of minutes. The mistress isn't back from town yet.'

I nodded absent-mindedly. Mary beat a retreat to the kitchen quarters and I went down the passage and opened the study door.

After the dusk of the passage, the evening sunshine that was pouring into the room made my eyes blink. I took a step or two across the floor and then stopped dead.

For a moment I could hardly take in the meaning of the scene before me.

Colonel Protheroe was lying sprawled across my writing table in a horrible unnatural position. There was a pool of some dark fluid on the desk by his head, and it was slowly dripping on to the floor with a horrible drip, drip, drip.

I pulled myself together and went across to him. His skin was cold to the touch. The hand that I raised fell back lifeless. The man was dead – shot through the head.

I went to the door and called Mary. When she came I ordered her to run as fast as she could and fetch Dr Haydock, who lives just at the corner of the road. I told her there had been an accident.

Then I went back and closed the door to await the doctor's coming.

Fortunately, Mary found him at home. Haydock is a good fellow, a big, fine, strapping man with an honest, rugged face.

His eyebrows went up when I pointed silently across the room. But, like a true doctor, he showed no signs of emotion. He bent over the dead man, examining him rapidly. Then he straightened himself and looked across at me.

'Well?' I asked.

'He's dead right enough – been dead half an hour, I should say.'

'Suicide?'

'Out of the question, man. Look at the position of the wound. Besides, if he shot himself, where's the weapon?'

True enough, there was no sign of any such thing.

'We'd better not mess around with anything,' said Haydock. 'I'd better ring up the police.'

He picked up the receiver and spoke into it. He gave the facts as curtly as possible and then replaced the telephone and came across to where I was sitting.

'This is a rotten business. How did you come to find him?'

I explained. 'Is – is it murder?' I asked rather faintly.

'Looks like it. Mean to say, what else can it be? Extraordinary business. Wonder who had a down on the poor old fellow. Of course I know he wasn't popular, but one isn't often murdered for that reason – worse luck.'

'There's one rather curious thing,' I said. 'I was telephoned for this afternoon to go to a dying parishioner. When I got there everyone was very surprised to see me. The sick man was very much better than he had been for some days, and his wife flatly denied telephoning for me at all.'

Haydock drew his brows together.

'That's suggestive – very. You were being got out of the way. Where's your wife?'

'Gone up to London for the day.'

'And the maid?'

'In the kitchen – right at the other side of the house.'

'Where she wouldn't be likely to hear anything that went on in here. It's a nasty business. Who knew that Protheroe was coming here this evening?'

'He referred to the fact this morning in the village street at the top of his voice as usual.'

'Meaning that the whole village knew it? Which they always do in any case. Know of anyone who had a grudge against him?'

The thought of Lawrence Redding's white face and staring eyes came to my mind. I was spared answering by a noise of shuffling feet in the passage outside.

'The police,' said my friend, and rose to his feet.

Our police force was represented by Constable Hurst, looking very important but slightly worried.

'Good evening, gentlemen,' he greeted us. 'The Inspector will be here any minute. In the meantime I'll follow out his instructions. I understand Colonel Protheroe's been found shot – in the Vicarage.'

He paused and directed a look of cold suspicion at me, which I tried to meet with a suitable bearing of conscious innocence.

He moved over to the writing table and announced:

'Nothing to be touched until the Inspector comes.'

For the convenience of my readers I append a sketch plan of the room.

He got out his notebook, moistened his pencil and looked expectantly at both of us.

I repeated my story of discovering the body. When he had got it all down, which took some time, he turned to the doctor.

'In your opinion, Dr Haydock, what was the cause of death?'

'Shot through the head at close quarters.'

'And the weapon?'

'I can't say with certainty until we get the bullet out. But I should say in all probability the bullet was fired from a pistol of small calibre – say a Mauser .25.'

I started, remembering our conversation of the night before, and Lawrence Redding's admission. The police constable brought his cold, fish-like eye round on me.

'Did you speak, sir?'

I shook my head. Whatever suspicions I might have, they were no more than suspicions, and as such to be kept to myself.

'When, in your opinion, did the tragedy occur?'

The doctor hesitated for a minute before he answered. Then he said:

'The man has been dead just over half an hour, I should say. Certainly

535

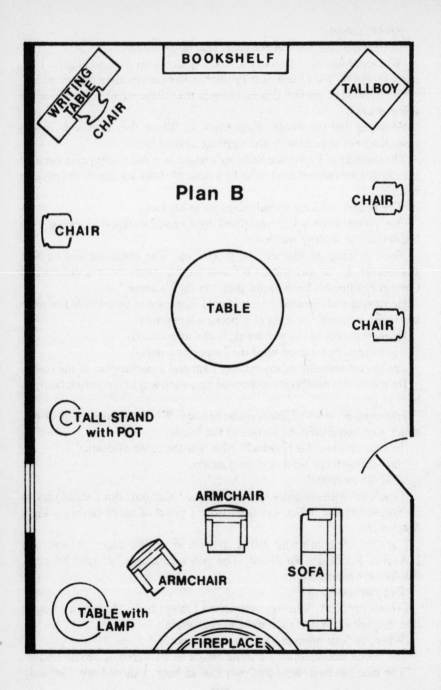

not longer.'

Hurst turned to me. 'Did the girl hear anything?'

'As far as I know she heard nothing,' I said. 'But you had better ask her.'

But at this moment Inspector Slack arrived, having come by car from Much Benham, two miles away.

All that I can say of Inspector Slack is that never did a man more determinedly strive to contradict his name. He was a dark man, restless and energetic in manner, with black eyes that snapped ceaselessly. His manner was rude and overbearing in the extreme.

He acknowledged our greetings with a curt nod, seized his subordinate's note-book, perused it, exchanged a few curt words with him in an undertone, then strode over to the body.

'Everything's been messed up and pulled about, I suppose,' he said.

'I've touched nothing,' said Haydock.

'No more have I,' I said.

The Inspector busied himself for some time peering at the things on the table and examining the pool of blood.

'Ah!' he said in a tone of triumph. 'Here's what we want. Clock overturned when he fell forward. That'll give us the time of the crime. Twenty-two minutes past six. What time did you say death occurred, doctor?'

'I said about half an hour, but –'

The Inspector consulted his watch.

'Five minutes past seven. I got word about ten minutes ago, at five minutes to seven. Discovery of the body was at about a quarter to seven. I understand you were fetched immediately. Say you examined it at ten minutes to – Why, that brings it to the identical second almost!'

'I don't guarantee the time absolutely,' said Haydock. 'That is an approximate estimate.'

'Good enough, sir, good enough.'

I had been trying to get a word in.

'About the clock –'

'If you'll excuse me, sir, I'll ask you any questions I want to know. Time's short. What I want is absolute silence.'

'Yes, but I'd like to tell you –'

'Absolute silence,' said the Inspector, glaring at me ferociously. I gave him what he asked for.

He was still peering about the writing table.

'What was he sitting here for?' he grunted. 'Did he want to write a note – Hallo – what's this?'

He held up a piece of note-paper triumphantly. So pleased was he with his

537

find that he permitted us to come to his side and examine it with him.

It was a piece of Vicarage note-paper, and it was headed at the top 6.20.

'Dear Clement' – it began – 'Sorry I cannot wait any longer, but I must . . .'

Here the writing tailed off in a scrawl.

'Plain as a pikestaff,' said Inspector Slack triumphantly. 'He sits down here to write this, an enemy comes softly in through the window and shoots him as he writes. What more do you want?'

'I'd just like to say –' I began.

'Out of the way, if you please, sir. I want to see if there are footprints.'

He went down on his hands and knees, moving towards the open window.

'I think you ought to know –' I said obstinately.

The Inspector rose. He spoke without heat, but firmly.

'We'll go into all that later. I'd be obliged if you gentlemen will clear out of here. Right out, if you please.'

We permitted ourselves to be shooed out like children.

Hours seemed to have passed – yet it was only a quarter-past seven.

'Well,' said Haydock. 'That's that. When that conceited ass wants me, you can send him over to the surgery. So long.'

'The mistress is back,' said Mary, making a brief appearance from the kitchen. Her eyes were round and agog with excitement. 'Come in about five minutes ago.'

I found Griselda in the drawing-room. She looked frightened, but excited.

I told her everything and she listened attentively.

'The letter is headed 6.20,' I ended. 'And the clock fell over and has stopped at 6.22.'

'Yes,' said Griselda. 'But that clock, didn't you tell him that it was always kept a quarter of an hour fast?'

'No,' I said. 'I didn't. He wouldn't let me. I tried my best.' Griselda was frowning in a puzzled manner.

'But, Len,' she said, 'that makes the whole thing perfectly extraordinary. Because when that clock said twenty past six it was really only five minutes past, and at five minutes past I don't suppose Colonel Protheroe had even arrived at the house.'

We puzzled over the business of the clock for some time, but we could make nothing of it. Griselda said I ought to make another effort to tell Inspector Slack about it, but on that point I was feeling what I can only describe as 'mulish.'

Inspector Slack had been abominably and most unnecessarily rude. I was looking forward to a moment when I could produce my valuable contribution and effect his discomfiture. I would then say in a tone of mild reproach:

'If you had only listened to me, Inspector Slack . . .'

I expected that he would at least speak to me before he left the house, but to our surprise we learned from Mary that he had departed, having locked up the study door and issued orders that no one was to attempt to enter the room.

Griselda suggested going up to Old Hall.

'It will be so awful for Anne Protheroe – with the police and everything,' she said. 'Perhaps I might be able to do something for her.'

I cordially approved of this plan, and Griselda set off with instructions that she was to telephone to me if she thought that I could be of any use or comfort to either of the ladies.

I now proceeded to ring up the Sunday School teachers, who were coming at 7.45 for their weekly preparation class. I thought that under the circumstances it would be better to put them off.

Dennis was the next person to arrive on the scene, having just returned from a tennis party. The fact that murder had taken place at the Vicarage seemed to afford him acute satisfaction.

'Fancy being right on the spot in a murder case,' he exclaimed. 'I've always wanted to be right in the midst of one. Why have the police locked up the study? Wouldn't one of the other door keys fit it?'

I refused to allow anything of the sort to be attempted. Dennis gave in with a bad grace. After extracting every possible detail from me he went out into the garden to look for footprints, remarking cheerfully that it was lucky it was only old Protheroe, whom everyone disliked.

His cheerful callousness rather grated on me, but I reflected that I was perhaps being hard on the boy. At Dennis's age a detective story is one of the best things in life, and to find a real detective story, complete with corpse, waiting on one's own front doorstep, so to speak, is bound to send a healthy-minded boy into the seventh heaven of enjoyment. Death means very little to a boy of sixteen.

Griselda came back in about an hour's time. She had seen Anne

Protheroe, having arrived just after the Inspector had broken the news to her.

On hearing that Mrs Protheroe had last seen her husband in the village about a quarter to six, and that she had no light of any kind to throw upon the matter, he had taken his departure, explaining that he would return on the morrow for a fuller interview.

'He was quite decent in his way,' said Griselda grudgingly.

'How did Mrs Protheroe take it?' I asked.

'Well – she was very quiet – but then she always is.'

'Yes,' I said. 'I can't imagine Anne Protheroe going into hysterics.'

'Of course it was a great shock. You could see that. She thanked me for coming and said she was very grateful but that there was nothing I could do.'

'What about Lettice?'

'She was out playing tennis somewhere. She hadn't got home yet.' There was a pause, and then Griselda said:

'You know, Len, she was really very quiet – very queer indeed.'

'The shock,' I suggested.

'Yes – I suppose so. And yet –' Griselda furrowed her brows perplexedly. 'It wasn't like that, somehow. She didn't seem so much bowled over as – well – terrified.'

'Terrified?'

'Yes – not showing it, you know. At least not meaning to show it. But a queer, watchful look in her eyes. I wonder if she has a sort of idea who did kill him. She asked again and again if anyone were suspected.'

'Did she?' I said thoughtfully.

'Yes. Of course Anne's got marvellous self-control, but one could see that she was terribly upset. More so than I would have thought, for after all it wasn't as though she were so devoted to him. I should have said she rather disliked him, if anything.'

'Death alters one's feelings sometimes,' I said.

'Yes, I suppose so.'

Dennis came in and was full of excitement over a footprint he had found in one of the flower beds. He was sure that the police had overlooked it and that it would turn out to be the turning point of the mystery.

I spent a troubled night. Dennis was up and about and out of the house long before breakfast to 'study the latest developments', as he said.

Nevertheless it was not he, but Mary, who brought us the morning's sensational bit of news.

We had just sat down to breakfast when she burst into the room, her cheeks red and her eyes shining, and addressed us with her customary lack

540

of ceremony.

'Would you believe it? The baker's just told me. They've arrested young Mr Redding.'

'Arrested Lawrence,' cried Griselda incredulously. 'Impossible. It must be some stupid mistake.'

'No mistake about it, mum,' said Mary with a kind of gloating exultation. 'Mr Redding, he went there himself and gave himself up. Last night, last thing. Went right in, threw down the pistol on the table, and "I did it," he says. Just like that.'

She looked at us both, nodded her head vigorously, and withdrew satisfied with the effect she had produced. Griselda and I stared at each other.

'Oh! It isn't true,' said Griselda. 'It *can't* be true.'

She noticed my silence, and said: 'Len, *you* don't think it's true?'

I found it hard to answer her. I sat silent, thoughts whirling through my head.

'He must be mad,' said Griselda. 'Absolutely mad. Or do you think they were looking at the pistol together and it suddenly went off?'

'That doesn't sound at all a likely thing to happen.'

'But it must have been an accident of some kind. Because there's not a shadow of a motive. What earthly reason could Lawrence have for killing Colonel Protheroe?'

I could have answered that question very decidedly, but I wished to spare Anne Protheroe as far as possible. There might still be a chance of keeping her name out of it.

'Remember they had had a quarrel,' I said.

'About Lettice and her bathing dress. Yes, but that's absurd; and even if he and Lettice were engaged secretly – well, that's not a reason for killing her father.'

'We don't know what the true facts of the case may be, Griselda.'

'You *do* believe it, Len! Oh! How can you! I tell you, I'm *sure* Lawrence never touched a hair of his head.'

'Remember, I met him just outside the gate. He looked like a madman.'

'Yes, but – oh! It's impossible.'

'There's the clock, too,' I said. 'This explains the clock. Lawrence must have put it back to 6.20 with the idea of making an alibi for himself. Look how Inspector Slack fell into the trap.'

'You're wrong, Len. Lawrence knew about that clock being fast. "Keeping the vicar up to time!" he used to say. Lawrence would never have made the mistake of putting it back to 6.22. He'd have put the hands somewhere possible – like a quarter to seven.'

541

'He mayn't have known what time Protheroe got here. Or he may have simply forgotten about the clock being fast.'

Griselda disagreed.

'No, if you were committing a murder, you'd be awfully careful about things like that.'

'You don't know, my dear,' I said mildly. 'You've never done one.'

Before Griselda could reply, a shadow fell across the breakfast table, and a very gentle voice said:

'I hope I am not intruding. You must forgive me. But in the sad circumstances – the very sad circumstances . . .'

It was our neighbour, Miss Marple. Accepting our polite disclaimers, she stepped in through the window, and I drew up a chair for her. She looked faintly flushed and quite excited.

'Very terrible, is it not? Poor Colonel Protheroe. Not a very pleasant man, perhaps, and not exactly popular, but it's none the less sad for that. And actually shot in the Vicarage study, I understand?'

I said that that had indeed been the case.

'But the dear vicar was not here at the time?' Miss Marple questioned of Griselda. I explained where I had been.

'Mr Dennis is not with you this morning?' said Miss Marple, glancing round.

'Dennis,' said Griselda, 'fancies himself as an amateur detective. He is very excited about a footprint he found in one of the flower beds, and I fancy has gone off to tell the police about it.'

'Dear, dear,' said Miss Marple. 'Such a to-do, is it not? And Mr Dennis thinks he knows who committed the crime. Well, I suppose we all think we know.'

'You mean it is obvious?' said Griselda.

'No, dear, I didn't mean that at all. I dare say everyone thinks it is somebody different. That is why it is so important to have *proofs*. I, for instance, am quite *convinced* I know who did it. But I must admit I haven't one shadow of proof. One must, I know, be very careful of what one says at a time like this – criminal libel, don't they call it? I had made up my mind to be *most* careful with Inspector Slack. He sent word he would come and see me this morning, but now he has just phoned up to say it won't be necessary after all.'

'I suppose, since the arrest, it isn't necessary,' I said.

'The arrest?' Miss Marple leaned forward, her cheeks pink with excitement. 'I didn't know there had been an arrest.'

It is so seldom that Miss Marple is worse informed than we are that I had taken it for granted that she would know the latest developments.

'It seems we have been talking at cross purposes,' I said. 'Yes, there has been an arrest – Lawrence Redding.'

'Lawrence Redding?' Miss Marple seemed very surprised. 'Now I should not have thought –'

Griselda interrupted vehemently.

'I can't believe it even now. No, not though he has actually confessed.'

'Confessed?' said Miss Marple. 'You say he has confessed? Oh! dear, I see I have been sadly at sea – yes, sadly at sea.'

'I can't help feeling it must have been some kind of an accident,' said Griselda. 'Don't you think so, Len? I mean his coming forward to give himself up looks like that.'

Miss Marple leant forward eagerly.

'He gave himself up, you say?'

'Yes.'

'Oh!' said Miss Marple, with a deep sigh. 'I am so glad – so very glad.'

I looked at her in some surprise.

'It shows a true state of remorse, I suppose,' I said.

'Remorse?' Miss Marple looked very surprised. 'Oh, but surely, dear, dear vicar, you don't think that he is guilty?'

It was my turn to stare.

'But since he has confessed –'

'Yes, but that just proves it, doesn't it? I mean that he had nothing to do with it.'

'No,' I said. 'I may be dense, but I can't see that it does. If you have not committed a murder, I cannot see the object of pretending you have.'

'Oh, of course, there's a reason!' said Miss Marple. 'Naturally. There's always a reason, isn't there? And young men are so hot-headed and often prone to believe the worst.'

She turned to Griselda.

'Don't you agree with me, my dear?'

'I – I don't know,' said Griselda. 'It's difficult to know what to think, I can't see any reason for Lawrence behaving like a perfect idiot.'

'If you had seen his face last night –' I began.

'Tell me,' said Miss Marple.

I described my homecoming while she listened attentively.

When I had finished she said:

'I know that I am very often rather foolish and don't take in things as I should, but I really do not see your point.

'It seems to me that if a young man had made up his mind to the great wickedness of taking a fellow creature's life, he would not appear distraught about it afterwards. It would be a premeditated and cold-blooded action and though the murderer might be a little flurried and possibly might make some small mistake, I do not think it likely he would fall into a state of agitation such as you describe. It is difficult to put oneself in such a position, but I cannot imagine getting into a state like that myself.'

'We don't know the circumstances,' I argued. 'If there was a quarrel, the shot may have been fired in a sudden gust of passion, and Lawrence might afterwards have been appalled at what he had done. Indeed, I prefer to think that this is what did actually occur.'

'I know, dear Mr Clement, that there are many ways we prefer to look at things. But one must actually take facts as they are, must one not? And it does not seem to me that the facts bear the interpretation you put upon them. Your maid distinctly stated that Mr Redding was only in the house a couple of minutes, not long enough, surely, for a quarrel such as you describe. And then again, I understand the colonel was shot through the back of the head while he was writing a letter – at least that is what my maid told me.'

'Quite true,' said Griselda. 'He seems to have been writing a note to say he couldn't wait any longer. The note was dated 6.20, and the clock on the table was overturned and had stopped at 6.22, and that's just what has been puzzling Len and myself so frightfully.'

She explained our custom of keeping the clock a quarter of an hour fast.

'Very curious,' said Miss Marple. 'Very curious indeed. But the note seems to me even more curious still. I mean –'

She stopped and looked round. Lettice Protheroe was standing outside the window. She came in, nodding to us and murmuring 'Morning.'

She dropped into a chair and said, with rather more animation than usual:

'They've arrested Lawrence, I hear.'

'Yes,' said Griselda. 'It's been a great shock to us.'

'I never really thought anyone would murder father,' said Lettice. She was obviously taking a pride in letting no hint of distress or emotion escape her. 'Lots of people wanted to, I'm sure. There are times when I'd have liked to do it myself.'

'Won't you have something to eat or drink, Lettice?' asked Griselda.

'No, thank you. I just drifted round to see if you'd got my beret here – a queer little yellow one. I think I left it in the study the other day.'

'If you did, it's there still,' said Griselda. 'Mary never tidies anything.'

'I'll go and see,' said Lettice, rising. 'Sorry to be such a bother, but I seem to have lost everything else in the hat line.'

'I'm afraid you can't get it now,' I said. 'Inspector Slack has locked the room up.'

'Oh, what a bore! Can't we get in through the window?'

'I'm afraid not. It is latched on the inside. Surely, Lettice, a yellow beret won't be much good to you at present?'

'You mean mourning and all that? I shan't bother about mourning. I think it's an awfully archaic idea. It's a nuisance about Lawrence – yes, it's a nuisance.'

She got up and stood frowning abstractedly.

'I suppose it's all on account of me and my bathing dress. So silly, the whole thing . . .'

Griselda opened her mouth to say something, but for some unexplained reason shut it again.

A curious smile came to Lettice's lips.

'I think,' she said softly, 'I'll go home and tell Anne about Lawrence being arrested.'

She went out of the window again. Griselda turned to Miss Marple. 'Why did you step on my foot?'

The old lady was smiling.

'I thought you were going to say something, my dear. And it is often so much better to let things develop on their own lines. I don't think, you know, that that child is half so vague as she pretends to be. She's got a very definite idea in her head and she's acting upon it.'

Mary gave a loud knock on the dining-room door and entered hard upon it.

'What is it?' said Griselda. 'And Mary, you must remember not to knock on doors. I've told you about it before.'

'Thought you might be busy,' said Mary. 'Colonel Melchett's here. Wants to see the master.'

Colonel Melchett is Chief Constable of the county. I rose at once.

'I thought you wouldn't like my leaving him in the hall, so I put him in the drawing-room,' went on Mary. 'Shall I clear?'

'Not yet,' said Griselda. 'I'll ring.'

She turned to Miss Marple and I left the room.

Colonel Melchett is a dapper little man with a habit of snorting suddenly and unexpected. He has red hair and rather keen bright blue eyes.

'Good morning, vicar,' he said. 'Nasty business, eh? Poor old Protheroe. Not that I liked him. I didn't. Nobody did, for that matter. Nasty bit of work for you, too. Hope it hasn't upset your missus?'

I said Griselda had taken it very well.

'That's lucky. Rotten thing to happen in one's house. I must say I'm surprised at young Redding – doing it the way he did. No sort of consideration for anyone's feelings.'

A wild desire to laugh came over me, but Colonel Melchett evidently saw nothing odd in the idea of a murderer being considerate, so I held my peace.

'I must say I was rather taken aback when I heard the fellow had marched in and given himself up,' continued Colonel Melchett, dropping on to a chair.

'How did it happen exactly?'

'Last night. About ten o'clock. Fellow rolls in, throws down a pistol, and says: "Here I am. I did it." Just like that.'

'What account does he give of the business?'

'Precious little. He was warned, of course, about making a statement. But he merely laughed. Said he came here to see you – found Protheroe here. They had words and he shot him. Won't say what the quarrel was about. Look here, Clement – just between you and me, do you know anything about it? I've heard rumours – about his being forbidden the house and all that. What was it – did he seduce the daughter, or what? We don't want to bring the girl into it more than we can help for everybody's sake. Was that the trouble?'

'No,' I said. 'You can take it from me that it was something quite different, but I can't say more at the present juncture.'

He nodded and rose.

'I'm glad to know. There's a lot of talk. Too many women in this part of the world. Well, I must get along. I've got to see Haydock. He was called out to some case or other, but he ought to be back by now. I don't mind telling you I'm sorry about Redding. He always struck me as a decent young chap. Perhaps they'll think out some kind of defence for him. After-effects of war, shell shock, or something. Especially if no very adequate motive turns up. I must be off. Like to come along?'

I said I would like to very much, and we went out together.

Haydock's house is next door to mine. His servant said the doctor had just come in and showed us into the dining-room, where Haydock was sitting down to a steaming plate of eggs and bacon. He greeted me with an amiable nod.

'Sorry I had to go out. Confinement case. I've been up most of the night, over your business. I've got the bullet for you.'

He shoved a little box along the table. Melchett examined it.

'Point two five?'

Haydock nodded.

'I'll keep the technical details for the inquest,' he said. 'All you want to know is that death was practically instantaneous. Silly young fool, what did he want to do it for? Amazing, by the way, that nobody heard the shot.'

'Yes,' said Melchett, 'that surprises me.'

'The kitchen window gives on the other side of the house,' I said. 'With the study door, the pantry door, and the kitchen door all shut, I doubt if you would hear anything, and there was no one but the maid in the house.'

'H'm,' said Melchett. 'It's odd, all the same. I wonder the old lady – what's her name – Marple, didn't hear it. The study window was open.'

'Perhaps she did,' said Haydock.

'I don't think she did,' said I. 'She was over at the Vicarage just now and she didn't mention anything of the kind which I'm certain she would have done if there had been anything to tell.'

'May have heard it and paid no attention to it – thought it was a car back-firing.'

I struck me that Haydock was looking much more jovial and good-humoured this morning. He seemed like a man who was decorously trying to subdue unusually good spirits.

'Or what about a silencer?' he added. 'That's quite likely. Nobody would hear anything then.'

Melchett shook his head.

'Slack didn't find anything of the kind, and he asked Redding, and Redding didn't seem to know what he was talking about at first and then denied point blank using anything of the kind. And I suppose one can take his word for it.'

'Yes, indeed, poor devil.'

'Damned young fool,' said Colonel Melchett. 'Sorry, Clement. But he really is! Somehow one can't get used to thinking of him as a murderer.'

'Any motive?' asked Haydock, taking a final draught of coffee and pushing back his chair.

'He says they quarrelled and he lost his temper and shot him.'

'Hoping for manslaughter, eh?' The doctor shook his head. 'That story doesn't hold water. He stole up behind him as he was writing and shot him through the head. Precious little "quarrel" about that.'

547

'Anyway, there wouldn't have been time for a quarrel,' I said, remembering Miss Marple's words. 'To creep up, shoot him, alter the clock hands back to 6.20, and leave again would have taken him all his time. I shall never forget his face when I met him outside the gate, or the way he said, "You want to see Protheroe – oh, you'll see him all right!" That in itself ought to have made me suspicious of what had just taken place a few minutes before.'

Haydock stared at me.

'What do you mean – what had just taken place? When do you think Redding shot him?'

'A few minutes before I got to the house.'

The doctor shook his head.

'Impossible. Plumb impossible. He'd been dead much longer than that.'

'But, my dear man,' cried Colonel Melchett, 'you said yourself that half an hour was only an approximate estimate.'

'Half an hour, thirty-five minutes, twenty-five minutes, twenty minutes – possibly, but less, no. Why, the body would have been warm when I got to it.'

We stared at each other. Haydock's face had changed. It had gone suddenly grey and old. I wondered at the change in him.

'But, look here, Haydock.' The colonel found his voice. 'If Redding admits shooting him at a quarter to seven –'

Haydock sprang to his feet.

'I tell you it's impossible,' he roared. 'If Redding says he killed Protheroe at a quarter to seven, then Redding lies. Hang it all, I tell you I'm a doctor, and I know. The blood had begun to congeal.'

'If Redding is lying,' began Melchett. He stopped, shook his head.

'We'd better go down to the police station and see him,' he said.

548

We were rather silent on our way down to the police station. Haydock drew behind a little and murmured to me:

'You know I don't like the look of this. I don't like it. There's something here we don't understand.'

He looked thoroughly worried and upset.

Inspector Slack was at the police station and presently we found ourselves face to face with Lawrence Redding.

He looked pale and strained but quite composed – marvellously so, I thought, considering the circumstances. Melchett snorted and hummed, obviously nervous.

'Look here, Redding,' he said, 'I understand you made a statement to Inspector Slack here. You state you went to the Vicarage at approximately a quarter to seven, found Protheroe there, quarrelled with him, shot him, and came away. I'm not reading it over to you, but that's the gist of it.'

'Yes.'

'I'm going to ask a few questions. You've already been told that you needn't answer them unless you choose. Your solicitor –'

Lawrence interrupted.

'I've nothing to hide. I killed Protheroe.'

'Ah! well –' Melchett snorted. 'How did you happen to have a pistol with you?'

Lawrence hesitated. 'It was in my pocket.'

'You took it with you to the Vicarage?'

'Yes.'

'Why?'

'I always take it.'

He had hesitated again before answering, and I was absolutely sure that he was not speaking the truth.

'Why did you put the clock back?'

'The clock?' He seemed puzzled.

'Yes, the hands pointed to 6.22.'

A look of fear sprang up in his face.

'Oh! that – yes. I – I altered it.'

Haydock spoke suddenly.

'Where did you shoot Colonel Protheroe?'

'In the study at the Vicarage.'

'I mean in what part of the body?'

'Oh! – I – through the head, I think. Yes, through the head.'

'Aren't you sure?'

549

'Since you know, I can't see why it is necessary to ask me.'

It was a feeble kind of bluster. There was some commotion outside. A constable without a helmet brought in a note.

'For the vicar. It says very urgent on it.'

I tore it open and read:

'Please – please – come to me. I don't know what to do. It is all too awful. I want to tell someone. Please come immediately and bring anyone you like with you. – Anne Protheroe.'

I gave Melchett a meaning glance. He took the hint. We all went out together. Glancing over my shoulder, I had a glimpse of Lawrence Redding's face. His eyes were riveted on the paper in my hand, and I have hardly ever seen such a terrible look of anguish and despair in any human being's face.

I remembered Anne Protheroe sitting on my sofa and saying:

'I'm a desperate woman,' and my heart grew heavy within me. I saw now the possible reason for Lawrence Redding's heroic self-accusation. Melchett was speaking to Slack.

'Have you got any line on Redding's movements earlier in the day? There's some reason to think he shot Protheroe earlier than he says. Get on to it, will you?'

He turned to me and without a word I handed him Anne Protheroe's letter. He read it and pursed up his lips in astonishment. Then he looked at me inquiringly.

'Is this what you were hinting at this morning?'

'Yes. I was not sure then if it was my duty to speak. I am quite sure now.' And I told him of what I had seen that night in the studio.

The colonel had a few words with the inspector and then we set off for Old Hall. Dr Haydock came with us.

A very correct butler opened the door, with just the right amount of gloom in his bearing.

'Good morning,' said Melchett. 'Will you ask Mrs Protheroe's maid to tell her we are here and would like to see her, and then return here and answer a few questions.'

The butler hurried away and presently returned with the news that he had despatched the message.

'Now let's hear something about yesterday,' said Colonel Melchett. 'Your master was in to lunch?'

'Yes, sir.'

'And in his usual spirits?'

'As far as I could see, yes, sir.'

'What happened after that?'

'After luncheon Mrs Protheroe went to lie down and the colonel went to his study. Miss Lettice went out to a tennis party in the two-seater. Colonel and Mrs Protheroe had tea at four-thirty, in the drawing-room. The car was ordered for five-thirty to take them to the village. Immediately after they had left Mr Clement rang up' – he bowed to me – 'I told him they had started.'

'H'm,' said Colonel Melchett. 'When was Mr Redding last here?'

'On Tuesday afternoon, sir.'

'I understand that there was a disagreement between them?'

'I believe so, sir. The colonel gave me orders that Mr Redding was not to be admitted in future.'

'Did you overhear the quarrel at all?' asked Colonel Melchett bluntly.

'Colonel Protheroe, sir, had a very loud voice, especially when it was raised in anger. I was unable to help overhearing a few words here and there.'

'Enough to tell you the cause of the dispute?'

'I understood, sir, that it had to do with a portrait Mr Redding had been painting – a portrait of Miss Lettice,'

Melchett grunted.

'Did you see Mr Redding when he left?'

'Yes, sir, I let him out.'

'Did he seem angry?'

'No, sir; if I may say so, he seemed rather amused.'

'Ah! He didn't come to the house yesterday?'

'No, sir.'

'Anyone else come?'

'Not yesterday, sir.'

'Well, the day before?'

'Mr Dennis Clement came in the afternoon. And Dr Stone was here for some time. And there was a lady in the evening.'

'A lady?' Melchett was surprised. 'Who was she?'

The butler couldn't remember her name. It was a lady he had not seen before. Yes, she had given her name, and when he told her that the family were at dinner, she had said that she would wait. So he had shown her into the little morning-room.

She had asked for Colonel Protheroe, not Mrs Protheroe. He had told the colonel and the colonel had gone to the morning-room directly dinner was over.

How long had the lady stayed? He thought about half an hour. The

551

colonel himself had let her out. Ah! Yes, he remembered her name now. The lady had been a Mrs Lestrange.

This was a surprise.

'Curious,' said Melchett. 'Really very curious.'

But we pursued the matter no further, for at that moment a message came that Mrs Protheroe would see us.

Anne was in bed. Her face was pale and her eyes very bright. There was a look on her face that puzzled me – a kind of grim determination. She spoke to me.

'Thank you for coming so promptly,' she said. 'I see you've understood what I meant by bringing anyone you liked with you.' She paused.

'It's best to get it over quickly, isn't it?' she said. She gave a queer, half-pathetic little smile. 'I suppose you're the person I ought to say it to, Colonel Melchett. You see, it was I who killed my husband.'

Colonel Melchett said gently:

'My dear Mrs Protheroe –'

'Oh! It's quite true. I suppose I've said it rather bluntly, but I never can go into hysterics over anything. I've hated him for a long time, and yesterday I shot him.'

She lay back on the pillows and closed her eyes.

'That's all. I suppose you'll arrest me and take me away. I'll get up and dress as soon as I can. At the moment I am feeling rather sick.'

'Are you aware, Mrs Protheroe, that Mr Lawrence Redding has already accused himself of committing the crime?'

Anne opened her eyes and nodded brightly.

'I know. Silly boy. He's very much in love with me, you know. It was frightfully noble of him – but very silly.'

'He knew that it was you who had committed the crime?'

'Yes.'

'How did he know?'

She hesitated.

'Did you tell him?'

Still she hesitated. Then at last she seemed to make up her mind.

'Yes – I told him . . .'

She twitched her shoulders with a movement of irritation.

'Can't you go away now? I've told you. I don't want to talk about it any more.'

'Where did you get the pistol, Mrs Protheroe?'

'The pistol! Oh, it was my husband's. I got it out of the drawer of his dressing-table.'

'I see. And you took it with you to the Vicarage?'

'Yes. I knew he would be there –'

'What time was this?'

'It must have been after six – quarter – twenty past – something like that.'

'You took the pistol meaning to shoot your husband?'

'No – I – meant it for myself.'

'I see. But you went to the Vicarage?'

'Yes. I went along to the window. There were no voices. I looked in. I saw my husband. Something came over me – and I fired.'

'And then?'

'Then? Oh, then I went away.'

'And told Mr Redding what you had done?'

Again I noticed the hesitation in her voice before she said 'Yes.'

'Did anybody see you entering or leaving the Vicarage?'

'No – at least, yes. Old Miss Marple. I talked to her for a few minutes. She was in her garden.'

She moved restlessly on the pillows.

'Isn't that enough? I've told you. Why do you want to go on bothering me?'

Dr Haydock moved to her side and felt her pulse.

He beckoned to Melchett.

'I'll stay with her,' he said in a whisper, 'whilst you make the necessary arrangements. She oughtn't to be left. Might do herself a mischief.'

Melchett nodded.

We left the room and descended the stairs. I saw a thin, cadaverous-looking man come out of the adjoining room and on impulse I remounted the stairs.

'Are you Colonel Protheroe's valet?'

The man looked surprised. 'Yes, sir.'

'Do you know whether your late master kept a pistol anywhere?'

'Not that I know of, sir.'

'Not in one of the drawers of his dressing-table? Think, man.'

The valet shook his head decisively.

'I'm quite sure he didn't, sir. I'd have seen it if so. Bound to.'

I hurried down the stairs after the others.

Mrs Protheroe had lied about the pistol.

Why?

After leaving a message at the police station, the Chief Constable announced his intention of paying a visit to Miss Marple.

'You'd better come with me, vicar,' he said. 'I don't want to give a member of your flock hysterics. So lend the weight of your soothing presence.'

I smiled. For all her fragile appearance, Miss Marple is capable of holding her own with any policeman or Chief Constable in existence.

'What's she like?' asked the colonel, as we rang the bell. 'Anything she says to be depended upon or otherwise?'

I considered the matter.

'I think she is quite dependable,' I said cautiously. 'That is, in so far as she is talking of what she has actually seen. Beyond that, of course, when you get on to what she thinks – well, that is another matter. She has a powerful imagination and systematically thinks the worst of everyone.'

'The typical elderly spinster, in fact,' said Melchett, with a laugh. 'Well, I ought to know the breed by now. Gad, the tea parties down here!'

We were admitted by a very diminutive maid and shown into a small drawing-room.

'A bit crowded,' said Colonel Melchett, looking around. 'But plenty of good stuff. A lady's room, eh, Clement?'

I agreed, and at that moment the door opened and Miss Marple made her appearance.

'Very sorry to bother you, Miss Marple,' said the colonel, when I had introduced him, putting on his bluff military manner which he had an idea was attractive to elderly ladies. 'Got to do my duty, you know.'

'Of course, of course,' said Miss Marple. 'I quite understand. Won't you sit down? And might I offer you a little glass of cherry brandy? My own making. A recipe of my grandmother's.'

'Thank you very much, Miss Marple. Very kind of you. But I think I won't. Nothing till lunch time, that's my motto. Now, I want to talk to you about this sad business – very sad business indeed. Upset us all, I'm sure. Well, it seems possible that owing to the position of your house and garden, you may have been able to tell us something we want to know about yesterday evening.'

'As a matter of fact, I *was* in my little garden from five o'clock onwards yesterday, and, of course, from there – well, one simply cannot help seeing anything that is going on next door.'

'I understand, Miss Marple, that Mrs Protheroe passed this way yesterday evening?'

'Yes, she did. I called out to her, and she admired my roses.'

'Could you tell us about what time that was?'

'I should say it was just a minute or two after a quarter past six. Yes, that's right. The church clock had just chimed the quarter.'

'Very good. What happened next?'

'Well, Mrs Protheroe said she was calling for her husband at the Vicarage so that they could go home together. She had come along the lane, you understand, and she went into the Vicarage by the back gate and across the garden.'

'She came from the lane?'

'Yes, I'll show you.'

Full of eagerness, Miss Marple led us out into the garden and pointed out the lane that ran along by the bottom of the garden.

'The path opposite with the stile leads to the Hall,' she explained. 'That was the way they were going home together. Mrs Protheroe came from the village.'

'Perfectly, perfectly,' said Colonel Melchett. 'And she went across to the Vicarage, you say?'

'Yes. I saw her turn the corner of the house. I suppose the colonel wasn't there yet, because she came back almost immediately, and went down the lawn to the studio – that building there. The one the vicar lets Mr Redding use as a studio.'

'I see. And – you didn't hear a shot, Miss Marple?'

'I didn't hear a shot then,' said Miss Marple.

'But you did hear one sometime?'

'Yes, I think there was a shot somewhere in the woods. But quite five or ten minutes afterwards – and, as I say, out in the woods. At least, I think so. It couldn't have been – surely it couldn't have been –'

She stopped, pale with excitement.

'Yes, yes, we'll come to all that presently,' said Colonel Melchett. 'Please go on with your story. Mrs Protheroe went down to the studio?'

'Yes, she went inside and waited. Presently Mr Redding came along the lane from the village. He came to the Vicarage gate, looked all round –'

'And saw you, Miss Marple.'

'As a matter of fact, he didn't see me,' said Miss Marple, flushing slightly. 'Because, you see, just at that minute I was bending right over – trying to get up one of those nasty dandelions, you know. So difficult. And then he went through the gate and down to the studio.'

'He didn't go near the house?'

'Oh, no! He went straight to the studio. Mrs Protheroe came to the door to meet him, and then they both went inside.'

Plan C

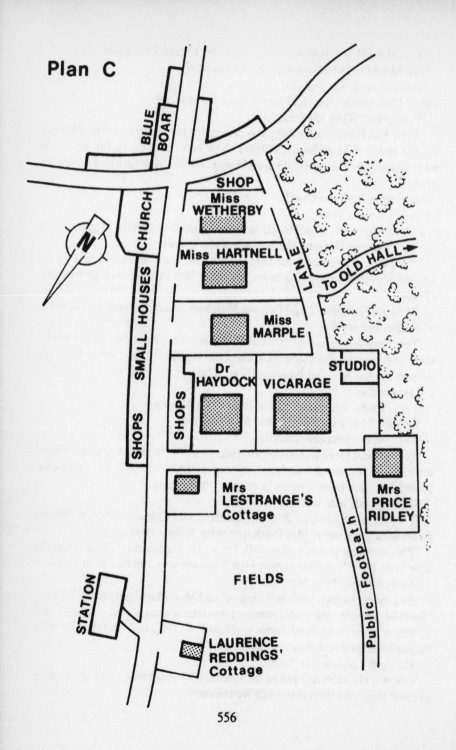

Here Miss Marple contributed a singularly eloquent pause.

'Perhaps she was sitting for him?' I suggested.

'Perhaps,' said Miss Marple.

'And they came out – when?'

'About ten minutes later.'

'That was roughly?'

'The church clock had chimed the half-hour. They strolled out through the garden gate and along the lane, and just at that minute, Dr Stone came down the path leading to the Hall, and climbed over the stile and joined them. They all walked towards the village together. At the end of the lane, I think, but I can't be quite sure, they were joined by Miss Cram. I think it must have been Miss Cram because her skirts were so short.'

'You must have very good eyesight, Miss Marple, if you can observe as far as that.'

'I was observing a bird,' said Miss Marple. 'A golden crested wren, I think he was. A sweet little fellow. I had my glasses out, and that's how I happened to see Miss Cram (if it was Miss Cram, and I think so), join them.'

'Ah! Well, that may be so,' said Colonel Melchett. 'Now, since you seem very good at observing, did you happen to notice, Miss Marple, what sort of expression Mrs Protheroe and Mr Redding had as they passed along the lane?'

'They were smiling and talking,' said Miss Marple. 'They seemed very happy to be together, if you know what I mean.'

'They didn't seem upset or disturbed in any way?'

'Oh, no! Just the opposite.'

'Deuced odd,' said the colonel. 'There's something deuced odd about the whole thing.'

Miss Marple suddenly took our breath away by remarking in a placid voice:

'Has Mrs Protheroe been saying that she committed the crime now?'

'Upon my soul,' said the colonel, 'how did you come to guess that, Miss Marple?'

'Well, I rather thought it might happen,' said Miss Marple. 'I think dear Lettice thought so, too. She's really a very sharp girl. Not always very scrupulous, I'm afraid. So Anne Protheroe says she killed her husband. Well, well. I don't think it's true. No, I'm almost sure it isn't true. Not with a woman like Anne Protheroe. Although one never can be quite sure about anyone, can one? At least that's what I've found. When does she say she shot him?'

'At twenty minutes past six. Just after speaking to you.'

Miss Marple shook her head slowly and pityingly. The pity was, I think, for two full-grown men being so foolish as to believe such a story. At least that is what we felt like.

'What did she shoot him with?'

'A pistol.'

'Where did she find it?'

'She brought it with her.'

'Well, that she didn't do,' said Miss Marple, with unexpected decision. 'I can swear to that. She'd no such thing with her.'

'You mightn't have seen it.'

'Of course I should have seen it.'

'If it had been in her handbag.'

'She wasn't carrying a handbag.'

'Well, it might have been concealed – er – upon her person.'

Miss Marple directed a glance of sorrow and scorn upon him.

'My dear Colonel Melchett, you know what young women are nowadays. Not ashamed to show exactly how the creator made them. She hadn't so much as a handkerchief in the top of her stocking.'

Melchett was obstinate.

'You must admit that it all fits in,' he said. 'The time, the overturned clock pointing to 6.22 –'

Miss Marple turned on me.

'Do you mean you haven't told him about that clock yet?'

'What about the clock, Clement?'

I told him. He showed a good deal of annoyance.

'Why on earth didn't you tell Slack this last night?'

'Because,' I said, 'he wouldn't let me.'

'Nonsense, you ought to have insisted.'

'Probably,' I said, 'Inspector Slack behaves quite differently to you than he does to me. I had no earthly chance of insisting.'

'It's an extraordinary business altogether,' said Melchett. 'If a third person comes along and claims to have done this murder, I shall go into a lunatic asylum.'

'If I might be allowed to suggest –' murmured Miss Marple.

'Well?'

'If you were to tell Mr Redding what Mrs Protheroe has done and then explain that you don't really believe it is her. And then if you were to go to Mrs Protheroe and tell her that Mr Redding is all right – why then, they might each of them tell you the truth. And the truth *is* helpful, though I dare say they don't know very much themselves, poor things.'

'It's all very well, but they are the only two people who had a motive for making away with Protheroe.'

'Oh, I wouldn't say that, Colonel Melchett,' said Miss Marple.

'Why, can you think of anyone else?'

'Oh! yes, indeed. Why,' she counted on her fingers, 'one, two, three, four, five, six – yes, and a possible seven. I can think of at least seven people who might be very glad to have Colonel Protheroe out of the way.'

The colonel looked at her feebly.

'Seven people? In St Mary Mead?'

Miss Marple nodded brightly.

'Mind you I name no names,' she said. 'That wouldn't be right. But I'm afraid there's a lot of wickedness in the world. A nice honourable upright soldier like you doesn't know about these things, Colonel Melchett.'

I thought the Chief Constable was going to have apoplexy.

His remarks on the subject of Miss Marple as we left the house were far from complimentary.

'I really believe that wizened-up old maid thinks she knows everything there is to know. And hardly been out of this village all her life. Preposterous. What can she know of life?'

I said mildly that though doubtless Miss Marple knew next to nothing of Life with a capital L, she knew practically everything that went on in St Mary Mead.

Melchett admitted that grudgingly. She was a valuable witness – particularly valuable from Mrs Protheroe's point of view.

'I suppose there's no doubt about what she says, eh?'

'If Miss Marple says she had no pistol with her, you can take it for granted that it is so,' I said. 'If there was the least possibility of such a thing, Miss Marple would have been on to it like a knife.'

'That's true enough. We'd better go and have a look at the studio.'

The so-called studio was a mere rough shed with a skylight. There were no windows and the door was the only means of entrance or egress. Satisfied on this score, Melchett announced his intention of visiting the Vicarage with the inspector.

'I'm going to the police station now.'

As I entered through the front door, a murmur of voices caught my ear. I opened the drawing-room door.

On the sofa beside Griselda, conversing animatedly, sat Miss Gladys Cram. Her legs, which were encased in particularly shiny pink stockings, were crossed, and I had every opportunity of observing that she wore pink striped silk knickers.

'Hullo, Len,' said Griselda.

'Good morning, Mr Clement,' said Miss Cram. 'Isn't the news about the colonel really too awful? Poor old gentleman.'

'Miss Cram,' said my wife, 'very kindly came in to offer to help us with the Guides. We asked for helpers last Sunday, you remember.'

I did remember, and I was convinced, and so, I knew from her tone, was Griselda, that the idea of enrolling herself among them would never have occurred to Miss Cram but for the exciting incident which had taken place at the Vicarage.

'I was only just saying to Mrs Clement,' went on Miss Cram, 'you could have struck me all of a heap when I heard the news. A murder? I said. In this quiet one-horse village – for quiet it is, you must admit – not so much as a picture house, and as for Talkies! And then when I heard it was Colonel

560

Protheroe – why, I simply couldn't believe it. He didn't seem the kind, somehow, to get murdered.'

'And so,' said Griselda, 'Miss Cram came round to find out all about it.'

I feared this plain speaking might offend the lady, but she merely flung her head back and laughed uproariously, showing every tooth she possessed.

'That's too bad. You're a sharp one, aren't you, Mrs Clement? But it's only natural, isn't it, to want to hear the ins and outs of a case like this? And I'm sure I'm willing enough to help with the Guides in any way you like. Exciting, that's what it is. I've been stagnating for a bit of fun. I have, really I have. Not that my job isn't a very good one, well paid, and Dr Stone quite the gentleman in every way. But a girl wants a bit of life out of office hours, and except for you, Mrs Clement, who is there in the place to talk to except a lot of old cats?'

'There's Lettice Protheroe,' I said.

Gladys Cram tossed her head.

'She's too high and mighty for the likes of me. Fancies herself the country, and wouldn't demean herself by noticing a girl who had to work for her living. Not but what I *did* hear her talking of earning her living herself. And who'd employ her, I should like to know? Why, she'd be fired in less than a week. Unless she went as one of those mannequins, all dressed up and sidling about. She could do that, I expect.'

'She'd make a very good mannequin,' said Griselda. 'She's got such a lovely figure.' There's nothing of the cat about Griselda. 'When was she talking of earning her own living?'

Miss Cram seemed momentarily discomfited, but recovered herself with her usual archness.

'That would be telling, wouldn't it?' she said. 'But she did say so. Things not very happy at home, I fancy. Catch me living at home with a stepmother. I wouldn't sit down under it for a minute.'

'Ah! but you're so high spirited and independent,' said Griselda gravely, and I looked at her with suspicion.

Miss Cram was clearly pleased.

'That's right. That's me all over. Can be led, not driven. A palmist told me that not so very long ago. No. I'm not one to sit down and be bullied. And I've made it clear all along to Dr Stone that I must have my regular times off. These scientific gentlemen, they think a girl's a kind of machine – half the time they just don't notice her or remember she's there. Of course, I don't know much about it,' confessed the girl.

'Do you find Dr Stone pleasant to work with? It must be an interesting job if you are interested in archaeology.'

'It still seems to me that digging up people that are dead and have been dead for hundreds of years isn't – well, it seems a bit nosy, doesn't it? And there's Dr Stone so wrapped up in it all, that half the time he'd forget his meals if it wasn't for me.'

'Is he at the barrow this morning?' asked Griselda.

Miss Cram shook her head.

'A bit under the weather this morning,' she explained. 'Not up to doing any work. That means a holiday for little Gladys.'

'I'm sorry,' I said.

'Oh! It's nothing much. There's not going to be a second death. But do tell me, Mr Clement, I hear you've been with the police all morning. What do they think?'

'Well,' I said slowly, 'there is still a little – uncertainty.'

'Ah!' cried Miss Cram. 'Then they don't think it is Mr Lawrence Redding after all. So handsome, isn't he? Just like a movie star. And such a nice smile when he says good morning to you. I really couldn't believe my ears when I heard the police had arrested him. Still, one has always heard they're very stupid – the county police.'

'You can hardly blame them in this instance,' I said. 'Mr Redding came in and gave himself up.'

'What?' the girl was clearly dumbfounded. 'Well – of all the poor fish! If I'd committed a murder, I wouldn't go straight off and give myself up. I should have thought Lawrence Redding would have had more sense. To give in like that! What did he kill Protheroe for? Did he say? Was it just a quarrel?'

'It's not absolutely certain that he did kill him,' I said.

'But surely – if he says he has – why really, Mr Clement, he ought to know.'

'He ought to, certainly,' I agreed. 'But the police are not satisfied with his story.'

'But why should he say he'd done it if he hasn't?'

That was a point on which I had no intention of enlightening Miss Cram. Instead I said rather vaguely:

'I believe that in all prominent murder cases, the police receive numerous letters from people accusing themselves of the crime.'

Miss Cram's reception of this piece of information was:

'They must be chumps!' in a tone of wonder and scorn.

'Well,' she said with a sigh, 'I suppose I must be trotting along.' She rose. 'Mr Redding accusing himself of the murder will be a bit of news for Dr Stone.'

'Is he interested?' asked Griselda.

Miss Cram furrowed her brows perplexedly.

'He's a queer one. You never can tell with him. All wrapped up in the past. He'd a hundred times rather look at a nasty old bronze knife out of those humps of ground than he would see the knife Crippen cut up his wife with, supposing he had a chance to.'

'Well,' I said, 'I must confess I agree with him.'

Miss Cram's eyes expressed incomprehension and slight contempt. Then, with reiterated goodbyes, she took her departure.

'Not such a bad sort, really,' said Griselda, as the door closed behind her. 'Terribly common, of course, but one of those big, bouncing, good-humoured girls that you can't dislike. I wonder what really brought her here?'

'Curiosity.'

'Yes, I suppose so. Now, Len, tell me all about it. I'm simply dying to hear.'

I sat down and recited faithfully all the happenings of the morning, Griselda interpolating the narrative with little exclamations of surprise and interest.

'So it was Anne Lawrence was after all along! Not Lettice. How blind we've all been! That must have been what old Miss Marple was hinting at yesterday. Don't you think so?'

'Yes,' I said, averting my eyes.

Mary entered.

'There's a couple of men here – come from a newspaper, so they say. Do you want to see them?'

'No,' I said, 'certainly not. Refer them to Inspector Slack at the police station.'

Mary nodded and turned away.

'And when you've got rid of them,' I said, 'come back here. There's something I want to ask you.'

Mary nodded again.

It was some few minutes before she returned.

'Had a job getting rid of them,' she said. 'Persistent. You never saw anything like it. Wouldn't take no for an answer.'

'I expect we shall be a good deal troubled with them,' I said. 'Now, Mary, what I want to ask you is this: Are you quite certain you didn't hear the shot yesterday evening?'

'The shot what killed him? No, of course I didn't. If I had of done, I should have gone in to see what had happened.'

'Yes, but –' I was remembering Miss Marple's statement that she had heard a shot 'in the woods'. I changed the form of my question. 'Did you

563

hear any other shot – one down in the wood, for instance?'

'Oh! That.' The girl paused. 'Yes, now I come to think of it, I believe I did. Not a lot of shots, just one. Queer sort of bang it was.'

'Exactly,' I said, 'Now what time was that?'

'Time?'

'Yes, time.'

'I couldn't say, I'm sure. Well after tea-time. I do know that.'

'Can't you get a little nearer than that?'

'No, I can't. I've got my work to do, haven't I? I can't go on looking at clocks the whole time – and it wouldn't be much good anyway – the alarm loses a good three-quarters every day, and what with putting it on and one thing and another, I'm never exactly sure what time it is.'

This perhaps explains why our meals are never punctual. They are sometimes too late and sometimes bewilderingly early.

'Was it long before Mr Redding came?'

'No, it wasn't long. Ten minutes – a quarter of an hour – not longer than that.'

I nodded my head, satisfied.

'Is that all?' said Mary. 'Because what I mean to say is, I've got the joint in the oven and the pudding boiling over as likely as not.'

'That's all right. You can go.'

She left the room, and I turned to Griselda.

'Is it quite out of the question to induce Mary to say sir or ma'am?'

'I have told her. She doesn't remember. She's just a raw girl, remember?'

'I am perfectly aware of that,' I said. 'But raw things do not necessarily remain raw for ever. I feel a tinge of cooking might be induced in Mary.'

'Well, I don't agree with you,' said Griselda. 'You know how little we can afford to pay a servant. If once we got her smartened up at all, she'd leave. Naturally. And get higher wages. But as long as Mary can't cook and has those awful manners – well, we're safe, nobody else would have her.'

I perceived that my wife's methods of housekeeping were not so entirely haphazard as I had imagined. A certain amount of reasoning underlay them. Whether it was worth while having a maid at the price of her not being able to cook, and having a habit of throwing dishes and remarks at one with the same disconcerting abruptness, was a debatable matter.

'And anyway,' continued Griselda, 'you must make allowances for her manners being worse than usual just now. You can't expect her to feel exactly sympathetic about Colonel Protheroe's death when he jailed her young man.'

'Did he jail her young man?'

'Yes, for poaching. You know, that man, Archer. Mary has been walking out with him for two years.'

'I didn't know that.'

'Darling Len, you never know anything.'

'It's queer,' I said, 'that everyone says the shot came from the woods.'

'I don't think it's queer at all,' said Griselda. 'You see, one so often hears shots in the wood. So naturally, when you do hear a shot, you just assume as a matter of course that it *is* in the wood. It probably just sounds a bit louder than usual. Of course, if one were in the next room, you'd realize that it was in the house, but from Mary's kitchen with the window right the other side of the house, I don't believe you'd ever think of such a thing.'

The door opened again.

'Colonel Melchett's back,' said Mary. 'And the police inspector with him, and they say they'd be glad if you'd join them. They're in the study.'

I saw at a glance that Colonel Melchett and Inspector Slack had not been seeing eye to eye about the case. Melchett looked flushed and annoyed and the inspector looked sulky.

'I'm sorry to say,' said Melchett, 'that Inspector Slack doesn't agree with me in considering young Redding innocent.'

'If he didn't do it, what does he go and say he did it for?' asked Slack sceptically.

'Mrs Protheroe acted in an exactly similar fashion, remember, Slack.'

'That's different. She's a woman, and women act in that silly way. I'm not saying she did it for a moment. She heard he was accused and she trumped up a story. I'm used to that sort of game. You wouldn't believe the fool things I've known women do. But Redding's different. He's got his head screwed on all right. And if he admits he did it, well, I say he did do it. It's his pistol – you can't get away from that. And thanks to this business of Mrs Protheroe, we know the motive. That was the weak point before, but now we know it – why, the whole thing's plain sailing.'

'You think he can have shot him earlier? At six-thirty, say?'

'He can't have done that.'

'You've checked up his movements?'

The inspector nodded.

'He was in the village near the Blue Boar at ten past six. From there he came along the back lane where you say the old lady next door saw him – she doesn't miss much, I should say – and kept his appointment with Mrs Protheroe in the studio in the garden. They left there together just after six-thirty, and went along the lane to the village, being joined by Dr Stone. He corroborates that all right – I've seen him. They all stood talking just by the post office for a few minutes, then Mrs Protheroe went into Miss Hartnell's to borrow a gardening magazine. That's all right too. I've seen Miss Hartnell. Mrs Protheroe remained there talking to her till just on seven o'clock when she exclaimed at the lateness of the hour and said she must get home.'

'What was her manner?'

'Very easy and pleasant, Miss Hartnell said. She seemed in good spirits – Miss Hartnell is quite sure there was nothing on her mind.'

'Well, go on.'

'Redding, he went with Dr Stone to the Blue Boar and they had a drink together. He left there at twenty minutes to seven, went rapidly along the village street and down the road to the Vicarage. Lots of people saw him.'

'Not down the back lane this time?' commented the colonel.

'No – he came to the front, asked for the vicar, heard Colonel Protheroe was there, went in – and shot him – just as he said he did! That's the truth of it, and we needn't look further.'

Melchett shook his head.

'There's the doctor's evidence. You can't get away from that. Protheroe was shot not later than six-thirty.'

'Oh, doctors!' Inspector Slack looked contemptuous. 'If you're going to believe doctors. Take out all your teeth – that's what they do nowadays – and then say they're very sorry, but all the time it was appendicitis. Doctors!'

'This isn't a question of diagnosis. Dr Haydock was absolutely positive on the point. You can't go against the medical evidence, Slack.'

'And there's my evidence for what it is worth,' I said, suddenly recalling a forgotten incident. 'I touched the body and it was cold. That I can swear to.'

'You see, Slack?' said Melchett.

'Well, of course, if that's so. But there it was – a beautiful case. Mr Redding only too anxious to be hanged, so to speak.'

'That, in itself, strikes me as a little unnatural,' observed Colonel Melchett.

'Well, there's no accounting for tastes,' said the inspector. 'There's a lot of gentlemen went a bit balmy after the war. Now, I suppose, it means starting again at the beginning.' He turned on me. 'Why you went out of your way to mislead me about the clock, sir, I can't think. Obstructing the ends of justice, that's what that was.'

'I tried to tell you on three separate occasions,' I said. 'And each time you shut me up and refused to listen.'

'That's just a way of speaking, sir. You could have told me perfectly well if you had had a mind to. The clock and the note seemed to tally perfectly. Now, according to you, the clock was all wrong. I never knew such a case. What's the sense of keeping a clock a quarter of an hour fast anyway?'

'It is supposed,' I said, 'to induce punctuality.'

'I don't think we need go further into that now, Inspector,' said Colonel Melchett tactfully. 'What we want now is the true story from both Mrs Protheroe and young Redding. I telephoned to Haydock and asked him to bring Mrs Protheroe over here with him. They ought to be here in about a quarter of an hour. I think it would be as well to have Redding here first.'

'I'll get on to the station,' said Inspector Slack, and took up the telephone.

'And now,' he said, replacing the receiver, 'we'll get to work on this room.' He looked at me in a meaningful fashion.

'Perhaps,' I said, 'you'd like me out of the way.'

The inspector immediately opened the door for me. Melchett called out:

'Come back when young Redding arrives, will you, Vicar? You're a friend of his and you may have sufficient influence to persuade him to speak the truth.'

I found my wife and Miss Marple with their heads together.

'We've been discussing all sorts of possibilities,' said Griselda. 'I wish you'd solve the case, Miss Marple, like you did the time Miss Wetherby's gill of picked shrimps disappeared. And all because it reminded you of something quite different about a sack of coals.'

'You're laughing, my dear,' said Miss Marple, 'but after all, that is a very sound way of arriving at the truth. It's really what people call intuition and make such a fuss about. Intuition is like reading a word without having to spell it out. A child can't do that because it has had so little experience. But a grown-up person knows the word because they've seen it often before. You catch my meaning, Vicar?'

'Yes,' I said slowly, 'I think I do. You mean that if a thing reminds you of something else – well, it's probably the same kind of thing.'

'Exactly.'

'And what precisely does the murder of Colonel Protheroe remind you of?'

Miss Marple sighed.

'That is just the difficulty. So many parallels come to the mind. For instance, there was Major Hargreaves, a churchwarden and a man highly respected in every way. And all the time he was keeping a separate second establishment – a former housemaid, just think of it! And five children – actually five children – a terrible shock to his wife and daughter.'

I tried hard to visualize Colonel Protheroe in the rôle of secret sinner and failed.

'And then there was that laundry business,' went on Miss Marple. 'Miss Hartnell's opal pin – left most imprudently in a frilled blouse and sent to the laundry. And the woman who took it didn't want it in the least and wasn't by any means a thief. She simply hid it in another woman's house and told the police she'd seen this other woman take it. Spite, you know, sheer spite. It's an astonishing motive – spite. A man in it, of course. There always is.'

This time I failed to see any parallel, however remote.

'And then there was poor Elwell's daughter – such a pretty ethereal girl – tried to stifle her little brother. And there was the money for the Choir Boys' Outing (before your time, vicar) actually taken by the organist. His wife was sadly in debt. Yes, this case makes one think so many things – too many. It's very hard to arrive at the truth.'

'I wish you would tell me,' I said, 'who were the seven suspects?'

'The seven suspects?'

'You said you could think of seven people who would – well, be glad of Colonel Protheroe's death.'

'Did I? Yes, I remember I did.'

'Was that true?'

'Oh! Certainly it was true. But I mustn't mention names. You can think of them quite easily yourself, I am sure.'

'Indeed I can't. There is Lettice Protheroe, I suppose, since she probably comes into money on her father's death. But it is absurd to think of her in such a connection, and outside her I can think of nobody.'

'And you, my dear?' said Miss Marple, turning to Griselda.

Rather to my surprise Griselda coloured up. Something very like tears started into her eyes. She clenched both her small hands.

'Oh!' she cried indignantly. 'People are hateful – hateful. The things they say! The beastly things they say . . .'

I looked at her curiously. It is very unlike Griselda to be so upset. She noticed my glance and tried to smile.

'Don't look at me as though I were an interesting specimen you didn't understand, Len. Don't let's get heated and wander from the point. I don't believe that it was Lawrence or Anne, and Lettice is out of the question. There must be some clue or other that would help us.'

'There is the note, of course,' said Miss Marple. 'You will remember my saying this morning that that struck me as exceedingly peculiar.'

'It seems to fix the time of his death with remarkable accuracy,' I said. 'And yet, is that possible? Mrs Protheroe would only have just left the study. She would hardly have had time to reach the studio. The only way in which I can account for it is that he consulted his own watch and that his watch was slow. That seems to me a feasible solution.'

'I have another idea,' said Griselda. 'Suppose, Len, that the clock had already been put back – no, that comes to the same thing – how stupid of me!'

'It hadn't been altered when I left,' I said. 'I remember comparing it with my watch. Still, as you say, that has no bearing on the present matter.'

'What do you think, Miss Marple?' asked Griselda.

'My dear, I confess I wasn't thinking about it from that point of view at all. What strikes me as so curious, and has done from the first, is the subject matter of that letter.'

'I don't see that,' I said. 'Colonel Protheroe merely wrote that he couldn't wait any longer –'

'*At twenty minutes past six?*' said Miss Marple. 'Your maid, Mary, had already told him that you wouldn't be in till half-past six at the earliest, and

569

he appeared to be quite willing to wait until then. And yet at twenty past six he sits down and says he "can't wait any longer".'

I stared at the old lady, feeling an increased respect for her mental powers. Her keen wits had seen what we had failed to perceive. It *was* an odd thing – a very odd thing.

'If only,' I said, 'the letter hadn't been dated –'

Miss Marple nodded her head.

'Exactly,' she said. 'If it *hadn't* been dated!'

I cast my mind back, trying to recall that sheet of notepaper and the blurred scrawl, and at the top that neatly printed 6.20. Surely these figures were on a different scale to the rest of the letter. I gave a gasp.

'Supposing,' I said, 'it wasn't dated. Supposing that round about 6.30 Colonel Protheroe got impatient and sat down to say he couldn't wait any longer. And as he was sitting there writing, someone came in through the window –'

'Or through the door,' suggested Griselda.

'He'd hear the door and look up.'

'Colonel Protheroe was rather deaf, you remember,' said Miss Marple.

'Yes, that's true. He wouldn't hear it. Whichever way the murderer came, he stole up behind the colonel and shot him. Then he saw the note and the clock and the idea came to him. He put 6.20 at the top of the letter and he altered the clock to 6.22. It was a clever idea. It gave him, or so he would think, a perfect alibi.'

'And what we want to find,' said Griselda, 'is someone who has a cast-iron alibi for 6.20, but no alibi at all for – well, that isn't so easy. One can't fix the time.'

'We can fix it within very narrow limits,' I said. 'Haydock places 6.30 as the outside limit of time. I suppose one could perhaps shift it to 6.35 from the reasoning we have just been following out, it seems clear that Protheroe would not have got impatient before 6.30. I think we can say we do know pretty well.'

'Then that shot I heard – yes, I suppose it is quite possible. And I thought nothing about it – nothing at all. Most vexing. And yet, now I try to recollect, it does seem to me that it was different from the usual sort of shot one hears. Yes, there was a difference.'

'Louder?' I suggested.

No, Miss Marple didn't think it had been louder. In fact, she found it hard to say in what way it had been different, but she still insisted that it was.

I thought she was probably persuading herself of the fact rather than actually remembering it, but she had just contributed such a valuable new outlook to the problem that I felt highly respectful towards her.

She rose, murmuring that she must really get back – it had been so tempting just to run over and discuss the case with dear Griselda. I escorted her to the boundary wall and the back gate and returned to find Griselda wrapped in thought.

'Still puzzling over that note?' I asked.

'No.'

She gave a sudden shiver and shook her shoulders impatiently.

'Len, I've been thinking. How badly someone must have hated Anne Protheroe!'

'Hated her?'

'Yes. Don't you see? There's no real evidence against Lawrence – all the evidence against him is what you might call accidental. He just happens to take it into his head to come here. If he hadn't – well, no one would have thought of connecting him with the crime. But Anne is different. Suppose someone knew that she was here at exactly 6.20 – the clock and the time on the letter – everything pointing to her. I don't think it was only because of an alibi it was moved to that exact time – I think there was more in it than that – a direct attempt to fasten the business on her. If it hadn't been for Miss Marple saying she hadn't got the pistol with her and noticing that she was only a moment before going down to the studio – Yes, if it hadn't been for that ...' She shivered again. 'Len, I feel that someone hated Anne Protheroe very much. I – I don't like it.'

I was summoned to the study when Lawrence Redding arrived. He looked haggard, and, I thought, suspicious. Colonel Melchett greeted him with something approaching cordiality.

'We want to ask you a few questions – here, on the spot,' he said.

Lawrence sneered slightly.

'Isn't that a French idea? Reconstruction of the crime?'

'My dear boy,' said Colonel Melchett, 'don't take that tone with us. Are you aware that someone else has also confessed to committing the crime which you pretend to have committed?'

The effect of these words on Lawrence was painful and immediate.

'S-s-omeone else?' he stammered. 'Who – who?'

'Mrs Protheroe,' said Colonel Melchett, watching him.

'Absurd. She never did it. She couldn't have. It's impossible.'

Melchett interrupted him.

'Strangely enough, we did not believe her story. Neither, I may say, do we believe yours. Dr Haydock says positively that the murder could not have been committed at the time you say it was.'

'Dr Haydock says that?'

'Yes, so, you see, you are cleared whether you like it or not. And now we want you to help us, to tell us exactly what occurred.'

Lawrence still hesitated.

'You're not deceiving me about – about Mrs Protheroe? You really don't suspect her?'

'On my word of honour,' said Colonel Melchett.

Lawrence drew a deep breath.

'I've been a fool,' he said. 'An absolute fool. How could I have thought for one minute that she did it –'

'Suppose you tell us all about it?' suggested the Chief Constable.

'There's not much to tell. I – I met Mrs Protheroe that afternoon –' He paused.

'We know all about that,' said Melchett. 'You may think that your feeling for Mrs Protheroe and hers for you was a dead secret, but in reality it was known and commented upon. In any case, everything is bound to come out now.'

'Very well, then. I expect you are right. I had promised the vicar here (he glanced at me) to – to go right away. I met Mrs Protheroe that evening in the studio at a quarter past six. I told her of what I had decided. She, too, agreed that it was the only thing to do. We – we said goodbye to each other.

'We left the studio, and almost at once Dr Stone joined us. Anne managed

572

to seem marvellously natural. I couldn't do it. I went off with Stone to the Blue Boar and had a drink. Then I thought I'd go home, but when I got to the corner of this road, I changed my mind and decided to come along and see the vicar. I felt I wanted someone to talk to about the matter.

'At the door, the maid told me the vicar was out, but would be in shortly, but that Colonel Protheroe was in the study waiting for him. Well, I didn't like to go away again – looked as though I were shirking meeting him. So I said I'd wait too, and I went into the study.'

He stopped.

'Well?' said Colonel Melchett.

'Protheroe was sitting at the writing table – just as you found him. I went up to him – touched him. He was dead. Then I looked down and saw the pistol lying on the floor beside him. I picked it up – *and at once saw that it was my pistol.*

'That gave me a turn. My pistol! And then, straightaway I leaped to one conclusion. Anne must have bagged my pistol some time or other – meaning it for herself if she couldn't bear things any longer. Perhaps she had had it with her today. After we parted in the village she must have come back here and – and – oh! I suppose I was mad to think of it. But that's what I thought. I slipped the pistol in my pocket and came away. Just outside the Vicarage gate, I met the vicar. He said something nice and normal about seeing Protheroe – suddenly I had a wild desire to laugh. His manner was so ordinary and everyday and there was I all strung up. I remember shouting out something absurd and seeing his face change. I was nearly off my head, I believe. I went walking – walking – at last I couldn't bear it any longer. If Anne had done this ghastly thing, I was, at least, morally responsible. I went and gave myself up.'

There was a silence when he had finished. Then the colonel said in a business-like voice:

'I would like to ask just one or two questions. First, did you touch or move the body in any way?'

'No, I didn't touch it at all. One could see he was dead without touching him.'

'Did you notice a note lying on the blotter half concealed by his body?'
'No.'

'Did you interfere in any way with the clock?'

'I never touched the clock. I seem to remember a clock lying overturned on the table, but I never touched it.'

'Now as to this pistol of yours, when did you last see it?'

Lawrence Redding reflected. 'It's hard to say exactly.'

'Where do you keep it?'

'Oh, in a litter of odds and ends in the sitting-room in my cottage. On one of the shelves of the bookcase.'

'You left it lying about carelessly?'

'Yes. I really didn't think about it. It was just there.'

'So that anyone who came to your cottage could have seen it?'

'Yes.'

'And you don't remember when you last saw it?'

Lawrence drew his brows together in a frown of recollection.

'I'm almost sure it was there the day before yesterday. I remember pushing it aside to get an old pipe. I think it was the day before yesterday – but it may have been the day before that.'

'Who has been to your cottage lately?'

'Oh! Crowds of people. Someone is always drifting in and out. I had a sort of tea party the day before yesterday. Lettice Protheroe, Dennis, and all their crowd. And then one or other of the old Pussies comes in now and again.'

'Do you lock the cottage up when you go out?'

'No; why on earth should I? I've nothing to steal. And no one does lock their house up round here.'

'Who looks after your wants there?'

'An old Mrs Archer comes in every morning to "do for me" as it's called.'

'Do you think she would remember when the pistol was there last?'

'I don't know. She might. But I don't fancy conscientious dusting is her strong point.'

'It comes to this – that almost anyone might have taken that pistol?'

'It seems so – yes.'

The door opened and Dr Haydock came in with Anne Protheroe.

She started at seeing Lawrence. He, on his part, made a tentative step towards her.

'Forgive me, Anne,' he said. 'It was abominable of me to think what I did.'

'I –' She faltered, then looked appealingly at Colonel Melchett. 'Is it true, what Dr Haydock told me?'

'That Mr Redding is cleared of suspicion? Yes. And now what about this story of yours, Mrs Protheroe? Eh, what about it?'

She smiled rather shamefacedly.

'I suppose you think it dreadful of me?'

'Well, shall we say – very foolish? But that's all over. What I want now, Mrs Protheroe, is the truth – the absolute truth.'

She nodded gravely.

'I will tell you. I suppose you know about – about everything.'

'Yes.'

'I was to meet Lawrence – Mr Redding – that evening at the studio. At a quarter past six. My husband and I drove into the village together. I had some shopping to do. As we parted he mentioned casually that he was going to see the vicar. I couldn't get word to Lawrence, and I was rather uneasy. I – well, it was awkward meeting him in the Vicarage garden whilst my husband was at the Vicarage.'

Her cheeks burned as she said this. It was not a pleasant moment for her.

'I reflected that perhaps my husband would not stay very long. To find this out, I came along the back lane and into the garden. I hoped no one would see me, but of course old Miss Marple had to be in her garden! She stopped me and we said a few words, and I explained I was going to call for my husband. I felt I had to say something. I don't know whether she believed me or not. She looked rather – funny.

'When I left her, I went straight across to the Vicarage and round the corner of the house to the study window. I crept up to it very softly, expecting to hear the sound of voices. But to my surprise there were none. I just glanced in, saw the room was empty, and hurried across the lawn and down to the studio where Lawrence joined me almost at once.'

'You say the room was empty, Mrs Protheroe?'

'Yes, my husband was not there.'

'Extraordinary.'

'You mean, ma'am, that you didn't see him?' said the inspector.

'No, I didn't see him.'

Inspector Slack whispered to the Chief Constable, who nodded.

'Do you mind, Mrs Protheroe, just showing us exactly what you did?'

'Not at all.'

She rose, Inspector Slack pushed open the window for her, and she stepped out on the terrace and round the house to the left.

Inspector Slack beckoned me imperiously to go and sit at the writing table.

Somehow I didn't much like doing it. It gave me an uncomfortable feeling. But, of course, I complied.

Presently I heard footsteps outside, they paused for a minute, then retreated. Inspector Slack indicated to me that I could return to the other side of the room. Mrs Protheroe re-entered through the window.

'Is that exactly how it was?' asked Colonel Melchett.

'I think exactly.'

'Then can you tell us, Mrs Protheroe, just exactly where the vicar was in the room when you looked in?' asked Inspector Slack.

'The vicar? I – no, I'm afraid I can't. I didn't see him.'

Inspector Slack nodded.

'That's how you didn't see your husband. He was round the corner at the writing-desk.'

'Oh! she paused. Suddenly her eyes grew round with horror. 'It wasn't there that – that –'

'Yes, Mrs Protheroe. It was while he was sitting there.'

'Oh!' She quivered.

He went on with his questions.

'Did you know, Mrs Protheroe, that Mr Redding had a pistol?'

'Yes. He told me so once.'

'Did you ever have that pistol in your possession?'

She shook her head. 'No.'

'Did you know where he kept it?'

'I'm not sure. I think – yes. I think I've seen it on a shelf in his cottage. Didn't you keep it there, Lawrence?'

'When was the last time you were at the cottage, Mrs Protheroe?'

'Oh! About three weeks ago. My husband and I had tea there with him.'

'And you have not been there since?'

'No. I never went there. You see, it would probably cause a lot of talk in the village.'

'Doubtless,' said Colonel Melchett dryly. 'Where were you in the habit of seeing Mr Redding, if I may ask?'

'He used to come up to the Hall. He was painting Lettice. We – we often met in the woods afterwards.'

Colonel Melchett nodded.

'Isn't that enough?' Her voice was suddenly broken. 'It's so awful – having to tell you all these things. And – and there wasn't anything wrong about it. There wasn't – indeed, there wasn't. We were just friends. We – we couldn't help caring for each other.'

She looked pleadingly at Dr Haydock, and that soft-hearted man stepped forward.

'I really think, Melchett,' he said, 'that Mrs Protheroe has had enough. She's had a great shock – in more ways than one.'

The Chief Constable nodded.

'There is really nothing more I want to ask you, Mrs Protheroe,' he said. 'Thank you for answering my questions so frankly.'

'Then – then I may go?'

'Is your wife in?' asked Haydock. 'I think Mrs Protheroe would like to see her.'

'Yes,' I said, 'Griselda is in. You'll find her in the drawing-room.'

She and Haydock left the room together and Lawrence Redding

with them.

Colonel Melchett had pursed up his lips and was playing with a paper knife. Slack was looking at the note. It was then that I mentioned Miss Marple's theory. Slack looked closely at it.

'My word,' he said, 'I believe the old lady's right. Look here, sir, don't you see? – these figures are written in different ink. That date was written with a fountain pen or I'll eat my boots!'

We were all rather excited.

'You've examined the note for finger-prints, of course,' said the Chief Constable.

'What do you think, colonel? No finger-prints on the note at all. Finger-prints on the pistol those of Mr Lawrence Redding. May have been some others once, before he went fooling round with it and carrying it around in his pocket, but there's nothing clear enough to get hold of now.'

'At first the case looked very black against Mrs Protheroe,' said the colonel thoughtfully. 'Much blacker than against young Redding. There was that old woman Marple's evidence that she didn't have the pistol with her, but these elderly ladies are often mistaken.'

I was silent, but I did not agree with him. I was quite sure that Anne Protheroe had had no pistol with her since Miss Marple had said so. Miss Marple is not the type of elderly lady who makes mistakes. She has got an uncanny knack of being always right.

'What did get me was that nobody heard the shot. If it was fired then – somebody *must* have heard it – wherever they thought it came from. Slack, you'd better have a word with the maid.'

Inspector Slack moved with alacrity towards the door.

'I shouldn't ask her if she heard a shot in the house,' I said. 'Because if you do, she'll deny it. Call it a shot in the wood. That's the only kind of shot she'll admit to hearing.'

'I know how to manage them,' said Inspector Slack, and disappeared.

'Miss Marple says she heard a shot later,' said Colonel Melchett thoughtfully. 'We must see if she can fix the time at all precisely. Of course it may be a stray shot that had nothing to do with the case.'

'It may be, of course,' I agreed.

The colonel took a turn or two up and down the room.

'Do you know, Clement,' he said suddenly, 'I've a feeling that this is going to turn out a much more intricate and difficult business than any of us think. Dash it all, there's something behind it.' He snorted. 'Something we don't know about. We're only beginning, Clement. Mark my words, we're only beginning. All these things, the clock, the note, the pistol – they don't make sense as they stand.'

I shook my head. They certainly didn't.

'But I'm going to get to the bottom of it. No calling in of Scotland Yard. Slack's a smart man. He's a very smart man. He's a kind of ferret. He'll nose his way through to the truth. He's done several very good things already, and this case will be his *chef d'oeuvre*. Some men would call in Scotland Yard. I shan't. We'll get to the bottom of this here in Downshire.'

'I hope so, I'm sure,' I said.

I tried to make my voice enthusiastic, but I had already taken such a dislike to Inspector Slack that the prospect of his success failed to appeal to me. A successful Slack would, I thought, be even more odious than a baffled one.

'Who has the house next?' asked the Colonel suddenly.

'You mean at the end of the road? Mrs Price Ridley.'

'We'll go along to her after Slack has finished with your maid. She might just possibly have heard something. She isn't deaf or anything, is she?'

'I should say her hearing is remarkably keen. I'm going by the amount of scandal she has started by "just happening to overhear accidentally".'

'That's the kind of woman we want. Oh! here's Slack.'

The inspector had the air of one emerging from a severe tussle.

'Phew!' he said. 'That's a tartar you've got, sir.'

'Mary is essentially a girl of strong character,' I replied.

'Doesn't like the police,' he said. 'I cautioned her – did what I could to put the fear of the law into her, but no good. She stood right up to me.'

'Spirited,' I said, feeling more kindly towards Mary.

'But I pinned her down all right. She heard one shot – and one shot only. And it was a good long time after Colonel Protheroe came. I couldn't get her to name a time, but we fixed it at last by means of the fish. The fish was late, and she blew the boy up when he came, and he said it was barely half-past six anyway, and it was just after that she heard the shot. Of course, that's not accurate, so to speak, but it gives us an idea.'

'H'm,' said Melchett.

'I don't think Mrs Protheroe's in this after all,' said Slack, with a note of regret in his voice. 'She wouldn't have had time, to begin with, and then women never like fiddling about with firearms. Arsenic's more in their line. No, I don't think she did it. It's a pity!' He sighed.

Melchett explained that he was going round to Mrs Price Ridley's, and Slack approved.

'May I come with you?' I asked. 'I'm getting interested.'

I was given permission, and we set forth. A loud 'Hie' greeted us as we emerged from the Vicarage gate, and my nephew, Dennis, came running up the road from the village to join us.

578

'Look here,' he said to the inspector, 'what about that footprint I told you about?'

'Gardener's,' said Inspector Slack laconically.

'You don't think it might be someone else wearing the gardener's boots?'

'No, I don't!' said Inspector Slack in a discouraging way.

It would take more than that to discourage Dennis, however.

He held out a couple of burnt matches.

'I found these by the Vicarage gate.'

'Thank you,' said Slack, and put them in his pocket.

Matters appeared now to have reached a deadlock.

'You're not arresting Uncle Len, are you?' inquired Dennis facetiously.

'Why should I?' inquired Slack.

'There's a lot of evidence against him,' declared Dennis. 'You ask Mary. Only the day before the murder he was wishing Colonel Protheroe out of the world. Weren't you, Uncle Len?'

'Er –' I began.

Inspector Slack turned a slow suspicious stare upon me, and I felt hot all over. Dennis is exceedingly tiresome. He ought to realize that a policeman seldom has a sense of humour.

'Don't be absurd, Dennis,' I said irritably.

The innocent child opened his eyes in a stare of surprise.

'I say, it's only a joke,' he said. 'Uncle Len just said that any one who murdered Colonel Protheroe would be doing the world a service.'

'Ah!' said Inspector Slack, 'that explains something the maid said.'

Servants very seldom have any sense of humour either. I cursed Dennis heartily in my mind for bringing the matter up. That and the clock together will make the inspector suspicious of me for life.

'Come on, Clement,' said Colonel Melchett.

'Where are you going? Can I come, too?' asked Dennis.

'No, you can't,' I snapped.

We left him looking after us with a hurt expression. We went up to the neat front door of Mrs Price Ridley's house and the inspector knocked and rang in what I can only describe as an official manner. A pretty parlourmaid answered the bell.

'Mrs Price Ridley in?' inquired Melchett.

'No, sir.' The maid paused and added: 'She's just gone down to the police station.'

This was a totally unexpected development. As we retraced our steps Melchett caught me by the arm and murmured:

'If she's gone to confess to the crime, too, I really shall go off my head.'

I hardly thought it likely that Mrs Price Ridley had anything so dramatic in view, but I did wonder what had taken her to the police station. Had she really got evidence of importance, or that she thought of importance, to offer? At any rate, we should soon know.

We found Mrs Price Ridley talking at a high rate of speed to a somewhat bewildered-looking police constable. That she was extremely indignant I knew from the way the bow in her hat was trembling. Mrs Price Ridley wears what, I believe, are known as 'Hats for Matrons' – they make a speciality of them in our adjacent town of Much Benham. They perch easily on a superstructure of hair and are somewhat overweighted with large bows of ribbon. Griselda is always threatening to get a matron's hat.

Mrs Price Ridley paused in her flow of words upon our entrance.

'Mrs Price Ridley?' inquired Colonel Melchett, lifting his hat.

'Let me introduce Colonel Melchett to you, Mrs Price Ridley,' I said. 'Colonel Melchett is our Chief Constable.'

Mrs Price Ridley looked at me coldly, but produced the semblance of a gracious smile for the colonel.

'We've just been round to your house, Mrs Price Ridley,' explained the colonel, 'and heard you had come down here.'

Mrs Price Ridley thawed altogether.

'Ah!' she said, 'I'm glad *some* notice is being taken of the occurrence. Disgraceful, I call it. Simply disgraceful.'

There is no doubt that murder is disgraceful, but it is not the word I should use to describe it myself. It surprised Melchett too, I could see.

'Have you any light to throw upon the matter?' he asked.

'That's your business. It's the business of the police. What do we pay rates and taxes for, I should like to know?'

One wonders how many times that query is uttered in a year!

'We're doing our best, Mrs Price Ridley,' said the Chief Constable.

'But the man here hadn't even heard of it till I told him about it!' cried the lady.

We all looked at the constable.

'Lady been rung up on the telephone,' he said. 'Annoyed. Matter of obscene language, I understand.'

'Oh! I see.' The colonel's brow cleared. 'We've been talking at cross purposes. You came down here to make a complaint, did you?'

Melchett is a wise man. He knows that when it is a question of an irate middle-aged lady, there is only one thing to be done – listen to her. When she has said all that she wants to say, there is a chance that she will listen to you.

Mrs Price Ridley surged into speech.

'Such disgraceful occurrences ought to be prevented. They ought not to occur. To be rung up in one's own house and insulted – yes, insulted. I'm not accustomed to such things happening. Ever since the war there has been a loosening of moral fibre. Nobody minds what they say, and as to the clothes they wear –'

'Quite,' said Colonel Melchett hastily. 'What happened exactly?'

Mrs Price Ridley took breath and started again.

'I was rung up –'

'When?'

'Yesterday afternoon – evening to be exact. About half-past six. I went to the telephone, suspecting nothing. Immediately I was foully attacked, threatened –'

'What actually was said?'

Mrs Price Ridley got slightly pink.

'That I decline to state.'

'Obscene language,' murmured the constable in a ruminative bass.

'Was bad language used?' asked Colonel Melchett.

'It depends on what you call bad language.'

'Could you understand it?' I asked.

'Of course I could understand it.'

'Then it couldn't have been bad language,' I said.

Mrs Price Ridley looked at me suspiciously.

'A refined lady,' I explained, 'is naturally unacquainted with bad language.'

'It wasn't that kind of thing,' said Mrs Price Ridley. 'At first, I must admit, I was quite taken in. I thought it was a genuine message. Then the – er – person became abusive.'

'Abusive?'

'Most abusive. I was quite alarmed.'

'Used threatening language, eh?'

'Yes. I am not accustomed to being threatened.'

'What did they threaten you with? Bodily damage?'

'Not exactly.'

'I'm afraid, Mrs Price Ridley, you must be more explicit. In what way were you threatened?'

This Mrs Price Ridley seemed singularly reluctant to answer.

'I can't remember exactly. It was all so upsetting. But right at the end – when I was really *very* upset, this – this – *wretch* laughed.'

'Was it a man's voice or a woman's?'

'It was a degenerate voice,' said Mrs Price Ridley, with dignity. 'I can only describe it as a kind of perverted voice. Now gruff, now squeaky. Really a very *peculiar* voice.'

'Probably a practical joke,' said the colonel soothingly.

'A most wicked thing to do, if so. I might have had a heart attack.'

'We'll look into it,' said the colonel; 'eh, inspector? Trace the telephone call. You can't tell me more definitely exactly what was said, Mrs Price Ridley?'

A struggle began in Mrs Price Ridley's ample black bosom. The desire for reticence fought against a desire for vengeance. Vengeance triumphed.

'This, of course, will go no further,' she began.

'Of course not.'

'This creature began by saying – I can hardly bring myself to repeat it –'

'Yes, yes,' said Melchett encouragingly.

' "*You are a wicked scandal-mongering old woman!*" Me, Colonel Melchett – a scandal-mongering old woman. "*But this time you've gone too far. Scotland Yard are after you for libel.*" '

'Naturally, you were alarmed,' said Melchett, biting his moustache to conceal a smile.

' "*Unless you hold your tongue in future, it will be the worse for you – in more ways than one.*" I can't describe to you the menacing way *that* was said. I gasped, "who are you?" faintly – like that, and the voice answered, "*The Avenger*". I gave a little shriek. It sounded so awful, and then – the person laughed. Laughed! Distinctly. And that was all. I heard them hang up the receiver. Of course I asked the exchange what number had been ringing me up, but they said they didn't know. You know what exchanges are. Thoroughly rude and unsympathetic.'

'Quite,' I said.

'I felt quite faint,' continued Mrs Price Ridley. 'All on edge and so nervous that when I heard a shot in the woods, I do declare I jumped almost out of my skin. That will show you.'

'A shot in the woods?' said Inspector Slack alertly.

'In my excited state, it simply sounded to me like a cannon going off. "Oh!" I said, and sank down on the sofa in a state of prostration. Clara had to bring me a glass of damson gin.'

'Shocking,' said Melchett. 'Shocking. All very trying for you. And the shot sounded very loud, you say? As though it were near at hand?'

'That was simply the state of my nerves.'

'Of course. Of course. And what time was all this? To help us in tracing the telephone call, you know.'

'About half-past six.'

'You can't give it us more exactly than that?'

'Well, you see, the little clock on my mantlepiece had just chimed the half-hour, and I said, "Surely that clock is fast." (It does gain, that clock.) And I compared it with the watch I was wearing and that only said ten minutes past, but then I put it to my ear and found it had stopped. So I thought: "Well, if that clock *is* fast, I shall hear the church tower in a moment or two." And then, of course, the telephone bell rang, and I forgot all about it.' she paused breathless.

'Well, that's near enough,' said Colonel Melchett. 'We'll have it looked into for you, Mrs Price Ridley.'

'Just think of it as a silly joke, and don't worry, Mrs Price Ridley,' I said.

She looked at me coldly. Evidently the incident of the pound note still rankled.

'Very strange things have been happening in this village lately,' she said, addressing herself to Melchett. 'Very strange things indeed. Colonel Protheroe was going to look into them, and what happened to him, poor man? Perhaps I shall be the next?'

And on that she took her departure, shaking her head with a kind of ominous melancholy. Melchett muttered under his breath: 'No such luck.' Then his face grew grave, and he looked inquiringly at Inspector Slack.

That worthy nodded his head slowly.

'This about settles it, sir. That's three people who heard the shot. We've got to find out now who fired it. This business of Mr Redding's has delayed us. But we've got several starting points. Thinking Mr Redding was guilty, I didn't bother to look into them. But that's all changed now. And now one of the first things to do is look up that telephone call.'

'Mrs Price Ridley's?'

The inspector grinned.

'No – though I suppose we'd better make a note of that or else we shall have the old girl bothering in here again. No, I meant that fake call that got the vicar out of the way.'

'Yes,' said Melchett, 'that's important.'

'And the next thing is to find out what everyone was doing that evening between six and seven. Everyone at Old Hall, I mean, and pretty well everyone in the village as well.'

I gave a sigh.

'What wonderful energy you have, Inspector Slack.'

'I believe in hard work. We'll begin by just noting down your own movements, Mr Clement.'

'Willingly. The telephone call came through about half-past five.'

'A man's voice, or a woman's?'

'A woman's. At least is sounded like a woman's. But of course I took it for granted it was Mrs Abbott speaking.'

'You didn't recognize it as being Mrs Abbott's?'

'No, I can't say I did. I didn't notice the voice particularly or think about it.'

'And you started right away? Walked? Haven't you got a bicycle?'

'No.'

'I see. So it took you – how long?'

'It's very nearly two miles, whichever way you go.'

'Through Old Hall woods is the shortest way, isn't it?'

'Actually, yes. But it's not particularly good going. I went and came back by the footpath across the fields.'

'The one that comes out opposite the Vicarage gate?'

'Yes.'

'And Mrs Clement?'

'My wife was in London. She arrived back by the 6.50 train.'

'Right. The maid I've seen. That finishes with the Vicarage. I'll be off to Old Hall next. And then I want an interview with Mrs Lestrange. Queer, her going to see Protheroe the night before he was killed. A lot of queer things about this case.'

I agreed.

Glancing at the clock, I realized that it was nearly lunch time. I invited Melchett to partake of pot luck with us, but he excused himself on the plea of having to go to the Blue Boar. The Blue Boar gives you a first-rate meal of the joint and two-vegetable type. I thought his choice was a wise one. After her interview with the police, Mary would probably be feeling more temperamental than usual.

On my way home, I ran into Miss Hartnell and she detained me at least ten minutes, declaiming in her deep bass voice against the improvidence and ungratefulness of the lower classes. The crux of the matter seemed to be that The Poor did not want Miss Hartnell in their houses. My sympathies were entirely on their side. I am debarred by my social standing from expressing my prejudices in the forceful manner they do.

I soothed her as best I could and made my escape.

Haydock overtook me in his car at the corner of the Vicarage road. 'I've just taken Mrs Protheroe home,' he called.

He waited for me at the gate of his house.

'Come in a minute,' he said. I complied.

'This is an extraordinary business,' he said, as he threw his hat on a chair and opened the door into his surgery.

He sank down on a shabby leather chair and stared across the room. He looked harried and perplexed.

I told him that we had succeeded in fixing the time of the shot. He listened with an almost abstracted air.

'That lets Anne Protheroe out,' he said. 'Well, well, I'm glad it's neither of those two. I like 'em both.'

I believed him, and yet it occurred to me to wonder why, since, as he said, he liked them both, their freedom from complicity seemed to have had the result of plunging him in gloom. This morning he had looked like a man with a weight lifted from his mind, now he looked thoroughly rattled and upset.

And yet I was convinced that he meant what he said. He was fond of both Anne Protheroe and Lawrence Redding. Why, then, this gloomy absorption? He roused himself with an effort.

'I meant to tell you about Hawes. All this business has driven him out of my mind.'

'Is he really ill?'

'There's nothing radically wrong with him. You know, of course, that he's had Encephalitis Lethargica, sleepy sickness, as it's commonly called?'

'No,' I said, very much surprised, 'I didn't know anything of the kind. He never told me anything about it. When did he have it?'

'About a year ago. He recovered all right – as far as one ever recovers. It's a strange disease – has a queer moral effect. The whole character may change after it.'

He was silent for a moment or two, and then said:

'We think with horror now of the days when we burnt witches. I believe the day will come when we will shudder to think that we ever hanged criminals.'

'You don't believe in capital punishment?'

'It's not so much that.' He paused. 'You know,' he said slowly, 'I'd rather have my job than yours.'

'Why?'

'Because your job deals very largely with what we call right and wrong – and I'm not at all sure that there's any such thing. Suppose it's all a question of glandular secretion. Too much of one gland, too little of another – and you get your murderer, your thief, your habitual criminal. Clement, I believe the time will come when we'll be horrified to think of the long centuries in which we've punished people for disease – which they can't help, poor devils. You don't hang a man for having tuberculosis.'

'He isn't dangerous to the community.'

'In a sense he is. He infects other people. Or take a man who fancies he's the Emperor of China. You don't say how wicked of him. I take your point about the community. The community must be protected. Shut up these people where they can't do any harm – even put them peacefully out of the way – yes, I'd go as far as that. But don't call it punishment. Don't bring shame on them and their innocent families.'

I looked at him curiously.

'I've never heard you speak like this before.'

'I don't usually air my theories abroad. Today I'm riding my hobby. You're an intelligent man, Clement, which is more than some parsons are. You won't admit, I dare say, that there's no such thing as what is technically termed, 'Sin,' but you're broadminded enough to consider the possibility of such a thing.'

'It strikes at the root of all accepted ideas,' he said.

'Yes, we're a narrow-minded, self-righteous lot, only too keen to judge matters we know nothing about. I honestly believe crime is a case for the doctor, not the policeman and not the parson. In the future, perhaps, there won't be any such thing.'

'You'll have cured it?'

'We'll have cured it. Rather a wonderful thought. Have you ever studied the statistics of crime? No – very few people have. I have, though. You'd be amazed at the amount there is of adolescent crime, glands again, you see. Young Neil, the Oxfordshire murderer – killed five girls before he was suspected. Nice lad – never given any trouble of any kind. Lily Rose, the little Cornish girl – killed her uncle because he docked her of sweets. Hit him when he was asleep with a coal hammer. Went home and a fortnight later killed her elder sister who had annoyed her about some trifling matter.

586

Neither of them hanged, of course. Sent to a home. May be all right later – may not. Doubt if the girl will. The only thing she cares about is seeing the pigs killed. Do you know when suicide is commonest? Fifteen to sixteen years of age. From self-murder to murder of someone else isn't a very long step. But it's not a moral lack – it's a physical one.'

'What you say is terrible!'

'No – it's only new to you. New truths have to be faced. One's ideas adjusted. But sometimes – it makes life difficult.'

He sat there, frowning, yet with a strange look of weariness.

'Haydock,' I said, 'if you suspected – if you knew – that a certain person was a murderer, would you give that person up to the law, or would you be tempted to shield them?'

I was quite unprepared for the effect of my question. He turned on me angrily and suspiciously.

'What makes you say that, Clement? What's in your mind? Out with it, man.'

'Why, nothing particular,' I said, rather taken aback. 'Only – well, murder is in our minds just now. If by any chance you happened to discover the truth – I wondered how you would feel about it, that was all.'

His anger died down. He stared once more straight ahead of him like a man trying to read the answer to a riddle that perplexes him, yet which exists only in his own brain.

'If I suspected – if I knew – I should do my duty, Clement. At least, I hope so.'

'The question is – which way would you consider your duty lay?'

He looked at me with inscrutable eyes.

'That question comes to every man some time in his life, I suppose, Clement. And every man has to decide in his own way.'

'You don't know?'

'No, I don't know . . .'

I felt the best thing was to change the subject.

'That nephew of mine is enjoying this case thoroughly,' I said. 'Spends his entire time looking for footprints and cigarette ash.'

Haydock smiled. 'What age is he?'

'Just sixteen. You don't take tragedies seriously at that age. It's all Sherlock Homes and Arsene Lupin to you.'

Haydock said thoughtfully:

'He's a fine-looking boy. What are you going to do with him?'

'I can't afford a University education, I'm afraid. The boy himself wants to go into the Merchant Service. He failed for the Navy.'

'Well – it's a hard life – but he might do worse. Yes, he might do worse.'

'I must be going,' I exclaimed, catching sight of the clock. 'I'm nearly half an hour late for lunch.'

My family were just sitting down when I arrived. They demanded a full account of the morning's activities, which I gave them, feeling, as I did so, that most of it was in the nature of an anticlimax.

Dennis, however, was highly entertained by the history of Mrs Price Ridley's telephone call, and went into fits of laughter as I enlarged upon the nervous shock her system had sustained and the necessity for reviving her with damson gin.

'Serve the old cat right,' he exclaimed. 'She's got the worst tongue in the place. I wish I'd thought of ringing her up and giving her a fright. I say, Uncle Len, what about giving her a second dose?'

I hastily begged him to do nothing of the sort. Nothing is more dangerous than the well-meant efforts of the younger generation to assist you and show their sympathy.

Dennis's mood changed suddenly. He frowned and put on his man of the world air.

'I've been with Lettice most of the morning,' he said. 'You know, Griselda, she's really *very* worried. She doesn't want to show it, but she is. Very worried indeed.'

'I should hope so,' said Griselda, with a toss of her head.

Griselda is not too fond of Lettice Protheroe.

'I don't think you're ever quite fair to Lettice.'

'Don't you?' said Griselda.

'Lots of people don't wear mourning.'

Griselda was silent and so was I. Dennis continued:

'She doesn't talk to most people, but she *does* talk to me. She's awfully worried about the whole thing, and she thinks something ought to be done about it.'

'She will find,' I said, 'that Inspector Slack shares her opinion. He is going up to Old Hall this afternoon, and will probably make the life of everybody there quite unbearable to them in his efforts to get at the truth.'

'What do you think *is* the truth, Len?' asked my wife suddenly.

'It's hard to say, my dear. I can't say that at the moment I've any idea at all.'

'Did you say that Inspector Slack was going to trace that telephone call – the one that took you to the Abbotts'?'

'Yes.'

'But can he do it? Isn't it a very difficult thing to do?'

'I should not imagine so. The Exchange will have a record of the calls.'

'Oh!' My wife relapsed into thought.

'Uncle Len,' said my nephew, 'why were you so ratty with me this morning for joking about your wishing Colonel Protheroe to be murdered?'

'Because,' I said, 'there is a time for everything. Inspector Slack has no sense of humour. He took your words quite seriously, will probably cross-examine Mary, and will get out a warrant for my arrest.'

'Doesn't he know when a fellow's ragging?'

'No,' I said, 'he does not. He has attained his present position through hard work and zealous attention to duty. That has left him no time for the minor recreations of life.'

'Do you like him, Uncle Len?'

'No,' I said, 'I do not. From the first moment I saw him I disliked him intensely. But I have no doubt that he is a highly successful man in his profession.'

'You think he'll find out who shot old Protheroe?'

'If he doesn't,' I said, 'it will not be for the want of trying.'

Mary appeared and said:

'Mr Hawes wants to see you. I've put him in the drawing-room, and here's a note. Waiting for an answer. Verbal will do.' I tore open the note and read it.

'Dear Mr Clement. – I should be so very grateful if you could come and see me this afternoon as early as possible. I am in great trouble and would like your advice.

Sincerely yours,

'Estelle Lestrange.'

'Say I will come round in about half an hour,' I said to Mary. Then I went into the drawing-room to see Hawes.

Hawes's appearance distressed me very much. His hands were shaking and his face kept twitching nervously. In my opinion he should have been in bed, and I told him so. He insisted that he was perfectly well.

'I assure you, sir, I never felt better. Never in my life.'

This was so obviously wide of the truth that I hardly knew how to answer. I have a certain admiration for a man who will not give in to illness, but Hawes was carrying the thing rather too far.

'I called to tell you how sorry I was – that such a thing should happen in the Vicarage.'

'Yes,' I said, 'it's not very pleasant.'

'It's terrible – quite terrible. It seems they haven't arrested Mr Redding after all?'

'No. That was a mistake. He made – er – rather a foolish statement.'

'And the police are now quite convinced that he is innocent?'

'Perfectly.'

'Why is that, may I ask? Is it – I mean, do they suspect anyone else?'

I should never have suspected that Hawes would take such a keen interest in the details of a murder case. Perhaps it is because it happened in the Vicarage. He appeared as eager as a reporter.

'I don't know that I am completely in Inspector Slack's confidence. As far as I know, he does not suspect anyone in particular. He is at present engaged in making inquiries.'

'Yes. Yes – of course. But who can one imagine doing such a dreadful thing?'

I shook my head.

'Colonel Protheroe was not a popular man, I know that. But murder! For murder – one would need a very strong motive.'

'So I should imagine,' I said.

'Who could have such a motive? Have the police any idea?'

'I couldn't say.'

'He might have made enemies, you know. The more I think about it, the more I am convinced that he was the kind of man to have enemies. He had a reputation on the Bench for being very severe.'

'I suppose he had.'

'Why, don't you remember, sir? He was telling you yesterday morning about having been threatened by that man Archer.'

'Now I come to think of it, so he did,' I said. 'Of course, I remember. You were quite near us at the time.'

'Yes, I overheard what he was saying. Almost impossible to help it with

590

Colonel Protheroe. He had such a very loud voice, hadn't he? I remember being impressed by your own words. That when his time came, he might have justice meted out to him instead of mercy.'

'Did I say that?' I asked, frowning. My remembrance of my own words was slightly different.

'You said it very impressively, sir. I was struck by your words. Justice is a terrible thing. And to think the poor man was struck down shortly afterwards. It's almost as though you had a premonition.'

'I had nothing of the sort,' I said shortly. I rather dislike Hawes's tendency to mysticism. There is a touch of the visionary about him.

'Have you told the police about this man Archer, sir?'

'I know nothing about him.'

'I mean, have you repeated to them what Colonel Protheroe said – about Archer having threatened him?'

'No,' I said slowly. 'I have not.'

'But you are going to do so?'

I was silent. I dislike hounding a man down who has already got the forces of law and order against him. I held no brief for Archer. He is an inveterate poacher – one of those cheerful ne'er-do-wells that are to be found in any parish. Whatever he may have said in the heat of anger when he was sentenced I had no definite knowledge that he felt the same when he came out of prison.

'You heard the conversation,' I said at last. 'If you feel it your duty to go to the police with it, you must do so.'

'It would come better from you, sir.'

'Perhaps – but to tell the truth – well, I've no fancy for doing it. I might be helping to put the rope round the neck of an innocent man.'

'But if he shot Colonel Protheroe –'

'Oh, if! There's no evidence of any kind that he did.'

'His threats.'

'Strictly speaking, the threats were not his, but Colonel Protheroe's. Colonel Protheroe was threatening to show Archer what vengeance was worth next time he caught him.'

'I don't understand your attitude, sir.'

'Don't you,' I said wearily. 'You're a young man. You're zealous in the cause of right. When you get to my age, you'll find that you like to give people the benefit of the doubt.'

'It's not – I mean –'

He paused, and I looked at him in surprise.

'You haven't any – any idea of your own – as to the identity of the murderer, I mean?'

591

'Good heavens, no.'

Hawes persisted. 'Or as to the – motive?'

'No. Have you?'

'I? No, indeed. I just wondered. If Colonel Protheroe had – had confided in you in any way – mentioned anything . . .'

'His confidences, such as they were, were heard by the whole village street yesterday morning,' I said dryly.

'Yes. Yes, of course. And you don't think – about Archer?'

'The police will know all about Archer soon enough,' I said. 'If I'd heard him threaten Colonel Protheroe myself, that would be a different matter. But you may be sure that if he actually has threatened him, half the people in the village will have heard him, and the news will get to the police all right. You, of course, must do as you like about the matter.'

But Hawes seemed curiously unwilling to do anything himself.

The man's whole attitude was nervous and queer. I recalled what Haydock had said about his illness. There, I supposed, lay the explanation.

He took his leave unwillingly, as though he had more to say, and didn't know how to say it.

Before he left, I arranged with him to take the service for the Mothers' Union, followed by the meeting of District Visitors. I had several projects of my own for the afternoon.

Dismissing Hawes and his troubles from my mind I started off for Mrs Lestrange.

On the table in the hall lay the *Guardian* and the *Church Times* unopened.

As I walked, I remembered that Mrs Lestrange had had an interview with Colonel Protheroe the night before his death. It was possible that something had transpired in that interview which would throw light upon the problem of his murder.

I was shown straight into the little drawing-room, and Mrs Lestrange rose to meet me. I was struck anew by the marvellous atmosphere that this woman could create. She wore a dress of some dead black material that showed off the extraordinary fairness of her skin. There was something curiously dead about her face. Only the eyes were burningly alive. There was a watchful look in them today. Otherwise she showed no signs of animation.

'It was very good of you to come, Mr Clement,' she said, as she shook hands. 'I wanted to speak to you the other day. Then I decided not to do so. I was wrong.'

'As I told you then, I shall be glad to do anything that can help you.'

'Yes, you said that. And you said it as though you meant it. Very few people, Mr Clement, in this world have ever sincerely wished to help me.'

592

'I can hardly believe that, Mrs Lestrange.'

'It is true. Most people – most men, at any rate, are out for their own hand.' There was a bitterness in her voice.

I did not answer, and she went on:

'Sit down, won't you?'

I obeyed, and she took a chair facing me. She hesitated a moment and then began to speak very slowly and thoughtfully, seeming to weigh each word as she uttered it.

'I am in a very peculiar position, Mr Clement, and I want to ask your advice. That is, I want to ask your advice as to what I should do next. What is past is past and cannot be undone. You understand?'

Before I could reply, the maid who had admitted me opened the door and said with a scared face:

'Oh! Please, ma'am, there is a police inspector here, and he says he must speak to you, please.'

There was a pause. Mrs Lestrange's face did not change. Only her eyes very slowly closed and opened again. She seemed to swallow once or twice, then she said in exactly the same clear, calm voice: 'Show him in, Hilda.'

I was about to rise, but she motioned me back again with an imperious hand.

'If you do not mind – I should be much obliged if you would stay.'

I resumed my seat.

'Certainly, if you wish it,' I murmured, as Slack entered with a brisk regulation tread.

'Good afternoon, madam,' he began.

'Good afternoon, inspector.'

At this moment, he caught sight of me and scowled. There is no doubt about it, Slack does not like me.

'You have no objection to the vicar's presence, I hope?'

I suppose that Slack could not very well say he had.

'No-o,' he said grudgingly. 'Though, perhaps, it might be better –'

Mrs Lestrange paid no attention to the hint.

'What can I do for you, inspector?' she asked.

'It's this way, madam. Murder of Colonel Protheroe. I'm in charge of the case and making inquiries.'

Mrs Lestrange nodded.

'Just as a matter of form, I'm asking everyone just where they were yesterday evening between the hours of 6 and 7 p.m. Just as a matter of form, you understand.'

'You want to know where I was yesterday evening between six and seven?'

'If you please, madam.'

'Let me see.' She reflected a moment. 'I was here. In this house.'

'Oh!' I saw the inspector's eyes flash. 'And your maid – you have only one maid, I think – can confirm that statement?'

'No, it was Hilda's afternoon out.'

'I see.'

'So, unfortunately, you will have to take my word for it,' said Mrs Lestrange pleasantly.

'You seriously declare that you were at home all the afternoon?'

'You said between six and seven, inspector. I was out for a walk early in the afternoon. I returned some time before five o'clock.'

'Then if a lady – Miss Hartnell, for instance – were to declare that she came here about six o'clock, rang the bell, but could make no one hear and was compelled to go away again – you'd say she was mistaken, eh?'

'Oh, no,' Mrs Lestrange shook her head.

'But –'

'If your maid is in, she can say not at home. If one is alone and does not happen to want to see callers – well, the only thing to do is to let them ring.'

Inspector Slack looked slightly baffled.

'Elderly women bore me dreadfully,' said Mrs Lestrange. 'And Miss Hartnell is particularly boring. She must have rung at least half a dozen times before she went away.'

She smiled sweetly at Inspector Slack.

The inspector shifted his ground.

'Then if anyone were to say they'd seen you out and about then –'

'Oh! but they didn't, did they?' She was quick to sense his weak point. 'No one saw me out, because I was in, you see.'

'Quite so, madam.'

The inspector hitched his chair a little nearer.

'Now I understand, Mrs Lestrange, that you paid a visit to Colonel Protheroe at Old Hall the night before his death.'

Mrs Lestrange said calmly: 'That is so.'

'Can you indicate to me the nature of that interview?'

'It concerned a private matter, inspector.'

'I'm afraid I must ask you tell me the nature of that private matter.'

'I shall not tell you anything of the kind. I will only assure you that nothing which was said at that interview could possibly have any bearing upon the crime.'

'I don't think you are the best judge of that.'

'At any rate, you will have to take my word for it, inspector.'

'In fact, I have to take your word about everything.'

'It does seem rather like it,' she agreed, still with the same smiling calm.

Inspector Slack grew very red.

'This is a serious matter, Mrs Lestrange. I want the truth –' He banged his fist down on a table. 'And I mean to get it.'

Mrs Lestrange said nothing at all.

'Don't you see, madam, that you're putting yourself in a very fishy position?'

Still Mrs Lestrange said nothing.

'You'll be required to give evidence at the inquest.'

'Yes.'

Just the monosyllable. Unemphatic, uninterested. The inspector altered his tactics.

'You were acquainted with Colonel Protheroe?'

'Yes, I was acquainted with him.'

'Well acquainted?'

There was a pause before she said:

'I had not seen him for several years.'

'You were acquainted with Mrs Protheroe?'

'No.'

'You'll excuse me, but it was a very unusual time to make a call.'

'Not from my point of view.'

'What do you mean by that?'

'I wanted to see Colonel Protheroe alone. I did not want to see Mrs Protheroe or Miss Protheroe. I considered this the best way of accomplishing my object.'

'Why didn't you want to see Mrs or Miss Protheroe?'

'That, inspector, is my business.'

'Then you refuse to say more?'

'Absolutely.'

Inspector Slack rose.

'You'll be putting yourself in a nasty position, madam, if you're not careful. All this looks bad – it looks very bad.'

She laughed. I could have told Inspector Slack that this was not the kind of woman who is easily frightened.

'Well,' he said, extricating himself with dignity, 'don't say I haven't warned you, that's all. Good afternoon, madam, and mind you we're going to get at the truth.'

He departed. Mrs Lestrange rose and held out her hand.

'I have chosen my part.'

'I am going to send you away – yes, it is better so. You see, it is too late for advice now. I have chosen my part.'

She repeated in a rather forlorn voice:

As I went out I ran into Haydock on the doorstep. He glanced sharply after Slack, who was just passing through the gate, and demanded: 'Has he been questioning her?'

'Yes.'

'He's been civil, I hope?'

Civility, to my mind, is an art which Inspector Slack has never learnt, but I presumed that according to his own lights, civil he had been, and anyway, I didn't want to upset Haydock any further. He was looking worried and upset as it was. So I said he had been quite civil.

Haydock nodded and passed on into the house, and I went on down the village street, where I soon caught up the inspector. I fancy that he was walking slowly on purpose. Much as he dislikes me, he is not the man to let dislike stand in the way of acquiring any useful information.

'Do you know anything about the lady?' he asked me point blank.

I said I knew nothing whatever.

'She's never said anything about why she came here to live?'

'No.'

'Yet you go and see her?'

'It is one of my duties to call on my parishioners,' I replied, evading to remark that I had been sent for.

'H'm, I suppose it is.' He was silent for a minute or two and then, unable to resist discussing his recent failure, he went on: 'Fishy business, it looks to me.'

'You think so?'

'If you ask me, I say "blackmail." Seems funny, when you think of what Colonel Protheroe was always supposed to be. But there, you never can tell. He wouldn't be the first churchwarden who'd led a double life.'

Faint remembrances of Miss Marple's remarks on the same subject floated through my mind.

'You really think that's likely?'

'Well, it fits the facts, sir. Why did a smart, well-dressed lady come down to this quiet little hole? Why did she go and see him at that funny time of day? Why did she avoid seeing Mrs and Miss Protheroe? Yes, it all hangs together. Awkward for her to admit – blackmail's a punishable offence. But we'll get the truth out of her. For all we know it may have a very important bearing on the case. If Colonel Protheroe had some guilty secret in his life – something disgraceful – well, you can see for yourself what a field it opens up.'

I suppose it did.

'I've been trying to get the butler to talk. He might have overheard some of the conversation between Colonel Protheroe and Lestrange. Butlers do sometimes. But he swears he hasn't the least idea of what the conversation was about. By the way, he got the sack through it. The colonel went for him, being angry at his having let her in. The butler retorted by giving notice. Says he didn't like the place anyway and had been thinking of leaving for some time.'

'Really.'

'So that gives us another person who had a grudge against the colonel.'

'You don't seriously suspect the man – what's his name, by the way?'

'His name's Reeves, and I don't say I do suspect him. What I say is, you never know. I don't like that soapy, oily manner of his.'

I wonder what Reeves would say of Inspector Slack's manner.

'I'm going to question the chauffeur now.'

'Perhaps, then,' I said, 'you'll give me a lift in your car. I want a short interview with Mrs Protheroe.'

'What about?'

'The funeral arrangements.'

'Oh!' Inspector Slack was slightly taken aback. 'The inquest's tomorrow, Saturday.'

'Just so. The funeral will probably be arranged for Tuesday.'

Inspector Slack seemed to be a little ashamed of himself for his brusqueness. He held out an olive branch in the shape of an invitation to be present at the interview with the chauffeur, Manning.

Manning was a nice lad, not more than twenty-five or six years of age. He was inclined to be awed by the inspector.

'Now, then, my lad,' said Slack, 'I want a little information from you.'

'Yes, sir,' stammered the chauffeur. 'Certainly, sir.'

If he had committed the murder himself he could not have been more alarmed.

'You took your master to the village yesterday?'

'Yes, sir.'

'What time was that?'

'Five-thirty.'

'Mrs Protheroe went too?'

'Yes, sir.'

'You went straight to the village?'

'Yes, sir.'

'You didn't stop anywhere on the way?'

'No, sir.'

'What did you do when you got there?'

'The colonel got out and told me he wouldn't want the car again. He'd walk home. Mrs Protheroe had some shopping to do. The parcels were put in the car. Then she said that was all, and I drove home.'

'Leaving her in the village?'

'Yes, sir.'

'What time was that?'

'A quarter past six, sir. A quarter past exactly.'

'Where did you leave her?'

'By the church, sir.'

'Had the colonel mentioned at all where he was going?'

'He said something about having to see the vet . . . something to do with one of the horses.'

'I see. And you drove straight back here?'

'Yes, sir.'

'There are two entrances to Old Hall, by the South Lodge and by the North Lodge. I take it that going to the village you would go by the South Lodge?'

'Yes, sir, always.'

'And you came back the same way?'

'Yes, sir.'

'H'm. I think that's all. Ah! Here's Miss Protheroe.'

Lettice drifted towards us.

'I want the Fiat, Manning,' she said. 'Start her for me, will you?'

'Very good, miss.'

He went towards a two-seater and lifted the bonnet.

'Just a minute, Miss Protheroe,' said Slack. 'It's necessary that I should have a record of everybody's movements yesterday afternoon. No offence meant.'

Lettice stared at him.

'I never know the time of anything,' she said.

'I understand you went out soon after lunch yesterday?'

She nodded.

'Where to, please?'

'To play tennis.'

'Who with?'

'The Hartley Napiers.'

'At Much Benham?'

'Yes.'

'And you returned?'

'I don't know. I tell you I never know these things.'

'You returned,' I said, 'about seven-thirty.'

599

'That's right,' said Lettice. 'In the middle of the shemozzle. Anne having fits and Griselda supporting her.'

'Thank you, miss,' said the inspector. 'That's all I want to know.'

'How queer,' said Lettice. 'It seems so uninteresting.'

She moved towards the Fiat.

The inspector touched his forehead in a surreptitious manner.

'A bit wanting?' he suggested.

'Not in the least,' I said. 'But she likes to be thought so.'

'Well, I'm off to question the maids now.'

One cannot really like Slack, but one can admire his energy.

We parted company and I inquired of Reeves if I could see Mrs Protheroe. 'She is lying down, sir, at the moment.'

'Then I'd better not disturb her.'

'Perhaps if you would wait, sir, I know that Mrs Protheroe is anxious to see you. She was saying as much at luncheon.'

He showed me into the drawing-room, switching on the electric lights since the blinds were down.

'A very sad business all this,' I said.

'Yes, sir.' His voice was cold and respectful.

I looked at him. What feelings were at work under that impassive demeanour. Were there things that he knew and could have told us? There is nothing so inhuman as the mask of the good servant.

'Is there anything more, sir?'

Was there just a hint of anxiety to be gone behind that correct expression?

'There's nothing more,' I said.

I had a very short time to wait before Anne Protheroe came to me. We discussed and settled a few arrangements and then:

'What a wonderfully kind man Dr Haydock is!' she exclaimed.

'Haydock is the best fellow I know.'

'He has been amazingly kind to me. But he looks very sad, doesn't he?'

It had never occurred to me to think of Haydock as sad. I turned the idea over in my mind.

'I don't think I've ever noticed it,' I said at last.

'I never have, until today.'

'One's own troubles sharpen one's eyes sometimes,' I said.

'That's very true.' She paused and then said:

'Mr Clement, there's one thing I absolutely *cannot* make out. If my husband were shot immediately after I left him, how was it that I didn't hear the shot?'

'They have reason to believe that the shot was fired later.'

'But the 6.20 on the note?'

'Was possibly added by a different hand – the murderer's.'

Her cheek paled.

'It didn't strike you that the date was not in his handwriting?'

'How horrible!'

'None of it looked like his handwriting.'

There was some truth in this observation. It was a somewhat illegible scrawl, not so precise as Protheroe's writing usually was.

'You are sure they don't still suspect Lawrence?'

'I think he is definitely cleared.'

'But, Mr Clement, who can it be? Lucius was not popular, I know, but I don't think he had any real enemies. Not – not that kind of enemy.'

I shook my head. 'It's a mystery.'

I thought wonderingly of Miss Marple's seven suspects. Who could they be?

After I took leave of Anne, I proceeded to put a certain plan of mine into action.

I returned from Old Hall by way of the private path. When I reached the stile, I retraced my steps, and choosing a place where I fancied the undergrowth showed signs of being disturbed, I turned aside from the path and forced my way through the bushes. The wood was a thick one, with a good deal of tangled undergrowth. My progress was not very fast, and I suddenly became aware that someone else was moving amongst the bushes not very far from me. As I paused irresolutely, Lawrence Redding came into sight. He was carrying a large stone.

I suppose I must have looked surprised, for he suddenly burst out laughing.

'No,' he said, 'it's not a clue, it's a peace offering.'

'A peace offering?'

'Well, a basis for negotiations, shall we say? I want an excuse for calling on your neighbour, Miss Marple, and I have been told there is nothing she likes so much as a nice bit of rock or stone for the Japanese gardens she makes.'

'Quite true,' I said. 'But what do you want with the old lady?'

'Just this. If there was anything to be seen yesterday evening Miss Marple saw it. I don't mean anything necessarily connected with the crime – that she would think connected with the crime. I mean some *outré* or bizarre incident, some simple little happening that might give us a clue to the truth. Something that she wouldn't think worth while mentioning to the police.'

'It's possible, I suppose.'

'It's worth trying anyhow. Clement, I'm going to get to the bottom of this business. For Anne's sake, if nobody's else. And I haven't any too much confidence in Slack – he's a zealous fellow, but zeal can't really take the place of brains.'

'I see,' I said, 'that you are that favourite character of fiction, the amateur detective. I don't know that they really hold their own with the professional in real life.'

He looked at me shrewdly and suddenly laughed.

'What are you doing in the wood, padre?'

I had the grace to blush.

'Just the same as I am doing, I dare swear. We've got the same idea, haven't we? *How did the murderer come to the study?* First way, along the lane and through the gate, second way, by the front door, third way – is there a third way? My idea was to see if there was any sign of the bushes being disturbed or broken anywhere near the wall of the Vicarage garden.'

'That was just my idea,' I admitted.

'I hadn't really got down to the job, though,' continued Lawrence. 'Because it occurred to me that I'd like to see Miss Marple first, to make quite sure that no one did pass along the lane yesterday evening whilst we were in the studio.'

I shook my head.

'She was quite positive that nobody did.'

'Yes, nobody whom she would call anybody – sounds mad, but you see what I mean. But there might have been someone like a postman or a milkman or a butcher's boy – someone whose presence would be so natural that you wouldn't think of mentioning it.'

'You've been reading G.K. Chesterton,' I said, and Lawrence did not deny it.

'But don't you think there's just possibly something in the idea?'

'Well, I suppose there might be,' I admitted.

Without further ado, we made our way to Miss Marple's. She was working in the garden, and called out to us as we climbed over the stile.

'You see,' murmured Lawrence, 'she sees everybody.'

She received us very graciously and was much pleased with Lawrence's immense rock, which he presented with all due solemnity.

'It's very thoughtful of you, Mr Redding. Very thoughtful indeed.'

Emboldened by this, Lawrence embarked on his questions. Miss Marple listened attentively.

'Yes, I see what you mean, and I quite agree, it is the sort of thing no one mentions or bothers to mention. But I can assure you that there was nothing of the kind. Nothing whatever.'

'You are sure, Miss Marple?'

'Quite sure.'

'Did you see anyone go by the path into the wood that afternoon?' I asked. 'Or come from it?'

'Oh, yes, quite a number of people. Dr Stone and Miss Cram went that way – it's the nearest way to the barrow for them. That was a little after two o'clock. And Dr Stone returned that way – as you know, Mr Redding, since he joined you and Mrs Protheroe.'

'By the way,' I said. 'That shot – the one you heard, Miss Marple. Mr Redding and Mrs Protheroe must have heard it too.'

I looked inquiringly at Lawrence.

'Yes,' he said, frowning. 'I believe I did hear some shots. Weren't there one or two shots?'

'I only heard one,' said Miss Marple.

'It's only the vaguest impression in my mind,' said Lawrence. 'Curse it all, I wish I could remember. If only I'd known. You see, I was so completely taken up with – with –'

He paused, embarrassed.

I gave a tactful cough. Miss Marple, with a touch of prudishness, changed the subject.

'Inspector Slack has been trying to get me to say whether I heard the shot after Mr Redding and Mrs Protheroe had left the studio or before. I've had to confess that I really could not say definitely, but I have the impression – which is growing stronger the more I think about it – that it was after.'

'Then that lets the celebrated Dr Stone out anyway,' said Lawrence, with a sigh. 'Not that there has ever been the slightest reason why he should be suspected of shooting poor old Protheroe.'

'Ah!' said Miss Marple. 'But I always find it prudent to suspect everybody just a little. What I say is, you really never *know*, do you?'

This was typical of Miss Marple. I asked Lawrence if he agreed with her about the shot.

'I really can't say. You see, it was such an ordinary sound. I should be inclined to think it had been fired when we were in the studio. The sound would have been deadened and – one would have noticed it less there.'

For other reasons than the sound being deadened, I thought to myself.

'I must ask Anne,' said Lawrence. 'She may remember. By the way, there seems to me to be one curious fact that needs explanation. Mrs Lestrange, the Mystery Lady of St Mary Mead, paid a visit to old Protheroe after dinner on Wednesday night. And nobody seems to have any idea what it was all about. Old Protheroe said nothing to either his wife or Lettice.'

'Perhaps the vicar knows,' said Miss Marple.

Now how did the woman know that I had been to visit Mrs Lestrange that afternoon? The way she always knows things is uncanny.

I shook my head and said I could throw no light upon the matter.

'What does Inspector Slack think?' asked Miss Marple.

'He's done his best to bully the butler – but apparently the butler wasn't curious enough to listen at the door. So there it is – no one knows.'

'I expect someone overheard something, though, don't you?' said Miss Marple. 'I mean, somebody always *does*. I think that is where Mr Redding may find out something.'

'But Mrs Protheroe knows nothing.'

'I didn't mean Anne Protheroe,' said Miss Marple. 'I meant the women servants. They do so hate telling anything to the police. But a nice-looking young man – you'll excuse me, Mr Redding – and one who has been unjustly suspected – oh! I'm sure they'd tell him at once.'

'I'll go and have a try this evening,' said Lawrence with vigour. 'Thanks for the hint, Miss Marple. I'll go after – well, after a little job the vicar and I are going to do.'

It occurred to me that we had better be getting on with it. I said goodbye to Miss Marple and we entered the woods once more.

First we went up the path till we came to a new spot where it certainly looked as though someone had left the path on the right-hand side. Lawrence explained that he had already followed this particular trail and found it led nowhere, but he added that we might as well try again. He might have been wrong.

It was, however, as he had said. After about ten or twelve yards any sign of broken and trampled leaves petered out. It was from this spot that Lawrence had broken back towards the path to meet me earlier in the afternoon.

We emerged on the path again and walked a little farther along it. Again we came to a place where the bushes seemed disturbed. The signs were very slight but, I thought, unmistakable. This time the trail was more promising. By a devious course, it wound steadily nearer to the Vicarage. Presently we arrived at where the bushes grew thickly up to the wall. The wall is a high one and ornamented with fragments of broken bottles on the top. If anyone had placed a ladder against it, we ought to find traces of their passage.

We were working our way slowly along the wall when a sound came to our ears of a breaking twig. I pressed forward, forcing my way through a thick tangle of shrubs – and came face to face with Inspector Slack.

'So it's you,' he said. 'And Mr Redding. Now what do you think you two gentlemen are doing?'

Slightly crestfallen, we explained.

'Quite so,' said the inspector. 'Not being the fools we're usually thought to be, I had the same idea myself. I've been here over an hour. Would you like to know something?'

'Yes,' I said meekly.

'Whoever murdered Colonel Protheroe didn't come this way to do it! There's not a sign either on this side of the wall, nor the other. Whoever murdered Colonel Protheroe came through the front door. There's no other way he could have come.'

'Impossible,' I cried.

'Why impossible? Your door stands open. Anyone's only got to walk in. They can't be seen from the kitchen. They know you're safely out of the way, they know Mrs Clement is in London, they know Mr Dennis is at a tennis party. Simple as A B C. And they don't need to go or come through the village. Just opposite the Vicarage gate is a public footpath, and from it you can turn into these same woods and come out whichever way you choose. Unless Mrs Price Ridley were to come out of her front gate at that particular minute, it's all clear sailing. A great deal more so than climbing over walls. The side windows of the upper storey of Mrs Price Ridley's house do overlook most of that wall. No, depend upon it, that's the way he came.'

It really seemed as though he must be right.

Inspector Slack came round to see me the following morning. He is, I think, thawing towards me. In time, he may forget the incident of the clock.

'Well, sir,' he greeted me. 'I've traced that telephone call that you received.'

'Indeed?' I said eagerly.

'It's rather odd. It was put through from the North Lodge of Old Hall. Now that lodge is empty, the lodgekeepers have been pensioned off and the next lodgekeepers aren't in yet. The place was empty and convenient – a window at the back was open. No fingerprints on the instrument itself – it had been wiped clear. That's suggestive.'

'How do you mean?'

'I mean that it shows that call was put through deliberately to get you out of the way. Therefore the murder was carefully planned in advance. If it had been just a harmless practical joke, the fingerprints wouldn't have been wiped off so carefully.'

'No. I see that.'

'It also shows that the murderer was well acquainted with Old Hall and its surroundings. It wasn't Mrs Protheroe who put that call through. I've accounted for every moment of her time that afternoon. There are half a dozen other servants who can swear that she was at home till five-thirty. Then the car came round and drove Colonel Protheroe and her to the village. The colonel went to see Quinton, the vet, about one of the horses. Mrs Protheroe did some ordering at the grocers and at the fish shop, and from there came straight down the back lane where Miss Marple saw her. All the shops agree she carried no handbag with her. The old lady was right.'

'She usually is,' I said mildly.

'And Miss Protheroe was over at Much Benham at 5.30.'

'Quite so,' I said. 'My nephew was there too.'

'That disposes of her. The maid seems all right – a bit hysterical and upset, but what can you expect? Of course, I've got my eye on the butler – what with giving notice and all. But I don't think he knows anything about it.'

'Your inquiries seem to have had rather a negative result, inspector.'

'They do and they do not, sir. There's one very queer thing has turned up – quite unexpectedly, I may say.'

'Yes?'

'You remember the fuss that Mrs Price Ridley, who lives next door to you, was kicking up yesterday morning? About being rung up on the telephone?'

'Yes?' I said.

'Well, we traced the call just to calm her – and where on this earth do you think it was put through from?'

'A call office?' I hazarded.

'No, Mr Clement. That call was put through from Mr Lawrence Redding's cottage.'

'What?' I exclaimed, surprised.

'Yes. A bit odd, isn't it? Mr Redding had nothing to do with it. At that time, 6.30, he was on his way to the Blue Boar with Dr Stone in full view of the village. But there it is. Suggestive, eh? Someone walked into that empty cottage and used the telephone, who was it? That's two queer telephone calls in one day. Makes you think there's some connection between them. I'll eat my hat if they weren't both put through by the same person.'

'But with what object?'

'Well, that's what we've got to find out. There seems no particular point in the second one, but there must be a point somewhere. And you see the significance? Mr Redding's house used to telephone from. Mr Redding's pistol. All throwing suspicion on Mr Redding.'

'It would be more to the point to have put through the *first* call from his house,' I objected.

'Ah, but I've been thinking that out. What did Mr Redding do most afternoons? He went up to Old Hall and painted Miss Protheroe. And from his cottage he'd go on his motor bicycle, passing through the North Gate. Now you see the point of the call being put through from there. *The murderer is someone who didn't know about the quarrel and that Mr Redding wasn't going up to Old Hall any more.*'

I reflected a moment to let the inspector's points sink into my brain. They seemed to me logical and unavoidable.

'Were there any fingerprints on the receiver in Mr Redding's cottage?' I asked.

'There were not,' said the inspector bitterly. 'That dratted old woman who goes and does for him had been and dusted them off yesterday morning.' He reflected wrathfully for a few minutes. 'She's a stupid old fool, anyway. Can't remember when she saw the pistol last. It might have been there on the morning of the crime, or it might not. "She couldn't say, she's sure." They're all alike!

'Just as a matter of form, I went round and saw Dr Stone,' he went on. 'I must say he was pleasant as could be about it. He and Miss Cram went up to that mound – or barrow – or whatever you call it, about half-past two yesterday, and stayed there all the afternoon. Dr Stone came back alone, and she came later. He says he didn't hear any shot, but admits he's absent-minded. But it all bears out what we think.'

'Only,' I said, 'you haven't caught the murderer.'

'H'm,' said the inspector. 'It was a woman's voice you heard through the telephone. It was in all probability a woman's voice Mrs Price Ridley heard. If only that shot hadn't come hard on the close of the telephone call – well, I'd know where to look.'

'Where?'

'Ah! That's just what it's best not to say, sir.'

Unblushingly, I suggested a glass of old port. I have some very fine old vintage port. Eleven o'clock in the morning is not the usual time for drinking port, but I did not think that mattered with Inspector Slack. It was, of course, cruel abuse of the vintage port, but one must not be squeamish about such things.

When Inspector Slack had polished off the second glass, he began to unbend and become genial. Such is the effect of that particular port.

'I don't suppose it matters with you, sir,' he said. 'You'll keep it to yourself? No letting it get round the parish.'

I reassured him.

'Seeing as the whole thing happened in your house, it almost seems as though you have a right to know.'

'Just what I feel myself,' I said.

'Well, then, sir, what about the lady who called on Colonel Protheroe the night before the murder?'

'Mrs Lestrange,' I cried, speaking rather loud in my astonishment.

The inspector threw me a reproachful glance.

'Not so loud, sir. Mrs Lestrange is the lady I've got my eye on. You remember what I told you – blackmail.'

'Hardly a reason for murder. Wouldn't it be a case of killing the goose that laid the golden eggs? That is, assuming that your hypothesis is true, which I don't for a minute admit.'

The inspector winked at me in a common manner.

'Ah! She's the kind the gentlemen will always stand up for. Now look here, sir. Suppose she's successfully blackmailed the old gentleman in the past. After a lapse of years, she gets wind of him, comes down here and tries it on again. *But*, in the meantime, things have changed. The law has taken up a very different stand. Every facility is given nowadays to people prosecuting for blackmail – names are not allowed to be reported in the press. Suppose Colonel Protheroe turns round and says he'll have the law on her. She's in a nasty position. They give a very severe sentence for blackmail. The boot's on the other leg. The only thing to do to save herself is to put him out good and quick.'

I was silent. I had to admit that the case the inspector had built up was plausible. Only one thing to my mind made it inadmissable – the personality of Mrs Lestrange.

'I don't agree with you, inspector,' I said. 'Mrs Lestrange doesn't seem to me to be a potential blackmailer. She's – well, it's an old-fashioned word, but she's a – lady.'

He threw me a pitying glance.

'Ah! well, sir,' he said tolerantly, 'you're a clergyman. You don't know half of what goes on. Lady indeed! You'd be surprised if you knew some of the things I know.'

'I'm not referring to mere social position. Anyway, I should imagine Mrs Lestrange to be a *déclassée*. What I mean is a question of – personal refinement.'

'You don't see her with the same eyes as I do, sir. I may be a man – but I'm a police officer, too. They can't get over me with their personal refinement. Why, that woman is the kind who could stick a knife into you without turning a hair.'

Curiously enough, I could believe Mrs Lestrange guilty of murder much more easily that I could believe her capable of blackmail.

'But, of course, she can't have been telephoning to the old lady next door and shooting Colonel Protheroe at one and the same time,' continued the inspector.

The words were hardly out of his mouth when he slapped his leg ferociously.

'Got it,' he exclaimed. 'That's the point of the telephone call. Kind of *alibi*. Knew we'd connect it with the first one. I'm going to look into this. She may have bribed some village lad to do the phoning for her. *He'd* never think of connecting it with the murder.'

The inspector hurried off.

'Miss Marple wants to see you,' said Griselda, putting her head in. 'She sent over a very incoherent note – all spidery and underlined. I couldn't read most of it. Apparently she can't leave home herself. Hurry up and go across and see her and find out what it is. I've got my old women coming in two minutes or I'd come myself. I do hate old women – they tell you about their bad legs and sometimes insist on showing them to you. What luck that the inquest is this afternoon! You won't have to go and watch the Boys' Club Cricket Match.'

I hurried off, considerably exercised in my mind as to the reason for this summons.

I found Miss Marple in what, I believe, is described as a fluster. She was very pink and slightly incoherent.

'My nephew,' she explained. 'My nephew, Raymond West, the author. He is coming down today. Such a to-do. I have to see to everything myself. You cannot trust a maid to air a bed properly, and we must, of course, have a meat meal tonight. Gentlemen require such a lot of meat, do they not? And drink. There certainly should be some drink in the house – and a siphon.'

'If I can do anything –' I began.

'Oh! How very kind. But I did not mean that. There is plenty of time really. He brings his own pipe and tobacco, I am glad to say. Glad because it saves me from knowing which kind of cigarettes are right to buy. But rather sorry, too, because it takes so long for the smell to get out of the curtains. Of course, I open the window and shake them well very early every morning. Raymond gets up very late – I think writers often do. He writes very clever books, I believe, though people are not really nearly so unpleasant as he makes out. Clever young men know so little of life, don't you think?'

'Would you like to bring him to dinner at the Vicarage?' I asked, still unable to gather why I had been summoned.

'Oh! No, thank you,' said Miss Marple. 'It's very kind of you,' she added.

'There was – er – something you wanted to see me about, I think,' I suggested desperately.

'Oh! Of course. In all the excitement it had gone right out of my head.' She broke off and called to her maid. 'Emily – Emily. Not those sheets. The frilled ones with the monogram, and don't put them too near the fire.'

She closed the door and returned to me on tiptoe.

'It's just rather a curious thing that happened last night,' she explained. 'I thought you would like to hear about it, though at the moment it doesn't seem to make sense. I felt very wakeful last night – wondering about all this sad business. And I got up and looked out of my window. And what do you think I saw?'

I looked, inquiring.

'Gladys Cram,' said Miss Marple, with great emphasis. 'As I live, going into the wood with a suitcase.'

'A suitcase?'

'Isn't it extraordinary? What should she want with a suitcase in the wood at twelve o'clock at night?'

'You see,' said Miss Marple, 'I dare say it has nothing to do with the murder. But it is a Peculiar Thing. And just at present we all feel we must take notice of Peculiar Things.'

'Perfectly amazing,' I said. 'Was she going to – er – sleep in the barrow by any chance?'

'She didn't, at any rate,' said Miss Marple. 'Because quite a short time afterwards she came back, and she hadn't got the suitcase with her.'

The inquest was held that afternoon (Saturday) at two o'clock at the Blue Boar. The local excitement was, I need hardly say, tremendous. There had been no murder in St Mary Mead for at least fifteen years. And to have someone like Colonel Protheroe murdered actually in the Vicarage study is such a feast of sensation as rarely falls to the lot of a village population.

Various comments floated to my ears which I was probably not meant to hear.

'There's vicar. Looks pale, don't he? I wonder if he had a hand in it. 'Twas done at Vicarage, after all.' 'How can you, Mary Adams? And him visiting Henry Abbott at the time.' 'Oh! But they do say him and the colonel had words. There's Mary Hill. Giving herself airs, she is, on account of being in service there. Hush, here's coroner.'

The coroner was Dr Roberts of our adjoining town of Much Benham. He cleared his throat, adjusted his eyeglasses, and looked important.

To recapitulate all the evidence would be merely tiresome. Lawrence Redding gave evidence of finding the body, and identified the pistol as belonging to him. To the best of his belief he had seen it on the Tuesday, two days previously. It was kept on a shelf in his cottage, and the door of the cottage was habitually unlocked.

Mrs Protheroe gave evidence that she had last seen her husband at about a quarter to six when they separated in the village street. She agreed to call for him at the Vicarage later. She had gone to the Vicarage about a quarter past six, by way of the back lane and the garden gate. She had heard no voices in the study and had imagined that the room was empty, but her husband might have been sitting at the writing-table, in which case she would not have seen him. As far as she knew, he had been in his usual health and spirits. She knew of no enemy who might have had a grudge against him.

I gave evidence next, told of my appointment with Protheroe and my summons to the Abbotts'. I described how I had found the body and my summoning of Dr Haydock.

'How many people, Mr Clement, were aware that Colonel Protheroe was coming to see you that evening?'

'A good many, I should imagine. My wife knew, and my nephew, and Colonel Protheroe himself alluded to the fact that morning when I met him in the village. I should think several people might have overheard him, as, being slightly deaf, he spoke in a loud voice.'

'It was, then, a matter of common knowledge? Anyone might know?'

I agreed.

Haydock followed. He was an important witness. He described carefully and technically the appearance of the body and the exact injuries. It was his opinion that the deceased had been shot at approximately 6.20 to 6.30 – certainly not later than 6.35. That was the outside limit. He was positive and emphatic on that point. There was no question of suicide, the wound could not have been self-inflicted.

Inspector Slack's evidence was discreet and abridged. He described his summons and the circumstances under which he had found the body. The unfinished letter was produced and the time on it – 6.20 – noted. Also the clock. It was tacitly assumed that the time of death was 6.22. The police were giving nothing away. Anne Protheroe told me afterwards that she had been told to suggest a slightly earlier period of time than 6.20 for her visit.

Our maid, Mary, was the next witness, and proved a somewhat truculent one. She hadn't heard anything, and didn't want to hear anything. It wasn't as though gentlemen who came to see the vicar usually got shot. They didn't. She'd got her own jobs to look after. Colonel Protheroe had arrived at a quarter past six exactly. No, she didn't look at the clock. She heard the church chime after she had shown him into the study. She didn't hear any shot. If there had been a shot she'd have heard it. Well, of course, she knew there must have been a shot, since the gentleman was found shot – but there it was. She hadn't heard it.

The coroner did not press the point. I realized that he and Colonel Melchett were working in agreement.

Mrs Lestrange had been subpoenaed to give evidence, but a medical certificate, signed by Dr Haydock, was produced saying she was too ill to attend.

There was only one other witness, a somewhat doddering old woman. The one who, in Slack's phrase, 'did for' Lawrence Redding.

Mrs Archer was shown the pistol and recognized it as the one she had seen in Mr Redding's sitting-room 'over against the bookcase, he kept it, lying about.' She had last seen it on the day of the murder. Yes – in answer to a further question – she was quite sure it was there at lunch time on Thursday – quarter to one when she left.

I remembered what the inspector had told me, and I was mildly surprised. However vague she might have been when he questioned her, she was quite positive about it now.

The coroner summed up in a negative manner, but with a good deal of firmness. The verdict was given almost immediately:

Murder by Person or Persons unknown.

As I left the room I was aware of a small army of young men with bright, alert faces and a kind of superficial resemblance to each other. Several of them were already known to me by sight as having haunted the Vicarage the

613

last few days. Seeking to escape, I plunged back into the Blue Boar and was lucky enough to run straight into the archaeologist, Dr Stone. I clutched at him without ceremony.

'Journalists,' I said briefly and expressively. 'If you could deliver me from their clutches?'

'Why, certainly, Mr Clement. Come upstairs with me.'

He led the way up the narrow staircase and into his sitting-room, where Miss Cram was sitting rattling the keys of a typewriter with a practised touch. She greeted me with a broad smile of welcome and seized the opportunity to stop work.

'Awful, isn't it?' she said. 'Not knowing who did it, I mean. Not but that I'm disappointed in an inquest. Tame, that's what I call it. Nothing what you might call spicy from beginning to end.'

'You were there, then, Miss Cram?'

'I was there all right. Fancy your not seeing me. Didn't you see me? I feel a bit hurt about that. Yes, I do. A gentleman, even if he is a clergyman, ought to have eyes in his head.'

'Were you present also?' I asked Dr Stone, in an effort to escape from this playful badinage. Young women like Miss Cram always make me feel awkward.

'No, I'm afraid I feel very little interest in such things. I am a man very wrapped up in his own hobby.'

'It must be a very interesting hobby,' I said.

'You know something of it, perhaps?'

I was obliged to confess that I knew next to nothing.

Dr Stone was not the kind of man whom a confession of ignorance daunts. The result was exactly the same as though I had said that the excavation of barrows was my only relaxation. He surged and eddied into speech. Long barrows, round barrows, stone age, bronze age, paleolithic, neolithic kistvaens and cromlechs, it burst forth in a torrent. I had little to do save nod my head and look intelligent – and that last is perhaps over optimistic. Dr Stone boomed on. He was a little man. His head was round and bald, his face was round and rosy, and he beamed at you through very strong glasses. I have never known a man so enthusiastic on so little encouragement. He went into every argument for and against his own pet theory – which, by the way, I quite failed to grasp!

He detailed at great length his difference of opinion with Colonel Protheroe.

'An opinionated boor,' he said with heat. 'Yes, yes, I know he is dead, and one should speak no ill of the dead. But death does not alter facts. An opinionated boor describes him exactly. Because he had read a few books,

614

he set himself up as an authority – against a man who has made a lifelong study of the subject. My whole life, Mr Clement, has been given up to this work. My whole life –'

He was spluttering with excitement. Gladys Cram brought him back to earth with a terse sentence.

'You'll miss your train if you don't look out,' she observed.

'Oh!' The little man stopped in mid speech and dragged a watch from his pocket. 'Bless my soul. Quarter to? Impossible.'

'Once you start talking you never remember the time. What you'd do without me to look after you, I really don't know.'

'Quite right, my dear, quite right.' He patted her affectionately on the shoulder. 'This is a wonderful girl, Mr Clement. Never forgets anything. I consider myself extremely lucky to have found her.'

'Oh! Go on, Dr Stone,' said the lady. 'You spoil me, you do.'

I could not help feeling that I should be in a material position to add my support to the second school of thought – that which foresees lawful matrimony as the future of Dr Stone and Miss Cram. I imagined that in her own way Miss Cram was rather a clever young woman.

'You'd better be getting along,' said Miss Cram.

'Yes, yes, so I must.'

He vanished into the room next door and returned carrying a suitcase.

'You are leaving?' I asked in some surprise.

'Just running up to town for a couple of days,' he explained. 'My old mother to see tomorrow, some business with my lawyers on Monday. On Tuesday I shall return. By the way, I suppose that Colonel Protheroe's death will make no difference to our arrangements. As regards the barrow, I mean. Mrs Protheroe will have no objection to our continuing the work?'

'I should not think so.'

As he spoke, I wondered who actually would be in authority at Old Hall. It was just possible that Protheroe might have left it to Lettice. I felt that it would be interesting to know the contents of Protheroe's will.

'Causes a lot of trouble in a family, a death does,' remarked Miss Cram, with a kind of gloomy relish. 'You wouldn't believe what a nasty spirit there sometimes is.'

'Well, I must really be going.' Dr Stone made ineffectual attempts to control the suitcase, a large rug and an unwieldly umbrella. I came to his rescue. He protested.

'Don't trouble – don't trouble. I can manage perfectly. Doubtless there will be somebody downstairs.'

But down below there was no trace of a boots or anyone else. I suspect that they were being regaled at the expense of the Press. Time was getting on, so we set out together to the station, Dr Stone carrying the suitcase, and I holding the rug and umbrella.

Dr Stone ejaculated remarks in between panting breaths as we hurried along.

'Really too good of you – didn't mean – to trouble you . . . Hope we shan't miss – the train – Gladys is a good girl – really a wonderful girl – a very sweet nature – not too happy at home, I'm afraid – absolutely – the heart of a child – heart of a child. I do assure you, in spite of – difference in our ages – find a lot in common . . .'

We saw Lawrence Redding's cottage just as we turned off to the station. It stands in an isolated position with no other houses near it. I observed two young men of smart appearance standing on the doorstep and a couple more peering in at the windows. It was a busy day for the Press.

'Nice fellow, young Redding,' I remarked, to see what my companion would say.

He was so out of breath by this time that he found it difficult to say anything, but he puffed out a word which I did not at first quite catch.

'Dangerous,' he gasped, when I asked him to repeat his remark.

'Dangerous?'

'Most dangerous. Innocent girls – know no better – taken in by a fellow like that – always hanging round women . . . No good.'

From which I deduced that the only young man in the village had not passed unnoticed by the fair Gladys.

'Goodness,' ejaculated Dr Stone. 'The train!'

We were close to the station by this time and we broke into a fast sprint. A down train was standing in the station and the up London train was just coming in.

At the door of the booking office we collided with a rather exquisite young man, and I recognized Miss Marple's nephew just arriving. He is, I think, a young man who does not like to be collided with. He prides himself on his poise and general air of detachment, and there is no doubt that vulgar contact is detrimental to poise of any kind. He staggered back. I apologized hastily and we passed in. Dr Stone climbed on the train and I handed up his baggage just as the train gave an unwilling jerk and started.

I waved to him and then turned away. Raymond West had departed, but our local chemist, who rejoices in the name of Cherubim, was just setting out for the village. I walked beside him.

'Close shave that,' he observed. 'Well, how did the inquest go, Mr Clement?'

I gave him the verdict.

'Oh! So that's what happened. I rather thought that would be the verdict.

Where's Dr Stone off to?'

I repeated what he had told me.

'Lucky not to miss the train. Not that you ever know on this line. I tell you, Mr Clement, it's a crying shame. Disgraceful, that's what I call it. Train I came down by was ten minutes late. And that on a Saturday with no traffic to speak of. And on Wednesday – no, Thursday – yes, Thursday it was – I remember it was the day of the murder because I meant to write a strongly-worded complaint to the company – and the murder put it out of my head – yes, last Thursday. I had been to a meeting of the Pharmaceutical Society. How late do you think the 6.50 was? *Half an hour*. Half an hour exactly! What do you think of that? Ten minutes I don't mind. But if the train doesn't get in till twenty past seven, well, you can't get home before half-past. What I say is, why call it the 6.50?'

'Quite so,' I said, and wishing to escape from the monologue I broke away with the excuse that I had something to say to Lawrence Redding whom I saw approaching us on the other side of the road.

CHAPTER 19

'Very glad to have met you,' said Lawrence. 'Come to my place.'

We turned in at the little rustic gate, went up the path, and he drew a key from his pocket and inserted it in the lock.

'You keep the door locked now,' I observed.

'Yes.' He laughed rather bitterly. 'Case of stable door when the steed is gone, eh? It is rather like that. You know, padre,' he held the door open and I passed inside, 'there's something about all this business that I don't like. It's too much of – how shall I put it – an inside job. Someone knew about that pistol of mine. That means that the murderer, whoever he was, must have actually been in this house – perhaps even had a drink with me.'

'Not necessarily,' I objected. 'The whole village of St Mary Mead probably knows exactly where you keep your toothbrush and what kind of tooth powder you use.'

'But why should it interest them?'

'I don't know,' I said, 'but it does. If you change your shaving cream it will be a topic of conversation.'

'They must be very hard up for news.'

'They are. Nothing exciting ever happens here.'

'Well, it has now – with a vengeance.'

I agreed.

'And who tells them all these things anyway? Shaving cream and things like that?'

'Probably old Mrs Archer.'

'That old crone? She's practically a half-wit, as far as I can make out.'

'That's merely the camouflage of the poor,' I explained. 'They take refuge behind a mask of stupidity. You'll probably find that the old lady has all her wits about her. By the way, she seems very certain now that the pistol was in its proper place midday Thursday. What's made her so positive all of a sudden?'

'I haven't the least idea.'

'Do you think she's right?'

'There again I haven't the least idea. I don't go round taking an inventory of my possessions every day.'

I looked round the small living-room. Every shelf and table was littered with miscellaneous articles. Lawrence lived in the midst of an artistic disarray that would have driven me quite mad.

'It's a bit of a job finding things sometimes,' he said, observing my glance. 'On the other hand, everthing is handy – not tucked away.'

'Nothing is tucked away, certainly,' I agreed. 'It might perhaps have

618

been better if the pistol had been.'

'Do you know I rather expected the coroner to say something of the sort. Coroners are such asses. I expected to be censured or whatever they call it.'

'By the way,' I asked, 'was it loaded?'

Lawrence shook his head.

'I'm not quite so careless as that. It was unloaded, but there was a box of cartridges beside it.'

'It was apparently loaded in all six chambers and one shot had been fired.'

Lawrence nodded.

'And whose hand fired it? It's all very well, sir, but unless the real murderer is discovered, I shall be suspected of the crime to the day of my death.'

'Don't say that, my boy.'

'But I do say it.'

He became silent, frowning to himself. He roused himself at last and said:

'But let me tell you how I got on last night. You know, old Miss Marple knows a thing or two.'

'She is, I believe, rather unpopular on that account.'

Lawrence proceeded to recount his story.

He had, following Miss Marple's advice, gone up to Old Hall. There, with Anne's assistance, he had had an interview with the parlourmaid. Anne had said simply:

'Mr Redding wants to ask you a few questions, Rose.'

Then she had left the room.

Lawrence had felt somewhat nervous. Rose, a pretty girl of twenty-five, gazed at him with a limpid gaze which he found rather disconcerting.

'It's – it's about Colonel Protheroe's death.'

'Yes, sir.'

'I'm very anxious, you see, to get at the truth.'

'Yes, sir.'

'I feel that there may be – that someone might – that – that there might be some incident –'

At this point Lawrence felt that he was not covering himself with glory, and heartily cursed Miss Marple and her suggestions.

'I wondered if you could help me?'

'Yes, sir?'

Rose's demeanour was still that of the perfect servant, polite, anxious to assist, and completely uninterested.

'Dash it all,' said Lawrence, 'haven't you talked the thing over in the servants' hall?'

This method of attack flustered Rose slightly. Her perfect poise

619

was shaken.

'In the servants' hall, sir?'

'Or the housekeeper's room, or the bootboy's dugout, or wherever you do talk? There must be *some* place.'

Rose displayed a very faint disposition to giggle, and Lawrence felt encouraged.

'Look here, Rose, you're an awfully nice girl. I'm sure you must understand what I'm feeling like. I don't want to be hanged. I didn't murder your master, but a lot of people think I did. Can't you help me in any way?'

I can imagine at this point that Lawrence must have looked extremely appealing. His handsome head thrown back, his Irish blue eyes appealing. Rose softened and capitulated.

'Oh, sir! I'm sure – if any of us could help in any way. None of us think you did it, sir. Indeed we don't.'

'I know, my dear girl, but that's not going to help me with the police.'

'The police!' Rose tossed her head. 'I can tell you, sir, we don't think much of that inspector. Slack, he calls himself. The police indeed.'

'All the same, the police are very powerful. Now, Rose, you say you'll do your best to help me. I can't help feeling that there's a lot we haven't got yet. The lady, for instance, who called to see Colonel Protheroe the night before he died.'

'Mrs Lestrange?'

'Yes, Mrs Lestrange. I can't help feeling there's something rather odd about that visit of hers.'

'Yes, indeed, sir, that's what we all said.'

'You did?'

'Coming the way she did. And asking for the colonel. And of course there's been a lot of talk – nobody knowing anything about her down here. And Mrs Simmons, she's the housekeeper, sir, she gave it as her opinion that she was a regular bad lot. But after hearing what Gladdie said, well, I didn't know what to think.'

'What did Gladdie say?'

'Oh, nothing, sir! It was just – we were talking, you know.'

Lawrence looked at her. He had the feeling of something kept back.

'I wonder very much what her interview with Colonel Protheroe was about.'

'Yes, sir.'

'I believe you know, Rose?'

'Me? Oh, no, sir! Indeed I don't. How could I?'

'Look here, Rose. You said you'd help me. If you overheard anything,

anything at all – it mightn't seem important, but anything ... I'd be so awfully grateful to you. After all, anyone might – might chance – just *chance* to overhear something.'

'But I didn't, sir, really, I didn't.'

'Then somebody else did,' said Lawrence acutely.

'Well, sir –'

'Do tell me, Rose.'

'I don't know what Gladdie would say, I'm sure.'

'She'd want you to tell me. Who *is* Gladdie, by the way?'

'She's the kitchenmaid, sir. And you see, she'd just stepped out to speak to a friend, and she was passing the window – the study window – and the master was there with the lady. And of course he did speak very loud, the master did, always. And naturally, feeling a little curious – I mean –'

'Awfully natural,' said Lawrence, 'I mean one would simply have to listen.'

'But of course she didn't tell anyone – except me. And we both thought it very odd. But Gladdie couldn't say anything, you see, because if it was known she'd gone out to meet – a – a friend – well, it would have meant a lot of unpleasantness with Mrs Pratt, that's the cook, sir. But I'm sure she'd tell you anything, sir, willing.'

'Well, can I go to the kitchen and speak to her?'

Rose was horrified by the suggestion.

'Oh, no, sir, that would never do! And Gladdie's a very nervous girl anyway.'

At last the matter was settled, after a lot of discussion over difficult points. A clandestine meeting was arranged in the shrubbery.

Here, in due course, Lawrence was confronted by the nervous Gladdie who he described as more like a shivering rabbit than anything human. Ten minutes were spent in trying to put the girl at her ease, the shivering Gladys explaining that she couldn't ever – that she didn't ought, that she didn't think Rose would have given her away, that anyway she hadn't meant no harm, indeed she hadn't, and that she'd catch it badly if Mrs Pratt ever came to hear of it.

Lawrence reassured, cajoled, persuaded – at last Gladys consented to speak. 'If you'll be sure it'll go no further, sir.'

'Of course it won't.'

'And it won't be brought up against me in a court of law?'

'Never.'

'And you won't tell the mistress?'

'Not on any account.'

'If it were to get to Mrs Pratt's ears –'

621

'It won't. Now tell me, Gladys.'

'If you're sure it's all right?'

'Of course it is. You'll be glad some day you've saved me from being hanged.'

Gladys gave a little shriek.

'Oh! Indeed, I wouldn't like that, sir. Well, it's very little I heard – and that entirely by accident as you might say –'

'I quite understand.'

'But the master, he was evidently very angry. "After all these years" – that's what he was saying – "you dare to come here –" "It's an outrage –" I couldn't hear what the lady said – but after a bit he said, "I utterly refuse – utterly –" I can't remember everything – seemed as though they were at it hammer and tongs, she wanting him to do something and he refusing. "It's a disgrace that you should have come down here," that's one thing he said. And "You shall not see her – I forbid it –" and that made me prick up my ears. Looked as though the lady wanted to tell Mrs Protheroe a thing or two, and he was afraid about it. And I thought to myself, "Well, now, fancy the master. Him so particular. And maybe no beauty himself when all's said and done. Fancy!" I said. And "Men are all alike," I said to my father later. Not that he'd agree. Argued, he did. But he did admit he was surprised at Colonel Protheroe – him being a church-warden and handing round the plate and reading the lessons on Sundays. "But there," I said, "that's very often the worst." For that's what I've heard my mother say, many a time.'

Gladdie paused out of breath, and Lawrence tried tactfully to get back to where the conversation had started.

'Did you hear anything else?'

'Well, it's difficult to remember exactly, sir. It was all much the same. He said once or twice, "I don't believe it." Just like that. "Whatever Haydock says, I don't believe it." '

'He said that, did he? "Whatever Haydock says"?'

'Yes. And he said it was all a plot.'

'You didn't hear the lady speak at all?'

'Only just at the end. She must have got up to go and come nearer the window. And I heard what she said. Made my blood run cold, it did. I'll never forget it. *By this time tomorrow night, you may be dead,*" she said. Wicked the way she said it. As soon as I heard the news, "There," I said to Rose. "There!" '

Lawrence wondered. Principally he wondered how much of Gladys's story was to be depended upon. True in the main, he suspected that it had been embellished and polished since the murder. In especial he doubted the accuracy of the last remark. He thought it highly possible that it owed its being to the fact of the murder.

He thanked Gladys, rewarded her suitably, reassured her as to her misdoings being made known to Mrs Pratt, and left Old Hall with a good deal to think over.

One thing was clear, Mrs Lestrange's interview with Colonel Protheroe had certainly not been a peaceful one, and it was one which he was anxious to keep from the knowledge of his wife.

I thought of Miss Marple's churchwarden with his separate establishment. Was this a case resembling that?

I wondered more than ever where Haydock came in. He had saved Mrs Lestrange from having to give evidence at the inquest. He had done his best to protect her from the police.

How far would he carry that protection?

Supposing he suspected her of crime – would he still try and shield her?

She was a curious woman – a woman of very strong magnetic charm. I myself hated the thought of connecting her with the crime in any way.

Something in me said, 'It can't be her!' Why?

And an imp in my brain replied: 'Because she's a very beautiful and attractive woman. That's why.'

There is, as Miss Marple would say, a lot of human nature in all of us.

CHAPTER 20

When I got back to the Vicarage I found that we were in the middle of a domestic crisis.

Griselda met me in the hall and with tears in her eyes dragged me into the drawing-room. 'She's going.'

'Who's going?'

'Mary. She's given notice.'

I really could not take the announcement in a tragic spirit.

'Well,' I said, 'we'll have to get another servant.'

It seemed to me a perfectly reasonable thing to say. When one servant goes, you get another. I was at a loss to understand Griselda's look of reproach.

'Len – you are absolutely heartless. You don't *care*.'

I didn't. In fact, I felt almost light-hearted at the prospect of no more burnt puddings and undercooked vegetables.

'I'll have to look for a girl, and find one, and train her,' continued Griselda in a voice of acute self-pity.

'Is Mary trained?' I said.

'Of course she is.'

'I suppose,' I said, 'that someone has heard her address us as sir or ma'am and has immediately wrested her from us as a paragon. All I can say is, they'll be disappointed.'

'It isn't that,' said Griselda. 'Nobody else wants her. I don't see how they could. It's her feelings. They're upset because Lettice Protheroe said she didn't dust properly.'

Griselda often comes out with surprising statements, but this seemed to me so surprising that I questioned it. It seemed to me the most unlikely thing in the world that Lettice Protheroe should go out of her way to interfere in our domestic affairs and reprove our maid for slovenly housework. It was so completely unLettice-like, and I said so.

'I don't see,' I said, 'what our dust has to do with Lettice Protheroe.'

'Nothing at all,' said my wife. 'That's why it's so unreasonable. I wish you'd go and talk to Mary yourself. She's in the kitchen.'

I had no wish to talk to Mary on the subject, but Griselda, who is very energetic and quick, fairly pushed me through the baize door into the kitchen before I had time to rebel.

Mary was peeling potatoes at the sink.

'Er – good-afternoon,' I said nervously.

Mary looked up and snorted, but made no other response.

'Mrs Clement tells me that you wish to leave us,' I said.

Mary condescended to reply to this.

'There's some things,' she said darkly, 'as no girl can be asked to put up with.'

'Will you tell me exactly what it is that has upset you?'

'Tell you that in two words, I can.' (Here, I may say, she vastly underestimated.) 'People coming snooping round here when my back's turned. Poking round. And what business of hers is it, how often the study is dusted or turned out? If you and the missus don't complain, it's nobody else's business. If I give satisfaction to you that's all that matters, I say.'

Mary has never given satisfaction to me. I confess that I have a hankering after a room thoroughly dusted and tidied every morning. Mary's practice of flicking off the more obvious deposit on the surface of low tables is to my thinking grossly inadequate. However, I realized that at the moment it was no good to go into side issues.

'Had to go to that inquest, didn't I? Standing up before twelve men, a respectable girl like me! And who knows what questions you may be asked. I'll tell you this. I've never before been in a place where they had a murder in the house, and I never want to be again.'

'I hope you won't,' I said. 'On the law of averages, I should say it was very unlikely.'

'I don't hold with the law. *He* was a magistrate. Many a poor fellow sent to jail for potting at a rabbit – and him with his pheasants and what not. And then, before he's so much as decently buried, that daughter of his comes round and says I don't do my work properly.'

'Do you mean that Miss Protheroe has been here?'

'Found her here when I come back from the Blue Boar. In the study she was. And "Oh!" she says. "I'm looking for my little yellow berry – a little yellow hat. I left it here the other day." "Well," I says, "I haven't seen no hat. It wasn't here when I done the room on Thursday morning," I says. And "Oh!" she says, "but I dare say you wouldn't see it. You don't spend much time doing a room, do you?" And with that she draws her finger along the mantelshelf and looks at it. As though I had time on a morning like this to take off all them ornaments and put them back, with the police only unlocking the room the night before. "If the vicar and his lady are satisfied that's all that matters, I think, miss," I said. And she laughs and goes out of the windows and says, "Oh! but are you sure they are?" '

'I see,' I said.

'And there it is! A girl has her feelings! I'm sure I'd work my fingers to the bone for you and the missus. And if she wants a new-fangled dish tried, I'm always ready to try it.'

'I'm sure you are,' I said soothingly.

'But she must have heard something or she wouldn't have said what she did. And if I don't give satisfaction I'd rather go. Not that I take any notice of what Miss Protheroe says. She's not loved up at the Hall, I can tell you. Never a please or a thank you, and everything scattered right and left. I wouldn't set any store by Miss Lettice Protheroe myself for all that Mr Dennis is so set upon her. But she's the kind that can always twist a young gentleman round her little finger.'

During all this, Mary had been extracting eyes from potatoes with such energy that they had been flying round the kitchen like hailstones. At this moment one hit me in the eye and caused a momentary pause in the conversation.

'Don't you think,' I said, as I dabbed my eye with my handkerchief, 'that you have been rather too inclined to take offence where none is meant? You know, Mary, your mistress will be very sorry to lose you.'

'I've nothing against the mistress – or against you, sir, for that matter.'

'Well, then, don't you think you're being rather silly?'

Mary sniffed.

'I was a bit upset like – after the inquest and all. And a girl has her feelings. But I wouldn't like to cause the mistress inconvenience.'

'Then that's all right,' I said.

I left the kitchen to find Griselda and Dennis waiting for me in the hall.

'Well?' exclaimed Griselda.

'She's staying,' I said, and sighed.

'Len,' said my wife, 'you *have* been clever.'

I felt rather inclined to disagree with her. I did not think I had been clever. It is my firm opinion that no servant could be a worse one than Mary. Any change, I consider, would have been a change for the better.

But I like to please Griselda. I detailed the heads of Mary's grievance.

'How like Lettice,' said Dennis. 'She couldn't have left that yellow beret of hers here on Wednesday. She was wearing it for tennis on Thursday.'

'That seems to me highly probable,' I said.

'She never knows where she's left anything,' said Dennis, with a kind of affectionate pride and admiration that I felt was entirely uncalled for. 'She loses about a dozen things every day.'

'A remarkably attractive trait,' I observed.

Any sarcasm missed Dennis.

'She *is* attractive,' he said, with a deep sigh. 'People are always proposing to her – she told me so.'

'They must be illicit proposals if they're made to her down here,' I remarked. 'We haven't got a bachelor in the place.'

'There's Dr Stone,' said Griselda, her eyes dancing.

'He asked her to come and see the barrow the other day,' I admitted.

'Of course he did,' said Griselda. 'She *is* attractive, Len. Even bald-headed archaeologists feel it.'

'Lots of S.A.,' said Dennis sapiently.

And yet Lawrence Redding is completely untouched by Lettice's charm. Griselda, however, explained that with the air of one who knew she was right.

'Lawrence has got lots of S.A. himself. That kind always likes the – how shall I put it – the Quaker type. Very restrained and diffident. The kind of woman whom everybody calls cold. I think Anne is the only woman who could ever hold Lawrence. I don't think they'll ever tire of each other. All the same, I think he's been rather stupid in one way. He's rather made use of Lettice, you know. I don't think he ever dreamed she cared – he's awfully modest in some ways – but I have a feeling she does.'

'She can't bear him,' said Dennis positively. 'She told me so.'

I have never seen anything like the pitying silence with which Griselda received this remark.

I went into my study. There was, to my fancy, still a rather eerie feeling in the room. I knew that I must get over this. Once give in to that feeling, and I should probably never use the study again. I walked thoughtfully over to the writing table. Here Protheroe had sat, red faced, hearty, self-righteous, and here, in a moment of time, he had been struck down. Here, where I was standing, an enemy had stood . . .

And so – no more Protheroe . . .

Here was the pen his fingers had held.

On the floor was a faint dark stain – the rug had been sent to the cleaners, but the blood had soaked through.

I shivered.

'I can't use this room,' I said aloud. 'I can't use it.'

Then my eye was caught by something – a mere speck of bright blue. I bent down. Between the floor and the desk I saw a small object. I picked it up.

I was standing staring at it in the palm of my hand when Griselda came in.

'I forgot to tell you, Len. Miss Marple wants us to go over tonight after dinner. To amuse the nephew. She's afraid of his being dull. I said we'd go.'

'Very well, my dear.'

'What are you looking at?'

'Nothing.'

I closed my hand, and looking at my wife, observed:

'If you don't amuse Master Raymond West, my dear, he must be very hard to please.'

My wife said: 'Don't be ridiculous, Len,' and turned pink.

She went out again, and I unclosed my hand.

In the palm of my hand was a blue lapis lazuli ear-ring set in seed pearls.

It was rather an unusual jewel, and I knew very well where I had seen it last.

I cannot say that I have at any time had a great admiration for Mr Raymond West. He is, I know, supposed to be a brilliant novelist and has made quite a name as a poet. His poems have no capital letters in them, which is, I believe, the essence of modernity. His books are about unpleasant people leading lives of surpassing dullness.

He has a tolerant affection for 'Aunt Jane', whom he alludes to in her presence as a 'survival'.

She listens to his talk with a flattering interest, and if there is sometimes an amused twinkle in her eye I am sure he never notices it.

He fastened on Griselda at once with flattering abruptness. They discussed modern plays and from there went on to modern schemes of decoration. Griselda affects to laugh at Raymond West, but she is, I think, susceptible to his conversation.

During my (dull) conversation with Miss Marple, I heard at intervals the reiteration 'buried as you are down here'.

It began at last to irritate me. I said suddenly:

'I suppose you consider us very much out of the things down here?'

Raymond West waved his cigarette.

'I regard St Mary Mead,' he said authoritatively, 'as a stagnant pool.'

He looked at us, prepared for resentment at his statement, but somewhat, I think, to his chagrin, no one displayed annoyance.

'That is really not a very good simile, dear Raymond,' said Miss Marple briskly. 'Nothing, I believe, is so full of life under the microscope as a drop of water from a stagnant pool.'

'Life – of a kind,' admitted the novelist.

'It's all much the same kind, really, isn't it?' said Miss Marple.

'You compare yourself to a denizen of a stagnant pond, Aunt Jane?'

'My dear, you said something of the sort in your last book, I remember.'

No clever young man likes having his works quoted against himself. Raymond West was no exception.

'That was entirely different,' he snapped.

'Life is, after all, very much the same everywhere,' said Miss Marple in her placid voice. 'Getting born, you know, and growing up – and coming into contact with other people – getting jostled – and then marriage and more babies –'

'And finally death,' said Raymond West. 'And not death with a death certificate always. Death in life.'

'Talking of death,' said Griselda. 'You know we've had a murder here?'

Raymond West waved murder away with his cigarette.

'Murder is so crude,' he said. 'I take no interest in it.'

That statement did not take me in for a moment. They say all the world loves a lover – apply that saying to murder and you have an even more infallible truth. No one can fail to be interested in a murder. Simple people like Griselda and myself can admit the fact, but anyone like Raymond West has to pretend to be bored – at any rate for the first five minutes.

Miss Marple, however, gave her nephew away by remarking:

'Raymond and I have been discussing nothing else all through dinner.'

'I take a great interest in all the local news,' said Raymond hastily. He smiled benignly and tolerantly at Miss Marple.

'Have you a theory, Mr West?' asked Griselda.

'Logically,' said Raymond West, again flourishing his cigarette, 'only one person could have killed Protheroe.'

'Yes?' said Griselda.

We hung upon his words with flattering attention.

'The vicar,' said Raymond, and pointed an accusing finger at me.

I gasped.

'Of course,' he reassured me, 'I know you didn't do it. Life is never what it should be. But think of the drama – the fitness – churchwarden murdered in the vicar's study by the vicar. Delicious!'

'And the motive?' I inquired.

'Oh! That's interesting.' He sat up – allowed his cigarette to go out. 'Inferiority complex, I think. Possibly too many inhibitions. I should like to write the story of the affair. Amazingly complex. Week after week, year after year, he's seen the man – at vestry meetings – at choir-boys' outings – handing round the bag in church – bringing it to the altar. Always he dislikes the man – always he chokes down his dislike. It's un-Christian, he won't encourage it. And so it festers underneath, and one day –'

He made a graphic gesture.

Griselda turned to me.

'Have you ever felt like that, Len?'

'Never,' I said truthfully.

'Yet I hear you were wishing him out of the world not so long ago,' remarked Miss Marple.

(That miserable Dennis! But my fault, of course, for ever making the remark.)

'I'm afraid I was,' I said. 'It was a stupid remark to make, but really I'd had a very trying morning with him.'

'That's disappointing,' said Raymond West. 'Because, of course, if your subconscious were really planning to do him in, it would never have allowed you to make that remark.'

630

He sighed.

'My theory falls to the ground. This is probably a very ordinary murder – a revengeful poacher or something of that sort.'

'Miss Cram came to see me this afternoon,' said Miss Marple. 'I met her in the village and I asked her if she would like to see my garden.'

'Is she fond of gardens?' asked Griselda.

'I don't think so,' said Miss Marple, with a faint twinkle. 'But it makes a very useful excuse for talk, don't you think?'

'What did you make of her?' asked Griselda. 'I don't believe she's really so bad.'

'She volunteered a lot of information – really a lot of information,' said Miss Marple. 'About herself, you know, and her people. They all seem to be dead or in India. Very sad. By the way, she has gone to Old Hall for the weekend.'

'What?'

'Yes, it seems Mrs Protheroe asked her – or she suggested it to Mrs Protheroe – I don't quite know which way about it was. To do some secretarial work for her – there are so many letters to cope with. It turned out rather fortunately. Dr Stone being away, she has nothing to do. What an excitement this barrow has been.'

'Stone?' said Raymond. 'Is that the archaeologist fellow?'

'Yes, he is excavating a barrow. On the Protheroe property.'

'He's a good man,' said Raymond. 'Wonderfully keen on his job. I met him at a dinner not long ago and we had a most interesting talk. I must look him up.'

'Unfortunately,' I said, 'he's just gone to London for the weekend. Why, you actually ran into him at the station this afternoon.'

'I ran into you. You had a little fat man with you – with glasses on.'

'Yes – Dr Stone.'

'But, my dear fellow – that wasn't Stone.'

'Not Stone?'

'Not the archaeologist. I know him quite well. The man wasn't Stone – not the faintest resemblance.'

We stared at each other. In particular I stared at Miss Marple.

'Extraordinary,' I said.

'The suitcase,' said Miss Marple.

'But why?' said Griselda.

'It reminds me of the time the man went round pretending to be the gas inspector,' murmured Miss Marple. 'Quite a little haul, he got.'

'An impostor,' said Raymond West. 'Now this is really interesting.'

'The question is, has it anything to do with the murder?' said Griselda.

'Not necessarily,' I said. 'But –' I looked at Miss Marple.

'It is,' she said, 'a Peculiar Thing. Another Peculiar Thing.'

'Yes,' I said, rising. 'I rather feel the inspector ought to be told about this at once.'

Inspector Slack's orders, once I had got him on the telephone, were brief and emphatic. Nothing was to 'get about'. In particular, Miss Cram was not to be alarmed. In the meantime, a search was to be instituted for the suitcase in the neighbourhood of the barrow.

Griselda and I returned home very excited over this new development. We could not say much with Dennis present, as we had faithfully promised Inspector Slack to breath no word to anybody.

In any case, Dennis was full of his own troubles. He came into my study and began fingering things and shuffling his feet and looking thoroughly embarrassed.

'What is it, Dennis?' I said at last.

'Uncle Len, I don't want to go to sea.'

I was astonished. The boy had been so very decided about his career up to now.

'But you were so keen on it.'

'Yes, but I've changed my mind.'

'What do you want to do?'

'I want to go into finance.'

I was even more surprised.

'What do you mean – finance?'

'Just that. I want to go into the city.'

'But, my dear boy, I am sure you would not like the life. Even if I obtained a post for you in a bank –'

Dennis said that wasn't what he meant. He didn't want to go into a bank. I asked him what exactly he did mean, and of course, as I suspected, the boy didn't really know.

By 'going into finance', he simply meant getting rich quickly, which with the optimism of youth he imagined was a certainty if one 'went into the city'. I disabused him of this notion as gently as I could.

'What's put it into you head?' I asked. 'You were so satisfied with the idea of going to sea.'

'I know, Uncle Len, but I've been thinking. I shall want to marry some day – and, I mean, you've got to be rich to marry a girl.'

'Facts disprove your theory,' I said.

'I know – but a real girl. I mean, a girl who's used to things.'

It was very vague, but I thought I knew what he meant.

'You know,' I said gently, 'all girls aren't like Lettice Protheroe.'

He fired up at once.

'You're awfully unfair to her. You don't like her. Griselda doesn't either.

633

She says she's tiresome.'

From the feminine point of view Griselda is quite right. Lettice *is* tiresome. I could quite realize, however, that a boy would resent the adjective.

'If only people made a few allowances. Why even the Hartley Napiers are going about grousing about her at a time like this! Just because she left their old tennis party a bit early. Why should she stay if she was bored? Jolly decent of her to go at all, I think.'

'Quite a favour,' I said, but Dennis suspected no malice. He was full of his own grievances on Lettice's behalf.

'She's awfully unselfish really. Just to show you, she made me stay. Naturally I wanted to go too. But she wouldn't hear of it. Said it was too bad on the Napiers. So just to please her, I stopped on a quarter of an hour.'

The young have very curious views on unselfishness.

'And now I hear Susan Hartley Napier is going about everywhere saying Lettice has rotten manners.'

'If I were you,' I said, 'I shouldn't worry.'

'It's all very well, but –'

He broke off.

'I'd – I'd do anything for Lettice.'

'Very few of us can do anything for anyone else,' I said. 'However much we wish it, we are powerless.'

'I wish I were dead,' said Dennis.

Poor lad. Calf love is a virulent disease. I forebore to say any of the obvious and probably irritating things which come so easily to one's lips. Instead, I said goodnight, and went up to bed.

I took the eight o'clock service the following morning and when I returned found Griselda sitting at the breakfast table with an open note in her hand. It was from Anne Protheroe.

'Dear Griselda, – If you and the vicar could come up and lunch here quietly today, I should be so very grateful. Something very strange has occurred, and I should like Mr Clement's advice.

Please don't mention this when you come, as I have said nothing to anyone.

With love,

Yours affectionately,

Anne Protheroe.'

'We must go, of course,' said Griselda.

I agreed.

'I wonder what can have happened?'

I wondered too.

'You know,' I said to Griselda, 'I don't feel we are really at the end of this case yet.'

'You mean not till someone has really been arrested?'

'No,' I said, 'I didn't mean that. I mean that there are ramifications, under-currents, that we know nothing about. There are a whole lot of things to clear up before we get at the truth.'

'You mean things that don't really matter, but that get in the way?'

'Yes, I think that expresses my meaning very well.'

'I think we're all making a great fuss,' said Dennis, helping himself to marmalade. 'It's a jolly good thing old Protheroe is dead. Nobody liked him. Oh! I know the police have got to worry – it's their job. But I rather hope myself they'll never find out. I should hate to see Slack promoted, going about swelling with importance over his cleverness.'

I am human enough to feel that I agree over the matter of Slack's promotion. A man who goes about systematically rubbing people up the wrong way cannot hope to be popular.

'Dr Haydock thinks rather like I do,' went on Dennis. 'He'd never give a murderer up to justice. He said so.'

I think that that is the danger of Haydock's views. They may be sound in themselves – it is not for me to say – but they produce an impression on the young careless mind which I am sure Haydock himself never meant to convey.

Griselda looked out of the window and remarked that there were reporters in the garden.

'I suppose they're photographing the study windows again,' she said, with a sigh.

We had suffered a good deal in this way. There was first the idle curiosity of the village – everyone had come to gape and stare. There were next the reporters armed with cameras, and the village again to watch the reporters. In the end we had to have a constable from Much Benham on duty outside the window.

'Well,' I said, 'the funeral is tomorrow morning. After that, surely, the excitement will die down.'

I noticed a few reporters hanging about Old Hall when we arrived there. They accosted me with various queries to which I gave the invariable answer (we had found it the best), that, 'I had nothing to say.'

We were shown by the butler into the drawing-room, the sole occupant of which turned out to be Miss Cram – apparently in a state of high enjoyment.

'This is a surprise, isn't it?' she said, as she shook hands. 'I never should have thought of such a thing, but Mrs Protheroe is kind, isn't she? And, of course, it isn't what you might call nice for a young girl to be staying alone at a place like the Blue Boar, reporters about and all. And, of course, it's not as though I haven't been able to make myself useful – you really need a secretary at a time like this, and Miss Protheroe doesn't do anything to help, does she?'

I was amused to notice that the old animosity against Lettice persisted, but that the girl had apparently become a warm partisan of Anne's. At the same time I wondered if the story of her coming here was strictly accurate. In her account the initiative had come from Anne, but I wondered if that were really so. The first mention of disliking to be at the Blue Boar alone might have easily come from the girl herself. Whilst keeping an open mind on the subject, I did not fancy that Miss Cram was strictly truthful.

At that moment Anne Protheroe entered the room.

She was dressed very quietly in black. She carried in her hand a Sunday paper which she held out to me with a rueful glance.

'I've never had any experience of this sort of thing. It's pretty ghastly, isn't it? I saw a reporter at the inquest. I just said that I was terribly upset and had nothing to say, and then he asked me if I wasn't very anxious to find my husband's murderer, and I said "Yes." And then whether I had any suspicions, and I said "No." And whether I didn't think the crime showed local knowledge, and I said it seemed to certainly. And that was all. And now look at this!'

In the middle of the page was a photograph, evidently taken at least ten years ago – Heaven knows where they had dug it out. There were large headlines:

'WIDOW DECLARES SHE WILL NEVER REST TILL SHE HAS
HUNTED DOWN HUSBAND'S MURDERER.

'Mrs Protheroe, the widow of the murdered man, is certain that the murderer must be looked for locally. She has suspicions, but no certainty. She declared herself prostrated with grief, but reiterated her determination to hunt down the murderer.'

'It doesn't sound like me, does it?' said Anne.

'I dare say it might have been worse,' I said, handing back the paper.

'Impudent, aren't they?' said Miss Cram. 'I'd like to see one of those fellows trying to get something out of me.'

By the twinkle in Griselda's eye, I was convinced that she regarded this statement as being more literally true than Miss Cram intended it to appear.

Luncheon was announced, and we went in. Lettice did not come in till half-way through the meal, when she drifted into the empty place with a smile for Griselda and a nod for me. I watched her with some attention, for reasons of my own, but she seemed much the same vague creature as usual. Extremely pretty – that in fairness I had to admit. She was still not wearing mourning, but was dressed in a shade of pale green that brought out all the delicacy of her fair colouring.

After we had had coffee, Anne said quietly:

'I want to have a little talk with the vicar. I will take him up to my sitting-room.'

At last I was to learn the reason of our summons. I rose and followed her up the stairs. She paused at the door of the room. As I was about to speak, she stretched out a hand to stop me. She remained listening, looking down towards the hall.

'Good. They are going out into the garden. No – don't go in there. We can go straight up.'

Much to my surprise she led the way along the corridor to the extremity of the wing. Here a narrow ladder-like staircase rose to the floor above, and she mounted it, I following. We found ourselves in a dusty boarded passage. Anne opened a door and led me into a large dim attic which was evidently used as a lumber room. There were trunks there, old broken furniture, a few stacked pictures, and the many countless odds and ends which a lumber room collects.

My surprise was so evident that she smiled faintly.

'First of all, I must explain. I am sleeping very lightly just now. Last night – or rather this morning about three o'clock, I was convinced that I heard someone moving about the house. I listened for some time, and at last got up and came out to see. Out on the landing I realized that the sounds came, not from down below, but from up above. I came along to the foot of these stairs. Again I thought I heard a sound. I called up, "Is anybody there?" But there was no answer, and I heard nothing more, so I assumed that my nerves had been playing tricks on me, and went back to bed.

'However, early this morning, I came up here – simply out of curiosity. And I found *this!*'

She stooped down and turned round a picture that was leaning against the wall with the back of the canvas towards us.

I gave a gasp of surprise. The picture was evidently a portrait in oils, but the face had been hacked and cut in such a savage way as to render it unrecognizable. Moreover, the cuts were clearly quite fresh.

'What an extraordinary thing,' I said.

'Isn't it? Tell me, can you think of any explanation?'

I shook my head.

'There's a kind of savagery about it,' I said, 'that I don't like. It looks as though it had been done in a fit of maniacal rage.'

'Yes, that's what I thought.'

'What is the portrait?'

'I haven't the least idea. I have never seen it before. All these things were in the attic when I married Lucius and came here to live. I have never been through them or bothered about them.'

'Extraordinary,' I commented.

I stooped down and examined the other pictures. They were very much what you would expect to find – some very mediocre landscapes, some olegraphs and a few cheaply-framed reproductions.

There was nothing else helpful. A large old-fashioned trunk, of the kind that used to be called an 'ark,' had the initials E.P. upon it. I raised the lid. It was empty. Nothing else in the attic was the least suggestive.

'It really is a most amazing occurrence,' I said. 'It's so – senseless.'

'Yes,' said Anne. 'That frightens me a little.'

There was nothing more to see. I accompanied her down to her sitting-room where she closed the door.

'Do you think I ought to do anything about it? Tell the police?'

I hesitated.

'It's hard to say on the face of it whether –'

'It has anything to do with the murder or not,' finished Anne. 'I know. That's what is so difficult. On the face of it, there seems no connection whatever.'

'No,' I said, 'but it is another Peculiar Thing.'

We both sat silent with puzzled brows.

'What are your plans, if I may ask?' I said presently.

She lifted her head.

'I'm going to live here for at least another six months!' She said it defiantly. 'I don't want to. I hate the idea of living here. But I think it's the only thing to be done. Otherwise people will say that I ran away – that I had a guilty conscience.'

'Surely not.'

'Oh! Yes, they will. Especially when –' She paused and then said: 'When the six months are up – I am going to marry Lawrence.' Her eyes met mine. 'We're neither of us going to wait any longer.'

'I supposed,' I said, 'that that would happen.'

Suddenly she broke down, burying her head in her hands.

'You don't know how grateful I am to you – you don't know. We'd said good bye to each other – he was going away. I feel – I feel so awful about Lucius's death. If we'd been planning to go away together, and he'd died then – it would be so awful now. But you made us both see how wrong it would be. That's why I'm grateful.'

'I, too, am thankful,' I said gravely.

'All the same, you know,' she sat up. 'Unless the real murderer is found they'll always think it was Lawrence – oh! Yes, they will. And especially when he marries me.'

'My dear, Dr Haydock's evidence made it perfectly clear –'

'What do people care about evidence? They don't even know about it. And medical evidence never means anything to outsiders anyway. That's another reason why I'm staying on here. Mr Clement, *I'm going to find out the truth.*'

Her eyes flashed as she spoke. She added:

'That's why I asked that girl here.'

'Miss Cram?'

'Yes.'

'You did ask her, then. I mean, it was your idea?'

'Entirely. Oh! As a matter of fact, she whined a bit. At the inquest – she was there when I arrived. No, I asked her here deliberately.'

'But surely,' I cried, 'you don't think that that silly young woman could have anything to do with the crime?'

'It's awfully easy to appear silly, Mr Clement. It's one of the easiest things in the world.'

'Then you really think –?'

'No, I don't. Honestly, I don't. What I do think is that that girl knows something – or might know something. I wanted to study her at close quarters.'

'And the very night she arrives, that picture is slashed,' I said thoughtfully.

'You think she did it? But why? It seems so utterly absurd and impossible.'

'It seems to me utterly impossible and absurd that your husband should have been murdered in my study,' I said bitterly. 'But he was.'

'I know.' She laid her hand on my arm. 'It's dreadful for you. I do realize that, though I haven't said very much about it.'

I took the blue lapis lazuli ear-ring from my pocket and held it out to her.

'This is yours, I think?'

'Oh, yes!' She held out her hand for it with a pleased smile. 'Where did you find it?'

But I did not put the jewel into her outstretched hand.

'Would you mind,' I said, 'if I kept it a little longer?'

'Why, certainly.' She looked puzzled and a little inquiring. I did not satisfy her curiosity.

Instead I asked her how she was situated financially.

'It is an impertinent question,' I said, 'but I really do not mean it as such.'

'I don't think it's impertinent at all. You and Griselda are the best friends I have here. And I like that funny old Miss Marple. Lucius was very well off, you know. He left things pretty equally divided between me and Lettice. Old Hall goes to me, but Lettice is to be allowed to choose enough furniture to furnish a small house, and she is left a separate sum for the purpose of buying one, so as to even things up.'

'What are her plans, do you know?'

Anne made a comical grimace.

'She doesn't tell them to me. I imagine she will leave here as soon as possible. She doesn't like me – she never has. I dare say it's my fault, though I've really always tried to be decent. But I suppose any girl resents a young stepmother.'

'Are you fond of her?' I asked bluntly.

She did not reply at once, which convinced me that Anne Protheroe is a very honest woman.

'I was at first,' she said. 'She was such a pretty little girl. I don't think I am now. I don't know why. Perhaps it's because she doesn't like me. I like being liked, you know.'

'We all do,' I said, and Anne Protheroe smiled.

I had one more task to perform. That was to get a word alone with Lettice Protheroe. I managed that easily enough, catching sight of her in the deserted drawing-room. Griselda and Gladys Cram were out in the garden.

I went in and shut the door.

'Lettice,' I said, 'I want to speak to you about something.'

She looked up indifferently.

'Yes?'

I had thought beforehand what to say. I held out the lapis ear-ring and said quietly:

'Why did you drop that in my study?'

I saw her stiffen for a moment – it was almost instantaneous. Her recovery was so quick that I myself could hardly have sworn to the movement. Then she said carelessly:

'I never dropped anything in your study. That's not mine. That's Anne's.'

'I know that,' I said.

'Well, why ask me, then? Anne must have dropped it.'

'Mrs Protheroe has only been in my study once since the murder, and then she was wearing black and so would not have been likely to have had on

640

a blue ear-ring.'

'In that case,' said Lettice, 'I suppose she must have dropped it before.' She added: 'That's only logical.'

'It's very logical,' I said. 'I suppose you don't happen to remember when your stepmother was wearing these ear-rings last?'

'Oh!' She looked at me with a puzzled, trustful gaze. 'Is it very important?'

'It might be,' I said.

'I'll try and think.' She sat there knitting her brows. I have never seen Lettice Protheroe look more charming than she did at that moment. 'Oh, yes!' she said suddenly. 'She had them on – on Thursday. I remember now.'

'Thursday,' I said slowly, 'was the day of the murder. Mrs Protheroe came to the study in the garden that day, but if you remember, in her evidence, she only came as far as the study window, not inside the room.'

'Where did you find this?'

'Rolled underneath the desk.'

'Then it looks, doesn't it,' said Lettice coolly, 'as though she hadn't spoken the truth?'

'You mean that she came right in and stood by the desk?'

'Well, it looks like it, doesn't it?'

Her eyes met mine serenely.

'If you want to know,' she said calmly, 'I never have thought she was speaking the truth.'

'And I *know you* are not, Lettice.'

'What do you mean?'

She was startled.

'I mean,' I said, 'that the last time I saw this ear-ring was on Friday morning when I came up here with Colonel Melchett. It was lying with its fellow on your stepmother's dressing-table. I actually handled them both.'

'Oh –!' She wavered, then suddenly flung herself sideways over the arm of her chair and burst into tears. Her short fair hair hung down almost touching the floor. It was a strange attitude – beautiful and unrestrained.

I let her sob for some moments in silence and then I said very gently:

'Lettice, why did you do it?'

'What?'

She sprang up, flinging her hair wildly back. She looked wild – almost terrified.

'What do you mean?'

'What made you do it? Was it jealousy? Dislike of Anne?'

'Oh! – Oh, yes!' She pushed the hair back from her face and seemed suddenly to regain complete self-possession. 'Yes, you can call it jealousy.

I've always disliked Anne – ever since she came queening it here. I put the damned thing under the desk. I hoped it would get her into trouble. It would have done if you hadn't been such a Nosey Parker, fingering things on dressing-tables. Anyway, it isn't a clergyman's business to go about helping the police.'

It was a spiteful, childish outburst. I took no notice of it. Indeed, at that moment, she seemed a very pathetic child indeed.

Her childish attempt at vengeance against Anne seemed hardly to be taken seriously. I told her so, and added that I should return the ear-ring to her and say nothing of the circumstances in which I had found it. She seemed rather touched by that.

'That's nice of you,' she said.

She paused a minute and then said, keeping her face averted and evidently choosing her words with care:

'You know, Mr Clement, I should – I should get Dennis away from here soon, if I were you I – think it would be better.'

'Dennis?' I raised my eyebrows in slight surprise but with a trace of amusement too.

'I think it would be better.' She added, still in the same awkward manner: 'I'm sorry about Dennis. I didn't think he – anyway, I'm sorry.'

We left it at that.

On the way back, I proposed to Griselda that we should make a detour and go round by the barrow. I was anxious to see if the police were at work and if so, what they found. Griselda, however, had things to do at home, so I was left to make the expedition on my own.

I found Constable Hurst in charge of operations.

'No sign so far, sir,' he reported. 'And yet it stands to reason that this is the only place for a *cache*.'

His use of the word cache puzzled me for a moment, as he pronounced it catch, but his real meaning occurred to me almost at once.

'Whatimeantersay is, sir, where else could the young woman be going starting into the wood by that path? It leads to Old Hall, and it leads here, and that's about all.'

'I suppose,' I said, 'that Inspector Slack would disdain such a simple course as asking the young lady straight out.'

'Anxious not to put the wind up her,' said Hurst. 'Anything she writes to Stone or he writes to her may throw light on things – once she knows we're on to her, she'd shut up like *that*.'

Like *what* exactly was left in doubt, but I personally doubted Miss Gladys Cram ever being shut up in the way described. It was impossible to imagine her as other than overflowing with conversation.

'When a man's an h'impostor, you want to know *why* he's an h'impostor,' said Constable Hurst didactically.

'Naturally,' I said.

'And the answer is to be found in this here barrow – or else why was he for ever messing about with it?'

'A *raison d'être* for prowling about,' I suggested, but this bit of French was too much for the constable. He revenged himself for not understanding it by saying coldly:

'That's the h'amateur's point of view.'

'Anyway, you haven't found the suitcase,' I said.

'We shall do, sir. Not a doubt of it.'

'I'm not so sure,' I said. 'I've been thinking. Miss Marple said it was quite a short time before the girl reappeared empty-handed. In that case, she wouldn't have had time to get up here and back.'

'You can't take any notice of what old ladies say. When they've seen something curious, and are waiting all eager like, why, time simply flies for them. And anyway, no lady knows anything about time.'

I often wonder why the whole world is so prone to generalize. Generalizations are seldom if ever true and are usually utterly inaccurate. I have a poor sense of time myself (hence the keeping of my clock fast) and Miss Marple, I should say, has a very acute one. Her clocks keep time to the minute and she herself is rigidly punctual on every occasion.

However, I had no intention of arguing with Constable Hurst on the point. I wished him good afternoon and good luck and went on my way.

It was just as I was nearing home that the idea came to me. There was nothing to lead up to it. It just flashed into my brain as a possible solution.

You will remember that on my first search of the path, the day after the murder, I had found the bushes disturbed in a certain place. They proved, or so I thought at the time, to have been disturbed by Lawrence, bent on the same errand as myself.

But I remembered that afterwards he and I together had come upon another faintly marked trail which proved to be that of the inspector. On thinking it over, I distinctly remembered that the first trail (Lawrence's) had been much more noticeable than the second, as though more than one person had been passing that way. And I reflected that that was probably what had drawn Lawrence's attention to it in the first instance. Supposing that it had originally been made by either Dr Stone or else Miss Cram?

I remembered, or else I imagined remembering, that there had been several withered leaves on broken twigs. If so, the trail could not have been made the afternoon of our search.

I was just approaching the spot in question. I recognized it easily enough and once more forced my way through the bushes. This time I noticed fresh twigs broken. Someone *had* passed this way since Lawrence and myself.

I soon came to the place where I had encountered Lawrence. The faint trail, however, persisted farther, and I continued to follow it. Suddenly it widened out into a little clearing, which showed signs of recent upheaval. I say a clearing, because the denseness of the undergrowth was thinned out there, but the branches of the trees met overhead and the whole place was not more than a few feet across.

On the other side, the undergrowth grew densely again, and it seemed quite clear that no one had forced a way through it recently. Nevertheless, it seemed to have been disturbed in one place.

I went across and kneeled down, thrusting the bushes aside with both hands. A glint of shiny brown surface rewarded me. Full of excitement, I thrust my arm in and with a good deal of difficulty I extracted a small brown suitcase.

I uttered an ejaculation of triumph. I had been successful. Coldly snubbed by Constable Hurst, I had yet proved right in my reasoning. Here without doubt was the suitcase carried by Miss Cram. I tried the hasp, but it was locked.

As I rose to my feet I noticed a small brownish crystal lying on the ground. Almost automatically, I picked it up and slipped it into my pocket.

Then grasping my find by the handle, I retraced my steps to the path.

As I climbed over the stile into the lane, an agitated voice near at hand called out:

'Oh! Mr Clement. You've found it! How clever of you!'

Mentally registering the fact that in the art of seeing without being seen, Miss Marple had no rival, I balanced my find on the palings between us.

'That's the one,' said Miss Marple 'I'd know it anywhere.'

This, I thought, was a slight exaggeration. There are thousands of cheap shiny suitcases all exactly alike. No one could recognize one particular one seen from such a distance away by moonlight, but I realized that the whole business of the suitcase was Miss Marple's particular triumph and, as such, she was entitled to a little pardonable exaggeration.

'It's locked, I suppose, Mr Clement?'

'Yes. I'm just going to take it down to the police station.

'You don't think it would be better to telephone?'

Of course unquestionably it would be better to telephone. To stride through the village, suitcase in hand, would be to court a probably undesirable publicity.

So I unlatched Miss Marple's garden gate and entered the house by the French window, and from the sanctity of the drawing-room with the door shut, I telephoned my news.

The result was that Inspector Slack announced he would be up himself in a couple of jiffies.

When he arrived it was in his most cantankerous mood.

'So we've got it, have we?' he said. 'You know, sir, you shouldn't keep things to yourself. If you'd any reason to believe you knew where the article in question was hidden, you ought to have reported it to the proper authorities.'

'It was a pure accident,' I said. 'The idea just happened to occur to me.'

'And that's a likely tale. Nearly three-quarters of a mile of woodland, and you go right to the proper spot and lay your hand upon it.'

I would have given Inspector Slack the steps in reasoning which led me to this particular spot, but he had achieved his usual result of putting my back up. I said nothing.

'Well?' said Inspector Slack, eyeing the suitcase with dislike and would be indifference, 'I suppose we might as well have a look at what's inside.'

He had brought an assortment of keys and wire with him. The lock was a cheap affair. In a couple of seconds the case was open.

I don't know what we had expected to find – something sternly sensational, I imagine. But the first thing that met our eyes was a greasy plaid scarf. The inspector lifted it out. Next came a faded dark blue overcoat, very much the worse for wear. A checked cap followed.

'A shoddy lot,' said the inspector.

A pair of boots very down at heel and battered came next. At the bottom of the suitcase was a parcel done up in newspaper.

'Fancy shirt, I suppose,' said the inspector bitterly, as he tore it open.

A moment later he had caught his breath in surprise.

For inside the parcel were some demure little silver objects and a round platter of the same metal.

Miss Marple gave a shrill exclamation of recognition.

'The trencher salts,' she exclaimed. 'Colonel Protheroe's trencher salts, and the Charles II tazza. Did you ever hear of such a thing!'

The inspector had got very red.

'So that was the game,' he muttered. 'Robbery. But I can't make it out. There's been no mention of these things being missing.'

'Perhaps they haven't discovered the loss,' I suggested. 'I presume these valuable things would not have been kept out in common use. Colonel Protheroe probably kept them locked away in a safe.'

'I must investigate this,' said the inspector. 'I'll go right up to Old Hall now. So that's why our Dr Stone made himself scarce. What with the murder and one thing and another, he was afraid we'd get wind of his activities. As likely as not his belongings might have been searched. He got the girl to hide them in the wood with a suitable change of clothing. He meant to come back by a roundabout route and go off with them one night whilst she stayed here to disarm suspicion. Well, there's one thing to the good. This lets him out over the murder. He'd nothing to do with that. Quite a different game.'

He repacked the suitcase and took his departure, refusing Miss Marple's offer of a glass of sherry.

'Well, that's one mystery cleared up,' I said with a sigh. 'What Slack says is quite true; there are no grounds for suspecting him of the murder. Everything's accounted for quite satisfactorily.'

'It really would seem so,' said Miss Marple. 'Although one never can be quite certain, can one?'

'There's a complete lack of motive,' I pointed out. 'He'd got what he came for and was clearing out.'

'Y – es.'

She was clearly not quite satisfied, and I looked at her in some curiosity. She hastened to answer my inquiring gaze with a kind of apologetic eagerness.

646

'I've no doubt I am *quite* wrong. I'm so stupid about these things. But I just wondered – I mean this silver is very valuable, is it not?'

'A tazza sold the other day for over a thousand pounds, I believe.'

'I mean – it's not the value of the metal.'

'No, it's what one might call a connoisseur's value.'

'That's what I mean. The sale of such things would take a little time to arrange, or even if it was arranged, it couldn't be carried through without secrecy. I mean – if the robbery were reported and a hue and cry were raised, well, the things couldn't be marketed at all.'

'I don't quite see what you mean?' I said.

'I know I'm putting it badly.' She became more flustered and apologetic. 'But it seems to me that – that the things couldn't just have been abstracted, so to speak. The only satisfactory thing to do would be to replace these things with copies. Then, perhaps, the robbery wouldn't be discovered for some time.'

'That's a very ingenious idea,' I said.

'It would be the only way to do it, wouldn't it? And if so, of course, as you say, once the substitution had been accomplished there wouldn't have been any reason for murdering Colonel Protheroe – quite the reverse.'

'Exactly,' I said. 'That's what I said.'

'Yes, but I just wondered – I don't know, of course – and Colonel Protheroe always talked a lot about doing things before he actually did do them, and, of course, sometimes never did them at all, but he did say –'

'Yes?'

'That he was going to have all his things valued – a man down from London. For probate – no, that's when you're dead – for insurance. Someone told him that was the thing to do. He talked about it a great deal, and the importance of having it done. Of course, I don't know if he had made any actual arrangements, but if he had ...'

'I see,' I said slowly.

'Of course, the moment the expert saw the silver, he'd know, and then Colonel Protheroe would remember having shown the things to Dr Stone – I wonder if it was done then – legerdemain, don't they call it? So clever – and then, well, the fat would be in the fire, to use an old-fashioned expression.'

'I see your idea,' I said. 'I think we ought to find out for certain.'

I went once more to the telephone. In a few minutes I was through to Old Hall and speaking to Anne Protheroe.

'No, it's nothing very important. Has the inspector arrived yet? Oh! Well, he's on his way. Mrs Protheroe, can you tell me if the contents of Old Hall were ever valued? What's that you say?'

Her answer came clear and prompt. I thanked her, replaced the receiver, and turned to Miss Marple.

'That's very definite. Colonel Protheroe had made arrangements for a man to come down from London on Monday – tomorrow – to make a full valuation. Owing to the colonel's death, the matter has been put off.'

'Then there *was* a motive,' said Miss Marple softly.

'A motive, yes. But that's all. You forget. When the shot was fired, Dr Stone had just joined the others, or was climbing over the stile in order to do so.'

'Yes,' said Miss Marple thoughtfully. 'So that rules him out.'

I returned to the Vicarage to find Hawes waiting for me in my study. He was pacing up and down nervously, and when I entered the room he started as though he had been shot.

'You must excuse me,' he said, wiping his forehead. 'My nerves are all to pieces lately.'

'My dear fellow,' I said, 'you positively must get away for a change. We shall have you breaking down altogether, and that will never do.'

'I can't desert my post. No, that is a thing I will never do.'

'It's not a case of desertion. You are ill. I'm sure Haydock would agree with me.'

'Haydock – Haydock. What kind of a doctor is he? An ignorant country practitioner.'

'I think you're unfair to him. He has always been considered a very able man in his profession.'

'Oh! Perhaps. Yes, I dare say. But I don't like him. However, that's not what I came to say. I came to ask you if you would be kind enough to preach tonight instead of me. I – I really do not feel equal to it.'

'Why, certainly. I will take the service for you.'

'No, no. I wish to take the service. I am perfectly fit. It is only the idea of getting up in the pulpit, of all those eyes staring at me . . .'

He shut his eyes and swallowed convulsively.

It is clear to me that there is something very wrong indeed with Hawes. He seemed aware of my thoughts, for he opened his eyes and said quickly:

'There is nothing really wrong with me. It is just these headaches – these awful racking headaches. I wonder if you could let me have a glass of water.'

'Certainly,' I said.

I went and fetched it myself from the tap. Ringing bells is a profitless form of exercise in our house.

I brought the water to him and he thanked me. He took from his pocket a small cardboard box, and opening it, extracted a rice paper capsule, which he swallowed with the aid of the water.

'A headache powder,' he explained.

I suddenly wondered whether Hawes might have become addicted to drugs. It would explain a great many of his peculiarities.

'You don't take too many, I hope,' I said.

'No – oh, no. Dr Haydock warned me against that. But it is really wonderful. They bring instant relief.'

Indeed he already seemed calmer and more composed.

He stood up.

'Then you will preach tonight? It's very good of you, sir.'

'Not at all. And I insist on taking the service too. Get along home and rest. No, I won't have any argument. Not another word.'

He thanked me again. Then he said, his eyes sliding past me to the window:

'You – have been up at Old Hall today, haven't you, sir?'

'Yes.'

'Excuse me – but were you sent for?'

I looked at him in surprise, and he flushed.

'I'm sorry, sir. I – I just thought some new development might have arisen and that was why Mrs Protheroe had sent for you.'

I had not the faintest intention of satisfying Hawes's curiosity.

'She wanted to discuss the funeral arrangements and one or two other small matters with me,' I said.

'Oh! That was all. I see.'

I did not speak. He fidgeted from foot to foot, and finally said:

'Mr Redding came to see me last night. I – I can't imagine why.'

'Didn't he tell you?'

'He – he just said he thought he'd look me up. Said it was a bit lonely in the evenings. He's never done such a thing before.'

'Well, he's supposed to be pleasant company,' I said, smiling.

'What does he want to come and see me for? I don't like it.' His voice rose shrilly. 'He spoke of dropping in again. What does it all mean? What idea do you think he has got into his head?'

'Why should you suppose he has any ulterior motive?' I asked.

'I don't like it,' repeated Hawes obstinately. 'I've never gone against *him* in any way. I never suggested that *he* was guilty – even when he accused himself I said it seemed most incomprehensible. If I've had suspicions of anybody it's been of Archer – never of him. Archer is a totally different proposition – a godless irreligious ruffian. A drunken blackguard.'

'Don't you think you're being a little harsh?' I said. 'After all, we really know very little about the man.'

'A poacher, in and out of prison, capable of anything.'

'Do you really think he shot Colonel Protheroe?' I asked curiously.

Hawes has an inveterate dislike of answering yes or no. I have noticed it several times lately.

'Don't you think yourself, sir, that it's the only possible solution?'

'As far as we know,' I said, 'there's no evidence of any kind against him.'

'His threats,' said Hawes eagerly. 'You forget about his threats.'

I am sick and tired of hearing about Archer's threats. As far as I can make

650

out, there is no direct evidence that he ever made any.

'He was determined to be revenged on Colonel Protheroe. He primed himself with drink and then shot him.'

'That's pure supposition.'

'But you will admit that it's perfectly probable?'

'No, I don't.'

'Possible, then?'

'Possible, yes.'

Hawes glanced at me sideways.

'Why don't you think it's probable?'

'Because,' I said, 'a man like Archer wouldn't think of shooting a man with a pistol. It's the wrong weapon.'

Hawes seemed taken aback by my argument. Evidently it wasn't the objection he had expected.

'Do you really think the objection is feasible?' he asked doubtingly.

'To my mind it is a complete stumbling block to Archer's having committed the crime,' I said.

In face of my positive assertion, Hawes said no more. He thanked me again and left.

I had gone as far as the front door with him, and on the hall table I saw four notes. They had certain characteristics in common. The handwriting was almost unmistakably feminine, they all bore the words, 'By hand, Urgent', and the only difference I could see was that one was noticably dirtier than the rest.

Their similarity gave me a curious feeling of seeing – not double but quadruple.

Mary came out of the kitchen and caught me staring at them.

'Come by hand since lunch time,' she volunteered. 'All but one. I found that in the box.'

I nodded, gathered them up and took them into the study.

The first one ran thus:

'DEAR MR CLEMENT, – Something has come to my knowledge which I feel you ought to know. It concerns the death of poor Colonel Protheroe. I should much appreciate your advice on the matter – whether to go to the police or not. Since my dear husband's death, I have such a shrinking from every kind of publicity. Perhaps you could run in and see me for a few minutes this afternoon.

Yours sincerely,

MARTHA PRICE RIDLEY.'

I opened the second:

'DEAR MR CLEMENT, – I am so troubled – so *excited* in my mind – to know what I ought to do. Something has come to my ears that I feel may be important. I have such a *horror* of being mixed up with the police in any way. I am so disturbed and distressed. Would it be asking too much of you, dear vicar, to drop in for a few minutes and solve my doubts and perplexities for me in the wonderful way you always do?

Forgive my troubling you,
            Yours very sincerely,
                        CAROLINE WETHERBY.'

The third, I felt, I could almost have recited beforehand.

'DEAR MR CLEMENT, – Something most important has come to my ears. I feel you should be the first to know about it. Will you call in and see me this afternoon some time? I will wait in for you.'

This militant epistle was signed 'AMANDA HARTNELL'.

I opened the fourth missive. It has been my good fortune to be troubled with very few anonymous letters. An anonymous letter is, I think, the meanest and cruellest weapon there is. This one was no exception. It purported to be written by an illiterate person, but several things inclined me to disbelieve that assumption.

'DEAR VICAR, – I think you ought to know what is Going On. Your lady has been seen coming out of Mr Redding's cottage in a surreptitious manner. You know wot i mean. The two are Carrying On together. i think you ought to know.

                                    A FRIEND.

I made a faint exclamation of disgust and crumpling up the paper tossed it into the open grate just as Griselda entered the room.

'What's that you're throwing down so contemptuously?' she asked.

'Filth,' I said.

Taking a match from my pocket, I struck it and bent down. Griselda, however, was too quick for me. She had stooped down and caught up the crumpled ball of paper and smoothed it out before I could stop her.

She read it, gave a little exclamation of disgust, and tossed it back to me, turning away as she did so. I lighted it and watched it burn.

Griselda had moved away. She was standing by the window looking out

652

into the garden.

'Len,' she said, without turning round.

'Yes, my dear.'

'I'd like to tell you something. Yes, don't stop me. I want to, please. When – when Lawrence Redding came here, I let you think that I had only known him slightly before. That wasn't true. I – had known him rather well. In fact, before I met you, I had been rather in love with him. I think most people are with Lawrence. I was – well, absolutely silly about him at one time. I don't mean I wrote him compromising letters or anything idiotic like they do in books. But I was rather keen on him once.'

'Why didn't you tell me?' I asked.

'Oh! Because! I don't know exactly except that – well, you're foolish in some ways. Just because you're so much older than I am, you think that I – well, that I'm likely to like other people. I thought you'd be tiresome, perhaps, about me and Lawrence being friends.'

'You're very clever at concealing things,' I said, remembering what she had told me in that room less than a week ago, and the ingenuous way she had talked.

'Yes, I've always been able to hide things. In a way, I like doing it.'

Her voice held a childlike ring of pleasure to it.

'But it's quite true what I said. I didn't know about Anne, and I wondered why Lawrence was so different, not – well, really not noticing me. I'm not used to it.'

There was a pause.

'You do understand, Len?' said Griselda anxiously.

'Yes,' I said, 'I understand.'

But did I?

653

I found it hard to shake off the impression left by the anonymous letter. Pitch soils.

However, I gathered up the other three letters, glanced at my watch, and started out.

I wondered very much what this might be that had 'come to the knowledge' of three ladies simultaneously. I took it to be the same piece of news. In this, I was to realize that my psychology was at fault.

I cannot pretend that my calls took me past the police station. My feet gravitated there of their own accord. I was anxious to know whether Inspector Slack had returned from Old Hall.

I found that he had, and further, that Miss Cram had returned with him. The fair Gladys was seated in the police station carrying off matters with a high hand. She denied absolutely having taken the suitcase to the woods.

'Just because one of these gossiping old cats had nothing better to do than look out of her window all night you go and pitch upon me. She's been mistaken once, remember, when she said she saw me at the end of the lane on the afternoon of the murder, and if she was mistaken then, in daylight, how can she possibly have recognized me by moonlight?

'Wicked it is, the way these old ladies go on down here. Say anything, they will. And me asleep in my bed as innocent as can be. You ought to be ashamed of youselves, the lot of you.'

'And supposing the landlady of the Blue Boar identifies the suitcase as yours, Miss Cram?'

'If she says anything of the kind, she's wrong. There's no name on it. Nearly everybody's got a suitcase like that. As for poor Dr Stone, accusing him of being a common burglar! And he has a lot of letters after his name.'

'You refuse to give us any explanation, then, Miss Cram?'

'No refusing about it. You've made a mistake, that's all. You and your meddlesome Marples. I won't say a word more – not without my solicitor present. I'm going this minute – unless you're going to arrest me.'

For answer, the inspector rose and opened the door for her, and with a toss of the head, Miss Cram walked out.

'That's the line she takes,' said Slack, coming back to his chair. 'Absolute denial. And, of course, the old lady *may* have been mistaken. No jury would believe you could recognize anyone from that distance on a moonlit night. And, of course, as I say, the old lady may have made a mistake.'

'She may,' I said, 'but I don't think she did. Miss Marple is usually right. That's what makes her unpopular.'

The inspector grinned.

'That's what Hurst says. Lord, these villages!'

'What about the silver, inspector?'

'Seemed to be perfectly in order. Of course, that meant one lot or the other must be a fake. There's a very good man in Much Benham, an authority on old silver. I've phoned over to him and sent a car to fetch him. We'll soon know which is which. Either the burglary was an accomplished fact, or else it was only planned. Doesn't make a frightful lot of difference either way – I mean as far as we're concerned. Robbery's a small business compared with murder. These two aren't concerned with the murder. We'll maybe get a line on him through the girl – that's why I let her go without any more fuss.'

'I wondered,' I said.

'A pity about Mr Redding. It's not often you find a man who goes out of his way to oblige you.'

'I suppose not,' I said, smiling slightly.

'Women cause a lot of trouble,' moralized the inspector.

He sighed and then went on, somewhat to my surprise: 'Of course, there's Archer.'

'Oh!' I said, 'You've thought of him?'

'Why, naturally, sir, first thing. It didn't need any anonymous letters to put me on his track.'

'Anonymous letters,' I said sharply. 'Did you get one, then?'

'That's nothing new, sir. We get a dozen a day, at least. Oh, yes, we were put wise to Archer. As though the police couldn't look out for themselves! Archer's been under suspicion from the first. The trouble of it is, he's got an alibi. Not that it amounts to anything, but it's awkward to get over.'

'What do you mean by its not amounting to anything?' I asked.

'Well, it appears he was with a couple of pals all the afternoon. Not, as I say, that that counts much. Men like Archer and his pals would swear to anything. There's no believing a word they say. *We* know that. But the public doesn't and the jury's taken from the public, more's the pity. They know nothing, and ten to one believe everything that's said in the witness box, no matter who it is that says it. And of course Archer himself will swear till he's black in the face that he didn't do it.'

'Not so obliging as Mr Redding,' I said with a smile.

'Not he,' said the inspector, making the remark as a plain statement of fact.

'It is natural, I suppose, to cling to life,' I mused.

'You'd be surprised if you knew the murderers that have got off through the soft-heartedness of the jury,' said the inspector gloomily.

'But do you really think that Archer did it?' I asked.

It has struck me as curious all along that Inspector Slack never seems to have any personal views of his own on the murder. The easiness or difficulty of getting a conviction are the only points that seem to appeal to him.

'I'd like to be a bit surer,' he admitted. 'A fingerprint now, or a footprint, or seen in the vicinity about the time of the crime. Can't risk arresting him without something of that kind. He's been seen round Mr Redding's house once or twice, but he'd say that was to speak to his mother. A decent body, she is. No, on the whole, I'm for the lady. If I could only get definite proof of blackmail – but you can't get definite proof of anything in this crime! It's theory, theory, theory. It's a sad pity that there's not a single spinster lady living along your road, Mr Clement. I bet she'd have seen something if there had been.'

His words reminded me of my calls, and I took leave of him. It was about the solitary instance when I had seen him in a genial mood.

My first call was on Miss Hartnell. She must have been watching me from the window, for before I had time to ring she had opened the front door, and clasping my hand firmly in hers, had led me over the threshold.

'So good of you to come. In here. More private.'

We entered a microscopic room, about the size of a hencoop. Miss Hartnell shut the door and with an air of deep secrecy waved me to a seat (there were only three). I perceived that she was enjoying herself.

'I'm never one to beat about the bush,' she said in her jolly voice, the latter slightly toned down to meet the requirements of the situation. 'You know how things go the rounds in a village like this.'

'Unfortunately,' I said, 'I do.'

'I agree with you. Nobody dislikes gossip more than I do. But there it is. I thought it my duty to tell the police inspector that I'd called on Mrs Lestrange the afternoon of the murder and that she was out. I don't expect to be thanked for doing my duty, I just do it. Ingratitude is what you meet with first and last in this life. Why, only yesterday that impudent Mrs Baker –'

'Yes, yes,' I said, hoping to avert the usual tirade. 'Very sad, very sad. But you were saying.'

'The lower classes don't know who are their best friends,' said Miss Hartnell. 'I always say a word in season when I'm visiting. Not that I'm ever thanked for it.'

'You were telling the inspector about your call upon Mrs Lestrange,' I prompted.

'Exactly – and by the way, he didn't thank me. Said he'd ask for information when he wanted it – not those words exactly, but that was the spirit. There's a different class of men in the police force nowadays.'

'Very probably,' I said. 'But you were going on to say something?'

'I decided that this time I wouldn't go near any wretched inspector. After all, a clergyman is a gentleman – at least some are,' she added.

I gathered that the qualification was intended to include me.

'If I can help you in any way,' I began.

'It's a matter of duty,' said Miss Hartnell, and closed her mouth with a snap. 'I don't want to have to say these things. No one likes it less. But duty is duty.'

I waited.

'I've been given to understand,' went on Miss Hartnell, turning rather red, 'that Mrs Lestrange gives out that she was at home all the time – that she didn't answer the door because – well, she didn't choose. Such airs and graces. I only called as a matter of duty, and to be treated like that!'

'She has been ill,' I said mildly.

'Ill? Fiddlesticks. You're too unworldly, Mr Clement. There's nothing the matter with that woman. Too ill to attend the inquest indeed! Medical certificate from Dr Haydock! She can wind him round her little finger, everyone knows that. Well, where was I?'

I don't quite know. It is difficult with Miss Hartnell to know where narrative ends and vituperation begins.

'Oh, about calling on her that afternoon. Well, it's fiddlesticks to say she was in the house. She wasn't. I know.'

'How can you possibly know?'

Miss Hartnell's face turned redder. In someone less truculent, her demeanour might have been called embarrassed.

'I'd knocked and rung,' she explained. 'Twice. If not three times. And it occurred to me suddenly that the bell might be out of order.'

She was, I was glad to note, unable to look me in the face when saying this. The same builder builds all our houses and the bells he installs are clearly audible when standing on the mat outside the front door. Both Miss Hartnell and I knew this perfectly well, but I suppose decencies have to be preserved.

'Yes?' I murmured.

'I didn't want to push my card through the letter box. That would seem so rude, and whatever I am, I am never rude.'

She made this amazing statement without a tremor.

'So I thought I would just go round the house and – and tap on the window pane,' she continued unblushingly. 'I went all round the house and looked in at all the windows, but there was no one in the house at all.'

I understood her perfectly. Taking advantage of the fact that the house was empty, Miss Hartnell had given unbridled rein to her curiosity and had

657

gone round the house examining the garden and peering in at all the windows to see as much as she could of the interior. She had chosen to tell her story to me, believing that I should be a more sympathetic and lenient audience than the police. The clergy are supposed to give the benefit of the doubt to their parishioners.

I made no comment on the situation. I merely asked a question.

'What time was this, Miss Hartnell?'

'As far as I can remember,' said Miss Hartnell, 'it must have been close on six o'clock. I went straight home afterwards, and I got in about ten past six, and Mrs Protheroe came in somewhere round about the half-hour, leaving Dr Stone and Mr Redding outside, and we talked about bulbs. And all the time the poor colonel lying murdered. It's a sad world.'

'It is sometimes a rather unpleasant one,' I said.

I rose.

'And that is all you have to tell me?'

'I just thought it might be important.'

'It might,' I agreed.

And refusing to be drawn further, much to Miss Hartnell's disappointment, I took my leave.

Miss Wetherby, whom I visited next, received me in a kind of flutter.

'Dear vicar, how truly kind. You've had tea? Really, you won't? A cushion for your back? It is so kind of you to come round so promptly. Always willing to put yourself out for others.'

There was a good deal of this before we came to the point, and even then it was approached with a good deal of circumlocution.

'You must understand that I heard this on the best authority.'

In St Mary Mead the best authority is always somebody else's servant.

'You can't tell me who told you?'

'I promised, dear Mr Clement. And I always think a promise should be a sacred thing.'

She looked very solemn.

'Shall we say a little bird told me? That is safe isn't it?'

I longed to say, 'It's damned silly.' I rather wish I had. I should have liked to observe the effect on Miss Wetherby.

'Well, this little bird told that she saw a certain lady, who shall be nameless.'

'Another kind of bird?' I inquired.

To my great surprise Miss Wetherby went off into paroxysms of laughter and tapped me playfully on the arm saying:

'Oh, vicar, you must not be so naughty!'

When she had recovered, she went on.

'A certain lady, and where do you think this certain lady was going? She turned into the Vicarage road, but before she did so, she looked up and down the road in a most peculiar way – to see if anyone she knew were noticing her, I imagine.'

'And the little bird –' I inquired.

'Paying a visit to the fishmonger's – in the room over the shop.'

I know where maids go on their days out. I know there is one place they never go if they can help – anywhere in the open air.

'And the time,' continued Miss Wetherby, leaning forward mysteriously, 'was just before six o'clock.'

'On which day?'

Miss Wetherby gave a little scream.

'The day of the murder, of course, didn't I say so?'

'I inferred it,' I replied. 'And the name of the lady?'

'Begins with an L,' said Wetherby, nodding her head several times.

Feeling that I had got to the end of the information Miss Wetherby had to impart, I rose to my feet.

'You won't let the police cross-question me, will you?' said Miss Wetherby, pathetically, as she clasped my hand in both of hers. 'I do shrink from publicity. And to stand up in court!'

'In special cases,' I said, 'they let witnesses sit down.'

And I escaped.

There was still Mrs Price Ridley to see. That lady put me in my place at once.

'I will not be mixed up in any police court business,' she said grimly, after shaking my hand coldly. 'You understand that, on the other hand, having come across a circumstance which needs explaining, I think it should be brought to the notice of the authorities.'

'Does it concern Mrs Lestrange?' I asked.

'Why should it?' demanded Mrs Price Ridley coldly.

She had me at a disadvantage there.

'It's a very simple matter,' she continued. 'My maid, Clara, was standing at the front gate, she went down there for a minute or two – *she* says to get a breath of fresh air. Most unlikely, I should say. Much more probable that she was looking out for the fishmonger's boy – if he calls himself a boy – impudent young jackanapes, thinks because he's seventeen he can joke with all the girls. Anyway, as I say, she was standing at the gate and she heard a sneeze.'

'Yes,' I said, waiting for more.

'That's all. I tell you she heard a sneeze. And don't start telling me I'm not so young as I once was and may have made a mistake, because it was Clara

659

who heard it and she's only nineteen.'

'But,' I said, 'why shouldn't she have heard a sneeze?'

Mrs Price Ridley looked at me in obvious pity for my poorness of intellect.

'She heard a sneeze on the day of the murder at a time when there was no one in your house. Doubtless the murderer was concealed in the bushes waiting his opportunity. What you have to look for is a man with a cold in his head.'

'Or a sufferer from hay fever,' I suggested. 'But as a matter of fact, Mrs Price Ridley, I think that mystery has a very easy solution. Our maid, Mary, has been suffering from a severe cold in the head. In fact, her sniffing has tried us very much lately. It must have been her sneeze your maid heard.'

'It was a man's sneeze,' said Mrs Price Ridley firmly. 'And you couldn't hear your maid sneeze in your kitchen from our gate.'

'You couldn't hear anyone sneezing in the study from your gate,' I said. 'Or at least, I very much doubt it.'

'I said the man might have been concealed in the shrubbery,' said Mrs Price Ridley. 'Doubtless when Clara had gone in, he effected an entrance by the front door.'

'Well, of course, that's possible,' I said.

I tried not to make my voice consciously soothing, but I must have failed, for Mrs Price Ridley glared at me suddenly.

'I am accustomed not to be listened to, but I might mention also that to leave a tennis racquet carelessly flung down on the grass without a press completely ruins it. And tennis racquets are very expensive nowadays.'

There did not seem to be rhyme or reason in this flank attack. It bewildered me utterly.

'But perhaps you don't agree,' said Mrs Price Ridley.

'Oh! I do – certainly.'

'I am glad. Well, that is all I have to say. I wash my hands of the whole affair.'

She leaned back and closed her eyes like one weary of this world. I thanked her and said goodbye.

On the doorstep, I ventured to ask Clara about her mistress's statement.

'It's quite true, sir, I heard a sneeze. And it wasn't an ordinary sneeze – not by any means.'

Nothing about a crime is ever ordinary. The shot was not an ordinary kind of shot. The sneeze was not a usual kind of sneeze. It was, I presume, a special murderer's sneeze. I asked the girl what time this had been, but she was very vague, some time between a quarter and half-past six she thought. Anyway, 'it was before the mistress had the telephone call and was took bad.'

I asked her if she had heard a shot of any kind. And she said the shots had been something awful. After that, I placed very little credence in her statements.

I was just turning in at my own gate when I decided to pay a friend a visit. Glancing at my watch, I saw that I had just time for it before taking Evensong. I went down the road to Haydock's house. He came out on the doorstep to meet me.

I noticed afresh how worried and haggard he looked. This business seemed to have aged him out of all knowledge.

'I'm glad to see you,' he said. 'What's the news?'

I told him the latest Stone development.

'A high-class thief,' he commented. 'Well, that explains a lot of things. He'd read up his subject, but he made slips from time to time to me. Protheroe must have caught him out once. You remember the row they had. What do you think about the girl? Is she in it too?'

'Opinion as to that is undecided,' I said. 'For my own part, I think the girl is all right.'

'She's such a prize idiot,' I added.

'Oh! I wouldn't say that. She's rather shrewd, is Miss Gladys Cram. A remarkably healthy specimen. Not likely to trouble members of my profession.'

I told him that I was worried about Hawes, and that I was anxious that he should get away for a real rest and change.

Something evasive came into his manner when I said this. His answer did not ring quite true.

'Yes,' he said slowly. 'I suppose that would be the best thing. Poor chap. Poor chap.'

'I thought you didn't like him.'

'I don't – not much. But I'm sorry for a lot of people I don't like.' He added after a minute or two: 'I'm even sorry for Protheroe. Poor fellow – nobody ever liked him much. Too full of his own rectitude and too self-assertive. It's an unlovable mixture. He was always the same – even as a young man.'

'I didn't know you knew him then.'

'Oh, yes! When we lived in Westmorland, I had a practice not far away. That's a long time ago now. Nearly twenty years.'

I sighed. Twenty years ago Griselda was five years old. Time is an odd thing . . .

'Is that all you came to say to me, Clement?'

I looked up with a start. Haydock was watching me with keen eyes.

661

'There's something else, isn't there?' he said.

I nodded.

I had been uncertain whether to speak or not when I came in, but now I decided to do so. I like Haydock as well as any man I know. He is a splendid fellow in every way, I felt that what I had to tell might be useful to him.

I recited my interviews with Miss Hartnell and Miss Wetherby.

He was silent for a long time after I'd spoken.

'It's quite true, Clement,' he said at last. 'I've been trying to shield Mrs Lestrange from any inconvenience that I could. As a matter of fact, she's an old friend. But that's not my only reason. That medical certificate of mine isn't the put-up job you all think it was.'

He paused, and then said gravely:

'This is between you and me, Clement. Mrs Lestrange is doomed.'

'What?'

'She's a dying woman. I give her a month at longest. Do you wonder that I want to keep her from being badgered and questioned?'

He went on:

'When she turned into this road that evening it was here she came – to this house.'

'You haven't said so before.'

'I didn't want to create talk. Six to seven isn't my time for seeing patients, and eveyone knows that. But you can take my word for it that she was here.'

'She wasn't here when I came for you, though. I mean, when we discovered the body.'

'No,' he seemed perturbed. 'She'd left – to keep an appointment.'

'In what direction was the appointment? In her own house?'

'I don't know, Clement. On my honour, I don't know.'

I believed him, but –

'And supposing an innocent man is hanged?' I said.

'No,' he said. 'No one will be hanged for the murder of Colonel Protheroe. You can take my word for that.'

But that is just what I could not do. And yet the certainty in his voice was very great.

'No one will be hanged,' he repeated.

'This man, Archer –'

He made an impatient movement.

'Hasn't got brains enought to wipe his finger-prints off the pistol.'

'Perhaps not,' I said dubiously.

Then I remembered something, and taking the little brownish crystal I had found in the wood from my pocket, I held it out to him and asked him what it was.

'H'm,' he hesitated. 'Looks like picric acid. Where did you find it?'

'That,' I replied, 'is Sherlock Holmes's secret.'

He smiled.

'What is picric acid?'

'Well, it's an explosive.'

'Yes, I know that, but it's got another use, hasn't it?'

He nodded.

'It's used medically – in solution for burns. Wonderful stuff.'

I held out my hand, and rather reluctantly he handed it back to me.

'It's of no consequence probably,' I said. 'But I found it in rather an unusual place.'

'You won't tell me where?'

Rather childishly, I wouldn't.

He had his secrets. Well, I would have mine.

I was a little hurt that he had not confided in me more fully.

CHAPTER 26

I was in a strange mood when I mounted the pulpit that night.

The church was unusually full. I cannot believe that it was the prospect of Hawes preaching which had attracted so many. Hawes's sermons are dull and dogmatic. And if the news had got round that I was preaching instead, that would not have attracted them either. For my sermons are dull and scholarly. Neither, I am afraid, can I attribute it to devotion.

Everybody had come, I concluded, to see who else was there, and possibly exchange a little gossip in the church porch afterwards.

Haydock was in church, which is unusual, and also Lawrence Redding. And to my surprise, beside Lawrence I saw the white strained face of Hawes. Anne Protheroe was there, but she usually attends Evensong on Sundays, though I had hardly thought she would today. I was far more surprised to see Lettice. Church-going was compulsory on Sunday morning – Colonel Protheroe was adamant on that point, but I had never seen Lettice at evening service before.

Gladys Cram was there, looking rather blatantly young and healthy against a background of wizened spinsters, and I fancied that a dim figure at the end of the church who had slipped in late, was Mrs Lestrange.

I need hardly say that Mrs Price Ridley, Miss Hartnell, Miss Wetherby, and Miss Marple were there in full force. All the village people were there, with hardly a single exception. I don't know when we have had such a crowded congregation.

Crowds are queer things. There was a magnetic atmosphere that night, and the first person to feel its influence was myself.

As a rule, I prepare my sermons beforehand. I am careful and conscientious over them, but no one is better aware than myself of their deficiencies.

Tonight I was of necessity preaching *extempore*, and as I looked down on the sea of upturned faces, a sudden madness entered my brain. I ceased to be in any sense a Minister of God. I became an actor. I had an audience before me and I wanted to move that audience – and more, I felt the power to move it.

I am not proud of what I did that night. I am an utter disbeliever in the emotional Revivalist spirit. Yet that night I acted the part of a raving, ranting evangelist.

I gave out my text slowly.

I came not to call the righteous, but sinners to repentance.

I repeated it twice, and I heard my own voice, a resonant, ringing voice unlike the voice of the everyday Leonard Clement.

I saw Griselda from her front pew look up in surprise and Dennis follow her example.

I held my breath for a moment or two, and then I let myself rip.

The congregation in that church were in a state of pent-up emotion, ripe to be played upon. I played upon them. I exhorted sinners to repentance. I lashed myself into a kind of emotional frenzy. Again and again I threw out a denouncing hand and reiterated the phrase.

'I am speaking to *you* . . .'

And each time, from different parts of the church, a kind of sighing gasp went up.

Mass emotion is a strange and terrible thing.

I finished up with those beautiful and poignant words – perhaps the most poignant words in the whole Bible:

'*This night thy soul shall be required of thee* . . .'

It was a strange, brief possession. When I got back to the Vicarage I was my usual faded, indeterminate self. I found Griselda rather pale. She slipped her arm through mine.

'Len,' she said, 'you were rather terrible tonight. I – I didn't like it. I've never heard you preach like that before.'

'I don't suppose you ever will again,' I said, sinking down wearily on the sofa. I was tired.

'What made you do it?'

'A sudden madness came over me.'

'Oh! It – it wasn't something special?'

'What do you mean – something special?'

'I wondered – that was all. You're very unexpected, Len. I never feel I really know you.'

We sat down to cold supper, Mary being out.

'There's a note for you in the hall,' said Griselda. 'Get it, will you, Dennis?'

Dennis, who had been very silent, obeyed.

I took it and groaned. Across the top left-hand corner was written: *By hand – Urgent.*

'This,' I said, 'must be from Miss Marple. There's no one else left.'

I had been perfectly correct in my assumption.

'DEAR MR CLEMENT, – I should so much like to have a little chat with you about one or two things that have occurred to me. I feel we should all try and help in elucidating this sad mystery. I will come over about half-past nine if I may, and tap on your study window. Perhaps dear Griselda would be so very kind as to run over here and cheer up my nephew. And Mr Dennis too, of course, if he cares to come. If I do not hear, I will expect them and will come over myself at the time I have stated.

'Yours very sincerely,

'JANE MARPLE.'

I handed the note to Griselda.

'Oh, we'll go!' she said cheerfully. 'A glass or two of homemade liqueur is just what one needs on Sunday evening. I think it's Mary's blancmange that is so frightfully depressing. It's like something out of a mortuary.'

Dennis seemed less charmed at the prospect.

'It's all very well for you,' he grumbled. 'You can talk all this highbrow stuff about art and books. I always feel a perfect fool sitting and listening to you.'

'That's good for you,' said Griselda serenely. 'It puts you in your place. Anyway, I don't think Mr Raymond West is so frightfully clever as he pretends to be.'

'Very few of us are,' I said.

I wondered very much what exactly it was that Miss Marple wished to talk over. Of all the ladies in my congregation, I considered her by far the shrewdest. Not only does she see and hear practically everything that goes on, but she draws amazingly neat and apposite deductions from the facts that come under her notice.

If I were at any time to set out on a career of deceit, it would be of Miss Marple that I should be afraid.

What Griselda called the Nephew Amusing Party started off at a little after nine, and whilst I was waiting for Miss Marple to arrive I amused myself by drawing up a kind of schedule of the facts connected with the crime. I arranged them so far as possible in chronological order. I am not a punctual person, but I am a neat one, and I like things jotted down in a methodical fashion.

At half-past nine punctually, there was a little tap on the window, and I rose and admitted Miss Marple.

She had a very fine Shetland shawl thrown over her head and shoulders and was looking rather old and frail. She came in full of little fluttering remarks.

'So good of you to let me come – and so good of dear Griselda – Raymond admires her so much – the perfect Greuze he always calls her . . . No, I won't have a footstool.'

I deposited the Shetland shawl on a chair and returned to take a chair facing my guest. We looked at each other, and a little deprecating smile broke out on her face.

'I feel that you must be wondering why – why I am so interested in all this. You may possibly think it's very unwomanly. No – please – I should like to explain if I may.'

She paused a moment, a pink colour suffusing her cheeks.

'You see,' she began at last, 'living alone, as I do, in a rather out-of-the-way part of the world, one has to have a hobby. There is, of course, woolwork, and Guides, and Welfare, and sketching, but my hobby is – and always has been – Human Nature. So varied – and so very fascinating. And, of course, in a small village, with nothing to distract one, one has such ample opportunity for becoming what I might call proficient in one's study. One begins to class people, quite definitely, just as though they were birds or flowers, group so-and-so, genus this, species that. Sometimes, of course, one makes mistakes, but less and less as time goes on. And then, too, one tests oneself. One takes a little problem – for instance, the gill of picked shrimps that amused dear Griselda so much – a quite unimportant mystery but absolutely incomprehensible unless one solves it right. And then there was that matter of the changed cough drops, and the butcher's wife's umbrella – the last absolutely meaningless unless on the assumption that the greengrocer was not behaving at all nicely with the chemist's wife – which, of course, turned out to be the case. It is so fascinating, you know, to apply one's judgment and find that one is right.'

'You usually are, I believe,' I said smiling.

'That, I am afraid, is what has made me a little conceited,' confessed Miss Marple. 'But I have always wondered whether, if some day a really big mystery came along, I should be able to do the same thing. I mean – just solve it correctly. Logically, it ought to be exactly the same thing. After all, a tiny working model of a torpedo is just the same as a real torpedo.'

'You mean it's all a question of relativity,' I said slowly. 'It should be – logically, I admit. But I don't know whether it really is.'

'Surely it must be the same,' said Miss Marple. 'The – what one used to call the factors at school – are the same. There's money, and the mutual attraction people of an – er – opposite sex – and there's queerness of course – so many people are a little queer, aren't they? – in fact, most people are when you know them well. And normal people do such astonishing things sometimes, and abnormal people are sometimes so very sane and ordinary. In fact, the only way is to compare people with other people you have known or come across. You'd be surprised if you knew how very few distinct types there are in all.'

'You frighten me,' I said. 'I feel I'm being put under the microscope.'

'Of course, I wouldn't dream of saying any of this to Colonel Melchett – such an autocratic man, isn't he? – and poor Inspector Slack – well, he's exactly like the young lady in the boot shop who wants to sell you patent leather because she's got it in your size, and doesn't take any notice of the fact that you want brown calf.'

That, really, is a very good description of Slack.

'But you, Mr Clement, know, I'm sure, quite as much about the crime as Inspector Slack. I thought, if we could work together –'

'I wonder,' I said. 'I think each one of us in his secret heart fancies himself as Sherlock Holmes.'

Then I told her of the three summonses I had received that afternoon. I told her of Anne's discovery of the picture with the slashed face. I also told her of Miss Cram's attitude at the police station, and I described Haydock's identification of the crystal I had picked up.

'Having found that myself,' I finished up, 'I should like it to be important. But it's probably got nothing to do with the case.'

'I have been reading a lot of American detective stories from the library lately,' said Miss Marple, 'hoping to find them helpful.'

'Was there anything in them about picric acid?'

'I'm afraid not. I do remember reading a story once, though, in which a man was poisoned by picric acid and lanolin being rubbed on him as an ointment.'

'But as nobody has been poisoned here, that doesn't seem to enter into the question,' I said.

Then I took up my schedule and handed it to her.

'I've tried,' I said, 'to recapitulate the facts of the case as clearly as possible.'

MY SCHEDULE

Thursday, 21st inst.

12.30 a.m. – Colonel Protheroe alters his appointment from six to six-fifteen. Overheard by half village very probably.

12.45 – Pistol last seen in its proper place. (But this is doubtful, as Mrs Archer had previously said she could not remember.)

5.30 (approx.) – Colonel and Mrs Protheroe leave Old Hall for village in car.

5.30 Fake call put through to me from the North Lodge, Old Hall.

6.15 (or a minute or two earlier) – Colonel Protheroe arrives at Vicarage. Is shown into study by Mary.

6.20 – Mrs Protheroe comes along back lane and across garden to study window. Colonel Protheroe not visible.

6.29 – Call from Lawrence Redding's cottage put through to Mrs Price Ridley (according to Exchange).

668

6.30–ɔ.35 – Shot heard. (Accepting telephone call time as correct.) Lawrence Redding, Anne Protheroe and Dr Stone's evidence seem to point to its being earlier, but Mrs P R probably right.

6.45 – Lawrence Redding arrives Vicarage and finds the body.

6.48 – I meet Lawrence Redding.

6.49 – Body discovered by me.

6.55 – Haydock examines body.

NOTE. – The only two people who have no kind of alibi for 6.30–6.35 are Miss Cram and Mrs Lestrange. Miss Cram says she was at the barrow, but no confirmation. It seems reasonable, however, to dismiss her from the case as there seems nothing to connect her with it. Mrs Lestrange left Dr Haydock's house some time after six to keep an appointment. Where was the appointment, and with whom? It could hardly have been with Colonel Protheroe, as he expected to be engaged with me. It is true that Mrs Lestrange was near the spot at the time the crime was committed, but it seems doubtful what motive she could have had for murdering him. She did not gain by his death, and the inspector's theory of blackmail I cannot accept. Mrs Lestrange is not that kind of woman. Also it seems unlikely that she should have got hold of Lawrence Redding's pistol.

'Very clear,' said Miss Marple, nodding her head in approval. 'Very clear indeed. Gentlemen always make such excellent memoranda.'

'You agree with what I have written?' I asked.

'Oh, yes – you have put it all beautifully.'

I asked her the question then that I had been meaning to put all along.

'Miss Marple,' I said. 'Who do you suspect? You once said that there were seven people.'

'Quite that, I should think,' said Miss Marple absently. 'I expect every one of us suspects someone different. In fact, one can see they do.'

She didn't ask me who I suspected.

'The point is,' she said, 'that one must provide an explanation for everything. Each thing has got to be explained away satisfactorily. If you have a theory that fits every fact – well, then, it must be the right one. But that's extremely difficult. If it wasn't for that note –'

'The note?' I said, surprised.

'Yes, you remember, I told you. That note has worried me all along. It's wrong, somehow.'

'Surely,' I said, 'that is explained now. It was written at six thirty-five and another hand – the murderer's – put the misleading 6.20 at the top. I think that is clearly established.'

'But even then,' said Miss Marple, 'it's all wrong.'

'But why?'

'Listen.' Miss Marple leant forward eagerly. 'Mrs Protheroe passed my garden, as I told you, and she went as far as the study window and she looked in and she didn't see Colonel Protheroe.'

'Because he was writing at the desk,' I said.

'And that's what's all wrong. That was at twenty past six. We agreed that he wouldn't sit down to say he couldn't wait any longer until after half-past six – so, why was he sitting at the writing-table then?'

'I never thought of that,' I said slowly.

'Let us, dear Mr Clement, just go over it again. Mrs Protheroe comes to the window and she thinks the room is empty – she must have thought so, because otherwise she would never have gone down to the studio to meet Mr Redding. It wouldn't have been safe. The room must have been absolutely silent if she thought it was empty. And that leaves us three alternatives, doesn't it?'

'You mean –'

'Well, the first alternative would be that Colonel Protheroe was dead already – but I don't think that's the most likely one. To begin with he'd only been there about five minutes and she or I would have heard the shot, and secondly, the same difficulty remains about his being at the writing-table. The second alternative is, of course, that he was sitting at the writing-table writing a note, but in that case it must have been a different note altogether. It can't have been to say he couldn't wait. And the third –'

'Yes?' I said.

'Well, the third is, of course, that Mrs Protheroe was right, and that the room was actually empty.'

'You mean that, after he had been shown in, he went out again and came back later?'

'Yes.'

'But why should he have done that?'

Miss Marple spread out her hands in a little gesture of bewilderment.

'That would mean looking at the case from an entirely different angle,' I said.

'One so often has to do that – about everything. Don't you think so?'

I did not reply. I was going over carefully in my mind the three alternatives that Miss Marple had suggested.

With a slight sigh the old lady rose to her feet.

'I must be getting back. I am very glad to have had this little chat – though we haven't got very far, have we?'

'To tell you the truth,' I said, as I fetched her shawl, 'the whole thing seems to me a bewildering maze.'

'Oh! I wouldn't say that. I think, on the whole, one theory fits nearly everything. That is, if you admit one coincidence – and I think one coincidence is allowable. More than one, of course, is unlikely.'

'Do you really think that? About the theory, I mean?' I asked, looking at her.

'I admit that there is one flaw in my theory – one fact that I can't get over. Oh! If only that note had been something quite different –'

She sighed and shook her head. She moved towards the window and absent-mindedly reached up her hand and felt the rather depressed-looking plant that stood in a stand.

'You know, dear Mr Clement, this should be watered oftener. Poor thing, it needs it badly. Your maid should water it every day. I suppose it is she who attends to it?'

'As much,' I said, 'as she attends to anything.'

'A little raw at present,' suggested Miss Marple.

'Yes,' I said. 'And Griselda steadily refuses to attempt to sack her. Her idea is that only a thoroughly undesirable maid will remain with us. However, Mary herself gave us notice the other day.'

'Indeed. I always imagined she was very fond of you both.'

'I haven't noticed it,' I said. 'But, as a matter of fact, it was Lettice Protheroe who upset her. Mary came back from the inquest in rather a temperamental state and found Lettice here and – well, they had words.'

'Oh!' said Miss Marple. She was just about to step through the window when she stopped suddenly, and a bewildering series of changes passed over her face.

'Oh, dear!' she muttered to herself. 'I *have* been stupid. So that was it. Perfectly possible all the time.'

'I beg your pardon?'

She turned a worried face upon me.

'Nothing. An idea that has just occurred to me. I must go home and think things out thoroughly. Do you know, I believe I have been extremely stupid – almost incredibly so.'

'I find that hard to believe,' I said gallantly.

I escorted her through the window and across the lawn.

'Can you tell me what it is that has occurred to you so suddenly?' I asked.

'I would rather not – just at present. You see, there is still a possibility that I may be mistaken. But I do not think so. Here we are at my garden gate. Thank you so much. Please do not come any further.'

'Is the note still a stumbling block?' I asked, as she passed through the gate and latched it behind her.

She looked at me abstractedly.

'The note? Oh! Of course that wasn't the real note. I never thought it was. Good-night, Mr Clement.'

She went rapidly up the path to the house, leaving me staring after her. I didn't know what to think.

Griselda and Dennis had not yet returned. I realized that the most natural thing would have been for me to go up to the house with Miss Marple and fetch them home. Both she and I had been so entirely taken up with our preoccupation over the mystery that we had forgotten anybody existed in the world except ourselves.

I was just standing in the hall, wondering whether I would not even now go over and join them, when the door bell rang.

I crossed over to it. I saw there was a letter in the box, and presuming that this was the cause of the ring, I took it out.

As I did so, however, the bell rang again, and I shoved the letter hastily into my pocket and opened the front door.

It was Colonel Melchett.

'Hallo, Clement. I'm on my way home from town in the car. Thought I'd just look in and see if you could give me a drink.'

'Delighted,' I said. 'Come into the study.'

He pulled off the leather coat that he was wearing and followed me into the study. I fetched the whisky and soda and two glasses. Melchett was standing in front of the fireplace, legs wide apart, stroking his closely-cropped moustache.

'I've got one bit of news for you, Clement. Most astounding thing you've ever heard. But let that go for the minute. How are things going down here? Any more old ladies hot on the scent?'

'They're not doing so badly,' I said. 'One of them, at all events, thinks she's got there.'

'Our friend, Miss Marple, eh?'

'Our friend, Miss Marple.'

'Women like that always think they know everything,' said Colonel Melchett.

He sipped his whisky and soda appreciatively.

'It's probably unnecessary interference on my part, asking,' I said. 'But I suppose somebody has questioned the fish boy. I mean, if the murderer left by the front door, there's a chance the boy may have seen him.'

'Slack questioned him right enough,' said Melchett. 'But the boy says he didn't meet anybody. Hardly likely he would. The murderer wouldn't be exactly courting observation. Lots of cover by your front gate. He would have taken a look to see if the road was clear. The boy had to call at the Vicarage, at Haydock's, and at Mrs Price Ridley's. Easy enough to dodge him.'

'Yes,' I said, 'I suppose it would be.'

673

'On the other hand,' went on Melchett, 'if by any chance that rascal Archer did the job, and young Fred Jackson saw him about the place, I doubt very much whether he'd let on. Archer is a cousin of his.'

'Do you seriously suspect Archer?'

'Well, you know, old Protheroe had his knife into Archer pretty badly. Lots of bad blood between them. Leniency wasn't Protheroe's strong point.'

'No,' I said. 'He was a very ruthless man.'

'What I say is,' said Melchett, 'Live and let live. Of course, the law's the law, but it never hurts to give a man the benefit of the doubt. That's what Protheroe never did.'

'He prided himself on it,' I said.

There was a pause, and then I asked:

'What is this "astounding bit of news" you promised me?'

'Well, it *is* astounding. You know that unfinished letter that Protheroe was writing when he was killed?'

'Yes.'

'We got an expert on it – to say whether the 6.20 was added by a different hand. Naturally we sent up samples of Protheroe's handwriting. And do you know the verdict? *That letter was never written by Protheroe at all.*'

'You mean a forgery?'

'It's a forgery. The 6.20 they think is written in a different hand again – but they're not sure about that. The heading is in a different ink, but the letter itself is a forgery. Protheroe never wrote it.'

'Are they certain?'

'Well, they're as certain as experts ever are. You know what an expert is! Oh! But they're sure enough.'

'Amazing,' I said. Then a memory assailed me.

'Why,' I said, 'I remember at the time Mrs Protheroe said it wasn't like her husband's handwriting at all, and I took no notice.'

'Really?'

'I thought it one of those silly remarks women will make. If there seemed one thing sure on earth it was that Protheroe had written that note.'

We looked at each other.

'It's curious,' I said slowly. 'Miss Marple was saying this evening that that note was all wrong.'

'Confound the woman, she couldn't know more about it if she had committed the murder herself.'

At that moment the telephone bell rang. There is a queer kind of psychology about a telephone bell. It rang now persistently and with a kind of sinister significance.

674

I went over and took up the receiver.

'This is the Vicarage,' I said. 'Who's speaking?'

A strange, high-pitched hysterical voice came over the wire:

'*I want to confess,*' it said. '*My God, I want to confess.*'

'Hallo,' I said, 'hallo. Look here you've cut me off. What number was that?'

A languid voice said it didn't know. It added that it was sorry I had been troubled.

I put down the receiver, and turned to Melchett.

'You once said,' I remarked, 'that you would go mad if anyone else accused themselves of the crime.'

'What about it?'

'That was someone who wanted to confess . . . And the Exchange has cut us off.'

Melchett dashed over and took up the receiver.

'I'll speak to them.'

'Do,' I said. 'You may have some effect. I'll leave you to it. I'm going out. I've a fancy I recognized that voice.'

I hurried down the village street. It was eleven o'clock, and at eleven o'clock on a Sunday night the whole village of St Mary Mead might be dead. I saw, however, a light in a first floor window as I passed, and, realizing that Hawes was still up, I stopped and rang the door bell.

After what seemed a long time, Hawes's landlady, Mrs Sadler, laboriously unfastened two bolts, a chain, and turned a key and peered out at me suspiciously.

'Why, it's Vicar!' she exclaimed.

'Good evening.' I said. 'I want to see Mr Hawes. I see there's a light in the window, so he's up still.'

'That may be. I've not seen him since I took up his supper. He's had a quiet evening – no one to see him, and he's not been out.'

I nodded, and passing her, went quickly up the stairs. Hawes has a bedroom and sitting-room on the first floor.

I passed into the latter. Hawes was lying back in a long chair asleep. My entrance did not wake him. An empty cachet box and a glass of water, half-full, stood beside him.

On the floor, by his left foot, was a crumpled sheet of paper with writing on it. I picked it up and straightened it out.

It began: '*My dear Clement* –'

I read it through, uttered an exclamation and shoved it into my pocket. Then I bent over Hawes and studied him attentively.

Next, reaching for the telephone which stood by his elbow, I gave the number of the Vicarage. Melchett must have been still trying to trace the call, for I was told that the number was engaged. Asking them to call me, I put the instrument down again.

I put my hand into my pocket to look at the paper I had picked up once more. With it, I drew out the note that I had found in the letter box and which was still unopened.

Its appearance was horribly familiar. It was the same handwriting as the anonymous letter that had come that afternoon.

I tore it open.

I read it once – twice – unable to realize its contents.

I was beginning to read it a third time when the telephone rang. Like a man in a dream I picked up the receiver and spoke.

'Hallo?'

'Hallo.'

'Is that you, Melchett?'

'Yes, where are you? I've traced that call. The number is –'

'I know the number.'

'Oh, good! Is that where you are speaking from?'

'Yes.'

'What about that confession?'

'I've got the confession all right.'

'You mean you've got the murderer?'

I had then the strongest temptation of my life. I looked at the anonymous scrawl. I looked at the empty cachet box with the name of Cherubim on it. I remembered a certain casual conversation.

I made an immense effort.

'I – don't know,' I said. 'You'd better come round.'

And I gave him the address.

Then I sat down in the chair opposite Hawes to think.

I had two clear minutes to do so.

In two minutes' times, Melchett would have arrived.

I took up the anonymous letter and read it through again for the third time.

Then I closed my eyes and thought . . .

CHAPTER 29

I don't know how long I sat there – only a few minutes in reality, I suppose. Yet it seemed as though an eternity had passed when I heard the door open and, turning my head, looked up to see Melchett entering the room.

He stared at Hawes asleep in his chair, then turned to me.

'What's this, Clement? What does it all mean?'

Of the two letters in my hand I selected one and passed it to him. He read it aloud in a low voice.

'My Dear Clement, – It is a peculiarly unpleasant thing that I have to say. After all, I think I prefer writing it. We can discuss it at a later date. It concerns the recent speculations. I am sorry to say that I have satisfied myself beyond any possible doubt as to the identity of the culprit. Painful as it is for me to have to accuse an ordained priest of the church, my duty is only too painfully clear. An example must be made and –'

He looked at me questioningly. At this point the writing tailed off in an undistinguishable scrawl where death had overtaken the writer's hand.

Melchett drew a deep breath, then looked at Hawes.

'So that's the solution! The one man we never even considered. And remorse drove him to confess!'

'He's been very queer lately,' I said.

Suddenly Melchett strode across to the sleeping man with a sharp exclamation. He seized him by the shoulder and shook him, at first gently, then with increasing violence.

'He's not asleep! He's drugged! What's the meaning of this?'

His eye went to the empty cachet box. He picked it up.

'Has he –'

'I think so,' I said. 'He showed me these the other day. Told me he'd been warned against an overdose. It's his way out, poor chap. Perhaps the best way. It's not for us to judge him.'

But Melchett was Chief Constable of the County before anything else. The arguments that appealed to me had no weight with him. He had caught a murderer and he wanted his murderer hanged.

In one second he was at the telephone, jerking the receiver up and down impatiently until he got a reply. He asked for Haydock's number. Then there was a further pause during which he stood, his ear to the telephone and his eyes on the limp figure in the chair.

'Hallo – hallo – hallo – is that Dr Haydock's? Will the doctor come round at once to High Street? Mr Hawes. It's urgent ... what's that? ... Well, what number is it then? ... Oh, sorry.'

678

He rang off, fuming.

'Wrong number, wrong number – always wrong numbers! And a man's life hanging on it. HALLO – you gave me the wrong number . . . Yes – don't waste time – give me three nine – *nine*, not five.'

Another period of impatience – shorter this time.

'Hallo – is that you, Haydock? Melchett speaking. Come to 19 High Street at once, will you? Hawes has taken some kind of overdose. At once, man, it's vital.'

He rang off, strode impatiently up and down the room.

'Why on earth you didn't get hold of the doctor at once, Clement, I cannot think. Your wits have all gone wool gathering.'

Fortunately it never occurs to Melchett that anyone can possibly have different ideas on conduct to those he holds himself. I said nothing, and he went on:

'Where did you find this letter?'

'Crumpled on the floor – where it had fallen from his hand.'

'Extraordinary business – the old maid was right about its being the wrong note we found. Wonder how she tumbled to that. But what an ass the fellow was not to destroy this one. Fancy keeping it – the most damaging evidence you can imagine!'

'Human nature is full of inconsistencies.'

'If it weren't, I doubt if we should ever catch a murderer! Sooner or later they always do some fool thing. You're looking very under the weather, Clement. I suppose this has been the most awful shock to you?'

'It has. As I say, Hawes has been queer in his manner for some time, but I never dreamed –'

'Who would? Hallo, that sounds like a car.' He went across to the window, pushing up the sash and leaning out. 'Yes, it's Haydock all right.'

A moment later the doctor entered the room.

In a few succinct words, Melchett explained the situation.

Haydock is not a man who ever shows his feelings. He merely raised his eyebrows, nodded, and strode across to his patient. He felt his pulse, raised the eyelid and looked intently at the eye.

Then he turned to Melchett.

'Want to save him for the gallows?' he asked. 'He's pretty far gone, you know. It will be touch and go, anyway. I doubt if I can bring him round.'

'Do everything possible.'

'Right.'

'He busied himself with the case he had brought with him, preparing a hypodermic injection which he injected into Hawes's arm. Then he stood up.

679

'Best thing is to run him into Much Benham – to the hospital there. Give me a hand to get him down to the car.'

We both lent our assistance. As Haydock climbed into the driving seat, he threw a parting remark over his shoulder.

'You won't be able to hang him, you know, Melchett.'

'You mean he won't recover?'

'May or may not. I didn't mean that. I mean that even if he does recover – well, the poor devil wasn't responsible for his actions. I shall give evidence to that effect.'

'What did he mean by that?' asked Melchett as we went upstairs again.

I explained that Hawes had been a victim of encephalitis lethargica.

'Sleepy sickness, eh? Always some good reason nowadays for every dirty action that's done. Don't you agree?'

'Science is teaching us a lot.'

'Science be damned – I beg your pardon, Clement; but all this namby pambyism annoys me. I'm a plain man. Well, I suppose we'd better have a look round here.'

But at this moment there was an interruption – and a most amazing one. The door opened and Miss Marple walked into the room.

She was pink and somewhat flustered, and seemed to realize our condition of bewilderment.

'So sorry – so very sorry – to intrude – good evening, Colonel Melchett. As I say, I am so sorry, but hearing that Mr Hawes was taken ill, I felt I must come round and see if I couldn't do something.'

She paused. Colonel Melchett was regarding her in a somewhat disgusted fashion.

'Very kind of you, Miss Marple,' he said dryly. 'But no need to trouble. How did you know, by the way?'

It was the question I had been yearning to ask!

'The telephone,' explained Miss Marple. 'So careless with their wrong numbers, aren't they? You spoke to me first, thinking I was Dr Haydock. My number is three five.'

'So that was it!' I exclaimed.

There is always some perfectly good and reasonable explanation for Miss Marple's omniscience.

'And so,' she continued, 'I just came round to see if I could be of any use.'

'Very kind of you,' said Melchett again, even more dryly this time. 'But nothing to be done. Haydock's taken him off to hospital.'

'Actually to hospital? Oh, that's a great relief! I am so very glad to hear it. He'll be quite safe there. When you say "nothing to be done", you don't mean that he won't recover?'

'It's very doubtful,' I said.

Miss Marple'e eyes had gone to the cachet box.

'I suppose he took an overdose?' she said.

Melchett, I think, was in favour of being reticent. Perhaps I might have been under other circumstances. But my discussion of the case with Miss Marple was too fresh in my mind for me to have the same view, though I must admit that her rapid appearance on the scene and eager curiosity repelled me slightly.

'You had better look at this,' I said, and handed her Protheroe's unfinished letter.

She took it and read it without any appearance of surprise.

'You had already deduced something of the kind, had you not?' I asked.

'Yes – yes, indeed. May I ask you, Mr Clement, what made you come here this evening? That is a point which puzzles me. You and Colonel Melchett – not at all what I should have expected.'

I explained the telephone call and that I believed I had recognized Hawes's voice. Miss Marple nodded thoughtfully.

'Very interesting. Very providential – if I may use the term. Yes, it brought you here in the nick of time.'

'In the nick of time for what?' I said bitterly.

Miss Marple looked surprised.

'To save Mr Hawes's life, of course.'

'Don't you think,' I said, 'that it might be better if Hawes didn't recover? Better for him – better for everyone. We know the truth now and –'

I stopped – for Miss Marple was nodding her head with such a peculiar vehemence that it made me lose the thread of what I was saying.

'Of course,' she said. 'Of course! That's what he wants you to think! That you know the truth – and that it's best for everyone as it is. Oh, yes, it all fits in – the letter, and the overdose, and poor Mr Hawes's state of mind and his confession. It all fits in – *but it's wrong* . . .'

We stared at her.

'That's why I am so glad Mr Hawes is safe – in hospital – where no one can get at him. If he recovers, he'll tell you the truth.'

'The truth?'

'Yes – that he never touched a hair of Colonel Protheroe's head.'

'But the telephone call,' I said. 'The letter – the overdose. It's all so clear.'

'That's what he wants you to think. Oh, he's very clever! Keeping the letter and using it this way was very clever indeed.'

'Who do you mean,' I said, 'by "he"?'

'I mean the murderer,' said Miss Marple.
She added very quietly:
'I mean Mr Lawrence Redding . . .'

We stared at her. I really think that for a moment or two we really believed she was out of her mind. The accusation seemed so utterly preposterous.

Colonel Melchett was the first to speak. He spoke kindly and with a kind of pitying tolerance.

'That is absurd, Miss Marple,' he said. 'Young Redding has been completely cleared.'

'Naturally,' said Miss Marple. 'He saw to that.'

'On the contrary,' said Colonel Melchett dryly. 'He did his best to get himself accused of the murder.'

'Yes,' said Miss Marple. 'He took us all in that way – myself as much as anyone else. You will remember, dear Mr Clement, that I was quite taken aback when I heard Mr Redding had confessed to the crime. It upset all my ideas and made me think him innocent – when up to then I had felt convinced that he was guilty.'

'Then it was Lawrence Redding you suspected?'

'I know that in books it is always the most unlikely person. But I never find that rule applies in real life. There it is so often the obvious that is true. Much as I have always liked Mrs Protheroe, I could not avoid coming to the conclusion that she was completely under Mr Redding's thumb and would do anything he told her, and, of course, he is not the kind of young man who would dream of running away with a penniless woman. From his point of view it was necessary that Colonel Protheroe should be removed – and so he removed him. One of those charming young men who have *no* moral sense.'

Colonel Melchett had been snorting impatiently for some time. Now he broke out.

'Absolute nonsense – the whole thing! Redding's time is fully accounted for up to 6.50 and Haydock says positively Protheroe couldn't have been shot then. I suppose you think you know better than a doctor. Or do you suggest that Haydock is deliberately lying – the Lord knows why?'

'I think Dr Haydock's evidence was absolutely truthful. He is a very upright man. And, of course, it was Mrs Protheroe who actually shot Colonel Protheroe – not Mr Redding.'

Again we stared at her. Miss Marple arranged her lace fichu, pushed back the fleecy shawl that draped her shoulders, and began to deliver a gentle old-maidish lecture comprising the most astounding statements in the most natural way in the world.

'I have not thought it right to speak until now. One's own belief – even so strong as to amount to knowledge – is not the same as proof. And unless one has an explanation that will fit all the facts (as I was saying to dear Mr

683

Clement this evening) one cannot advance it with any real conviction. And my own explanation was not quite complete – it lacked just one thing – but suddenly, just as I was leaving Mr Clement's study, I noticed the palm in the pot by the window – and – well, there the whole thing was! Clear as daylight!'

'Mad – quite mad,' murmured Melchett to me.

But Miss Marple beamed on us serenely and went on in her gentle ladylike voice.

'I was very sorry to believe what I did – very sorry. Because I liked them both. But you know what human nature is. And to begin with, when first he and then she both confessed in the most foolish way – well, I was more relieved than I could say. I had been wrong. And I began to think of other people who had a possible motive for wishing Colonel Protheroe out of the way.'

'The seven suspects!' I murmured.

She smiled at me.

'Yes, indeed. There was that man Archer – not likely, but primed with drink (so inflaming) you never know. And, of course, there was your Mary. She's been walking out with Archer a long time, and she's a queer-tempered girl. Motive *and* opportunity – why, she was alone in the house! Old Mrs Archer could easily have got the pistol from Mr Redding's house for either of those two. And then, of course, there was Lettice – wanting freedom and money to do as she liked. I've known many cases where the most beautiful and ethereal girls have shown next to no moral scruple – though, of course, gentlemen never wish to believe it of them.'

I winced.

'And then there was the tennis racquet,' continued Miss Marple.

'The tennis racquet?'

'Yes, the one Mrs Price Ridley's Clara saw lying on the grass by the Vicarage gate. That looked as though Mr Dennis had got back earlier from his tennis party than he said. Boys of sixteen are so very susceptible and so very unbalanced. Whatever the motive – for Lettice's sake or for yours, it was a possibility. And then, of course, there was poor Mr Hawes and you – not both of you naturally – but alternatively, as the lawyers say.'

'Me?' I exclaimed in lively astonishment.

'Well, yes. I do apologize – and indeed I never really thought – but there was the question of those disappearing sums of money. Either you or Mr Hawes must be guilty, and Mrs Price Ridley was going about everywhere hinting that you were the person in fault – principally because you objected so vigorously to any kind of inquiry into the matter. Of course, I myself was always convinced it was Mr Hawes – he reminded me so much of that unfortunate organist I mentioned; but all the same one couldn't be absolutely *sure* –'

'Human nature being what it is,' I ended grimly.

'Exactly. And then, of course, there was dear Griselda.'

'But Mrs Clement was completely out of it,' interrupted Melchett. 'She returned by the 6.50 train.'

'That's what she *said*,' retorted Miss Marple. 'One should never go by what people say. The 6.50 was half an hour late that night. But at a quarter-past seven I saw her with my own eyes starting for Old Hall. So it followed that she must have come by the earlier train. Indeed she was seen; but perhaps you know that?'

She looked at me inquiringly.

Some magnetism in her glance impelled me to hold out the last anonymous letter, the one I had opened so short a time ago. It set out in detail that Griselda had been seen leaving Lawrence Redding's cottage by the back window at twenty past six on the fatal day.

I said nothing then or at any time of the dreadful suspicion that had for one moment assailed my mind. I had seen it in nightmare terms – a past intrigue between Lawrence and Griselda, the knowledge of it coming to Protheroe's ears, his decision to make me acquainted with the facts – and Griselda, desperate, stealing the pistol and silencing Protheroe. As I say – a nightmare only – but invested for a few long minutes with a dreadful appearance of reality.

I don't know whether Miss Marple had any inkling of all this. Very probably she had. Few things are hidden from her.

She handed me back the note with a little nod.

'That's been all over the village,' she said. 'And it did look rather suspicious, didn't it? Especially with Mrs Archer swearing at the inquest that the pistol was still in the cottage when she left at midday.'

She paused a minute and then went on.

'But I'm wandering terribly from the point. What I want to say – and believe it my duty – is to put my own explanation of the mystery before you. If you don't believe it – well, I shall have done my best. Even as it is, my wish to be quite sure before I spoke may have cost poor Mr Hawes his life.'

Again she paused, and when she resumed, her voice held a different note. It was less apologetic, more decided.

'That is my own explanation of the facts. By Thursday afternoon the crime had been fully planned down to the smallest detail. Lawrence Redding first called on the vicar, knowing him to be out. He had with him the pistol which he concealed in that pot in the stand by the window. When the vicar came in, Lawrence explained his visit by a statement that he had made up his mind to go away. At five-thirty, Lawrence Redding telephoned from the North Lodge to the vicar, adopting a woman's voice (you remember what a good amateur actor he was).

'Mrs Protheroe and her husband had just started for the village. And – a very curious thing (though no one happened to think of it that way) – Mrs Protheroe took no handbag with her. Really a *most* unusual thing for a woman to do. Just before twenty past six she passes my garden and stops and speaks, so as to give me every opportunity of noticing that she has no weapon with her and also that she is quite her normal self. They realized, you see, that I am a noticing kind of person. She disappears round the corner of the house to the study window. The poor colonel is sitting at the desk writing his letter to you. He is deaf, as we all know. She takes the pistol from the bowl where it is waiting for her, comes up behind him and shoots him through the head, throws down the pistol and is out again like a flash, and going down the garden to the studio. Nearly anyone would swear that there couldn't have been time!'

'But the shot?' objected the colonel. 'You didn't hear the shot?'

'There is, I believe, an invention called a Maxim silencer. So I gather from detective stories. I wonder if, possibly, the sneeze that the maid, Clara, heard might have actually been the shot? But no matter. Mrs Protheroe is met at the studio by Mr Redding. They go in together – and, human nature being what it is, I'm afraid they realize that I shan't leave the garden till they come out again!'

I had never liked Miss Marple better than at this moment, with her humorous perception of her own weakness.

'When they do come out, their demeanour is gay and natural. And there, in reality, they made a mistake. Because if they had really said goodbye to each other, as they pretended, they would have looked very different. But you see, that was their weak point. They simply *dare* not appear upset in any way. For the next ten minutes they are careful to provide themselves with what is called an alibi, I believe. Finally Mr Redding goes to the Vicarage, leaving it as late as he dares. He probably saw you on the footpath from far away and was able to time matters nicely. He picks up the pistol and the silencer, leaves the forged letter with the time on it written in a different ink and apparently in a different handwriting. When the forgery is discovered it will look like a clumsy attempt to incriminate Anne Protheroe.

'But when he leaves the letter, he finds the one actually written by Colonel Protheroe – something quite unexpected. And being a very intelligent young man, and seeing that this letter may come in very useful to him, he takes it away with him. He alters the hands of the clock to the same time as the letter – knowing that it is always kept a quarter of an hour fast.

The same idea – attempt to throw suspicion on Mrs Protheroe. Then he leaves, meeting you outside the gate, and acting the part of someone nearly distraught. As I say, he is really most intelligent. What would a murderer who had committed a crime try to do? Behave naturally, of course. So that is just what Mr Redding does not do. He gets rid of the silencer, but marches into the police station with the pistol and makes a perfectly ridiculous self-accusation which takes everybody in.'

There was something fascinating in Miss Marple's resumé of the case. She spoke with such certainty that we both felt that in this way and in no other could the crime have been committed.

'What about the shot heard in the wood?' I asked. 'Was that the coincidence to which you were referring earlier this evening?'

'Oh, dear, no!' Miss Marple shook her head briskly. '*That* wasn't a coincidence – very far from it. It was absolutely necessary that a shot should be heard – otherwise suspicion of Mrs Protheroe might have continued. How Mr Redding arranged it, I don't quite know. But I understand that picric acid explodes if you drop a weight on it, and you will remember, dear vicar, that you met Mr Redding carrying a large stone just in the part of the wood where you picked up that crystal later. Gentlemen are so clever at arranging things – the stone suspended above the crystals and then a time fuse – or do I mean a slow match? Something that would take about twenty minutes to burn through – so that the explosion would come about 6.30 when he and Mrs Protheroe had come out of the studio and were in full view. A very safe device because what would there be to find afterwards – only a big stone! But even that he tried to remove – when you came upon him.'

'I believe you are right,' I exclaimed, remembering the start of surprise Lawrence had given on seeing me that day. It had seemed natural enough at the time, but now ...

Miss Marple seemed to read my thoughts, for she nodded her head shrewdly.

'Yes,' she said, 'it must have been a very nasty shock for him to come across you just then. But he turned it off very well – pretending he was bringing it to me for my rock gardens. Only –' Miss Marple became suddenly very emphatic. 'It was the wrong sort of stone for my rock gardens! And that put me on the right track!'

All this time Colonel Melchett had sat like a man in a trance. Now he showed signs of coming to. He snorted once or twice, blew his nose in a bewildered fashion, and said:

'Upon my word! Well, upon my word!'

Beyond that, he did not commit himself. I think that he, like myself, was impressed with the logical certainty of Miss Marple's conclusions. But for the moment he was not willing to admit it.

Instead, he stretched out a hand, picked up the crumpled letter and barked out:

'All very well. But how do you account for this fellow Hawes! Why, he actually rang up and confessed.'

'Yes, that was what was so providential. The vicar's sermon, doubtless. You know, dear Mr Clement, you really preached a most remarkable sermon. It must have affected Mr Hawes deeply. He could bear it no longer, and felt he must confess – about the misappropriations of the church funds.'

'What?'

'Yes – and that, under Providence, is what has saved his life. (For I hope and trust it *is* saved. Dr Haydock is so clever.) As I see the matter, Mr Redding kept this letter (a risky thing to do, but I expect he hid it in some safe place) and waited till he found out for certain to whom it referred. He soon made quite sure that it was Mr Hawes. I understand he came back here with Mr Hawes last night and spent a long time with him. I suspect that he then substituted a cachet of his own for one of Mr Hawes's, and slipped this letter in the pocket of Mr Hawes's dressing-gown. The poor young man would swallow the fatal cachet in all innocence – after his death his things would be gone through and the letter found and everyone would jump to the conclusion that he had shot Colonel Protheroe and taken his own life out of remorse. I rather fancy Mr Hawes must have found that letter tonight just after taking the fatal cachet. In his disordered state, it must have seemed like something supernatural, and, coming on top of the vicar's sermon, it must have impelled him to confess the whole thing.'

'Upon my word,' said Colonel Melchett. 'Upon my word! *Most* extraordinary! I – I – don't believe a word of it.'

He had never made a statement that sounded more unconvincing. It must have sounded so in his own ears, for he went on:

'And can you explain the other telephone call – the one from Mr Redding's cottage to Mrs Price Ridley?'

'Ah!' said Miss Marple. 'That is what I call the coincidence. Dear Griselda sent that call – she and Mr Dennis between them, I fancy. They had heard the rumours Mrs Price Ridley was circulating about the vicar, and they thought of this (perhaps rather childish) way of silencing her. The coincidence lies in the fact that the call should have been put through at exactly the same time as the fake shot from the wood. It led one to believe that the two must be connected.'

I suddenly remembered how everyone who spoke of that shot had described it as 'different' from the usual shot. They had been right. Yet how hard to explain just in what way the 'difference' of the shot consisted.

Colonel Melchett cleared his throat.

'Your solution is a very plausible one, Miss Marple,' he said. 'But you will allow me to point out that there is not a shadow of proof.'

'I know,' said Miss Marple. 'But you believe it to be true, don't you?'

There was a pause, then the colonel said almost reluctantly:

'Yes, I do. Dash it all, it's the only way the thing could have happened. But there's no proof – not an atom.'

Miss Marple coughed.

'That is why I thought perhaps under the circumstances –'

'Yes?'

'A little trap might be permissible.'

689

CHAPTER 31

Colonel Melchett and I both stared at her.

'A trap? What kind of a trap?'

Miss Marple was a little diffident, but it was clear that she had a plan fully outlined.

'Supposing Mr Redding were to be rung up on the telephone and warned.'

Colonel Melchett smiled.

' "All is discovered. Fly!" That's an old wheeze, Miss Marple. Not that it isn't often successful! But I think in this case young Redding is too downy a bird to be caught that way.'

'It would have to be something specific. I quite realize that,' said Miss Marple. 'I would suggest – this is just a mere suggestion – that the warning should come from somebody who is known to have rather unusual views on these matters. Dr Haydock's conversation would lead anyone to suppose that he might view such a thing as murder from an unusual angle. If he were to hint that somebody – Mrs Sadler – or one of her children – had actually happened to see the transposing of the cachets – well, of course, if Mr Redding is an innocent man, that statement will mean nothing to him, but if he isn't –'

'Well, he might just possibly do something foolish.'

'And deliver himself into our hands. It's possible. Very ingenious, Miss Marple. But will Haydock stand for it? As you say, his views –'

Miss Marple interrupted him brightly.

'Oh, but that's theory! So very different from practice, isn't it? But anyway, here he is, so we can ask him.'

Haydock was, I think, rather astonished to find Miss Marple with us. He looked tired and haggard.

'It's been a near thing,' he said. 'A very near thing. But he's going to pull through. It's a doctor's business to save his patient and I saved him, but I'd have been just as glad if I hadn't pulled it off.'

'You may think differently,' said Melchett, 'when you have heard what we have to tell you.'

And briefly and succinctly, he put Miss Marple's theory of the crime before the doctor, ending up with her final suggestion.

We were then privileged to see exactly what Miss Marple meant by the difference between theory and practice.

Haydock's views appeared to have undergone a complete transformation. He would, I think, have liked Lawrence Redding's head on a charger. It was not, I imagine, the murder of Colonel Protheroe that so stirred his rancour.

It was the assault on the unlucky Hawes.

'The damned scoundrel,' said Haydock. 'The damned scoundrel! That poor devil Hawes. He's got a mother and a sister too. The stigma of being the mother and sister of a murderer would have rested on them for life, and think of their mental anguish. Of all the cowardly dastardly tricks!'

For sheer primitive rage, commend me to a thoroughgoing humanitarian when you get him well roused.

'If this thing's true,' he said, 'you can count on me. The fellow's not fit to live. A defenceless chap like Hawes.'

A lame dog of any kind can always count on Haydock's sympathy.

He was eagerly arranging details with Melchett when Miss Marple rose and I insisted on seeing her home.

'It is most kind of you, Mr Clement,' said Miss Marple, as we walked down the deserted street. 'Dear me, past twelve o'clock. I hope Raymond has gone to bed and not waited up.'

'He should have accompanied you,' I said.

'I didn't let him know I was going,' said Miss Marple.

I smiled suddenly as I remembered Raymond West's subtle psychological analysis of the crime.

'If your theory turns out to be the truth – which I for one do not doubt for a minute,' I said, 'you will have a very good score over your nephew.'

Miss Marple smiled also – an indulgent smile.

'I remember a saying of my Great Aunt Fanny's. I was sixteen at the time and thought it particularly foolish.'

'Yes?' I inquired.

'She used to say: "The young people think the old people are fools; but the old people *know* the young people are fools!" '

691

There is little more to be told. Miss Marple's plan succeeded. Lawrence Redding was not an innocent man, and the hint of a witness of the change of capsule did indeed cause him to do 'something foolish'. Such is the power of an evil conscience.

He was, of course, peculiarly placed. His first impulse, I imagine, must have been to cut and run. But there was his accomplice to consider. He could not leave without getting word to her, and he dared not wait till morning. So he went up to Old Hall that night – and two of Colonel Melchett's most efficient officers followed him. He threw gravel at Anne Protheroe's window, aroused her, and an urgent whisper brought her down to speak with him. Doubtless they felt safer outside than in – with the possibility of Lettice waking. But as it happened, the two police officers were able to overhear the conversation in full. It left the matter in no doubt. Miss Marple had been right on every count.

The trial of Lawrence Redding and Anne Protheroe is a matter of public knowledge. I do not propose to go into it. I will only mention that great credit was reflected upon Inspector Slack, whose zeal and intelligence had resulted in the criminals being brought to justice. Naturally, nothing was said of Miss Marple's share in the business. She herself would have been horrified at the thought of such a thing.

Lettice came to see me just before the trial took place. She drifted through my study window, wraith-like as ever. She told me then that she had all along been convinced of her stepmother's complicity. The loss of the yellow beret had been a mere excuse for searching the study. She hoped against hope that she might find something the police had overlooked.

'You see,' she said in her dreamy voice, 'they didn't hate her like I did. And hate makes things easier for you.'

Disappointed in the result of her search, she had deliberately dropped Anne's ear-ring by the desk.

'Since I *knew* she had done it, what did it matter? One way was as good as another. She *had* killed him.'

I sighed a little. There are always some things that Lettice will never see. In some respects she is morally colour blind.

'What are you going to do, Lettice?' I asked.

'When – when it's all over, I am going abroad.' She hesitated and then went on. 'I am going abroad with my mother.'

I looked up, startled.

She nodded.

'Didn't you ever guess? Mrs Lestrange is my mother. She is – is dying, you know. She wanted to see me and so she came down here under an assumed name. Dr Haydock helped her. He's a very old friend of hers – he was keen about her once – you can see that! In a way, he still is. Men always went batty about mother, I believe. She's awfully attractive even now. Anyway, Dr Haydock did everything he could to help her. She didn't come down here under her own name because of the disgusting way people talk and gossip. She went to see father that night and told him she was dying and had a great longing to see something of me. Father was a beast. He said she'd forfeited all claim, and that I thought she was dead – as though I had ever swallowed that story! Men like father never see an inch before their noses!

'But mother is not the sort to give in. She thought it only decent to go to father first, but when he turned her down so brutally she sent a note to me, and I arranged to leave the tennis party early and meet her at the end of the footpath at a quarter past six. We just had a hurried meeting and arranged when to meet again. We left each other before half-past six. Afterwards I was terrified that she would be suspected of having killed father. After all, she *had* got a grudge against him. That's why I got hold of that old picture of her up in the attic and slashed it about. I was afraid the police might go nosing about and get hold of it and recognize it. Dr Haydock was frightened too. Sometimes, I believe, he really thought she had done it! Mother is rather a – desperate kind of person. She doesn't count consequences.'

She paused.

'It's queer. She and I belong to each other. Father and I didn't. But mother – well, anyway, I'm going abroad with her. I shall be with her till – till the end ...'

She got up and I took her hand.

'God bless you both,' I said. 'Some day, I hope, there is a lot of happiness coming to you, Lettice.'

'There should be,' she said, with an attempt at a laugh. 'There hasn't been much so far – has there? Oh, well, I don't suppose it matters. Goodbye, Mr Clement. You've been frightfully decent to me always – you and Griselda.'

Griselda!

I had to own to her how terribly the anonymous letter had upset me, and first she laughed, and then solemnly read me a lecture.

'However,' she added, 'I'm going to be very sober and Godfearing in future – quite like the Pilgrim fathers.'

I did not see Griselda in the rôle of a Pilgrim father.

She went on:

'You see, Len, I have a steadying influence coming into my life. It's coming into your life, too, but in your case it will be a kind of – of rejuvenating one – at least, I hope so! You can't call me a dear child half so much when we have a real child of our own. And, Len, I've decided that now I'm going to be a real "wife and mother" (as they say in books), I must be a housekeeper too. I've bought two books on Household Management and one on Mother Love, and if that doesn't turn me out a pattern I don't know what will! They are all simply screamingly funny – not intentionally, you know. Especially the one about bringing up children.'

'You haven't bought a book on How to Treat a Husband, have you?' I asked, with sudden apprehension as I drew her to me.

'I don't need to,' said Griselda. 'I'm a very good wife. I love you dearly. What more do you want?'

'Nothing,' I said.

'Could you say, just for once, that you love me madly?'

'Griselda,' I said – 'I adore you! I worship you! I am wildly, hopelessly and quite unclerically crazy about you!'

My wife gave a deep and contented sigh.

Then she drew away suddenly.

'Bother! Here's Miss Marple coming. Don't let her suspect, will you? I don't want everyone offering me cushions and urging me to put my feet up. Tell her I've gone down to the golf links. That will put her off the scent – and it's quite true because I left my yellow pullover there and I want it.'

Miss Marple came to the window, halted apologetically, and asked for Griselda.

'Griselda,' I said, 'has gone to the golf links.'

An expression of concern leaped into Miss Marple's eyes.

'Oh, but surely,' she said, 'that is most unwise – just now.'

And then in a nice, old-fashioned, lady-like, maiden-lady way, she blushed.

And to cover the moment's confusion, we talked hurriedly of the Protheroe case, and of 'Dr Stone,' who had turned out to be a well-known cracksman with several different aliases. Miss Cram, by the way, had been cleared of all complicity. She had at last admitted taking the suitcase to the wood, but had done so in all good faith, Dr Stone having told her that he feared the rivalry of other archaeologists who would not stick at burglary to gain their object of discrediting his theories. The girl apparently swallowed this not very plausible story. She is now, according to the village, looking out for a more genuine article in the line of an elderly bachelor requiring a secretary.

As we talked, I wondered very much how Miss Marple had discovered our latest secret. But presently, in a discreet fashion, Miss Marple herself supplied me with a clue.

'I hope dear Griselda is not overdoing it,' she murmured, and, after a discreet pause, 'I was in the bookshop in Much Benham yesterday –'

Poor Griselda – that book on Mother Love has been her undoing!

'I wonder, Miss Marple,' I said suddenly, 'if you were to commit a murder whether you would ever be found out.'

'What a terrible idea,' said Miss Marple, shocked. 'I hope I could never do such a wicked thing.'

'But human nature being what it is,' I murmured.

Miss Marple acknowledged the hit with a pretty old-ladyish laugh.

'How naughty of you, Mr Clement.' She rose. 'But naturally you are in good spirits.'

She paused by the window.

'My love to dear Griselda – and tell her – that any little secret is quite safe with me.'

Really Miss Marple is rather a dear . . .